THE *Valiant* HEARTS

ROMANCE COLLECTION

9 Stories of Love Put to the Test

THE *Valiant* HEARTS ROMANCE COLLECTION

MaryLu Tyndall, Kathleen Y'Barbo
Kristin Billerbeck, Darlene Franklin,
Pamela Griffin, JoAnn A. Grote, Colleen L. Reece
Janet Spaeth, Jennifer Rogers Spinola

BARBOUR BOOKS
An Imprint of Barbour Publishing, Inc.

By Dim and Flaring Lamps ©2001 by Colleen L. Reece
Misprint ©2005 by Kathleen Y'Barbo
Beauty from Ashes ©2012 by MaryLu Tyndall
Buttons for Birdie ©2013 by Darlene Franklin
Dreamlight ©2006 by Janet Spaeth
Black Widow ©2013 by Jennifer Rogers Spinola
Birth of a Dream ©2012 by Pamela Griffin
Home Fires Burning ©2001 by JoAnn A. Grote
Bayside Bride ©2001 by Kristin Billerbeck

Print ISBN 978-1-63409-672-0

eBook Editions:
Adobe Digital Edition (.epub) 978-1-63409-867-0
Kindle and MobiPocket Edition (.prc) 978-1-63409-868-7

Unless otherwise indicated, scripture quotations are taken from the King James Version of the Bible.

This book is a work of fiction. Names, characters, places, and incidents are either products of the author's imagination or used fictitiously. Any similarity to actual people, organizations, and/or events is purely coincidental.

Published by Barbour Books, an imprint of Barbour Publishing, Inc., P.O. Box 719, Uhrichsville, OH 44683, www.barbourbooks.com

Our mission is to publish and distribute inspirational products offering exceptional value and biblical encouragement to the masses.

 Member of the
Evangelical Christian
Publishers Association

Printed in Canada.

Contents

By Dim and Flaring Lamps

by Colleen L. Reece

Author's Note

The Civil War, also called "The War between the States," divided families and pitted brother against brother. Each side fought for a *cause*: the North to free the slaves and preserve the Union, and the South to maintain a way of life begun by those who pioneered and won their lands against immeasurable odds.

Some incidents in *By Dim and Flaring Lamps* are based on stories handed down in my family for more than a century—legends of boys in their teens and grizzled men who, at day's end, often laid down their weapons and crossed battle lines. They played cards, swapped tobacco, and told stories about their homes, all the time knowing the next day they would again fight one another.

Music played an important part in the conflict. Southern Johnny Rebs lustily sang, "Oh, I wish I was in Dixie. . ."—a song used against Abraham Lincoln when he ran for president in 1860. (Five years later, after the Civil War ended, Lincoln had a band play "Dixie" at the White House.)

Julia Ward Howe gave the North "The Battle Hymn of the Republic," inspired by visits to military camps near Washington, D.C., shortly after the war started.

Colleen

Chapter 1

I have seen Him in the watchfires of a hundred circling camps;
They have builded Him an altar in the evening dews and damps;
I can read His righteous sentence by the dim and flaring lamps,
His day is marching on.
— "Battle Hymn of the Republic" by Julia Ward Howe; 2nd stanza; 1861

Hickory Hill, Virginia
October 25, 1860

An inquisitive, late-afternoon sunbeam sneaked between the thin muslin curtains of the upstairs hall's west window in Dr. Luke Danielson's modest but spotless home. It roved over plain white walls brightened by occasional watercolor landscapes, and highlighted a cross-stitched sampler that read: *How far that little candle throws his beams! So shines a good deed in a naughty world.*[1] The sunbeam danced on until it reached a heavy mirror mounted on the wall next to the staircase leading to the ground floor. There it lingered, for all the world as if it had finally found something worthy of its full attention.

The massive mirror gave the slim, blue-calico-clad figure poised at the top of the staircase an auburn-haired twin, a twin with sparkling blue eyes that often changed to mysterious green, depending on the wearer's gown. Both image and original displayed a few tiny, gold-dust freckles on their lightly tanned, tip-tilted noses—the result of forgetting to shade creamy skin from the sun by wearing tiresome hats.

The gleaming glass also reflected Lucy Danielson's right-hand grasp of the smooth, highly polished banister rail, a definite threat to good intentions. "Young ladies should rest one hand lightly and sweep down the stairs," she muttered.

Knowing she should put aside her childish ways on this, her fifteenth birthday, Lucy loosened her grip. She was almost a woman. Why, some of her friends were married and taking on airs. Lucy grimaced. *She* would never do so. "I may become a woman, but I won't stop being a girl," she vowed.

She sighed, then with a quick change of mood, curved her left hand, smirked, and took a single mincing step forward. The next moment, she made the mistake of allowing her gaze to linger on the tempting banister. Its beautifully grained surface served as a silent reminder of countless journeys made since Lucy first eluded Mammy Roxy's watchful care and discovered the new, wonderful means of descent. Numerous scoldings and threats (that never

1   William Shakespeare

materialized) to tell the child's beloved father, "Daddy Doc," hadn't kept Lucy from engaging in the forbidden activity.

She closed her eyes in order to better fight temptation. A girl who had accompanied her father on his rounds ever since she was old enough to sit in the buggy beside him had no business sliding down banister rails. Lucy laughed. The joyous sound echoed in the quiet hall. How many times had Mammy scolded, "It ain't fittin' for you to be takin' that chile into all kinds of unsav'ry places, Dr. Luke. It just ain't fittin'!"

Lucy's big, blond Scandinavian father always just laughed. He usually listened to Roxy, who had become nurse and substitute mother on the day Dr. Luke's cherished wife died while birthing their only child. Yet on this one thing he remained firm. "I don't take Lucy anywhere that will endanger her health," he patiently explained over and over. "It's also the only way I can be with my daughter. Hickory Hill folks run me ragged; you know that." He covered a yawn with the strong hand, which could be gentle as a mother's touch when needed, and smiled at Roxy.

"Those same folks is plumb scandalized," Roxy reminded him. She rolled her dark eyes. "Just last week Miz Tarbell said 'twas plain shockin' to see a girl-chile sittin' on the seat of a doctor's buggy and goin' into sickrooms."

"That was last week." Dr. Luke grinned like an urchin triumphantly harboring a secret weapon. "A few days later, that same Miz Tarbell admitted Lucy's small but firm hands 'do a powerful lot to ease away miz'ry in the head.'"

Roxy threw her voluminous white apron over her head, and the doctor added, "Don't worry, Roxy. Lucy has wanted to be a nurse for as long as either of us can remember." His blue eyes glistened. "She will make a fine one. The child brings light and happiness simply by stepping into a room. She comes by it naturally. Both of our names mean 'bringer of light.'" His face turned somber. "Would that we could bring even more light into the darkness! Doctors and nurses fight ignorance and superstition as much as actual illness."

◆ ◆ ◆

The distant slam of a door returned Lucy to the present. She blinked moisture from her uselessly long lashes. A rush of love for her father and Mammy Roxy swept through her. Would she ever be as good as they thought she already was?

Probably not. She had inherited too much of her carefree Irish mother's bubble and bounce.

She glanced at the tempting rail again, intending to overcome its silent invitation. Instead, she recalled the exciting *whoosh* created by her rapid downward progress—her momentary kinship with birds flying wild and free. Most of all, she remembered the satisfying *thud* of her slippered feet when she landed in the small, sunlit entryway below.

The memories proved Lucy's undoing. She glanced to her right. To her left. She looked out the sun-touched window and made sure no one was entering or leaving the adjoining single-story building her father used for his medical and surgical practice. October lay over the land like a benediction, warm and soft as the feather bed in which Lucy slept. Good. No one was in sight. Her father had been called out earlier but refused to take her with him. "Birthday girls need to be home getting beautiful," he had teased.

"My stars, who can be beautiful when they have red hair?" Lucy had burst out.

"Your mother was. *Fiona* means fair. She was and you are. Inside and out."

His words pounded in Lucy's brain but were soon vanquished by the desire for mischief that surged through her. This time she made no attempt to squelch it. The "almost a woman," who planned to never cease being a girl, bundled her wide skirts and many petticoats around her. She catapulted down, down, down in a ride more glorious than any she remembered.

"Honey-chile? Is that you?"

The rich voice, followed by heavy footsteps, drowned out the sound of Lucy's landing *thud*. She set herself to rights and whispered an unrepentant prayer of thanks for not being caught. An irreverent thought followed. Did God have banisters alongside the heavenly golden stairs Roxy and her caretaker husband, Jackson Way, sometimes sang about climbing?

The door leading to the large Danielson kitchen opened. A massive woman stepped into the hall. The dark face beneath Roxy's spotless white turban held suspicion. So did the folding of her hands across the familiar white apron that protected her print work dress. "What you up to, Miss Lucy?"

Oh dear. Mammy seldom called her charge Miss Lucy, except to strangers. *Better try to distract her.* "Nothing important. Mammy, will you please tell me The Story before it's time to dress for my birthday dinner? Who is coming, anyway?"

"Who says birthday dinner?" Roxy planted her hands on her hips and glared, but her twitching lips betrayed excitement at what Lucy knew lay ahead. "If you was havin' a dinner, and I ain't sayin' so, who d'you think would be comin'?"

Lucy swallowed a grin at the success of her diversionary tactics and tried to suppress the blush she felt creeping up from the soft white collar of her gown. "You 'ain't sayin' ' not, either," she mimicked. "Why else did you order me out of the kitchen and dining room today? I'll wager the table is already set." She danced across the hall in a whirl of skirts and threw her arms around her nurse and friend.

She waltzed Roxy across the hall until the older woman protested, "Stop, chile! You'll be the death of me yet." She pulled free and rested one hand on Lucy's shining auburn hair. The corners of her mouth turned down. "Tryin' to s'prise you's like tryin' to put salt on a bird's tail. And the same folks've been comin' year after year."

"I know," Lucy admitted. She felt a rush of tears crowd behind her eyelids, as they did each time she wheedled Roxy into repeating the tale more romantic to her fifteen-year-old heart than those in any storybook or novel. "Tell me The Story again, Mammy. It's the best birthday present of all."

"I done tol' you that tale more times than there's stars in the sky," Roxy protested. Yet a special look came into her eyes, and she allowed Lucy to lead her into a small, carpeted sitting room, made bright with fall foliage Lucy had gathered and arranged earlier in the day. She plumped heavily down on a settee and smiled at her charge.

Lucy dropped to a tapestry-covered footstool and leaned against Roxy's knee, her favorite position for The Story. "Now, Mammy." She closed her eyes, listening for words she knew by heart.

◆   ◆   ◆

The day Laird and Isobel Cunningham's only son was born, the prosperous Virginia plantation owner devised a plan cunning enough to make his frugal Scottish ancestors chortle with glee. He would begin searching at once for a suitable wife for young Jeremiah, thereby ensuring a large dowry for the Cunningham coffers and expanding Hickory Manor's wide borders.

But, alas, his son's first glimpse of Lucy Danielson dealt a deathblow to Laird Cunningham's hopes. Jeremiah gazed at Lucy's fair skin, shining red curls, sometimes blue, sometimes sparkling green eyes—and promptly declared his intentions to marry her!

At this point in the story, Lucy felt the same thrill she experienced no matter how many times she heard about that fateful day. Her heart pounded, thinking of Jere Cunningham and his daring.

Roxy's body shook with mirth when she said, "Honey-chile, you took one look at Master Jere when he come in the room and honed in on him like a bee heads for a flower. When your fingers touched his hand, why, they just tangled themselves 'round and 'round his heartstrings."

"Shameless," Lucy put in from the depths of Roxy's capacious lap, where she had hidden her burning face. "Why didn't you teach me better?"

Roxy's deep laughter sounded as if it came from her toes, as Dr. Luke wrote that it must. She ignored the question she had heard a hundred times before and continued with The Story. "Folks gathered 'round laughed and laughed, your daddy most of all."

"Why, Mammy?" Lucy asked, as usual.

"You already knows," Roxy scolded, also as usual. "Master Jere were only six and it were only your first birthday."

Lucy wondered if Roxy could hear her wildly thumping heart but remained silent. A gentle hand smoothed the rebellious auburn curls that insisted on going their own wayward way. The older woman's rich voice went on. "Chile, that were fourteen year ago." She hesitated, then added significantly, "Folks done stopped their laughin' a long time ago."

Lucy looked up in time to see Roxy nod and to catch the knowing expression that filled the shining face. "You young 'uns ain't changed a mite. There ain't nothin' in this world goin' to sep'rate you."

A feather of fear brushed the listening girl's heart, which skipped a beat. "Laird Cunningham would, if he could. *He* didn't laugh that day."

The life-wrinkles at the corners of Roxy's expressive mouth deepened, and she shook her head. "Hmp-um. I reckon the milk of human kindness done soured in that man. Now Jackson Way heard tell he's already combin' the countryside lookin' for suitors for Miss Jinny." Roxy rolled her eyes and grunted, "And her not yet fourteen."

Lucy sat bolt-upright. "Suitors? Jinny? *I* never had suitors."

Roxy's laugh rolled out again. "That's 'cause all the boys know you belongs to Master Jere. Ain't he been takin' you ridin' and sleddin' and lookin' after you since you could crawl? Whyfor you want suitors? Hmm?"

Lucy cocked her head to one side, a habit that signified deep thought. "I didn't say I *wanted* suitors, Mammy. Just that I didn't have any." She grinned at the answering frown.

"Don't you go hankerin' after brass when you done got pure gold," Roxy warned. "Ain't no boy 'round Hick'ry Hill better than Master Jere."

Lucy felt warm blood course through her veins. A tantalizing image of the tall young man her childhood playmate had become crept into her mind. "I know," she whispered.

The sound of buggy wheels shattered the special moment they had shared and sent Lucy flying to the window. "My stars! Daddy Doc's home already." She leaped to her feet and hurled her disheveled self through the hall and out the front door, to enthusiastically welcome home one of the two men most important in her charmed, secure world.

Chapter 2

A war-cry yell like those heard in battles between early Virginia settlers and Indians mingled with the steady drum of hooves beating on the well-traveled road from Hickory Manor to Hickory Hill. The next instant, a magnificent black stallion with a rider bent low over his neck topped a knoll overlooking the plantation. They stopped, turned, and faced the wide valley below, as they always did on their way to and from the village.

"Good boy." Jere Cunningham relaxed his set jaw, patted his thoroughbred's neck, slid from the saddle, and tossed the reins over Ebony's head. No need to tie the horse taught as a colt to stand with reins hanging. One arm thrown across Ebony's neck, the strong young man surveyed the land he loved.

Horse and rider's vantage point offered an unsurpassed view. The three-story mansion, in all its white-columned glory, crouched amidst manicured lawns, well-cared-for flower beds, and a stand of hickory trees from which the plantation took its name. Late-afternoon sunlight gilded the walls of Jere's home. It changed glistening white to soft gold, enhancing the beauty. Pride stirred within his heart.

"Mother's doing," he muttered to Ebony, who nickered and nosed him in response. "Father cares far more for land than for buildings. Land and money," he bitterly added. Yet the familiar sense of permanency emanating from the heart of Hickory Manor swelled within him. Anger over Jere's recent confrontation with his father lessened. The peace he always experienced in this particular spot gradually stilled his twanging nerves.

A vision of his lovely patrician mother danced in the still air. Jere drew in an unsteady breath and shot a silent prayer of thanks upward. How much Isobel Cunningham had passed on to her son! From her had come the crisp, golden brown locks that waved across his wide forehead. The ruddy color in his cheeks that even his deep tan couldn't hide. The farseeing eyes that stole their brightness from Scottish lochs reflecting the bluest heavens.

Jere had also inherited his mother's love of books, especially the "Auld Book," as his Scottish ancestors called the Bible. Most important, she had led Jere to the Lord when he was first old enough to understand God's infinite love. "If you had been the only person who ever lived, Jesus would still have come, so that you might one day live with Him," Isobel quietly told her listening son.

Jere never forgot the childish words with which he asked Jesus to live in his heart and help him to "be a good boy." They served him in good stead when trials came. The stern control Laird Cunningham exercised over himself, his household, the many slaves who served him, and especially his only son seldom slipped. The occasions when it did were legendary.

The elder Cunningham unfortunately bequeathed both his love for the plantation and his stubbornness to his only son. Many times Jere flinched at his father's rock-hard determination to control his life. Jere never let it show. Laird Cunningham despised weakness and rode roughshod over opposition, believing he was duty-bound to direct others in the way they ought to go.

On most such occasions, Jere silently met his father's stern gaze, then went his own way. Today in the drawing room had been different. Jere shrank from the memory raw in his mind and deliberately concentrated on the vast Cunningham domain. It stretched as far as he could see in every direction. Beautifully cared-for fields ribboned with lazy streams swept to low hills that were backed by distant mountain ridges. The hum of bees heavy with pollen harmonized with voices from the whitewashed cabins that housed the Cunningham slaves. Voices now raised in a familiar spiritual. No ramshackle dwellings marred Hickory Manor. Each tidy cabin had its cow, garden, and patch of flowers.

Jere turned up his nose in disgust. Some of the neighbors' slave quarters were disgraceful, little more than shacks. He furrowed his brow. The one time he protested the deplorable conditions to his father, Laird Cunningham shook his head and sternly reminded, "How he treats his slaves is each man's responsibility. We treat ours well, but we are not our brothers' keepers."

We should be. The words remained unspoken but never completely disappeared into the land of forgotten conversations. They popped up at odd times, leaving Jere depressed without knowing what to do about his feelings.

A cloud slid across the sky, blotting out the sun and Jere's temporary peace. He sighed, unable to laugh off or ignore the incident that had sent him galloping away from home and his father's presence. Resentment rose like bile. Jere flung his head back and stared at a distant, blue-hazed mountain. "Sorry I couldn't hold my tongue, God. I can't and won't marry Harriet Conrad, even though she would bring a dowry as large as her feet to the house of Cunningham."

He paused, wishing God would tell him, *I don't expect you to marry her.* The heavens remained silent. Jere chuckled. What had he expected? A lightning bolt? Why ask for reassurance when he already had it? His heart had confirmed his convictions a hundred, nay, a *thousand* times since the day he would remember if he lived to be older than Methuselah. In the space between heartbeats, he had taken measure and staked his claim to Lucy Danielson. For fourteen years he'd remained unshaken in the face of his father's continuing disbelief that a six-year-old's fanciful attachment would be strong enough to carry into manhood.

Jere expelled an exasperated breath and set his mouth in a grim line. Father had brought the subject up again today. His steely gaze had bored into his son, who dreaded hearing the timeworn arguments and accusations he knew by heart.

"You're twenty years old," he stated through thinned lips, paying out the words the way a miser reluctantly parts with his gold. He glared at Jere, seated in the richly upholstered chair on the opposite side of the great marble fireplace. "Old enough to put aside this abominable obsession with the Danielson child, and—"

Jere closed his mind against the rest of the speech. *Child? In many ways,* he admitted to himself. A hundred glimpses of her laughing face when she followed or led him into mischief flooded his brain. Lucy calmly removing her shoes and wading stocking-footed in the creek when she knew it would scandalize Mammy Roxy. Lucy sneaking tidbits to a mongrel dog through the open window behind her at a formal dinner. Lucy filling his heart with her antics and obvious adoration. Even though no vow of love had been declared between them, her incredible blue-green eyes showed awareness of the bonds that shut out any possibility of either Jere or her marrying anyone else.

His father's grating voice interrupted the thought. "Can you imagine *Lucy Danielson* as mistress of all this?" He carelessly gestured around the tastefully furnished drawing room.

"Unless she changes completely, and I see little hope of that. . . ." He paused and raised a skeptical eyebrow. "She will never be mature enough to properly grace any man's home, let alone a man of your station."

The sleeping protest Jere had stifled more times than he could remember roused, shook itself, and roared like a cannon. "Mature enough!" Jere felt his eyes burn and knew they flashed blue fire at his father. "She's mature enough to accompany Dr. Luke on his rounds. Mature enough for everyone in Hickory Hill and miles around—except you—to recognize that she has been given the gift of healing! Mature enough to know from childhood that nursing is her calling and to have studied all she could get her hands on, plus learning from Dr. Luke." Pride choked off his tribute. He observed the consternation in his father's face at the unexpected outburst but retrieved his voice and heedlessly rushed on.

"Every day Lucy tries to live up to the standard set by her heroine, Florence Nightingale. You must know the courageous 'lady with the lamp' and her assistants overcame unspeakable conditions in the Turkish barracks used as a hospital during the Crimean War. Miss Nightingale saved the lives of countless British soldiers." He paused. "Lucy has already helped save lives right here."

"The Nightingale woman disgraced her father and broke his heart."

Jere sprang to his feet so abruptly, his heavy chair crashed to the polished floor. He stepped forward, unable to hold back words he had wanted to speak a million times. Words he had swallowed because of the commandment to honor his father and mother. "Thank God Dr. Luke isn't such a man! He respects his daughter enough to let her choose her own life."

The older man slowly and deliberately raised himself from his chair. His fixed gaze never wavered from his son's face. "Some of us can afford to be more choosy," he grimly pointed out. "Lucas Danielson has little land and fewer possessions to leave future generations. Your mother and I have given our lives to the establishing of Hickory Manor. In many ways, it *is* our lives."

Yours, not mother's, Jere thought. *She would be happy no matter how little she had. Although she enjoys her home, what really matters to Mother is serving God and her family.*

"Jinny will be suitably betrothed at the proper time," Laird droned on in a voice as devoid of emotion as if he were describing the selling of a farm animal.

Jere opened his mouth to protest, then shrugged. Why bring his younger sister's future into the argument? Doing so at this point meant prolonging Father's tirade, something Jere hated and avoided whenever possible.

Today it wasn't possible. In the same calculated tones, the master of Hickory Manor announced, "You will be twenty-one next August. As you know, you stand to inherit a goodly section of land. If between now and then you consent to wed Harriet Conrad, all will be well. I have approached her father on your behalf." The words fell like cold, hard pebbles into the pool of silence that Jere stonily maintained. "Conrad and his daughter are both agreeable to the union."

"Agreeable?" Furious at the suggestion, Jere lost the last of his self-control. "Not to me. I absolutely refuse to marry that simpering lummox!"

Laird's great hands balled into fists. His face grew mottled. "Enough! No woman will be spoken of so in this household."

"You are right, sir. I shouldn't have ridiculed Miss Conrad, any more than you should belittle Lucy Danielson." He hesitated, then decided that since all-out war must ultimately be declared, it might as well happen. Father could never be any angrier than right now, after having had his principles thrown into his teeth.

"I'm sorry I can't live up to what you expect of me, but I wouldn't marry Miss Conrad if she were the only woman on earth. I will also never marry in order to increase our holdings. You married for love. So will I." Jere searched the granitelike face for any sign of softening. He found none. Years of pride and ambition had evidently erased Father's memories of the young man he once was.

Jere took a deep breath and freed himself from the invisible shackles he'd felt tightening around him ever since the conversation began. Should Father carry out his implied threat of disinheriting, perhaps even disowning, his natural heir, it meant losing both land and dreams. Yet something deep in Jere's soul compelled him to say, "I've loved Lucy Danielson since childhood. I always will. Marrying another would be akin to sacrilege. God and Dr. Luke willing, I plan to offer Lucy a betrothal ring one year from today."

His father laughed unpleasantly. "Which she will naturally accept. What girl wouldn't leap at the opportunities you offer?" He ignored Jere's murmur of protest. "I repeat my ultimatum. Either you marry Miss Conrad on or before your twenty-first birthday, or I shall not be responsible for the consequences."

Jere didn't trust himself to say more. He bolted from the room and from the house as if pursued by a thousand devils. A few minutes later, he mounted Ebony and galloped away, seething with the unfairness of it all. Just before he reached the rising ground leading to his favorite knoll, his pent-up emotions exploded into a war cry that echoed across the valley and bounced off the distant hills.

◆ ◆ ◆

Ebony poked his nose against his master's shoulder and whinnied, shattering Jere's reverie. How long had he been standing atop the knoll? He gazed at the westering sun. Rose-purple streaks heralded the near approach of dusk. Jere vaulted into the saddle and headed for Hickory Hill. Should he remain in the village after completing his errand and go straight to the Danielson home at the appointed time, thereby escaping another meeting with Father?

A hasty survey of his rumpled riding clothes scotched the idea. No gentleman would appear at his ladylove's birthday soiree in such condition, even though she had seen him far more disheveled many times. *Social conventions sometimes bring more trouble than they are worth,* he thought bleakly.

"Nobody knows the trouble I've seen," Jere sang mournfully, urging Ebony into a ground-devouring trot, then a canter, followed by a gallop. "Nobody knows but Jesus. . . ." He thought of the many times he'd heard field hands sing the haunting words, supposedly written by an unknown slave or slaves. Somehow their poignancy had never touched him as much as they did now. He sang on,

"Sometimes I'm up, sometimes I'm down,

Oh, yes, Lord;

Sometimes I'm almost to the ground,

Oh, yes, Lord."

Inexplicably comforted, Jere reached the outskirts of the village. He slowed Ebony to a trot and turned him toward the least likely place one would expect to find a gift for fifteen-year-old Lucy Danielson's birthday: the blacksmith shop.

Chapter 3

The grime-covered face of the village blacksmith brightened when Jere and Ebony halted before the smithy. A wide smile broke out, like whitecaps against a dark reef. "I was beginning to wonder if you'd forgotten our little secret." He removed a bulky package from the corner. "It's just as you wanted it."

Jere's usual high spirits returned. He leaped from the saddle and eagerly accepted the package, hefting its weight and grinning. "How did it turn out?"

"Perfect. Just perfect." The smile grew even larger. "Miss Lucy's gonna get the surprise of her life." The blacksmith chuckled gleefully and rubbed his hamlike hands, obviously enjoying the conspiracy. "Smart as she is, I predict that little lady will never guess what's in the package— not the way you had me wrap it. Your folks coming in for her birthday supper, as usual?"

"Yes." Jere tucked the heavy package in his saddlebag and paid the previously agreed-on price for his purchase. "As usual."

"Lemme see; it's been nigh onto fourteen years, ain't it?" Rolls of flesh nearly hid the twinkling eyes. "Folks ain't forgot the way you stood there straight as a wooden soldier when Miss Lucy toddled over to you. Or how you told the world what you wanted, right then and there." His joyful bellow rang out louder than the sound of hammers and anvil with which he plied his trade. He slapped his leather apron. "I hear tell you ain't changed your mind."

"Would you?" Jere demanded, already knowing the answer.

"No, siree. You're the second luckiest feller around."

"Second luckiest? Why not the luckiest?" Jere demanded.

"The way I figure is, I got me the best lass in the world. I've had her for more than thirty years. That makes Miss Lucy second." He scratched his balding head and his expression changed. "My wife wouldn't have made it through that bad spell of ague if it hadn't been for that child, which she ain't anymore. Dr. Luke was run off his feet taking care of sick folks. He didn't have time to stay with just one person. Miss Lucy waltzed into our house like she owned it. She told me what to do and made sure I did it." Gratitude added a touch of beauty to the rugged features. "There's nothing I wouldn't do for her. The whole village feels the same way." The big man cleared his throat. "That goes for you, too, son."

A bittersweet feeling threatened Jere's composure. Why couldn't Father admit Lucy's worth, when so many others recognized it and loved her for serving? *Or mine,* he mentally added. Family loyalty sealed his lips from uttering words that would betray the lord of the manor's attitude. Besides, folks—including the blacksmith—would find out soon enough. He'd wager Ebony against a swaybacked nag that before morning, news of his heated argument with Father would romp through the peaceful valley on tattletale feet. Each telling would add spice and lurid details until the tale had only passing acquaintance with truth.

Jere grinned in spite of himself. By the time the story traveled full circle through village and neighboring plantations then back to Hickory Manor, he'd be cast as everything from the prodigal son to Sir Galahad, depending on who repeated the gossip and how many times.

He gripped the blacksmith's hand, then swung into the saddle. "Thanks. I couldn't have done this without you, but you already know that."

The blacksmith swiped one hand across his face. "Yeah, but it won't be me who gets Miss Lucy's undying gratitude." His eyes glistened. "Wish I could be a mouse in a corner when she starts peeling away that paper."

His laggard customer just laughed. A touch of heels to Ebony's sides sent them racing down the wide street toward home. The last thing he needed tonight was another lecture about cutting the family's time for leaving short. "This is Lucy's birthday, and she has a right to be happy," he told the stallion.

Ebony snorted, extended his powerful legs, and headed for Hickory Manor.

They reached the stables at last light. Jere tossed the reins to a waiting stable boy, hid his package in the carriage the family used for more formal occasions, and hurried toward the house. He reached his room undetected and rang for hot water. After his bath, the dark-suited gentleman with the gleaming white shirtfront who stood brushing his sunny hair before the glass atop his chiffonier, bore little resemblance to Ebony's carelessly attired rider. Jere admitted without conceit that he would do and bounded downstairs after a servant tapped at his door and informed him the family was ready and waiting in the "libr'y."

Laird Cunningham raised one eyebrow but said nothing. Isobel, lovely in pale blue, smiled a welcome. Jinny curtseyed, her rose-pink skirts swaying with the motion. Alerted by his father's coldly stated plan for Jinny, Jere felt a protective surge of concern. He silently vowed she would not be sacrificed on the altar of greed. If Father ever attempted to force Jinny into a marriage not of her own choosing, Jere would thwart his plans. Even if it meant carrying her so far away that Father would never find her. God forbid it would come to that.

"You're staring at me as if you'd never seen me before," Jinny accused.

"I've never seen you look so beautiful," her brother told her.

She blushed until her surprised face matched her gown. "Why, Jere! You never use pretty words to me. Is it because—I mean, you act different."

"I never before realized how quickly you are growing up," he said soberly, wondering if his fear for her future showed in his eyes or in his voice.

Perhaps it had, for some of Jinny's radiance dimmed. Uncertainty crept into her face, and her gaze followed Jere's quick look at their father. With a rustle of skirts, she ran to Isobel and unnecessarily smoothed a wisp of her carefully arranged hair. "You're the one who looks beautiful. Doesn't she, Father?"

Jere hated the appraising look that came into his father's eyes before he bowed to his wife and said, "Mrs. Cunningham is always pleasing to behold." Why didn't he admit Mother was even lovelier than Jinny?

Jere held his sister's cloak while his father did the same for Mother. Donning his own, Jere trailed the others out the front door and down the steps to the waiting carriage. At first, Jinny excitedly chattered about the evening ahead. Her father's rigidity and lack of response soon silenced her. The rest of the journey was accomplished in total stillness, broken only when they reached Hickory Hill.

"I hope you acquired a gift suitable for the occasion," Laird Cunningham said in a voice that showed he had grave doubts about that very thing.

Jere knew the comment was directed at him but clung to his determination to make this a happy occasion for Lucy and refused to rise to the bait. Jinny quickly replied, "Oh, my, yes!

Mother and I sent away for a copy of Mr. Dickens's *A Christmas Carol*. Lucy has read her copy so many times, it is almost worn out."

"A quite suitable gift," her father mocked. "Especially for one obviously fond of frittering away valuable time on idle tales."

"That will be quite enough, Mr. Cunningham," Isobel said in a voice cold enough to freeze icicles. "*A Christmas Carol* is no idle tale. It offers great value to those who read it. I suggest you do so before criticizing those who have."

Jinny gasped. Jere wanted to cheer. He could count on one hand the times his mother had stood up against her husband in their children's presence. The last time had been so long ago, Jere couldn't remember the reason. He did remember shock at his father's reaction. A cool stare, then, "As you wish, my dear."

How would Father respond this time? Jere's lips twitched when Laird Cunningham hesitated, then said in a colorless voice, "As you wish, my dear," before irritably telling Jinny, "If you must make rude noises, Virginia, do cover your mouth."

A lace-adorned hand flew to obey, but Jere gave wordless thanks for the darkness he felt sure hid satisfaction dancing in his sister's expressive eyes.

His suspicions were confirmed when they reached the Danielson home and he helped Jinny from the carriage. She lingered long enough for their parents to reach the porch door and be out of earshot, then giggled and quoted, " 'The smallest worm will turn being trodden on. . . .' "

Jere squeezed her arm in relief. "Lord Clifford to the king in *Henry VI, Part 3*." Jinny was growing up, but she hadn't completely crossed the borders of childhood. Yet if she were still a child, why did he feel he had gained an ally, a staunch friend who would prove herself invaluable in coming days?

Pondering the strange thought, Jere ceremoniously followed his parents into the Danielson entryway, where a beaming Jackson Way took their cloaks. A loud gasp turned all heads toward Jinny, staring openmouthed at the staircase leading to the upper floor.

"What did I tell you, Virginia?" Laird Cunningham hissed, face red with annoyance. "Have you no manners whatsoever?" The next moment, his gaze followed his daughter's. His jaw dropped. He rubbed one hand across his eyes like someone awakening from a deep sleep and being unsure of his surroundings.

A small smile played over Isobel's sensitive lips. She laid a gentle hand on her son's dark sleeve and unobtrusively pointed with the other.

Jere turned his back on his thunderstruck father and looked up. In the next few seconds, he felt himself running a gamut of emotions, from shock to wonder, pride to humility. Two long strides put him at the foot of the staircase. He rested a strong hand on the carved top of the newel—and waited.

◆　◆　◆

A short time before Jere Cunningham stepped into the family carriage at Hickory Manor, Roxy reverently held up a gown the same hue as November sunlight and Lucy's bedroom walls. "Mmm, mmm, this do be fine," she crooned. "The finest ever you had." She carefully dropped the garment over Lucy's head and fastened the row of tiny buttons from the modest neckline to the girl's slender waist. She spread the gown's ruffled skirt over her charge's many petticoats. Lucy scorned the heavy wire and whalebone crinolines her friends wore. She claimed they "squished her innards," and she absolutely refused to put herself through such torture for the sake of fashion.

Roxy leaned against a dark wooden bedpost. "Honey-chile, 'twouldn' s'prise me if your real mammy is lookin' down from heaven this very minute. I s'pect Miss Fiona's bustin' with pride and pointin' you out to the angels."

Lucy gazed at the silken-clad figure in the bedroom mirror. "Do you really, truly think so, Mammy?" Her lips trembled. She tried to blink back tears conjured up by the precious image of a mother she only knew through pictures and what she'd been told by others. Despite her best efforts, one spilled.

Roxy brushed it away with a gentle dark finger. "I does, and I reckon Master Cunningham's goin' to think you're just as fine." She pursed her lips. "Only trouble is, my chile's done gettin' all growed up." A shadow crossed the face peering over Lucy's shoulder and into the mirror. A sigh escaped.

"Don't you want me to grow up, Mammy?" Lucy tremulously asked.

"I does and I doesn't," was the cryptic answer. "Now, run along. It's time for the comp'ny." She placed her hands on her hips and stood with arms akimbo. "And don't be forgettin' what Dr. Luke always says."

"I won't." Heart overflowing with happiness, Lucy whirled toward Roxy and mimicked Dr. Luke, " 'Handsome is as handsome does.' " The sound of carriage wheels set her heart to thumping. "They're here, Mammy!" She ran into the hall and rustled her way to the top of the staircase, with Roxy close behind.

"No slidin' down, you hear?"

Lucy's imp of mischief, perpetually poised for action, tempted her to do just that. She'd love to see Laird Cunningham's face if she landed at the bottom just as he stepped inside the front door! Lucy firmly shook her head. Tonight, she would be a lady. She wouldn't embarrass Daddy Doc before a man he persisted in keeping as a friend, although Lucy couldn't for the life of her see why.

One hand lightly touched the railing. One dainty slipper reached for the first step, then hesitated. Something about the moment made her long to hold it close forever. To stay at the top of the stairs, secure in Mammy's care. To savor the aroma of roasting meat, the tang of wood smoke from the fireplace, and the bustle in the entryway below, as Jackson Way proudly took away the guests' cloaks.

Don't be foolish, she told herself. *This is just another birthday, even if you do have a new, becoming gown. You're as bad as Mammy with her "does and doesn't" want you to grow up. Next thing, you'll be having the vapors.* She laughed and shook her head so vigorously, the curls Roxy had insisted on pinning into a cluster threatened to escape their moorings and come tumbling down. The action freed her senses, and her reluctance to move vanished.

A loud gasp from below caught Lucy's attention. She gazed down at Jinny, lovely as a wild rose. At frowning Laird Cunningham, whose change of countenance more than repaid the forfeiture of a downward plunge. At his wife, whose smiling eyes and mouth warmed Lucy's heart.

Last of all, she faced Jere, standing next to the newel. Lucy had never seen him so elegant and refined. Where was her playmate of former years? Gone forever, replaced by the man whose hair looked molten gold in the lamplight, whose blue eyes held admiration and love.

She caught her breath at the indescribable sweetness of the look. A feeling far stronger than all the comradeship and adoration she had freely given her friend stirred in Lucy's heart. She squared her shoulders and, step by graceful step, made her way downstairs to take her place where she knew she belonged: at Jere Cunningham's side.

Chapter 4

I t came like a storm in summer. Unexpected. Unwanted. Unnecessary. Afterward, Jere censured himself for failing to observe small-cloud warnings, starting with his father's expression when Lucy first appeared. Never again could he dismiss her as a child. In all probability, she would continue to lapse into childlike behavior now and then, but the radiance and grace shown tonight proved her worthy of the heir of Cunningham.

Jere noticed little else. The change in Lucy's dress and demeanor was enough to distract any man. Her modest home sparkled with lamplight and laughter. It provided a fitting setting for the capable young woman at the opposite end of the table from Dr. Luke. Quiet orders to Jackson Way resulted in a succession of vittles. Great platters of pink Virginia ham. Luscious yellow sweet potatoes. Collard greens. Beaten biscuits light enough to float from the lace-covered dining room table, accompanied by home-churned butter and a variety of preserves. Jackson Way beamed and kept a seemingly endless supply coming until all at last protested they could eat no more.

As if on cue, Roxy demoted her husband from the role of waiter to table clearer. She herself carried in the *pièce de résistance*—Lucy's birthday cake. Seven layers high and swathed in delicate frosting whiter than Roxy's turban, it even brought a grunt of approval from Laird Cunningham.

"Roxy, you've outdone yourself," Dr. Luke solemnly told her after his first generous bite. "Every year your cake gets better. This one really is the best."

She beamed, spoiling any attempt at modesty. "Mmm, mmm. Strange how folks be so full, yet have space for cake." A burst of laughter greeted her sally. Roxy bowed her head and backed out of the room, voice swelling in song.

"My Lord calls me,
He calls me by the lightnin';
The trumpet sounds within-a my soul,
I ain't got long to stay here."[2]

The rich voice faded kitchenward.

Laird's features congealed. "How dare she sing that abominable song? When are you going to sell her and Jackson Way and get decent house servants?"

Dr. Luke laughed outright. "Lucy and I prefer loyalty and excellent service, music included. We couldn't get along without Roxy and Jackson Way." He smiled down the length of the table at his daughter.

Laird raised an expressive eyebrow. "She shows insolence and lack of respect to you and your guests," he carped. "Correct me if I'm mistaken—I'm sure I am not; that song was first used during the Nat Turner Rebellion, right here in Virginia in 1831. It was and continues to serve as a signal for secret meetings of slaves, escape plans, and other nefarious behavior."

2   Negro spiritual, chorus

◆ ◆ ◆

Consternation choked off Jere's protest. How despicable of his father to introduce such an unpleasant topic of conversation at such a time!

Laird continued, lecturing as if the others were historical illiterates. He sounded like he was reading from a textbook. "It's one of the biggest blots on Virginia history. A black slave and preacher, leading sixty to seventy slaves. Sixty whites died, including the family of the man who owned Turner!"

"Let's not forget the one hundred innocent slaves killed by angry whites," Dr. Luke quietly reminded. "Including everyone in Roxy and Jackson Way's family. The two of them barely escaped with their lives. Now, I believe it's time to repair to the parlor for coffee. I must confess that I prefer the small sitting room, but this is an occasion. We shall do Lucy honor by sitting on less comfortable chairs."

"Not at all," she protested. Laughter swept color back into the cheeks that had turned pale a few minutes earlier. "We will use the sitting room, as usual."

"Good." Dr. Luke stood. "Ladies, if you please. Come, Laird."

Jere felt reprieved. Tonight wasn't the first time the lord of the manor had publicly objected to Dr. Luke about Roxy and Jackson Way's lack of formality.

Yet he had never before gone this far. Mother's set face and tightly compressed lips betrayed the fear she would say far too much if she stepped in. If only Father would hold his terrible tongue! Jere had little hope of such a miracle. Laird Cunningham hated not having the last word.

It happened as Jere feared. Minutes after the party seated themselves in the other room and Lucy served coffee from the polished tray that awaited them, Laird returned to his obsession like a deer to a salt lick. He took a sip of midnight black liquid and declared, "Really, Lucas. You *must* do something about this impossible situation."

He paused to let the command sink in. "If not for your sake, then do it for the the rest of us. There's already unrest in the slave quarters. The shameful way you allow your blacks to rule the roost is common talk. It can't help encouraging rebellion in others. God knows we have more than enough of that, ever since the pack of lies called *Uncle Tom's Cabin* was published eight or nine years ago.

"The way I hear it, the Stowe woman came prancing down here breathing fire and chock-full of her Northern ideas.[3] She poked around until she found a few mistreated slaves, which, unfortunately, can be done if you look hard enough. Then she headed back to where she should have stayed in the first place and wrote the book." He clenched his free hand. "I tell you this. If war between North and South ever comes, it will largely be that meddlesome woman's fault!"

Lucy stirred in her chair and started to speak. Dr. Luke warned her with the look Jere had seen dozens of times before in volatile circumstances. A muscle twitched in his cheek. He ignored the latter part of the tirade and addressed Laird's earlier comments. "You call my treatment of Roxy and Jackson Way shameful. Hardly." His Scandinavian blue eyes flashed, but his impeccable manners held. "It is true they serve us, but there is neither bond nor free in this household."

A triumphant smile curled Laird's thin lips. "You inherited Roxy and Jackson Way from your parents. Call them anything you like. They are still slaves."

3   Harriet Beecher Stowe (1851–52)

"No, they are not." The flat denial hung in the tense air. "Slaves are subject to their masters. Servants choose where and whom they will serve."

Match to powder keg. Laird looked jolted. Coffee spilled from the cup he clutched in shaking hands. "Sir, *don't tell me you've freed Roxy and Jackson Way!*" Horror punctuated every word.

"I have. They've had their manumission papers for years. They are free to go at any time." Dr. Luke's eyes glowed. "Thank God there has never been any question about them wanting to leave Lucy and me. They consider us the family they lost through revenge."

Laird Cunningham looked dumbstruck. Jere silently compared him with Dr. Luke. Both God-fearing. Both hardworking. Yet one lived by the letter of the law, one by its spirit. It made the latter the stronger man.

For the second time that day, Isobel Cunningham asserted herself, in the same steely voice she had used a few hours earlier. "Gentlemen, we will speak of other things." Her tone permitted no disagreement and was in sharp contrast to the loving smile she aimed at Lucy. "Today should be happy, my dear, not a time for airing grievances. You must open your presents before we take our leave. Jinny, I believe you insisted on carrying ours in your reticule?"

"Y–yes." She shot a frightened glance at her father and scurried to get it.

Jere watched Lucy unwrap her gift, hoping with all his heart the evening would end without another incident. His heart went out to Lucy, valiantly attempting to gather the remaining fragments of her birthday joy into a semblance of the real thing.

"Thank you so much," she said, clasping *A Christmas Carol* with both hands. Honest pleasure shone in the eyes more blue than green tonight, because of her pale yellow gown. Her few tiny freckles glinted like specks of gold. "Now I know why Jinny stared so at my tattered copy some time ago."

Jere bit his lip. How gallantly she carried on! *She always will,* a small voice inside him reminded. *No matter where she is or what she faces, Lucy Danielson will carry on, with banners.*

Isobel turned to her son. "I believe Jere has a gift for you, as well."

He had purposely left it in the carriage, planning to bring it in at the proper time and bestow it on the girl he loved. Now Jere rebelled at the idea. In spite of the Danielsons' efforts to restore normalcy, tarnish lay over the celebration. He could not bear to present the special gift on which he had spent so much time and effort in such circumstances. If Father dishonored his choice, Jere would not be able to control his temper. Lucy and Dr. Luke had gone through enough tonight. They should not be forced to endure a row that would make the Cunningham men's earlier altercation pale by comparison.

Laird spoke for the first time since his wife intervened. "Well?"

A quick glance around the room alerted Jere to the fact that everyone present recognized it as a challenge. He rose to his feet and forced a smile. "Sorry, Lucy. I don't have your gift with me." He didn't. It was still in the carriage.

Quick understanding sprang to her eyes. "It's all right. You can drop by tomorrow. It will give me something to look forward to."

He had never been prouder of her than at that moment. Not even when he had stood at the bottom of the staircase and watched her come down and stand beside him. He stood, took her hand, and formally bowed. "Until tomorrow."

"Must you go? You haven't seen Daddy Doc's gift," Lucy said reproachfully. Some of the sparkle came back into her face. "It's a book, too. A wonderful book about famous persons, such as George Washington, Thomas Jefferson, and Benjamin Franklin. It also has stories about people who are important right now, such as Abraham Lincoln."

Jere cringed. In her eagerness to ease the tension, Lucy had unwittingly chosen the worst subject possible. Laird Cunningham hated and feared Lincoln, an antislavery Republican. He idolized Democrat Stephen A. Douglas, who contended each state or territory had the right to choose whether they would be slave or free. Great had been Laird's rejoicing when Douglas defeated Lincoln for a United States Senate seat in 1858. Loud was his outcry after the May 1860 Republican National Convention chose Lincoln as their candidate.

To make matters worse, the Democratic party had been weakened by splitting into factions. Northern Democrats nominated Douglas for president. The Southern proslavery wing, angry with Douglas, nominated Vice President John Breckinridge, now serving with President Buchanan. A fourth party, the Constitutional Union party, nominated former Tennessee Senator John Bell.

For months, Laird Cunningham and other concerned plantation owners made dire predictions about the future if Lincoln became president. Now only twelve days remained until the November 6 Election Day. Jere shuddered to think what his home atmosphere would be like should Lincoln win. Or what struggles Virginia and the rest of the country would face. Talk of secession by several Southern states already ran rampant. What would Lincoln do if the South rose up in defense of her way of life and tried to leave the Union?

Jere thought of the warning given in Matthew 12:25: *"And Jesus knew their thoughts, and said unto them, Every kingdom divided against itself is brought to desolation; and every city or house divided against itself shall not stand."*

A hollow feeling grew in him. Tonight had seen the fulfillment of the Scripture in small part. Laird Cunningham's attitude had created a rift in the two families' long-held friendship. Lucy's innocent remark had widened it. Now more than ever, the lord of the manor would vehemently oppose any alliance between the houses of Cunningham and Danielson.

At last they were in the carriage and headed toward Hickory Manor. Laird unclamped his tight lips and said, "You made a fool of yourself tonight, Jeremiah. Only a simpleton attends a birthday celebration empty-handed. Not that the girl needed anything from you. She appeared perfectly satisfied with your mother and sister's gift. And, of course, her book about Lincoln." He spat out the name like a morsel of spoiled food.

Jinny clutched her brother's arm, but Isobel sat up straight. "It is not my son who played the fool, Mr. Cunningham. No *gentleman* transgresses the laws of hospitality as you did tonight." Her stinging words fell like ice pellets.

Jere waited for the inevitable explosion. Stopping an unpleasant conversation was one thing. A slur against Father's conduct was far more serious. The blood of proud Scottish chiefs flowed in his veins, and his greatest vanity lay in being considered every inch a gentleman.

"How dare you speak so to me?" Laird inquired in a deadly voice.

She didn't give an inch. "I dare because I must. No man should be allowed to act in such a manner. We shall continue this discussion in private."

Jinny was right. For better or worse—and all indications pointed to the latter—the worm had turned. For the second time that day, Jere Cunningham wanted to stand up and cheer.

Chapter 5

Hickory Hill, Virginia
April 12, 1861

Lucy Danielson fingered the collar of the simple dark cotton dress she wore when assisting her father. Her hands dropped to the towering stack of sun-dried sheets and towels fresh from washing in strong soap and boiling water. Her mind far away, Lucy automatically began folding them and stowing them away in the storage area adjoining her father's examining room.

She looked out the open window, rejoicing in the warm April day. How long ago her disastrous fifteenth birthday celebration seemed! " 'Weeping may endure for a night, but joy cometh in the morning,'" she softly quoted. "Psalm 30:5."

Her hands stilled. A small smile tugged at her lips. Joy hadn't come on the morning of October 26 as she had expected. All day she waited for Jere Cunningham to keep his promise and bring her gift. She had almost given up on him when he and Ebony dashed into the Danielson yard in the late afternoon. Storm clouds darkened his blue eyes as he stepped inside the front door. "I'm sorry. I couldn't get here any sooner." Lucy suspected from the firm set of Jere's lips and jaw that there had been another altercation with his father, perhaps concerning a certain red-haired Danielson girl. She was incensed. Why must Laird Cunningham be so set against her? So what if she didn't have wealth and lands? Wasn't a heart full of love enough? She felt a blush begin at her collar and move upward, so she quickly led Jere into the small sitting room. "It's all right. I'm just glad you came." In an attempt to erase the anger in his face, she planted her hands on her hips and demanded, "All right, Jeremiah Marcus, Jerabone, Markabone, Napoleon Bonaparte Cunningham, where's my present?"

Her tactic worked. Jere threw his head back and snickered loudly. "Aren't you ever going to forget that?"

"No one in Hickory Hill except your father is ever going to forget it," she taunted. "I never did understand how he kept from hearing about it." She bit her lip. She actually did know. Village sympathies had always lain with son, not father. In addition, few people cared or were brave enough to risk the lord of the manor's wrath by reporting Jere's shortcomings.

Lucy returned to her attack. "The idea! Telling the brand-new schoolmaster your name was Jeremiah Marcus, Jerabone, Markabone, Napoleon Bonaparte Cunningham on the very first day he walked into the classroom and took roll."

Jere's eyes gleamed with memories and mischief. "Don't scold. I was only ten. Besides, I couldn't resist testing the new schoolmaster."

"You didn't even *try* to resist," she accused. "It's a wonder he didn't punish you severely."

"He was a good scout." Jere chuckled, the last shreds of trouble disappearing from his face. "He just stood there all solemn and tall until everyone stopped laughing. Then he quietly

said, 'That's an awfully long name, Jeremiah. Do you mind being called something shorter?' "
Jere grinned sheepishly. "No one moved a muscle. I felt like crawling under a table but managed to mumble, 'Call me Jere, please.'

"The teacher's mouth twitched. 'Very well,' he said. Then he grinned and began laughing. The whole room joined in." Jere smiled at the memory. In an apparent burst of high spirits, he grabbed Lucy's hands and whirled her around the entryway.

"Stop stalling," she told him after she caught her breath from the wild dance and could speak again. She pulled her hands free and scowled, knowing her uptilted lips spoiled any attempt at sternness. "I want my present. Now."

Jere folded his arms across his chest. His eyes sparkled with the ten-year-old mischief that had prompted the schoolroom incident. "Really, Miss Danielson, your curiosity is mighty unbecoming for a proper young lady."

"So when have I ever been a proper young lady?" she asked.

He gave her a dazzling smile. "You were last night. Surely Roxy and Dr. Luke told you that, as well as your mirror. 'Mirror, mirror, on the wall, who's the fairest. . . ?' " He bowed from the waist in a grandiloquent manner.

Lucy's heart bounced at the open admiration in his gaze when he straightened up. "Thank you ever so much, kind sir." She spread her green-checked gingham skirts and curtseyed low in imitation of a coy Southern belle. "I do declare, sir. I remember a certain gentleman promising that same proper young lady a present." Lucy fluttered her eyelashes. Ugh. How could her girlfriends bear to act so? It made her feel like a ninny.

Jere threw his hands into the air. "I surrender. Sit down and I'll bring it in."

He strode out and returned a few minutes later carrying a good-sized package, which he carefully deposited in her lap.

Lucy touched it with an exploring finger. "It's heavy." She took off the outer wrappings and revealed a box. She opened it and found more wrappings. Another box. "What is this? A treasure hunt?"

"You might say so." Jere chortled. A suspicious glance showed he was thoroughly enjoying her bewilderment.

Lucy continued removing wrapping and boxes until, "A brick?" she said disbelievingly. "You gave me a *brick* for my birthday?" She stared at the heavy, offensive object lying off-center in the bottom of the last box.

"You mean you don't like my present?" Jere laughed until tears rolled. "You could at least be polite and pretend."

Lucy cocked her head to one side and silently surveyed his oh-so-innocent face. Did the silly brick hold a special significance? Was it his way of hinting that someday they would build a home together, using the brick for a cornerstone? The thought sent another rush of blood to her already overheated cheeks. "Is it. . .does it. . .I mean, is there a reason for giving me a brick?" she finally asked in a very small voice.

He lifted one eyebrow. "Oh, yes. A very special reason."

Lucy couldn't move. *My stars. Is Jere about to declare his intentions? Again? If he does, what shall I do? What should I say? Heroines in novels faint at such moments, but I can't imagine myself swooning.*

She was spared the painful decision of how to answer when after a long pause Jere told her, "The brick is actually camouflage for your real present."

Lucy didn't know whether to be glad or relieved. The strange new feelings of the night before suffered a setback and mild disappointment, but part of her didn't want things to change between them. "There's nothing else in the box."

"Oh, but there is. Reach to the very bottom, alongside the brick," he said in a voice that showed he was as excited as she. Lucy obeyed and took out a hard something swathed in more paper. She discarded the final wrappings and a small box appeared. Lucy hesitated, heart pounding. The box was just large enough to hold a ring. Lucy swallowed. Now what? *Please, God, help me not to make a fool of myself,* she prayed.

"Open it, Lucy," Jere whispered.

With trembling fingers, she followed directions. The contents of the box made her gasp. A small brooch lay on a nest of soft cotton. Not a jeweled or antique brooch, but one far more precious to Lucy—a tiny lamp hammered from metal and burnished to a soft glow. The pin was a miniature replica of the lamp carried by Florence Nightingale that Lucy had seen in pictures. She picked it up and held it in the palm of her hand. "Oh, Jere!" Tears spilled. "How could you ever find such a perfect gift?"

"I didn't find it. I made it for you." His intense blue gaze never left her face. "I've been working on it for months, whenever I could steal a few minutes from chores at Hickory Manor. My friend, the blacksmith, taught me how and kept my secret." He cleared his throat. A slight uncertainty crept into his face.

"The blacksmith says I crafted it so well, it will last forever. You can pass it down to our—your children and grandchildren." Color crept up to the golden brown hair across his forehead.

Lucy knew that if she didn't do something, anything, she would burst into tears of joy and be unable to tell Jere why. She quickly pinned the brooch just above her heart and impulsively sprang from her chair. A few steps took her to Jere. She threw her arms around him, rose to the tips of her soft-soled slippers, and kissed him. Then, with a gasp at her brazen action, she darted into the entryway, unceremoniously leaving her astounded guest frozen to the spot.

◆　◆　◆

A flash of red and the call of a cardinal to his mate just outside the open window rudely interrupted Lucy's woolgathering. Her face burned, as it did each time she remembered the kiss. Her fingers stole again to her collar and gently stroked the tiny lamp's smooth surface. She had worn the brooch day and night since the day she received it.

Lucy chuckled to herself. The kiss wasn't all she remembered about that fateful afternoon. Or the lamp pin. Jere's dumbfounded expression when she kissed him never failed to bring a smile to her heart and lips. Thank goodness Jere was gentleman enough not to remind her of how forward she had been! She knew he hadn't forgotten the incident, any more than she could forget. His just-biding-my-time expression and occasional comment that sixteen was a good age for a girl to become betrothed, preferably to someone a few years older, made clear his love for her, without pledging vows of eternal devotion. The love that hadn't changed since he was a boy of six.

"I'm the one who has changed, God," she whispered. "I feel years older than I was just six months ago. If Jere brings me a ring on my next birthday and Daddy Doc agrees, I'll be the happiest girl who ever lived. You've blessed me so much. Help me be worthy of Jere and a good mother to his children."

She hesitated, wanting to cling to the sunny moment, knowing only too well that shadows and perhaps darkness lurked just around the next bend in life's road. "Father, so much has happened in such a short time that sometimes I feel the world has gone crazy."

When had the fog of anxiety first begun to cloud her normally bright skies? Lucy thought back to her birthday dinner. Laird Cunningham had all but accused Mammy Roxy and Jackson Way of being part of some dark and devious plot. To do what, Lucy had no idea. Escape? Hardly, when they were free to leave any time they chose. Slaves, including some on neighboring plantations, might use the song "Steal Away" as a signal. Not Mammy. When she sang about the Lord calling her and a trumpet sounding in her soul, she expressed the deep faith she had passed on to her charge in good measure. The words, *I ain't got long to stay here,* reflected her yearning for heaven and the family who had been so cruelly torn from her and Jackson Way long ago.

The seeds of depression planted in Lucy's heart that birthday evening had been temporarily overshadowed by the gift of the lamp pin. Yet they sprouted alarmingly on November 6, when Abraham Lincoln won the presidency of the United States. Consternation sped through Hickory Hill. Talk of Virginia leaving the Union intensified, especially after South Carolina actually seceded. A month later, Alabama, Florida, Georgia, Louisiana, and Mississippi followed suit.

The flames of independence flared even higher when the six states sent representatives to Montgomery, Alabama, in February. There they formed the Confederate States of America and elected Mississippian Jefferson Davis as their president. Two days before Lincoln was inaugurated in March, Texas became part of the Confederacy.

In his inaugural address, Lincoln wisely omitted any mention of threatening immediate force against the South. However, he firmly stated that the Union would stand forever. He would use the nation's full power to hold federal possessions in the South. This infuriated many. Virginia teetered on the edge of secession.

The tenth state to be admitted to the Union was greatly divided on whether to remain with the Union or join the Confederacy. So was Hickory Hill. Secession became such an issue between families and friends that many "done chose up sides and are about to start throwin' rocks at each other," as Jackson Way put it.

Lucy and her father kept their opinions to themselves. "I'm a physician, not a politician," Dr. Luke protested, when pressed by warring factions. "God put me here to patch up folks. He gave me Lucy to help. We have a full-time job, just doing what we're meant to do."

Yet just the night before, the troubled doctor had privately confessed to his daughter, "I don't know how much longer Virginia will remain neutral. We have hotheads on both sides." A somber hue marred his usually cheerful countenance. "It's like the sword of Damocles, suspended over our heads and hanging by a single hair. It won't take much to break the hair and free the sword. I fear what will happen when it comes plunging down."

Lucy suddenly felt cold, even though sunlight streamed in the window as brightly as ever. A long time ago, she'd heard a granny-woman say she felt like something was walking across her grave. Lucy hadn't understood what the woman meant. Now she did. If the sword fell, it could destroy all she held dear.

A few hours later, her worst fears were realized.

Chapter 6

Footsteps in the entryway outside the cozy sitting room where Lucy sat reading took her away from King Arthur's court and into the present. She raised her head and frowned. The steps sounded shambling, not sure and crisp, like Daddy Doc's firm stride. Was something wrong with him?

The door flew open. Lucy jumped to her feet as her father reeled into the room, blond hair awry, face whiter than the sheets and towels Lucy had folded earlier. A tornado of dread swept through her. "What's wrong? Are you sick?"

"Sick at heart." Pain contorted his face and dulled the blue of his eyes to gray. Lucy recognized the look from times she had seen her father give the best of his skills in an attempt to save a life, only to face defeat in the end.

Her father dropped heavily into a chair. He stared straight at Lucy, but she felt he wasn't really seeing her. "Word just came. The Confederate forces have fired on Fort Sumter, the federal military post in the Charleston, South Carolina, harbor."

Lucy felt herself stiffen. "What does it mean?"

A glazed look further dulled his eyes. "War. Misery, suffering, needless death. North against South. Brother against brother. Friend against friend. God help us all—and forgive the sins that have led to this terrible thing!"

His outburst shocked Lucy to the core. Even in critical situations, she had never heard him speak so. "Why?" she cried. "There must be a way to stop it."

"The time for that is past. It ended with the firing of the first shot."

Horrified by the hopelessness in his voice, a sob rose to Lucy's lips and escaped. She blindly fled to her father, who opened his arms and encircled her. She felt the peace of his embrace—along with something else: his need to receive comfort, not just give it. "God won't allow war to come," she faltered, desperately trying to reassure herself as well as her father but knowing how unconvincing she sounded. "He doesn't want people killing each other."

The arms about her tightened. "No, Lucy. He doesn't. Yet men choose to take control instead of leaving the world in His hands. God gave us agency. When we make terrible choices, He stands aside and lets us suffer the consequences."

"Sometimes He intervenes."

"Yes." Dr. Luke held her away from him and looked down into her wet eyes. "We can pray this will be one of those times." His lips thinned to a straight line. "It's hard enough fighting ignorance and superstition and sickness. If war comes, we will be forced to tend hundreds of victims of man's folly."

"You don't think war will come to Hickory Hill!" Lucy freed herself and slid to her knees in front of his chair. "It can't. It just can't," she brokenly protested. "Our valley is so peaceful." She put her hands over her ears, vainly attempting to silence the imagined sound of cannons, the cries for help from the wounded.

Dr. Luke gently removed her hands and cradled them in his own. "I'm terribly afraid today's action by South Carolina will inflame Virginians to the point of secession," Dr. Luke told her. "The worst thing is, both North and South believe they have a cause worth fighting for, even dying."

"Who cares about causes?" Lucy flared. "We are all part of the same country. How can a cause be important enough to make us go to war against ourselves?" She anxiously searched her father's face for help in understanding the precarious position into which the country she loved had fallen.

"Many wonder the same thing," her father said. Some of the blue returned to his eyes, but none of their usual sparkle. "It is a dangerous thing when both sides believe they are right. That is what's happening now. The North is committed to freeing the slaves and preserving the Union. The South will fight to maintain a way of life begun by those who pioneered and won their lands through suffering and hardship. Only God knows how or when it will end."

He dropped Lucy's hands and stroked her hair. "You need to face the worst. If war comes, as I feel it will, our lives will never be the same." He paused before adding, "Neither will Jere's. If I know Laird Cunningham, and I believe I do, he will move heaven and earth to ensure his son fights for the Confederacy."

"No!" Lucy shrieked. She bounded to her feet and glared down at her father. "If he wants war, *he* should be the one to go fight it, not his son. Jere can't go. I won't let him!" More protective of the man she loved than a wildcat guarding her cubs, Lucy felt herself wave good-bye to lingering childhood.

"How does Jere feel about it?" Dr. Luke asked.

Lucy's defiance crumpled. She would fight Laird Cunningham to the death, but if Jere chose to go, she would be helpless. "I don't know. Oh, Daddy Doc, how can such things be?"

◆   ◆   ◆

Lucy's poignant cry resounded across the valley and echoed off the distant ridges above Hickory Hill. They grew even louder three days later when Lincoln ordered Union troops to reclaim Fort Sumter. The South saw it as a declaration of war. Soon Arkansas, North Carolina, and Tennessee joined the Confederacy.

So did Virginia, in spite of vehement protests by those in the western counties. Strongly loyal to the Union, they threatened to leave Virginia and become a separate state.[4] Southern patriots branded them as traitors.

Once Virginia joined the Confederacy, Jere Cunningham's life became a living hell. Laird Cunningham continually harped on the need for Jere to enlist in the "Cause."

"Would to God I weren't desperately needed here," he lamented. "Since I am, you must go in my place."

Jere didn't know what to do. The desire to please his father for once in his life warred with his own convictions. "Or lack of convictions," he told Dr. Luke one day while waiting for Lucy to come downstairs. "I see right and wrong on both sides." He buried his head in his hands. When he raised it, he felt his mouth twist into a grimace. "Our preacher told me it was my duty to serve. He said God would give the South victory over the oppressors. My God isn't Northern *or* Southern. Claiming He is on one side is simply an excuse to justify war."

4   This separation led to the eventual statehood of West Virginia in 1863.

"My heart goes out to you," Dr. Luke quietly told him. "I wish I had the answer. Instead, I struggle over my own place of service. I'd like nothing better than to stay right here. I doubt it will be possible." He gripped Jere's hand.

Lucy's quick footsteps on the stairs effectively ended the conversation, but not Jere's dilemma. It worsened one afternoon a few weeks later when his father called him into the drawing room. In the past months, Jere had grown to hate the room that had seen so many quarrels. Every tick of the mantel clock prolonged the battles. Strange. Until now he had never noticed how relentlessly it marked time. Now he groaned. What new torment had Father dreamed up?

Laird Cunningham's latest ploy far exceeded Jere's wildest fears and imaginings. He carefully seated himself in the chair across from the one his son occupied. His colorless eyes gleamed. "I have a proposition for you, Jeremiah." He fitted the tips of his fingers together and made a teepee before aiming a calculating look toward Jere. "Do you still hope to marry the Danielson girl?"

Jere clutched at his frayed temper with all his might. "Yes, I intend to marry *Miss Danielson*, when the time is right for both of us."

"I am ready to withdraw my objections—on one condition."

Jere's heart leaped at the first statement, plummeted with the second. Father never traded unless sure he would best his opponent. "That condition is. . . ?" He marveled that the words could crowd out of his suddenly dry throat.

Another long, searching look probed the depths of Jere's soul. He had the feeling eternity hung in the balance. Then Laird said, "If you will enlist and serve your country, I will no longer oppose your ill-advised choice of mate. It will not take long for the South to drive the enemy from her lands. I fully expect this ill-conceived impertinence to end long before your birthday in August."

He paused to let his proposition sink in before folding his arms across his chest and tucking his stubborn chin deeper into his high collar. "You will come home having done your God-given duty. You will be twenty-one. The land set aside for you will be ready and waiting. If you present the betrothal ring as planned, Dr. Danielson will insist on his daughter having a year in which to prepare for her marriage. During that time, you will build a fitting home for the woman you intend to wed."

Once long ago, Jere and Ebony had been caught in a hailstorm that pelted them with ice balls the size of walnuts. In the few minutes before they reached shelter, both were bruised and battered. So it was now. Each word bruised Jere's spirit and battered against reason. What a diabolical plan, yet how canny! With his usual unerring instinct, Father had ferreted out Jere's weak spot: Lucy. Now he had made clear that he intended to use it to conquer his rebellious son.

"Well?" The word cracked like a horsewhip.

Jere steadily eyed the father he loved but could not please, no matter how hard he tried. What if he acceded to the lord of the manor's wishes and enlisted? What if he refused? The questions smoldered in his soul, then burst into a raging flame. He had to know the answers, no matter how terrible they might be.

"Speak up, boy. What's it to be? Will you do as I command?"

Jere took a deep breath, held it, then slowly expelled it. "If I refuse. . . ?"

Rage changed the granite-hard face to an ugly mask. "Should you be half-witted enough to cross me in this, you will henceforth be no son of mine. I will have no part of you. The land earmarked for you will be given to the man Jinny marries." Laird stood and strode to the door on giant steps, turned, and flung back, "You have one week to decide. Seven days from now you will pack and leave Hickory Manor. Either you will take up arms for your country or go wherever you choose, so long as it is out of my sight. I cannot force you to leave Hickory Hill, but I give you fair warning."

He shook a long, bony finger at his son. "If you stay, no neighbor will hire you. I will see to that. If we meet on the street, I shall neither recognize you nor speak." Again he paused, then fired the most significant weapon in his arsenal. "I shall also forbid your mother and Jinny to have anything more to do with you."

White-hot fury brought Jere to his feet. "Only a coward threatens from behind women's skirts." Scorn underlined each word. "Nothing on earth, including you, can keep me from Mother and Jinny. Do you think they will allow it? Lord of the manor you may be; lord of creation you are not." His voice rang in the silent room. If the truth sounded a death knell to reconciliation with Father, so be it.

Laird Cunningham turned apoplectic. "How dare you speak to me like this?" he thundered. "It is a commandment of God that you honor your father.[5] I myself taught you His precepts."

Jere didn't give an inch. "They also require me to honor my mother. Forsaking her would not show honor." Another accusation poured out. "The Bible also warns, 'Fathers, provoke not your children to anger, lest they be discouraged.' "[6]

His father remained rigid, yet Jere had the feeling he had suddenly shrunk in stature and grown hollow. Pity welled up in Jere. It softened his voice. "Father, I haven't yet said I won't fight." He ignored the hope flickering in the watching eyes. "I know your offer to set aside your feelings about Lucy was not easy. I thank you for making it. On the other hand, she can't be a pawn. Or a carrot dangled before my nose to make me do your will." He spread his hands wide.

"Don't you see? I have to decide my own course. We are talking about my conscience and my life, Father. Consider. What if you send your only son into battle and he comes home to lie in the family plot? How will you feel?"

Laird straightened his shoulders. The look of a fanatic came into his face. "If that comes to pass, and I pray to God it never shall, I can always be proud I had the courage to do what was right. You have one week to decide." The first hint of emotion he had shown during the entire conversation roughened his voice. "If you cannot serve for the girl's sake or for that of your country, go for your mother and sister. If war reaches Hickory Manor and I am killed, they will not be safe from invaders." He turned on his heel and marched out, closing the door behind him as firmly as he'd closed off any chance of compromise.

Jere could not help respecting his father for the valiant fight he was making on behalf of what he undeniably believed was right. He walked to the fireplace, cold and empty now, and leaned his head against the mantel. If only Father's passion were directed toward anything but "the Cause"!

The door opened behind him. *Please, God, don't let it be Father,* Jere silently pleaded. *I can't talk with him any longer just now. I must have time to think.*

5   Exodus 20:12
6   Colossians 3:21

A rustle of silken skirts brought his head up. He turned. His mother stood at his side. "Jeremiah, you must follow your heart." Her soft lips quivered and the hand below her lace-edged sleeve found its way into her son's. "No matter how high the cost, *you must do what you believe is right.*"

He clutched her fingers, wishing he was a carefree child again, not a man facing the hardest, most important decision of his life. His cry of despair rose to the high drawing room ceiling. "What *is* right? If I only knew!"

Isobel Cunningham mournfully shook her head. The mantel clock continued its merciless ticking. Seconds. Minutes. Hours. Each pushing the troubled son of the house of Cunningham closer to his moment of decision.

Chapter 7

Late in the afternoon of the sixth day following Laird Cunningham's edict, Jere and Lucy rode to the knoll overlooking the peaceful valley they both loved. Dismounting, they stood side by side, united by years of companionship. Hickory Manor lay tranquil in the sunlight. At that moment, the possibility of battle one day marring its serenity seemed unreal.

Long moments passed before Lucy turned to the tall young man who had transferred his blue gaze from the valley to her face. So much love and pain showed in his eyes, she wondered how her heart could go on beating. At last she spoke. "You know what your decision means."

"I know."

She didn't cry out or attempt to sway him. She didn't know if his choice was right or wrong. She only knew the boyishness he had retained in spite of reaching manhood was gone, perhaps forever. She mourned its passing, even while recognizing that the upheaval of their secure world required both Jere and she herself to put aside childish things and become man and woman.

Jere had not told her of his soul struggle and nightlong vigils. Lucy had also kept vigil in the sleepless hours, not knowing what to say to God at this momentous time. The night before, she stole from bed in the darkest hour and made a light. She returned to her pillowed nest with her Bible. It fell open to Psalm 119:105—"Thy word is a lamp unto my feet, and a light unto my path." Again she tried to pray, to ask for that light. She felt her petition barely reached the ceiling.

"Please, God, help me," she whispered. After a short while, something Daddy Doc said long ago crept into her troubled mind. Lucy remembered the day as clearly as if it was yesterday. She sat next to her father in the buggy, a small child content to be going on rounds with him. She was curious about the world and God and Daddy Doc's faith in Someone he couldn't see. "Does God hear every prayer? Even the littlest, tiniest one?" she anxiously asked.

"Oh my, yes," her father told her. "He hears all kinds of prayers. Ones we speak, and ones we just think and don't say out loud." Dr. Luke chuckled, a sound as warm as the sunlight on his fair hair. "God hears written-down prayers, too. Many of the songs we sing are really prayers." He began to sing.

"O God, our help in ages past,
    Our hope for years to come,
Our shelter from the stormy blast,
    And our eternal home!"[7]

Lucy never forgot that special moment, with sunlight on her face and Daddy Doc close beside her. Every remembrance of his rich voice raised in a hymn of praise, which she felt surely reached the heavens, set chills playing tag up and down her spine. Now she idly turned the pages of her Bible, reading verses here and there until one Scripture leaped from the page and etched itself into her brain.

"And the Lord answered me, and said, Write the vision, and make it plain. . . ."[8]

The rest of the sentence blurred. Lucy's heart threatened to burst from her chest. She had prayed for help. Was this God's answer?

She scrambled from bed, heedless of the cool breeze blowing in the open window and fluttering the thin sleeves of her nightgown. She dared not chance disturbing her father, so she crept down the hall guided by pale moonlight streaming in the window near the head of the staircase. For once, Lucy didn't even consider sliding to the entryway below but descended step by cautious step.

A few minutes later, she gathered writing materials and curled up in her favorite chair in the small sitting room, not bothering to close the door. What she planned to do wouldn't rouse her father. A thick book with blank pages lay in her lap, one she had intended to use for recording patient visits. Daddy Doc wouldn't care if she used it for a worthy purpose. After a time of thought, Lucy started writing.

Dear God,

Daddy Doc says songs are written-down prayers, and that You hear every one. I am having a hard time telling You how I feel, so I was just wondering: Will You hear my prayer if I put it in a letter to You?

A little while ago, I asked You to help me, and I found the verse about writing. I don't know if it is Your answer, but right now it is so much easier to talk to You on paper. Everything is so confusing. The war. Jere and his father. Even Hickory Hill has changed. At church last Sunday some of the families who have always sat together took seats as far away from each other as possible and scowled across the aisle.

Lucy was so engrossed in her task, she didn't realize she was no longer alone until a slight sound drew her gaze to the open doorway. Her father stood rubbing his eyes in amazement. "I thought I heard a noise. What is Miss Nightingale Danielson doing out of bed in the middle of the night? Doesn't she know my best nurse needs her rest?" He looked at the blank book. Understanding came into his eyes. "A letter to Jere?"

"No. A letter to God." She waited, hoping he would grasp what she couldn't fully explain, even to herself.

"A fine idea, Lucy. I am sure any means that helps us approach our heavenly Father is acceptable to Him. Go on with your letter." Dr. Luke cleared his throat and quietly left the room.

In the wee morning hours, Lucy slipped back to bed, carrying the book. Little did she realize she'd just written the first of many letters to God, letters that would sustain and give her hope in the perilous times ahead.

◆　◆　◆

The last six days had also taken their toll on Jere. Keenly aware of his father's marking time, he spent hours alone with Ebony on their favorite knoll. He watched the slaves on the

8　Habakkuk 2:2

plantation, noting how well-cared-for they were. What would happen should they be freed? Used to others being responsible for their welfare, could they survive if set adrift? Yet Jere's soul rebelled at taking up arms against the Union, even in defense of the only way of life he knew.

He turned to the Scriptures for help and found it in James 1:5, a familiar verse: "If any of you lack wisdom, let him ask of God, that giveth to all men liberally, and upbraideth not; and it shall be given him." Instead of stopping, as he usually did, he read the next verse. "But let him ask in faith, nothing wavering. For he that wavereth is like a wave of the sea driven with the wind and tossed."

The words haunted him. What would tomorrow and all the tomorrows bring? To him, to Lucy, to North and South? He ceased to waver and made his choice.

Only God could know the outcome, but Jere shuddered just thinking about it.

Now he laid his arm across Lucy's slim shoulders. "It means separation," he quietly told her. "No one can predict for how long." His heart quelled at the thought. How could he stand days and months apart from the bright-haired lass he loved more than anything in the world except God? "I'll come back, Lucy."

"I know." She turned from the valley and looked into his eyes. "I'll be here waiting." Her voice broke.

Jere gathered her into his arms and bent his head. How ironic! Their first mutual kiss—bittersweet with memories and fear of the future—was also good-bye. Lucy clung to him for a moment, then freed herself and stumbled to her horse.

They silently rode from their meeting place to Hickory Hill, Lucy's promise warm between them. The tiny lamp pin glinted on the collar of her blouse. Neither spoke when Jere wheeled Ebony in front of her home and goaded him into a dead run. Yet if he lived to be a hundred, he'd never forget his last blurred sight of her. Head high, although Jere knew her heart was breaking, Lucy flung one hand toward the sky in a valiant gesture of farewell. Only the knowledge that he had chosen the one course open to him kept Jere from turning back.

◆ ◆ ◆

Supper at the Cunninghams' that night was a miserable affair. Jinny poked at her food until Laird ordered, "Either eat it or let the servants take it away."

Jere longed to defend his sister but refrained. Tension in the dining room was already thick enough to slice. With a reassuring glance for his drooping sister and a prayer for the coming interview, Jere said, "I'm finished, as well."

His father threw down his linen napkin and rose. "Then I suggest we excuse ourselves from the ladies and repair to the drawing room. Tomorrow is the seventh day, as I'm sure you recall."

Jere searched the stern face for any sign of weakening. There was none. He sighed, stood, and opened the fray. "Mother, Jinny, I want you to be present."

Laird's eyes darkened. "As you wish." He led the way to the scene of so many recent battles between father and son. Isobel and Jinny sat side by side on a settee. Laird seated himself in his usual chair. After a moment's hesitation, Jere took the one opposite. He preferred to stand, but it would not be permitted. Doing so would offer too much advantage over his opponent. Regret went through him. And anger. Why must Father be considered an enemy? Jere jerked back to the present. Now was no time to ponder long-held resentments and wrongs.

Every tick of the clock beat into his brain. "Sir, I ask you to do me the courtesy of hearing me out before speaking." His father folded his arms across his chest and nodded, but the grim set of his jaw warned that storms lay ahead.

With another quick prayer for help, the impassioned feelings built through six long days of inward strife rolled out. "You have ordered me to fight for my country. This I am prepared to do. I will live up to the letter of the law in your command, but not the spirit." Jere saw the quick relief that sprang to his father's watching eyes, then died aborning.

"The word 'country' means more than just the South to me. America is my homeland—a nation forged by all those who gave their lives to settle it. How can I fight men whose ancestors died the first hard year at Plymouth? Or at Valley Forge?" He paused for breath, then rushed on. "Jesus said, 'Every kingdom divided against itself is brought to desolation; and every city or house divided against itself shall not stand.'⁹ Father, if this country is split in two, it shall surely fall, perhaps to foreign powers. I cannot be part of its destruction."

Slow understanding crept into Laird Cunningham's stone-gray eyes. His face congealed. "You, my only son, intend to turn traitor and join the Yankees? To arm yourself and perhaps kill friends and kin, as others are doing?" A hint of froth came to his lips. "*Would to God I had never lived to see this day!*"

Jere leaped to his feet and forestalled the tirade he knew would come. "Never! I shall join Northern forces with the stipulation I shall not be forced to bear arms. Thanks to Dr. Luke and Lucy, I know the rudiments of medicine. I can bind up wounds and care for the injured. I am strong and can carry litters. By serving my country this way, I will be saving life, not taking it."

Laird Cunningham stood. "Do you honestly think you will be allowed to play war under your own terms?" Scorn dripped from every word. "What a fool! The first time you refuse to carry a weapon *and to use it against your own,* you will be court-martialed. Or shot without the formality of a court-martial."

Jere didn't budge. "Were I to fight for the Confederacy, I'm sure that would be true. However, I am voluntarily enlisting under the explicit understanding I will not bear arms. I will also demand and receive a written, signed statement to that effect from a commander in charge. Otherwise, I shall not enlist. Conscientious objectors have been exempted to non-combatant positions since Colonial times, when men were forced to serve in their colony's militia."

"Are you such a dunce that you aren't aware you must belong to some pacifist religious group to claim such status?" Laird taunted.

Jere deliberately kept his voice steady. "Under normal circumstances, yes. In my case, no. I cannot and will not break God's commandment not to kill."

His father squared his shoulders. "Conscientious objectors. They are even worse than Yankees! Cowards, all of them, unwilling to fight like other men. . ."

Isobel Cunningham rose with a rustle of skirts. Her face was whiter than her delicate gown. "Be still!" she commanded in a voice like low, rolling thunder. "You shall not say such things in my presence. No man willing to carry the wounded from the front lines of battle is a coward! Far from it. It takes more courage to go armed with nothing save the protection of Almighty God, than equipped with weapons." Twin spots of red burned in her cheeks like circles of paint on a stark white ground.

9   Matthew 12:25

"Mr. Cunningham, I wish to speak with you alone and at once. Virginia, Jeremiah, you may be excused."

Brother and sister somehow made it out of the room. Jere regained his wits enough to say, "Father may forbid contact with me once I leave the house. Tell Mother I will send word through the blacksmith." He embraced Jinny. "Hurry upstairs and don't come down in the morning. I couldn't bear it."

"All right." She kissed his cheek, leaving a wide wet streak, then fled.

Jere never knew what his mother said to the lord of the manor. Only Isobel appeared the next morning to wish her son Godspeed. But before nightfall, the valley grapevine had reached into every hut and mansion with its shocking news: Jeremiah Cunningham had ridden away to join the Union army.

Chapter 8

Lucy Danielson did not receive an engagement ring on her sixteenth birthday. Caught in the upheaval of the world she had taken for granted, the significance of the day she had looked forward to dwindled. How could she be happy with Jere far away?

It was all Lucy could do to poke down Mammy Roxy's delectable fried chicken and luscious cake. She pasted on the best smile she could manage for the sake of Daddy Doc, Mammy, and Jackson Way, whose anxious gazes betrayed their deep concern for her. Yet all the while, she missed Jere Cunningham so badly she wanted to cry.

Lucy had received a few scrawled letters from Jere. Knowing him as she did, she saw beyond the forced cheerfulness to his turmoil of soul, his rebellion against the conflict rending country and families. Lucy filled her answers with hope that the fighting would soon end, although Daddy Doc warned her it wouldn't happen. Both sides had too much at stake to allow a quick end to the war that should never have begun.

After supper, Lucy and her father settled down in their cozy room. A bright fire crackled and cast an orange glow on the walls. Peace slowly stole into the troubled girl's heart. The next moment, a quick look into her father's grave face made her sigh. "What is it?" she asked.

Dr. Luke didn't act surprised at her perception. He leaned forward and fixed his steady gaze on his daughter's face. "I've fought it for weeks, but now I know what I must do, Lucy. I have no choice but to leave Hickory Hill and serve at the front." His somber face showed the struggle he had gone through. "I also feel I should not go alone."

Lucy sat up straight, heart pounding. "You mean. . . ?"

"I believe you will be safer with me at the front than if I were to leave you here. God knows I can make use of your willing hands and heart." A twisted smile came to his lips. "This is your chance, Miss Nightingale Danielson. Will you go serve with your father and help him patch up the wounded? It won't be easy."

"I will," Lucy vowed. She slipped from her chair and knelt beside him.

Dr. Luke's strong hand rested on her shining head. "There's a catch. You are far too young and lovely to be a regular nurse. You must dress as a boy." He tugged at a curl. "Are you willing to sacrifice your beautiful hair?"

Lucy blinked hard and she sprang to her feet. "Do you think I'd let any silly curls keep me from serving, when Jer—that is, others—are giving up everything?" she fiercely demanded. "I'll have Mammy cut my hair tomorrow." She laughed. "It will hurt her more than it will me!"

Lucy predicted wisely. Roxy was scandalized when Dr. Luke told her what he planned. She threw her hands into the air and exclaimed, "You're takin' my chile off to the *war?* Lord have mercy on us all!" She sniffled with every snip of the scissors and bathed her charge's shorn head with her tears.

A few days later, Dr. Luke and Lucy rode away in their well-equipped buggy, leaving their loyal servants to look after things. Dr. Luke's parting orders were, "If you are ever in danger, don't try to protect the property. You're far more important to us than the house or even my offices."

Lucy waved until they reached a bend in the road, then set her face forward. How long would it be before they returned? Weeks? Months? *Years?* her heart questioned. For one traitorous moment she wanted to stop the buggy and go back. Plenty of folks in Hickory Hill needed their skills. Why should they leave their own people to the uncertain ministrations of the retired doctor who had reluctantly agreed to carry on while the Danielsons were gone?

Daddy Doc evidently sensed her hesitation, for he said, "It isn't too late for you to turn back, Lucy. I can make arrangements for you to leave Virginia and stay with friends where there is little likelihood of fighting."

"Would you go with me?" she burst out, ashamed, but knowing she must ask.

He shook his head. "No. Our heavenly Father has called me to serve according to His will. I can do nothing less than obey Him."

A wave of love drowned Lucy's fears. She would not desert Daddy Doc. " 'Entreat me not to leave thee,' " she shakily quoted, " 'or to return from following after thee: for whither thou goest, I will go. . . .' "[10]

One hand left the reins and patted Lucy's hand. "Thank you, my darling." Dr. Luke lightened the emotion-charged moment by adding, "We have to decide what to call you. I don't know any boys named Lucy. Hmmm. We're Danielson and Danielson. I'll call you by our last name."

"All right." Lucy removed the wide-brimmed hat that shaded her eyes and let the cool late-fall air riffle her short hair. New name. New haircut. New life. The future was irrevocably sealed. She would look back no more. She bounced on the buggy seat, some of her naturally high spirits returning. "All my life I've wanted to help make a difference," she confided to her father. "Now I will have the chance." She shivered. "I only hope I can meet the test."

"You can and will," he reassured. "God will give us strength to accomplish whatever tasks we face and help us keep on giving our best long after we feel we can do no more."

◆　◆　◆

Dr. Luke's words stayed with Lucy. She clung to them, as the Southern field hospital unit she and her father had joined followed the sounds of battle across the Virginia landscape. Lucy sometimes felt if she had to watch the tents come down one more time, then wearily crawl into the Danielson buggy and relocate closer to the ever-shifting front, she would scream.

She never did, although the excellent training she had received from Daddy Doc a lifetime earlier hadn't prepared her for the ravages of war. Many times Lucy was sickened by what she was called on to do. She often responded to her father's quiet, "Danielson, I need you" purely from habit. Yet again and again, God provided the strength to keep on, to care for the wounded and comfort the dying.

Had Florence Nightingale felt the way Lucy did when she made her nightly rounds with her dim lamp? Powerless to stem the tide of injured but glad for the solace she could offer? The thought brought consolation and a renewed determination to give her best to men and boys, some no older than she. She faithfully followed her father's orders, and those given by Mary, the crusty, gray-haired nurse who had automatically assumed command over the newcomer when the Danielsons arrived at the front.

10   Ruth 1:16

Months later, Lucy wiped sweat from her forehead and stumbled to her blanketed cot. She had just finished assisting Daddy Doc and Mary with a nasty piece of surgery, one a less-skilled surgeon would never have attempted. Because of the three dedicated workers, a young soldier's life had been saved.

For what purpose, God? Lucy wrote in her journal later that night. *We dress their wounds, set their broken limbs, patch them up, and send them back into battle. The boy we saved today was brought in a few weeks ago. We did our best, then and now. Others we care for don't return. Is there really any use in saving lives that will only be lost in the end? I secretly rejoice when those we care for are disabled enough to be sent home, at least for a time. There is always a chance the war will end before they are healed enough to be able to fight again.*

Lucy slowly closed her journal. Some of her greatest help came from two sources: her letters to God and the fact that she saw Jere Cunningham's face superimposed on every suffering Confederate or Yankee soldier she treated. One night, when she was so weary she could barely keep her eyes open, Lucy fancied she saw the face of Christ looking at her from a nearby cot, waiting His turn for the help she could give. Daddy Doc wept when she shared the experience, and he reminded her that all they did for those in their care was also done for Jesus.

Somewhere in the second—or was it the third?—year of the war that Lucy felt had begun an eternity earlier, the tired nurse lost track of what day or week it was. Hickory Hill had receded into the mists of the past, real only when rare news came. Jinny Cunningham wrote that her father had sent her and her mother north to keep them safe from possible danger. She thought it hypocritical of him to seek the North's protection for his family while condemning the North for the war.

Jere's blacksmith friend later sent word that Hickory Manor had been stripped by the Billy Yanks, although the mansion itself still stood. No one knew what had become of Laird Cunningham. The blacksmith added that Hickory Hill had so far escaped invasion. Roxy and Jackson Way were keeping the Danielson home in such a constant condition of readiness, one would think they expected Dr. Luke and Lucy home any minute.

The news about the Cunninghams saddened Lucy, but some of her old grin returned when she told her father the part about Mammy and Jackson Way. His sudden smile brightened Lucy's day.

The war ground on. Both North and South instituted a draft system. Once enthusiasm for the war faded, volunteer enlistments had dramatically decreased. Persons and places were in the news. Northern generals Ulysses Grant and William Sherman. Southern counterparts Robert E. Lee and Stonewall Jackson. Chilling tales of battles ran rampant. Bull Run, also known as Manassas. Shiloh. The gory battle of Antietam. Fredericksburg and Chancellorsville. Gettysburg. A never-ending stream of wounded and dying poured into the Danielsons' care.

Other news trickled to the front. Lucy and Dr. Luke laughed when hearing the qualifications from a circular: "No woman under thirty years need apply to serve in government hospitals. All nurses are required to be very plain-looking women. Their dresses must be brown or black, with no bows, no curls or jewelry, and no hoop skirts."

"Wonder what the recruiter would think of you?" the good doctor teased.

Lucy ruefully looked at her worn clothing. "Not much, I'm afraid." She turned toward him, noting the fatigue in his face, the early streaks of gray in his hair. The sparkle in his fine eyes remained undimmed, however. She sighed in relief. As long as Daddy Doc could keep going, so could she.

Women were also making their mark. Mary ("Mother") Bickerdyke went to the front wearing a calico dress, heavy boots, and sunbonnet. According to rumor, when she was challenged about not having an official commission, she retorted, "I have received my authority from the Lord God Almighty." Officials dared not dispute her claim.

Florence Nightingale remained Lucy's heroine. After serving in Crimea, Miss Nightingale had become a world authority on the scientific care of the sick. The United States sought her advice on setting up military hospitals.

Another selfless woman offered further inspiration to Lucy. Clara Barton, also without an official commission, began carrying supplies to the front and nursing the wounded on the battlefields soon after the war started. Her work gained national attention and appreciation. She was given the title *Angel of the Battlefield.* Garbed in a plain skirt and jacket, she was determined to serve but struggled. She was quoted as saying she had contended long and hard with her conscience. The appalling fact that she was a woman whispered in one ear; the groans of those who needed her thundered in the other.

Lucy understood her feelings. If Mammy could see her "honey-chile" in the primitive surroundings where need overcame maidenly modesty, she would roll her eyes and throw her apron over her head!

◆ ◆ ◆

Jere's letters became more despondent and less frequent. He no longer attempted to hide his true feelings. One letter almost broke Lucy's heart.

> *Tonight some of the Johnny Rebs crossed the lines after the fighting ended for the day. We gathered around our campfires. Some swapped tobacco and played cards. Others simply talked. Of home. Of families. There was little speculation about when the war might end or the war itself.*
>
> *I thought I would die of pain when they left. Tomorrow, or the next day, I may be called on to bind up the wounds or help set the shattered bones of some of those here tonight. My countrymen, whose only desire is for this to be over so they can go home. Oh, Lord, how long?*

Jere's cry of despair echoed in Lucy's heart. She kissed the single page and tucked it into her journal next to his previous letters, worn thin from handling. How thick her journal had become. How revealing. Brief notes about the war and the Danielsons' place in it snuggled among rare bits of humor and Lucy's precious letters to God. Together they painted a painfully accurate picture of life since she left Hickory Hill.

Lucy clutched her journal, knowing she would keep it long after the war ended. Someday she would pass it on to future generations. God forbid any of them would face experiences similar to her own! If they did, perhaps the precious journal would offer the same strength to them as it had to her.

Chapter 9

It was Jere's last letter. Plagued by fear, Lucy continued to write to him. Was Jere dead, victim of a bullet fired by a Johnny Reb with whom he had spent the evening? Struck down by a Billy Yank's stray shot?

The thought terrified Lucy more than the war raging around her. She spent every free moment in prayer. She searched the Scriptures and clung to the Twenty-third Psalm, receiving comfort each time she quoted it to those in her care.

The fourth verse, "Yea, though I walk through the valley of the shadow of death, I will fear no evil: for thou art with me; thy rod and thy staff they comfort me," took on special meaning. The shadow of death hung low. Yet Lucy knew God was still in control. His rod, a shepherd's cudgel, was stout enough to drive off enemies; His staff, far-reaching enough to pull His children back from danger. No harm could befall them unless God permitted it.

Lucy shared her deepening faith one evening when she and Daddy Doc had a few minutes free. "Knowing God really is in control changes everything," she said. "That's what keeps you going, isn't it?"

Dr. Luke gathered her in his arms and held her close. Hot tears fell on the kerchief that kept Lucy's curly hair out of her eyes. She had discarded her disguise soon after reaching the front and proving herself so invaluable, no one, not even Mary, protested her presence. She regretted abandoning the more practical male attire but soon discovered the wounded often appreciated a woman's presence, even one clad in simple dark dresses with white collars and cuffs.

"No man ever had a better daughter," Dr. Luke said hoarsely. "I am proud of you. I know God must be, too." He released her and stumbled away.

Lucy watched him go with brimming eyes. It was the first time she had seen him shed tears. Her work-worn fingers stole to her collar and the tiny lamp pin that adorned it. She needed no mirror to picture its glow, bright through constant touching. It warmed her fingers and her soul.

Just like the service we give for Christ's sake, her heart whispered. Tears gave way to peace, and that night Lucy slept deeply. It was well, for the rest and peace fortified her for what was yet to come.

A few days later, she received a long-delayed message from the Hickory Hill blacksmith. Jeremiah Cunningham was officially listed as missing in action.

A time of waiting began. A time of "hanging on to God's coattails for dear life," as Lucy wrote in her journal. A time of losing her life for the sake of others and finding it again; of sensing that Someone walked beside her. A time of predictions that the war must soon end. The Union army supposedly had grown to more than a million soldiers, five times the number of Confederate soldiers. Rumor claimed that a full 10 percent of those on both sides had deserted. Sickened of fighting, they simply laid down their arms and started their long journeys home.

A bedraggled letter from Jinny Cunningham brought both hope and fresh concern. Jere and several comrades had been captured and sent to a prison camp. Some had been wounded, but Jere had miraculously escaped injury.

Lucy saw her father's worried look. Survival in the pest-ridden camps was as precarious as on the battlefield. "Jere has something in his favor," Dr. Luke comforted. "Prison camps can always use those with medical knowledge." He smiled. "At least you know where he is. Now you can write to him."

"Yes. Except Jinny's letter is dated weeks ago." Still, hope fluttered in Lucy's heart like a moth dancing in the wind that night when she wrote her letter. It overflowed with joy for Jere being alive. Lucy forced back sleep and didn't stop writing until her lamp dimmed, sputtered, and went out. Her last waking act was to smile and touch her own lamp, carefully pinned to her high nightgown collar.

◆　◆　◆

Jere Cunningham slowly pulled a worn blanket over a dead soldier's face, one of a half-dozen lads in their teens who had died that week. Confederate gray or Union blue, the same red blood spilled on the battlefields and stained the nation.

What felt like an eternity earlier, Jere and his friends had been captured in a surprise attack. Jere cocked an eyebrow. In the time it took to reach the Southern prison camp, at least he'd be free from the stench of powder and death.

Unfortunately, the long, jolting ride also provided time for Jere to relive the past. It unrolled like a scroll in his mind. How sure of himself he had been that final morning at Hickory Manor. How cocky to think he could dictate to the Union army! Except for the grace of God and a Northern surgeon. . .

Jere grinned. He and Ebony had headed straight for the closest Union encampment. In accordance with Jere's well-laid plan, they were captured. "I came to enlist," Jere said. "Take me to your commanding officer."

The patrol who had discovered him gaped. Their leader sneered. "Count on it." He led the way, with Jere sandwiched between him and his men.

Once in camp, Jere stepped from the saddle. A grizzled sergeant approached him after a rumbling exchange with the patrol. "You want to enlist, you hightail it to the other side of the war, sonny." He cursed.

"No, sir," Jere said in a loud voice. "My conscience doesn't permit me to bear arms for either side. I won't take life, but I can help save it. I know basic medicine and can serve as a litter bearer or a surgeon's assistant."

"Just what might your name be?" the sergeant demanded in icy tones.

Jere stifled the perverse desire to retort, "It might be Tom Thumb or Jeremiah Marcus, Jerabone, Markabone, Napoleon Bonaparte Cunningham, but it ain't."

He disciplined a grin. The doughty sergeant was no good-natured schoolmaster with whom to trifle. "Jeremiah Cunningham. Hickory Hill, Virginia."

"Well, Mr. Jeremiah Cunningham, what makes you think the Union army can be told what to do by a Johnny Reb?" the sergeant barked.

"If I were a rebel I wouldn't be here."

Mistrust sprang into the pale eyes. "You would if you were a spy." He spat. "I'm betting that's what you are."

"I am no spy." Jere raised his voice until it rang throughout the encampment. "I demand to see your commanding officer. *Now.*"

Pitting belligerence against belligerence followed by a silent prayer had paid off. A camp doctor clad in bloodstained clothing erupted from a nearby tent. He had obviously heard the altercation. "For the love of God," he yelled, "if this man has medical skill, I don't care if he's Southern or purple! I'll take full responsibility for him!" He gripped Jere's shoulder and unceremoniously shoved him into the commanding officer's tent.

Gimlet eyes must have seen Jere's sincerity. A half hour later, he was given an ironclad, special-consideration contract with the Union army.

◆　◆　◆

Heartaches and horrors followed, tempered by joy over saved lives. The thought of Lucy facing the same situations gripped Jere's heart and gave him strength. Days and months limped into a blur of years. The loss of Ebony to a covetous officer hit Jere hard. He couldn't speak of it, even to Lucy, whose letters he read until they fell apart at the creases. He memorized what his weary brain could retain, preparing for a time when no letters came.

Now Jere bowed his head, wondering, as he had done the fateful day he was captured: Could even the Almighty salvage anything good from the carnage? He pondered the question until one day a startling thought came. Wasn't his being in the prison camp proof God cared for the sick and dying? Cared enough to send Jeremiah, "appointed by Jehovah," to give soul comfort, even when the lack of medicine and supplies hampered proper physical care?

The conviction revitalized him. He began to share his faith with all who would listen. "God loves us so much He sent Jesus to die in our place," he stated. Truth rang in every word. "If we accept God's gift and invite Jesus into our hearts, our souls will never die." Jere threw his head back and laughed. Laughed at the squalor, the privation, the misery. "Men, *we will never have to fight again. We will live in heaven in peace. Forever.*"

Some responded to the sheer force of Jere's belief. Conditions in the prison camp worsened, but a powerful new influence was at work. No walls could keep out the hope of the gospel of Christ when preached by a man who knew and loved his God. Was it for this Jere had ridden away on his faithful horse, Ebony? Could this be the good God had foreseen during all Jere's terrible arguments with Father, the agonizing years of war, his separation from family and Lucy?

Jere felt reborn. Like a child who discovers a bright new world outside his doorstep, his first thought was: *I must go tell my father.* He could not. Shackled by duty, he pushed himself even harder to relieve suffering. One day he collapsed, victim of the unspeakable conditions. He didn't know or care that General Robert E. Lee formally surrendered to General Grant at Appomattox on April 9, 1865. Five days later, the world reeled from the news of President Lincoln's assassination. Jere's world reeled with fever, so high and debilitating, the grave-faced doctor who finally came shook his head and moved on. Jere didn't know how or when he was removed from the prison camp to an overflowing hospital that offered a shade better care than the camp.

Deep inside his tortured body, a spirit made strong by trials refused to give up. Jere slowly began to rally. At last he opened his eyes and stared at the unfamiliar ceiling, then dropped into a natural sleep. He awakened to find a man at his bedside. Jere recoiled, certain he had lost his sanity and was seeing ghosts.

The man knelt by his bed and took Jere's wasted hands in his. A voice Jere had never forgotten spoke in a tone he'd never before heard. "Jeremiah. Son. God knows you have good reason, but please, don't turn away from me!"

You? Here? It was too much to comprehend. Weakened by all he'd gone through, Jere bowed his head. The dam that had withstood coldness and injustice broke. A flood came, carrying away the debris of bitterness.

Later, he learned his father's story. When the invaders neared Hickory Manor, Laird took refuge in a large hickory tree. He watched his home being stripped of all but the family silver, previously buried. A former slave, now wearing Union blue, shouted, "We'll show Old Man Cunningham. Burn the house!"

"Hold it!" a grizzled sergeant had barked from below Laird's perch. "There's a surgeon's assistant at my former company named Cunningham. He's from around here. Good man. Saved a lot of Yankee lives. March on!"

Jere gasped, but his father continued. The enemy rode away. In the dead of night, Laird dug up as much of the family silver as he could carry. He made his way to Boston. Isobel and Jinny had just learned of Jere's whereabouts. "I spent weeks trying to obtain your release," he brokenly said. "Now the war is over. God has forgiven this stubborn Scotsman. So have Isobel and Jinny. Can you?"

"I forgave you the moment I realized God brought good from our conflict."

Laird smiled. "As soon as you get well, we'll go home. If the government confiscates Hickory Manor, as it may, so be it. We'll start over." A twinkle brightened his gray eyes. "With a new redheaded member of the family."

◆　◆　◆

The war was over, but nineteen-year-old Lucy's battle raged on. Where was Jere? Her letters to the prison camp had come back unopened.

After the Danielsons' last patient was gone, they packed the buggy and left for home. Lucy dreaded going. Would they find desolation, ruin, a town ravaged by war like the ones they passed? Finally realizing that no more wounded and dying pleaded for her help, Lucy closed her eyes and asked for strength before they reached the village.

"Wake up, Lucy. Look. Oh, Lucy, look!" Dr. Luke's voice broke.

She opened her eyes and stared toward Hickory Hill. It had been spared and lay peaceful in the sunlight. They reached the Danielson home. The fragrance of roses and beeswax greeted Lucy when she rushed into the entry hall. "Mammy?" she screamed. "Jackson Way?"

"Honey-chile, is that *you?*" Roxy stepped into the hall and clasped Lucy to her white-aproned bosom. "The Lord be praised!" she shouted. "Your mammy was afeared she'd never see her chile again!"

"I'm home, Mammy." Blinding tears choked off Lucy's words.

She heard steps behind her, then a laughing voice said, "My name is Jeremiah Marcus, Jerabone, Markabone—oh, hang it all, Lucy, the fighting's over, with Father as well as the country. When will you marry me?"

She tore herself free from Mammy's arms and whirled. The man she loved stood just inside the doorway. She searched his face. Laughter couldn't hide how he had aged, but the love in his blue eyes shone steady and true.

Lucy slowly removed the lamp pin from her collar. She pinned it on his ragged shirt. "Soon, Jere," she whispered. "Very soon."

COLLEEN L. REECE was born and raised in a small western Washington logging town. She learned to read by kerosene lamplight and dreamed of someday writing a book. God has multiplied Colleen's "someday" book into more than 150 titles that have sold six million copies. Colleen was twice voted Heartsong Presents' Favorite Author and later inducted into Heartsong's Hall of Fame. Several of her books have appeared on the CBA Bestseller list.

Misprint

by Kathleen Miller Y'Barbo

Thank You, Jesus, for finding me
and for helping me locate chapter two.
This one is for the cheerleaders.
You know who you are.
And for Judy, companions for lunch and life.
We made it!
Finally, many, many thanks
to my dear friend Janice Thompson,
who gave more than I could ever ask of her in time
and prayers to see this book into print.

Chapter 1

Friday, June 29, 1860

T ruly, Penney, I'll just m–m–make a mistake, I know it." Helen Morgan shook her head and took two steps back toward the safety of her little desk in the far corner of the newspaper office.

"If I can set type, anyone can." Penney Brice scurried back to the table holding the bits and pieces of letters that would form tomorrow's edition of the *Golden Gate Gazette*. "With both of us working together, we'll finish the changes to the front page in half the time." She paused to shrug. "Of course, I'll understand if you're too busy."

Busy.

Ever since she'd accepted employment as the sole bookkeeper at the *Gazette*, her life had been one series of busy moments after the other. Not that she looked upon her chosen profession as work, for nothing could be further from the truth.

To Helen, the process of collecting the numbers and fitting them into orderly categories and columns was an occupation that bordered on a mission. Other than in the Lord, she'd never found any greater satisfaction in all her twenty-seven years than in her recent work at the *Gazette*. Finding immense comfort in the solitude her employment offered was an added bonus.

Helen leaned against the door's ornately carved wooden frame and watched Penney bend over a tray of letters. With swift movements, Penney picked out letters and set them in place, oblivious to the stifling heat. Before her eyes, Helen watched tomorrow's headline take shape.

The process did look quite simple. Any imbecile should be able to spell sufficiently to place the correct letters in a line to form words and sentences. Surely. . .

Helen's hopeful musings ground to an abrupt halt. The words of her late father, James Elliston Morgan, the honorable senator from the great state of Texas, rang through her head as her fingers grasped the door frame. "You'll never manage it, Helen," she heard the great orator declare. "Unfortunately, you've inherited your charming mother's temperament and deficit of abilities." Always, once the pronouncement was made, a proper pause ensued, followed by the postscript of "may the Lord rest her dear departed soul."

The last time she'd heard her father's words, she chimed in with a response long held in check. "I daresay Mother has finally found her rest with the Lord, as she surely did not find it here in this life."

Of course she'd chosen the most inopportune time to assert her newfound outspokenness. One does not besmirch one's father's relationship with one's mother publicly, least of all at his inaugural dinner. Surely the dear ladies and gentlemen of the Austin elite spoke in hushed tones about the senator's rebellious daughter for many years afterward.

For Helen the evening had produced a twofold result. First, she'd been shipped off for "finishing back East," which meant spending the last year of her second decade with a pair of maiden great-aunts who adored her but cast as little care on her whereabouts as they did on their gray-striped tomcat. Second, she'd discovered that when the senator spoke, he stated the truth. As surely as if the Lord Himself had said the words, the edict regarding Helen's competence had hit home and stuck.

She'd not only inherited Mama's temperament and abilities, she'd taken what was in her mother an endearing inability to finish the slightest detailed task correctly and perfected it, adding a general aberration for people and public places and a horrible tendency to stutter when nervous. Outside of adding and subtracting numbers, Helen Morgan was a total, un-adulterated failure at every new venture she attempted.

So why in the world did she find herself gravitating toward the typesetting table and her dear friend Penney?

She mustered a smile and listened with no small measure of concern as Penney began to instruct her on the fine art of typesetting. "Surely someone will be sorry that I've taken on this task."

"Don't be silly, Helen." Penney thrust a tray full of metal letters in her direction and smiled. "Anyone who can make sense of all those numbers will find this job terribly easy."

Half an hour later, Helen had all but given up on being any sort of serious help to dear Penney. To the contrary, it seemed as though Penney spent half the energy doing twice the work while Helen struggled to match each letter, each sentence, and each paragraph to the copy Mr. Madison left them. Still, she'd managed to do a decent job of it, a fact she noted with an equal measure of pleasure and surprise.

"Honestly, Penney, I don't know how you do this day after day." Helen stretched to relieve the ache in her back. "I believe I'd go stark raving mad after the first week."

Ever cheerful, Penney smiled and tossed her curls. "Oh, it's not as terrible as that. Besides, I'm just biding my time," she said with a wink.

Penney made no secret of the fact that, while she had taken a job at the *Gazette* as a typesetter, she had no intention of staying in the position indefinitely. Beneath that pretty and youthful exterior beat the heart of a reporter of serious news.

Helen shuddered. Imagine interviewing unknown persons for a living, speaking to strangers as if they were familiar, or worse, chasing down a story from a reluctant perpetrator of crime. Why, sometimes it was all Helen could do to make small talk with one of Mr. Madison's advertisement sponsors or, worse, one of her roommates' gentleman friends. Imagine wanting to do these things on a regular basis.

Shaking off the awful thought, she went back to her work with renewed vigor. The sooner she finished this task, the sooner she could get back to her familiar world of columns and balances.

"Just as I predicted." Penney reached behind her back to untie her apron. "We're done, and in half the time."

"We are, aren't we?" Truthfully, Helen had been so immersed in her work, she'd failed to notice the passage of time.

"I knew you would be good at this," Penney said. "You're good at everything you attempt."

Helen bit back a comment and smiled. How little her dear friend knew, and yet it felt nice to think someone found her competent. Wouldn't Father have been surprised?

◆ ◆ ◆

Monday, July 2, 1860

The first workday of July, and already the heat had him bested. Henry Hill removed his hat and stepped into the welcoming dimness of the Chandler Building's outer lobby, then headed for the stairs, slouching off his formal jacket as he climbed the risers by twos.

"If it were any hotter, bullets would start firing on their own," he said with a chuckle as he touched the revolver hidden under his vest with his left hand. A man in his position had to be careful, thus the firearm, though thankfully Henry had found no reason lately to have need for the weapon.

When he reached the second floor, he paused to find his handkerchief and mop his brow. A man less inclined to his work would have removed himself to the mountains weeks ago or at least taken a holiday someplace where an egg would not fry on the roof. Many had done just that, including his law partner, Asa Chambers, but Henry had business that precluded any vacation, now or in the future.

How could he be about the business of making a difference, of righting wrongs in this city, if he forsook his duties to find solace in the redwoods? Henry straightened his spine and neatly folded his handkerchief back into place in his vest pocket, then pushed open his office door. No, it would not do for the future mayor of San Francisco to retreat in the face of something as minor as a little warm weather.

A trickle of perspiration teased his forehead. Henry reached for his handkerchief again. At this rate he would need another one before noon.

"I certainly hope it's not this hot on Independence Day. I'll have a time with my speech if it is."

His speech. Henry made a note to take another look at the speech he'd be delivering on Independence Day. Too bad Asa would not be there to witness the festivities. After all, he'd spent the better part of two days helping Henry craft the message that would provide the official launch of the mayoral race. Asa Chambers was a friend indeed.

Casting a glance at his friend's portrait, hanging alongside his in the foyer, Henry had to chuckle. He would have preferred the money paid to the artist to have gone to charity. Asa's father, however, insisted on footing the bill. Asa called them masterpieces. Henry just thought they were pretentious.

Shutting the door behind him, Henry hung his hat on the coatrack, then carefully arranged his jacket to hang beside it. Finally he removed the key from his vest pocket and unlocked the topmost desk drawer on the left, then placed his revolver beneath his Bible and slid the drawer closed. After returning the key to his pocket, he checked the time. Exactly half past nine.

"Excellent," he whispered.

He always arrived precisely half an hour before his first appointment of the day, time enough to place a sizable dent in the teetering pile of papers bordering the northernmost corner of his desk. Once upon a time, Henry would never have thought of allowing such a mess in his office. But then, once upon a time, he hadn't set his cap for the mayor's job.

Mayor Henry Hill.

The phrase gave him pause each time he considered it. He'd entered the election with much prayer and still much trepidation. Dared he actually assume that God would call him to lead a city? Some days, when life bore down on him, he doubted.

The hardscrabble way he'd come up in the world most certainly gave Henry an edge in the election, as well as empathy for the unrepresented masses who collected in the less glamorous parts of the city. No matter how long he lived, he would never forget what it was like to go to bed hungry or to wake up to a rat the size of a small dog chewing on the bedpost—or worse, on him. If the Lord allowed his victory, Henry would do his best to see that no other child had to live in such abhorrent conditions.

San Franciscans would never know from whence Henry Hill came. His change of name and adoption at the age of seven by the wealthy and tenderhearted Anna Hill, heiress to the Hill shipping fortune, precluded any questions regarding his background. Anna's story of taking in her late sister Violet's son had been accepted without question, especially given her status as a childless unmarried woman with a love of children and a long list of charities to her credit.

What Anna failed to mention was that her late sister had died destitute and estranged from the family, who had refused to accept the man who fathered her only son. Where that man was now was anyone's guess.

"A good name is rather to be chosen than great riches, and loving favor rather than silver and gold." His favorite verse and the words by which he lived. With the Lord's help, Eli Barnes would never return to besmirch the name Henry had worked so hard to keep from tarnishing.

But what if Eli Barnes did return? What if his opponent's cronies were able to track him down? Would the voters of San Francisco still accept attorney Henry Hill as a candidate once they laid eyes on the ne'er-do-well who sired him?

"God is in control," he whispered.

Bypassing a folded note and a pair of newly delivered letters that were most likely invitations to some social event, he reached for the topmost paper on the stack and dove in to the intricacies of law, both his passion and his respite from thoughts too unpleasant to bear. Every time he tackled a question of legal jurisprudence, he thanked God for choosing him to be a defender of the less fortunate. With His help, Henry would soon be in a position to provide aid and assistance on a much larger scale.

Moments later, or so it seemed, a soft knock captured his attention. Henry rose and ushered the first of several dozen clients into his office. By the time he'd finished with the last one, darkness had long since settled over the city. As he opened the desk drawer to retrieve his revolver, he saw the Bible.

"Where were You today, God?" he whispered as he shrugged into his coat, donned his hat, and stepped into the foyer. "Or rather, why didn't I find time to look for You?"

Henry made the climb down the back stairs, knowing he'd find an answer to that last question but fearing he would also make the same mistake tomorrow. Someday, when the pressures of his life were lessened a bit, maybe he would find the time to earnestly search for God's presence. In the meantime, a hasty prayer and a promise for better days to come were the best Henry could offer. After all, he had a city to lead.

"No, Lord, that's not right. You'll be doing the leading. I'll just take the orders and do my best to follow."

Chapter 2

W hat a nice man, that Mr. Hill," Penney said with a sigh as she and Helen strolled away from the Fourth of July festivities. "He really seems to care about people."

"I suppose."

Helen linked arms with Penney as they strolled past the darkened windows of the *Gazette* and turned toward home. In truth, while she'd found the man's message both uplifting and God-honoring, the man himself was much more interesting. A strange feeling, this vague attraction to one so handsome and unapproachable, thus she reasoned it must be ignored.

No good would come of entertaining fanciful thoughts of romance with any fellow, much less one so far beyond her in ambition. The Bible claimed it far better to live a quiet life, and Helen held this in no dispute. In fact, the verse in the fourth chapter of 1 Thessalonians was among her favorites: *"And that ye study to be quiet, and to do your own business, and to work with your own hands."*

Ah yes, *quiet*. Helen's definition of the well-lived life.

Imagine making one's livelihood from public displays, such as this evening. Helen shuddered despite the lingering warmth of the day. A worse lot in life, she could not imagine.

"Mr. Hill has such exciting plans for helping the poor," Penney said as the pair stepped gingerly across a particularly muddy spot in the street. "He seems like someone who will give a voice to people like us."

"People like us?" Helen looked down into the kind face of her friend. How little Penney knew about the life Helen led before making her way to San Francisco. While she hadn't been untruthful about her privileged past, neither had she spoken in any detail. As far as her three friends knew, Helen Morgan was an average woman with an average life, and this suited Helen just fine.

"Yes, the common folk," Penney said, punctuating the statement with a smile. "He did seem quite sincere."

"I suppose," she repeated.

No need in telling her perpetually optimistic friend that in all likelihood Henry Hill was just like all politicians, as blustery as the wind and just as difficult to find in times of need. *An opinion poorly timed and quickly given bore no good return.* Words of wisdom from Father that had served Helen well through the years.

Helen smiled. Perhaps someday when she met him in heaven, she would tell Father she'd listened to each and every speech he'd delivered, albeit discreetly and selectively. Wouldn't he be surprised?

"Oh my." Penney stopped short and gave Helen a stricken look. "My reticule. I must have left it back at the celebration."

"Are you sure?" she called to Penney's retreating form. "Maybe you just forgot to bring it."

"No, I'm sure I had it when we were sitting beside the stage, and then I. . ." Penney's voice trailed off as she turned the corner. Helen rushed to catch up, nearly bowling down a well-dressed matron and her slightly younger escort.

"Forgive me," Helen said as she rushed past the pair. "It seems as though my friend has lost her—"

"Handbag?"

The question brought her to a halt. Helen whirled about to face the speaker. There he stood, the politician himself, so close she could practically read the swirling initial on his gold signet ring and count the buttons on his expensively tailored formal coat.

Center stage, the man—what was his name?—appeared quite dashing, but here, so near, dashing was but a pale version of his true description.

The gentleman in question thrust a dark object toward Helen. "I believe this is what your friend is seeking."

Helen nodded, thankfully rendered mute, and forced her fingers to close around the item. What was it? Something soft, made of velvet, with a fringe that tickled her palm. She stole a glance at her still-outstretched hand. Ah, yes, Penney's reticule.

Helen lifted her gaze and found the politician and the woman staring expectantly. She should speak, should say something—anything. But about what? Ah, yes, the handbag.

The moment she made the determination, her fingers rebelled and released their grip. Helen watched as Penney's handbag slipped out of her reach and landed with a *thud* in the muck.

"Dear," the woman said, "are you ill?"

"I–i–ill?" Helen forced her lips closed and swallowed hard, then took a deep breath and exhaled slowly. With concentration, she managed to focus on the politician's companion. "Thank you. No, I'm fine."

Dark eyes smiled back from a kind face, slightly weathered by a sum of years that seemed to have treated her most kindly. "Perhaps we could see you home then?" She gave the politician an almost imperceptible nudge in the rib with her elbow.

"Yes," he said quickly as he once again retrieved the velvet bag and thrust it into her hand. "Yes, do accompany us, Miss. . ."

"Morgan." She tightened her fingers around the reticule and tried not to jump with joy that the single word hadn't come out as a string of unintelligible gibberish.

The woman offered her gloved hand. "How do you do, Miss Morgan? I'm Anna Hill."

Helen somehow completed the exchange of pleasantries without further embarrassment, then took a step backward. "Thank you, but I—I—I really must go." She tested her footing on the uneven thoroughfare and found it lacking. Her ankle turned, and a sharp pain preceded a humiliating stumble forward. The politician immediately came to her aid.

"Dear, do assist the young lady to the buggy. I shan't imagine she will be going home on her own."

Ignoring the urge to flee, Helen called upon the manners she'd learned at her mother's knee and prayed her faulty phrasing could enunciate the words she needed to say. "Thank you, but it isn't necessary t–t–to—"

"Nonsense," argued the matron as she bustled toward a rather elegant carriage parked just ahead.

Somehow Helen felt herself moving forward, placing one foot ahead of the other and progressing toward the selfsame coach. Had she gathered any senses, she might have resisted. Rather, Helen fell into step beside the gentleman and stared at his hand on her arm, the signet ring with the swirling double *H* on his hand, and finally, into the eyes of her escort.

As her gaze locked with the politician's, she froze. *What's come over me?*

Helen cleared her throat and enunciated slowly. "Do unhand me, sir."

The gentleman removed his hand and frowned. "Forgive me," he said, although the apologetic sentiment did not quite match his amused expression.

When he looked away, Helen turned and fled without so much as a proper farewell.

"Helen?" Penney asked as Helen approached. "You found my reticule. I don't know what I would have done if I'd lost it."

"Actually, I didn't find it." She paused to gesture toward the politician now walking toward them. "He did."

"Why, isn't that the fellow from this afternoon?" She waved her reticule in his direction. "Mr. Hill? I'm ever so grateful for you—"

"Don't give it another thought," he said, approaching with one hand hidden beneath his coat. As he strode past, barely sparing a glance toward her and Penney, Helen noticed a glint of silver under the politician's formal coat.

A revolver.

Nothing particularly out of order about that. San Francisco could be a dangerous town, and one would assume a man of Mr. Hill's caliber would deem protection necessary. Of course, one could also assume that a man who practically raced away from his companion with his hand atop his revolver might be heading for trouble rather than protecting himself from it.

"Well, he certainly seemed to be in a rush," Penney said as she linked arms with Helen. "Indeed he did."

Chapter 3

Miss Morgan, there's been some late-breaking news, and I'd like very much if you would edit the copy then help the typesetter in working this article into the front page." Mr. Madison thrust a hastily scribbled paper in her direction, and she caught it just before it floated to the floor. "Facts are sketchy, so work with what we know. I'm meeting with the chief in a few minutes, but I don't expect he'll have anything new to say until the arrest is made public. In the meantime, I know it's late, but I expect you girls to get this edition in print posthaste. Can't let the other papers beat us to the story."

Helen rose and watched Mr. Madison rush toward the door. "I've left the headline to you," he called as he donned his hat. "Make it a good one."

"Yes, sir." She lowered her gaze to the paper in her hand and began to read.

"What is it?" Penney called from her spot at the typesetting table.

"Big news," Helen said, imitating Mr. Madison's distinctive voice. "We're to get the edition out as soon as possible in his absence." She shrugged and glanced around the empty newsroom. "Looks like I'm your only help."

Penney smiled. "Then let's get to it. What do we have that's so important?"

Helen laid the paper in front of Penney. "A murder. Someone named Frank Bynum was killed last night. They found his body this afternoon hidden behind the livery."

"Frank Bynum? That name sounds familiar," Penney said.

"Well, I've never heard of him, but that doesn't mean a thing." Helen paused. "Oh my. Is this the fellow who found your handbag? The one who's running for mayor?"

Penney leaned closer. "No, his name was Henry Hill. The fellow who's going to be arrested for the crime is named Henry Hall. See?"

"Well, that's a relief. He did seem like a nice fellow." *Even if he is a politician.*

Helen reached for a handful of letters and began assembling the headline while Penney deftly pieced together the body of the text. In short order, the changes had been made to the front page, the sensational news taking the place of a less important story. Helen wiped her hands on her apron and smiled. "That certainly went quickly, didn't it?"

"Yes, it did." Penney smiled. "Two heads are always better than one."

"I'm just glad I could help." Penney had no idea how very much Helen meant the sentiment. Her days of incompetence seemed destined to be over, and the successful completion of tasks such as this gave her hope that someday she might feel capable to take on larger ones.

◆ ◆ ◆

Friday, July 6, 1860

Henry Hill pounded his fist on the table and nearly upset his adoptive mother's favorite Wedgwood coffee service. He had certainly upset her.

True to her nature, the dear woman said nothing in anticipation of the explanation she demanded with the lift of a dark brow. On another day, he might have taken heed of her warning look, might have voiced the apology she silently demanded, but not today.

Not with his career and his campaign lying in tatters. Not after having his evening ruined by a cryptic note handed to Asa during the speech and the possibility of meeting with his long-lost father that thankfully had never taken place.

"Heads will roll, Mother." He pushed away from the table and tossed his napkin onto the offending tabloid, effectively hiding the headline that all of San Francisco had most certainly seen by now.

"Surely you exaggerate, dear." She reached beneath the lump of cloth to retrieve the *Gazette*. Once again her brows rose, this time as her gaze scanned the front page, only to stop on the bold print of the day's headline: HENRY HILL BELIEVED RESPONSIBLE FOR JULY 4TH DEATH OF WEALTHY BUSINESSMAN FRANK BYNUM.

"Oh my." His mother carefully folded the paper in half and set it aside before lifting her gaze to meet his. Brown eyes blinked hard, and it seemed as though a tear fought for escape. "Oh my," she repeated.

"Indeed."

Henry took a deep breath and fought for composure. He forced a weak smile, then reached into his vest pocket to snap open his pocket watch. While he didn't give a fig for what time the blasted thing said, he hoped the action might make her believe he considered the morning's upset to be finished. A woman so delicate and dear need not be unduly troubled.

Nor did she need to know he planned to right this wrong posthaste.

Better for her to believe he intended to spend his morning like all the others, hard at work rather than berating some editor for a misprint that could very well have cost him the election.

Slipping the watch back into his pocket, Henry turned his attention to his mother. "If you will excuse me, I'll be off now."

Mother frowned. "Promise me you will think before you act and pray before you think."

"If only I had a vote for every time you've spoken those words, I should truly prevail as mayor." Henry gathered up the newspaper, then leaned down to kiss the top of his mother's head, inhaling the soft scent of violets. "Perhaps you should do the praying for me."

"For you and for the poor soul you intend to unleash your wrath upon at the *Gazette*." Her words chased him out the door and into the dreary San Francisco morning.

"Surely she doesn't think I would—"

"To the office, sir?" The aged driver, one of Mother's many "rescue projects," turned as best as his arthritic back would allow and narrowed his dark eyes. His wrinkled face offered no expression until he lifted a bushy brow. "Or did you have business elsewhere this morning?"

He'd obviously read the *Gazette*. "Where else would I go this time of morning, James?" he asked as he climbed into the buggy.

James turned about to grasp the reins with gnarled hands, then set the horse in motion. "The office it is, then." In short order, he began whistling the first of many hymns that made up his morning concert.

Most mornings Henry either barely tolerated or completely ignored the musical stylings of his driver, but today he found both most difficult to accomplish. Was he wrong, or had James intentionally raised his volume higher than normal?

As the buggy bounced along, Henry cast a glance at the folded paper on the seat beside him. Most citizens of San Francisco were acquainted with the murder victim, if not personally, then by reputation. Bynum's money came from sources both unknown and seemingly unlimited in their nature. His style was often bold and brash, and his largesse was not limited to the tawdry taverns and bawdy houses he was reputed to own. He was known to place large sums of cash or bags of gold on the doorsteps of the local orphanage or bawdy houses or in public spots around town, then laugh along with his cronies as children fought adults for a portion of the stake.

Some found this game amusing, while others offered the donations as proof of the man's soft heart and sterling character. Henry was not among either camp.

Asa once mentioned the possibility of Chambers and Hill representing the Bynum fellow in a series of real estate deals. Henry felt it would never do for the future mayor of San Francisco's law firm to represent such a character, especially when people like Frank Bynum were the very ones Henry intended to run out of town should he be elected. Thankfully he had a friend as well as a partner in Asa Chambers. The representation was never offered, and nothing further had been spoken on the subject.

Henry tucked the offending paper under his arm and climbed out of the buggy, then gave a cursory wave to the driver and turned toward his office. When the rig clattered out of sight, Henry whirled about and headed for the newspaper office.

As he strode toward his destination, he forced out the occasional greeting to future constituents, including an elderly gentleman who grasped hold of Henry's arm and waxed poetic on the rough political waters in the States for the better part of ten minutes. After assuring the man he would look into his concerns, Henry finally wrenched free and continued on.

As he neared the *Gazette*, he straightened his shoulders and picked up his pace. No matter his mood, the campaign had to be foremost in his mind at all times. A bit of irritation at a misprint might not be remembered come election time, while a ready smile and the willingness to listen to his constituents would.

Or *was* it a misprint? Thus far, Russell Madison had kept the *Gazette* out of the political fray. Perhaps this was his subtle way of endorsing the opposition. Henry stopped short at the errant thought.

By the time he caught sight of the newspaper office, the thought had become a real concern, and he'd worked up quite a head of steam. Now to find the guilty party and unleash a bit of that steam, starting with the Madison fellow.

◆　◆　◆

Despite the threat of rain, it was a beautiful morning. Helen had been at work nearly an hour, awakened well before dawn by the strangest of dreams. Someone chased her through the streets of San Francisco, some small unnamed and unseen person carrying a white object in his tiny hand and bent on an unidentified evil deed. Exhausted, she finally gave up on sleep and dressed for work, fearing her dream might end—and not happily—should she return to her slumber.

She'd arrived at the paper to find Mr. Madison bent over his desk, pen in hand. Being an absurdly early riser and generally the first on the job had its perks. Today the habit had caused her to be targeted for a special assignment: manning the front desk and attending to matters until Mr. Madison returned from yet another early morning meeting with the police chief.

Helen took to the task with trepidation. She tucked her receipts beneath her arm and reached for her stool. Perhaps she could get a bit of work done rather than standing about and merely looking foolish.

Teetering on the edge of the stool to keep from revealing her crinolines, she reached for the first of many receipts awaiting her attention. "Doesn't he realize I have a mountain of receipts that have to be—"

The doors crashed open, and an enraged man stalked toward her. She jumped and almost fell backward. Receipts went flying about like leaves in a strong wind.

The politician.

Straightening her skirts, Helen reached for the edge of the counter to steady herself. *Crash.* She jumped and whirled about to see the stool where she had formerly perched on its side atop the debris, a victim of her swirling crinolines. A late-falling receipt from a supplier back East fluttered past her nose and landed atop her shoe as she pressed her hands against her sides to still the movement of her skirt.

With care, she returned her attention to the red-faced man on the other side of the counter. Had she actually found him attractive upon their first meeting? Perhaps a dose of kindness would counteract his ire. When she mustered a smile, he answered with a frown.

"May I help you?" came out in a series of squeaks.

The politician slammed a folded newspaper between them, and Helen jumped yet again. "I demand to speak to Mr. Madison at once."

"He's out," Helen managed to say.

"Then I shall speak to the person in charge immediately." He leaned forward, eyes narrowed, vein pulsing on his temple. "A member of this establishment has committed a grievous error that must be corrected at once."

Something inside froze. Helen opened her mouth, but nothing came out. She tried again to no avail, then attempted prayer. *Lord, please help me,* was all she could manage.

The politician pounded his fist on the counter and leaned closer. Helen took a step back and collided with the leg of the overturned stool. This time her attempts to right herself were a bit more successful and no more furniture or office receipts were sacrificed. Only her pride and her shin suffered.

"Madam, have you not heard me? I insist on speaking to the person in command of this enterprise at once."

"It is I, s–s–sir." She gulped, eyes closed. "What can I do f–f–for you?"

Silence.

Helen opened her eyes to see the politician smiling. The anger that contorted his face had abated slightly, although no one short of a daft fool would mistake him for a happy man.

"No, dear," he said in a curt voice, "it's your employer to whom I wish to speak. Now, run and fetch him."

Of all the nerve. "I am in charge."

A complete sentence. *Thank You, Lord.*

"Am I to understand that *you* are running this publication?"

Rather than risk further humiliation struggling with words that refused to emerge, Helen settled for a nod, then added a smile as a postscript. For a moment, the strategy seemed to work. The man's tense features relaxed, he took a less threatening stance, and he even spared her what looked to be the beginning of a smile.

"Dare I ask? Have I not met you before?"

Quite the welcome shift in topic. "Why, yes, actually." She nodded. "You see, my friend and I were attending the Fourth of July festivities, and at their conclusion, Penney left her handbag behind. You and your. . ."

"Mother," he supplied.

"Yes, well," Helen said as she reached down to right the stool. "You and your mother were kind enough to retrieve the handbag."

The politician reached down to retrieve a pair of receipts and set them onto the counter beside the newspaper. "So you are employed by this establishment then?"

Helen settled on the stool and folded her hands in her lap. "I am."

He gave her a sideways look. "In a supervisory role?"

"Well, actually, I am a bookkeeper, but Mr. Madison just asked me to—"

Without warning, his countenance changed. "Then you, Madam Supervisor," he said slowly, "owe me a public apology and an explanation of this." He swept his hand across the newspaper's headline. "And along with the apology and the explanation, I demand the idiot who did this be fired forthwith."

Fired?

Anger simmered, then quickly hit the boiling stage. How dare this. . .this *politician* treat her in such a manner? Why, if she weren't a lady and the daughter of a politician herself, she would. . .

"Madam, are you daft?" His voice rose well beyond the proper tone, summoning Penney from the back.

"Well, hello, Mr. Hill." Penney smiled and wiped her hands on her apron. "Is there a problem?"

"Problem?" He held his volume in check, but his tone sounded deadly as he returned his gaze to Helen. "Do me the favor of reading this headline, please."

Helen turned the paper around and stared at the boldface type announcing a break in the investigation of the biggest murder to hit San Francisco in years. Mr. Madison had been rightly proud to have been the first in San Francisco to run the story, prouder still to have her read the copy and deliver the corrected manuscript to Penney before it went to press. She looked up to see the politician staring at her intently.

"Do you see the problem with this headline, Madam Supervisor?"

Once more she read the words spanning the top of the morning edition before handing it back to him. "No, actually it looks fine to me."

"I see." He nodded and studied the headline before looking up at Penney and then at Helen. "Can either of you tell me the name of the fellow the police are seeking?"

"I believe that would be Henry Hall, sir," Penney said.

"Henry Hall." The politician seemed to contemplate the name a moment before spreading the paper out on the counter. "Then pray tell me whether that is the appellation you see here?"

Penney leaned against Helen and took the paper. Her lower lip quivered as she read the name aloud. "Henry Hill." She looked up at the politician and let the paper drop onto the counter. "Oh no," she whispered.

Helen snatched up the paper. "Henry Hill." Her gaze met his. "That's you."

"Yes, madam, it is."

"Oh my."

"I'm sure there's a reasonable explanation, sir," Penney said. "This is probably one of those silly coincidences and not a mistake at all. Let me go get the copy Mr. Madison gave us, and I'll show you."

Penney's bright smile belied the tear Helen noted on the woman's cheek. How dare that *man* make her friend cry over something obviously coincidental?

As her friend scurried toward the back of the building, Helen took a deep breath and exhaled slowly—one of Mother's tricks for remaining a lady when the words you desire to speak would brand you otherwise. Feeling reasonably confident she held a measure of control, Helen leaned forward and spread this morning's copy of the *Gazette* between them. She took her time meeting his gaze and held it a bit longer than polite society might deem proper.

"Are you *sure* you're not a suspect, Mr. Hill?"

His glare precluded further argument. This time when he leaned forward, Helen took a step back even though the sturdy counter filled the space between them.

"Are you sure this is *really* a misprint?"

Her gasp of surprise must have had the desired effect, for the politician turned on his heels and strode away. "Make the necessary changes or face prosecution, madam," he called as he reached the door.

"Sir," she called to his retreating back, "to be sure, this situation must be very distressing for you, but I f–f–fail to see how this sort of behavior will accomplish—"

"Here it is," Penney called as she rounded the corner and thrust the edited copy of Mr. Madison's story into Helen's hand. "I told you the headline was right. I spelled it just like it shows on Mr. Madison's notes." She stopped short and looked around. "Where did he go?"

Helen shrugged and set the copy on the counter. "Wherever bad-mannered politicians hide when they're not upsetting nice people." She touched Penney's sleeve. "I'm sorry he made you cry."

Penney shook her head. "I'm just glad it was all a mistake. It must be very upsetting to be running for an important political office and then learn that a murderer shares your name."

Helen watched Penney return to her work, then knelt to retrieve the receipts littering the floor. Amy arrived with Jennie trailing a few steps behind. Both greeted Helen before heading toward the back of the building. Helen checked the clock. Almost nine. Mr. Madison would probably return soon as well.

As long as that awful Mr. Hill did not return.

"What an angry fellow," she said under her breath as she collected the last of the slips of paper. "He'll never be elected to anything with that attitude."

She picked up the copy to set it aside and a name caught her eye. Not the name in the headline, Henry Hill, which Helen had written at Mr. Madison's request, but the one appearing in the second sentence of Mr. Madison's story.

"Early this very evening, the citizens of San Francisco were presented with the name of the possible culprit of the murder of one of our fair fellows. Law enforcement personnel are searching for one Henry Hall. . . ."

Helen let the paper drop. "Oh no."

Chapter 4

Henry walked past the newspaper offices twice in the half hour since his confrontation with the green-eyed woman, and both times his heart told him to go in and apologize for his rude behavior. So did his conscience.

Why he'd strolled past without stopping, without doing what he knew he should, defied reason. To be certain, he owed both women an apology, for he'd surely made the little one cry, but something about his exchange with the tall one set his jaw—and his heart—on edge.

She made him want to be right.

He shook his head and went back to work on his writ. No, that wasn't it. Henry began to twirl his pen.

She made him want to be. . .

Enough foolishness.

With force, he reapplied pen to paper and attempted to continue with the writ he'd set to drafting. Instead of coherent and intelligent words filling the page, his pen stalled, and so did the eloquent phrasings.

What in the world was wrong? Even the incident with the counterfeit note from his father hadn't caused him as much uneasiness as this.

He dropped his pen and watched a nasty splat of ink decorate a corner of the page. He'd spend another hour redrafting the document for sure, longer if he continued to let his thoughts wander.

Leaning back in his chair, Henry laced his fingers behind his head and closed his eyes. No doubt whatever ailed him, its source was the woman.

Rather bookish, that one, and well past the age of employment. To be blunt, the first time he met her she'd barely made an impression. Why, until she mentioned the fact, he hadn't realized the woman at the *Gazette* was the same one whom he had met days earlier on the street.

He met so many people these days. A hazard of his chosen profession—or at least the profession he hoped would choose him. What's a politician without an office to hold?

Better off.

A strange thought. Did he really question God's plan for him to pursue the mayor's office?

Henry heard her before he actually saw her. She called his name, stiffly and formally, and with the slightest hint of a stutter.

Opening his eyes, he saw the object of his thoughts standing in the doorway. She wore yellow. Why hadn't he noticed before?

"Do come in, Miss. . ."

"Morgan." She wrung her hands together, then clasped them behind her back. "M—m—may I intrude for a moment?"

He stood a bit too quickly and pushed away from the desk, then gestured to the chair nearest him. "Do sit down."

Miss Morgan waved away his invitation with a sweep of her gloved hand and fixed her attention somewhere behind him. As she exhaled, she met his gaze with a direct look. Her dark brows furrowed.

"Forgive me," she said with excruciating care. "I am. . ." She paused and closed her eyes, then opened them slowly. Henry made the absurd observation that they were green and fringed with dark lashes.

"Sir, I bear complete responsibility for the m—m—m—misprint. I assure you it was unintentional."

His heart sank, and so did he, landing in his chair with an unceremonious *thud*. "I assure you, Miss Morgan, that it is I who should be begging your forgiveness. My behavior was terribly and inexcusably rude."

The lady looked a bit perplexed. "I beg to differ, sir. You see I—I—I know a bit about the workings of a political campaign and a m—m—m—mistake of this magnitude that could cast aspersions on the candidate, well. . ." She paused and looked as if she'd spoken more than she intended.

The lady knows about politics? Interesting.

Henry let the silence fall thick between them, a lawyer's courtroom trick designed to cause the other party to speak rather than bear the quiet. It didn't work. Instead Miss Morgan turned on her heels and walked out without so much as a word of good-bye.

He sat for a very long time, pondering the situation and going over each word of their conversation. Somewhere his plan to apologize had gotten derailed, but he hadn't the slightest idea how to get it back on track.

The rest of the morning passed slowly with work done in fits and starts. Finally, when the clock in the anteroom rang the noon hour, he donned his coat and hat and stuffed what he could of the work on his desk into his valise. If he couldn't force his ability to concentrate into submission at his desk, perhaps he could tackle the job on the long walk home and be of some good to his clients after a proper lunch. Mother would be happy with his decision to work the afternoon away in his study rather than return to the office.

The better to drag him off to the opera or some dreadfully boring dinner all the sooner.

Henry smiled, took the back stairs two at a time, and emerged into the alley. As the door closed behind him, he realized he'd left his revolver locked in his desk drawer. He pulled on the knob. Locked tight.

Casting a glance up at the second-floor window of his office suite, Henry contemplated his choices. He could go around the block to reenter the building through the front door, or he could forget all about retrieving the revolver today. Opting for the latter, he turned to head east toward home. At Coromundel Street, he briefly considered a side trip to the *Gazette*. What would he say to her? Worse, how would he handle a casual appearance at the paper when his last visit had been anything but polite?

To be certain, apologies had been exchanged, but Henry still felt something had been left unsaid, some deed undone. If only he could ascertain just what that was.

At Baker Street, he veered to the right and began the steep climb toward its intersection with Decatur Avenue. "Thank You, Lord, for cooler temperatures today."

"You ought to be thanking the Lord that him and me don't shoot you dead right here on the street."

Henry whirled around to find himself face-to-face with two masked thugs pointing revolvers at him. The tallest of the pair, a man with more scars than teeth, lowered his weapon to wrench away the valise. The other one pressed his gun against Henry's forehead.

As Henry watched the man rifle through legal papers and court documents, he waited for his opportunity to use his own gun on the petty thieves. The gun he had left back in his office. His heart sank.

"There ain't nothin' in there worth takin'." Toothless tossed the valise at Henry's feet, and several documents slid into the street. A particularly important writ landed unceremoniously in a puddle alongside the silver pen his mother had given him when he graduated from law school.

"Just shoot him and get it over with," Shorty said.

Get it over with.

No. Not today. Squaring his shoulders, Henry prepared to use the only weapon he had left—his fists. Toothless leaned in close and narrowed his eyes. Shorty pulled back on the trigger with a loud *click.*

Henry refused to allow fear to cloud his thinking. If this was how God planned for him to go to heaven, then so be it. If not, then all the better. He'd take them both at once if he had to.

The tall fellow poked at Henry's chest with his free hand. "Funny, you don't look like a man who don't pay his debts." Toothless stood so near that his rancid breath blew toward him in waves. "So me and him are gonna give you a chance to pay up."

"Pay up?" Henry searched his mind for the identity of the thugs. Had he represented one of them before? Worse, had he prosecuted them? "I don't know what you're talking about."

Not the most brilliant statement but a decent stall nonetheless.

Shorty giggled. His gaze shifted from Henry to Toothless, and he giggled again. His fingers never moved, and neither did the gun.

"Look, fellows, whoever this interloper is that you seek, I assure you it is not I." Henry notched up his smile and focused on Toothless, whom he'd decided was the leader of the pair. "I'm not without resources." He paused a moment to let the idea sink in, all the while deciding where on the thug's body to aim his first punch. "So what do say you on this? Put those guns away, and we'll discuss this like gentlemen. Perhaps I can lead you to the person you seek."

"Gentlemen?" Toothless snorted. "That's a funny one. It truly is." His eyes narrowed. "Gentlemen don't forget when they owe somebody, though, do they?"

"My point exactly." Henry's left hand itched to connect with the criminal's jaw. "I assure you I've not forgotten any debts," he said as he waited for just the right moment.

"Maybe we oughta help him remember." Shorty's forefinger danced inches away from the trigger, which from Henry's perspective looked enormous. "You got paid for something, and you didn't deliver. Now you gotta pay that money back."

"What are you talking about?"

Toothless leaned closer. "Maybe you should ask your—"

"Hello? Mr. Hill, is that you?"

Henry tore his attention from the gun to the approaching pedestrian and groaned. The lady wore yellow and carried a folded newspaper under her arm.

"She a friend of yours?" Toothless leered at Helen, and Henry fought the urge to capture the thug's attention with his fists. With Miss Morgan so close, however, he could hardly risk the possibility of her being robbed by the hooligans as well—or worse, being shot.

"A friend?" He shook his head. "Hardly. The woman has caused me nothing but grief."

◆　◆　◆

Helen slowed her pace and clutched the paper to her chest. It was warm, but the heat she felt on her face didn't come from the temperature or the steep climb up Baker Avenue.

Mr. Hill's companions whirled about and snapped to attention, hands behind their backs. An interesting pair, those two, and nothing like the fellows she expected the politician to keep company with. Perhaps they were clients.

The taller one wore a dark coat that seemed absurdly heavy for the temperate weather, while the other, a short man with a thin patch of sandy hair and what seemed to be a perpetual grin, dressed in a more conservative suit befitting a professional of some sort. Only his shoes seemed out of place, rough work boots more fit for the field than the city.

Helen returned her attention to the politician, who looked ready to bolt and run at any moment. Of course, he was a busy man, and she'd taken up far too much of his time today.

"Forgive me for intruding once again," she said, "b–b–but Mr. Madison asked that I deliver this personally."

"No intrusion at all, miss." The short one widened his grin. "In fact, it's a right pleasure."

Henry Hill said nothing.

Her gaze landed on the overturned valise and the documents spilling into the street. The taller of the strangers must have noticed, for he stuffed something into the pocket of his coat, then quickly reached to right the briefcase and stuffed muddy papers inside. He handed the briefcase back to Mr. Hill, and the pair exchanged a terse look. "We'll be in touch," she heard the tall one say.

Perhaps these were clients with whom Mr. Hill was upset. There certainly seemed to be no camaraderie among them.

Whatever the situation, none of the three men looked particularly happy to see her. Of the three, Mr. Hill seemed to be the most bothered by her presence. Truly he looked more piqued than he had this morning at the paper. Perhaps she shouldn't have greeted the politician or interrupted what looked to be a street-side business meeting. It *was* behavior of the most daring caliber, at least for her.

Still, Mr. Madison had selected her to deliver a copy of this afternoon's special edition of the *Gazette* to Mr. Hill immediately. Considering the magnitude of her mistake, a bit more humiliation was nothing.

She took a few more halting steps and thrust the paper in Mr. Hill's direction. He stared at her hand as if it were a foreign object. Finally he lifted his gaze to meet hers. The irritation on his face hadn't reached his eyes. No, something else lay there. Was she mistaken, or did he flash a warning with those dark eyes?

"I–i–it's this afternoon's special edition," she finally said before stabbing the newspaper toward him. "I'll not b–b–bother you further."

His curt nod served as an answer. Helen did not linger. Instead she walked back to the *Gazette* at a brisk pace, all the while praying this encounter with Henry Hill would be her last.

She cast a quick glance over her shoulder as she turned onto Freedman's Street and saw that the three gentlemen had already parted ways. The strange pair was headed south at a brisk pace, but Mr. Hill still stood where she'd left him, one hand shading his eyes from the noonday sun and the other on his hip.

He was staring in her direction.

Chapter 5

Henry spent most of Saturday and Sunday thinking about *not* thinking about Helen Morgan. It was absurd, this feeling he had that somehow he had not seen the last of the timid woman. He breathed deep of the musty air and dropped his valise on his desk. "Ridiculous."

With the retraction satisfactorily printed in Friday's special edition of the *Gazette* and an update regarding the search for tavern owner Henry Hall as this morning's headline, it seemed as though Henry's tarnished image had been repaired.

"What's ridiculous?"

Henry reached for his revolver and laid aim before he could blink. When he saw Asa Chambers in his sights, he put away his gun and gave his friend a hearty slap on the back. At nearly his height, Asa wore his weight across his shoulders and in arms that belonged on a boxer rather than a lawyer.

He punched one of those beefy arms for good measure. "You scared the life out of me, Asa."

"And almost out of me." Asa took the punch with good-natured grace, then leaned against the edge of Henry's desk.

"How'd the speech go?"

Henry shrugged. "Fine, I suppose. The crowd seemed to applaud in all the right places, although I did skip around a bit."

His friend leaned back in the chair and fixed his gaze on the window behind Henry. "I suppose you're wondering why I'm back in San Francisco before the end of the month."

Henry settled into his chair and steepled his hands. "The thought *had* occurred to me."

Asa plopped down in a chair across from the desk and closed his eyes. His fingers drummed a rhythm on his knees, and his foot pounded a restless accompaniment. Since childhood, or at least from the age of eight, when Henry had first been introduced to his best friend, Asa Chambers had been in motion. To stop moving meant he'd fallen asleep.

"Too much to do back here," he said slowly. "And absolutely nothing worthwhile to do up there."

"Translated, my friend, that means what?"

He opened his eyes. "That means I couldn't spend another minute up there when you needed me here to help with your campaign."

"That's the sorriest excuse I've ever heard." Henry chuckled. "I can't believe your father let you go."

"Well, actually, he thinks I'm on an extended fishing trip." Asa slowed his drumming long enough to study his nails. "I figure that will buy me at least two weeks here in the city."

He gave Henry a sideways look. "What? We are fishing for votes, aren't we?"

"Excuse me, sirs," a small voice called. "There be a note for you."

Henry rose to follow the voice, only to find the lobby vacant. He darted into the hall to find it empty as well. A single sheet of white paper, folded in half, crunched beneath his feet, and Henry bent to retrieve it.

"Who was that?" Asa called from his perch in Henry's office.

"Don't know," Henry said. "But he left this."

He settled into his chair and opened the note. *Pay your debt, or Miss Morgan will pay for you*, it said in an elegant script. As befitting a missive from a coward, the note bore no signature. *Interesting.*

Henry threw the chair back and stormed to the door, ignoring his hat and coat. Friday he thought he'd convinced the thugs that they'd gone after the wrong man. Further, he'd convinced himself he'd been the random victim of street hoodlums and nothing more. Obviously he'd underestimated the thugs. To cast aspersions on his good name was one thing, but to threaten an innocent woman was quite another.

Asa followed him out into the hall. "Where are you going?"

"To the chief of police. This has gone far enough."

An hour later, standing outside the chief's office with Asa, Henry tried not to let his anger show. While the chief had given the impression of being appropriately disturbed by the letter, he'd all but laughed off Henry's concern for Miss Morgan's safety and ignored Asa's concerns altogether.

The chief put off the note and the message on the handkerchief to political jealousy at the least and political trickery at worst. He promised to investigate but made the statement with little enthusiasm. His parting words had been to leave the worrying to the police department.

While logic told Henry he should do as the policeman suggested and let law enforcement handle the problem, intuition told him he should at least warn Miss Morgan of the possible danger. An informed person generally took fewer risks.

A bell sounded in the distance, signaling a packet boat's arrival in the harbor. Overhead a pair of seabirds circled, their calls punctuating the dull roar of carriages and horse traffic on busy Coromundel Street.

"Well," Asa said, "what do you intend to do now?"

Henry inhaled the pungent odor of horses and the sea and shrugged. "I'm not sure."

Asa took him by the arm and darted across Coromundel Street. "Forget about the woman. You've got an office to win, and I've only got two weeks to help you win it. What say you to a meeting of the minds back at the office? I've got some ideas for winning this election that I'd like to go over with you."

Shaking off his friend's grip, Henry turned away and headed for the offices of the *Gazette* two blocks away. "Later," he called to Asa as he rounded the corner. "I've got something more important to attend to first."

Outside the newspaper building, Henry froze. His encounters with Miss Morgan, although surprisingly frequent, had not been particularly pleasant. To be blunt, the cause lay with him, and he knew it.

Perhaps he'd better take a different tack on this visit. He stared at his reflection in the window and caught himself frowning. Immediately he pasted on a smile and strode inside.

He would be pleasant, state his concern for the lady, and be on his way. The less attention paid to his visit, the better, and his duty to a fellow citizen would be done.

The elderly woman behind the counter was not Miss Morgan. A setback, albeit a minor one, he decided as he upped his smile a notch and tipped his hat. "Is Miss Morgan about?" he inquired. "I'd like a moment with her, please."

With a nod, the woman scurried away in a whirl of skirts and crinolines, nearly knocking over a stool in her haste. A moment later she returned with another young woman. "Miss Morgan's been sent on an errand," the petite blond said. "Perhaps you'd prefer to wait here."

Henry cast a glance behind her and saw a gaggle of young women, three to be factual, staring at him and whispering. One smiled while the other two nodded. The blond turned and gave them a look that sent them all scampering back to their work.

"Ah, no, actually I'm wondering if perhaps you could give me an idea of where Miss Morgan's errands might take her. It might be more convenient to find her rather than to wait here." He stared pointedly at the women, who whirled about and went back to their work. "I wouldn't want to be a bother."

Moments later, Henry was heading toward the harbor, where he'd been told Miss Morgan had been sent to retrieve bundles of newspapers and other parcels sent from back East. He spied the object of his concern wearing blue and making her way across the uneven boards of the sidewalk, a small army of urchins following in her wake. Each carried something—a box or a paper-wrapped package or some other container. Miss Morgan marched ahead, whistling, of all things. Her hat bobbed as she walked, and a blue ribbon bounced and fluttered in the breeze.

Rather than disturb the little parade, Henry stuck to the shadows and watched as the motley group made its way down the other side of the street. Occasionally, Miss Morgan would stop and offer a handkerchief to one or a smile to another. When the party turned the corner and disappeared, Henry picked his way across the muddy street and hugged the buildings to keep out of sight.

At Freedman's Street, he froze. Just across the way he saw a familiar face. Toothless. As Miss Morgan's group headed north, so did he. When they made an abrupt turn to the east, he did the same.

A block away from the *Gazette*, Henry saw the glint of what appeared to be a pistol in Toothless's hand. "You there," he called as he pushed past a pair of matrons and an elderly coachman to barge into the busy street. Toothless glanced in his direction, but Henry couldn't tell if he'd actually heard Henry's cry. Too much traffic and noise separated them. When Henry made his way past carriages and horses to reach the other side, Toothless was gone.

At least temporarily.

Thankfully the little parade had stopped on the steps of the *Gazette*, oblivious to the incident. Henry leaned against the side of the mercantile and watched Miss Morgan receive each urchin's package, then reward him with a coin. When all members of the group had dispersed, Miss Morgan began to stack the items to carry inside. The bundles listed dangerously toward the street, and several seemed about to burst at the seams.

Miss Morgan looked as though she could use some assistance. A perfect invitation to an accidental meeting. Henry smoothed his lapels and strolled as casually as he could toward the woman in blue. Until he could make other arrangements, he'd just have to see to Miss Morgan's safety himself.

"Well, good morning," he said with a politician's practiced smile. "Fancy meeting you again."

◆　◆　◆

Helen jumped, and a paper-wrapped parcel went flying, nearly hitting a farmer square in the back of his head. Mr. Hill showed his athletic prowess by catching the bundle before it landed on the sidewalk—or the farmer. A quick flip of the politician's wrist, and the item lay in her arms once more.

"Thank you," she managed to whisper, "b–b–but I can manage, really."

"Nonsense."

He nodded to a passing citizen, who called him by name, then turned his attention back to her. Helen made the silly observation that his eyes were just a shade lighter than his hair. His smile seemed just for her, as if he'd created it special and saved it just for this moment. She shook off the romantic notion and squared her thoughts and her shoulders as she watched Mr. Hill heft an inordinately large pair of boxes onto his left shoulder.

"Where do you want these, Miss Morgan?"

"No, really," she said as she scurried behind him. "You'll hurt yourself."

Ignoring her comment, he set off toward the door. "You cannot leave these packages on the street corner, and I've seen the womenfolk this paper deems suitable for employment. While they are pleasant to view, not a single one of them, yourself included, could be termed particularly muscular."

Not like you. Her face flushed with heat. *What a simpering idiot I've become.*

Before she could protest further, the politician had deposited the packages on the counter and returned to gather up an armload of items. She followed his lead, removing a box or two from the steps while he stole her breath by taking twice as many on each trip.

"What is going on?" Penney called as Helen dropped a box of newspapers atop the heap on the counter.

"I'll just put these on the floor," Mr. Hill said as he positioned a pair of small barrels against the wall and strode back outside.

Penney smiled. "Why, Helen, it looks like you've found a knight in shining armor."

The heat in her cheeks turned up a notch. "Oh, hush."

Penney giggled. "I *would* help, but then the job wouldn't take nearly as long, and your knight would have to disappear back to the castle far too soon." She said the last of the words just as Mr. Hill walked back in with another armload of items.

"Something wrong?" he asked as he straightened his hat and pressed his hand over his lapel.

"No, nothing," both women said at once.

He gave them a quizzical look, then headed back to his work. Penney's giggles followed Helen as she ducked back outside.

In short order, the items were stacked inside, and Helen found herself standing on a busy sidewalk staring at one of the most public figures in San Francisco. Perspiration glistened at his temples, and his damp hair clung to his forehead beneath his hat. His starched collar hung a bit limp, and a smudge of dirt decorated his right cheek. As heat-wilted and mussed up as Henry Hill looked, the politician was still the handsomest man she'd seen in quite a long time.

He shifted his weight from one foot to the other, arms crossed. Helen braved eye contact only to look away. On the street, a horse nickered, a patron of the local mercantile shouted a salutation to a passerby, and a pair of nicely dressed young ladies offered Mr. Hill a giggle and a greeting.

All the while he kept his gaze fixed on her.

Say something.

"I don't know how I would have m–m–managed without your help, Mr. Hill." *Wonderful, Helen. You sound like a simpering idiot. And a Morgan does not simper.*

The politician looked around as if he was trying to find someone. "My pleasure, I assure you," he mumbled.

Helen followed his gaze and saw nothing but the usual collection of San Franciscans going about their daily business. Something caught his attention, and he seemed instantly distracted by it. Only a tug at his watch chain and the checking of the time on a gold pocket watch seemed to change his focus.

Did he have an appointment elsewhere? Helen tried not to feel disappointment. Of course her knight in shining armor had just been an ordinary man coming to her aid. No ordinary man, she corrected, but a busy attorney and possibly the next mayor.

"I've kept you from your duties far too long, s–s–sir."

He seemed surprised that she spoke. "What? No, you see. . ." He paused and cast another quick glance over his shoulder before surprising her by turning his dark gaze on her. "Forgive me," he said.

"We seem to be saying that to each other quite regularly."

Another long silence fell between them. Finally, Mr. Hill cleared his throat and placed his hand on her arm. "With your permission, I would like to change that."

She shook her head. "I don't understand. What do you mean?"

"What I mean is, I would like very much if. . ."

Another maddening pause. Helen had to remind herself to breathe.

"Forgive me," he said, then chuckled. "If only I had a vote for every time I've said that to you."

"And I to you, Mr. Hill." She took a step backward and winced when her shin collided with the steps. "So now that we have that s–s–settled, I'm afraid I really must return to work."

Chapter 6

Henry stood on the sidewalk like a fool and tried to think of something witty to say. What was it about this woman?

"Wait!" he called, but the doors had already closed behind her. He looked around and saw nothing untoward. No thugs lurking in the shadows or other oddities held him there. Why then did he follow Helen Morgan inside the offices of the *Gazette*, the very place where he'd humiliated himself venting his anger only days ago?

To keep her safe, he decided as he picked his way through the packages and barrels to reach the counter. Once the thugs had been caught, he and Helen Morgan would part ways. Until then, he had a duty to protect the innocent woman he'd unintentionally involved in a potentially dangerous situation.

"Excuse me," he called, but instead of Miss Morgan answering his call, another young lady appeared from behind the boxes. He vaguely remembered her as the woman whose handbag he'd retrieved from the Independence Day celebration. The same woman he'd upset along with Miss Morgan on his last visit to the newspaper.

"Hello, I'm Penney. May I help you?" she asked brightly.

If only he hadn't made such a fool of himself before. Where to start?

Penney leaned against the counter and gave him a sideways look. "Is there something wrong?"

"Actually, yes," he said. "I owe you an apology. I was terribly rude before, and I—"

"Don't give it another thought." The woman waved away his concerns with a sweep of her hand. "I would be upset if I were in your shoes, too."

"Yes, well, thank you." He tried to effect a casual demeanor. "Would Miss Morgan be about?"

"About what?" Penney covered her mouth with her hand and giggled. "Sorry," she said a moment later. "I couldn't help that one. Why don't I go and fetch Helen?"

She disappeared, and soon Henry heard whispers coming from somewhere behind the boxes. The whispers became a bit louder, a bit more insistent. One voice belonged to the young woman, the other, he decided, must be Miss Morgan. Unfortunately, any understanding of the words spoken escaped him.

And then Penney returned. Alone. "I'm sorry, Mr. Hill. I told her she had a visitor, but I can't seem to budge her from her desk."

So, he'd been spurned. Worse things had happened, to be sure, and yet it stung. "I see."

Penney's face brightened. "So there's nothing left to do but go to her. Follow me."

Henry followed Penney through a maze of desks and chairs and the odd table or two until she turned abruptly. There, in the farthest corner of the building, sat a desk that looked very much like his—piled with papers organized in neat but towering stacks. Atop one stack was a thick volume of Shakespeare's tragedies, and beside another lay a battered copy of Jane

Austen's *Sense and Sensibility*.

So the woman knew about politics *and* enjoyed Shakespeare. Interesting.

Behind the desk sat the object of his concern—and consternation. When she saw him, she stood.

"Penney!" Her cheeks flushed the most interesting shade of pink as she crossed her arms over her chest. "You know I don't want visitors back here."

"Mr. Hill is not a visitor, are you, Mr. Hill?"

"I know you're busy, Miss Morgan." Henry stepped forward as much to garner Miss Morgan's attention as to shield Penney from her coworker's ire. "I assure you I'll be brief."

Her countenance softened a bit, but the color remained high in her cheeks. "All right." She began to drum her fingers on the surface of her desk. "Be brief, then."

"Have dinner with me."

"Dinner?" Penney and Miss Morgan said the word at the same time.

"Yes," Penney said with a grin.

"No, thank you," Miss Morgan answered a second later. "I have plans."

"Nonsense," Penney said. "What time?"

"Penney!" Helen protested. "I demand you both remove yourselves at once." She turned her wrath on poor Penney, who merely broadened her smile. "I can accept my own dates, thank you very much."

"Then you *do* accept," Henry said. "Excellent. I'll call for you at half past seven so we can dine before the opera."

"Dinner and the opera? Wait, you don't even know where I live," he heard as he stepped outside.

◆　◆　◆

Helen narrowed her eyes and stared at Penney. "I cannot believe you actually made a date for me, in my presence. I am not a child. I can answer for myself."

Penney shrugged. "Oh, you answered for yourself," she said as she turned and began to walk away. "You just gave the wrong answer, so I corrected it a bit."

"Corrected it a bit?" Helen followed Penney back to the typesetting table. "I'd say that telling a man I would have dinner with him when I specifically said I would not is somewhat more than 'correcting it a bit.'"

"Oh, now don't be angry." Penney reached for the tray of letters and began to arrange them on the table. "It's just one evening, and he *does* seem to be a nice fellow." She pressed her palms to the table and looked Helen in the eye. "Besides, what did you have planned that would be more fun than having dinner with one of the most eligible bachelors in San Francisco?"

"For your information, I had planned to finish *Sense and Sensibility* this evening."

"Jane Austen again?" Penney rolled her eyes like a petulant child. "Dear, I love Miss Austen's novels as much as the next person, but I will never choose one of her books over the possibility of a lovely evening of male companionship."

"Who's spending a lovely evening with a male companion?"

The pair whirled around to see Mr. Madison standing at the door.

"Helen," Penney said quickly. "She has plans for the evening with a gentleman caller."

Helen slid Penney a warning look. Was her friend blushing? She shook her head.

With that, she began to make her way back to the solace of her little corner. Perhaps a few hours with her receipts and numbers would fade the humiliation she now felt. To her surprise, Mr. Madison appeared at her desk a moment later.

"I didn't mean to embarrass you, Miss Morgan."

She waved away his apology and picked up a pencil. "There will be no 'lovely evening,' because the man doesn't even know where I live."

"Actually," Mr. Madison said slowly, "he does now."

Helen dropped her pencil and watched it roll onto the floor. "What do you mean?"

Mr. Madison grinned and began to study his ink-stained nails. "I told him."

◆ ◆ ◆

Somehow, Helen managed to get through the afternoon, although she knew she'd spend the next morning double-checking each column she'd added to be certain the tallies came out right. At a quarter to six, with Penney's prodding, she dropped her pencil into the drawer and reached for her reticule. Slipping *Sense and Sensibility* inside, she rose to walk past Penney and the others with as much dignity as she could manage.

She'd almost reached the door when Penney came rushing up, her shawl pulled over her shoulders and her handbag under her arm. "I'm going with you," she said as she pushed on the door and strolled outside.

"On the date?" Helen asked.

"No, silly," Penney said. "I'm going back home to help you get ready."

"I assure you I'm quite capable of dressing myself," Helen said, but a short while later, standing in the room she shared with Penney, she began to doubt the truth of that statement. It seemed as though each dress Helen pulled out of the armoire was rejected by Penney. Finally her friend sent Helen off for a perfumed bath while she picked out a "suitable outfit."

"You'd think I was headed for an audience with the queen," she muttered as she sank into lavender-scented water.

"I just want everything to be perfect," Penney called.

Helen submerged herself in the warm water up to her chin. "Why?" she called. "Are you worried I might not get another chance?"

Penney arrived with a towel and an uncharacteristic frown. "No, but I am worried that you won't *accept* another chance."

At ten minutes to seven, Helen donned a green frock that had been languishing in the back of her armoire. Leftover from her days back East, the dress was one she couldn't bear to part with and yet had never expected to have use of again.

Father had issued his only compliment of her adult years in regard to that frock. "Why, Helen," she remembered him saying, "you look stunning, simply stunning."

She also remembered waiting for the qualifying "but" that always came after a kind word from her father. When he merely stood transfixed and smiled, she marked the moment both in her journal and in her mind. She also promised herself she would keep the dress forever.

Penney fussed with Helen's hair until Helen could stand it no more. "Enough, Penney," she said as she attempted to stand.

Her friend placed her hands on her shoulders and pressed her back into her chair. "A few minutes more and no longer, I promise." She struggled to tame an obstinate strand into submission, then tied in a green ribbon. "There, all done." She handed Helen the mirror. "What do you think?"

Helen peered into the mirror, and her breath caught in her throat. Her hair, always hidden beneath serviceable hats or pinned out of the way, fell in curls and wound around a ribbon perfectly matched in color to her dress. A lump gathered in her throat, and tears stung her eyes.

Penney knelt beside Helen. "What's wrong?" she asked, her face stricken.

"No one's done this for me in such a long time," Helen whispered.

Her friend looked confused. "What do you mean?"

She took Penney's hand in hers. "My mother used to play with my hair for hours. She would braid it and tie it in ribbons, anything we could think of to do with it. When I tired of letting her fix my hair, I would take a turn with hers. After she died, there was no one to fix my hair. At least no one who could do it like she did." A sob caught and held just out of reach. "I miss her tonight."

"Oh, Helen," Penney whispered. "I'm so glad we're friends."

A knock at the door sent Penney scurrying. Helen followed a step behind, her heart pounding.

"Go back in there this instant, Helen Morgan," Penney said. "Don't you know the first thing about courting?"

"No," Helen said, "actually I don't." She pressed past Penney to touch the doorknob, her reticule dangling from her arm. "And furthermore, I have no desire to learn."

Penney placed her hand over Helen's and drew her back from the door. In a deft motion, she removed the reticule from Helen's arm and opened it.

"Just as I thought," she said and made little clucking sounds of disapproval. "One does not bring Miss Austen on an evening out with a gentleman." She pulled Helen's copy of *Sense and Sensibility* out of the handbag and placed it on the table nearest the door. "Now, if you insist, go ahead and open the door, but if I had things my way, I'd send you off to the other room and make Mr. Hill wait a bit. It never looks good to be too anxious, if you know what I mean."

"No, I don't know what you mean. Now if you'll excuse me." Helen opened the door and lost her breath, all in one hurried moment.

The politician wore black, and he carried the loveliest bouquet of flowers she'd ever seen. If only she could form the words to thank him.

Instead, she squeaked something that she hoped would pass for gratitude and let Penney take over. Somehow, the flowers ended up in water, and she ended up in a lovely coach with a handsome politician heading down Coromundel Street to dinner and the opera.

As Mr. Hill gave directions to the driver, a hymn-singing fellow of lengthy years, she couldn't help but think that this was a scene that even Miss Austen couldn't have written.

Chapter 7

Things were not turning out at all as Henry had planned. He cast a glance to his right. No, indeed, not at all.

First, someone had shanghaied the mousy Miss Morgan and replaced her with the spectacular creature swathed in green silk and seated beside him. Second, rather than the smell of newsprint and ink as he'd half-expected, she wore the most lovely fragrance of flowers, spice, and something else, a scent he couldn't put his finger on and yet knew he would always remember. And third, his normally charismatic ability to charm his constituents into lengthy conversation apparently did not apply to Helen Morgan.

Indeed, somewhere in his great scheme to protect the frail and innocent newspaperwoman, things had gone seriously awry. He had to do something fast before he became the one in need of protection.

"I'm pleased you could join me tonight, Miss Morgan."

"Thank you," he thought she mumbled.

He shifted positions to better see her. A lacy fretwork of light and shadows teased her face, bringing softness to the angle of her chin and the tilt of her nose. Aristocratic fingers were clenched in her lap, knuckles white, and she stared straight ahead as if looking toward a destiny for which she felt no particular joy.

Silence, a politician's worst enemy, fell between them. A reminder that this was not a real date failed to soothe his bruised self-esteem. Real or not, he had to set the situation to rights. He decided to try another tack.

"I generally take my meals with a law book." He inserted an off-the-cuff chuckle to lighten the mood. "Not nearly as pleasant a companion as you, I daresay."

Inwardly, Henry groaned. *You sound like an idiot, Hill.* He forced his smile up a notch and waited for a reaction from his guest.

At first nothing. She merely clenched and unclenched her fists until he thought she might slug him. Then, slowly, she met his gaze with eyes as green as her dress.

"I'm p–p–pleased to know I'll not be asked to meet high standards, Mr. Hill."

He waited for her smile to match his, for some indication she'd made the statement in jest. It never appeared. Gradually he gave up the pretense of sociability and settled back into the seat.

James began to hum an off-key rendition of "Camptown Races" as the first drops of rain hit the roof of the coach. Soon the downpour began in earnest.

Henry continued to steal covert glances at his companion, who now seemed to be oblivious to his presence. This was shaping up to be the longest night of his life.

And it had barely begun.

◆ ◆ ◆

He keeps staring. That was all Helen could think as she rode along in uncomfortable silence. The stillness was barely broken by small talk and inconsequential discussions of law books and the stormy weather, which bore down around them. It followed them into the restaurant, a lovely eatery on the far end of Montgomery Street famed for its seven-course meals and decadent dessert menu.

Like as not, the food would be wasted on her tonight.

Once inside and settled at a table, Helen studied her nails and contemplated the length of the torture this evening looked to become. Meanwhile, her companion greeted a seemingly endless stream of well-wishers, pausing only to whisper instructions to a waiter. Occasionally he would introduce her as his friend, once as his companion, but more often that not, she simply remained "Miss Morgan" to those who ventured forth.

As no comment seemed necessary, Helen remained quiet and listened to the men talk politics. An unhappy reminder of the first two decades of her life. *Smiling girl decorates table for politician.* A headline worthy of her life if not worthy of the newspaper.

Helen sighed. Why hadn't she returned the book to its place in her reticule, or better yet, stayed home to read in the privacy of her room? Just wait until she returned home. She would make sure that neither Penney nor the others ever coerced her into an evening out with a man again.

Her foray into the world of dating was done. At least she had the opera to look forward to.

"I noticed you read Jane Austen," the politician said in a rare moment without an audience. Her shock must have registered on her face, for he continued. "I'm sorry. Am I wrong? I just assumed as much since I saw *Sense and Sensibility* on your desk."

"Oh?"

He nodded and lifted his glass, then took a sip. "Personally I prefer *Northanger Abbey*."

Finally, a topic worthy of discussion. Perhaps this evening might be saved yet.

Helen leaned forward and shook her head, warming to the topic. "I beg to differ, Mr. Hill. Why, the complexity of the plot alone makes it far superior to—"

"Henry Hill, you old scalawag, is that you?"

And so it went, the moment so fleeting had absconded with her companion. Some gray-bearded gentleman had Mr. Hill's attention and would likely hold it for a while from the looks of things. Helen leaned back in her chair and crossed her arms over her chest. It seemed as though her duty tonight would be to remain awake and keep her smile propped up. Other than this, her companion seemed to have no need of her.

The waiter approached and signaled to Mr. Hill, who answered with a nod. "Forgive me, Nigel," Mr. Hill said to the elderly man, "but I'm afraid the lady and I are late for an appointment."

An appointment? We haven't had dinner yet.

Helen tamed her surprise and rose along with her companion while her heart sank. She'd made such a poor impression on the man that he'd decided to rid himself of her company before the food even arrived. In her youth she'd had a few social outings with gentlemen callers, some of which were less than memorable, but none had ended *before* dinner. Just wait until she saw Penney.

"Shall we?" The politician grasped her elbow and guided her through a maze of tables to. . .what was this? The kitchen?

Chaos greeted her, along with a wall of stifling heat. To her left, a dozen men in suits dashed about in a complicated ballet while another dozen raced about, providing a symphony of sounds with their pots and pans. When taken together, the chaos fell into order, and the food went out to the guests, or so it seemed.

"Miss Morgan?" Helen turned to follow the sound of her name, only to find the waiter standing there. Mr. Hill was nowhere in sight. Her heart sank, even though this was the ending she'd expected. Evidently the job of finding her a way home had fallen to the waiter. "Please follow me."

She obliged, but rather than heading out the back door, Helen found herself climbing a rather rickety set of back stairs that emerged onto a large room that seemed to be some sort of storage area. Beyond the barrels and crates, she found Mr. Hill awaiting her at a table set beside a window that afforded a view of Montgomery Street and the ocean beyond.

Or it would have had the rain not been beating a rhythm against the cracked panes of glass.

Mr. Hill pushed back a rather plain wooden kitchen chair and helped her settle into her seat before taking his place beside her. The waiter snapped his fingers, and a parade of dark-suited men, some of whom she recognized from the kitchen, paraded in, carrying trays bulging with food.

"Forgive me, Miss Morgan," Mr. Hill said as the last of the trays was placed on a pair of crates that served as a sideboard, "but this was the only way I could have an uninterrupted conversation with you."

"I see." Discomfort of another sort snaked up her spine, and the room seemed to shrink.

The politician seemed to sense her lack of enthusiasm. "Mr. Kent and his staff will be with us at all times, so I assure you there will be no impropriety." He paused and leaned back in his chair. "If you feel the least bit uncomfortable, I assure you other arrangements can be made, or I can take you home."

Warm candlelight mixed with the glow of a large whale oil lamp and bounced across the scarred wooden floorboards and danced up the walls to meet in the center of the ceiling. In lieu of a fancy tablecloth, someone had appropriated a bright red-and-white quilt. There was nothing about this room that felt uncomfortable, and strangely, neither did she.

"No," she said softly. "This will be fine."

"Excellent." He motioned for the staff to begin serving the first course. "Now I believe we were discussing the fact that *Northanger Abbey* far exceeds *Sense and Sensibility* in all aspects of the story."

Helen squared her shoulders and gave him a sideways look. "We were discussing nothing of the sort," she said with mock sternness.

Somehow the courses came and went. Helen ate little and talked almost as much as she listened. The politician, as it happened, was quite well read.

By the time dessert was served, Helen had learned that Shakespeare and James Fenimore Cooper were his favorite authors, that he was currently reading *A Tale of Two Cities*, and that he had large passages of *Last of the Mohicans* and the Bible memorized.

To her amazement, Henry Hill was actually quite a fascinating fellow. He also had an appetite. He'd partaken of all seven courses, then ordered dessert—the house specialty: apple dumpling. Each course was delivered by the dour-looking waiter, who retired between courses to the corner of the room, where he had a stack of newspapers at the ready.

While they rested between courses, Mr. Hill paused in his discourse regarding his mayoral aspirations to stare into Helen's face. "You indicated once that you were familiar with the workings of a political campaign."

She froze, stricken. "D–d–did I?"

"Well, not in so many words," he said slowly. "But there was a suggestion that perhaps you'd had some experience in that arena."

Helen's mouth went dry, and she reached for her glass of water. The politician must have sensed her unease, for he placed his hand over hers. It was warm, this masculine hand, while hers felt like ice. She stared at the swirling *H*s atop the gold signet ring and slowly let out a pent-up breath.

What do I say, Lord? she found herself asking.

The truth, came the soft response.

So she told him. Speaking in fits and starts, she told the politician the whole story. About her father and her mother and the dear women who took care of her. She found that once she began to tell it, the story refused to stop until she told it all. Finally she reached the part where she attended her father's funeral and then headed West to the place her mother had once read her a story about. The first train out of Texas had brought her to San Francisco. God, however, had brought her to church and to the three friends she'd made there, friends with whom she now worked at the *Gazette*.

When she finished, she realized she'd said far too much. Covering her embarrassed frown with her napkin, she pretended to dab at the corners of her mouth. Mr. Hill removed the napkin from her hand and brought her fingers to his lips for a brief moment.

"I have a story, too, Miss Morgan, and I've never told a soul," he said softly, each breath blowing warm against her fingertips. "I believe I would like to share it with you." He met her gaze. "Would that be terribly improper?"

Her heart rose to her throat, and she found the words she wanted to say lodged there as well. "I would be honored to hear your story," she finally managed.

An eternity later, images of a young boy living in abject poverty, a youth saved by a loving aunt, and a grateful young man making a promise to the Lord filled her mind. "Thank you for sharing this," she said through a shimmering of tears. "Now I see why you feel so strongly about helping the less fortunate."

He nodded and leaned toward her. "I've never felt comfortable sharing that story with anyone. Even my best friend, Asa, hasn't heard all of it." He entwined his fingers with hers once more, and this time he held them to his chest. She could practically feel the beating of his heart as she seemed pulled toward him. "To think this all started because. . ."

"Because of what?"

"Never mind."

Her lips were inches from his when she realized she was about to kiss him.

Or rather, he was about to kiss her.

"Dessert is served!" the waiter called.

Helen jumped and nearly fell out of her chair. She cast a covert glance at Mr. Hill, who seemed just as shaken. He allowed the waiter to serve each of them, then handed her the dessert fork. "Prepare to be amazed," he said with a grin.

I already am. She tore herself away from his gaze to stab at the decadent dessert.

One taste of the melt-in-your-mouth pastry and spicy sweet apple inside, and she groaned. "Oh, this is better than reading a book," she said, then blushed when she realized she'd spoken the words aloud.

Mr. Hill laughed. "I daresay that is the best compliment I've heard in a long time. What say you, Mr. Kent?"

The waiter smiled and nodded, then went back to his newspaper.

Their desserts quickly disposed of, the pair returned to a much safer and less personal topic, their debate of the merits of Shakespeare's comedies over his tragedies. While Helen favored the tragedies, the politician tended to prefer the comedies, which led to a lively discussion.

Helen never noticed the passing of time until she suppressed a yawn. "I'm terribly sorry," she said with a start as Mr. Hill checked his pocket watch, then quickly rose.

She settled beside him in the coach, keeping a respectable distance. By the time the coach made its way through the drizzling rain and arrived at her doorstep, it was nearly midnight. Tomorrow she would have a difficult time making numbers add up and totals come out correctly.

No matter, she decided as she bade the politician good-bye at the door with a polite handshake and practically floated inside. What was a little exhaustion when the evening had been so perfect? As the door closed behind her, she could hear Mr. Hill's driver whistling a rather unique rendition of "Hail, Columbia."

It came as no surprise that Penney sat just inside the door, pretending to read her Bible. She might have gotten away with it had the book not been upside down. When Helen walked past without a word, Penney gave up all pretenses and followed her into the bedroom.

"So?"

She slipped out of her green dress and returned it to the back of the armoire, suppressing a smile. "So *what?*"

Penney huffed, feigning annoyance as she slipped under the covers and gave the pillow a vicious plumping. "Look, I didn't wait up half the night just to hear nothing. How did it go?"

Helen slipped into her nightdress and sank onto her bed, threading her fingers behind her head. She let a long moment pass, then sighed. "It was wonderful," she said as she extinguished the lamp.

Telling Penney was like reliving the evening, and as she spoke, she tried to remember each detail. She'd nearly fallen asleep when she realized that they'd forgotten all about their tickets to the opera.

Chapter 8

The next morning Helen arrived at the *Gazette* with a troubled heart. What seemed impossibly romantic last night seemed more like a dream today, and in her experience, dreams never survived the light of day. Whatever insanity possessed Mr. Hill last night would most certainly be gone today.

With that thought uppermost in her mind, she tackled the day's work with a lackluster attitude. By noontime, her strength was gone, and so was her ability to add, subtract, and generally make sense of receipts and invoices. Somewhere between breakfast and midmorning tea, she'd put a name to the malady that held her in its grasp: love.

It certainly never seemed as though the characters in Jane Austen's novels were as miserable as she; still, she recognized all the signs. Dropping her pencil, she leaned forward on her elbows and rested her chin in her hands. She'd seen the strange symptoms in Jennie and Amy, but she never expected to catch the infirmity herself.

"Love," she whispered. "Ridiculous."

"What's so ridiculous?"

Helen looked up to see Jennie standing beside her desk. "He's a politician, and I'm just a woman who adds numbers. I hate crowds, and he craves them. He makes these beautiful speeches, and I, well, sometimes I can't even get a word to come out properly." She lowered her head and studied the pile of receipts, already blurring from unshed tears. "It's just not what I expected."

"Do you think love is what I expected when I met Nick, or what Amy expected to find with Evan?" Jennie smiled. "Love is usually the last thing anyone who falls into it imagines will happen. That's what makes it so special."

Helen shrugged. "But I've only spent one evening with him, and we're so different. It makes no sense."

Her friend knelt beside the desk and took Helen's hand in hers. "Helen, how long do you figure it takes God to decide who we're to spend our lives with?"

"An instant, I suppose. I've never actually thought about it."

Jennie patted her hand then rose. "And maybe not thinking about it is the way the Lord wants it."

"What do you mean?"

"In Genesis, He says He will make a helper for man. Do you think God asked Eve if anything made sense when He put her in the Garden of Eden, pointed her toward Adam, and told her to go be a helper?"

Helen smiled. She couldn't argue with her friend's logic. "No, I don't suppose He did."

"Then who are we to doubt when He points us to the man He's created for us?" She paused. "Even if it doesn't make sense to us sometimes, it makes perfect sense to Him."

◆ ◆ ◆

It made absolutely no sense.

Henry carried the thought around inside his head, but it failed to drown out his need to see Helen Morgan again. He told himself he was just protecting her until the men who'd threatened her life were caught, but deep down he knew better.

One evening with the green-eyed woman had seared his heart forever.

He was in love.

It made no sense.

"What's all the groaning about?" Asa sauntered in and leaned against the door frame.

Henry cleared his throat and reached for his pen. "Nothing," he said. "Just more work than I wanted to tackle today."

"Ah, I see." He remained there, leaning, looking past Henry to stare out the window where sunshine streamed in. Finally he shook his head. "I suppose my fishing trip's going to have to come to an end soon. Today, I think."

"Yes, I thought it might," Henry said as he reached for the topmost document in the stack. "But on the bright side, July will be over soon. Your banishment will end before you know it."

When Asa did not respond, Henry looked up to see he'd already gone.

By lunchtime, he'd wandered out, intending to merely stroll past the *Gazette*. Of course he ended up inside and returned to his office with plans for another evening out with Miss Morgan. This time they might actually attend the opera. He might actually kiss her as well.

That night the music was superb, the company delightful. Helen wore the green dress again, disguised by a lovely shawl, but he would have never let on that he noticed. Most of the time they sat in silence, holding hands and trading covert glances. At the end of the evening, with James whistling an irritating rendition of "Home Sweet Home," Henry walked Helen to the door and in a moment of stupidity, bravery, and insanity, held her in his arms and kissed her.

He expected her to slap him. He certainly deserved as much. Instead, she kissed him back, then raced inside, embarrassed. The next morning he sent flowers and a lovely dress from the mercantile that he'd been unable to resist. Pale pink—it reminded him of the color in her cheeks when he kissed her.

She kept the flowers but returned the dress along with a note stating her appreciation but explaining that she was unable to keep such a personal gift. He returned the gift to her with another note, this one explaining why he chose that particular color. Not only did she keep the dress, but she also wore it that night to the symphony along with a flower from the bouquet pinned in her hair.

By the end of the second week, they had not only attended the opera, but they'd also had two picnics, visited church together, enjoyed two evenings at the symphony, endured an afternoon's sail on the choppy bay, and finally last night, had dinner with his mother.

That memory burned stronger than any of the others. Of course, Anna loved Helen immediately. There had been no doubt that she would.

Tomorrow he would see Helen again. He would ask her to become his wife.

◆ ◆ ◆

Thursday, July 19, 1860

They sat at the same table in the same little room upstairs. Henry made sure every detail was perfect, even to the point of rehearsing the grand finale of the evening with the restaurant's owner. While his plan to have the ring embedded in the apple dumpling had been nixed by both the owner and the cook, Henry did manage to talk the waiter into cooperating with his alternate plan.

Anticipating Helen's surprise at finding an engagement ring slipped over the stem of her fork kept Henry on edge all day. By the time he and Helen arrived at the restaurant, she suspected something was in the offing. When she spied the ring, she burst into tears.

Henry dropped to one knee beside her and searched for the eloquent speech he'd memorized. It was gone. In its place, he found these words: "Helen Morgan, do me the honor of becoming my wife."

His beloved looked at the ring, then lifted her gaze to meet his. Her eyes brimming with tears and her cheeks the color of her dress, she looked away. "It's lovely, Henry," she said softly. "I d–d–don't know what to say."

He grasped both her hands in his. "Say yes, Helen."

For a long moment, silence fell between them. Henry felt sure his heart would burst before he heard the words that would make him the happiest man in San Francisco.

Thank You, God, for giving me Helen. Now, would You please make her say something?

"I can't marry you, Henry." She jumped up and ran out the door. Henry climbed to his feet and watched her go.

"That's not exactly what I had in mind, Lord."

Racing down the stairs and through the maze of tables in the main dining room, Henry ignored the calls of friends, constituents, and political allies. He had to find Helen. He pushed past the doors to emerge on the sidewalk, then froze in his tracks. Helen was being hurled into a buggy, which sped away down Montgomery Street. Holding the reins was an all-too-familiar man: Toothless.

Henry climbed into the saddle of the first horse he could reach and set off after the buggy. The chase led him through the city's center, then east toward the water. At the edge of the bay, the buggy stopped abruptly by a stand of eucalyptus. Two dark-clad men spilled out, but Helen remained inside.

If something happens to Helen, Lord, I will die, too. So unless You want the both of us at Your door, please do something.

Dismounting, Henry reached beneath his jacket for the revolver. Before either man could take aim, Henry had fired off two shots. He strode past the two crumpled and groaning forms to lift a distraught Helen from the buggy. She nestled against his chest and let the tears flow.

"They said you owed them money," she said between deep gulps for air. "They told me you took money to guarantee a win in the election and then killed Frank Bynum so you didn't have to pay it back."

"Shhh," he whispered. "Those are lies. You didn't believe them, did you?"

Helen shook her head. "No, but—"

The clatter of horses' hooves interrupted her. A moment later, the chief of police and several of his deputies rode into sight.

"Thank the good Lord you're here, Chief," Henry said.

The chief reined in his horse and looked down at Henry. "Arrest the lot of 'em, boys," he said.

A pair of deputies dismounted and headed toward Toothless and his accomplice while a third pushed Helen away to place restraints on Henry's wrists. When Henry protested, the deputy raised his club, and the world went black.

Chapter 9

I don't care what the police say. I know Henry's not guilty." Helen tried to remain calm as she sat across the desk from the chief of police, the very man who had ordered Henry's arrest.

The chief offered a condescending smile. "I applaud your loyalty, Miss Morgan, but the facts do not lie." He leaned back in his chair. "Those two fellows he shot worked for Frank Bynum. When their boss turned up dead, they figured they would make a little money out of the deal by trying to shake down Mr. Hill for some of the gold he'd been given."

She focused on her hands rather than look directly at the chief. "That makes no sense. Henry already has plenty of money."

The chief laughed. "In my line of work, I've learned that no one ever has enough money. Besides that, it wasn't just the money that made him do it. You see, Henry Hill needed votes more than he needed gold. Bynum offered him the votes, sweetened the deal with the money, and then got in the way of a bullet from Henry Hill's gun when Hill backed out of the deal."

White-hot anger boiled just beneath the surface. How dare this man accuse Henry of such things? "That's not true," she said through a clenched jaw.

"Lady, I've got a receipt made out to one Henry Hill for the sale of a diamond pin to a jeweler in Los Angeles. Cleaning lady found it when she moved the filing cabinet in the office. The jeweler has identified the pin as an identical copy of the one missing from Frank Bynum's body. To top things off, Henry Hall, the tavern owner we'd pegged as the gunman, was found dead in a shallow grave. Looks like he'd been there awhile, which means he couldn't have pulled the trigger on Bynum."

He handed her the paper, and she read it while her heart sank. A moment later, she collected her thoughts. Henry was innocent. That she knew.

"Where did you get this?"

"His partner found it in his office. Said it was behind a filing cabinet."

"It could have been planted there."

His face softened. "Look, I know you care about Henry. I like him, too. Trouble is, he's a crook."

Again her anger flared. "P–p–prove it," she said as she rose and tossed the offensive document onto the desk.

The chief pushed back from the desk and stood. "Why don't *you* prove he *isn't* a crook?"

Helen stormed out of the police station determined to do just that. Her Henry was not mixed up with thugs and hoodlums. He was a good man. But how to prove it? She smiled and turned toward Montgomery Street and Henry's office.

Perhaps a bit of sleuthing would turn up a clue to exonerate Henry. She took the back stairs up to the second floor and slipped inside the offices of Chambers and Hill as quietly as possible. Noises from downstairs floated up through the floor, but Helen soon found the offices to be empty. She stole past the portraits of Henry and his partner and hurried to Henry's office to begin her search. Something, anything had to be found to prove him innocent.

"Well, what do we have here?"

Helen nearly jumped out of her skin, and her heart raced. She whirled around to find Henry's partner, Asa Chambers, standing in the doorway. She recognized him from the portrait in the foyer.

"I'm terribly sorry. I'm Helen, Henry's fiancée." She cringed as she said it.

She should be his fiancée if it weren't for her selfishness. If only she'd told him she feared she wouldn't be the wife he needed rather than running away.

Helen pushed those thoughts aside and gave thanks that the Lord had sent help. Soon she could tell Henry everything. Soon she would ask his forgiveness and accept his offer, if it still stood. Soon perhaps she *would* be his fiancée.

"Henry told me you were away on holiday, Mr. Chambers."

His smile upped a notch, but his posture tensed. "I guess you weren't expecting me."

"Actually, no," she said, "but as long as you're here, perhaps you could help me."

She pressed past him to head for the filing cabinet in the foyer where the receipt had been found. Kneeling to open the bottom drawer, she found it stuck. She pulled hard, and the drawer flew open. An oversized book, one she recognized as an accounting ledger, slid forward with a *thud*. She picked it up and held it in her lap. "I'm looking for any sort of evidence that will help to prove that Henry—"

The air went out of her mid-sentence, and it took a moment to register that Asa Chambers had his hand wrapped around her throat. The ledger fell to the floor as Asa lifted her to her feet. On the opened page, she could see the names of certain prominent San Franciscans with numbers written beside them.

Contributions or bribes? She might never know, but she'd do what she could to see that Henry—and the police—found out.

"We're both on the s–s—same side, Mr. Chambers. Why don't you let me go so we can talk about this?"

"You should never have seen that ledger. I honestly hoped it wouldn't come to this." Asa began to move her toward Henry's office. "Henry's my friend. I worked too hard to make sure he won the race, and now look what you've done."

"What *I've* done?" Helen choked off the last of the statement when Asa's beefy arm closed around her waist.

She jabbed at him with her elbows. He only laughed.

"You weren't the right wife for him anyway."

Asa turned her around to face him, then slammed her back against the wall. Through the haze of pain, Helen could see the vein on the side of his forehead throb, could smell the sweet macassar oil in his hair.

His lips twisted into a scowl. "He needs someone who can be an asset to him, someone who can talk and not be an embarrassment."

The truth. There it hung in the narrow space between them. For one brief moment in this horrendous conversation, Asa Chambers was right.

His eyes narrowed. The vein in his forehead pulsed faster.

And then she remembered Jennie's words: "Who are we to doubt when He points us to the man He's created for us?"

"Who are we to doubt?" she whispered as she summoned all the strength, all the fight, she could muster. A well-placed kick, and he loosened his grip; another, and he crumpled to the floor, taking her with him. Helen slid from his grasp and ran as fast as her crinolines would allow, slowing only to retrieve the ledger.

She cast a glance back to see Asa climb to his feet, then fall once more. Pausing only long enough to gauge the distance to the main stairs and Montgomery Street beyond, she ducked down the back stairs. Hanging on with one hand, the ledger tucked under her arm, Helen raced down the stairs. A few steps from the bottom, she turned to see how close her captor had come to catching her.

No one was there.

She stopped and tried to catch her breath, then started to giggle. It was irrational. Ridiculous. Yet all Helen could feel was exhilaration that she'd bested Asa Chambers. With the ledger in hand, Henry would be freed and all would be well.

Click. "Give me the ledger."

Helen turned around slowly to face Asa Chambers. He held a revolver inches from her forehead.

"The ledger, Miss Morgan. I want it—"

A shot rang out, and his face registered surprise, then shock. A second later he crumpled in a heap at Helen's feet. She looked beyond the wounded man to see Henry rushing toward her.

He gathered her in his arms and carried her out to his carriage. His driver looked frantic as he jumped up to open the carriage door. "What in the world happened back there, Mr. Hill? I done heard gunshots. Took all I had to keep the hosses from runnin' off."

Henry grasped Helen's hand, searched her face. "Did he hurt you?"

Gulping for air, she managed to say, "No. How did you get here? Why aren't you in jail?"

"When the chief explained the enormity of their crimes, the thugs who kidnapped you were only happy to oblige and tell the whole story."

"Which is?"

"Which is that Asa was behind the whole thing." Henry looked away, pained. "He sold the promise of my political influence to anyone who would pay and hired those two to make sure the payments reached him."

Helen reached for his hand and held it tight. "But why did they come after you?"

"When the Bynum fellow asked for proof of my cooperation in the scam, Asa had none to provide. Bynum had already paid up, so he asked for his gold to be returned. So did a few other people, which put Asa in quite a financial bind."

"But I thought he was fairly well-to-do."

Henry shook his head. "No, his *father* is well-to-do. Asa is still waiting for his share of the fortune."

"Oh." Helen drew closer to Henry.

"Asa sent those thugs after me and ultimately after you to try to collect money to pay his debts. Bynum got impatient, and it cost him his life." He held her against his chest, studied her for a moment, then held her tight again. "You know I love you, Helen, and I'm terribly sorry you had to be involved in this."

"I love you, too, Henry, and a *wife* should be involved in her husband's life, good or bad."

"A wife?"

When he leaned back to look at her, she nodded. "Yes, if the offer is still good."

"Oh yes, the offer's most definitely still good." He kissed her soundly, then paused and looked away. "I have to see to Asa. Regardless of what he's done, he's my friend. Do you understand?"

"Yes," she said. "But please be careful."

"I will." He turned to his driver. "See that she stays here, James, and be on the ready. Mr. Chambers may need to be transported to the hospital."

◆　◆　◆

Wednesday, July 25, 1860

Helen leaned back in her chair and allowed her gaze to fall on the remains of their dinner. As in the two times before, Henry insisted they dine privately, with only the lead waiter, Mr. Kent, and his army of waiters as chaperones.

"Something wrong?" Henry reached for her hand and held it against his chest. "You look a bit pensive."

Helen giggled. "Pensive? Not exactly. Overfed, perhaps."

"You barely ate enough to feed a bird, my darling," he said. "Don't tell me you're not going to have dessert."

"Apple dumpling?"

Henry winked. "Exactly what I had in mind." He motioned for the waiter, who scurried off down the stairs.

Helen leaned against Henry's shoulder and closed her eyes. The night was perfect. Almost. "How's Asa?"

"Asa?" She felt his shoulders heave. "Asa's healthy as a horse, but he'll walk with a limp for a while."

She pulled away to stare into his eyes. "You could have killed him, you know. A less understanding man might have. You did the right thing. Now it's in the hands of the judge."

Henry ducked his head. "I suppose."

"Dessert is served!"

The waiter placed two steaming apple dumplings on the table before them, then retreated to his place by the stairs. A second later he hid himself behind yesterday's copy of the *Golden Gate Gazette*.

While Henry dug in to his dessert, Helen weighed the fork in her hand but did not take a bite. The last time her fork had been adorned with a beautiful ring tied up in a green ribbon. How different things might have been if she'd just said yes the first time. With time to consider the situation, Henry probably had come to the conclusion that he'd do better finding a wife who was an asset to his political career instead of a hindrance.

"Do I have to finish yours, too?"

THE *Valiant* HEARTS ROMANCE COLLECTION

Helen looked over at Henry's empty plate and contemplated the real threat of losing her apple dumpling to him. While he pretended to reach for her plate, she stuck her fork in and pulled out. . .a ring?

"Henry? What's this?"

He dropped the fork into the pitcher of water and fished out a beautiful—and clean—engagement ring adorned with one oversized emerald and circled in diamonds. He dropped to one knee. "Helen Morgan, will you do me the honor of becoming my wife?"

For a moment she sat stunned. Finally, she found her voice. "But, Henry, I stutter, I hate crowds, and I completely disagree with your preferences in the works of Shakespeare and Jane Austen. What sort of wife would I make for the next mayor of San Francisco?"

"The only sort I want."

Epilogue

THE *GOLDEN GATE GAZETTE*
Thursday, July 26, 1860

CANDIDATE FOR MAYOR HENRY HILL TO WED MISS HELEN MORGAN OF THE
GOLDEN GATE GAZETTE

Henry Hill, noted attorney and candidate for San Francisco mayor, wishes to announce his engagement to the lovely Helen Morgan, an employee of our own *Golden Gate Gazette*. The *Gazette* wishes to congratulate Mr. Hill on his fine choice of a wife, and the future Mrs. Hill on her decision not to continue her brief but illustrious career as a crime fighter. In response, Miss Morgan replies that being the wife of a politician will be adventurous enough for her.

APPLE DUMPLINGS SAN FRANCISCO STYLE

Ingredients:
- 2 tablespoons of butter
- 2 tablespoons of sugar
- 1 teaspoon nutmeg
- 1 teaspoon vanilla
- 2 teaspoons cinnamon
- ½ teaspoon grated orange zest
- 1 cup raisins
- 8 large apples
- 1 piecrust, unbaked
- White of one egg

Topping:
- 1–2 tablespoons sugar
- 1 teaspoon cinnamon

Mix together butter, sugar, nutmeg, vanilla, cinnamon, grated orange zest, and raisins. Core apples and stuff butter mixture inside. Cut piecrust into circles and wrap apples completely with crust. Twist dough closed on top and trim excess. The dumpling should look like a small bag. Place each apple in a custard cup (a large muffin tin is an acceptable substitute) and brush with egg white. Sprinkle with topping and bake in 350-degree oven for 30–45 minutes or until crust is brown (time will vary depending on size of apples).

Bestselling author **KATHLEEN Y'BARBO** is a multiple Carol Award and RITA nominee of more than sixty novels with almost two million copies in print in the US and abroad. A tenth-generation Texan, she has been nominated for a Career Achievement Award as well a Reader's Choice Award and is the winner of the 2014 Inspirational Romance of the Year by *Romantic Times* magazine.

Kathleen is a paralegal, a proud military wife, and an expatriate Texan cheering on her beloved Texas Aggies from north of the Red River. Connect with her through social media at www.kathleenybarbo.com.

Sadie's Secret, a Secret Life of Will Tucker historical romantic suspense novel, is in stores now, as is *Firefly Summer*, the first in the contemporary Pies, Books & Jesus Book Club!

Beauty from Ashes

by MaryLu Tyndall

Dedication

To anyone who has been scarred by life, both on the inside and on the outside.

To console those who mourn in Zion, to give them beauty for ashes, the oil of joy for mourning, the garment of praise for the spirit of heaviness; that they may be called trees of righteousness, the planting of the LORD, that He may be glorified.

ISAIAH 61:3 NKJV

Chapter 1

The Shaw Plantation, outside Williamsburg, Virginia, May 23, 1865

Permelia Shaw's stomach growled. Wrapping her arms around her waist, she gazed out the front parlor window. Evening shadows fell upon the cedar and birch trees, coating them in a dull, lifeless gray. Gray like the Confederate uniforms that had been conspicuously absent from Williamsburg these past three years.

Except those that were torn and covered in blood.

A moan rumbled from her belly again. Though she'd eaten an hour ago, the meager fare had not been enough to assuage her hunger—a recurring condition during this horrendous war. Four years was a long time, a lifetime for a young girl who had been only nineteen at the beginning. A lifetime in which she had grown from a pampered daughter of a wealthy plantation owner to a mature woman who could fend for herself.

"I'm hungry." Sitting upon the flowered sofa, her sister, Annie, voiced Permelia's thoughts. "Jackson said he'd come by with some meat today."

Permelia rubbed the blisters on her palms and gazed down at the dirt beneath her fingernails, trying to gather what patience she had left after her long day's work. "It is not right to take food from that man, Annie."

"Oh fiddle. Who cares?" her sister whined.

Spinning around, Permelia made her way to the mantel. Striking a match, she lit the gilt-bronze sconces on either side of the fireplace. Golden light spilled into the parlor, chasing away the gloom and cascading over Annie's lavender taffeta evening gown. No matter the war, no matter their destitute condition, Annie always dressed to perfection.

Just like their mother had done. A quality sorely lacking in Permelia. Sorrow dragged her to sit beside her sister, who drew her lips together in one of her perfectly adorable pouts.

"Without Jackson's help"—Annie thrust out her chin—"we wouldn't have been able to keep our furniture, our gowns, and most of our things. Not to mention the occasional pig and rabbit he brings for supper."

Permelia touched her sister's arm. "But it's wrong to entertain his affections, Annie. Not only is he the enemy, but you're engaged."

"I haven't heard from William in over three years." Annie waved a hand through the air. "For all I know, he is dead."

Permelia's heart collapsed. "You shouldn't say such a thing. You haven't heard from him because you stopped writing to him." She slid her hand into a pocket she'd sewed inside her skirts, where the hard shape of the coin brought her comfort—hope that he was still alive, though his last letter had been dated eight months ago.

Annie's eyes moistened. She lowered her chin. "It was this war. I couldn't bear the thought of him on the battlefield."

"There, there." Permelia flung her arm around her sister's shoulders and drew her close. "It is, indeed, a hard thing to consider." She knew that fear all too well for she had thought of nothing else for three years. What she couldn't understand was how her sister could abandon the man she loved in his darkest hour. When he needed most to read her comforting, loving words. But Annie was different from Permelia. More sensitive to such brutalities.

Drawing a handkerchief from her sleeve, Annie dabbed her eyes. "Why hasn't Jackson come to call in over two days?"

The quick shift of topic from William to Jackson made Permelia wonder who the tears were really for. "Now that the war is over, perhaps he's gone home." At least she hoped so. The Union soldier was all charm and good looks. A man who had taken advantage of Annie in her weakened condition.

"How can you say that?" Shrugging from Permelia's embrace, Annie rose and straightened out the braided ruffles of her gown. "He said he loves me. He said he would never leave me."

Though the words bristled over Permelia, she studied her sister, trying to understand. The war, the Union occupation of their town, both had taken so much from Annie. Including Colonel William Wolfe, a month before their wedding. No wonder Annie had rushed into the arms of the first man who offered her his protection and love. Yet. . .

"Jackson shouldn't say such things when you are betrothed to another." Permelia held out a hand toward her sister. "Besides, never fear, I'm sure William will arrive any day now."

Annie swerved about, her hoop skirt nearly knocking over a porcelain vase on the table—one of the objects Mr. Jackson Steele had returned to them. "Everyone leaves me. Papa left me, then Samuel. Then William."

Rising, Permelia eased beside her sister and took her hand, swallowing down a burst of her own sorrow as she remembered the letter from President Davis announcing the death of their father at Cross Keys. And the one that followed informing them that their brother, Samuel, was listed as missing in action. They'd never heard from him again and could only assume the worst.

"Then Mama last year." Annie faced Permelia, her eyes swimming. "I cannot lose Jackson, too."

Permelia squeezed her sister's hand. "Many have lost much during this war. Some their entire family and homes. We have each other. And God. He has taken good care of us."

"*I* have taken care of us." Annie tugged her hand away. "By accepting Jackson's courtship. Otherwise those Yankees would have stolen everything we had."

Permelia's jaw tensed. "So I suppose my toiling in the fields every day is of no consequence?"

Annie's eyes softened, and she gave a gentle smile. "Don't be cross, Permi." Turning, she traversed the room, then settled back on the sofa. Her smile faded beneath a heavy sigh. "Oh, what are we to do?"

"We are doing fine. Thank goodness Papa left the plantation to us in the event we should lose both Samuel and Mama. Besides, we have Martha, Elijah, and Ruth to help."

"Slaves," Annie said with contempt.

"How can you say that?" Permelia took a seat beside her sister. "They are family now. This is their home, too. With Elijah's help, we will plant tobacco like Papa did and start all over again."

"Us?" Annie's face scrunched into a knot. "Women growing tobacco?"

"Why not? Wouldn't it be wonderful to be so independent? To run this plantation by ourselves and answer to no one?"

"I hate this dull, old plantation. All I want is to get married." Annie gazed out the window.

Permelia studied her sister, wondering how they could be so different, wondering how Annie could so easily throw away a liberty that few women enjoyed. If their brother did not return, whoever Annie married would inherit all the land. Permelia had accepted that fact. But for now, she relished her freedom, relished being in charge of the plantation that had meant so much to her father—and now to her.

"Ah, William," Annie said dreamily. "So successful, so wealthy, and *so* handsome."

Permelia smiled. "And honorable and kind and good. He is still all those things, Annie. If God permitted him to live, he'll be here soon to marry you."

"Do you really think so?" Annie's eyes regained their sparkle.

"Yes." Though the thought both elated and pained Permelia. Elated her that William lived. Pained her that he would never be hers.

"Then I shall marry him and live in New York, wealthy and happy and strolling the streets on the arm of the most handsome man in the city." Annie sat up straight and spread her skirts around her. "He is handsome, isn't he, Permelia?"

"Yes, very." Permelia's face heated, and she turned away. Handsome indeed, but so much more than that.

While her sister went on about all the cotillions, plays, and concerts she and William would attend, and the attention they would draw as they sauntered down the Boulevard in New York, Permelia returned to her spot at the window. Darkness settled over the Virginia landscape. A slight breeze stirred the hair dangling about her neck, bringing with it the scent of wild violet and moist fern. Pulling the coin from her pocket she caressed it lovingly—the coin William had given Annie in Central Park as a vow of their love the night the war had separated their families. Permelia had carried it on her person ever since Annie had tossed it out her window in a fit of rage. She brushed her fingers over the engraving on the back:

"Love never fails. W.W. Central Park."

She prayed that was true. For if William ever came to claim his bride, Permelia would need all the power of her love for both William and Annie to keep her own heart from crumbling.

◆　◆　◆

William Wolfe nudged his weary horse down the path. Weary like him. Removing his cap, he wiped the sweat from his brow. His head throbbed, his back ached, and his legs cramped from riding for five days, stopping only long enough to sleep. He must see Annie. He couldn't wait another day. Another minute. Even for a quick bath and shave in Williamsburg to remove the stench from his clothes. Besides, the condition of the town had spurred him onward: the crumbling buildings, whiskey-drinking loafers, and hundreds of graves dotting the churchyards. Not to mention the hate-filled looks of the citizens as he rode past in his Union uniform. He'd heard Williamsburg had been occupied by Union forces since early in the war. But what he hadn't expected was that his fellow soldiers would have caused so much destruction. His only hope was that the pernicious Union arm had not stretched as far as the Shaw plantation, an hour outside of town.

Darkness transformed the landscape into a battlefield of prickly monsters and sinister dwarfs. Or perhaps it was just his war-weary mind. William rubbed the back of his neck. An owl pealed a *hoot, hoot* from his right, sending a chill over his skin. He chuckled. He'd faced the enemy head-on in battle. Was he now afraid of the dark?

Or perhaps exhaustion and excitement had befuddled his mind. Regardless of the late hour, he must see Annie. He must ensure her safety. He must know if she still loved him.

And whether she would still love him after she saw his face.

William swept fingers over the ripples of burned flesh on his right cheek. Though numb to the touch, the pain of molten iron lingered in an agonizing memory.

He was no longer handsome. He was disfigured, a monster. Wounded on the outside and on the inside in a war that he could not wrap a shred of sense around. A war in which he'd seen thousands of his fellow Americans die.

Ducking beneath a low-hanging branch, William released a heavy sigh and patted the bundle stuffed in his coat pocket. Dozens of letters from his beloved Annie. Letters that made him believe she would love him no matter what he looked like. Letters that had exposed a heart so pure, so loving, it astounded him that he'd not seen it in her before.

Rounding a large oak, his eyes beheld the Shaw plantation house. Still standing! Three Greek-style columns guarded a wide front porch on the first and second levels. Moonlight dripped from the roof like silver rain, making it seem surreal—an ancient palace in another world. Yet the lantern light flickering from the parlor window and in one of the upstairs rooms spoke of an earthly reality. Of living, breathing people inside.

William nudged his horse onward. "We're almost there, fellow."

The beast begrudgingly complied, even heightening its pace as the gravel crunched beneath its hooves, mimicking the pounding of William's heart. He halted before the house, slid from his saddle, straightened his coat, and slowly made his way up the stairs to stand before the door.

He raised his hand to knock when he heard the distinct cock of a gun, a booted footfall, and the words in a female voice. "Stop right there or I'll shoot you dead where you stand."

Chapter 2

The musket shook in Permelia's hand. The intruder turned his head in her direction, but she could not make out his face. What she could make out was that he was tall and muscular. And that he wore a Union uniform. All three things together portended disaster. She had spotted him from the window, sent a trembling Annie upstairs to rouse Elijah from his bed, then grabbed her gun and sneaked around the side of the house.

"I said, don't move. I know how to use this."

"I have no doubt of that, miss." His voice was low and rich, like the soothing sound of a cello. Somewhere deep within her, it nipped a memory. A pleasant one, for her heart took up a rapid beat. He lifted his hands in the air, revealing the gleam of a saber hanging at his side.

"Who are you, and what do you want?" Permelia demanded.

"Miss Shaw?" He addressed her as if he was making a social call. "Is that you?"

Again the voice eased over her like warm butter. She gulped, attempting to steady the musket. "And who, sir, are you?"

Lowering his arms, he took a step toward her. Memories assailed her exhausted mind—memories of Union soldiers rampaging through her home, tossing everything they could find into sacks: jewelry, silverware, expensive vases and figurines, her father's collection of East Indian tobacco. All accompanied by the sound of her mother wailing in the distance.

And one soldier in particular who wasn't satisfied with only objects. Whose eyes burned with lechery as he crept toward Permelia in her chamber.

"It's me, William." *William.* The name echoed through the night air as if traveling through molasses. Permelia shook her head, corralling her terrifying thoughts.

The soldier took another step toward her. *No, not again!* She must defend her family. Her sister, herself.

She fired the musket.

The crack split the dark sky. The man ducked. His horse neighed. Smoke filled the air, burning her nose, her mouth. Grabbing the gun, he ripped it from her hands. But instead of assaulting her, he wrapped his arms around her and held her tight. He smelled of gunpowder and sweat and earth.

"It's all right, Miss Shaw. It's me, William. You're safe now." The comforting words drifted upon that familiar voice, sparking hope within her. *William?* Against all propriety, she melted into him, never wanting the dream to end. For surely it must be a dream. The same one that had made her endless nights bearable these past years.

But then he was gone. A *whoosh* of chilled air sent a shiver through her.

"What you doin' there!" Elijah shoved William back and leveled a pistol at his chest. Martha, ragged robe tossed over her nightdress, appeared in the doorway, lantern in hand, their twelve-year-old daughter, Ruth, behind her.

William raised his hands again. "Whatever happened to Southern hospitality?" He chuckled and a quizzical look came over Elijah's face.

Shaking off her stupor, Permelia charged forward. "It's all right, Elijah." She nudged his pistol aside. "It is Colonel William Wolfe, Annie's fiancé."

"Then why did you shoot at 'im, miss?" Elijah studied William but did not release his firm grip on the weapon.

"I was about to ask the same question," William said, his tone playful.

Permelia faced him, his expression still lost to her in the shadows. "I'm so sorry, Colonel Wolfe. I didn't know it was you."

"Quite all right, Miss Shaw." He lowered his hands. "I've grown used to being shot at."

"Well, I'll be." Martha held up her lantern and moved forward. "Annie's fiancé. We thought you was dead." The light crept over the porch and up his blue trousers, blinking off his saber and the three gold buttons on his cuff, and brightening the red sash about his waist.

"I am happy to report otherwise." William dipped his head.

"Elijah, put down that gun," Martha scolded.

Recognition loosened the overseer's features. "Good to see you, Colonel." He lowered the weapon.

Martha took another step forward. Light from the lantern slid over William's steady jaw, regal nose, penetrating eyes, and glimmered off the epauletts on his shoulders.

The breath caught in Permelia's throat. She'd dreamed of him for so many nights, she could hardly believe he stood before her all flesh and man.

But then Martha's smile faded. Ruth turned away and retreated into the house. Elijah's eyes widened.

William raised a hand to his right cheek, hidden from Permelia's view.

"Let's not stand here staring at the poor man. Do come in, Colonel." Permelia swept past him, leading the way into the parlor. "Annie will be beyond herself with delight."

Delight that now spiraled through Permelia, igniting all her senses.

Dragging off his hat, William stepped through the doorway. Elijah grabbed the musket and took a spot beside his wife, while Ruth clung to the shadows beyond the stairway. All three lowered their eyes to the floor. Something they hadn't done since before Lincoln's proclamation had freed them from their chains.

Whatever was wrong with everyone?

Closing the door, Permelia tried to settle her erratic breathing. *William was alive!* Not only alive but standing in her foyer. She studied him while his back was turned, trying to gain her composure. Light from an overhead chandelier cascaded over him, accentuating the war-honed muscles stretching the fabric of his coat. Hair the color of rich coffee grazed his stiff collar, curling at the tips.

Why would her heart not settle? He came for Annie. Not for her. Taking a deep breath, Permelia moved to face him.

The first thing she noticed was the depth of pain in his eyes. The second, that the right half of his face hung in shivered purple flesh. What was left of Permelia's breath escaped her lungs. She stifled the gasp that tried to force its way to her lips. His jaw stiffened, and he looked down, fumbling with his hat.

Permelia took a step toward him. His eyes met hers. Those brown eyes, deep and rich like the soil within a lush forest. The same eyes she remembered. Yet not the same. The haughtiness, the innocent exuberance, was gone, replaced by wisdom and deep sorrow. Her own eyes burned. For the agony he must have endured. For the pain, the heartache.

"Martha, would you please go get Annie?" Permelia said.

"I'll put some tea on." Elijah grabbed Ruth and pulled her from the room as Martha headed upstairs.

William attempted a smile. "You are not repulsed?"

Permelia shook her head. "No. Of course not." Shocked. Grieved. She wanted to tell him that he could never repulse her, but the words faltered on her lips. "I cannot imagine what you must have endured. How did it happen?"

William shifted his boots over the marble floor. "An exploding cannon."

Permelia threw a hand to her mouth. "Oh my. When?"

"Nearly nine months ago."

So that was why his letters had stopped. "When I—Annie didn't hear from you, we feared the worst."

◆   ◆   ◆

Miss Permelia's eyes flooded with concern as she reached up to touch William's face. He shrank away, uncomfortable. Yet she kept her eyes upon him. She did not run away in horror as so many others had done. That alone gave him hope. A hope that had stirred at the mention of Annie's name. A hope that kept him rooted in place, willing to risk allowing her to see him in full light.

And perhaps, dare he hope, to look at him in the same way her sister was doing right now. Not in pity, but with concern, and something else that gave him pause. He shrugged it off when he heard light footfalls on the stairs. The swoosh of satin and the lacy bottom of a gown materialized. The steps increased. The gown bounced, and the angel appeared.

His Annie.

Hair like gold silk was pinned back from a face that rivaled perfection: alabaster skin, pink lips, luminous blue eyes. Curls danced over the nape of her neck with each graceful movement down the stairs. She raised her gaze to his. Her smile washed away. The flame in her eyes turned to ice. An ice that froze her in place. She drew a hand to her chest.

William's heart shriveled.

"William?" Annie managed to breathe out in a halting sob.

"I'm afraid so." Though he wanted to turn away, to spare her the horrendous sight, he kept his gaze steady upon her, waiting—waiting to see love sweep away the shock and horror in her eyes.

Instead she lowered her chin and turned her face away. Gripping the banister, she wobbled.

Risking her repulsion, William vaulted the steps between them and grabbed her by the waist before she fell. She stiffened at his touch. Permelia reached her other side, and after exchanging a compassionate look with William, led her sister down the stairs and into the parlor.

William hesitated, his insides crumbling. Should he follow? Was he welcome? But Permelia's gentle smile beckoned him onward.

The servant woman he remembered as a slave brought tea and William chose a cushioned seat in the shadows. Annie sat on the sofa, staring at the cold hearth.

Permelia approached him. "Colonel, please join us." She gestured toward one of the chairs in the center of the room. "It's only the shock, I'm afraid."

"Please call me William." He heaved a sigh. "And I won't be staying."

Annie's eyes shot his way.

Permelia smiled. "Don't be silly, William. You've no doubt had an arduous journey and are welcome to stay with us as long as you wish." She made her way to the table and began pouring tea.

"Either way, I have only a week before I must report back for duty." William shifted in his seat. His gaze wandered to the door, silently chastising himself. He'd put his selfish desire to see Annie above any thought of how the sight of him would shock her. Now he'd upset her. Which was the last thing he'd wanted to do. He should leave.

Miss Permelia handed her sister a cup. "William must stay. Isn't that right, Annie?"

A visible sob shook his beloved Annie. Sipping the tea, she set it down with a delicate clank as his future, his heart, hung precariously on her response.

"Of course, William. We'll not hear another word about it." Annie's sweet voice brought his gaze back to her, where he was graced with one of her smiles. A smile that warmed him down to his toes—as it always used to do. Hope stirred. Then grew stagnant again as she added, "But surely you must return to your regiment?" It wasn't so much the question but the expectation in her tone that set William aback.

"After the terms of surrender were signed, my commanding officer granted me a month's leave." He coughed. "To settle my affairs."

Annie spread her skirts around her in a festoon of velvet braids and ruffles. "You must forgive me, William." She raised the back of her hand to her mouth, sorrow crumpling her features. "Seeing you. . .like this. . .it is such a shock."

Miss Permelia gave her sister an odd look before she settled into a chair between them. "William was injured in the war, Annie."

"Of course. I can see that," Annie snapped. Then the sharp lines of her face softened. "I'm so sorry, William. I hope you didn't suffer."

Not nearly as much as he was suffering now. "No, not overmuch."

Rising, Annie swooshed to the mantel, eyeing the gilded clock and bronze figurines sitting atop it. "We feared you had died." Yet there was no fear in her voice.

Permelia sipped her tea. "It is very good to see you, William."

"Yes, of course." Annie forced a smile, tried to look at him, then glanced back at the mantel.

Unease prickled over William, his thoughts traveling to his last visit to the Shaw estate—when he'd been welcomed with open arms, enjoyed the richest foods, the Southern charm of Mrs. Shaw, and the hustle and bustle of a prosperous tobacco plantation. "Where are your mother and father? Your brother?" William sipped the bitter tea. He never did enjoy it without sugar.

"They are all gone." Miss Permelia stared at the teacup in her lap. "Except perhaps Samuel. We do not yet know his fate."

"I hate this detestable war! It's taken everything from me!" Annie fisted her hands beneath lacy cuffs.

Gone. William nearly dropped his cup. Instead, he set it down on the table beside him and rose. He longed to swallow Annie up in his arms, comfort her. "How? When? Why didn't you tell me in your letters?"

Annie's brow crumpled.

Permelia shifted in her seat. "Father died at Cross Keys. And Mother became ill and joined him last year."

"So it is just the two of you here?"

"And Elijah, Martha, and Ruth," Miss Permelia said.

Sorrow, coupled with alarm, assailed William. "How have you managed?"

Annie sank to the sofa in a sob, drawing a handkerchief to her eyes.

"Better than most." Miss Permelia moved to sit beside her sister. "We keep a garden and Elijah hunts. In addition, by God's grace, we hope to harvest our first crop of tobacco this year." Golden specks of hope and sincerity sparked in her eyes.

William wondered why he'd never noticed how beautiful they were before.

"We've had to sacrifice so much." Annie's voice broke, tearing at his heart.

A lump formed in his throat. "I'm so sorry. You never mentioned it." He could only surmise that in her selfless love, Annie had wanted to keep him from worrying while he was on the battlefield. Warmed by the thought, he gazed about the room, noting the rosewood center table, painted porcelain vases, gilded mirror and assorted oil paintings hanging on the wall, and the mahogany Grecian sofa upon which Annie sat. "But how were you able to keep so many of your nice things?"

Clutching her handkerchief, Annie straightened her back and glanced out the window. "We've made friends with some of the Union soldiers."

"Ah, then we are not all such bellicose toads?" William chuckled.

A smile flickered then faded on Annie's lips. "Why have you returned, William?" Her eyes swept to his. And finally remained.

And it gave him the impetus to answer her question.

"To marry you, Annie. If you'll still have me."

Chapter 3

Permelia set the candle atop her dressing bureau and knelt beside the trunk at the foot of her bed. Her heart felt as heavy and dark as the sultry night lurking outside her window—a night that barely entertained a whisper of a breeze to stir the curtains framing the leaded glass. Silver moonlight spilled upon the woven rug and toyed with the hem of her gown as if trying to improve her mood.

Wiping moisture from her eyes, she chastised herself. She should be happy for her sister. Happy that William had returned to claim her as his bride. Deep down, she *was* happy for Annie. Although at the moment, that joy seemed smothered by her own selfish agony. *Please forgive me, Lord.*

Oh, why hadn't Annie answered William's question? If he had asked Permelia to marry him, she would have leaped into his arms on the spot. Instead, Annie had promised to discuss his proposal tomorrow and promptly left the parlor. Perhaps she engaged in some sort of amorous dalliance, as she often liked to do with men—flirtatious behavior Permelia had never quite mastered.

She opened the trunk and drew her mother's shawl to her nose. The slight hint of jasmine still lingered on the cashmere. She breathed it in, wishing her mother were still in her chamber a few steps down the hallway. Though they'd never been close—not like her mother and Annie had been—Permelia missed her terribly. And if there was ever a time she needed a mother's advice, it was now. Now, when her heart was a jumble of discordant thoughts and feelings. Most of which she'd never experienced before.

Setting the shawl aside, she pulled out the bundle of letters and held them against her chest.

Ah, William! He was here! She could hardly believe it.

The air stirred outside her window, fluttering leaves and entering her room to caress her face—as she had longed to do with William's. To caress away his pain, kiss away his scars. Lowering the bundle to her lap, she brushed her fingers over the crinkled vellum. Such sweet words they had shared, such intimacies, dreams, and hopes.

A tear slid down her cheek and plopped onto the paper. She quickly dabbed it with her sleeve, lest it destroy one precious word. But these letters were not meant for her. William thought he had been writing to Annie. When he penned each word, each loving phrase, it was Annie's face that filled his thoughts, his heart.

Not Permelia's.

"Oh, Lord, I never meant to deceive him. Please forgive me." She squeezed her eyes shut as more tears escaped. She had only meant to comfort him. To give him hope in the midst of the horrors of war. Words from someone who cared. But when William had mistook her signature, *P. A. Shaw*, for Annie, and his letter had been so filled with joy at hearing from her, Permelia hadn't the heart to tell him that Annie had given up writing to him.

That she had turned her affections to another.

Then the years passed and the letters continued, and Permelia found herself waiting for each missive with giddy expectation. For out from the penned words, emerged a hero. A man of honor, nobility, and courage. Yet with a kind, gentle heart and a wit that never failed to make her smile.

And she had fallen in love with him.

But now, he had come for Annie. As it should be. Permelia should be thankful that she had been able to offer William some solace during his darkest hours. Placing a gentle kiss on the bundle, she put them back in the chest, covered them with her mother's shawl, and closed the lid. At least she would always have his letters. No one could take away the precious words she'd shared with William.

A cloud swallowed up the moonlight, leaving her with only the flicker of a single candle to chase away the gloom.

God, help me to forget him. Help me to be happy for him and Annie. If not, she feared she would shrivel up and die.

◆　◆　◆

William stood beside the men under his command. Ten companies in all. Behind them, Union soldiers lined up like incoming waves before a storm. Early morning fog shrouded the field in a white veil, muffling the sounds of boots on grass, the cocking of rifles. The heavy breaths of jittery soldiers. The frenzied thud *of their hearts.*

The crack, crack, crack *of gunfire split the mist. A flock of birds fluttered into the sky and disappeared.*

"Fire!" William shouted. The soldiers raised their guns and ignited thunderous pandemonium. Enemy bullets whined past William's ears. "Forward march!" The men parted the tall grass. Yellow flashes sparked in the distant mist.

The air filled with smoke and screams and ear-pounding explosions. William grabbed the man to his right to usher him forward. He toppled to the dirt. A red pool bubbled from his chest. His eyes gaped toward heaven in vacant shock.

William crumbled beside him.

The boy was only eighteen. William had met his mother back in Philadelphia and had promised her he'd look out for him. Brushing his fingers over the boy's eyes, he closed them forever.

A cannonball struck the ground nearby. The shock sent William flying. He landed in mud. Pain throbbed in his shoulder. A loud buzzing filled his ears. Accompanied by the thump, thump *of his heart. Shaking his head, he looked up just in time to see the tip of a Rebel saber headed for his chest.*

William snapped his eyes open. The blur of thick timbers crisscrossing the ceiling came into focus. The *cluck, cluck* of a chicken sounded. Where was he? He shot up and gazed over the gloomy room. Sunlight speared through small glass windows on either side of a door, which stood slightly ajar. A chicken perched in the entryway, staring at him. She clucked, bobbed her head up and down, then ruffled her back feathers and left.

He snorted. Even a chicken couldn't stand the sight of him.

Tossing his legs over the side of the cot, William raked both hands through his hair and drew in a deep breath, wondering when the nightmares would stop. He rubbed his sore neck and took in the one-room house that had once been the slave quarters. At least that's what Miss Permelia had told him when she and Elijah had escorted him there last night. Since it wouldn't be proper for him to stay in the main house, and the overseer's quarters had been burned to the ground last year, this was all they had to offer. Little did Miss Permelia know that compared to where he'd been sleeping the past four years, these quarters might as well be a room at the Fifth Avenue Hotel in New York.

He struggled to his feet, stretched out the aches still resident from his long ride, and made his way to the washbasin with one thought in mind. *Annie.* After making himself as presentable as possible, he intended to spend the day with her. Woo her and charm her like he used to do before this hellish war had separated them. He stopped to ensure the letters were still safe in the coat he'd slung over the back of a chair. He drew them out, flipped open his knapsack, and gently placed them inside. Better not to carry them around and risk losing them.

For to him, they were the essence of the woman he loved and the reason his sentiments for Annie had grown so deeply, despite his extended absence—despite her reaction to him last night.

Cringing at the memory, he made his way to the basin Elijah had filled with water. How could he blame her? Perhaps William should have written of his arrival. Perhaps he should have written about his scars. Deep down, he supposed he'd hoped they wouldn't matter; he'd hoped the woman he'd grown to love wouldn't care.

But what he hadn't considered was how much suffering Annie had faced in the past four years. Besides, when he'd posed his question of marriage last night, she had not turned him down. In fact, he thought he saw a spark of love in her eyes.

Halting before the worn chest of drawers, William gazed at his reflection in the mirror. Sunlight rippled over his puckered flesh, accentuating the purple divots and the pale, distended skin. He slammed his eyes shut. Would he ever get used to the sight? How could he expect someone as beautiful as Annie to love such a monster?

After washing and shaving, he donned a fresh uniform, minus his coat, and headed outside. The smell of freshly turned dirt, horseflesh, and wild oregano combined in an oddly pleasant scent as his glance took in the wide expanse of the plantation. Behind the main house stood the kitchen, dairy, and smokehouse. Off in the distance the barn rose stark before the encroaching forest. To its right stood the stables, once brimming with horses, but now eerily silent.

Laughter drew his gaze to a field to his left. He halted at the sight of a woman, hoe in hand, tending the soil beside Elijah. Curiosity drew him toward her. Surely Miss Permelia hadn't meant that *she* worked in the fields. Absurd!

Yet, as he came closer, his suspicions were confirmed, for there she stood, dirt smudged on her arms and neck and perspiration beading on her brow. The hem of her cotton skirt was gathered and tucked within her belt, revealing a soiled petticoat and ankle boots covered in mud. But it was the healthy color of her cheeks and the way the sun flung golden ribbons through the brown hair dancing about her waist that drew William's attention.

Shielding her eyes, she gazed up at him and quickly lowered the folds of her gown. "William, good morning. Did you sleep well?" The red on her cheeks darkened.

Elijah leaned on his shovel. "I always slept well in that house. Lots o' good memories in there."

William flinched, wondering how a slave could have any good memories. "I did sleep well. Thank you." He stared at her aghast. "This is hardly suitable work for a young lady." His voice came out more pretentious than he intended.

"I beg your pardon, Colonel, but this particular lady does not wish to starve. Nor see her sister starve. I hardly think that either of those options would be more suitable than this breach of propriety."

The way she tossed her pert little nose in the air made him want to chuckle. Instead he cleared his throat. "Forgive me. I meant no insult."

"Quite all right." She set her hoe aside and stomped toward him, dirt clumping on her boots. "We've already planted the carrots, chard, green onions, and basil." She pointed to another large field next to what used to be the storehouse, if William's memory served, where tiny green sprouts dotted the fresh earth.

"And what are you planting here?"

"Tobacco." Lifting the brim of her straw bonnet, she gazed over the field. "Our first attempt. Now that the war is over, we hope to be able to make some profit from it like Papa did."

William wondered how they would manage all the work it required to process tobacco but dared not ask. He had a feeling this resolute woman already had a plan.

She wiped her face, leaving a smudge of dirt. William found it adorable. "You must be hungry," she said.

He should be. He hadn't eaten since early yesterday. But his stomach had been nothing but a cyclone of nerves since he'd arrived. "In truth, no. I would, however, like to see Annie."

Elijah chuckled.

Miss Permelia gazed at the sun. "I fear you'll have a few hours' wait. She never rises before noon."

William jerked at the statement, concern flooding him. "Does she suffer from some malady?"

Permelia shook her head. "It's the war. It has taken a toll on her, I'm afraid."

William frowned. "A toll I only increased with my sudden appearance last night."

Permelia looked at him, neither avoiding the scarred side of his face, nor flinching at the sight of it. "I'm sorry for her reaction, Col—William. She's not been herself lately." She gestured toward the small brick house, where ribbons of smoke spiraled from the chimney. "Help yourself to biscuits and coffee in the kitchen. Martha and Ruth will be happy to see you." Gathering her skirts, she headed toward the main house. "Forgive me, but I haven't the time to entertain you properly. I must get cleaned up and head into town."

Wiping his arm over his forehead, Elijah returned to his work.

"Alone?" William shouted after her.

She faced him. "I need to take the wild blueberries Elijah and I picked this morning to sell at market, and"—she hesitated—"attend to another matter."

"Unescorted?" William could not conceive of a woman traveling alone during such tremulous times.

"I have no choice, Colonel. Elijah is needed here." Her tone was clipped as she marched toward the house.

This time he couldn't help but chuckle. Turning, she gazed at him quizzically. "And just what is so amusing?"

William caught up to her. "You call me 'colonel' when you become cross."

"I do?" She laughed. "But I'm not cross. It's just that many things have changed since your last visit." She continued onward.

He walked beside her. "If you'll permit me, I'd love to accompany you. Though I am not on duty, I should report my presence to Lieutenant Lee, the provost marshal." Besides, he found himself longing to spend more time with this fascinating woman, a woman who didn't shy away from dirt, hard labor, or working side by side with a freed slave.

"I'd be delighted." Her blue eyes flashed with an emotion he could not place before she turned away.

Five hours later, William strode down the Duke of Gloucester Street in Williamsburg, ignoring the sordid glares from both the citizens and returning Confederate soldiers. He could hardly blame them. He had reported to Lieutenant Lee and found him to be a pompous buffoon, who no doubt had entertained himself by reigning terror over the poor inhabitants.

Tipping his hat at a passing lady and her child, William continued onward, noting how she cringed when she saw his face and hurried to the other side of the street. How different from the way he'd been received by ladies before the war. He pictured himself, dressed in his velvet cape and top hat, strolling down the Boulevard in New York City, showered with the flirtatious smiles of ladies who all but swooned as they passed him by.

Yet he was the same man as before. Perhaps even a better man for all he'd endured.

His glance took in the buildings along the side of the road, and he realized Williamsburg had endured much as well. Yards once filled with flowers stood trampled and vacant, outbuildings had been burned, porches lay neglected and crumbling. Gaping holes glared at him from walls like angry eyes where windows and doors had once stood.

A group of Confederate soldiers, bandages around the arms and legs of their stained uniforms, loitered in front of Vest's store. The sharp scent of alcohol stung William's nose as he passed. Their gazes locked upon him like a dozen rifles, following him down the street and making him think that it hadn't been such a good idea to wear his uniform.

He quickened his pace to the Baptist Church, where Permelia had said to meet her. Church. He hadn't stepped inside a real church in years—only attended services when it was required of him in the army. And even then, he had ceased to listen to the sermons. He still believed in God. But if he had to admit it, William supposed he was angry at a God who would allow the misery he'd witnessed on the battlefield. Men torn forever from their families. Young boys mutilated, their lives ripped from them before they'd even lived. And for what?

The United States would continue on as before. Yes, the slaves were freed—as evidenced by the many Negro freedmen walking the streets, receiving nearly as much scorn as William. But had the war really been about slavery? Or was it about men grasping for the same things that had caused all the conflicts throughout time: greed and power?

Shoving his cap farther on his head to shadow his scars as much as possible, he wiped the sweat from his neck. May, and already the unbearably hot Virginia summer was forcing its way onto citizens who had suffered enough. Looking forward to a reprieve from the sun, he entered the foyer of the church.

He halted as if he'd slammed into a brick wall.

What he had expected to see was a group of people kneeling in prayer or listening to the endless droll of some parson demanding recompense for the damages done by the North. Or perhaps a group of the faithful gathered to complain and whine about the occupation. Instead his eyes landed on a pile of amputated limbs stacked in the corner like discarded pieces of rotting wood. A horde of flies swarmed around them. William's stomach vaulted.

He forced his eyes to cots that lined a room where pews must have once stood. The injured, maimed, and sickly writhed upon them like churning, restless waves at sea. Women in bloodstained aprons, carrying buckets and bandages, flitted between the patients, ministering to their needs. A stench he'd only smelled once before, on the battlefield of Chancellorsville, where the Union had lost over fourteen thousand men, assaulted him—the sour, putrid smell of death. Hand pressed to his belly, William stepped outside for air before he made a fool of himself.

"William." He turned around to see Permelia wiping her hands on her stained apron and looking at him with concern. "Are you unwell?"

Forcing a smile, William gathered his resolve. "No. Forgive me. I hadn't expected. . ."

"To see so many injured?" She brushed strands of hair from her face. Red stains marred her fingers.

"No, not here, in a church."

She glanced over her shoulder at the mayhem, genuine sorrow on her face. "We have been tending the wounded here ever since the war began." She sighed. "Despite the peace, the injured still pour in."

Moans shot from the open door, drawing William's gaze to a Union uniform draped over the bottom of a cot. He blinked. "Both sides?"

She gave him an incredulous look. "Of course. God loves Yankees, too, William." One corner of her mouth lifted.

He smiled, delighting in the sparkle in her eyes, present despite the misery surrounding her. After all she'd suffered and lost, after shouldering the burden of providing for her and her family, she still took time to help others. "How often do you assist here?"

"Twice a week, or as needed. The doctor sends for me if we receive a large number of wounded."

A woman called to her from within the church. Excusing herself, Permelia dashed off, promising to meet him outside as soon as possible.

Happy to oblige her, William wandered around the church grounds, stopping at the west side of the building, where group graves marked the passing of many soldiers from this world.

"We ran out of space for them." Permelia's voice startled him, and he caught the mist in her eyes before she turned away.

He wanted to apologize, wanted to erase the pain from her face. But instead he offered his arm and led her away from the church.

◆ ◆ ◆

Guilt assailed Permelia as she wandered down the street on the arm of her sister's fiancé. Not guilt in the act, for it was innocent enough, but guilt that she enjoyed William's company so much—his voice, his words, his touch. Thrilled that he had offered her his arm. Proud to be walking by his side, despite the belligerent gazes scouring them. Throughout the occupation, many of Williamsburg's citizens had grown to loathe the Yankees. With God's grace, Permelia saw them as mere humans on the other side of a nonsensical dispute that had been caused by man's foolish sinfulness.

Adjusting her bonnet, she peeked at William sauntering beside her. The way the fringed epaulettes perched on his broad shoulders shimmered in the sun, the brass buttons lining his long blue coat, his leather belt and baldric, the red sash about his waist, the service sword at his side. And she had never seen a more handsome figure. Though she had tried to quell her reaction to his close proximity, she'd finally given in to the flutter in her belly and the *thump* of her heart and decided she might as well enjoy this time with him. Soon he and Annie would be gone. To New York City, where they would marry, have a bevy of children, and live a happy life together.

On the wagon ride into town, he had hardly spoken, and Permelia sensed a deep sorrow within him. She longed to discuss the things they'd written of in their letters but dared not. Though she knew him intimately, he treated her as a mere acquaintance. But of course, to him, she was. It pained her nonetheless. So she'd spent the hour sneaking glimpses of him, admiring the assertive way he sat, directing the horses, the way his hair, the color of rich earth, fluttered against his collar. The stiff angle of his jaw and chin. And his deep-set eyes, so full of pain she longed to wrap her arms around him. Now, walking beside her in his crisp Union blues, he carried himself with an authority that set her at ease, a protectiveness that made her feel safe.

And she hadn't felt safe in a long time.

"It grieves me to see your fair town in this condition," he said as a horse and carriage rattled by, stirring up dust.

Permelia glanced over to the spot where the hotel had once stood. "Every vacant house was torn down by the soldiers for wood. They stripped the ones left standing of anything valuable." She nodded to Mrs. Milligan, who was standing in her yard, eyeing them with curiosity. Permelia strolling on the arm of a Union officer would certainly give the elderly gossip something to talk about.

"I apologize for what my fellow soldiers have done, Permelia. It appears they have not behaved as gentlemen." Genuine sorrow tainted his voice. He laid his hand upon hers tucked within the crook of his elbow.

A thrill spun in her belly. "Some have been quite kind. But it seems war brings out the worst in men."

He gave her a look that said he understood that fact all too well. "Still, I am both astonished and overjoyed that the Yankees, as you call them, left your home unharmed."

"They didn't at first. We quite feared for our lives." Permelia shivered as memories of those first few weeks of occupation marched across her thoughts. "But God took care of us. He has blessed us greatly."

William seemed surprised at her statement, but he only offered her a smile in reply.

Up ahead, a familiar face twisted a knot in Permelia's gut. *Jackson.* She wished Annie could see him now as he flirted with two young, attractive ladies. Upon spotting her, he started her way, his pointed gaze taking in William like a hawk would newfound prey. When his eyes focused on William's face, he flinched, halted before them, and offered a salute with languid enthusiasm.

"Good day, Jackson," Permelia said, wiggling her nose at the cedar oil he'd sprinkled in his hair.

"Miss Permelia." He removed his hat and dipped a bow.

"Sergeant Jackson Steele, may I present Colonel William Wolfe."

Jackson stood at attention, staring at William's coat. "Welcome, Colonel. I had not heard of additional officers arriving."

"At ease, Sergeant." William seemed unaffected by the man's inability to gaze upon his face. "I am not on duty at the moment. Though I do not find it surprising that you are not made aware of the movement of every officer." His tone had turned superior.

Jackson's eyes narrowed at the insult. Easing his stance, he slid his fingers over the oiled hair at his temples. "Regardless, it is good to see Miss Permelia on the arm of a gentleman. I've warned her more than once that she is fast becoming an old spinster."

Heat rose on Permelia's neck that had nothing to do with the hot sun beating down on them.

William cleared his throat.

"I fear you are mistaken," Permelia began. "William is but an acquaintance." How could she tell the man the truth? But it must come out sooner or later. Though she wasn't overly fond of Jackson, she didn't wish to hurt him, either. "In fact," she continued, "you should know that he is Annie's fiancé from New York, come to claim her."

For the first time since she'd known Jackson, the supercilious facade slipped from his face. Yet, what replaced it terrified Permelia. Pure hatred. He slid a finger over his mustache and stretched his shoulders beneath his blue coat as if shrugging off the information. Once again the mask of imperious charm stiffened his features. He forced a smile, revealing a row of gleaming teeth that reminded Permelia of a horse neighing its displeasure.

"Well, that is quite impossible, Colonel," he said, "since Annie is already engaged to me."

Chapter 4

Y ou can't avoid him forever, Annie." Permelia spun around from her spot by the chamber window.

"Tighter, Ruth." Annie gripped the bedpost as the young Negro girl yanked on the lacings of her corset. Fear of displeasing her mistress was still resident in her wide eyes, though she'd been freed three years ago.

"I am quite aware of that, dear sister, which is why I intend to take a stroll with him today." Annie twisted her lips. "That is far too tight, stupid girl."

Ruth's hands shook.

Permelia approached, gave Ruth a sympathetic look, and took over the lacing. "Ruth, would you please assist your mother in the kitchen?" After the young girl left, Permelia finished the binding and helped Annie on with her petticoats. "Ruth is no longer our slave, Annie. You mustn't be so cruel to her."

"Oh, fiddle. I know. I'm sorry." Annie adjusted her crinoline. "I'm just so tired. And seeing William has been so. . .so difficult."

Permelia frowned. "I would think you'd be thrilled to finally see him." As Permelia was. Far too thrilled.

"Of course I am." Annie puckered her lips as Permelia assisted her with her final muslin petticoat before draping her skirt over the top.

"Then why have you been feigning illness these past two days?" Permelia planted her hands at her hips and gave her sister a look of reprimand.

"Oh Permi." Annie dropped onto her bed, fluffing out her silver-blue skirts around her. "He's just so hard to look upon."

Permelia had no such difficulty. With a sigh she strolled back to the window, preferring to watch William working in the fields than to see her sister's pouting face. Shovel in hand and stripped to the waist, he helped Elijah dig irrigation ditches. The sun glistened off his powerful chest and arms, both rippling beneath the exertion. Her belly fluttered, and she hugged it in an effort to stifle the pleasant feelings, all the while growing accustomed to them. She had also grown accustomed to the absence of hunger pains since William had arrived. For he'd purchased a fresh pig and enough rice and grain to feed them for a month.

Annie's voice whined behind Permelia like an annoying gnat, but she couldn't tear her gaze from William. The son of a wealthy shipbuilder, a graduate of West Point, and an officer in the Union army, out working in the fields beside an ex-slave. Laughter rose on the wind as he and Elijah shared a joke. Permelia smiled. Perhaps the war had indeed changed him.

"I fear you are mistaken, Annie, about his appearance. He's not hard to look upon at all." The thoughts filling Permelia's mind slipped off her lips unawares. She nearly gasped at her sensuous tone—a tone that drew her sister to the window, where she followed Permelia's gaze down to William. An unusual look contorted her features. Almost like jealousy. But that couldn't be. Annie would never be jealous of Permelia.

As if reading her thoughts, Annie flounced to the dressing glass and cocked her head, sending her golden curls bouncing as she admired her reflection. "You know what I mean, Permi. His face. It's hideous."

"You shouldn't say such things. It's him you love, not his face, Annie."

Her sister didn't answer. Instead she held a string of pearls around her neck. "Can you hook these?" The necklace Jackson Steele had given her, no doubt stolen from some other Virginia woman.

"You shouldn't wear those."

"Why not? They are beautiful."

"They are too fine a gift from a man who isn't your fiancé."

"What does that matter?"

If Annie didn't know, Permelia wouldn't tell her. Besides, when did her sister ever listen to her? Permelia latched the hook.

Annie swerved about, sending her skirts swaying back and forth like a church bell. "Stop being such a sanctimonious sprite, Permi. You always were so perfect. Never did anything wrong, anything dangerous. Don't you want to live a little, enjoy life?" A devilish gleam sparkled in her eyes.

Permelia squelched her rising frustration at the insignia she'd been branded with since childhood. Even the children in town had teased her when she wouldn't join them in their shenanigans. She hadn't wanted to disappoint her parents. She wanted to make everyone happy. To not hurt anyone's feelings. But she'd been a hopeless failure at that as well. "Of course I want to enjoy life. But you don't have to be evil to do so."

"But you can be a bit naughty now and then." One side of Annie's rosy lips lifted in a mischievous grin. "Come now, I'll wager you've never kissed a man."

Permelia swallowed and dropped her gaze to the wool rug.

"No, of course you haven't." Annie gave a ladylike snort and laid a hand on her heart, gazing upward. "Kissing a man is so heavenly."

Permelia gasped. "Don't tell me you've kissed Jackson?"

"Of course I have." Annie pinned silk flowers in her hair.

Permelia rubbed her arms and gazed back at William in the field. Her heart ached for him. While he had been fighting on the battlefield, his fiancée was in another man's arms.

"There's no harm in a simple kiss," Annie continued with a pout.

Permelia eased back the curtains as a breeze fluttered the lace at her neckline and helped cool her anger toward her sister. "Now that William is here, you should reserve your affections solely for him."

"I don't know if I can kiss him, Permi," Annie whined and crossed the room, plopping back onto her bed. "He's so. . ." She shuddered, and Permelia knelt before her, grasping her hands.

"Annie, of course you can. He's beautiful inside. I assure you, you will grow so accustomed to the scars, you'll hardly notice them." As Permelia had done these past few days. Forced to entertain William in Annie's absence, she had enjoyed every minute of their time together—despite his constant inquiries about Annie. Yet the pain in his voice had prompted Permelia to do all she could to encourage Annie to rekindle their relationship.

Though it tore Permelia up inside.

"He must leave in a few days, Annie. And you never gave him your answer."

Annie leaned on the bedpost. "Is it possible to love two men?"

"I have no idea." Rising, Permelia eased a lock of Annie's hair from her forehead. "But you can't be engaged to two men. You need to call it off with Jackson."

"Hmph. I already tried." Annie folded her lips, then cast Permelia a venomous look. "And I know you told him about William."

Permelia began to straighten the pillows on Annie's bed. "I had no choice." Perhaps she should have told her sister about the encounter in town. But wait. Permelia stared at Annie. "What do you mean, you tried already? Tell me Jackson hasn't come to call."

Annie sashayed to her dressing table and dabbed perfume on her neck. "He came by last night, after you retired."

"Highly inappropriate."

"Don't be silly." Annie's voice was patronizing. "I assured him that I hadn't made up my mind yet." She paused, glancing at her reflection in the dressing glass again. "Jackson is so handsome, so charming, so romantic." She sighed. "But he has no money."

Pamela rubbed the ache rising behind her temples. Sometimes she felt as though she didn't know her sister at all. "You're promised to William. Please give him a chance." Though the thought broke her heart, Permelia wanted to see William happy above all else.

And from all indications, he truly loved Annie.

Annie adjusted her skirts. "I've never seen Jackson quite so enraged. Though I don't know why. I informed him about William years ago." She faced Permelia. "I simply can't know what's he's going to do. He all but declared he will not let me go without a fight. Isn't that romantic?"

At the look of excitement in her sister's eyes, Permelia spun back around. Jackson Steele was not a man to be trifled with. She recalled the way he had glared at William in town as if he were an enemy on the battlefield. A knot formed in Permelia's throat. Certainly the man wouldn't harm William. Would he?

◆　◆　◆

A warm spring breeze wafted over William as he strolled along the stone path marking the outskirts of the Shaw plantation. The scent of dogwood and cedar filled the air as the honeyed voice of Annie filled his ears, bringing him a contentment he'd not felt since he arrived in Virginia. Not only had Annie finally recovered from her illness, but she agreed to spend some time alone with him. Just like they used to do when he'd come courting, walking this same path, arm in arm.

Although the scenery had changed.

Fields that used to be brimming with tobacco plants lay overgrown with weeds. Instead of the chatter of activity, whinny of horses, grate of ploughs, and laughter of children, only the buzz of insects and the chirp of birds accompanied the tap of their shoes over the thistle-infested flagstone.

Yet with Annie's delicate hand once again on his arm, his mind wandered back to former days, to a happier time when they had strolled down the bustling streets of New York, drawing the gazes of society matrons all abuzz at their famed courtship. William

Wolfe, inheritor of Wolfe Shipbuilding and the most handsome eligible bachelor in town. Ah, yes, those were grand days!

"I'm most pleased you are feeling better, Annie."

Adjusting her parasol against the hot sun, she smiled but did not meet his gaze. "I am not sure what came over me." She hesitated. "It is truly good to see you, William."

See him? Since they'd left the house, she hadn't *seen* him at all. Not once had she looked his way. Though he couldn't attest to the same. In fact, he couldn't keep his eyes off her. The way the sunlight glittered off her skin and hair in a shower of brilliant diamonds, her lips the shade of the wild geraniums doting the landscape, moist with dew. He swallowed the desire to kiss them. Though he had taken such liberties in New York, he felt no such offer extended to him here. At least not yet. And not before he discovered who this Jackson fellow was and why he was under the mistaken notion that he was engaged to Annie. But he'd wait to pursue that topic. William did not wish to spoil the first happy moment he and Annie had shared since his arrival.

"This war has done no disservice to your beauty, dear. You are the picture of loveliness as always."

Voices drew his gaze to Miss Permelia helping Elijah load the wagon with vegetables to exchange in town for much-needed supplies. Absent from the younger sister were the sparkling jewels, the bead-laced coiffure, the bell skirt that fairly floated over the ground. Instead, with loose hair flowing down her back, Permelia wore a simple cotton gown fringed in nothing but dirt.

"Why, how kind of you to say, William." Annie giggled, drawing his gaze back to her.

He kissed her forehead, inhaling her fragrance of lilac. A fragrance that brought back memories of the last time he saw her on Bow Bridge in Central Park four years ago. He could picture them so clearly standing on the snowy bridge: the way her distraught sighs had emerged in sweet puffs upon the icy winter air, her glistening eyes so full of love, her father's carriage in the distance waiting to take her back to Virginia, and William commanded to report to his captain that afternoon and be sent off to fight.

"I cannot stand to be apart from you," she had said, falling into his embrace. *"I hate this war already. Why can't we be married now?"*

William had reluctantly nudged her back. Taking her shoulders, he'd studied her face, trying to memorize each line and curve, the graceful shape of her nose, her thick lashes now wet with tears. *"Because your father will not permit us to marry until this war is over."* Reaching into his pocket, he'd pulled out the coin and handed it to her.

"What is this?"

"My pledge to you, darling."

She examined the engraving. "It says 'Love never fails. W.W. Central Park.' " A tear slipped down her cheek.

He wiped it away. "This coin is my pledge to marry you on this very spot as soon as the war is over."

"Oh William." She stood on her tiptoes and smothered him with kisses.

Even now, four years later, William warmed at the memories. Especially with her once again by his side. "Where is that coin I gave you?"

Pushing away from him, she fingered the top of a tall weed. "I have it somewhere. I don't remember." She started walking again.

William's jaw tightened. *Don't remember?* Did his pledge to marry her mean so little?

A group of wood swallows flitted between the limbs of a mighty oak to William's left, serenading them in a celebratory chorus. Or was it a warning?

The silence stiffened between them, and William sought the words to ask her once again if she would accompany him to New York. If she still wished to marry him.

Perhaps sensing the oncoming question, she began chattering about all the difficulties she had endured during the war.

A squirrel halted on the path ahead of them and stared at them curiously before scurrying away.

Taking her hand, he slid it in the crook of his elbow once again. "I cannot imagine what you suffered, darling. I wish I had been here to help, to comfort you, when you heard of your father's death."

"And we were left defenseless." She sobbed, though no tears filled her eyes. "All our slaves ran off. Can you believe it?" She flashed a glance at him but quickly averted her eyes. He remembered that expression of hers so well, like a spoiled little girl who didn't get her way. It used to charm him. But now, he found it oddly annoying.

He halted. "All men have a right to live free, Annie."

Huffing, she snapped her parasol shut. "Of course I know that." She leaned her head on his shoulder. "But it was so frightening, William. Just Permi and me. And then the soldiers ransacked our house, I feared for our. . ." She bit her lip. "Well, you know. . . . I feared they would. . ."

Gripping her shoulders, William turned her to face him. "Did they?"

She lowered her chin. "No. But Permi shot one of them."

"Shot?" He glanced at Permelia hefting a small crate onto the back of a wagon.

"Yes, it was horrifying."

Horrifying for Permelia, no doubt. He glanced at the pearls around Annie's neck and her elaborate gown. "Yet you seem to have kept most of your nice things."

"Only because of Ja—well, a lady needs such fripperies, William." She gave him a coy smile, her gaze avoiding the scarred side of his face. "How else am I to charm my fiancé when he arrives?"

Which fiancé? William wondered. "Because of Mr. Jackson Steele, you meant to say."

Her lips slanted, and she continued forward.

William wiped the sweat from the back of his neck. "I met him in town. The man swears you are engaged to him."

Halting beneath the shade of a hickory tree, she turned her back to him. "You do not understand. I had to ensure our survival."

Agony caught in her voice, lowering William's defenses. He was behaving like a jealous ogre. He touched her shoulders. She didn't recoil. Turning her around, he took her in his arms. "Forgive me, Annie. I didn't mean to distress you."

She looked up at him, then out onto the fields, her eyes blue jewels in a creamy pond. "While Permi grows her meager crops, it is I who's been forced into frightening alliances with the enemy."

"Of course, darling. I'm behaving the cad." Though William could not entirely understand why she had to go as far as espousing herself to Jackson, he *did* understand the desperate measures one had to take during wartime to survive.

She laid her head on his chest and sniffled. "The sacrifices I've made. And here you accuse me of. . .of. . ."

"I am truly sorry." He caressed her back, wondering why his body did not react to the press of her curves—a sensation he had longed to feel during the endless years of war. But it was her letters that had kept him going. Her sweet letters—filled with words that had caused him to fall even more deeply in love with her.

Chapter 5

Flirtatious laughter spilled from the front parlor. Halting at the door, Permelia took a moment to brace her heart before entering the room, tea service in hand. She knew what her eyes would see. What they had seen all day. Her sister clinging to William, chattering and fluttering her fan about like a lovesick bird—like she always did when eligible men were present.

Any eligible man.

Earlier Permelia had been forced to witness the amorous playacting as the couple strolled about the plantation grounds. Now, in early evening, the heartrending performance continued incessantly in the house.

Silently begging God's forgiveness for her jealousy and for the strength to endure the night, Permelia set the tray down and gazed at the couple sitting side by side on the sofa. She supposed the sight would settle better with her if William looked at all pleased. But a perpetual glimmer of suspicion and unease had sparked in his eyes ever since they'd entered the house.

Completely unnoticed by Annie, of course, who continued to regale him with gossip from town.

"You don't need to do that, Permi. That's why we have Martha and Ruth." Annie waved her fan in Permelia's direction.

"Martha and Ruth are otherwise occupied preparing our supper." Permelia forced a smile and handed William his tea. "For which we have you to thank, William. I must say, we haven't had such abundance in years."

Taking his glass, William's eyes locked with hers. Something flickered within them she could not place. But whatever it was, it sent her heart thumping. Turning, she strolled to the open window. Shadows drizzled over the trees like molasses, transforming their bright greens into a dull gray. A breeze cooled the perspiration on her neck. Absently slipping her hand into her pocket, she fingered the coin, the feel of it helping to assuage her sorrow. She'd meant to give it back to Annie but had forgotten. Or had she? She couldn't imagine being without it. Besides the letters, it was her only link to William. A link that had shamelessly fed her fantasy all these years that he'd pledged his love to her instead of Annie.

Which was ludicrous, of course.

She sipped her tea. A burst of mint followed the cool liquid down her throat.

"So, dear William, tell me how your family fares?" Annie asked. "Were you able to visit them after the war?"

"Indeed. I paid them a visit before traveling here. They are all well."

"And your family's shipbuilding business. Did it suffer much during the hostilities?"

Permelia spun around and lowered herself into a chair.

William glanced toward her, sending a thrill through her once again. "Quite the opposite, in fact," he said. "War increases the need for sturdy, well-built ships. My father informed me production has nearly doubled." He'd abandoned his uniform for civilian clothes: black trousers stuffed within knee-high boots, a gray waistcoat over a simple white shirt, a black neck cloth neatly tied about his throat. Yet even without the epaulettes and stripes, his commanding presence permeated the room.

"I am so pleased to hear it." Annie flashed one of her beguiling smiles and sipped her tea. "You'll no doubt be taking over the business in a few years as your father promised?"

"That is my plan." Again, he looked at Permelia. She averted her eyes. Why was he torturing her so?

His answer seemed to please Annie as she squirmed in delight, sending her curls bouncing over the nape of her neck. Candlelight shimmered over her cream-colored gown and reflected a luminous glow from the pearls at her neck and ears and the beads adorning her hair. Even her turquoise eyes glittered like the sea under a noon sun.

Permelia glanced down at her plain, soiled gown, suddenly wishing she could fade into the velvet fabric of her chair. After working in the fields, traveling to town and back, and spending an hour helping Martha in the kitchen, she had forgotten to change for supper.

Running a hand through his hair, William leaned back on the sofa and gazed at Annie as she continued prattling. How could Permelia blame him for being so enchanted with Annie's beauty?

Or was he?

Setting down her tea, Permelia studied the odd expression on his face, which harbored more confusion than admiration. Annie would have noticed it, too, if she took the time to look at him. But even sitting on his unscarred side, she barely glanced his way.

Permelia, on the other hand, found it increasingly difficult to tear her gaze from him. In fact, she hardly noticed his rippled flesh anymore.

Annie pouted. "How nice to hear that not everything was destroyed by this horrid war. Why, we have struggled for so long, I cannot imagine living without worrying every day how we are to survive."

William laid a hand over hers. "When we are married, you need never concern yourself with such things again." He turned to Permelia. "And of course I will institute a good overseer for the plantation. You will be well cared for here."

"You are too kind." Emotion burned in Permelia's throat, and she gazed down at her hands folded in her lap. She was truly happy for Annie and William. Their marriage would be good for everyone. So would be happy, and Permelia would not have to worry about money ever again. Then why were her insides flopping like a fish caught in a jumbled net of jealousy? Just being with them, watching them together, drained the life from her soul. She had always prided herself on her kindness, her charity, and her obedience to God. What was wrong with her?

Standing, she intended to excuse herself to see about supper when the front door slammed open. Boot steps pounded over the marble foyer, and all eyes turned to see Sergeant Jackson Steele appear in the doorway.

◆　◆　◆

William rose slowly. Something on the man's face had him reaching for the sword at his hip. Which was absent, of course.

Jackson's sword, however, was not. In fact, the polished metal winked at William in the final rays of the setting sun angling through the window.

Permelia gasped.

Annie froze. Her eyes took on a skittish look. "Whatever are you doing here, Jackson?"

The man sauntered into the parlor as if he'd been there a thousand times before. "I came to set things straight." Dressed in a freshly pressed dark uniform with light blue stripes, he held his cap in one hand while the other hovered precariously over the hilt of his sword. Sharp gray eyes scanned the room with impunity from within a finely sculptured face.

Annie struggled to stand. "Jackson, may I introduce William Wo—"

"We've met, love." Jackson sneered.

Love. The hair on the back of William's neck stood at attention.

Pressing down her skirts, Annie sashayed toward the intruder. "This is hardly the time, Jackson." She clutched his arm and attempted to tug him out the door.

"Let him speak," William said. It was fine time he discovered the truth. Annie certainly wasn't being forthright. And Permelia, sweet Permelia, never said a disparaging word about anyone.

Disgust at William's scarred face reflected in Jackson's eyes. "Annie and I are engaged, Colonel." He took Annie's hand and threaded it through his outstretched arm. "And I insist you leave at once. It isn't proper for you to be lodging with two unattached women."

Pulling away from Jackson, Annie's face paled. She lifted a hand to her forehead while Permelia rushed to her side.

"You would be well advised to curb your tone when speaking to a superior, Sergeant," William said as both confusion and fury rampaged through him.

"You pull rank on me in so personal a matter?" He gave a tight grin. "Very well, I will alter my tone, but that does not alter the truth that Annie is still engaged to me."

William glanced at his fiancée, hoping she'd tell the man the truth, but she seemed to be having trouble breathing. "The lady tells a different story, Sergeant. As I understand it, she offered you her kind regard in exchange for protection from vandalism. That is all."

Jackson snorted. "'Kind regard'. Is that what she's calling it?" A salacious gleam sparked in his eyes as they swept over Annie.

William took a step toward him. Sword or not, he would put this mongrel in his place if he dared say another word to impugn Annie's reputation.

"Please go, Jackson," she breathed out as Permelia led her to a chair.

"Not until you tell him the truth, love."

"There is no need for an altercation," Permelia pleaded. "I'm sure we can work this out."

"Indeed we can," Jackson said, gesturing toward William, "if this man leaves." He raised his brows toward Annie. "Love, do tell the colonel."

Annie stared at William, her wide eyes brimming with tears. Her lips trembled. Her gaze bounced between William and Jackson. She opened her mouth, then slammed it shut. Finally, clutching her skirts, she darted from the room. The pitter-patter of her shoes and the whimper of her tears echoed down the stairs.

Jackson glared at William. "If you aren't gone by tomorrow, I assure you, sir, you will regret my acquaintance."

"I fear it is too late for that, Sergeant." William returned his glare.

"We shall see." Shoving his hat atop his head, Jackson spun around and stormed from the room. A second later the front door slammed with an ominous *thud.*

William glanced at the stairs where Annie had fled. Should he follow her? Comfort her? Demand the truth? But no, that wouldn't be proper.

Permelia sank into the chair her sister had vacated. "Please forgive her, William. I warned her not to entertain that man's affections. But. . . Well, she's endured so much pain."

"No more than you, and you haven't aligned yourself with a blackguard."

She gave a bitter chuckle. "I'm afraid that option was not open to me. I lack both the charm and the beauty of my sister." She pressed her hands over her skirts as if trying to smooth the wrinkles and remove the stains.

William found the action adorable. He wanted to tell her that she was wrong on both counts. He wanted to tell her that he'd been unable to keep his eyes from her ever since she'd walked into the room. Now, gazing at her sun-pinked cheeks and the way the loose strands of her cinnamon-colored hair wisped across her neck, his heart took an odd leap.

"Besides, God has protected us," she said, "not Jackson."

As if drawn by an invisible rope, William took a step toward her. "Such resilient faith."

She graced him with a smile. "Isn't it trials that strengthen our faith? I'm sure you found much solace in God's presence during the war."

William swallowed. "Quite the opposite." He rubbed his mutilated cheek, numb to the touch. "I could not reconcile a loving God with the horrors I witnessed."

Gripping the chair, she stood, her forehead wrinkling. "Do not say such things, William. You cannot blame God for man's failings."

William stared at her, studying her humble stance, her graceful neck and delicate jaw. Before he could stop himself, he reached for her hand and laced his fingers through hers. "You make me want to believe that."

Her eyes flitted between his like skittish doves afraid to land. Fear and a yearning that surprised him flashed across them. She tried to say something, but the air between them had vanished, replaced by her scent of wildflowers and sunshine. He drew in a deep breath and caressed her hand, his body thrilling at the feel of her skin. "Why do I feel as though I know you so well, Permelia?" He sighed. "While Annie seems like a stranger to me."

"Please don't say such things." She tugged her hand from his, making him regret his honesty. "Annie doesn't mean to be cruel. She is confused, hurting." She looked away.

"Why do you always make excuses for her behavior?" Reaching up, he touched her chin and brought her gaze back to his. A curl fell across her cheek. He eased it behind her ear, running his thumb over her skin—soft like the petal of a rose.

A tremble ran through her. She closed her eyes.

And William's restraint abandoned him. He lowered his lips to hers. Moist and soft. Just as he had imagined them. But what he had not imagined was how welcoming they would be. The room dissolved around him. Nothing mattered but Permelia and the press of her lips on his, her sweet scent, her taste. Then she pulled away, but ever so slightly. Their breath mingled in the air between them. What was he doing? He tried to shake off her spell, but it wrapped around his heart, refusing to let go.

She raised her gaze to his, candlelight reflecting both confusion and desire.

He ran the back of his hand over her cheek, longing to draw out the precious moment. Pressing his lips on hers once again, he pulled her close.

A footfall padded outside the parlor.

Followed by a gasp.

Permelia pushed away from him. Remorse screamed from her eyes before she darted from the room.

◆ ◆ ◆

Tossing off her quilt, Permelia swung her legs over the bed and lit a candle. She'd spent the past several hours listening to the wind whistling past her window, the distant *hoot* of an owl, and the creak of the house settling. Or was someone else up and moving about? She gave up trying to tell. Regardless, sleep eluded her. Along with her sanity and possibly her salvation.

She had kissed William! She'd allowed him to touch the bare skin of her hands, her cheek. Her lips.

Shame lowered her gaze to the sheen of moonlight covering the wooden floor. There was no excuse for her behavior. She knew that. She had begged God for His forgiveness. Had prayed it had all been a dream. But the tingle that still coursed through her body told her otherwise.

When William had grabbed her hand, her heart had all but stopped. She should have pulled away then. Should have resisted him. Then when he had caressed her cheek, her breath escaped. And she couldn't move.

But when his lips had met hers, Permelia's world exploded in a plethora of sensations: the scratch of his stubble on her chin, his masculine scent filling her nose, his warm breath caressing her cheek. She felt as though she were another woman in another world. A world where William loved her, not Annie.

Thank God a noise from the foyer had stopped them or who knows how far into debauchery she would have sunk.

Sliding from her bed, Permelia hugged herself and started toward the window. But why had William kissed her? She could make no sense of it. No doubt it was simply an emotional response, a need for comfort in the face of Jackson's threats and Annie's rejection.

Hinges creaked behind her. A loud crash sent her heart into her throat. She spun around to see the door bouncing off the wall and Annie charging into the room like an angry apparition. Setting her candle down, she approached Permelia, her eyes molten steel.

And Permelia knew she had seen William kiss her. She tried to back away, but Annie raised a hand and struck her across the cheek. "How dare you?"

Pain radiated across Permelia's face and down her neck. Laying a hand on her stinging skin, she lowered her gaze. "I'm sorry. I. . .he. . .I don't know how it happened." A sob caught in her throat. "Oh Annie, I'm so sorry. It was nothing." But she lied even now. William's kiss had meant everything. Even so, she was nothing but a shameless hussy—a woman who had kissed another woman's fiancé.

"You're sorry! That's all you have to say for yourself?" Annie's voice boiled. "I've been pacing my room all night trying to figure out how my loving sister could justify kissing my fiancé."

Permelia had no answer. No excuse. Gathering her resolve, she finally looked at her sister, absorbing the scorn, the hatred searing in her eyes. Permelia deserved it all. The vision of her sister blurred beneath a torrent of tears.

The fury on Annie's face faded, replaced by a haunted look. "Wasn't it enough that you stole Father's heart from me? That he always loved you more than me?"

"That isn't true." Permelia took a step toward her, her mind reeling.

Annie spun around, sending her silk night robe twirling in the moonlight. She lowered her head and sobbed. "Yes it is. And you know it. Perfect little Permelia." She waved a hand over her shoulder. "Papa's eyes always lit up when you came in the room."

Permelia's heart sank. She'd never realized. Everyone adored Annie. All the young boys at school. All her friends. Mother. "I'm so sorry, Annie, I didn't—"

Annie's eyes flashed. "William doesn't love you." Her gaze traveled over Permelia with disdain. "How could he love someone like you?" Then with a lift of her chin, she floated from the room on a puff of white silk.

The slam of the chamber door thundered through Permelia's heart. Her legs gave way. Sinking to the floor, she dropped her head into her hands and sobbed. How could she have missed Annie's pain all these years? The rejection she had felt from their father? While Permelia had relished in her father's adoration, Annie's heart had been breaking. Selfish, insensitive girl. Permelia pounded the carpet with her fists, watching her tears fall and sink into the stiff fibers. Finally, hours later, she collapsed in a fit of exhaustion.

The sweet trill of birds drifted on the first glow of dawn. Permelia woke with a start. Struggling to stand, she brushed the tear-caked hair from her face and gazed out the window. Across the fields, darkness retreated from the advancing light.

And she remembered that God's mercy was new every morning.

"Thank You, Lord. Thank You for Your mercy and forgiveness."

Now she must do her best to gain Annie's. And to be a better sister. A better follower of Christ.

But one thing was for sure. For the remainder of William's time at the plantation, Permelia must do everything in her power to avoid him.

Chapter 6

Rubbing his eyes, William entered the dining room, lured by the smell of coffee and biscuits and the hope that he'd have a chance to speak with Permelia about their kiss. A kiss that had kept him up most of the night. A kiss that still lingered like a sweet whisper on his lips. A kiss he should never have stolen. A touch of her skin he should never have enjoyed. All behaviors so unlike him. Behaviors that were no doubt caused by the weariness of war, coupled with the pain of Annie's inability to look at his face.

He sighed. Regardless of his attraction to Permelia, he had vowed to marry Annie. And a Wolfe never went back on his word.

Approaching the buffet table, William poured a cup of coffee when a sound brought his gaze to the door. Pressing down the sides of her skirt, Annie flounced into the room. Her bright eyes glanced over him but did not remain.

"William, I hoped to find you here."

He froze, stunned by her presence so early in the morning.

"Well, don't just stand there, William." She tilted her head, a coy smile on her lips. "Tell me how beautiful I look." She sashayed toward him. "Like you used to do."

William sipped his coffee, admiring the way the sunlight caressed her golden hair. "You know how beautiful you are, Annie. You need no affirmation from me." He stepped aside as she poured herself a cup of tea, a pleased look on her face. Had she always been this vain?

He cleared his throat. "What I'd like to know is the truth, Annie."

"About what?" She plucked a biscuit from a tray, grabbed her tea, and moved to the table.

"You know about what." His gaze followed her, though he found no allure in the bow-like pout on her lips or the sway of her silk bustle. "I refer to Jackson Steele. You left before answering the sergeant's question."

She waited for him to pull out her chair. "Why, William, I've already told you why I befriended the man."

After seating her, William retrieved his coffee from the buffet and sat opposite her. "Somehow he seems to have gotten the wrong impression."

"Indeed. He's become quite obstinate." She bit her biscuit.

"Perhaps because you refuse to tell him the truth. Or perhaps it's me to whom you're lying?" He raised his brows.

"How can you suggest such a thing?" Sky-blue eyes locked upon his, then shifted to the right side of his face. Gulping, Annie looked away.

Oddly, her aversion no longer pained him. He thought of the familiar way Jackson had gazed at her. The way he had called her "love" still rankled William, but not in the way it should.

"I find Sergeant Steele's intimate tone with you most inappropriate."

"What are you implying?" Her eyes misted. Four years ago, those glistening tears would have brought him to his knees before her, begging her forgiveness.

Instead they pricked his suspicion. "Nothing. I demand honesty. And that you choose one of us."

"Why, William, I have chosen." Yet the wobble in her voice did not convince him. She set down her biscuit and dabbed a napkin over her lips. "Let's go for a picnic today, shall we? Perhaps if we spent time together. . .like old times." She gave a sad smile and gazed out the window before facing him again.

William finished his coffee, setting the cup a bit too hard on the table. Perhaps she was right. Perhaps he had expected too much from someone as delicate as Annie—expected her to accept his disfigurement as if everything was still the same. He chastised himself for his impatience. Beneath all the fluff and Southern charm lurked a woman of substance, of character, and of faith—the woman he had fallen in love with through her letters. Perhaps it would just take time for that part of her to surface.

And for the first time since he arrived, Annie seemed willing to try.

Permelia entered the room. Tossing his napkin on the table, William stood, an unavoidable smile spreading across his lips.

She flinched as if shocked to find them there. A breeze toyed with the hem of her lacy petticoat. She'd arranged her hair in one long braid that hung down the front of her gown. Her eyes latched upon his, then quickly sped away as a pink hue crept up her neck onto her face.

"Oh Permi." Annie rose, pressed down her skirts, and glided to William's side. Flinging her arms about his neck, she kissed him on the cheek. His good cheek, of course. "William and I are going to take the carriage out for a picnic today. Aren't we, William?"

William blinked, confused at the sudden display of affection. "Just for a short while," he conceded. "However, Miss Permelia, I fully intend to help you and Elijah with the chores." He *wanted* to help with the chores.

Permelia gazed out the window. "Do not concern yourself, William. You and Annie need time to become reacquainted." Yet, she wouldn't look at her sister. That, coupled with the palpable tension in the room since her arrival, made William wonder if the noise he'd heard in the foyer last night had been Annie.

"Besides, Elijah and I are going into town." Permelia turned to leave.

The room threatened to grow cold in her absence. "To help at the hospital?" William asked.

She halted but did not turn around. "I teach Negro children to read and write at the church once a week." Then she disappeared, the *clip* of her boots fading down the hallway.

Annie released his arm and sighed. "Have you ever heard such a thing? A few years ago, a person could be hanged for teaching slaves. Why ever do Negros need to read and write anyway?"

◆　◆　◆

Dragging the stool to his bedside, William set the lantern atop it and sat on his straw-stuffed mattress. A night breeze wafted through his window, bringing with it a reprieve from the day's heat and the scent of wild violet and hay. Despite the pleasant evening, William had been unable to fall to sleep. He untied the bundle of letters in his hand and opened the first one. Holding it up to the light, he scanned the elegant pen and sweet words of his precious Annie:

Dearest William,

Your last letter brought me great joy as well as deep sorrow. Joy to know that you survived your last battle and sorrow to hear of the death of your friend, Major Mankins. I know how much his good company meant to you, and I grieve alongside you for the loss. May God fill you with His comfort as you continue to fight this senseless war. Know that you are not alone in your suffering. I cry along with you and long for the day when I can cry in your arms. Tears of joy instead of pain.

You asked how we fared here under the occupation. I suppose now that word has reached you of the fate of Williamsburg I can mention our predicament. I did not wish to burden you with our meager problems when you had so much responsibility weighing upon your shoulders. But let me allay your fears, dear William. The Shaw plantation stands, and we are all well. God's wings of protection cover us, and in Him we abide.

Please know you are not alone. God and my love are with you always.

Oh brave, wise William. You are ever in my heart and prayers. . . . Annie

Releasing a heavy sigh, William gently folded the letter and set it on top of the others on his bed. Confusion stormed through him, muddling his thoughts and twisting his heart. Nothing made sense anymore.

He'd spent the day with Annie. First they'd taken a carriage ride through the country, followed by a lovely picnic beside a creek, and finally ending with afternoon tea in her father's library.

And he could find no trace of the kindhearted, humble, godly woman in these letters in the primped, vainglorious Annie.

Though her attitude toward him had vastly improved.

Though she seemed more accepting of his appearance.

Had she always been this way? Or had the war changed her? Perhaps the war had changed him. He dropped his head into his hands and scrubbed his face.

Even worse, all the while Annie chittered and chattered about this and that, William's thoughts had been on Permelia. Though Elijah accompanied her into town, he wondered how she fared, what she was doing, whom she spoke to.

Whether she thought of him.

And teaching Negro children to read and write. Her kindness astounded him. In all his prior visits to the Shaw plantation, why had he not noticed her? Had he been so dazzled by Annie's beauty that he'd been blinded to the golden heart within her sister?

But he had no choice now. He was espoused to Annie. And to break off the engagement would bring irreparable shame to her, not to mention to his family. The Wolfe honor was as solid as the ships they built.

And just as unsinkable.

Picking up the letters, he pressed them against his chest. He must set aside his foolish admiration of Permelia and trust that eventually the real Annie would shine forth. Hopefully before he had to leave in two days to report to his commanding officer. He would love to have his engagement settled by then so he could enlist his mother to begin arrangements for the ceremony in New York while he served his remaining months in the army.

Mind cluttered with these thoughts, William lay back on his bed, arms beneath his head, when the faint whinny of a horse and stomp of hooves wandered over his ears. Odd. He'd helped Elijah secure the two remaining horses in the stables for the night. Unease slithered over him. Shrugging it off to exhaustion, he sat up, tied a cord around the letters, and packed them away in his knapsack. He strode to the window. Wind stirred the leaves of an elm tree, causing them to shiver in an eerie cacophony. Well past midnight, the main house loomed dark and large in the distance.

Light flickered in an upstairs room.

William scratched his chin. Who else would be up at this hour?

Shaking his head, he started back to his bed when a woman's scream pierced the night.

◆　◆　◆

An odd sensation crept through Permelia's slumberous mind, stirring her consciousness. A sensation of danger, of warning. But she didn't want to wake up. It had taken her far too long to fall asleep after her long day of trying to avoid William and Annie. A scuffing sound prickled her spine. Her stomach complained. Begging off with an excuse of a headache, she'd forsaken her supper, not able to tolerate watching Annie unleash the full flood of her charm and flirtation on William. Knowing it was merely an act to prove to Permelia where William's true affections lay.

Permelia sighed, her mind now fully awake. She opened her eyes. Movement focused her gaze to the right. The dark silhouette of a man stood by her bed. A clawlike hand reached for her throat.

Permelia screamed.

Skin, thick and scabrous and smelling of tobacco and sweat, slammed over her mouth. She tasted blood and fear. Pain throbbed in her chin, her gums. Her cries for help clumped in her throat. The glint of moonlight on steel revealed a knife in his other hand, floating over her bed like the scythe of the Grim Reaper.

"Well, if it ain't the prim and proper Miss Shaw." His voice spiked with angry sarcasm. "I'm goin' to take away my hand. If you so much as utter a peep, I'll slit your throat. Understood?"

Lifting a harried prayer to the Lord, Permelia nodded. Blood thundered in her ears. Was this to be her end? A violent death?

He removed his grip on her mouth, waving the knife before her. His face blurred in the darkness, but she felt his gaze scouring over her. "Yankee lover!" He spat to the side. "Where is that stinkin' Yankee hiding? Tell me now, or I'll finish you off in your bed."

A thud sounded on the floorboards behind the man, followed by a commanding voice. "Looking for me?"

Chapter 7

Relief flooded Permelia at the sound of William's voice. But terror quickly returned. The intruder swung about, knife clutched in his hand. Moonlight coated William in milky light. He stood by the door, arms crossed over his chest as if he were attending a country ball, not confronting an armed assailant.

Permelia struggled to sit.

The man took a step toward William, a sordid chuckle emerging from his lips.

William spread his arms out. "If it's me you're looking for, here I am. Leave the lady be."

He carried no weapons. Fear for William's safety choked Permelia's sense of self-preservation, sending her leaping from the bed in search of anything with which to strike the man.

He must have heard her, for he swerved about and grabbed her by the waist.

"Let me go!" She struggled, trying to pound him with her fists, but he tightened a meaty arm around her chest and arms, pinning her to him.

He pressed the knife to her throat. Pain pinched her skin. Something warm trickled down her neck.

William's confident stance transformed into one of fury. "What do you want?"

"We want you, Colonel."

"We?"

"Me and the soldiers of the Confederate Seventeenth Infantry Regiment." His hot breath wafted over Permelia's neck. "At least those who are left."

"And what do you want with me?"

"We was there. At the Second Manassas. We lost forty-eight men that day. Good men."

A flicker of emotion sparked in William's eyes.

"Ah yes." The soldier snickered. "We know you were there, too, commanding your Yanks to slaughter us."

William's jaw hardened. "We were all forced to do our duty that day, sir. The war is over." He gestured with his hand. "Lower the knife."

"It will never be over, Colonel." Spite dripped from the man's lips. "You will leave with me now. We have a lynching party ready for you. An' I'll bring the lady along so you'll behave."

Permelia's breath came quick and hard. The knife pierced deeper into her skin.

"No need, sir." William took a step forward. "Leave her here. I'll come with you."

"No, William!" Her words garbled beneath the press of the blade.

William swallowed. "Very well. Just don't harm her." His tone was conciliatory, but a fire ignited in his eyes. They narrowed. Stretching his jaw, he headed for the door.

The intruder followed him. "Easy now, Colonel. One false move and I'll gut her."

Permelia's legs grew numb.

Something flashed in her vision. *Slam. Thud.* The assailant groaned. Yelping, he fell away from her. Pain burned across her throat. She gasped and raised a hand to the cut. William shook his hand from the strike. Stumbling, the man attempted to regain his composure, but William was already on him. He jerked him up by the collar and slugged him across the face. The knife flew from the man's hand, clanking to the floor.

The assailant's face twisted into a maniacal mixture of fear and fury. He rose to his impressive stature, even towering over William. Terrified, Permelia dropped to the floor and groped for the knife.

Yet William's expression remained confident. "Leave now, sir, while you are still able."

The man wiped blood from his jaw. "I came for you, and I'm not leaving without you."

William released an exasperated sigh. The man charged him. Permelia gasped. She shrank into the corner. In movements quicker than her eyes could follow, William blocked three of the man's strikes, then leveled one of his own into his belly. The man bent over clutching his middle. He barreled toward William again. William grabbed his head and slammed him into the far wall. The *snap* of wood cracked the air. The assailant toppled to the ground. William seized him by the shirt and jerked him to his feet. The man held up his arms to block the next strike.

Clutching him with one hand, William dragged him out the door. Permelia found the knife and followed him. She halted at the top of the stairs, her legs nearly folding beneath her. She heard the man's boots thumping down each tread, saw the front door open in a flood of moonlight, and watched as William tossed him onto the porch.

Elijah appeared beside her, lantern in hand. "What's happening, miss?"

"An intruder. Go help William." She pointed below, sending Elijah racing down the stairs. Not that William needed any help, however. Clutching the banister, she followed him.

"Who put you up to this?" William demanded, gripping the man by the collar. "Who told you I was here?"

The man cowered. His chest heaved. Blood spilled from his swollen lip.

Elijah set the lantern on the railing and stepped beside William.

"Who sent you?" William asked again. Permelia had never heard his voice so full of rage.

"Steele." The man seethed.

Permelia's breath escaped her. She leaned on the door frame.

"Jackson Steele?" William asked. "Isn't he also a Yank?"

"Not one who slaughtered my friends."

Yanking him down the porch stairs, William shoved him to the ground. "You tell Sergeant Steele that if he has an argument with me, he's welcome to come and issue a proper challenge. Soldier to soldier."

The man struggled to his feet and wiped a hand over his mouth.

William's face became flint. "If I ever see you here again, you'll be the one hanging from a tree."

Turning, the man slinked away, muttering "Yankee lover" under his breath.

Elijah rubbed the back of his neck. "Sorry I didn't hear nothin' till a few minutes ago. I was dead asleep."

"It's quite all right, Elijah." William's gaze followed the intruder. "No harm done."

Elijah started down the stairs. "I'll make sure he leaves."

Permelia stepped onto the porch. Her knuckles hurt, and she released her tight grip on the knife.

William's shoulders lowered as he shook off the stiff cloak of a warrior.

A breeze fluttered his hair, his shirt, and toyed with the hem of her nightdress. She hugged herself, gazing at him. She'd never seen anything like it before. The way he had dispatched the man with such skill and confidence. He'd protected her. Saved her life. Her heart didn't know whether to embrace the thrill of his chivalry or shrink from the terror of her ordeal. She chose the former. Especially when he turned around and rushed to take her in his arms.

Halting, he grabbed the handle of the knife. "I'll take that." The kindness reappeared in his voice.

Happily relinquishing it, Permelia's legs wobbled, and William took her waist and drew her near. She collapsed in his arms. Muscles, strong and hard, surrounded her, encasing her in a safe fortress.

"You are safe now, sweet Permelia. Sweet, sweet Permelia."

She drew in a deep breath of his scent and leaned her cheek on his chest. "You saved me. I thought. . .I thought I was. . .I thought that man. . ."

"Shh, dearest. All is well."

And surrounded by William's arms, feeling the rapid beat of his heart against her cheek, she believed all was well indeed.

Until a startled cry jerked her away from him, and she turned to see Annie, lantern in hand, crystalline hair tumbling like a silken waterfall over her robe, standing in the foyer.

Her jealous glare bore into Permelia.

Throwing a hand to her forehead, she closed her eyes and started to swoon.

Abandoning Permelia, William dashed toward Annie just in time to grab the lantern and capture her in his arms before she toppled to the marble floor.

◆　◆　◆

William settled a sniffling Annie onto the sofa in the parlor, then struck a match and lit the oil lamp sitting on the table. A golden glow flickered over the room, sparkling the tears sliding down her cheeks. Holding a hand out to him, she beckoned him to sit beside her. "It is all so horrible, William. An intruder in our house? Utterly terrifying. Do tell me what happened."

With her pink nose, golden hair cascading over her silk robe, her full lips, she truly was a beauty. He remembered how she could captivate him with one glance of those blue eyes, one lift of those moist lips.

But he felt nothing as she gazed at him now, her eyes settling on the left side of his face. Instead he glanced toward the door where Permelia had announced she'd go make some tea. He longed for her return, longed to know how she fared after her harrowing ordeal.

"Oh William, I need you." Annie's sob drew his attention. Taking her trembling hand in his, he sat beside her.

"Just an angry, bitter soldier returning from the battlefield, I'm afraid." He wouldn't tell her about Jackson. It would only upset her further and serve no purpose. William would have to deal with the man on his own.

Footsteps sounded, and he knew Permelia had entered. He knew because the innocent sheen hardened over Annie's eyes as they shot toward the door.

"Here we are. Perhaps this will settle our nerves." Permelia set down the tray and began pouring tea into a trio of china cups. Her hand quivered, spilling some of the hot liquid, and

William longed to grab it, caress it. Kiss it. She raised her gaze to his. Pain and confusion stretched a cord between them, locking their eyes in place.

Annie cleared her throat, snapping William from his trance. She accepted the cup from Permelia. "Thank you, Permi. No need to stay up. I'm sure you're exhausted."

Permelia touched the thin red line etched across her throat. She'd tossed a gown over her nightdress, but the lace peeked out from her neckline and hem. William remembered the way she'd clutched the knife and followed him downstairs. So brave.

"Yes, I am rather tired." She smiled.

Concern punched William's heart, and he leaned forward on his knees. "Would you like me to attend to that?" He gestured toward her wound. "I acquired some medical experience during the war."

"No." Permelia looked down. "I can take care of it, thank you."

Annie moaned. "Are we safe here, William?" She clutched his arm and drew him back toward her. "Will the intruder return?"

He patted her hand. "Never fear, I will guard the house while you and Permelia sleep."

"Sleep! I could never after such a horrifying event. Oh, do stay with me, William." She puckered her lips as a child would when begging a father for a treat.

William turned to face Permelia. To tell her she must stay with them, as well.

But she was gone.

◆　　◆　　◆

Hiking her skirts into her belt, Permelia knelt beside the row of cabbage and began pulling weeds from around the tender plants. Why did weeds always grow among the good sprouts, sucking the life from them? Her precious cabbage wouldn't stand a chance at surviving if she didn't come out here daily to pluck the offenders. She was reminded of the parable Jesus told of the wheat and the tares. The wheat represented God's beloved children, and the tares were those who didn't know Him—those destined to be pulled and tossed into the fire. As she was doing now. Yanking one particularly thorny interloper, she threw it atop a growing pile in her bucket then wiped her sleeve across her forehead. The afternoon sun lashed her with hot rays as the air weighed upon her, heavy with moisture.

But the work had to be done or they would not have enough food come winter. That was, unless William and Annie married. Another reason why Permelia should stay away from him. Then why did the prospect make her so sad? She inched down the row of plants and plucked another weed. Better to keep busy. Better to keep her mind off of William. Off of Annie. And off of the threats made against him last night. Perhaps it was for the best that he was leaving soon. She'd never survive if any harm came to him.

Her thoughts sped to his chivalrous rescue last night. And the way she'd felt so safe and loved in his arms. Her heart swelled. But she quickly squelched it. She must not think of such things.

She hadn't seen William or Annie all day. They were no doubt entertaining themselves in the parlor or strolling about the grounds. Reigniting their love. Planning their wedding.

Yanking another weed, Permelia tossed it in her pail and stood, pressing a hand on her back. A man emerged from the tree line at the edge of the plantation. A light-skinned man. Her heart jolted. She grabbed the rifle lying atop the dirt, cocked it, and leveled it at the intruder. Fear set every nerve on edge as the seconds brought him more clearly into view. His confident gait. The wide spread of his shoulders. Dark hair spilling from beneath his hat.

William.

She lowered the rifle.

He hefted his gun onto his shoulder. Two rabbits swung from the barrel. With a wide grin, he halted before her. "Permelia." Her name emerged from his lips as if it were precious to him.

She brushed dirt from her skirts. "I thought you were with Annie."

His eyes wouldn't leave her. "I left before dawn to hunt."

"So I see. How kind of you."

He stepped toward her. His fingers brushed the bandage at her throat. "How are you?"

Shaking off the daze caused by his touch, she retreated. "It is nothing. Thanks to you."

"When I saw that knife at your throat"—he gulped and drew a breath—"I was so frightened."

She looked away.

He leaned toward her. "I couldn't bear the thought of losing you." His breath caressed her cheek. He smelled like cedar and hay.

Permelia's heart sped. Was it possible this man returned her affection? She searched his face: his dark, imposing eyes; strong jaw; straight nose; and the rippled flesh on his right cheek. She longed to kiss away the scars. "You shouldn't say such things." Confusion tumbled her thoughts until she couldn't separate reason from desire. And that's what frightened her the most.

"I know. Forgive me." Resignation weighted his voice as he squinted toward the house. "I'm leaving tomorrow."

Permelia's heart sank.

"Before I leave, I will insist Annie tell me whether she still wishes to marry me."

"She'd be a fool not to." The words had escaped her lips before Permelia could stop them.

"No, I'm afraid I've been the fool." He cupped her cheek, and she leaned into his rough hand.

If only for a moment. Just one moment. So, he did feel something for her. Her heart took up a rapid pace again. But no. She stepped back. Whatever was between them, they must end it now. She was about to tell him just that when the *thuump, thu-ump* of a galloping horse drew their gazes to the front of the main house. A rider dressed in Union blues hastened down the tree-lined path and jerked his horse to a halt before the front porch. Sliding from the saddle, Jackson Steele grabbed his sword from his pouch, spotted them in the field, and shouted.

"I've answered your call, Wolfe! A duel to the death!"

Chapter 8

Permelia gaped at Jackson, not trusting her ears with the words she'd just heard. *A duel?* William's jaw knotted. He faced her with determination. "Where is Elijah?"

Permelia swallowed. "In town."

"Gather Martha and Ruth and get inside the house."

"But what are you going to do?"

Gripping his rifle, he marched toward the slave quarters, the rabbits swaying from the gun's barrel with each step. "Ensure Annie is still inside and then bolt the doors and windows."

"Surely you aren't thinking of—"

He swung about. The stern look on his face clipped the words from her lips. "Take your gun, and do not leave the house. No matter what." His brows drew into a stern line. "That's an order."

For the first time Permelia imagined what the men under William's command must have felt when they stared into those commanding eyes, ignited with intent and purpose.

But she wasn't under his command.

She spun around and stormed toward Jackson, leveling her gun upon the knave. "Leave my property at once, sir, or I will fire upon you."

Jackson planted his sword in the dirt and leaned on the hilt. "Hiding behind a woman, eh, Wolfe?"

The heavy gun shook in her grip. Her hands grew moist. Perspiration slid down her back. But she wouldn't relent. She couldn't let this man hurt William. Or ruin their lives as he seemed intent on doing.

She heard the crunch of gravel behind her. William appeared at her side. Placing a hand on the barrel of her gun, he gently lowered it, admiration in his gaze. "I must settle this once and for all, don't you see, Permelia?" His voice, gentle at first, hardened with conviction. "The man will simply come back at another time. Most likely after I've left and you're here all alone." He brushed a thumb over her jaw.

"And I couldn't stand for that." He flattened his lips. "Now do as I say." Then turning, he stomped away.

Permelia gave Jackson a venomous look. He chuckled. Clutching her rifle, she headed toward the kitchen house. Fear curdled in her belly. She could barely gather her thoughts. *Oh, Lord, please protect William. Please let no one die today.*

Within minutes, Permelia hurried a wide-eyed Martha and jittery Ruth in through the back entrance of the main house. After checking on Annie, who was sulking in the library, Permelia bolted all the doors then dashed to the front window of the parlor. She leaned the rifle against the wall and rubbed her aching hand.

Sunlight glared off Jackson's saber as he swung it before him with ease. Attired in his dress uniform, complete with blue-striped coat lined with brass buttons, it was obvious he had complete confidence in his skills and intended to use the entire heinous performance as a means to impress Annie.

"I wish Elijah were here," Martha said as she took her daughter's hand and stood to the left of the window.

Annie swept into the room. "What is all the fuss about?" She pushed back the curtains and cocked her head.

"Jackson has called William out to a duel." Permelia bit her lip as an idea sprang into her mind. "Perhaps you could stop them, Annie?"

"Why would I do that?" Annie peered out the window. Her eyes lit up. "They are dueling over me." She released a satisfied sigh. "How romantic, don't you think?"

Martha clucked her tongue but gave no other indication of the disgust written on her face.

Permelia cringed. "How can you say such a thing? One of them could get hurt, possibly killed."

"Oh, fiddle. Boys will be boys." Annie plucked out her fan and fluttered it around her face. "It's hot in here. Open the window. I want to hear what's going on."

"William said not to." Permelia gripped her sister's arm. "Please, Annie. You must stop this."

Annie looked at her as if she'd lost her mind before tugging from her grasp.

The sight of William drew Permelia's gaze back out the window. He stormed into view, his service sword in hand. He stopped to speak to Jackson, hopefully to try to talk some sense into him. *Please, Lord, let him succeed.*

"I'm going onto the porch. I can't see anything from here," Annie announced, exiting the room before Permelia could protest.

The front door opened and angry voices rode upon a burst of heated wind. Grabbing the rifle, Permelia instructed Martha to stay put, then followed Annie.

"Next time, don't send one of your lackeys to do your dirty work for you." William tossed his hat onto the dirt and flung his sword out before him.

Jackson smiled and opened his arms wide. "Your wish is my command, Colonel."

"You could have injured one of the ladies," William added.

"A Confederate would not injure his own."

"Tell that to Permelia. Your man held a knife to her throat."

Jackson's gaze shot to Permelia and then over to Annie, still batting her fan about her face.

"Jackson, whatever are you doing?" Annie feigned disapproval. "You stop misbehaving at once." Her flippant tone brought a smile to Jackson's lips.

Bile lurched into Permelia's throat.

"You look stunning, love." Jackson dipped a bow. "I fear I must inform this man of our engagement in the only language he understands."

William faced Annie, anger rumbling across his features. "If the lady would break off our engagement and tell me to leave, we could avoid this foolishness."

Annie seemed to falter beneath both men's gazes. She leaned against the post.

Permelia whispered prayers that her sister would finally speak the truth. "Tell them, Annie, for goodness' sake, before someone gets hurt."

Annie slapped her fan shut and flattened her lips, glancing up at the sky as if it contained the answer. "I don't rightly know what to say."

Permelia closed her eyes, trying to corral her anger. This was all just a game to her sister. "Choose one of them, dear sister, or your choice will be made for you," she seethed.

Annie tilted her head. "Then let it be made. And may the best man win."

William ran a hand through his hair and snorted his disgust. He turned to Jackson. "Regardless, you attempted to have me murdered in my bed. And now you dare challenge me. I cannot allow such an affront to pass."

Jackson leaned on his sword. "To the death then? Or until one of us forfeits." He snickered.

Annie gasped. Her wide eyes shot to Permelia as if she only now understood the deadly implications.

But it was too late. With a *swoosh* of his blade, Jackson sauntered to William, leveling it at his chest.

William slapped the offending sword away with an ominous *ching* and eyed his opponent. Jackson circled him then swept down on William's right. Blade met blade with a resounding *clang* that filled the air and sent a shiver through Permelia.

William flung his sword back and forth with speed and agility, countering each of Jackson's blows. Jackson halted. Sweat shone on his handsome brow. William charged forward. Their blades rang together as he forced Jackson back over the dirt.

Permelia pressed a hand over her rattling chest.

Jackson's face reddened. "You're more skilled than I thought, Colonel."

"And you're not nearly as skilled as I thought."

Hatred fumed from Jackson's eyes. "We shall see." He spun about and dipped to William's left, striking him on the leg. A red stripe appeared across his trousers.

Both Permelia and Annie gasped at the same time. Permelia glanced at her sister, wondering if she truly cared for William, but Annie's eyes were riveted on Jackson.

"Ahha!" Jackson boasted, strolling in a circle of victory as he caught his breath.

William, however, seemed barely out of breath. Neither did he seem concerned. Instead he lunged toward Jackson, this time lifting his blade high. Caught off guard, Jackson turned and met the attack with equal force, their blades locking. William grunted as he forced the man backward, then shoved him against the bark of a tree.

The arrogant grin slipped from Jackson's face, replaced by fear.

"Don't hurt him, William," Annie whined.

William shoved his blade toward Jackson's shoulder. The man slipped away. The point stuck in the tree.

William tried to pull it free.

Jackson grinned, slowly approaching him like a cougar on wounded prey.

Abandoning the blade, William plucked a knife from his boot and faced Jackson.

"Perhaps you'll forfeit the fight, Colonel, and leave Virginia immediately?" Jackson sneered. "Rather that than suffer a humiliating death in front of the ladies."

William wiped the sweat from his brow. "Not until you promise the same."

Jackson slashed toward William.

William leaped out the way. No fear, no emotion at all, registered on his face. Just the confident expression of a warrior.

"I grow tired of this dance, Colonel." Jackson's face hardened and he stormed toward

William in a vicious onslaught. He thrust the tip of his blade toward William's chest.

Permelia screamed.

◆　◆　◆

Tucking in his arm, William dipped and rolled across the dirt, landing on his feet. He thrust his boot in the air, knocking Jackson's blade from his hand and sending him sprawling to the ground. Before the man could recover, William picked up the sword and leveled the tip against Jackson's pristine blue coat. The man's eyes erupted into volcanoes of hatred. "Go ahead, Colonel. Kill me." He gulped for air, thrusting out a defiant chin.

"No!" A woman's scream filled the air as Annie dashed down the stairs and knelt before Jackson, shielding him with her billowing skirts.

Stunned, William backed up and lowered his sword. So Annie did love Jackson, after all. Sudden pain throbbed in William's thigh. His legs gave out and he sank to the ground. In an instant, an angel appeared beside him, embracing him, her tears dampening his cheeks. Like an elixir they stirred his soul back to life. Permelia. Plucking her handkerchief from within her pocket she pressed it on his wound. Terror, relief, and something else he couldn't place burned in her gaze. "I was so worried, William."

He reached up and wiped the tears from her cheeks. Over her shoulder, Jackson rose to his full height. Annie clutched his arm. Jealous fury faded from his features, replaced by a conciliatory respect. He dipped his head slightly. "You have won fairly, Colonel. And because I still have my life, I will honor my vow to never call on Annie again." He kissed her cheek, his face somber and determined. Then, nudging her aside, he mounted his horse and rode away.

Lifting a hand to her mouth, Annie fled into the house, hysterical sobs trailing in her wake.

Permelia helped William to his feet. Grabbing his sword, he sheathed it and drew her close, kissing her forehead.

"I've never seen such bravery, William." Permelia leaned against his shirt. "Forgive Annie. When she calms down, she'll see things differently, I'm sure."

"I'm not of the same mind." William huffed. Why did this sweet woman always try to spare his feelings and defend her sister? Releasing Permelia, he wiped the hair from her face. He should tell her what his heart was bursting to say. That he loved her. That he wanted to marry her, not Annie. He opened his mouth to do so when a glare blinded his eyes, drawing his gaze to something on the ground. Leaning over, he picked up a coin. His coin. Shock sped through him.

He flipped it over. The coin he'd given Annie as a pledge of their love and marriage. He gazed at Permelia, confused.

Her eyes shifted from the coin to him. Her face paled.

"Where did this come from?" he asked.

She glanced down.

Placing a finger under her chin, he lifted her gaze to his. "I know you won't lie to me."

"It must have fallen from my pocket."

He stepped back, more shocked than angry. Annie had already made her sentiments quite clear. But what of Permelia? Yes, she had kissed him, and he thought he'd seen affection in her eyes more than once. But perhaps that was simply his desperate yearning for it to be true. Now he longed to hear the words from her mouth. "Why was it in your pocket?"

But instead of answering him, her lip quivered and her eyes filled with tears. Then clutching her skirts, she dashed into the house.

◆　◆　◆

Permelia slammed the door of her chamber and fell into a heap on the floor. Dropping her head into her hands, she sobbed. Sobbed to release the terror that had gripped her as she'd watched Jackson and William duel. Sobbed to release the shame of her feelings for him. Sobbed because she couldn't tell him the real reason she kept the coin in her pocket. If he discovered that Annie had tossed it from the window, that she thought so little of it, William would be wounded far deeper than the cut on his thigh. Oh, why hadn't she given the coin back to Annie? Why had she been so selfish? *Thank You, Lord, for protecting him. But please send him and Annie to New York to marry. I do not think I can stand this torture anymore.*

Opening her trunk, she pulled out the letters and held them to her nose. They smelled of gunpowder and William. Wailing filtered down the hall from Annie's chamber, pricking Permelia's guilt. She should go to her. Comfort her. But she knew her sister's tears were for Jackson. Confusion tore through Permelia as desire and duty fought their own duel within her. She covered her ears but could not muffle her sister's sobs. Finally Permelia left the room, went downstairs and out the back door. A walk about the grounds would do her good, clear her mind, give her a chance to hear from God.

◆　◆　◆

William approached Permelia's chamber door. It stood slightly ajar, yet no sounds came from within. He knew he shouldn't be sneaking about a lady's bedchambers, but his tormented thoughts would allow him no peace until he found out the truth of where Permelia's sentiments lay. More importantly, why had she run away when he found the coin? He must know, and he must know tonight. For tomorrow he had to leave, report back to his commanding officer, serve out his remaining months in the army.

He eased the door aside. "Permelia." No answer. He inched inside, gave a quick scan of the room, and upon finding it empty, moved to the foot of a four-poster bed, decorated with a simple quilt. A dressing table and mirror stood against the far wall beside an armoire. On the other side of the room, a writing desk, littered with pens, paper, and a Bible sat beneath the window.

Pain lanced through his thigh, and he pressed a hand over the wound. At least the bleeding had stopped. A burst of wind blew through the window, stirring something on the floor. Paper crinkled, and William knelt to find a bundle of letters tied with a thread beside an open trunk. Gathering them, he started to place them back in the chest when their familiarity struck him.

His heart stopped. Sliding the first one out from the cord, he unfolded it and scanned the words.

His letters. His letters to Annie.

The *tap tap* of steps and a tiny gasp drew William's gaze to the door, where Permelia stood, her hair tousled by the wind and smelling of wildflowers and horses. He held the letters up to her, unable to speak, unable to find the words. Unsure if he found them, that they'd be very kind. He could think of only one reason she would have them. Anger replaced confusion in his gut. Anger that this woman, this precious woman he thought he loved, had betrayed him!

Chapter 9

Permelia entered her chamber. A tremble threatened to buckle her legs. "I can explain." William held up the bundle of letters, one of them open in his hand. "Why do you have the letters I wrote to Annie?"

Permelia tried to speak, but the words knotted in her throat. He would hate her if he knew. And she couldn't bear that.

He glanced at the letters then back at her, shock and pain drawing lines on his forehead. "You."

Making her way to the bedpost, Permelia clung to it, afraid her legs would crumple beneath her.

"You wrote the letters I received," he repeated.

She couldn't meet his gaze. Couldn't bear the agony in his voice, let alone the pain she would see in his eyes. "Not all."

"How many?" The agony turned to anger. He marched toward her and thrust the letters in her face. "How many?"

She flinched. "I started writing you after the occupation." She finally raised her gaze to his. "I didn't mean to deceive you, William. You mistook my P. A. Shaw for Annie."

Fire burned in his eyes. "So my mistake gave you license to pretend to be your sister?"

A tear slid down her cheek. She batted it away. "I hoped only to spare your feelings."

"Spared from wha—" William jerked as if someone struck him. "Of course. Annie stopped writing to me." He took up a pace, his boots thundering over the wooden floor. "When Jackson Steele came into town, no doubt."

Though longing to ease his pain, Permelia clung to the bedpost and said nothing. All her attempts to spare him, to comfort him, had only caused him more grief in the end.

"You lied to me." He halted. The rage on his face stabbed her heart. "You should have told me the truth."

"I couldn't." She managed past the sorrow bunching in her throat. "You were out on the battlefield, enduring horrors beyond imagination. How could I tell you that your fiancée fell in love with another man?"

He snorted and ran a hand through his hair. "Sweet, sweet Permelia." He spat the words as if they were a curse. His eyes latched upon the letters. His face reddened. "I shared such intimacies with you."

"And I, you." Things she had never shared with anyone.

He shook his head. "And the coin?" He plucked it from his waistcoat pocket and held it up. Sunlight angled through the window and sought it out, setting it aglow. "Did Annie toss this aside as easily as she did our love?"

Permelia wiped another tear with the back of her hand and sank onto the bed.

"Why did you have it?" he demanded.

What did it matter now if she told him the truth? He was lost to her anyway. "I carried

144

it because it made me feel close to you."

He flinched, his eyes narrowing.

"Because I love you." She looked up at him, his visage blurred through her tears.

Her words seemed to loosen the tightness in his face. But then his eyes narrowed again. "Love doesn't deceive." Tossing the letters into the trunk, he stormed from her chamber.

◆　◆　◆

William pulled his stool to the rickety dresser and sat, releasing a heavy sigh. Light from a single candle flickered over the blank sheet of paper, daring him to write. But words escaped him. At least the right words. He propped his elbows on the dresser and dropped his head into his hands. A breeze from the slave quarters' window wafted around him, bringing the scent of primrose as katydids chirped a nighttime chorus.

He must leave first thing in the morning. And he had no idea what to do about Annie. Or Permelia. Or if he should do anything at all. Even if he resigned his commission, it would be months before he could return to Virginia. He raked both hands through his hair. Why didn't Annie simply break off their engagement? She'd made her feelings quite clear. And though he'd attempted to speak with her all day, she'd refused to see him.

His thoughts drifted to Permelia. She said she loved him. At the time he was too angry to let the words sink into his heart. But now, a thrill sped through him at the knowledge. Pushing back the stool, he made his way to his knapsack and took out the letters. He gently thumbed through them, remembering all the sweet words, the comforts, the fears, the laughs they contained. He had fallen in love with the woman in these letters. At least now he could make sense of the disparity between that woman and Annie. Permelia, sweet Permelia. Even the reason for her deception had been selfless and loving. It had taken him most of the day to break through his pride and fully understand that. He drew the letters to his chest.

He did love her. More than anything. He longed to go to her, tell her he understood her reasons for deceiving him. But it wouldn't be right to declare his love while he was still engaged to Annie. And now he had no time left to sort out the mess between them all.

Oh, God, what am I to do? He uttered his first prayer in years, spurred on by Permelia's unyielding faith—the way she spoke so lovingly, so reverently of her Father in heaven despite the tragedies that had struck her.

A breeze from the window stirred the dust at his feet. A cloud moved. Moonlight flooded him. He fell to his knees. "Forgive me, God, for abandoning You when I needed You the most. For being angry at You."

"I have always been with you, son."

William scanned the room for the source of the words. But no one was there. No one but him and God. "I've been such a fool." But he wouldn't be a fool anymore. From now on, he would talk to God often, praise Him daily. "I need Your help, God. Please tell me what to do."

"Love never fails."

The words swirled around him, stirring his faith and guiding his thoughts.

Finally he stood, straightening his shoulders. He knew exactly what to do. "Thank You, God." Then setting the letters down, he slipped onto the stool once again.

And began to write.

◆ ◆ ◆

A glow shifted over Permelia's eyelids, growing brighter and brighter. A chorus of birds filled her ears. She popped her eyes open. Jerking upright, she glanced toward the window. The early blush of dawn had long since passed, giving rise to a bright midmorning sun. Rubbing her eyes, she leaped from the bed, slid into her slippers, tossed her robe about her, and dashed out the door. She'd stayed up far too late last night, pacing her chamber, crying and praying, until she'd finally given everything over to God and accepted His will—whatever that turned out to be. Even if it meant life without William. Afterward, a peace had settled on her, and she had fallen fast asleep.

But she had wanted to at least say good-bye to William. To tell him how sorry she was one last time. Hurrying down the stairs, she flung open the front door and made her way to the slave quarters. Darting inside the open door, she scanned the room. It was empty. All William's things were gone. Her heart as heavy as a brick, she dashed to the stables where she discovered what she had already guessed. His horse was nowhere to be seen.

William was gone.

Tears spilled down her cheeks as she dragged herself back into the main house and sat upon the sofa in the parlor. Numb. Dazed. Her mind reeled with sorrow. He hadn't even said good-bye. But after what she'd done, what did she expect?

Something winked at her from the table, drawing her gaze. The coin, sitting atop a folded piece of paper. She grabbed it, fingering the gold as a smile played on her lips. At least she still had the coin. Laying it aside, she picked up the letter. The words *Annie and Permelia* were written on the outside. Her chest tightened.

Shuffling noises brought her gaze to the door. Annie entered, her eyes puffy and red and her hair askew. She gave Permelia a seething look then dropped into a chair. "I suppose you're happy now."

Permelia gripped the letter, longing to open it, desperate to know what it said. "Why would I be happy?"

"Now that Jackson is gone forever."

"I'm not happy, Annie. I didn't want them to fight at all." She touched Annie's arm. "I'm truly sorry you are so upset."

Annie sighed and played with a ring on her finger.

"You should know that William left," Permelia said.

Annie's brow wrinkled. "Without saying good-bye?"

"You wouldn't even see him yesterday."

"I was upset." She pouted. "Now what am I to do? You've gone and chased off both my good prospects!"

Permelia would be angry if the accusation weren't so absurd.

"What is that?" Annie pointed at the letter.

"It's from William, addressed to both of us."

Scooting to the edge of her seat, Annie snatched it from Permelia, scanned it for a moment, then began to read out loud:

Dearest Annie and Permelia,
  Forgive me for not saying good-bye, but under the circumstances, I thought it best to leave without causing further heartache. I plan to serve the remainder of my time in

the army and then resign my commission at the end of the year. I have but one final request of you both. Search your hearts and decide what each of you truly wants. Honor forbids me to choose between you, so I have left the outcome in the hands of God. Should one of you decide you love this disfigured warrior enough to marry me, then meet me on Bow Bridge in Central Park on January 1st of next year at noon. I will be waiting.

William

Permelia's hands trembled. She clasped them together in her lap as Annie gaped at her. "Do you think he is serious?"

"It would seem so." Permelia couldn't help but cling to the hope that, should Annie decide not to meet him, William would be hers. Surely this proved that he loved her. Otherwise, why would he have included her in the ultimatum? He loved her! Her breath caught in her throat.

"So, he would accept you as his wife?" Annie's face scrunched.

"Is it so hard to believe?"

Standing, Annie sauntered about the room, her silk night rail streaming behind her.

Permelia stood. "If you break the engagement, Annie, I'm sure William will not hold Jackson to his vow."

"Of course I know that." Annie waved a hand in the air.

"Why can't you simply choose? Don't you see the mess you've created?"

Annie spun to face her. "How can I choose between great wealth and great attraction?"

"You mean beauty. If William wasn't scarred, you'd have no trouble deciding."

"Oh, fiddle. You just want William's money for yourself."

Permelia shook her head, her heart plummeting at her sister's accusation. How could she tell Annie that she loved William? How could her sister understand something so deep and abiding? Yet why, oh why, was Permelia's future, her very life, in the hands of her selfish sister?

Love never fails.

The words settled on her heart, chasing away her fears. God's love for Permelia never failed. And no matter what He had planned for her, it would be for her good and His glory. Even if it meant that Annie married William. No, Permelia's future was not in her sister's hands, but safely tucked within God's.

She faced her sister. "What are you going to do, Annie?"

◆　◆　◆

Flipping up the collar of his wool cloak, William blew into his hands as he ascended the bridge, retracing the footprints he'd left in the snow only moments ago. His nervous breath puffed around his face. He'd been waiting for this day for seven months. Could hardly believe it had arrived. And now that it had, he wondered at the sanity of the ultimatum he'd left Permelia and Annie. He crested the bridge, swiped off the snow on the railing, and watched it tumble into the icy river below.

Tumble down like his dreams would if this day did not turn out as he hoped. He pulled his pocket watch from his waistcoat and glanced at the time. Nearly noon. Soon the months of waiting would end, and he would know who would become his wife. Or if he would have a wife at all. He glanced in both directions. A group of children built a snowman in the field beyond the river, their playful laughter bubbling through the crisp air. Sunlight glinted off freshly fallen snow and sparkled off icicles hanging from bare tree limbs. A lady and gentleman approached from the left. William tipped his hat. At the sight of his face, the woman's smile fell from her lips. She turned away.

He turned toward the river again. Would the pain of people's revulsion ever fade?

The sound of bells, clack of carriages, and stomp of horses' hooves drifted on muted conversations coming from New York City. A distant clock chimed the time. Each resounding clang tightened William's nerves. Finally the twelfth one sounded. He shoved off from the railing and began his trek down the other side of the bridge.

Then he saw her.

A woman coming toward him on the shaded path. Billowing lavender skirts peeked out from her long wool mantle. Her hands disappeared inside a furry muff while a wide-brimmed bonnet hid the color of her hair.

Oh, Lord, let it be brown.

Let it be Permelia, sweet Permelia. Though he had resigned himself to God's will, it had been Permelia who had filled his thoughts, his dreams, these long months. It had been Permelia he longed for. Loved with all his heart.

A heart that now thrashed in his chest with each step she took.

He tried to go to her, but his feet were frozen in place. His heavy breath puffed about his face, clouding his vision.

She moved into the sunlight. And stopped. Straining, William made out the details of her face.

◆　◆　◆

Permelia stepped into the sunshine. The trembling that had begun when she'd first spotted William increased in fervor. Accompanied by a racing heart. She could hardly believe her eyes. There he was! On the bridge just like he'd said he would be. And as handsome as ever in his black velvet-trimmed cape and high silk hat. But why wasn't he moving? Why wasn't he coming to her?

She stopped, her heart constricting. Perhaps he had hoped to see Annie instead. Perhaps he was overcome with disappointment. She glanced over her shoulder, wondering if she should leave, but when she faced him again, recognition flashed across his eyes and a wide smile spread upon his lips. He hastened forward, arms wide.

Grabbing her skirts, Permelia darted toward him and fell into his embrace. Thick arms circled her in a cocoon of strength and warmth. She drew a deep breath of his scent. William. At last. She could hardly believe it. Easing her away, he cupped her face in his hands and swept his gaze over her as if memorizing every detail. "I'm so happy it's you, Permelia." He wiped her tears with his thumb. "I hoped, I prayed it would be you."

Permelia's laughter broke in between sobs. "You did?"

"Of course. I love you, Permelia. I love you." Leaning over, he pressed his lips to hers. At first gentle and soft, like the flutter of a butterfly, his warm breath caressed her cheek. Heat sped through her, swirling in her belly. Her legs quivered. Then he deepened the kiss. Like a man desperate for more of her. Permelia's world spun. He tasted of spice and William, and she wished the moment would never end.

He withdrew.

"I love you, too, William," she said. "I always have."

He tenderly brushed a curl from her cheek. "But tell me, what of Annie?"

Permelia bit her lip. How would he take the news? Did he still care for her?

His brows drew together. "She is ill?"

"Not as far as we know. You see, my brother arrived home and—"

"That is wonderful news." He lifted one of her hands and kissed it.

"Not for Annie, I'm afraid," Permelia said. "He forbade her to marry Jackson. Said the man was a hooligan."

William snorted. "A good judge of character, this brother of yours."

"Indeed." Permelia smiled.

"What of Elijah, Martha, and Ruth?"

"Samuel hired them, along with many other workers. Thanks be to God, the plantation is doing quite well." Permelia couldn't keep her eyes off William, afraid he would vanish like the mist rising off the frozen river. Her thoughts shifted to Annie, and she frowned. "However, I'm afraid Annie ran away with Jackson anyway."

William flinched. "Eloped?"

Permelia nodded, happy when she saw no pain, no sorrow, in his eyes.

"She always was a bit pernicious." He chuckled.

Permelia looked down. "I fear for her well-being. In truth, I miss her."

He brushed a thumb over her cheek. "Then we shall pray for their happiness."

Reaching inside her muff, Permelia pulled out the coin and held it out to him. "I believe this is yours, sir?"

He smiled then closed her hand over it. "I know it was intended for Annie, but it would honor me if you would keep it. As my pledge to love you forever."

Emotion burned in her throat. But before she could find her voice to respond, he lowered himself on one knee. Brown eyes, brimming with joy and expectation, stared up at her. "Will you marry me, Permelia?"

She caressed his scarred cheek, hardly daring to believe his words. "Yes. Oh yes, indeed."

Mist covered his eyes as he rose and lifted her in his arms, spinning her around and around. Their laughter mingled in the air above them as Permelia gazed into the sky and thanked God for William, for his love, and for proving to her that, indeed. . .

Love never fails.

MARYLU TYNDALL, a Christy Award finalist and bestselling author of the Legacy of the King's Pirates series, is known for her adventurous historical romances filled with deep spiritual themes. She holds a degree in math and worked as a software engineer for fifteen years before testing the waters as a writer. MaryLu currently writes full-time and makes her home on the California coast with her husband, six kids, and four cats. Her passion is to write page-turning, romantic adventures that not only entertain but open people's eyes to their God-given potential. MaryLu is a member of American Christian Fiction Writers and Romance Writers of America.

Buttons for Birdie

by Darlene Franklin

If any man be in Christ, he is a new creature:
old things are passed away;
behold, all things are become new.
2 Corinthians 5:17

Chapter 1

Birdie Landry smoothed her gloved hand over the sign one of her sewing circle friends had made for her: FRESH EGGS CHEAPER BY THE DOZEN. She could picture it now, sitting inside the window of Finnegan's Mercantile, drawing customers in to buy her eggs from Ned.

I'm doing Ned Finnegan a favor. Gerard's, the other general store in town, didn't offer eggs. Birdie could have danced for joy when Miss Kate agreed that she could raise chickens on the property. She figured she would have enough eggs to pay for her room at the boardinghouse Miss Kate ran in addition to the diner, and then sell the extras for cash at the mercantile.

Those two-and-a-half-dozen hens represented the first step in bringing Birdie's dreams for her mission project to life. She hoped and prayed that Ned wouldn't hold her past against her.

No, Birdie told herself. Her friends—imagine, calling the daughter of a pastor a friend—kept reminding her that she was a child of the King. As in the fairy tales she had loved when she was a girl, that made her a princess. Unlike the stories, she didn't expect Prince Charming to ride up and save her.

Mr. Finnegan treated her with respect, like any other woman who frequented his store. Mr. Gerard had frequented the Betwixt 'n' Between on more than one occasion, although he had never requested Birdie's services.

Every day Birdie was reminded of her former occupation as she walked the streets of Calico. No matter what route she traveled from the boardinghouse, she passed one of her former clients' homes. Mrs. Fairfield, the pastor's wife, encouraged her to pray for the men and the families involved. She called it heaping coals of fire on their heads.

Like the pretty white house standing to her right. The bank president lived in that place. Birdie kept her eyes open as she prayed, hoping to imprint the image of new summer grass and children at play on the lawn over the sight of the man in his long underwear.

The door to the house opened, and Birdie crossed the street. She tugged her sunbonnet forward and kept her gaze focused on her feet. No one else appeared in her line of vision as she turned onto Main Street. Because of the early hour, earlier than most people came to the store, she hoped to catch Mr. Finnegan before he had any customers.

Spotting the deputy sheriff heading down the street, Birdie ducked into the doorway of the mercantile. Mr. Finnegan smiled at her as he unlocked the door. His slight build and kind face matched his occupation.

He opened the door wide and stood back so she could enter. "Good morning, Miss Landry! You're up and about early today."

He said that every time she came, although he must guess her reasons for the hour. She shifted the bag holding the sign from one arm to the other and prayed for courage.

"I see you have something in your bag already. Are you wanting to trade?" He walked to his register and leaned forward on his elbows.

With that unexpected opening, Birdie stammered a bit in her response. "No. I mean, yes, I hope to, in the future." She drew a breath.

"Sit a spell and tell me what you have in mind." He led her to a table at the back of the store underneath a sign that promised a fresh cup of coffee. Without asking, he poured some into a dainty china cup and then refilled his usual mug. "Did you bring some of Miss Kate's doughnuts, by any chance?"

Birdie spread out the extra pastries Miss Kate had sent with her. Mr. Finnegan took one, broke it in half, and dunked it in his coffee. "Delicious."

He turned the bag in Birdie's direction. "Go ahead and take one."

Birdie shook her head. "Thank you, but I already had some for breakfast."

Ned arranged the rest on a tray, fingers tapping on a sheet of paper as he counted up the total. "Tell her I'll add the credit to her account. People do love her doughnuts and cookies. But you didn't come here just to bring Miss Kate's doughnuts." He invited her proposition with a smile. "I always welcome a chance to examine new merchandise."

New merchandise. Birdie's mind fled to the day Nigel Owen had used those words to introduce her to a man he promised would be gentle with her. She shoved that thought out of her mind, reminding herself that to her knowledge, Ned Finnegan had never set foot in a saloon.

◆　◆　◆

Ned waited for Birdie—he thought of her as Birdie, as pretty as a cardinal, with hair to match—but she seemed in no hurry to speak her mind. He sent up a quick prayer for wisdom.

Pulling something out of her bag, she laid it on her lap. He resisted the temptation to take a peek. She looked at him briefly before returning her attention to her coffee cup. "You already carry my ready-made dresses, so I have no right to ask anything more from you."

Ned's heart twisted. She acted like she didn't quite trust him, and why should she, after all she had endured at the hands of evil men? *"Give her time,"* God's still, small voice urged him. So he kept his voice to a strict, businesslike enthusiasm. "You have done me a service. I sold the first dress you brought in here in two days' time, and I've had several requests for more." He folded his hands on the table. "I would be happy to take anything you create with your needle."

Once again the sunbonnet lifted, and he caught sight of those vivid blue eyes, as wide and as innocent as the midday sky, in spite of everything she had gone through. "Thank you for that, and I plan on bringing you more soon. But I have another proposition for you. You see, I have the opportunity to buy some laying hens. . . ." She stalled.

"You're wondering if I would be interested in buying eggs." Ned's mind raced around possibilities. Gerard didn't carry eggs. He calculated he could charge three cents for two eggs. "What price did you have in mind?"

She looked at him again. "I was wondering if you would pay a dime for a half dozen?" She looked away, as if unwilling for him to examine her face.

He would need to adjust his prices, but he didn't hesitate. "Twenty cents a dozen, a penny apiece if you have more or less on a given day." He offered his hand, and she shyly shook it.

"Now can I see what you have in that bag?" He kept his voice light, but she had aroused his curiosity.

"I'm afraid I presumed upon your kindness." She placed the object in her lap on the table between them.

Reading the sign, Ned laughed. "I am honored that you would offer me this business opportunity. I'll put it in the window right away. When do you expect the hens to start laying?"

Birdie kept her eyes on Ned while she explained her timetable for setting up the hen-house, filling it with birds, and letting them settle into their new environment. "I'll check back with you in a week."

"Good. Until then. . .do you need any fabric? Thread? Feed?"

Birdie opened her mouth, closed it, then glanced away as she said, "I don't have the funds for more than the feed."

Tempted to respond with a "put it on account," Ned considered how to help her without offending her pride. Somehow God had smoothed Birdie's ruffled feathers enough to accept Aunt Kate's offer of a roof over her head and daily food. Kate's relationship to Gladys Polson, one of Birdie's friends, helped. Ned had experienced Birdie's prickly pride firsthand. But God's love compelled him to try again.

Something Ned had heard tickled his memory. He pulled out his account books and scanned the lines. When he couldn't make out the ragged words, he pulled his glasses from the top of his head to his eyes. He didn't like the way he looked wearing them, but no one as lovely as Birdie Landry would ever look twice at someone as homely as he was, whether he wore glasses or not.

He found the entry and turned the ledger so Birdie could see. "Several of my customers are eagerly awaiting your next ready-to-wear dresses. Mrs. Olson is so eager, in fact, that she paid in advance so we would hold the next dress for her. I can use your share of the money for the supplies you need." He held his breath, hoping she would agree.

"Mrs. Olson?" Birdie's eyebrows furrowed. "My regular dress pattern might not fit. I want to be sure she is pleased with the product. Besides—" Sighing, she rested her fingers on the counter where the sewing notions were kept. "It's not good business to accept pay before the work is done. That's what happens when farmers borrow money against their crops. They end up losing the land." Such a sad look came over her face that Ned wondered if she had experienced that herself. Maybe that had forced her away from home and into a place like the Betwixt 'n' Between. "I don't like to accept money before I've done the work."

Ned had an answer for that. "That's the way I usually do my business. Get horseshoes on my Ellie, I pay the blacksmith before he starts. When I added a backroom to the store, I paid for expenses right up front."

"Get a meal at Miss Kate's, and you pay after you eat the meal," Birdie shot back. "I know the Bible says if a man doesn't work, he doesn't eat." Her back straightened. She had drawn her line in the sand, and she wouldn't cross over it.

Ned could quote half a dozen verses that talked about taking care of widows, orphans, and the poor, but Birdie would argue she didn't fit into any of those categories. Taking his glasses off the bridge of his nose, he scratched his head with an earpiece. "Tell you what. Do you have enough material and whatnots to make something for a baby? A quilt, a christening gown? My sister. . ." Heat crept into his face. He was uneasy discussing such an intimate matter. But he kept his voice steady. "She's in a delicate condition, and I've been thinking about what to give her. Anything you make would be a marvelous gift. You could probably fix that up quick, and then you'd have money for additional supplies." He kept his eyes locked on hers, willing her to agree.

Birdie returned his stare, her features not betraying her thoughts. She had a good face for poker. At last a rare smile burst out, bathing Ned with the first rays of sunrise. "I have some scraps that would be perfect for a baby quilt. When would you like it?"

Ned's niece or nephew wasn't due for six months, but Birdie didn't need to know that. "As soon as you can finish."

Birdie curled her fingers against her hands one by one, as if she was calculating the hours. "I should be able to finish it by a week from this Saturday." Her smile faded like the last hint of color on the horizon at the end of the day. "Thank you for your business, Mr. Finnegan." With a final nod of her head, she left his store.

Most men would do almost anything to put another one of those smiles on Birdie's face. With God's help, Ned hoped to be the one who did.

Chapter 2

T hese are all the scraps I have." Gladys handed a bag of fabric to Birdie. "I had set these aside to show to all of you before you told me about the baby quilt. If you find anything you can use, please take it off my hands. And here are the threads I pulled out from the seams, in case you can use them as well." She dropped a spool half full of thread into the bag of scraps without waiting for Birdie's answer.

Since Birdie and the others shared alike when they had extra bits of sewing materials, she didn't refuse the offer. The materials in the bag personified the adage her ma had branded on her mind: "Use it up, wear it out, make it do, or do without." But no matter how Ma scrimped, they never had enough. Pa drank money as soon as he got ahold of it.

Birdie reached for the spool and dropped it into her basket. Sorting through the scraps she had gathered, she decided on a pinwheel pattern in yellows, greens, and lavender. She had enough white fabric to mix with the others without purchasing anything else. "I've dealt with some stubborn men in my time, but I've never met anyone as bad as Mr. Finnegan. He wasn't going to let me go until he found a way to give me money."

The other women exchanged glances, and Annie laughed out loud. She examined a square Birdie had already finished. "He's not *giving* you anything. You've put a lot of hours into this quilt already. I couldn't make anything so fine in a month of Saturdays." She turned it over and examined the tiny knots on the back. "And to think you did this with leftover thread. You are a gifted seamstress."

Birdie's spirits lifted at the kind words. She had used those skills to repair dresses for the other girls at the Betwixt 'n' Between. Then there came a time when she didn't ever want to pick up a needle again. That changed after Mrs. Fairfield talked her into joining the Ladies Sewing Circle and she'd made friends with the women in this room. Ruth described the surprising turn of events as God turning something bad into something good.

"You're smiling." Gladys spoke like someone taking notes for class or a report to her newspaper editor fiancé, Haydn Keller.

"So spill the news." As usual, Annie was more straightforward. "You're smiling like Christmas Day."

Birdie cut one of Annie's scraps of fabric into two squares while she considered her answer. "It's something Ruth said about God making something good out of something bad."

"That comes from Romans," Ruth said. " 'And we know that all things work together for good to them that love God, to them who are the called according to his purpose.' "

"Or that verse in Isaiah about beauty for ashes." Gladys nodded.

Birdie looked at each woman, seeing the love in their eyes. When she first ran to the parsonage after fleeing the Betwixt 'n' Between, she half-expected the pastor, or his wife, to throw her out. At the time, she was desperate enough to try anything. "I never imagined myself in a place like this, making something for a baby, working among friends." Tears she bottled up while at the saloon clung to her eyelashes, as they often did these days. "God is *so* good."

Annie laid aside her knitting needles long enough to pat her arm. "Yes He is. Even my Bear has learned that much."

Strange how these mission projects had led to love for Gladys and then for Annie. Birdie held no such illusions for her own future. Men wanted purity in a wife, and she had given that up a long time ago. Even Christians had to live with the consequences of earlier bad choices.

The four of them bent their heads over their sewing and knitting. "Who are you making those for, Annie?" Gladys asked. "Seems like you've made enough socks to keep everyone in that fort in socks for a whole week."

"Not quite." Annie laughed. "They get holes in them, or they get lost in the laundry, or a new soldier comes. Jeremiah lets me know, and I don't mind at all. And what about you? You're making yourself another wedding quilt and not allowing us to work on it with you."

Ruth stitched endless arrays of diapers, sheets, and other items to give to people who came to the church in need of help. Guilt tickled Birdie's conscience, and Ruth tilted her head. "Now what's bothering you?" Her gray eyes softened.

"You're all working on your mission projects for free. And Ned is going to pay me for this." Birdie lifted the corner of the quilt.

Annie and Gladys exchanged a look. At Gladys's nod, Annie said, "You ask too much of yourself, Birdie. The three of us are blessed to live with our parents. You pay for your lodging—"

"No I don't. I help Miss Kate, that's all."

"If you didn't live there, she would pay you for your help. She pays me when I help out at the diner," Gladys said.

That fact was the only reason Birdie accepted the room. She felt better now that she had the laying hens and could offer as many eggs as Miss Kate needed for the diner.

Ruth said, "You won't accept help in getting your supplies, so you have to make money somehow to start on the clothes you want to give to your friends."

When Birdie sighed this time, peace lifted her heart like a feather on the wind. "I always feel so much better after we get together."

"That's why God tells us not to forget about gathering together. It's easier to wander away from Him when we're alone." Ruth finished stitching the sheet she was working on and turned down the top, starting a floral embroidery along the edge. "How is your mission project going?"

"So-so." When they first discussed projects in January, Birdie knew exactly what she wanted to do: help other girls stuck at the Betwixt 'n' Between. But doing that required so many things she didn't have yet. A small house they could share together. Proper clothing. Work. Safety. All of that took money. Ever since childhood, money had been the problem. God had provided for all her needs, just as He promised. Was she wrong to want more so that she could help others?

Ruth worked a leaf pattern on the sheet. "It will all work out in God's time. But it can be hard to wait." She pulled her needle and thread through the fabric. "I keep telling myself the same thing, while I wonder when God will show me what He wants me to do."

Ruth already did plenty by helping her parents with the church ministries. But she wanted something more personal, a specific person or situation.

Annie tied off a finished sock and stuck her needles through the remainder of the ball of yarn. "I'm done for the day. I need to leave soon to meet up with the Peates. Before I go, do we have any more prayer requests?"

Birdie enjoyed this part of their meetings the most, although she was still too shy to pray in front of the others. "We should pray for Mr. Finnegan's sister, and the baby."

"And Jeremiah told me one of the new soldiers is having a hard time adapting. Jeremiah is afraid he might desert." Annie never gave the names of the soldiers she asked prayer for, and she didn't this time.

Gladys slipped her needle into the fabric of the quilt top. "Haydn says the snowstorm damaged a few soddies. We should pray for those families."

They had discussed their personal prayer concerns many times. Today they had touched on Mr. Keller's health (improving), beaus for Ruth and Birdie (in spite of their objections), Ruth's hopes for the upcoming school year, and salvation and so much more for Birdie's friends.

Ruth finished the leaf she was working on and put the sheet away. "I'll start." They put away their projects and closed their eyes in prayer.

Prayer. Birdie had seen too many answers in the short months she had been a Christian to doubt its power. As each woman prayed for Birdie's friends by name, she could believe good things would happen. God would make something good out of something bad.

If only her faith remained as solid during the middle of the night.

◆ ◆ ◆

Ned prided himself on not revealing his emotions on his face. A successful store owner couldn't afford to offend potential customers. But Birdie's question today left him speechless. He recovered quickly. "You want red flannel? To make long johns?"

"I can make them for less money than they spend buying them from the catalog. Better quality, too." If Birdie was a store owner like Gerard, she would be rubbing her hands in anticipation of potential sales. "What I want to know is if you'll carry them in your store." Her smile indicated she expected an automatic yes answer.

Of course Birdie had seen men's undergarments, although Ned had shut his mind to that part of her past. But this venture would drag her back to the past and not the future she planned. Wouldn't it?

The light went out in her eyes, and Ned realized he had waited too long with his answer. "Never mind. I'll make money other ways." She handed him the day's basket of eggs. As she had promised, two dozen good-sized eggs each day.

He gave her forty cents. "This is enough for a couple of lengths of flannel." His voice sounded strangled to his ears as he lifted the bolt onto the cutting table. The scissors lay in the table drawer, and he busied himself with sharpening the blades while he waited for her instructions. After he marshaled his features into agreement, he lifted his face. "You're right, they would sell well."

When she didn't object, he nipped the edge of the material and cut in a straight line. "Do you need thread?"

Birdie shook her head and asked, "Do you think it's a bad idea?"

Her eyes told him she wanted a serious answer. He took his time slipping the scissors back into the drawer. When he looked at her again, the folded fabric lay between them like an exhibit ready to convict her in court. "I believe it's fine as long as no one knows who's making them. I haven't told anyone who's making the ready-made dresses, but I don't know if it's a secret. Some people might add four and four and make ten."

Ned's spirits flagged as Birdie's shoulders slumped, hunched over as if in defeat. She wouldn't look at him. The moment stretched like taffy, until Ned feared the fragile bond of trust between them would stretch too far and break. *What do I say, Lord?*

"Wait."

Ned put together the additional supplies Birdie needed for the long johns, offering his support in spite of his reservations. Once finished, he set the materials on the counter between them and waited. One moment she was slumped over, staring at the floor. In an instant, she changed. Straightening her back so that her shoulders made a proud line, she lifted her chin and looked him face-on. "Pastor Fairfield and his missus tell me that I have to avoid even the appearance of evil, because people will assume the worst. They also warned me that I might be tempted to return to my old ways. Tell me, Mr. Finnegan, is making long underwear for soldiers the kind of behavior they meant?"

His mouth suddenly dry, Ned could only nod. Popping a lemon drop into his mouth, he worked up enough saliva to speak. In the few seconds that took, he could see the tremble in Birdie's shoulders as she maintained her composure, trying to appear as if his answer didn't matter one way or the other.

"I'm sorry, Miss Landry. But it seems that way to me." Ned had to find some way to ease the defeat he'd read in her earlier posture. The smile that he had practiced on grouchy customers came in handy. "Annie Bliss is part of your sewing circle, right?"

Birdie nodded.

"She's made connections with the commander's wife at the fort. Together they might come up with a way to keep your role anonymous. Maybe she could even pretend she's the one making the underwear."

The starch left Birdie, and her nod wasn't forced. "I'll do that. I'll also ask Mrs. Fairfield for her suggestions." Her face returned to its usual placid expression, and she turned to exit the door.

"Don't you want the fabric?" Ned called to her departing back.

In the doorway, she turned. "I will once I have my answer."

That woman had enough pride and determination to build Rome in a day. Spunk, people would call that quality in someone else. She had used it to survive her past, and it gave her the courage to start over again now.

She was everything Ned was not, and he liked her all the more for it.

Chapter 3

T hank you for agreeing to meet with me in town." In spite of wearing her most modest dress, a deep blue that buttoned up the neck and at her wrists, the hem only far enough off the floor to avoid dragging in the dirt, Birdie felt stripped as Mrs. Peate fixed steady eyes on her.

"I am honored that you would ask me to help with another one of your missions. God has done some amazing things through our friend Annie." She nodded across the table where Annie and Gladys were seated. Mrs. Fairfield had joined them this morning, as well.

"Here is some fresh coffee." Miss Kate bustled out of the diner kitchen.

Finding a place to meet had proved problematical. They all agreed from the beginning that the meeting should not take place at the fort. Annie had said, "They figured out I was making their mittens, hats, and scarves because they saw me at the fort. That, and the fact I was spending so much time with Jeremiah." A small giggle testified to her present happiness.

If they met at Miss Kate's boardinghouse, another resident might see Mrs. Peate there and make the very connection they wanted to avoid. Miss Kate had suggested an alternative: They could meet at the diner an hour before opening. If someone happened to see them sitting quietly in the corner, they would assume the women were Gladys's or Miss Kate's guests.

Birdie's stomach twisted like a pretzel as she wondered whether the business opportunity she had conceived was of the Lord or of the devil.

Once all five ladies had settled at the table, sipping coffee and eating hot biscuits, they turned their eyes on Birdie. She spooned sugar into her coffee and stirred it, stalling for time. Ever since Ned questioned the wisdom of her enterprise, she had suffered a torrential rain of doubt.

Miss Kate appeared at the door again. "Just go ahead and tell them, dearie."

"That's my aunt Kate," Gladys grimaced. "She loves getting into our business. All with the kindest of motives, of course. She practically forced Haydn on me."

"And look how that turned out." Annie grinned. "So unfortunate that you discovered the man God wants you to marry."

Birdie decided to speak before they got sidetracked with matrimonial pursuits. "That doesn't matter, since there is no man involved in this matter." Her thoughts ran guiltily to Ned, his kindness and the way he championed her to the community. "At least, there is no man in particular."

"Stop speaking in puzzles." Mrs. Fairfield took her first sip of coffee. "My dear Mr. Fairfield always tells me to begin at the beginning."

Birdie could do that. "Ever since I became a Christian, I've dreamed of helping other girls get away from that place. When I was invited to join the sewing circle, I believed God had given me a sign. One of the first things the women need is modest clothing."

"What a lovely thought." Mrs. Peate nodded approvingly. "The captain often says a man feels the most like a soldier when he's wearing his dress uniform. Changing the look of the outside helps to change how you feel on the inside, even though the Lord values what's inside a man."

Bacon sizzled in the kitchen, and Birdie's stomach growled. She placed a light hand on her midsection as if that would stop the sound.

Miss Kate brought a tray with steaming bowls of oatmeal. "I'll have bacon and eggs for you in a minute."

"We didn't intend to make you work." Birdie's stomach didn't agree.

"Nonsense. Since it's already cooked, go ahead and eat."

Mrs. Peate ate a few bites of oatmeal. "That woman is a genius with food." She dabbed her mouth with a napkin. "I love your idea, but I don't understand how the men of the fort are involved."

Now came the hard part. Birdie didn't want to complain, but. . . "I've made money sewing since I became a Christian. God has provided for all my needs, but it takes everything I make to pay for my living expenses and supplies. Recently Miss Kate agreed to let me keep laying hens to make money a little faster."

Mrs. Peate ate a few more mouthfuls before Birdie started up again.

"I had another idea to increase my earnings. I thought about all those single men at the fort and wondered where they get their long underwear. If they would buy their long underwear from me, I could use the extra money. When I asked Mr. Finnegan for red flannel, he acted like it was a bad idea."

Mrs. Fairfield sighed, and Birdie froze, wondering what it meant.

When she didn't speak, Birdie continued. She turned to Annie and said, "I did wonder if *you* wanted to take on this business, since you already know the men. You could make a little extra money." She struggled to keep her expression neutral. If their secret was discovered, people wouldn't question Annie as much as they would someone with Birdie's past.

Miss Kate brought in bacon and eggs, and Annie turned her attention to her plate, her face a delicate pink. She speared a bite of eggs before she answered. "I'll stick to making things with my knitting needles."

The others nodded, and Birdie had a sinking sensation in her heart. The thought of a man's underwear made Annie uncomfortable. Birdie couldn't remember the last time she'd experienced embarrassment. No wonder Ned talked about the appearance of evil.

Mrs. Fairfield looked at Birdie with so much compassion that tears jumped to Birdie's eyes. "It's a bad idea. I shouldn't have asked," she said.

Mrs. Peate set her slice of bacon aside. "It's an admirable idea. From what I've seen of the men's laundry, they could use some new things. Why don't I think about the situation and see what we can do?"

"In the meantime, start sewing, so you can sell them as soon as we've figured it out," Annie said.

Birdie shook her head. If she bought supplies before she knew she had a buyer, she might waste money. Even though she hoped to speed up the process of making extra money, she needed to wait for God's timing.

"If the work makes you uncomfortable, you shouldn't pursue it. God will give you what you need," Mrs. Fairfield said. She reached out and squeezed Birdie's hand. "But the plan is a sound one, if that is what you feel led to do. Just remember, you're not on your own."

But Birdie had a hard time believing that. She had been on her own, all her life.

◆　◆　◆

Ned kept the red flannel hidden on the shelf beneath the cash register, waiting for Birdie to ask for it. Morning after morning, she walked into the store, dropped off her eggs, and took her money without asking for the flannel.

The bell over the door jangled. Birdie swung into the room and set the basket by the cash register with renewed light shining in her eyes. "Four of my hens dropped an extra egg today. I have enough money to buy what I need to make a dress."

Ned headed for the shelf of calicoes. "What do you have in mind?" How would the town respond to a pair of ex-saloon girls trying to make an honest living? Saloon supporters would object to the loss of "talent," and the Pharisees in town would object to their presence in church. If Ned was honest with himself, he'd admit he had reservations also.

Birdie followed him and hesitated by some of the fancier fabrics, a pretty beige silk that would look wonderful with her red hair, a fine wool on sale for a good price because it didn't sell well during the heat of summer. If he thought she would agree, he would offer it to her for the same price as the calico.

Next she passed behind Ned and studied the solid-colored cotton, the least expensive fabric. A frown creased her face, and she surveyed the calicoes, choosing a brown with white flowers, the plainest calico he had. She took the admonition to dress modestly very seriously, but even ugly fabric couldn't hide her beauty. "I'll take two lengths of this, with half a length of the brown." She pointed to a bolt of cotton.

Ned set out the box with sewing notions for her to examine, and she choose thread and a handful of buttons. "This is wonderful. Michal has indicated she's ready to leave as soon as I have a dress ready."

Another customer came in, and Ned left Birdie for a few minutes to measure out potatoes and flour. After the lady left, Birdie brought the supplies to the counter. "How much is it?"

"I'm glad you can do this at last." Ned told her the total and made change for her. He glanced at the shelf below the register, his hand touching the bundle of flannel still waiting for her. He picked it up and set it down next to the calico. "I would like for you to take this. A bonus for being a good supplier and customer. Since I already cut the flannel, I can't sell it to someone else."

The light in Birdie's eyes dimmed. "Thank you, but no. I decided against doing that. I'll pay you for the flannel, of course."

"Nonsense." Ned shook his head. "You never bought it."

"While we're talking. . . ," Birdie started.

Another customer entered and Birdie cuddled the fabric against her chest. He expected her to disappear with the same quiet stealth that dictated most of her movements. But she waited for the new customer to finish her business and leave the store before she addressed Ned again.

"You've had a busy morning."

"Business has been good lately." Although Ned welcomed the trade, he knew Birdie felt uncomfortable unless the store was empty.

"I've noticed that. Do you need additional help?" She tugged the fabric against her side and stared at her fingers before looking up again. "You're already doing so much for me that I feel guilty for asking."

"You can ask me anything." Ned's heart sped a little at the thought of what Birdie might ask of him.

"It's my friend. She'll need a job, and I wondered if you could use an assistant."

Ned scratched his head. "So far I've kept up with the extra business. I can't really afford to pay anyone."

Birdie's face fell, and she turned away. He should never have mentioned money.

"Of course. I should have realized. . . Never mind. God will provide. That's what Mrs. Fairfield always says." With that, she scooted out the door.

◆　◆　◆

Birdie slumped at the street corner, away from the window where Ned could see her. *I can't stay here long. I can't start crying my eyes out while I'm in public, where anyone can see.* She called on the iron backbone that had seen her through so many difficult times. After a minute, she raised her face, free of tears, and walked down the street as if she had a right to be there. Once in the boardinghouse, she raced up the stairs to her room and flung herself across the bed and allowed the sobs to shake her body.

I'm worthless, no matter what Pastor Fairfield says. No one believes in my dream. Why should they?

She had thought Ned was different, but he didn't want anything to do with a dirty saloon girl any more than anyone else did. God and Pastor Fairfield might see Birdie with new eyes, but no one else did. She allowed herself to hope that the members of the sewing circle liked her as well as their friendship suggested. "But not Ned." With that final thought, she burrowed her head into the pillow, allowing her tears to soak the fabric.

Get up. We don't allow any bawling in here. Customers come for a pretty face, not one all puffy from tears. The voice of Nigel Owen from the Betwixt 'n' Between intruded in Birdie's thoughts, as loud as if he were in the room with her.

Here, take some of this. It will take the edge off. Nigel had offered Birdie whiskey after her first customer humiliated her and bruised her in places she had scarcely known existed. She drank it that one time but then felt even worse. Never again. After that, she hid her true feelings, smiling on the outside while crying on the inside.

The new Birdie had no problem crying, but she held on until she could escape to a private place before she let go. Unable to put any more into words, she repeated the same three names—Annie, Gladys, Ruth—over and over. At last the tears stopped and she sat up.

The Bible on her nightstand opened to the eighth chapter of Romans, one Mrs. Fairfield said offered her great encouragement when she got discouraged. Birdie had read the chapter so often she almost had it memorized. She especially liked the verses about the Holy Ghost lifting up her heart "with groanings which cannot be uttered" and how neither height nor depth nor life nor death could separate her from the love of God. She reread the familiar words and clasped her Bible to her chest. She still couldn't believe the God of all the universe loved her like that.

A single tear dropped, and Birdie wiped it away. Exchanging the Bible for a brush, she ran it through her nearly waist-length hair, a hundred strokes. After she had calmed somewhat, she splashed water on her face until she had cooled, and looked into the mirror. Fiery hair framed her face, paler than usual except around the eyes, which were puffy and red. The puffy eyes didn't matter to her, and she knew they didn't matter to God, but Miss Kate would cluck over her. Birdie might skip lunch altogether. Why eat? She wasn't hungry.

Instead, she took her Bible and sat in a chair by the window, sipping from a glass of water and reading first one psalm then another, soaking in the promises and expressing the outrage the psalmist felt.

After a while, Birdie heard Miss Kate's heavy tread on the stairs. Her landlady's voice followed a light knock on the door. "I brought you some soup, dearie. Please open your door."

Birdie closed her Bible and stood, deciding she could tell Miss Kate about what happened. She had shown an amazing amount of discretion. Crossing the room, Birdie opened the door. "Come in."

Miss Kate surveyed the room, dwelling on the soaked pillow and Birdie's face. "Dearie, what has upset you so much?"

Chapter 4

Haydn Keller held the latest edition of the *Calico Chronicle* where Ned could see it through the window. A glance at the clock told Ned he had about a quarter of an hour before his first customers would arrive. *Perfect*. He unlocked the door, and Haydn rushed in.

"I still can't get used to Calico having a newspaper of our own." Ned had advertised in the paper from the first edition two months ago, and the decision had more than paid for itself the first week. But this week's paper held some special information.

The headline above the fold on the front page grabbed Ned's attention first. Local Entrepreneur to Join Business Interests with Restaurateur. The article promised upcoming nuptials between Haydn's grandfather and Miss Kate Polson before the end of the year. Haydn's smile made Ned laugh.

"If I can't feature my own grandfather when he announces his plans to get married, when can I?" Haydn clapped Ned on his back.

Ned perused the article. Gladys's outreach had helped the childhood sweethearts to reconnect. If Haydn's description of Gladys made her sound a little prettier, a tad more talented, who could blame him? "When are you going to announce your own wedding?"

"All in good time, all in good time." Haydn rubbed his hands together, and Ned caught the glimmer in his eyes.

Ned continued perusing the article. "You don't mention the sewing circle." He looked at Haydn for an explanation.

He shrugged. "Both Annie and Birdie have reasons to keep their projects quiet, and as far as I know, Ruth hasn't chosen hers yet. Gladys said they preferred to keep their names out of it."

So Haydn didn't print all the news all the time, instead showing sensitivity. Ned found his ad on the bottom right-hand corner of the center page. Coming Soon: Ready-Made Clothing for Every Need for Both Men and Women. Pictures of men's long johns appeared in the ad, as well as of ladies' dresses.

Ned had thought long and hard about how to promote ready-made long johns without drawing attention to Birdie. The idea of advertising in the paper wouldn't let go. He could gauge interest and, hopefully, assuage Birdie's fears. "Perfect. Is this my copy?"

Haydn nodded. "Good luck. We're praying that you get a good response." He looked at the clock. "Well, I'd better get going and deliver the rest of the papers." He headed for the door.

Haydn timed his paper to print on Friday, for customers who came to town to shop on Saturday. The challenge of anticipating his customers' needs intrigued Ned. In some ways, he faced the same dilemmas Birdie did. Maybe he could teach her how to plot a profit-and-loss sheet.

As the customers lined up outside his door, Ned remembered Birdie's suggestion to hire one of the saloon girls. That move would probably attract the wrong kind of customer.

God's advice to Samuel to look at the inside of a man whispered in Ned's mind, but he pushed it aside as he helped first one customer then another. The biggest crowd passed through after the diner closed for the day. Soldiers had come to town in anticipation of another social event, similar to the ones held earlier in the spring. Several headed in his direction. Did he dare hope they would express interest in men's underwear?

Lieutenant Arnold, who was in the store with Annie Bliss by his side examining dish patterns, noticed them as well. "Let me know if any of that lot gives you trouble."

Ned scratched his head. "I'll keep that in mind. Thanks." Peering out the door, he spotted Birdie, her hair covered with a sunbonnet, hiding in the alley beside the diner. Ned couldn't be sure, but he thought she was reading the paper. He hoped the advertisement would come as a welcome surprise.

She glanced up long enough for him to see the scowl on her face. When she saw the soldiers headed for the store, she disappeared from view before he crossed the room. Sighing, he let the men enter. "I'm fixing to close up shop pretty soon."

The soldiers were uniformly youthful, perhaps as young as sixteen, full of liquor and looking for a fight. Ned recognized a couple of them from the beer-infused brawl at the box lunch social a few months ago. Had they learned nothing?

Always professional, Ned forced himself to serve them with a smile. He didn't carry any items that would shame the buyer or the seller. As the men browsed, he asked, "May I help you find something?"

"Do you have any sarsaparilla?"

Ned nodded. "I do. Let me get it for you. How many of you want some?" He began pouring drinks from his soda fountain as fast as he could. "Could I interest you in large pickles?" He pointed to the barrel, hoping they would make their purchases and leave before Birdie decided to come another time.

Like children set loose in the store, the soldiers bought a variety of penny candies. One hesitated, torn between licorice and lemon drops, while the rest waited at the window. One of them, the oldest, if the extra creases in his trousers suggested years of use, whistled. "Well, looky there." He pointed across the street. "I didn't know them ladies came out in the daytime."

Ned's heart sank, but he stayed his distance, not wanting to draw extra attention to the object of the soldier's whistle.

The soldier who had requested sarsaparilla glanced at Birdie and shook his head. "Don't get your hopes up. They say the lady is out of business."

Birdie hastened down the street, out of Ned's line of vision. He couldn't imagine how she felt, all those men watching her walk down the street.

"Gentlemen, are you finished?" Ned asked, desperate to draw their attention away from Birdie.

"Sure." The last soldier asked for lemon drops but kept his head craned, looking over his shoulder for a final glimpse of Birdie.

Ned had change ready even before the soldier handed over his silver dollar. "If you hurry, you'll get to the town square in time for the horseshoe pitch."

"I'll beat you there," a blond-haired lad said.

Relief flooded Ned as they headed in the opposite direction from Birdie, but he felt bad about what had happened. Once again, she had removed herself from a social event rather than draw attention to herself or the hosts. *Not this time.* She had headed in the direction of the boardinghouse. Ned had never approached her there, but maybe now was the time.

After Ned locked the day's earnings in his cash box, he dashed out the back door and hurried along the fastest route to Aunt Kate's house. Birdie entered the house while he was still halfway down the street.

To his surprise, Aunt Kate came up behind him. "Oh dear. I had to return for my second basket of cookies, and I saw Birdie race up the steps like a scared rabbit. Do you know what happened?"

"If I had to guess, I would say she saw someone from her past."

"Oh, the poor thing. When will people accept who she is now and stop worrying about her old life?" Miss Kate shook her head as she opened the door for the two of them.

Ned peeked in the front parlor before following Miss Kate down the hall, glancing into any room that had an open door. They ended in the kitchen at the back, determining they were the only people on the first floor. A piece of newspaper stuck out from the oven. Ned opened the door and saw that the page with the ad was already charred around the edges, although the front page remained intact. "I understand congratulations are in order."

"Thank you." Miss Kate flushed a becoming pink before noticing the charred pages. "That's strange." She raised questioning eyes in Ned's direction.

Sighing, Ned snatched the paper from the fire. "I expect you'll want several copies. Too bad this one is burned. Do you mind if I go upstairs and see if Birdie will come down and talk with me?"

"Go on with you. You can use the front parlor. I'll be sending up prayers that you can get through to her."

◆　◆　◆

Birdie heard the firm tread of Ned's step as he climbed the stairs and reached the second floor. She knew it was Ned, because she'd overheard his conversation with Miss Kate. But did she want to speak with him? The assurance God gave Joshua when he was faced with a frightening situation jumped into her mind. *Don't be afraid, for I am with you.*

Uncertain, she waited midway between the settee by the window and the door. The knock came, followed by Ned's voice. "It's me, Ned. Ned Finnegan."

Her feet walked in that direction as if God Himself moved them, and she opened the door a couple of inches. "How can I help you?"

"Please come downstairs so we can talk. The house is empty except for Aunt Kate. We can sit in the front parlor without worry of anyone overhearing us."

Anyone passing by might catch sight of them talking and link their names together, anyone not at the town square, that was. "You should be at the fair."

His smile slipped at her nonresponsive answer. He shrugged as if it didn't matter, and she joined him in the hall. Wordlessly, she passed him and started down the stairs. Instead of the front room, she went to the sewing room at the back of the house. An unusual setting for a visit, but she couldn't think of another community room besides the parlor and the kitchen. She entered, pushing aside boxes of fabric and adding a couple of pins to her pin cushion before she took her favorite spot. Sunshine streamed through the window and illuminated her work space for most hours of the day.

Ned shifted a bag of scraps from the only other chair in the room and sat across from her. His arms hung loosely by his sides, and he tapped his leg with the newspaper without speaking. A faint sheen of sweat dotted his forehead, as if he had rushed to follow her to the boardinghouse. At last he spoke, his voice cool, as if he came calling every day. "Miss Landry, I know this is the last minute, but would you do me the honor of accompanying me to the fair today?"

Surprised by the question, Birdie blurted out, "No, I couldn't. I can't."

His eyes blinked closed, but when they opened again, his steady blue eyes studied her. "Do you object to my company, or do you want to avoid the people of this town?"

Embarrassment that didn't trouble Birdie when thinking about men's underwear flushed through her body, heating her cheeks.

"I saw you when the soldiers came into the store. The leader was one of the trouble-makers at the first box social. Don't let him steal the joy of the day from you. He's a fool who doesn't know any better." Ned lifted an arm, as if to reach out and comfort her, but then dropped it to his lap.

Birdie surveyed the room, seeking an answer. She could plead work; she had almost finished the first dress for her friend Michal. But the man addressing her deserved better than that.

Ned opened the newspaper, folded so she could see the inside pages. "I'm sorry I was so harsh about your plans for the red flannel. I wanted you to see this." He handed her the paper.

She read every word of the advertisement for Finnegan's Mercantile again, including the offer for ready-made clothes "for every need." Heat refused to leave her face, but she forced herself to meet Ned's eyes, the unspoken question trembling on her lips.

He met her gaze head on, a small smile lifting the corners of his mouth. "I couldn't get your idea out of my mind. You have a good head for business; I've noticed that before." He held the paper in the empty space halfway between their chairs. "And you are the best seamstress I know. Please forgive me? I do need your help, and I welcome your company at the picnic."

Surprise, pleasure, and frustration warred in Birdie without a clear winner. Ned waited her out, not pressing her for an answer. "I still don't have enough money to pay for the supplies." She fell back on her original objection to accepting payment before completing the work.

"That's the beauty of doing it this way. For now, and later as well, if you prefer, I am hiring you as my seamstress. Imagine you lived in a city and I hired you to work at my garment factory. It's the same principle, only you will do a much better job. We can talk about changing the terms later if you prefer."

"You want me to be your employee. Except I'll be working at home." What a kind, *sensible* thing to do, even if she resisted the idea of working for a man ever again. This was different. Ned wanted her to work for him using a skill she had acquired as a young girl, unlike the last man who offered her a job. The problem of delivery remained, however. If she brought long johns to the store, people would talk. The swirl of pleasure she felt in the offer melted away. "I would have to deliver them to you. People would guess."

"Aunt Kate can bring them in, or even Mrs. Fairfield. No one will question either one

THE Valiant HEARTS ROMANCE COLLECTION

of them." He inched forward in his chair, halving the distance between them, stopping short of making her uncomfortable. His whisper was intimate enough to carry over the inches between them. "And I am looking forward to the day that you can walk down the street with your head held high."

He had handed her innermost dreams to her on a plate. She could only nod her head. As soon as her chin dipped a quarter of an inch, he slipped the flannel package onto her work-table and extended his hand. "You can start practicing that today if you will come with me."

Chapter 5

Mesmerized by Ned's blue eyes, Birdie let him lead her to the kitchen. "May we escort Calico's newest affianced lady to the picnic?" Ned bowed as he said the words.

A blush danced across Miss Kate's face, smoothing and adding wrinkles in equal measure. "I didn't know you had such a way with words, Ned. But I hear my ride approach." She raced across the floor and peeked between the curtains. Birdie caught a glimpse of a four-wheeled brougham. Her landlady clapped her hands together. "Norman must have rented it from the livery. I told him to bring a wagon so I could carry baskets to the picnic. But he went all fancy on me."

"You are one blessed woman." Miss Kate's newfound happiness gladdened Birdie. She rejoiced with Gladys and Annie as well. She had no one but herself to blame for the choices that made marital bliss an impossibility for her. She squeezed her eyes shut. *Lord, shut my ears as well, to the harmful things people may say about me or Ned today. He is too nice a gentleman for rumors to dirty his reputation.*

Birdie rummaged up a smile. "Let's go."

Nodding his head in satisfaction, Ned swept Birdie out the door as Mr. Keller climbed the steps to greet his fiancée. From Gladys's description, Birdie had pictured Mr. Keller as a frail, elderly man in poor health. Love had restored so much vim and vigor, he could almost have passed for Haydn's father.

He tipped his hat in her direction, as if she was a lady deserving his respect. "Good afternoon. Miss Landry, isn't it?"

If everyone in town treated her like Mr. Keller did, Birdie might enjoy herself today. With a lighter heart than she thought possible when she raced home, her heart skipped ahead of them as Ned led her to the town square. He used the shortest path, the one Birdie avoided at all costs.

Birdie's steps slowed then came to a paralyzed stop in front of the Betwixt 'n' Between, with the fear of a prisoner approaching her jail cell. How many hours had she spent imagining herself anywhere but the room she occupied above the saloon?

"Keep on walking," Ned urged. "Don't give them the satisfaction of thinking they have any more power over you." He increased the pressure on her elbow until she moved in step with him.

A few feet farther, she hesitated again. A slender, pale figure loitered in the shadowed corner of the saloon, young Michal Clanahan. When Michal saw Birdie, her eyes widened, and she beckoned for her attention.

Ned hadn't seen the exchange. His attention was focused ahead of them, where the sounds of a lively fair beckoned. Birdie wanted to enjoy the company of the good man at her side, but she had to help Michal. *"She is the first one of many."* God's voice sounded clear in her heart, and she came to a complete stop.

"Mr. Finnegan. . ."

"I'd be honored if you called me Ned." He took another step but stopped when she planted her feet. "We're almost there."

"Michal, the girl I told you about, is waiting over there." Birdie looked at him, willing him to understand. "I'm not certain, but I think she's asking for help."

◆ ◆ ◆

Ned had taken the route past the saloon on purpose. Birdie needed help to shake free of her past, and he hoped God had given him the job. But he hadn't expected to be made a partner in Birdie's desire to rescue soiled doves.

Before he could formulate a response, Birdie's hand slipped from his grasp. "I've got to find out what's wrong." With a furtive glance around, she raced along the side of the building that held the bar. It was without windows; no one could see her.

Ned hesitated, uncertain. Should he follow? Should he go on ahead? Instinct told him to move away from the front of the saloon, where he might attract unwanted attention. As he was turning away, the saloon doors swung open and a barrel-chested man sauntered outside. Nigel Owen, the saloon owner. Ned's guts twisted. At all costs, he had to divert Owen's attention from the back of the saloon.

The saloon owner gulped a mouthful of fresh air before he clipped a cigar and stuffed it in his mouth. "Finnegan, isn't it?"

Ned nodded. Did Owen know anything about his association with Birdie? "Are you talking to me?"

"I sure am." Owen gestured for Ned to join him in the shadows on the porch. "Come on over here so's we can speak like civil people."

Birdie disappeared behind the next building, her friend in tow. Ned forced his difficult-customer smile on his face. "You must be Mr. Owen." He took a couple of short steps, stopping a considerable distance from the saloon. Standing that close to the establishment made him uncomfortable. *This is for Birdie.*

"How's your business doing these days?" Owen lit the cigar and puffed on it, and Ned changed positions so the smoke wouldn't blow in his face. "They've been dragging a little bit at the Betwixt 'n' Between, I have to tell you. Us businessmen have to stick together."

Us businessmen? Ned didn't have anything in common with the saloon owner. "I have no complaints." *Maybe God is getting ahold of the people of Calico and leading them away from the debauchery you represent.*

Owen frowned, brushing ash from his vest. "I saw your advertisement for long johns."

Ned stared at him, not wanting this man to read anything in his expression. "Would you like to order some?"

Owen laughed at that. "Not a'tall, but I wondered if you know who I can ask to sew up some pretty dresses for my girls."

He must have guessed. "I would not ask that of anyone I know."

"That's too bad. I lost my best girl recently, and I don't have anybody who can make things like she did." Owen puffed on the cigar again and waved it in Ned's direction. "I expect to get some extra customers tonight, with all the soldiers in town today."

Ned's stomach soured, but Owen's face remained pleasant. "I'd best get back inside and see if any trouble's brewing. Next time you head my way, first drink's on the house." Wiggling the cigar, he disappeared inside, the doors swishing behind him.

Patting his pockets as if searching for something, Ned forced himself to stay put until Owen was no longer visible. Shrugging his shoulders as if giving up, he spun around and headed to the town square. This new business might keep Birdie occupied for the rest of the day, and he wouldn't hunt her down. She had needed months to accept him as an ally; there was no telling how the new girl would react to the sight of him.

Nevertheless, Ned stayed alert for any sign of Birdie. Because of the fair, not many places remained open. He sauntered around the perimeter of the square, looking for someone he could join without them asking what he had been doing. Why he was late. On one side, the livery remained open, renting vehicles like the brougham and offering free pony rides. Gerard's General Store also kept its doors open. Ned walked by without stopping to chat.

City Hall and the jail occupied the third side of the town square, leaving only the fourth side, where the church was located. Ned's boots scuffed the dirt, and he wondered if he could find Pastor Fairfield. He spotted Ruth wrestling with a water barrel near the church. She raised her hand in greeting. "Mr. Finnegan! So good to see you."

"Let me carry that for you." Ned grabbed the barrel from her. While he set it up next to the water pump outside the parsonage, he scanned the area for any sign of Birdie. The church seemed like the most logical place for her to seek sanctuary for Michal.

Ruth placed her hands on the pump. "It's clear something is bothering you. Can I help, or do you want me to get my father for you?"

He waited for water to splash into the barrel to cover their conversation.

"Over here." Birdie's gentle voice broke through the silence. She crouched at the back corner of the parsonage, waving them over. Ned saw no sign of the girl who had called to her.

The summons caused no change in Ruth's expression. She stopped pumping and headed for the kitchen door, and Ned followed.

"A friend of mine needs help," Birdie began without preamble when they reached her. "Since your parents helped me last time, I didn't think they would mind." She nodded at Ned. "Thank you for keeping that man away from us. We didn't know how we would get away."

Ruth opened the door, and Ned held it while the two women went inside. A pale-faced girl who looked young enough to still be in the classroom waited for them in the windowless pantry. Her tawdry dress and sad eyes told a different story.

Ned shut the door, and Ruth closed the curtains over the sink. "We're safe. No one can see inside."

The girl shuffled forward, her eyes on Ned.

"You don't have to worry about Mr. Finnegan. He's never been to that place." Birdie gestured Michal forward and held the chair for her at the table. "These are true friends, Michal."

Michal risked a glance at each of them before her eyes sought her lap again.

Ruth looked at Birdie, inviting an explanation.

"Michal met me outside of that place today." Birdie swallowed, as if finding it difficult to continue.

Ruth took over. "Are you involved in Birdie's former line of work?" How she asked such a question in quiet, even tones, escaped Ned. He wouldn't be able to put his mouth around it without sputtering.

The girl lifted her head at the question, looking at them with eyes as wide and blue as a newborn baby's. "Oh no, ma'am." Red slapped her face as she lowered it again. "At least not yet."

Birdie put her arm around Michal's shoulders, but she kept her gaze steady on the other two. "Up until tonight, that man has only asked Michal to sing." She patted her back. "She has the voice of an angel. But today he received a special request for someone new."

"And he said. . .he said"—the words seeped out from the cave Michal had made with her shoulders and head—"that tonight I would have to start earning my keep." At that she lifted her head. "I had to get away. I ran outside, not knowing where I could go, and then I saw Miss Birdie. . .and I knew I was meant to go to her."

"And I brought her here." Birdie leaned over, pulling Michal's head against her shoulder as the younger girl shook with unheard tears.

"And I'm so glad you did. First thing, let's get you over to the church. Even Mr. Owen respects the church as a sanctuary. Or the sheriff does. He refused to fetch Birdie, and he won't trouble Michal either." Suiting action to her words, Ruth draped a cape over Michal's shoulders before they hurried between buildings.

Birdie slipped her hand through the crook of Ned's elbow and smiled up at him as if they were like any other couple enjoying a quiet moment at the fair. They strolled through the front door of the church, which was left unlocked during the day in case someone came in need of solitude and spiritual refreshment.

As he and Birdie stepped into the cool darkness of the sanctuary, Ned's eyes needed a moment to adjust. The door to a back room, where mothers could retire with their infants during the service, stood open, and Ruth gestured them forward.

The furnishings of the room interested Ned. The presence of rocking chairs didn't surprise him, but he hadn't expected a mattress.

Birdie must have followed the direction of his surprised look. "When I first came to the church, Mrs. Fairfield brought me here. She told me that from time to time strangers in need of a quiet place to stay come to their door, and I was far from the first person to take advantage of their hospitality."

Ruth straightened from adding a blanket and pillow to the mattress. "I hate to leave you here, Michal, but if I stay away much longer, people may wonder what happened to me. I'll come back later, with my parents, if that's all right with you."

"I can't thank you enough," Michal said.

Ruth exited the church the same way she came in, through a back door. Birdie sat on a rocker. "I'd like to stay." She looked at Ned. "I'll go out with you, in case anyone saw us come in together. Then I'll return through the back door." She smiled at Michal. Fear fought with courage in the look the girl sent Ned's way.

"I'll leave you alone to get settled while I wait in the sanctuary." Ned took a seat at the front, leaning his elbows on his knees and folding his hands in prayer. God had led him deeper into Birdie's plans than he ever intended to go. His questions felt trapped by the roof, unable to make it to heaven. He reached in the hymn rack for a Bible and leafed through a few psalms, stopping at Psalm 27: "Wait on the LORD: be of good courage, and he shall strengthen thine heart; wait, I say, on the LORD."

He'd been waiting all summer, but God didn't say how long he had to wait. His human mind wanted a limit, but maybe waiting was like forgiving a man seventy times seven: no limits given. All right.

As he leaned forward to put the Bible back in place, the front door swept open, letting in a blinding ribbon of daylight and revealing a barrel-chested man.

Chapter 6

Owen's body cast a long shadow down the center aisle. "Finnegan." The oily tone of his voice made him sound suspicious. "What are you doing here by yourself?"

A hundred different responses ran through Ned's mind. He rose to his feet and dusted off his trousers in a habit picked up in cleaning his store. "Mr. Owen. I don't believe I've seen you in church before."

Owen scowled, and Ned clamped his mouth shut before he antagonized the man. "But of course you are welcome. I come in here from to time to have a quiet conversation with the Lord."

"Talking with God ain't what's on my mind." Owen rotated, taking in the side windows, the lectern, and piano up front. "Who plays the piano for your meetings?"

"Mrs. Fairfield is quite accomplished. We are blessed."

"Preacher's wife." Owen made it sound like a cursed profession as he walked down the aisle to the piano. "My Ruby's never played a church song in her life. She knows all the popular songs though. She only needs to hear it once and she can play it right away." He plunked on a single key. The note rang in crystal clarity in the almost-empty room, sounding an alarm as clearly as a bell steeple.

Owen glanced at the door to the left of the lectern and headed in that direction. Did the man intend to take a tour of the church?

"If you're looking for the preacher, he's at the fair. I spotted him on the square while I was coming here," Ned said.

"He's not the one I'm after. I'm looking for one of the mares from my stable."

Of all the euphemisms for the world's oldest profession, "stable" was one of the worst, implying that women were animals and not men's helpmates nor created in the image of God.

Ned's face must have reflected his distaste, because Owen laughed. "I know you don't take advantage of my girls, but I treat 'em good. One of them got her dander up, that's all. I'm going to talk her back, gentle-like." Cold, calculating blue eyes raked Ned from head to toe. "Maybe you seen her. A pretty little thing, bouncing brown curls and bright blue eyes, stands about yea tall?"

Even though Michal had looked anything but bright and bouncy, the description fit her well enough. What to do? Lie outright? Claim sanctuary?

The side door that led to the parsonage swung open, and Pastor Fairfield came in. "Mr. Owen, I saw you come in and wondered if you needed my help."

Owen's eyes narrowed. "The same as last time. I'm looking for one of my girls."

Genuine surprise appeared on the pastor's face. "Any one of them is welcome here, but none has come recently."

Ned kept his shoulders down, willing himself not to betray the two women only a few feet away from them.

"I repeat, the women are welcome to come and go here as they please. You have no business here. I must ask you to leave." In spite of the pastor's mild expression, his presence provided as solid a barrier to Owen's intrusion as any of the soldiers at the fair.

Owen took a step back. "I can't prove it. Not today." He planted his feet on the polished wooden floor. Pointing his finger the way a marksman would look down the scope of his rifle, first he singled out the pastor, then Ned. "Your preaching is interfering with a legitimate business. It can't continue. No sir. I won't stand for it."

"You're not fighting us, Mr. Owen. You're fighting God," Pastor Fairfield said.

Ned moved to the pastor's side, shoulder to shoulder at the forefront of the battle lines. He breathed in the pastor's bravery. "You must realize you can't win this battle. Go out the way you came in."

Owen shifted his gaze to Ned. "Your God may reign supreme here, but there's other times and places. You can't keep an eye on your store every minute of every day."

With that final volley, Owen turned on his heels and marched out the door, sunshine once again flooding the church as his back disappeared from view.

The pastor looked outside. "He's gone." Shutting the door, he walked slowly down the center aisle. "Now, tell me what's going on."

◆ ◆ ◆

Birdie listened to the confrontation between the men. Ruth had returned to warn them of Owen's approach. Once the saloon owner left, Birdie straightened from the frozen posture she had taken at the keyhole. "He's left."

"Praise the Lord," Ruth murmured. Releasing the arm that she had around Michal's shoulders, she gestured for Birdie to come over. "You stay here while I catch my father up on what's happening."

The two women traded places, and Ruth left. Birdie flashed back to the day she had arrived at the church, as scared as Michal was right now. She put an arm around the girl's shoulders and pulled her close. "You'll be all right." Later she would tell Michal how she had escaped, how faithful God was in providing for every need she had, how God had made her over anew. Right now Michal only wanted to avoid returning to the Betwixt 'n' Between before morning. "The Fairfields are good folks. You'll be safe as long as you're here."

Ned was guarding them. Birdie treasured that thought close to her heart. Pastor Fairfield had recently preached about the honor roll of Bible heroes. She would add Ned to the list—an ordinary man who did extraordinary things because they were the right things to do.

Ruth slipped into the room. "I hate to leave you again, but people are expecting to see me at the fair. If I don't go back, they might ask uncomfortable questions."

"I'll stay." Even as the words jumped out of Birdie's mouth, an unspoken disappointment tugged at her heart, guilt traipsing along behind. When Ned invited her to the fair, she had dared hope for something. . .more.

What kind of Christian was she? God had given her the very thing she longed for, the opportunity to help Michal escape before the worst happened, and here she was, thinking about her own hopeless desires.

Ruth looked at her with something approaching compassion in her eyes. "Then go out and talk with Mr. Finnegan before I leave. He's pacing like the caged bear I saw in Lincoln." She bent over and whispered in Birdie's ear. "God will bless your faithfulness."

Birdie delayed a moment, checking the folds of her dress before going into the church.

"Ned. . .Mr. Finnegan, I mean." The heat she had tamped down swept through her body.

"I like it when you call me Ned." An understanding smile tugged at his mouth. "You need to stay here with Miss Clanahan." Shifting his feet, he hesitated. "God is using you, Miss—"

"If I call you Ned, you should call me Birdie." Would he think she was too forward?

"Miss Birdie." His face broke into a wide smile. "Thank you for allowing me the privilege of using your given name." He leaned forward an inch before pulling back. "God has blessed your desire to help your friends. He has important things for you to do, much more important than anything I might want. With your permission, I will take you to dinner at the diner one night next week."

The disappointment in Birdie's heart melted away at his kind words. "I would like that. Thank you for understanding."

"I will stay as long as necessary, in case Owen returns."

At the door, Ned turned around as if to fill his eyes with her image before he waved a final good-bye. Nodding, Birdie withdrew into the bedroom.

◆　◆　◆

The promised dinner didn't happen for almost an entire week, but Birdie didn't mind. Michal spent a couple of days in the back room while Birdie worked day and night finishing her dress. Last night, after Michal had donned a hooded cape, Ruth had walked with her to Miss Kate's boardinghouse, as bold as peacocks. The sheriff kept a close eye on them, making sure no one bothered them, and the move happened without incident.

Half an hour remained until Ned would arrive. Michal turned one direction and another, studying her reflection in the mirror. "Oh Birdie, I've never had anything so fine."

"All I did was show on the outside the beautiful person you are inside—a beautiful, innocent girl forced to make her living the only way she could." Birdie circled Michal, studying her work critically. Did she need to add another button at the back neckline? No, she decided. Finishing the dress had taken all the money she'd saved from selling eggs to Ned, and she hadn't even started on the long johns. Every day she thanked God for providing a way for her dreams to come true.

"I'll start on the long johns tonight." Michal had proven as skilled with needle and thread as her voice was beautiful. At just the right time, God had given Birdie more work than she could do by herself.

"Thank you." Birdie spared a look at the mirror, wishing God had given her a different color hair. She had to cover it to walk anywhere without notice.

"Yoo-hoo, Miss Landry." One of Miss Kate's tenants called up the stairs. "Your young man is here."

"You'd better go." Michal threaded her needle and knotted the end. "I hope someone as nice as Mr. Finnegan courts me someday."

Courting? Something had given Michal the wrong impression, but Birdie wouldn't argue the point. "You will. God has just the right young man out there." Birdie spoke with an assurance she didn't feel, but for this young, unsullied girl, marriage was still a possibility. She tied a blue sunbonnet that matched the shade of flowers on her dress under her chin.

Ned waited at the bottom of the stairs. When the squeak of the top step announced her presence, he glanced up, joy shining in his eyes. "Birdie."

Birdie's tongue tangled. He had asked her to call him Ned, but that felt too informal.

Her stuttering tongue stumbled, and what came out was "Mister. . .Ne–Ninnegan." She covered her mouth, embarrassed at the mistake.

He laughed. "Just Ned. Please." He placed his foot on the bottom stair and reached for her. "Aunt Kate has promised us a perfectly cooked chicken dinner."

"And no one cooks chicken like Miss Kate." Birdie accepted his arm as he led her out the door, where the same carriage Mr. Keller had rented on the day of the fair waited for them.

"You rented the brougham?" Maybe he *was* courting her. Fear sent cold tentacles down Birdie's arms, and she was grateful for the long sleeves in spite of the warm summer twilight.

"Of course." Ned helped her onto the seat as if he rented a carriage every day. "I felt bad for making you face down your former place of employment last Saturday." He climbed beside her, and they started forward.

"That's all right. If God hadn't brought us there at that time, who knows what would have happened to Michal?"

"We'll have to trust God has no one else for you to rescue this evening."

Birdie spotted Haydn Keller walking Gladys home. Gladys's face beamed total happiness, inviting Ned and Birdie to join the party.

The brougham took all the space in front of the diner. When Ned handed Birdie down from the seat, she half expected a red carpet to spread out under her feet. Never had she ridden in anything so fine. A couple of curious faces glanced at them then turned away, and she breathed a sigh of relief.

Ned led her to a table at the side of the diner, where she could sit with her back to the rest of the room, looking out a window. Miss Kate bustled out of the kitchen, carrying her coffeepot. "Oh good, you're here. I've got some fresh chicken fried up just now, and some of my best shortcake biscuits. Thank you for sending me the extra eggs today, Mr. Finnegan. I used every one of them in making the custard. Dessert's on me." She winked and bustled back into the kitchen.

Eggs? Dessert on the house? Fiddling with the strings of her sunbonnet, Birdie glanced at the chalkboard where Miss Kate had listed the day's specials. *Custard dessert 25 cents*—almost the same amount he'd paid her for a dozen eggs only a few hours ago. She folded her bonnet and laid it beside her.

"Aunt Kate likes to tell everyone what to eat, doesn't she?" Ned brought the coffee cup to his lips, oblivious to the anger coursing through Birdie's body.

"You sold eggs to Miss Kate. *My* eggs."

Ned's mouth formed a perfect O. "She ran out this morning and asked if I had any left. It's happened a couple of other times."

"How much did you sell the eggs to her for?

Ned stared at the table instead of meeting her eyes. "Twenty cents a dozen."

"The same amount you pay me for eggs."

Ned's smile turned into a grimace, and he nodded his head.

Birdie wasn't sure who upset her more—Miss Kate, for buying eggs from Ned when Birdie would gladly have given her whatever she needed, or Ned, for charging the same amount to his customers that he paid her, not making any profit on their business exchange after all.

Miss Kate reappeared, chicken, mashed potatoes, and carrots steaming from two plates. She placed the first plate in front of Birdie with a flourish. Next she served Ned, but he didn't look at either one of them, his chin pushing against his chest. "Oh my. Let me pull up a chair."

No one disobeyed Miss Kate when she used that tone, and Birdie moved to her right. The cook plunked beside her and took both Birdie's and Ned's hands in her own. "You two young ninnies. You're not going to let any little thing keep you apart, are you?"

Chapter 7

Birdie's feet moved of their own volition, ready to take flight away from the mockery Ned and Miss Kate made of her efforts toward independence. Ned wrapped his intentions in a nicer package than Owen did, that was all. Like all the men she had ever known, he wanted to control her. What he and Aunt Kate didn't seem to realize was that if she accepted charity, if she depended on someone else, she would never know if she could make her own way. What if she were tossed out on the street again, forced to find work in another place like the Betwixt 'n' Between—or even worse? "I won't take charity."

The bell over the door jangled, and Miss Kate left to greet the new customer.

"I have to make my own way. Why can't anyone understand that?" Birdie glared at the butter melting on her plate. Should she be polite and eat the meal she now had no appetite for? Or could she simply walk out? She started to turn around to ask Miss Kate to wrap up her plate so the food wouldn't go to waste.

"Don't." Ned's voice dug barbs into her soul. "You don't want him to see you."

"Well, well, well. Look who's here, sitting as pretty as you please."

Owen. Birdie froze, the hair on the back of her neck standing on end. Why, oh why, had she agreed to come to the diner with Ned, as if she had the same right as anybody else to have a nice meal in a public place?

Silence fell across the diner, and a heavy tread crossed the wooden boards.

"Mr. Owen, why don't you sit over here?" Miss Kate did her best to divert his attention.

"Why, that isn't necessary. I'm sure there's room for me at Birdie's table."

Ned shot to his feet and blocked Owen's path to Birdie. "Miss Landry and I are enjoying a quiet meal. I suggest you do the same."

Birdie's nose wrinkled at the odor of stale sweat, whiskey, and cigar smoke that followed Owen like a miasma, and she choked as acid rose in her throat. She pressed the napkin to her mouth and willed herself not to turn around, but she couldn't stop herself.

Owen stood a little higher on his toes and peered at Birdie over Ned's shoulder. "I just want a conversation, real friendly-like, with the lady."

"She's with me." Ned's voice deepened until Birdie could hardly recognize it.

Neither man moved. Miss Kate went from table to table, refilling water glasses and topping off coffee cups. She spoke quietly to the customers, and slowly the chatter of conversation resumed. She squeezed behind the two men and whispered in Birdie's ear, "Eat. Don't let him rattle you."

Birdie didn't know how she could chew, let alone swallow the bite, but she knew Miss Kate was right. She dipped her spoon into fluffy mashed potatoes smothered in creamy gravy that would slide down her throat without effort.

Miss Kate stood by the table until Birdie took a few bites. Then, nodding approvingly, she faced the two men. "Mr. Owen, if you have no intention of eating here tonight, I must ask you to leave." For someone without a grouchy bone in her body, her voice bordered on angry.

With a single swift move, Owen ducked between Ned's slender frame and Miss Kate's more ample figure and came face-to-face with Birdie. "You can't hide from me forever, girl. I know you had something to do with Michal's disappearance, and you're gonna tell me where she is." Satisfied with his final volley, he swung in a circle and marched out the door.

The need for pretense gone, Birdie dropped her fork on her plate. She grabbed for the water glass to ease the dryness in her throat. A few customers sent surreptitious glances her way, but most kept their eyes on their plates or on each other.

Ned, her champion, sat, and the iron that had armed him gradually left. He brought a chicken leg to his mouth and crunched on the crispy coating. "I know you want to leave, and I don't blame you. But you should wait until that man goes back to whatever hole he slithered out of. And please, don't go anywhere alone for the next few days. He's angry and frustrated because you're winning skirmishes you and the Almighty have started. He wants to strike back."

As much as Birdie wanted to make her own way, she recognized the difference between self-reliance and foolishness. Nodding her agreement, she dug her knife and fork into the chicken thigh. The flavorful dark meat went agreeably down her throat, and the sweet custard pie made from the extra eggs slid down without effort. Ned ate more than she did, chasing the crumbs around his plate. Neither one of them spoke beyond "Pass the salt, please."

Birdie took advantage of the quiet to formulate a plan. While Ned cleaned his plate, she folded her napkin in her lap and made herself look at him. "I know you want to help. But I have to make my own way. If you respect me at all, I beg you, let me do business in the way I see fit."

Ned's mouth opened and shut before he shrugged his shoulders in resignation. "I'll give you eighteen cents a dozen, if that will make you happy."

"Five cents for four eggs, or a penny an egg for less than that." She pinned him with her eyes.

Squirming at first, again he nodded his head.

Birdie had kept an account of every egg she'd sold to Ned, and the number stuck in her head. She knew exactly how much she needed to reimburse him. She had spent most of the money already, on the fabrics and whatnots to make another dress for Michal, as well as fabric for another dress for Shannon, another woman ready to leave Owen's employ. How could she pay Ned back?

As Birdie tied her sunbonnet under her chin, she wondered at the futile gesture. Owen had recognized her on the street in spite of the hat. In any case, she couldn't have kept it on after she took her seat.

Once they made their way into the street, the setting sun continued beating on her head. Whistling softly, Ned used an alternate route to drive the brougham to the boardinghouse. When he acted like this, attuned to her inner feelings, protecting her, she could almost forget the things he wanted to do that threatened her independence. Part of her, more than she wanted to admit, hated to hurt him, to strain the relationship growing between them. Then she remembered the way his patronizing her had dimmed the shine from her new life. She couldn't afford to be that dependent on any man ever again.

They reached the boardinghouse before she worked up the courage to tell him her decision. The porch swing invited her to enjoy a few stolen minutes with Ned, but they would be vulnerable to watching eyes. Ned must have sensed her unease, because he guided her around the side of the house where beautyberry bushes hid them from passersby but kept them within sight of the house windows.

Ned dropped his hand from her elbow. "You're upset with me. I'm ready to listen."

Birdie took a deep breath. How could she explain her abhorrence of depending on a man when she couldn't quite explain it to herself? "This is something I have to do by myself. Not with your help or Miss Kate's. God's help, maybe." She allowed herself a small smile.

"But you yourself want to help your friends. We—I—care about you. You've come so far in the past year, all on your own. It's all right to accept a gift."

"I can't explain it." Birdie shook her head. "If I had the money to pay you back today, I would give it to you. But I spent it already, on the fabric I bought yesterday. I won't accept any payment for the long johns or the eggs until I pay you back."

◆　◆　◆

"It's not that much." *Weak, Ned, that's weak. Tell her you refuse payment of any kind.*

"I'll check my records to make sure of the amount." Her face relaxed a little bit. "But I've counted it over and over, every penny and nickel and dime."

Ned counted to ten. He could list any number of reasons, from spiritual to practical, to prove her wrong, but God's small voice told him to let it go. Staying silent was difficult when all he wanted to do was to take Birdie in his arms and beg her to let him help. "It's no hardship, you know. God has blessed my business." A previous discussion popped into his head. Following up on her suggestion could do no harm. "My business has picked up, and I could use a clerk to help me. Would you like the job?"

Before he finished voicing the question, color raced into Birdie's face and she backed up a step. "Not me. I'm busy sewing. But one of the girls is real good with numbers, and I think she's ready to leave. As soon as. . ." The same defeated expression he had seen on her face earlier returned.

"Would Miss Clanahan be interested?"

The expression on Birdie's face gave Ned her answer before she spoke. "She's shy, in spite of everything she's been exposed to. She's handy with a needle, though. She's already helping me with the long johns." A small smile lightened her face.

As long as the women lived with Aunt Kate, they wouldn't go hungry. Ned thanked the Lord for that much. "I will let you do this, Birdie. But don't you try to repay me one penny more than one cent apiece. You're not the only one who keeps records."

The window curtains twitched, reminding Ned of how long they had lingered outside talking. The sky had deepened to the dark blues of twilight. A single strand of red hair dangled across Birdie's forehead and cheek. His fingers itched to tuck it behind her ear, but before he could untangle his fisted hand, she found it and took care of it.

"Thank you for standing up to that man tonight." Birdie played with the strings of her sunbonnet, and he wished she would remove it and reveal her glorious hair. "I will see you in the morning, when I bring the eggs." A frown line creased the bridge of her nose. "The next time Miss Kate needs eggs, send her to me. Please. She should know she only has to ask."

Ned nodded in resignation. Even when he and Aunt Kate came up with the idea of her buying eggs from the store for the diner instead of asking Birdie for more, he had known this day would come. "I will."

"Until tomorrow, then." Walking away, she removed the bonnet from her head, and the final golden fingers of sunset set her head afire.

Miss Birdie Landry might not accept his money. But there had to be something more he could do to help.

God would show him the way.

Chapter 8

How's this one?" Ned held up an empty jar from the top shelf for Gladys's inspection. "Perfect." Gladys accepted it and tied a bow in a red-and-white check around the mouth of the jar. On the outside she pasted a sign drawn on fine drawing paper that simply said: Buttons. She giggled. "Birdie will never guess what you have in mind. And she can't complain about this." She gave the jar a prominent place between the cash register and a container of lemon drops on the front counter. "Between Aunt Kate, Mrs. Fairfield, and me, this jar will be full in no time at all."

"And the button count will be a real contest. Everyone will win." Ned climbed down from the ladder. "I hope people will want to help."

"Mr. Keller has enough money to make things happen. In fact, he wants to be the first contributor. I'll buy some buttons, and you can put any change into Birdie's account." She pulled a ten-dollar bill from her pocket and studied the array of buttons with the sewing notions. "I know she loves pearl-like buttons, but they're a little more expensive. So I'll get wooden buttons in all different sizes and shapes, as well as in all different colors."

As soon as Ned counted out the buttons, Gladys dropped them into the jar, where they hit the bottom with a *ping*. "You said you have some buttons at home that you wanted to add?"

Emptying his pockets, Ned dropped a dozen or so buttons of assorted colors into the jar. "If I find more, I'll add them."

Gladys tacked another sheet of drawing paper next to the jar.

Button Contest. Bring any buttons that you have at home and add them to the jar. On July 1st–3rd, guess the number of buttons in the jar. The winner will be announced during the Independence Day festivities. Grand prize: a bag of lemon drops and a yard of your favorite fabric

"I never would have thought of lemon drops." Ned popped one in his mouth.

"The children will be excited. They'll pester their mothers, who will remember the buttons. Mrs. Fairfield said they've done the same kind of thing at church. Get the children to come and the adults will follow."

Ned scratched his head. "Did it work?"

"It must have." Gladys shrugged. "She wouldn't have suggested it otherwise."

The bell rang, and the door swung open. "Oh, you have a customer." Birdie spoke so quietly that Ned could hardly hear her.

"It's just me, Birdie, come on in. I wanted to talk with you anyhow." Gladys winked at Ned. "You're just the right person to help with this campaign."

"What is that?" Birdie came to the front. "Fifteen eggs today."

She waited while Ned counted them. "Fifteen it is." He nodded at the button jar. "I'm asking folks to bring whatever extra buttons they have, ones that they find on the ground or that they took off a shirt after it wore out."

"There are some in here already." Birdie leaned over and studied the contents of the jar. "You're off to a good start. Let me check and see if I have any. If I do, I'll bring them with me tomorrow."

Behind Birdie, Gladys smothered a laugh. "So you want the lemon drops?" She let out her laugh this time.

"If I win, I'll give the candy to Ruth for her schoolchildren. And fabric always comes in handy." She tapped on the countertop. "I expect to have three pairs of long johns ready by Friday if anyone inquires after them."

"That's good." Ned nodded. "You're getting a lot done with Miss Clanahan's help."

That brought a smile to Birdie's face.

"God is already using you to accomplish the mission He called you to do. I'm happy for you," Ned said.

Birdie's smile dimmed. "I don't think there's enough sewing for more than the two of us. Girls leaving the life need so much—clothes, jobs, a home." She fixed her gaze at a point far away down the street, out to the farms lying east of town.

Gladys said with a smile, "I have an idea about finding jobs."

Birdie spun around. "What's your idea?" Turning to Ned, she said, "Gladys was the one who suggested the mission projects idea for our group. She's a bit of a dreamer."

Gladys laughed and hugged Birdie in a sisterly embrace. "I hope you approve of this new idea." She glanced at Ned for confirmation to speak, and he nodded. "Actually, this is Haydn's idea. Ned here needs help in the store a few hours a day." She lifted her hand and started counting on her fingers. "I'd like to stop working at the diner after I get married, so Aunt Kate will need help. Mrs. French just had twins; she could use an extra pair of hands. There are other people who are willing to pay a small salary for someone to help them out."

"But most people won't want to have a saloon girl helping them, will they?"

"We won't know if we don't ask. Pastor Fairfield is preaching about being salt and light in the world, so God is already preparing our hearts." Gladys bounced up and down in her excitement. "And Haydn would like to write articles about each girl."

Birdie shook her head sharply.

"Listen to her before you say no." Ned heard the pleading note in his voice. When she wouldn't accept his help, he had hoped she would accept a suggestion from one of the other circle members.

"Haydn will use aliases. He'd love to tell their stories, but that is up to each lady. And he won't describe them either, so no one will be able guess who is who."

"I don't understand. How does this help them find jobs?" Birdie hadn't run away yet. Ned took comfort in that.

"The focus of each article will be the life story of each woman, with perhaps a mention of the work they would like to do."

Birdie shook her head thoughtfully. "A lot of the girls are in that place because they don't think they have anything to offer. But maybe I could match the services needed and the girls' skills, since I know them."

"Yes!" Gladys clapped her hands.

"What if they don't want to speak with Mr. Keller?"

Birdie was weakening! Ned cheered internally.

"He would tell you what questions to ask, and you could tell him the girls' answers. We don't want to make anyone feel uncomfortable. Mrs. Fairfield will speak with the people needing help to make sure none of the women encounters another Nigel Owen."

Birdie shivered, and Ned touched her shoulder. When she didn't shrug his hand away, he left it there as he breathed a prayer. *Please say yes.*

"I'll ask them." Her smile highlighted light pink dimples in her cheeks. "You've put a lot of thought into this. Thank you."

◆ ◆ ◆

Birdie splashed cold water on her face to wake herself up and pulled her hair back in a simple bun. Michal had already donned her new dress and was running a brush through her hair.

They heard a knock, and Miss Kate spoke through the door. "May I come in?"

"Yes," Birdie said.

The doorknob turned, and savory aromas accompanied Miss Kate into the bedroom. She set a steaming bag on the bed. "Ham biscuits and sausage rolls. I made extra, so you can take them for the other girls to eat."

For her landlady's sake, Birdie would try to eat. If everyone in Calico had Miss Kate's kind heart, Birdie wouldn't have any doubts about their plans for helping the girls.

But then, if everyone in Calico had Miss Kate's kind heart, the Betwixt 'n' Between would have gone out of business years ago. A piece of advice Mrs. Fairfield gave Birdie jumped into her head: look at others with God's eyes. That was the only way she could find her way to forgive men like Owen, men who had used and abused her.

"God sure has His hand on you," Miss Kate said. "The way Shannon came to church on Sunday, after the night she must have had. And then you could ask her to invite everyone who wanted to, to come to the meeting this morning."

The very hour of the meeting—four in the morning—spoke to the desperate circumstances of the women. It was late enough for the saloon to have closed down and its employees to be settled in their beds. And it was early enough that the girls hoped to leave without attracting Owen's attention.

Michal was already eating a biscuit. "This is delicious, Miss Kate. The girls will enjoy your home-cooked food." She ate every bite as if she didn't know when she would receive another meal. Meals were a haphazard affair at the Betwixt 'n' Between, cold leftovers snatched whenever they had a moment. Some girls turned to drinking their meals. Ones with an alcohol problem, like Michal's best friend, Susanna, would face even greater challenges than Birdie had if they were able to escape their present circumstances.

"Your three friends are all waiting in the kitchen. I gave them a bite to eat. Come on down when you're ready." The door shut behind Miss Kate as she left. For a woman of ample proportions, she was able to move quickly and quietly.

Birdie tied her blue sunbonnet over her hair and helped Michal into her cloak. Michal was still fearful to leave the safety of the boardinghouse. She hugged the bag of sandwiches and rolls close to her chest under the cover of her cloak.

Birdie's bag held only one item: the dress she had been able to finish. Only a single dress. Two more dresses were done except for the finishing touches—buttons and lace, matching thread for some invisible seam work. So little to show for so much work. Since she was now paying double for room and board—even though Miss Kate protested against it—she needed longer than she'd hoped to finish paying Ned back.

Candles cast a soft light on Birdie's friends' faces. Ruth hugged Michal as if they were longtime friends and introduced her to Annie and Gladys. Michal glanced up briefly from underneath the cover of her hood. "Glad to meet you."

"We are honored that you let us come." Annie's smile invited the world to join in. "Between the four of us, we hope we can address any concerns the ladies have."

Ruth gathered their dishes and put them in the sink. "Let's leave so we can be there when the others arrive. My mother is already at the church, ready to greet any early comers."

Her friends' kindness brought warmth to Birdie's heart but did little to ward off the chill of the early morning. She was grateful for the shawl draped around her shoulders. They walked in silence, Ruth, Gladys, and Annie surrounding Birdie and Michal, until they turned in the direction of the church side of the town square. A small light testified that someone in the parsonage was awake. "Papa said he would pray for us during our meeting," Ruth said.

So many people had helped to make this happen. Besides the sewing circle, Miss Kate, Pastor and Mrs. Fairfield, and Lieutenant Arnold had participated.

Ned. Birdie refused to think about him right now. One by one the women slipped into the side door of the church. Mrs. Fairfield rose from her seat on the front pew, embraced Birdie, and turned to Michal. "And you must be Michal. A shiny new jewel in the crown of our Lord. Please know how welcome you are here in our midst."

Michal colored, and Birdie remembered how uncomfortable Mrs. Fairfield's outspokenness had made her at first.

"And what is that I smell? Breakfast from Aunt Kate?"

"Ham biscuits and sausage rolls." Michal handed them to the pastor's wife.

"Excellent! I brought over a pot of coffee and some biscuits, but Aunt Kate's food is such a delight. Now, come this way. The room will be slightly crowded, but no one can see us in there." Mrs. Fairfield opened the door to the same room where Birdie and Michal had first taken refuge. "I'll stay out here in case anyone comes along later."

Birdie took the lead, entering the room first. One step inside transported her back to the Betwixt 'n' Between. Unwashed bodies, cloying floral scents, whiskey, cigar smoke—all of those smells and more, with girls in varying degrees of undress. She shut her eyes and stopped just short of pinching her nose, long enough for the unpleasant memories to diminish. Once again she repeated those beautiful words about God's love to herself. *For I am persuaded, that neither. . .things present, nor things to come. . .shall be able to separate us from the love of God, which is in Christ Jesus our Lord.* Mrs. Fairfield had added "nor things in the past." God wouldn't hold her past against her after she asked Him to forgive her. Something about her sins being buried in the deepest seas. She lifted her head high in the love of her Savior and prepared to meet the women He had called her to help.

Chapter 9

A handful of women crowded next to each other on the far bench. Naomi. Orpah. Both names, Ruth had told her, came from the book of Ruth in the Bible. Shannon, who was ready to leave today. Susanna, a Southern belle pushed west by the Civil War and its aftermath. She had taken Birdie under her wing, protected her as much as she could, and comforted her after customers got too rough. Michal had told Birdie that Susanna had also taken the blows dished out by Owen when Birdie ran away. Tears at the memories burned Birdie's eyes, and all her earlier fears fled, replaced by a courage unknown to her.

She glanced at the second bench, left free for the church ladies. She turned her back on the empty bench and laid a gentle hand on Susanna's shoulder. "Do you mind if I sit here?"

Eyes blurry from a night of excess peered at the sunbonnet on Birdie's head. "Birdie, 'sthat you?"

Here, in this room, Birdie had no need to hide herself. She removed the bonnet and shook her hair around her shoulders. "It's me, Susanna."

"I always did say your hair was like the sunrise." Susanna lifted a tentative hand, and Birdie leaned forward, letting her friend run fingers through her hair. "All that color without help from the henna bottle. You'se a lady now."

With those words, the women around Birdie shrank back. She reached as far as she could in both directions, until she touched each woman. "I'm no more or less a lady than ever I was. What has changed is that God has made me new. I'm a new creation. Nothing from the past can hold me back."

"That's all good and fine for you, Birdie. But nothing's gonna change for a gal like me." Naomi shook her head, even though a hopeful light beamed from almost black eyes, her dusky coloring and dark features suggesting Indian blood.

Love flooded Birdie's heart, mixed with a desire for these women to accept the good news of Jesus as shown by the people of Calico. "God's love is for anyone, anytime, anywhere. The Good Book says we were still Jesus' enemies when He died for us. One of His best ladies was a prostitute once upon a time. He loves us, all of us."

Michal handed out Miss Kate's breakfast. Before long, a knock at the door interrupted her, and Mrs. Fairfield came in. Birdie introduced her two sets of friends to one another.

Shannon sank against the wall. It was almost time to go back.

Another time Birdie would tell more of the old, old story. Right now these women needed an escape plan. "This is what we have in mind. Miss Fairfield and Miss Polson came up with a plan to help you find work if you decide you're ready to leave the Betwixt 'n' Between. I'll let Miss Polson explain."

The women listened with interest until Gladys mentioned the interviews that Haydn wanted to conduct. "A man interviewing me? How do I know he's not fixing to run and tell Owen all about our plans?" Orpah's lips made a thin line.

Birdie met Orpah's glare. "If you don't want to speak with Mr. Keller, you can talk with me. We won't give out your names or anything else you want to keep personal."

Orpah frowned but didn't say anything further. Naomi voiced her objections. "I don't have any clothes I can wear in normal society. I can't wear something like this." She gestured to the dress she had arrived at the saloon in, only a couple of months after Birdie. The hem rose higher on her ankle than was considered proper, and the cloth strained across her chest. The clothes the others wore were in even worse condition.

Birdie hastened to reassure her. "I'm working on dresses for you so you have something decent to wear about town." The single dress in her bag seemed so small in comparison to the need. "I only have one ready now, but I hope to have more ready soon." As soon as she could buy buttons, bric-a-brac, all those finishing details.

"You always wuz right handy with a needle and thread," Susanna said.

"So can we all leave right now?" Naomi asked. "Or do we have to leave one at a time? Owen might take it out on whoever's left behind." Her voice wobbled, but her gaze remained focused on Birdie.

Fear and joy fought within Birdie's racing heart. This was what she wanted—wasn't it?—but whatever would they do with four women all at once? Five, if they counted Michal.

Be not afraid. Birdie took in God's promise along with Mrs. Fairfield's nod. "Anyone who is ready to leave right now can stay here at the church until we find places for you all to go." Miss Kate had said to bring anybody along to the boardinghouse who wanted to come, but she didn't know if even that indomitable lady could handle four strangers all at once. "You can stay here in privacy, and there's plenty of good food to eat."

Orpah stopped chewing on her sausage roll and nodded in appreciation.

"It will be one of us who brings your food and helps you get away to a safe place." Annie handed the bag of rolls around again.

"We'll get some menfolk to keep watch. The sheriff's a good man, and so is my fiancé, Haydn Keller." A smile of unbridled joy shone in Gladys's eyes. "And Annie's lieutenant and Pastor Fairfield. And Ned Finnegan."

"I'll introduce them to you so you won't get scared when they come around." Mrs. Fairfield crossed the room in a few steps and stood in front of Susanna and took her hand. "I'm the pastor's wife, Hannah Fairfield. I'm pleased to meet you, Susanna." Mrs. Fairfield didn't seem to notice the torn fingernails or the reek of whiskey coming from Susanna's clothes. She went down the line, greeting each woman by name. "The parsonage is right next door, straight out the side door. If something happens that worries you, day or night, come right over and tell us about it." She offered a cloak and bonnet she had draped across her arm to Naomi. "This is yours if you'd feel better about wearing it when it's time for you to come. I know it's hot in here, but you should be out of here in a day or two."

"What if Owen comes looking for us? He's already breathing fire after losing Birdie and his songbird." Naomi spoke as if Owen's violence was a fact of life. For her, it was.

"He'll have to get past a whole host of angels—human and heavenly—to get to you. And the church is a sanctuary even Owen won't violate." As she pressed each of their hands, Birdie saw courage rising in each woman's heart. "But we'd best leave for now, before someone has reason to question what all of us are doing at the church at this hour. Gladys, Michal, why don't you head out first?"

Birdie gathered her hair into a knot at the back of her neck and tied her sunbonnet on before draping her shawl across her shoulders. "I have one more dress that is almost finished.

I'll bring it over as soon as I get the buttons." How she wished she could finish the other dresses more quickly.

She opened the door and slipped out after Gladys and Michal. A familiar figure waited at the front door. Ahead of her, Michal drew back, and Birdie touched her arm. "Don't worry. That's Mr. Finnegan."

◆　◆　◆

At the sound of female voices, Ned squinted into the early-morning sun pouring in the east-facing windows. *Birdie.* He hustled down the center aisle and met her halfway. "I thought I'd better come in case Owen figured out what was happening and tried to bother you."

Dependable. Kind. Brave. Any number of words could describe Ned Finnegan, even if the gun in his arm looked as out of place as a storekeeper's apron on a soldier. "Thank you, Ned."

The door opened, and Haydn scurried in. "Is everything all right?"

At Haydn's appearance, Michal drew back. Birdie said, "This is Mr. Keller, Gladys's intended. He's a good man."

Ned nodded at Birdie. "I'll walk you and Miss Clanahan home while Haydn escorts Miss Polson and Miss Bliss."

"Let's get moving, then, before it gets any later." But before Birdie could continue down the aisle, the front door opened and the preacher stood on the threshold. "He's on his way with his men."

Chapter 10

Pastor Fairfield didn't have to explain who he meant.

"I'll go get the sheriff." Haydn raced to the side door.

"Get back." Ned urged the women to safety.

Not quite steady on his feet, Owen pushed past the pastor, his men close behind. The gun he held was all the more dangerous in the hands of a drunken man.

"They're here. You can't tell me they're not. There's three of them right there, although what they're doing in church is a pretty story. Maybe your man of the cloth here isn't all you expect him to be."

"Why, you." Birdie spoke from behind Ned. She hadn't retreated to the room after all.

"Get down." Ned fought to keep fear out of his tone.

"I'll get 'er back sooner or later, but she ain't my concern this morning. Imagine my surprise when I headed downstairs for a pick-me-up, to find my faithful Susanna missing. Checked the cribs upstairs, and there's four gone, new this morning gone." Owen hurtled himself forward, almost falling down, righting himself when he grasped the back pew. "Bring 'em out nice and peaceable, and we won't have any argument between us."

"Over my dead body." Ned's voice rang out loud and clear. He might be a shopkeeper, but he had learned how to shoot on the farm as a boy.

"Nigel Owen!" Pastor Fairfield used a deep voice that could have scared the devil himself out of hell. "I have told you before. You have no business here. This is God's house."

Ned darted a glance at the pastor. Dressed in a pair of pants held up by suspenders, and with nothing more than a Bible in his hands, he still radiated unmistakable authority, the general of this spiritual fortress.

"Well, Pastor, so you keep saying. But you're interfering with a legitimate business. Those women signed contracts to work at the Betwixt 'n' Between. They have to come back."

Behind him, Ned heard Birdie grunt. She had told him about the marks the girls made on those contracts when they were too drunk to know what they were doing.

The side door opened and Sheriff Carter strode in. "Not unless I say so." He also trained his rifle on Owen. "In fact, I hear tell the town council is ready to put the vote to make Calico dry on the next ballot. If you know what's best for you, you'll skedaddle out of town before you lose your shirt altogether."

Owen stumbled forward a step, discharging his weapon as he flopped about. It hit a rafter high above him.

Ned's finger pressed on the trigger, and the bullet hit Owen right where he aimed it—at his right shoulder, to wing him, not to kill. Owen slumped on the floor and howled. "I wasn't shooting at you!" He screamed curses.

Sheriff Carter ran down the side aisle, keeping his rifle ready to shoot if necessary. He kicked Owen's gun away and handcuffed his hands together. "Tell it to the judge—after we all tell him how you started a gunfight in this house of worship. That'll be right after we get a doctor to fix you up." Dragging Owen to his feet, he paused by the door. "The rest of you better leave before I find a reason to drag you along with your boss."

"They all follow his lead." Birdie came up beside Ned as the men filed out the front door. "None of them has enough courage to come after us here without him. We're free." She pulled the sunbonnet from her head. "We're finally free. How perfect, to celebrate our personal freedom on the Fourth of July."

As the sheriff escorted Owen out of the church, Haydn headed for the back room and Ned crossed the front to the pastor. "I'm sorry for the gunfire, pastor."

"Don't worry. You were protecting what is most important to you except for the Lord Himself." He smiled at Birdie. "I'll join the ladies in the room."

Ned pulled Birdie close to him, closer than he ever had before, and she settled comfortably against his chest. He breathed in the floral scent of her brilliant hair. He could face a hundred lions for this woman.

Michal coughed, reminding him that although Ned had so much to tell Birdie, now was neither the time nor the place. He relaxed his hold on Birdie, and she took one hesitant step backward. "I need to get back to Miss Kate's. To let her know about her company coming." Even as she spoke, her eyes studied his features one by one, as if memorizing them.

◆ ◆ ◆

"You'll see me later today. I promise." A tenderness Birdie couldn't believe possible shone from Ned's eyes as he smiled down at her.

"Of course. When I bring you the eggs." Dropping her eyes, she stepped past Ned on her way to the door.

"And when I announce the winner of the button jar contest."

Birdie's laughter rang as she and Michal headed for the door. "I plan on being there."

"If you don't come, I'll come down and get you myself." She laughed again. "But now I'll walk you home."

Later that morning, Michal had no interest in the button drawing. "It's too soon for me, Birdie. But you go, with your Mr. Finnegan. Enjoy yourself."

Birdie walked down Main Street, striding confidently past the Betwixt 'n' Between. A good-sized crowd had gathered in front of Ned's store. He should be pleased.

Ned noticed her approach and motioned her forward. For some reason, he began to clap. Soon everyone joined in.

Birdie stopped in midstep. They couldn't be clapping for her—could they? Ned motioned again for her to join him in front of the store. "Now we can get started."

Light laughter rippled across the crowd.

"First I'll announce the winner of the counting contest. The person who will be leaving here with all the lemon drops she can eat, as well as a length of my prettiest calico, is the sheriff's wife, Enid Carter."

A young boy ran ahead and reached Ned first. "I'll take the lemon drops, please."

"That is up to your mother." Ned tossed a single lemon drop to the child, who caught it in midair.

"Thank you, Mr. Finnegan. For everything." Mrs. Carter walked back to her husband amid generous applause.

"And now. . .for the most important part of the day." Ned reached behind him and lifted the nearly full jar of buttons over his head. "Who gets to keep all these buttons that I've collected?"

Voices called from all over the crowd. "Miss Landry." "Miss Birdie." A few small children began chanting "Miss Landry" until everyone joined in.

Birdie looked at Ned, not understanding what was happening.

He handed her the jar of buttons. "Here is a gift from the people of Calico, to you. All of the buttons you'll need for a lot of dresses, as well as a sizable credit to your account for any other supplies you need, from concerned citizens."

The din of applause and hurrahs gave Ned and Birdie a cocoon of privacy. She found a tag attached to a red-and-white gingham bow around the top of the jar. She unfolded it and read the single sentence twice before looking at Ned.

"You don't think I'd let a few buttons come between me and the woman I love, do you?" Ned's grin was as spectacular as fireworks on the Fourth of July. "So. Will you marry me?"

All the defenses Birdie had built against a man's love crumbled. "Yes." Her answer was both a capitulation and an exultation.

Ned claimed Birdie's lips.

The crowd cheered even louder, their approval touching Birdie's heart like the ping of a button hitting the bottom of the jar.

Bestselling author **DARLENE FRANKLIN**'s greatest claim to fame is that she writes full-time from a nursing home. She lives in Oklahoma, near her son and his family, and continues her interests in playing the piano and singing, books, good fellowship, and reality TV in addition to writing. She is an active member of Oklahoma City Christian Fiction Writers, American Christian Fiction Writers, and the Christian Authors Network. She has written over fifty books and more than 250 devotionals. Her historical fiction ranges from the Revolutionary War to World War II, from Texas to Vermont. You can find Darlene online at www.darlenefranklinwrites.com

Dreamlight

by Janet Spaeth

Dedication

For Paulette Dvorak, with my love

"O thou of little faith, wherefore didst thou doubt?"

Matthew 14:31 KJV

Chapter 1

T he first rays of daylight stole across the garden as Francie Woods slipped through the thick green bushes that surrounded the foliaged area. She lifted her dark green skirt to an unmaidenly midcalf height and silently hurried on bare feet down the stone-tiled path.

The garden had been her favorite place since she'd first arrived on Mackinac Island one week before. Somehow God seemed closer there—and her stories and drawings came easier in the midst of the garden.

Near the center of the garden, morning glories coiled up a white-painted, slatted bower. The garden was an eclectic mixture of native plants and those that had come with her aunt, carefully uprooted from the Detroit home, packed with tenderness for their journey, and replanted here on Mackinac Island. This plot with its curving walkways and granite fountain was Aunt Dorothea's pride and joy on the island.

Francie dropped to a crouch and flipped open her sketchbook. Through the soft light of dawn, the sketches of yesterday's pansies, their faces remarkably humanlike, seemed to come alive.

But that wasn't what interested her now. She turned to an unmarked page but didn't write. Instead, she balanced in her stooped position, intently watching the morning glories.

Finally the magical moment began. The white flowers unfolded as the sun brightened, until, at last, they were totally opened.

Francie's fingers flew across the page, recording the process. Later, after she'd had her breakfast, she would visit with the family for a while before her morning walk to the shore. Right now, though, her attention was on the drawing before her.

The sun rose into its full radiance, and in the background, the muffled sounds of the island coming awake drifted to her. Inside Sea Breeze, the summer home of her aunt and uncle, she could hear the strains of "A Mighty Fortress Is Our God" hummed in Middle Meg's strong alto.

"Francie! Francine Woods!" Cousin Marie's voice rang out from the back porch. "Breakfast is ready, and Grandmama Christiana will have your head if you're late!"

Francie added a few quick lines to her picture and stood. "Coming!"

She hurried into the house and slid into her chair at the table, tucking her sketchbook under her and self-consciously patting her hair to make sure she wasn't any more disheveled than usual. It was a battle she fought daily—and generally lost.

Middle Meg, whose song had ended, winked at her as she poured tea in the delicate blue and white china cup at Francie's place, and Francie knew that the maid was aware of her time in the garden.

The first night there, Aunt Dorothea had explained Middle Meg's name. There were three generations of servants in the family, and all the women were named Margaret but called Meg. Old Meg and Young Meg were still in Detroit, tending to the main house and Uncle Leonard, who came to Mackinac Island whenever his banking business would let him. Middle Meg, her ruddy face always wreathed in a smile, took capable care of all of the others on the island.

"What are your plans for the day?" Aunt Dorothea asked Marie as she stirred her tea.

"Plans?" Marie laughed. "Francie and I will go for our morning walk."

Grandmama Christiana snorted. "You're probably going over to that nasty pit. I tell you, in my day, nice girls didn't stand around watching men at work. That's trouble looking right back at you, and don't say I didn't warn you."

Aunt Dorothea reached across the table and patted the elderly woman's hand. "Now, now, I'm sure that Marie and Francine will conduct themselves like the ladies they are, won't you, girls?"

"Yes, ma'am," they chorused, but as Marie looked at Francie, she rolled her eyes.

"You know the Grand Hotel is going to open in a month, so it's hardly a pit, not any longer," Marie declared. "It's extraordinarily large and very elegant."

Grandmama Christiana merely sniffed in response.

"Will you be stopping at the Carltons' house for your embroidery lesson?" Aunt Dorothea asked. "It's so nice of Annabelle to share her talents with you."

Grandmama Christiana nodded knowingly and turned her piercing dark gaze on Marie. "Embroidery is a lady's art, and you're wise to learn it. Now, that's the way a young woman should spend her time, not gallivanting around."

Francie nearly choked on her toast as Marie looked down and rolled her eyes surreptitiously.

"Yes, Grandmama Christiana," Marie said with an artificial meekness, and Aunt Dorothea adeptly steered the conversation to a safer discussion of daylilies.

Marie caught Francie's attention with a subtle wave of her napkin, and soon the two were out of the house and walking along the dusty path.

"I can't help it if the road to the Carltons' cottage goes right past where the Grand Hotel is being built, now can I?" Marie winked at her.

Francie smiled. The shortest route to the Carltons' home did, in fact, *not* go past the construction area, but she didn't say so.

Marie batted at a low-hanging branch. "I love Grandmama Christiana, but she came from another century. If she had her way, I'd be wrapped head to toe in black crepe."

This was a time to keep silent, Francie knew. The elderly woman was outspoken and crusty, but the twinkle in her eyes that were as black as polished onyx told Francie that she was probably not as cantankerous as she appeared.

Her cousin's steps slowed. "Is it terrible, having your parents gone so much? I know you've been in a boarding school, and now you're here and they're in South America." Her porcelain brow furrowed.

Francie had answered this question so many times that the response was practiced. "Yes, it's difficult, but they're doing God's work."

"I can't imagine being a missionary," Marie said. "You'd live in the worst conditions. There wouldn't be any stores, really, and I suspect the food is dreadful."

"It's not that bad. I went with my parents for a while. Some of the houses we lived in would seem primitive to you, I suppose, but in many parts of the world, Sea Breeze would be the home of several families. And the shops. . .the food. . . We spent time in China, and the stores and the food were exotic and tremendous. Every place has a unique beauty, given by the Master Artist."

She'd had similar conversations before, and each time, it drove home how different her life had been from most American girls and how it had made her find ways to amuse herself. Fortunately she'd discovered her vivid imagination and an artistic talent that might have otherwise gone untapped.

"Not having your parents around must seem strange."

"Not to me," Francie answered. "I'm used to it. I'd probably find it strange if they were suddenly around me—just as odd as you'd find it if your parents left to travel the world."

Marie shrugged. "Possibly." Then she laughed lightly. "Papa is so rarely here on the island, and when we're in Detroit, he's always off to some business or social matter. At times, it seems like he might as well be in Spain."

Francie didn't answer. There was no way to explain it, the longing that ate at her while her parents were gone. Of course they were in God's hands, doing His work, and she wouldn't begrudge them that. There were times, though, when she wished they would swoop in and carry her away and the three of them could spend time just walking and talking and being together.

But Marie was on to another subject. "So, at this boarding school you went to, did you get to see any fellows? At Miss Helena's, which was the day school I attended in Detroit, every Friday we had what she called 'Cotillion,' when we met with students from Briarhurst, the men's school. We had to make 'polite conversation.'" Marie stretched out the words in a terrible French accent and snorted in a totally unladylike manner. "Miss Helena was French when she wanted to be, but rumor had it that she came from Des Moines."

"We didn't have anything like that," Francie answered, with the unspoken addition of *fortunately*. Making "polite conversation" sounded dreadful. "We were kept quite sequestered."

"I don't believe I would care for that at all," Marie answered vaguely. Her interest seemed to have been diverted by the hive of activity where the hotel was being built.

As her cousin's steps slowed, Francie took the opportunity to lean over and study a cluster of trillium. The three petals of the lovely white flower rising from the three glossy green leaves were, her mother had once told her, a reminder of God's love for His people and what He expected them to do. Not only Father, Son, and Holy Ghost, she'd said, but Faith, Hope, and Charity.

The trillium was a beautiful flower and one of the first of the year to bloom.

"You and your flowers." Marie sighed, but there was no rancor in her words. "I'd rather look at—"

Her sentence was interrupted as a horse drawing a wagon clip-clopped along the path.

"Miss Harris!" The driver of the vehicle pulled back on the reins, and the horse stopped. "You're out early this fine summer morning."

Francie didn't move out of the shadow but instead watched Marie. The sideways tilt to her head and the faint smile on her cousin's face told her that this wasn't the first time the two had met on this road, and Marie's next words confirmed it.

"No earlier than usual, as you might know. A walk clears the mind and prepares it for the day ahead." Francie watched with a growing fascination as Marie overtly flirted with the man in the cart. "You should try it sometime."

Instead of being offended, the driver smiled broadly and laughed. "Yes, Princess Marie,

I shall do just that." And with a snappy salute, he clicked the reins smartly, and the wagon left them.

"Princess Marie?" Francie asked as he drove away. "Who was that man?"

Marie turned to her, a blush climbing her neck. "Just one of the workmen here who thinks he's being charming when in fact he's being overly fresh."

"You should report him to his supervisor," Francie said.

Marie, though, shook her head and laughed, a lovely sound that reminded Francie of a wind chime. "Francie, dear, if I reported every man who spoke to me, the hotel would never be built, and I'd have that on my conscience until the end of time."

"I don't know. . ." Francie began. "Maybe we should take another road to go to the Carltons' to avoid them then."

"Oh, you goose, I'm just teasing you. That fellow was harmless. I've seen him several times already, and he's simply being friendly." Her cousin touched Francie's arm. "But please don't mention this to Grandmama Christiana. She'd forbid both of us to leave the house, and we'd have to spend the entire summer stuffed inside that airless parlor, fanning ourselves and making 'polite conversation.'"

Just the week she'd been there had been long enough for Francie to recognize the truth in Marie's words. She could imagine the elderly woman's reaction when she learned Marie had been speaking with a workman. In all likelihood, the two young women would spend the rest of the summer inside Sea Breeze, safe from the advances of brash fellows.

"Anyway," Marie continued, leading her down the hill to the main street, "I want to stop in at the shops on our way to the Carltons' house. I'd like to get some fudge to take to Mrs. Carlton as a thank-you for teaching me to embroider. I'm really enjoying it—"

Francie listened to her cousin's chatter with only half her attention. She'd adored Marie since they'd been children playing together during summers at their grandparents' farm in southern Michigan. Marie, with her ebony hair and flashing dark eyes, was three years older than Francie, and her sophistication was appealing, even to a small girl. Now the distinction was more marked, but Marie was still as kind to the young admirer as she had been when Francie was six.

"Don't look now," Marie whispered, "but we're being followed."

Francie snapped back to attention. "We are? By whom? Is it that fellow in the cart?" Something cold and wet pushed into Francie's hand. "What on earth? Oh, will you look at this!"

A large yellow dog had joined them and was now happily investigating the smells of Francie's clothing. "To whom does he belong?" she asked Marie.

"He has the run of the island, but he's not the best-mannered creature," her cousin answered. "His name is Emerson, and he belongs at the carriage stables."

"He'll likely find his way back home when we get to the shops," Francie said, patting the dog's furry head. "But in the meantime, you're welcome to walk with us, Emerson."

The line of shops was like a wonderland on this early summer morning, and Emerson deserted them to investigate the activities. Shopkeepers called to each other as they opened their doors and shined windows and swept out the thresholds of the stores.

A lovely aroma drifted out into the street, and Francie melted. There was only one thing in the world that smelled as exquisite as that. *Chocolate.* It was her weakness, the one temptation that struck her deeply.

Marie pulled her into the source of the lovely smell. "This fudge is incredible."

The scent inside the store was even more extraordinary. Rich chocolate and cream mingled with butter into a luscious blend that tantalized her taste buds. Marie popped a sample into Francie's mouth. "Well, what do you think?"

"Mmm." There weren't words to describe the flavor of the fudge, and she didn't try. "Mmm."

Marie purchased two slices of the fudge, one for Mrs. Carlton and one to bring home. "Mama has a weakness for Mackinac Island fudge." Her dark eyes twinkled. "Although, to tell the truth, Grandmama Christiana is the one who's most fond of it, although she'll never admit it."

They strolled back onto the street, admiring the window displays until Marie's steps slowed.

"Let's go in here," she urged. "Come on!"

The beautiful scent of chocolate was replaced by leather and oil and metal. Francie voiced her objection immediately. "Certainly you don't need anything from here, unless you need to get new snowshoes!" She pointed to the woven snowshoes hanging on the wall.

"No, silly, I want you to meet someone. Thomas! Thomas!" She motioned to a young man in the back of the room. "You can't hide back there. I saw you come in here."

The man came toward them, a frown wrinkling his forehead over his small glasses. "Miss Harris, I can assure you that I was not hiding. I was obtaining a packet of nails to mend a wayward board in my study." He opened his hand as if to prove his words.

"Thomas, this is my cousin, Francine Woods. She's spending the summer with us. Be nice to her."

His gasp was audible. "Be nice! Why—!" He sputtered wordlessly.

Francie bit her lip to keep from laughing. If only he wouldn't react so strongly to Marie's teasing, he'd have an equal hand here.

He looked like a pleasant-enough fellow. His hair was a mass of sandy brown curls that looked as if he ran his fingers through it in exasperation several times a day, and his complexion was clear and a bit sunburned.

"Francie," Marie said, "this is Thomas Carlton. You'll probably see him quite a bit on the island. He's Annabelle Carlton's son."

"I'm delighted to meet you," Francie said, feeling a dreaded flush creep up her neck as he turned toward her with vague surprise, as if he'd forgotten she was there. His tawny eyes studied her briefly.

"You're Marie's cousin, are you? You don't look like her."

Heavy silence hung in the air, and Francie knew that she was getting even redder. It was true that Marie's exotic black hair and dark eyes often overwhelmed Francie's light brown hair and blue eyes, but lingering in the reflected brightness of Marie's beauty had always been enough.

Marie's easy laugh broke the awkward moment. "Fortunately for her, I'd say, she doesn't look anything like me. Now be a good fellow and say hello to Francie."

Something that could have been a smile twitched his lips, and he laid the nails on the counter. Taking her hand, he bowed slightly. "My pleasure, Miss Woods. I hope I'll have the honor of meeting you again."

With those words, he turned and walked out of the store, his handful of nails still on the polished wooden surface. Through the window, they saw the big yellow dog trot after him for a way before coming back to flop in front of the fudge store.

"Thomas seems nice," Francie commented. She motioned toward his intended purchase, still on the counter. "Though a bit forgetful, it seems."

"He's just come from school," her cousin told her as they trailed out of the store. "I suspect his mind is still in his books."

"There could be worse places, I suppose, to have one's mind than in books." As much as she enjoyed the morning walks with Marie, she was anxious to return to the garden, where the morning dew was drying on the flowers' faces.

"Look!" Marie pointed toward the end of the road. "He'll think we're following him, but I have an embroidery lesson with his mother in a few minutes. If we walk quickly, we can catch up with him. Thomas! Wait!"

The morning was already warming quickly, and droplets of sweat beaded Francie's face. A tendril of her rather carelessly caught-up bun had escaped and trailed down her neck.

This certainly wasn't the first impression she wanted to make.

"We're going to your house," Marie panted, a bit out of breath from rushing after him.

"Oh! Mother is teaching both of you?"

"No," Francie said. "Just Marie. I'm actually going back to Sea Breeze."

"Not a needlewoman, I take it?"

"I can sew a competent seam, but beyond that, I'm all thumbs." Why did he stare at her so intently? She tucked the wayward strand of hair back into place self-consciously, and it immediately fell back down.

"When is your father coming to the island?" Marie asked, with a sideways, amused glance at them both.

"He might be here tomorrow," Thomas answered. "He's a minister, supposedly retired because of his health, but you would never know it from his schedule. In the summer, especially, he fills in at various churches in need. He's in Lansing now."

"I'm sure you'll be glad to have him back home," Francie said. "I know how much you must miss him when he's away."

"Francie's parents are missionaries," Marie explained quietly. "They're in Brazil right now and won't be back until November."

"Missionaries? Really?" He leaned in a bit closer. He smelled like soap and freshly washed cotton. "Our lives are a bit parallel, aren't they?"

She paused and nodded. "We both have parents who have given their lives to serving the Lord."

"And do you?" His words were but a breath. "Do you give your life to serving your Lord?"

"I do." She spoke resolutely. "Perhaps not as a missionary but I do my best to live my life as God intends me to."

He nodded. "I see."

They walked in silence until they were at the entrance to the Carlton house. "Would you like to come in?" he asked. "I can offer you a glass of cool tea."

She shook her head. "No, thank you. I'm going back to Sea Breeze to do some work."

"Work?" His glance darted from her to Marie and then back again.

"Francie is an artist," Marie explained. "She's painting in Mama's garden."

Francie watched in amazement as he began to smile, slowly at first and then widely.

"Painting! Oh, my! Painting!"

The young man had clearly lost his mind. *Perhaps,* Francie thought, *he hasn't been at school at all, but in a home for the disturbed.*

"What is so funny?" Marie asked.

He touched Francie's head and turned it to the side. His fingertip traced a line under her ear to her chin. "I'd wondered where this streak had come from. I thought perhaps Mr. and Mrs. Harris had hired a charwoman."

"What *are* you talking about?"

He showed her his forefinger, now covered with a dark gray powder. "This. I gather you were using charcoals this morning?"

Suddenly she understood why he'd been staring at her earlier. She scrubbed at her neck, trying to eliminate the last vestiges of the morning's foray into the garden.

"You must think I'm a terrible mess." She knew her face was flushed a deep brick red. "I generally try to make myself more presentable when I go out into the public eye, trust me."

He shook his head. "I'm certain that you do, Miss Woods. I suspect a smudge of paint or charcoal is the risk one takes when one ventures into the visual arts."

Behind him, Marie aped his stiff demeanor, and Francie had to stifle the smile that bubbled up despite her embarrassment.

"It is, indeed, Mr. Carlton. I'm glad to have met you, and I'm sure our paths will cross again."

She bobbed a faint curtsey and walked away, not at all certain that he understood what had just transpired. . .or that she did either.

◆ ◆ ◆

Thomas stood at the window of his room at his parents' cottage on Mackinac Island. From here, on the second story, he could see the rooftop of Sea Breeze. It was only a short distance between the two houses, but today that distance seemed like a million miles.

Francine Woods. She was an odd woman—perhaps odd wasn't the best word, he acknowledged. She had the shyness of someone who had been cloistered at a boarding school, but he caught notes of an independent streak and an irrepressible sense of humor.

At the university, he studied literature and politics and philosophy. His parents had taught him religion and etiquette, and from his early occupation as a shop clerk before starting school, he had acquired the basics of a business knowledge.

Yet nothing had truly prepared him to be adept in a world full of people who trusted intuition and celebrated imagination. The truth was, he had no creativity at all. He couldn't sing, and piano lessons had been painful. His feeble attempts at sketching were pitiful. He hadn't a story or a fable of his own in his mind.

He didn't comprehend it. It simply didn't make sense, this imagination stuff. Life was made of facts, of real things, like a rock or a pen or a chair. That he understood. But why—or how—someone would work for hours on a painting of a boat when he could work for half the time on painting the boat itself so it would be more seaworthy. . . .

Thomas stared out the window, unseeing, as he thought of Francie. Perhaps he'd stop by Sea Breeze one day soon—just to see what her paintings were like and to investigate this mysterious artistic process. The fact that she had eyes as blue as Lake Huron itself had nothing to do with it, he told himself sternly. *Nothing at all.*

Chapter 2

"Francie, do you mind if we don't go on a walk this morning?" Marie brushed her long dark hair and wound it into a soft bun atop her head. "I'm going to the Carltons' house early today, but I don't want to leave you alone with nothing to do."

Francie shook her head. "I'll find something to do. I like exploring the island, plus Aunt Dorothea's garden is wonderful. The pansies are in bloom."

Marie shook her head. "As long as I live, I'll never see what you see when you look at the garden. It's just a bunch of flowers, and most of them can't be picked and brought into the house, since they wilt away almost instantly. What's so special about a pansy anyway?"

"Oh, I love the deep purple of the petals. They're like velvet. Plus, they have faces."

Marie laughed. "That's right. I remember when we were little, we'd go out into the garden and look at the pansy faces. I'd hold a dandelion under your chin to see if you liked butter—and you always did. And we'd pull the petals off the daisies—*He loves me, he loves me not.*"

"Even when we didn't have beaus!"

Their laughter continued as they went down the stairs to breakfast where Middle Meg was dishing up oatmeal.

"Eat hearty," Grandmama Christiana ordered from her chair. "Oatmeal is good, healthy food."

Though Francie adored oatmeal, especially with raisins sprinkled on top, Marie did not, and she let everyone know it.

"I cannot abide this stuff," she said, pushing it away. "It's horse food mixed with water."

The elderly woman leaned forward and pounded a bony fist on the table. "You need to eat it."

Aunt Dorothea swept into the room, pushing a last pin into her hair. "I overslept, and I don't know why. Oh, Middle Meg, you've given my oatmeal to Marie." She took the offending bowl from Marie and put it in her own place at the table. "There. Marie, would you rather have some toast?"

Grandmama Christiana sniffed. "If she were my child, she'd eat the oatmeal and be happy with it."

Aunt Dorothea patted her shoulder. "Yes, dear. Say, do you all realize that Leonard is coming in today? At least he's hoping to."

Francie smiled as the wind blew right out of Grandmama Christiana's sails. The older woman was extremely proud of her son. "He is? Today? Really?" Her wrinkled face settled into a placid expression. "It'll be so nice to see him again. So nice."

"Rev. Carlton might be arriving today, too," Francie said. "I met Thomas yesterday, and he mentioned that."

Aunt Dorothea nodded as she slid into her chair. "They could be on the same boat, and if they are, I hope one of them has the sense to know it's time to get themselves off when it pulls up. Those two, once they get to talking, they lose track of everything else. That reminds me, by the way, that I need to talk to Middle Meg about tonight's dinner. I want it to be special."

The conversation moved to a discussion of the evening's menu, with minor bickering between Aunt Dorothea and her mother-in-law. Soon Marie left to go to the Carltons', and Francie was able to escape into the garden.

Her sketchbook was filling quickly. In her hands, a dandelion became a tousle-haired child. Roses were the skirts of the enchanted ball gowns for imaginary fairies, and a lily of the valley stalk with its white-cupped flowers became wedding bells for the marriage of a beetle and a caterpillar.

As she drew the pictures, a story emerged, and she tucked her knees up to her chin. They were silly stories and sillier drawings, but she loved them; and the more she drew, the better the details became.

"Francie! Francie!" Aunt Dorothea stood at the back door of Sea Breeze. "Lunch!"

Reluctantly Francie shut the book and tucked it under her arm. As she entered the kitchen, she yelped happily. "Uncle Leonard! You *are* here!"

He swept her in a tight hug. "Francine, you're looking very well! Boarding school must have agreed with you."

"Mackinac Island is agreeing with me," she said.

"It's beautiful, isn't it?" he agreed. "Are you having a good time? Is my Marie being nice to you?"

She laughed. "Marie is always nice to me; you know that. She's at the Carltons' house now."

"Dorothea tells me she's learning to embroider from Mrs. Carlton." He grinned. "A valuable skill, I assume. Why aren't you joining her?"

She wrinkled her nose. "You could give me a whole faculty of needlewomen, and I still couldn't learn. I can do the basics, but that's it; honestly, that's all I care to do."

He guffawed. "You're a great girl, Francie. You're still doing your drawings, I hear."

"I am. I'm especially grateful for Aunt Dorothea's garden. I could sit out there all day and draw."

He patted her shoulder. "Ah, Francie's Fancies, right?"

Her stomach knotted into a tight ball. The dreadful nickname for her sketches still stung. She knew Uncle Leonard loved her—they all did—but none of them took her artwork as anything but triviality. To them, her pictures and stories were simply frivolities. Marie's embroidery was treated with more seriousness.

Dinner that evening was a joyous burst of activity, when everyone gathered together to welcome Uncle Leonard to the island. He explained to them that Rev. Carlton's interim pastor duties had been extended due to a death in his congregation, so they hadn't traveled together.

Marie shot Francie a wink and said sweetly, "That's too bad. Thomas was so looking forward to seeing him. Perhaps Francie can visit with him and keep him occupied until Rev. Carlton comes home. They can discuss church issues, I'm sure."

"Marie Harris, that is enough!" Grandmama Christiana glared at the young woman. "Your behavior is inappropriate. I'm sure that if Thomas and Francie talk, the subject matter will be elevated and of the highest standards."

Francie focused on moving the peas on her plate into a neat pile, and Aunt Dorothea rescued the conversation by discussing the church activities on Mackinac Island, a subject that satisfied Grandmama Christiana.

After a special dessert of strawberries and cream heaped on rich slabs of pound cake, the family retired to the wraparound porch, while the sounds of Middle Meg's clearing the table clattered in the background with a steady yet muted cadence, accompanied by her rendition of a medley of hymns.

"Ah." Uncle Leonard sighed as he sank into one of the wicker chairs. "There is nothing quite like the breeze right off the lake here."

He closed his eyes and put his feet up on the pedestal footstool. Aunt Dorothea dropped into the seat beside him. "It's good to have you here, dear. Time on the island will do you a world of good." She touched his arm. "You've been working so hard."

Francie perched on the far side of the porch and watched the two. Her aunt and uncle were clearly in love, and she appreciated their subtle signals to each other. They weren't the kind to show their affection in public, but these silent communications were endearing.

"I have to work hard," her uncle replied. His hair had begun to thin noticeably, and his right foot jiggled a staccato beat. In all of Francie's memories, she couldn't find one in which he didn't show some sign of nervous energy. Aunt Dorothea was just his opposite, calm and serene. Nothing seemed to ruffle her.

"I'm going for a walk," Marie called from the steps as she tied the yellow ribbons of her straw hat under her chin.

"A walk? This time of the day?" Grandmama Christiana thumped her way onto the wooden slats of the porch with her cane. "You're not going over to that nasty hotel place, are you?"

Under the brim of her hat, Marie rolled her eyes at Francie. "No, I'm not going to the hotel, and it's not nasty."

"Humph." The elderly woman plopped into the large chair at the top of the stairs with a meaningful glare at Aunt Dorothea. "No child of mine would traipse around unattended." She pointed her cane at Francie. "Go with her."

"I'll be fine by myself," Marie said. "I'll be—"

"Francie, go with Marie, please." Aunt Dorothea's voice remained composed, unperturbed.

"Mama—"

How amazing it is, Francie thought, *that there can be unseen and unheard fireworks, but that's exactly what is going on.* Mother and daughter didn't even look at each other, but the argument was obvious and the message clear.

Francie jumped off the railing and picked up the sketchbook. She never knew what kind of opportunity might present itself. "Marie, I could use a nice stroll."

As soon as they turned at the bend in the road, Marie sighed loudly. "That woman thinks we live in the midst of danger and intrigue here. Can you imagine any place as safe as Mackinac Island? And what is her quibble with the Grand Hotel?"

"I can't imagine," Francie admitted, pausing to admire a small rabbit that stopped to stare at them from behind a patch of trillium. "I suppose she might be worried about the men over at the fort being a bad influence on us, but I can't imagine them being unruly."

"Well," Marie declared, "they certainly aren't about to leap out at me and seize me off the path. Nothing that exciting would happen here."

"Marie! Don't say such a thing!"

"The old shrew. Oh, I'm sorry, Francie. You know I don't mean it. I'm just grumbling. Here I am, twenty-two and practically an old maid, and Grandmama Christiana would like to keep me in swaddling clothes until I'm laid in my grave."

"It must seem like that. Where would you like to go tonight? Shall we just wander?"

"I'd like to go to the Carltons' house. I think I left my embroidery there, and I would like to put in a few stitches tonight before I retire to sleep."

Francie frowned. "I'm sure you had your bag with you when you came in."

Marie shrugged and pulled on an overhanging branch, bringing it low and releasing it so it snapped as it flew back into place. "I must not have. I'll only be a moment."

They weren't far from the Carlton home, and as they turned into the entrance road, a figure separated from the gathering shadows.

"Thomas! You scared us!" Marie shook her finger at him.

"My apologies." He bowed slightly toward them both. "It's a fine evening, isn't it? I understand that Mr. Harris has come onto the island."

"Yes, he has. It's been wonderful to see Uncle Leonard again," Francie said.

"He was instrumental in getting me into Harvard." Thomas straightened his jacket, almost self-consciously it seemed to her.

"That's right," she said. "He went to school there. I didn't know you were at Harvard. What are you studying?"

"Excuse me," Marie interjected. "You two go ahead and visit while I go inside and see if I can find my embroidery bag."

Thomas took Francie's elbow. "I understand you enjoy gardens. Let me show you the family garden. I have to say it's not as nice as Dorothea's, but it's still quite pleasant."

He spoke like a textbook, she realized as they toured the small garden area. This might be a disadvantage of immersing oneself so completely in one's studies.

"These roses," he told her, "were brought from my grandparents' house in Grand Rapids. They've adapted amazingly, considering the climatic difference. They're tea roses, I believe."

"I love tea roses. They would be—" She broke off and leaned over to bury her face in the blooms. She absolutely could not share with him what she had been about to say, that these tiny blossoms would be perfect for the wedding she was planning, especially since the bridal pair were chipmunks in one of her stories.

He looked at her curiously, his golden eyes catching the early evening sun, but he didn't press her to finish her statement. "And here," he continued smoothly, "will eventually be a line of lilac bushes, but they need to mature before they'll be as showy as we'd like."

As they moved through the garden, the sun began to sink and the shadows lengthened, swaying as the breeze ruffled the surrounding trees and the leaves of the larger bushes.

"It's almost as if God were walking here in the evening," she said in a hushed voice.

He nodded but didn't comment at first. "You have an interesting view of God," he said at last.

"He is my best friend. You must have a similar relationship with Him, I suspect. After all, your father is a minister."

They paused in front of a small fountain. Water spilled from a pitcher-bearing cherub and splashed into an alabaster bowl. A cricket chirped, and Francie thought idly that if she could remember the formula for determining the temperature by counting cricket chirps, she would know how warm the day was.

"Do you enjoy your studies?" she asked him, trying desperately to make conversation and fill the silent corners of the night.

"I do. It's quite varied, and I find myself challenged by my professors and the readings. There's also a fine library at Harvard, and I'm taking advantage of it and reading beyond that which is assigned. Reading, in and of itself, can be quite an education."

Somewhere a night bird called, and the underbrush rustled just beyond the garden.

"It's almost noisy out here," she said with a smile.

"When the sun sets entirely, it's a real cacophony," he agreed.

"Speaking of the sun setting, I should find Marie so we can go home."

At the edge of the garden, he paused. "I've enjoyed this time with you, Francie, and I hope our paths will cross again."

What did he mean by that? Was he proposing a friendship, or was it more that that? Unfortunately living in a boarding school had kept her inexperienced, and she didn't have the faintest idea how to proceed with finding out.

She was spared having to deal with it at all when Marie chose that moment to come around the back of the house and join them. "My bag isn't here. Francie, we'd better get back or else Grandmama Christiana will snap off our heads."

"We wouldn't want that to happen," Thomas said. "I'll walk you back. Surely your grandmama can't object to that."

Marie hooted. "I wouldn't count on that."

During the short stroll home, Marie sang softly and Francie was content to listen to her. Her cousin had a lovely voice, and her version of "Abide With Me" was the perfect way to close the evening.

The family was still on the porch. "It's too pleasant to go inside," Aunt Dorothea explained. "I could fall asleep out here with the breeze blowing so gently."

"You'd certainly have sweet dreams," Thomas said with a slight smile. He turned toward Francie and Marie. "Ladies, it's been a pleasure to visit with you this evening." He nodded and disappeared in the deepening darkness.

"What did you talk about?" Grandmama Christiana's disembodied voice floated from the shadowed center of the porch. "Did he discuss his father's work?"

"No," Marie answered, "he didn't."

"Did you talk about his studies at the university?"

"No, not that either."

"Then what *did* you discuss?" Disapproval rang through the elderly woman's words.

"I'm not the one to ask," Marie said. "He talked to Francie, not me." She flashed a teasing smile at Francie and ran lightly inside the house.

"Flowers," Francie said. "We talked about flowers."

◆　◆　◆

Thomas leaned against the fountain. Night had covered the island completely, but sleep refused to come.

He hadn't been surprised when she'd said that about God in the garden. He just hadn't known what to say in response.

The truth was, he'd never thought of it that way. So here he stood, long after he should have been soundly asleep, standing in the midst of the garden and listening for his Lord.

A puff of wind lifted the flowers of the large-leafed plant beside him. He had no idea what it was; his knowledge of botany was limited to roses and daisies and other obvious flowers. Just as quickly as it came, the tiny gust vanished. Then the clusters of tea roses dipped, and soon the breeze passed to another part of the garden, until it seemed as if each growing thing had been caressed by the zephyr.

Could it be—? He dismissed the thought immediately. That was what Francie Woods would say. He shook his head. He was a university man. He dealt in facts, with proof, with truths.

And yet he was a man who believed in God.

It had always been enough. His faith was the one thing at odds with his schooling, but somehow he had always managed to make room for them both.

There were some other stirrings in his soul, too, which he hadn't felt before, and they had something to do with Miss Francie Woods.

He rubbed his forehead. His normally ordered life was becoming quite involved. The oddest part was that, whenever he thought of the source of that complication, he found himself smiling.

Smiling! He had spent exactly twenty-two minutes with the young woman—and the fact that he knew the time worried him just a bit—yet she had, with uncanny ease, made herself a part of his life.

Chapter 3

The fern moved slightly, and Francie held her breath as a tiny rabbit selected a tender stalk of grass and ate it. She was on another solitary walk. Marie, it turned out, was an early riser, and she was often already on her morning stroll when Francie woke up.

Overhead, a bird called, and the rabbit froze in place, its teeth still chewing industriously. How her fingers itched to record the moment on paper, but she was afraid to reach for her sketchbook lest the movement startle the rabbit.

Around her, the island was alive with the bustle of activity. She could hear the *clop* of hooves on the path and the squeak of wagon wheels. It was probably someone working on the Grand Hotel, like the fellow she and Marie had met the other day.

The hotel was amazing to her. She'd missed the initial days of its building, but it was growing at an incredible rate. Despite Grandmama Christiana's dire warnings, she managed to pass by the hotel daily.

It would open soon. The excitement was pervasive and as the day grew closer, the residents of the island watched with anticipation.

She couldn't bear to disturb the rabbit, but her legs were cramping from crouching off the road to study the animal. She'd have to move soon.

A sound from the road alarmed the rabbit, and it dropped the remainder of the grass stalk and scampered into the underbrush. Francie rose to her feet, wincing as she realized that one of her legs had gone to sleep.

It was only a cart bearing workmen to the hotel construction site, with Emerson, the yellow dog, running behind it. Francie looked with longing at the empty spot under the ferns where the rabbit had been. She sighed and made her way back to Sea Breeze, where a quiet garden awaited her.

Soon she was settled in Aunt Dorothea's garden, away from the activity of the hotel construction. The petunias, with their rich earthy aroma, were opened to the morning sunshine.

In Francie's hands, the petunias were transformed on paper into hats for tiny wrens. The story began to unfold in her mind as she drew the birds celebrating a summer birthday.

She sketched rapidly, capturing each bird's personality as it appeared on paper. As she did, she softly whistled the birdsong she'd heard earlier.

"You do that very well."

Her hand twitched in surprise, and she pulled it off the paper just in time to keep from drawing a stray line across her sketch. "Thomas!"

He reached down and took the sketchbook from her. "You did this?"

She nodded. "Yes." As she began to stand, he reached down and helped her to her feet.

"You have quite a talent."

"Thank you very much." She dusted stray bits of grass and dirt from the skirt of her dress.

"These birds are extremely realistic. I'm not sure, however, that they would wear flowers upended on their heads." He held the drawing out at arm's length and studied it with a bemused expression on his face.

"These do. They're having a birthday party."

"A birthday party?"

"Yes."

"Do you really think birds have parties?"

"Do you think they don't?"

Her quick response was teasing, but he didn't smile immediately. Then he laughed and said, "Oh, I see. You have an artist's overactive imagination."

She responded, somewhat stiffly. "Did you come to the garden for a specific reason? Or did you just want to insult me?"

"Insult?" He stared at her. "I've insulted you? Trust me, I didn't mean to."

"Perhaps you didn't intend to," she said evenly, "but I don't think of my artistic ability as an 'overactive imagination.' I see it as a gift—a gift from God."

"Our Lord provides us with His bounty," he said. "Certainly, as a minister's son, I'm aware of that." Was there a trace of bitterness in his voice? She must be misinterpreting it.

"You don't approve of my sketches, I gather." She'd met with amused tolerance from her family, but this was different.

"It's not whether I approve or not," he answered. "I must admit, however, that I am not at all artistically endowed."

"We have all been gifted differently. I know that God has given you talents that are uniquely yours."

His lips thinned into a straight line. "When I draw a cat, it looks like a horse. When I sing, dogs howl. My poetry sounds as if I am unlearned. Gifts? I think not."

"You have others."

"For someone who's just met me, you seem to have a comprehensive knowledge of who I am and what I'm like. I find that interesting."

"You are God's child," she said simply. "That's enough."

A faint smile softened his lips. "So what, Miss Francie Woods, do you believe are my gifts?"

"I wouldn't know," she responded a bit primly. This conversation was on the verge of getting quite personal, but as the child of missionaries, she was always ready to share God's presence. "In the book of Jeremiah, though, we can read that God has plans for us."

He nodded. "True." Then he grinned. "I never dispute the Word of the Lord."

"You're a smart man." *God, please help me with the words I need to touch this man's heart*, she prayed. The pain she heard—or thought she heard—in his voice struck her heart. "We all have been blessed with those traits which make us special to each other—and to Him. Not all gifts are artistic. What about the gift of healing? Of listening? Of reaching out? There are so many I cannot even begin to think of them all, let alone name them."

"Even for one such as I?"

"I do know this—you are an intelligent man. That is a gift, indeed, don't you think?"

"Perhaps. Perhaps not." He looked directly at her, and in his golden eyes, she saw only confusion. "Perhaps it is a burden of insurmountable proportions."

And with those enigmatic words, he turned and walked out of the garden.

◆   ◆   ◆

Thomas's feet led him aimlessly through the summertime glory of Mackinac Island. Horses leading carts of visitors clip-clopped their way past him, but he barely noticed them, so deep in thought was he.

At last, the path led him to the Grand Hotel. The construction site buzzed with activity, and he joined the others who had stopped to look at the progress. The yellow dog he had seen earlier moved through the group, gobbling up the occasional bit of bread that fell to the ground from an onlooker's hand.

"This is the best thing to happen to Mackinac Island," said one man, and another agreed.

"It's a mistake, a terrible mistake." Thomas couldn't stop the words that popped out of his mouth.

The small group of observers grew silent, and they all turned to look at him. "Why would you say that?" asked one man.

He might as well finish what he started, although from the looks he was getting, it was clear that he should never have said anything.

He frowned at the hotel. "This is Mackinac Island. It's not New York City. Who's going to stay in this hotel?"

"Visitors," boomed the man next to him. "Mark my words, we'll have more folks coming over if they have a spectacular place like the Grand Hotel in which to stay."

Thomas harrumphed. "More people coming here? Sorry, but I just don't see it. As sure as the sun rises every morning in the east, this hotel is going to go down in the island's history as a massive misstep."

"You don't know that," one voice in the crowd shot back.

"I know enough business theory to—"

One man stepped forward. Thomas recognized him as the owner of one of the shops, a well-respected and outspoken member of the community. The businessman hooked his thumbs in his suspenders and began to speak.

"To do what? Start a hotel? Ha. Everything you know, you learned in school."

A murmur of assent ran like a current through the gathering, and the shop owner continued. "Let me tell you, young fellow, you may be living a life of grace and money, enough to buy you a university education, but that's not going to teach you anything of value in this life. People aren't theories, and no matter how hard you try, they're going to resist being pigeonholed by your cockamamy 'theories,' which are, to tell the truth, not much more than great big guesses."

Thomas couldn't do more than stand, cemented in his spot, while the man spoke. The worst part was, he had excellent points. Much of what he said was valid.

It had been easy in his studies to get swept up in the theories without recognizing what they were—not absolute laws but educated guesses made upon studying general trends. His professors would cluck at his amateurish application of what they'd tried to teach him.

He didn't respond to the men who confronted him—what was there to say?—and at last, they muttered among themselves and then dispersed.

Thomas studied the hotel again, trying to see what others did. Opportunity? Growth potential? The future of Mackinac Island?

No matter how he looked, he saw nothing more than an expensive venture based upon financial faith. There was only one thing that faith was acceptable in, and that was his relationship with his Creator. Other than that, relying on projections was foolish.

Not unlike relying on theories?

Francie had said that his intelligence was a gift from God, but when he asked too many questions, and each question spawned even more, he could only see his intelligence as an encumbrance.

He felt a weight at his side and looked down. The yellow dog that had been outside the store the day he'd met Francie was leaning against him and gazing up at him with soulful liquid eyes.

"So what do you think, old fellow?" he asked the dog, tentatively scratching the top of the animal's head. "You probably think it's a good idea. A hotel means more pats on the head, and more scraps of food thrown your way."

The dog didn't answer, and Thomas sighed. "There's not much difference between us then, is there? We all want pretty much the same thing—a bit of fond recognition and some sustenance."

A carriage approached, and the dog's ears perked up.

"Go on," he told the dog, and the animal jogged after the carriage, his plumy tail held high.

Thomas, his mind spinning, took one long, last look at the hotel before turning on his heel and stalking away.

◆ ◆ ◆

The evening had been especially solitary for Francie. Marie had gone to bed right after dinner, pleading a headache. Aunt Dorothea was in the parlor, tatting a doily, while Grandmama Christiana snored softly in the chair beside her. Even Middle Meg had gone to her room early, a new novel sticking out from the pocket of her apron. Francie said her good nights and headed upstairs.

In the night air, sounds carried with amazing clarity. Francie crouched at the dormer window, letting the rising breeze ruffle her hair as she brushed it out before sleep. This window, a tiny little thing, looked out over the garden, and she loved to look at the darkened setting from above the second story.

Perhaps it was the quiet, the insulation from the sounds of life below, that made her feel a bit closer to God. Tree branches, heavy with leaves, rustled in front of her, so close that if she reached out, she could touch them.

Dearest God, I feel my life changing. Now, more than ever, I need Your steady hand on my shoulder.

She'd never had a beau. Such things hadn't been a part of her life. Of course, she had thought about it, dreamed of love and marriage and a family, but that had stayed just that—a dream.

Thomas Carlton was fascinating to her. His stilted speech, his worried frown, his extensive schooling—all made her eager to learn more about him.

But she knew she needed to be careful. The boarding school had teemed with rumors of those girls who'd fallen hard for the first man to come their way, whether his intention had been friendship or romance. Too often their hearts had been broken and their reputations stolen.

Not that Thomas would do either of those things to her—nor had he given her any solid indication that he was being more than polite. Still. . .

She put down the brush and leaned her chin in her hands. It was nice to be able to dream again. She stared at the shadowed garden.

The breeze stirred her hair again, and she pulled it back, preparing to braid it loosely for sleep. As she started the plait, something moved in the garden.

It was too big for a rabbit or a bird. The yellow dog would never move this carefully. Could it be a deer?

She leaned forward and tried to make it out as it slipped through the garden. Silhouetted against the moonlight, the figure was clearly not a deer. It was a person. She couldn't make out at this distance if it was male or female.

The wraithlike shape slipped through the far reaches of the garden, back where the lilacs were ending their blooming. It paused, made a move back, then forward, as if hesitating which way to go.

It darted from tree to bush, and then, as quickly as it appeared, it vanished.

Francie's heart—and her thoughts—raced. What had she seen? She didn't believe in ghosts, but on the other hand, she *had* seen something she couldn't explain.

The door behind her creaked open, and she spun around, fear turning her blood to ice. Her pencils scattered around her feet.

"Francie?" It was Aunt Dorothea. "Dear, are you up here?"

"Yes." The word came out as a whisper.

"Are you all right? Your voice sounds odd."

Francie managed a faint laugh. "You startled me, that's all."

"I'm sorry. I heard a sound up here, and I wanted to make sure that those silly squirrels hadn't taken up house in here again. We had such trouble with them last year."

"No squirrels," Francie said, gathering up the fallen pencils. "Just me."

"Are you sure you're feeling well?" asked Aunt Dorothea. The small lamp she held cast eerie flickering shadows across her face. "Goodness, girl, you're as white as a ghost!"

Chapter 4

The late-night mysterious garden visitor was nearly forgotten in the early morning clatter of Sea Breeze. Middle Meg was singing her usual mélange of songs, but this time she'd strayed from her usual repertoire of hymns. Francie suppressed a smile as the family employee easily segued from "My Bonnie Lies Over the Ocean" to "Annie Laurie."

Marie, her ebony eyes glimmering mischievously, said in a low aside to Francie, "Today's musical theme must be Scottish women."

Grandmama Christiana cleared her throat noisily, but Francie noticed that a tiny smile curled the edges of her normally tight lips. "Marie, I neglected to tell you that I found your embroidery bag by the garden gate yesterday. It's in my room now, on my bureau. You may retrieve it after breakfast."

"Thank you," Marie answered eagerly. "I thought I'd left it at the Carltons', but apparently it was here all the time. I'm delighted you found it!"

For a moment, Francie thought she might have found a clue to the shadowy figure's identity, but she realized that the bag had been lost before she'd seen the ghostlike image; the two couldn't possibly be connected.

Aunt Dorothea sailed into the room with a great swish of her full taffeta skirt. "Good morning, loved ones," she caroled. "Do you like my new dress? Leonard brought it with him, and Middle Meg, the dear, made the last of the alterations to it."

Marie scooted her chair back. "It's quite an interesting color. Not purple, not black. Plum, I guess?"

"I believe that's it indeed." Aunt Dorothea dropped a kiss on each of their heads. Marie smiled, and Grandmama Christiana grimaced slightly.

"Where is Leonard today?" Grandmama Christiana demanded. "Is he still asleep?"

Aunt Dorothea poured herself a cup of tea as she answered. "Oh, not at all. He was up long before any of us. He was planning to go to the Grand Hotel."

Grandmama Christiana sniffed. "Why is he going to *that* place?"

"Why, he has business there, of course. His bank had something to do with the funding."

"Dreadful!" The older woman looked distressed.

Aunt Dorothea put down her teacup and faced her mother-in-law. "Christiana, why do you dislike the hotel so much?"

"Well," Grandmama Christiana began, "it's going to be noisy."

"Noisy?" Marie guffawed in a very unladylike manner. "Once the thing is built, the island will go back to its usual blandness. Personally I like the excitement, even if it does mean hammers and saws."

Her grandmother ignored her and continued, "And I worry about the kind of people it's bringing in."

"Now, I must object to that," Aunt Dorothea said. "That's not—"

"I mean—" Grandmama Christiana's words shot out like bullets "—the young men who are swinging those hammers and manning those saws." She glanced first at Marie and then at Francie. "Those young men have nothing but a good time on their minds."

Marie flung her napkin onto her plate and pushed back her chair so fiercely that it fell back with a loud crash. "Enough of that! Enough! I am not a child, and I am not foolish! Please give me the respect of treating me appropriately!"

With those angry words, she grabbed Francie by the arm and pulled her along.

Francie had only a flashing view of Aunt Dorothea's astonished face and Grandmama Christiana's horrified expression before she and Marie tore through the kitchen.

"I'm sorry—" Francie tried to tell Middle Meg as they nearly knocked her over on their way out, but to her surprise, the rotund woman grinned broadly and winked.

What a strange house this is, Francie thought—*and how wonderful!*

◆ ◆ ◆

Overcast skies and choppy waters greeted Thomas at the ferry's side. The passengers who disembarked looked a bit queasy, and many gripped the railing with white-knuckled hands.

But one man, his thinning hair in wet disarray, bounded toward him, a wide smile creasing his sunburned cheeks. "Thomas!"

"Father, it's good to see you again." The words were true. His father had an energy that brightened any room.

Rev. Carlton wrapped his son in a bear hug, ignoring the water-drenched jacket he wore. "And I am delighted to see you, too. I must say, though, it's so good to be on terra firma again."

"The ride was rough, I gather," Thomas commented.

"Praise God, we made it. And I don't use our Lord's name lightly. There were times when I thought we would capsize, but between the skill of the ferryman and the grace of God, we managed only to get a tad waterlogged from the spray."

They loaded Rev. Carlton's bag and trunk into the small carriage and began their way back to the house. They had just passed the last shop when a large yellow dog darted in front of their cart, and Thomas had to pull back on the reins. His father slid forward, catching himself before losing his seating entirely.

The animal didn't even stop to look at them but continued in its quest for the squirrel that vanished behind one of the storefronts.

"I haven't seen that dog before," Rev. Carlton said as he righted himself.

"Are you hurt?" Thomas asked him, and as soon as his father assured him that he was all right, Thomas continued. "I don't know who that dog belongs to. I've seen it twice before, but then I've only been here a very short time myself."

"It's a handsome animal," his father said. "Whoever owns it is fortunate indeed."

"Fortunate? We could have been killed!" Thomas expostulated. "The dog needs some sterner supervision."

To his amazement, his father laughed and reached across the seat to hug him. "Thomas, you've led a far-too-sheltered life. Supervising a dog, indeed!"

◆ ◆ ◆

The next week passed in a flurry of dinners and guests at Sea Breeze. More than ever, Francie realized how special Uncle Leonard's time with them was. Not only was his family glad to see him, the entire island community took the time to drop by and visit.

Francie's head spun with the flurry of activity, and the only time her life seemed at all settled was within the cool sanctuary of Aunt Dorothea's garden.

There, flowers danced onto the pages of her sketchbook. A caterpillar in a top hat bowed to a ladybug with an oversized satchel. Two daisies put their heads together in a smiling pose. On a hollyhock stem, a family of bees clad in striped trousers gathered nectar.

This was her haven. As her fingers captured the pictures her imagination created, she spoke with God. *I'm a bit confused. I don't know how to act around boys—around men. There's a young man—oh, You know him—Thomas Carlton. He's interesting to me, but I don't know how or why, and I certainly don't know what to do. Is he a friend? Or—oh, dearest God, please help me know—is there more to it than that?*

God answered her in this quiet spot, perhaps not the way some would imagine, but with a calming reassurance that she was loved; despite all the cares and worries of the world, that was what mattered the most.

Her book soon filled with drawings. By the end of each evening, she scaled the steps to the quiet room with the tiny dormer window that looked out on her enchanted garden, and, no matter how tired she was, she absorbed the wonders of the garden in the shaded evening light.

And each night, her shadowed mysterious figure returned. Francie leaned as far forward as she could until her face was pressed against the glass and her breath made faint clouds on the pane, but the moonlit shape remained just out of her visual reach.

Finally, just as she was about to leave and go to her bed, another movement in the garden caught her attention. It was another form, gliding in to join the first.

She held her breath and watched, entranced, as the two shapes met, embraced, and separated. Then, together they merged into the darkest areas of the garden and vanished.

Who were they? What were they?

Francie hugged her knees to her chest and pondered what she'd seen. Although her imagination created whimsical situations that could never happen, she knew the difference between them and reality. She never expected to see a fairy wearing a petunia blossom as a skirt, and equally she never thought to see a specter—no, two specters—in the garden.

Ghosts? No, never. That was as likely as her flower-clad fairy. Such things simply did not exist.

Certainly her creative mind hadn't pulled them from her daydreams, had it? Francie bit her lip as she mulled over that possibility. No, she decided, what she had seen was too real to be a capricious fabrication.

She stared out the window at the garden, now free of any ethereal forms. What she saw was simply a nighttime garden, bathed in the moonlight. A kind of sadness struck at her heart. What if someone else were aware of the garden's visitors? What would become of the two apparitions that came from separate sides of the greenery, met, and left?

She almost didn't want to find out their identities, at least not yet. Having a mystery of her very own proved to be exciting and thrilling.

Francie smiled. Life was getting quite interesting.

Chapter 5

"Thomas, is there any chance you can look at the fence in back?" Mrs. Carlton's voice floated up from the bottom of the stairs.

He put a marker in the book he was reading, a treatise on the physical matter of the universe, and laid it aside. He knew his mother didn't want him just to look at the fence; she was expecting him to do some sort of repair.

"I'll be right there," he called back, as he gave the book a parting pat. He'd found it a fascinating study, and he left it reluctantly. But his mother needed his help, and that was more important.

"I'm sorry," she said when he joined her. "One of the slats is down, and a dog has been in and out all day, digging wildly." She grinned at him. "You don't suppose there are bones under the grass, do you?"

"I'm fairly sure there aren't," he answered, trying to match her light tone, "unless someone lost track of a cemetery and we've managed to build right on it."

She shuddered dramatically. "Do me a favor, Thomas, and after you nail the fence piece back, see if you can repair the damage to the lawn, too. Now, I'd better hurry back inside. Marie Harris is due any minute for an embroidery lesson."

If Marie is coming, Francie might be with her, an internal voice whispered to him, *and if Marie's with your mother, you might be pressed into occupying Francie.* The thought made him smile—and hurry in his task.

He went to the shed in the back where the tools were kept, found a hammer and a handful of nails, and located the section of the fence that was broken. Already the day was heating up, so he took off his jacket and draped it over the fence post.

Fortunately, this job seemed to be fairly easy. Nailing a board was something he could do. Beyond that, carpentry was out of his league.

The problem became readily apparent. The dog in question, a yellow Labrador retriever—the same animal that had almost upset them when his father had arrived—had no intention of leaving him alone to make the repair. Instead, it leaped joyfully around him, licking his face and putting its paws on his shoulder. When Thomas hammered, the dog apparently thought he was playing and tried to knock the hammer out of his hands.

Pushing the dog away just increased the canine's interest in Thomas's activities. He put all his energy into fixing the fence, and as he swung the final blow at the nail, the hound lunged and with a *thump*, tipped Thomas onto his back.

"No! No!" Even as he objected, Thomas started to laugh as the dog planted its huge paws on his shoulders and licked his face enthusiastically.

"Need some help?" Francie's voice sounded from the path that ran behind the Carlton home.

Of all the times for her to come along, this had to be the moment. He wished the earth would open and swallow him whole.

"Is this beast yours?" he asked as he tried to avoid the dog's slurps.

"No, he isn't. Marie told me he belongs to the fellow who owns the carriage tours, though. I think he calls the dog Emerson."

Hearing his name, the dog stopped licking Thomas's face and sprinted happily to Francie, who chuckled and let the dog greet her. She picked up a stick and hurled it down the clearing behind the fence, and the dog charged after it. "I'll take him back to the carriage stables. I don't know if he's never tied up or if he is some kind of an escape artist, but he's always being brought back to his owner, like a wayward child."

Thomas quickly stood up and tried to dust himself off. His shirt collar was awry, and there were scuff marks on his sleeves and shoulders where the dog had placed his paws. "I'm not making a very good impression, I'm afraid," he apologized.

To his amazement, she shook her head. "On the contrary, you've made a very good impression. It was wonderful to hear you laugh. Plus anyone who'll let a dog slobber over him has to be a good fellow."

"I didn't exactly *let* him," Thomas pointed out. "This beast is huge, and whatever Emerson wants, apparently Emerson gets."

The dog returned with the stick, dropped it at Francie's feet, and waited with obvious anticipation for her to throw it again.

"I've created a monster," she said, her voice bubbling with amusement. "I suspect Emerson will want me to throw this stick all afternoon."

The dog barked sharply and pawed at the stick, then tilted his head and looked at Francie beseechingly.

"He certainly knows how to look appealing," Thomas said. "I wonder if dogs do that naturally or if they learn it."

"It's a God-given gift," she replied, leaning over to scratch behind Emerson's ears. "There isn't a puppy alive that wasn't born with the ability to steal our hearts. They all have those melting eyes."

"You must be a dog owner," he commented, thinking about someone else who was terribly close to stealing his heart.

"No," she said. A shadow passed over her face but vanished as Emerson shoved his head into her knee. She obligingly picked up the stick and tossed it for him again. "I've never had a dog."

"You seem so natural with this brute, though."

"I've always wanted a dog, and Emerson is not a brute. He's as innocent and playful as a child."

Thomas watched Emerson bound back to them with the stick in his mouth. "A big child, perhaps," he admitted.

She laughed as one of Emerson's ears flopped over the top of his head. "I've lived overseas or in boarding schools my whole life. When we lived in China, I had a squirrel that I was taming—or trying to tame—but I didn't get far enough to be able to say it was my pet."

This woman was fascinating. Who would think of a squirrel as a pet? He had to find out more. "How were you taming it?"

"I laid a nut or cracker on the ground and waited as the squirrel stole it. Each day, I moved the treat closer to me, until eventually it would take the tidbit from my fingertips."

"That was rather dangerous," he reproved. "Squirrels carry nasty diseases. What if it had bitten you?"

Emerson barked, and she obliged by throwing the stick again. "I was so desperate for a pet that it was a chance I was willing to take. Plus," she added, dimpling, "I was nine. That kind of logical thinking was not my strong point."

He tried not to frown. At nine, he would never have approached a squirrel and would certainly never have encouraged one to come to him.

"Have you had any pets?" she asked. "A cat, perhaps? A parakeet?"

"No. Cats make me sneeze, and a parakeet requires too much care."

"A fish?" she suggested.

He shook his head. "No. Not even a goldfish. I'm afraid I get so involved in my studies that I don't have time to care for an animal."

"I suppose that's true," she commented as Emerson returned, stick in mouth, and sat expectantly for her attention. "They do require a commitment, but the love you'd get back would certainly be worth it, I'm sure."

Francie pretended to wrestle the stick from the dog. "Look at this," she continued. "He trusts me. He doesn't know me from Mother Goose, but he understands that I'm not going to hurt him. He has faith."

Something seemed to be stuck in his throat. He couldn't respond, and, truth be told, he didn't have any words to say if he had been able to speak.

There was no way she could have known the impact of what she'd just said, yet the fact was that her words cut to the bone. He'd always struggled with the conflict of what he saw and what he felt. As a minister's son, his pain had been particularly difficult.

Doubting Thomas.

Yet standing beside the fence, his clothing disheveled and his pride disintegrated, he wanted what others had. More than anything, he wanted that. He wanted the ability to believe completely.

In Francie's guileless blue eyes, so clear with uncompromised faith, he saw the dreadful image of his misgivings. He knew he was frowning—again—but he didn't seem to be able to stop himself. This morning as he'd shaved, he'd noticed that what had been tiny lines in his forehead, caused by hours of studying, had deepened to carved grooves.

He was too young for that. He knew it, and he could not stop it.

Francie was gazing at him with a look that told him she'd spoken to him and was awaiting an answer. Unfortunately he'd been so caught up in his own concerns that he hadn't heard her speak. "Excuse me?" he managed to say, hating the flush that crept up his neck.

"I'm going to take Emerson back to the stables."

"Now?"

The dog pawed at her leg. "I think I'd better," she said, "or I'll be here all day, tossing this stick until my arm falls off."

He couldn't let her leave. "I'll go with you," he offered, trying not to think about his soiled clothing. Fortunately his jacket would cover the worst of the stains, and he shrugged into it quickly.

"It's not necessary," Francie said, her cheeks a bit pinker than he'd remembered.

Thomas stopped buttoning his jacket in midmotion. "If you don't want me to come along—" he began, but she interrupted him.

"On the contrary. Please come. I'd appreciate the company."

They walked toward the stables, discussing the books they'd read. His heart leaped for joy when he found out that she, too, liked Tennyson. " 'The Charge of the Light Brigade' is so exciting," she told him fervently. "It's got to be one of my favorite Tennyson poems."

He preferred Tennyson's romantic works, but he would never admit it, so he nodded and agreed. "I usually wouldn't think that war could be fodder for poetry, but that work is riveting."

Their path to the stables took them past the site of the Grand Hotel. "Look at that," Francie breathed, stopping to take a look. Emerson sat beside her, apparently ready for a break from his labors. "Isn't it extraordinary? I've never seen anything quite like it, and I hear that the turnout for the opening is supposed to include all sorts of famous people."

Thomas couldn't stop a frown from forming. "I'm afraid I can't share your opinion of the place."

"Why on earth not?" she asked, running her fingers across the top of Emerson's head.

"It's wasteful." Even as the words emerged from his lips, he wanted to recall them. He knew he sounded priggish and self-righteous, but he spoke the truth. "How can they expect to fill those rooms? This is a tiny island."

"More people will come to stay—"

"Chicago and New York and Boston have splendid hotels," he pointed out. "Have you ever stayed at the Palmer House in Chicago? Now, there's a tremendous hotel. Why, the barbershop, I've heard, is paved with silver dollars."

Francie's smile was faint but polite. "I've heard that story about the silver dollars in the barbershop, but I must confess that I've never had the fortune to stay at the Palmer House so I haven't seen it. In fact, I've never been to Chicago."

If he could have managed to kick himself, he would have done so gladly. Of course she wouldn't have been able to stay at a hotel as expensive as the Palmer House. He hadn't either. What he knew of the luxurious hotel was simply what he'd heard from others.

He studied her face covertly as she watched the hotel site. The last thing he wanted to do was hurt her.

"Do you really think the owners will be able to rent all the rooms?" he asked, trying desperately not to sound judgmental.

She turned to face him. "Why not? It's a lovely building."

"But isn't it rather—daring?"

To his amazement, she answered, "I hope so."

For once, he didn't have an argument ready. Daring? Somehow *Francie* and *daring* didn't seem to go together. Or maybe it was *Thomas* and *daring* that didn't go together.

The conversation didn't progress further, for at that moment Emerson barked at a worker who came close to them. Francie recognized him as the fellow who had spoken to Marie that day on the path.

He smiled at them both, patted the yellow Labrador on the head, and left without saying a word.

"I think he knew Emerson," Thomas said.

"I suspect Emerson knows everybody on the island," Francie retorted, laughing as the dog watched the construction worker leave. From the way the dog looked back and forth at them and the laborer, it was clear he was torn between which one to follow. "If we're to get this pup home, we'd better take him. Otherwise, I fear he'll go with that man."

She urged Emerson to come with them, and the dog, after one last longing look at the retreating back of the hotel worker, trotted along beside them.

The stables were dark and humid. Thomas automatically pulled back at the intense smell of the horses, but Francie didn't seem to have any problem with going on in. "I have your dog," she called, and a man came out of a dark stall, wiping his face on his grimy arm.

"Emerson! Were you visiting folks today?" he asked in a deep voice. The dog leaped happily on his broad chest in greeting. "Yes, you're a good boy; yes, you are."

"That's a beautiful dog you have there," Francie said.

How could she be so cheerful in the presence of such an overwhelming stench? Thomas tried not to inhale any more than necessary. If there was any satisfaction to be found in the moment, it was that his clothes needed to be cleaned anyway, so the smell was just added cause.

"Aw, thanks, but he's not my dog," the man said. "He's a hanger-on, as near as I know. This feller's been here since I can remember."

"Does he belong to the owner?" Thomas asked. "Somebody must be feeding him. He's hardly skin and bones."

The stableman shook his head. "We all feed him. He's not the owner's dog; I can tell you that. I guess he likes the stables because they're warm, and you know, I think he likes the company of the horses."

Thomas glanced at Francie. Her face was soft, and her eyes were luminous in the golden rays of sunlight that broke through the slats in the door. Little flecks of straw floated in the air like miniature shards of gold. Even in this lowly setting, she looked like a princess.

As she looked down at the dog, which now lay sprawled across the floor of the stable at her feet, he wished that he could gather up the hound and hand it to her as a gift.

Silly, that's what he was. Women wanted jewels and furs and expensive perfume, not a vagabond dog sprawled on the floor of a stable, his fur patchy with dirt and smelling of horses.

Francie raised her head and smiled. "Isn't he beautiful?"

Beautiful? He turned his head to take one more look at Emerson, and—no, it wasn't possible. Or was it? Could the dog have just winked at him?

Chapter 6

"R everend Carlton, would you offer the blessing?" Aunt Dorothea asked.

The Carltons had joined the Harris family for dinner, and the leaf had been put in the table to accommodate them all. To Francie's right sat Marie, and to her left, Thomas.

"I'd be honored," Reverend Carlton responded. "Might we join hands as we petition and thank our Lord?"

Marie readily grasped Francie's right hand, and Thomas lightly took her left as the minister began the prayer. "Dearest Lord, we are gathered together as family and friends to share the fruits of Thy bounty. We thank Thee for Thy generous gifts, so many of which are laid upon this table. We thank Thee for the gift of food, which nourishes our bodies. We thank Thee for the gift of shelter, which protects us from the storms of life. We especially thank Thee for the gift of companionship and love, which feeds our souls and strengthens our hearts."

Marie squeezed Francie's hand at those words, and unexpected tears sprang to Francie's eyes. She'd missed being with her family this past year; Aunt Dorothea and Uncle Leonard, Cousin Marie, and even Grandmama Christiana had welcomed her into their lives without hesitation, and their openness had filled an aching void. They had taken her into their home—and their hearts—and treated her as if she'd always been there.

Reverend Carlton had just pronounced the "amen" when Middle Meg bustled into the room with the side dishes. Soon plates, bowls, and platters were being passed around the table, and conversation was buoyant and happy. In the background, Middle Meg sang a rousing rendition of "Oh! Susanna" from the kitchen.

The dinner was wonderful, as was anything that Middle Meg cooked, baked, or stirred. Francie devoted herself to thick slices of honeyed ham, piles of buttered corn, and warm sweet rolls dripping with jelly, until her stomach was stuffed as full as it could possibly be.

Middle Meg served coffee and tea and left an apple pie and a stack of sugar cookies in the middle of the table, although everyone vowed there was not a smidgen of room left for more food in their bellies. "Just in case," Middle Meg said with a wink as she placed the platters in the middle of the table. "You never know. You just never know."

Francie groaned. She wanted nothing more than a nap, but unless she nodded off in her teacup—which was seeming like a greater possibility as the moments of "polite conversation" ensued—she was destined to stay at the table for a while longer.

Talk turned quickly to the Grand Hotel. Francie felt Thomas stiffen beside her, and her drowsiness evaporated. *Please, God, don't let Thomas argue. This has been a lovely day. Nothing should spoil it.*

Out of the corner of her eye, she watched him. He sat stick-straight, occasionally opening his mouth a bit and then, seemingly thinking better of speaking, closing it. Small splotches of red began to grow on his cheeks.

Uncle Leonard boomed, "The hotel is bound to be a success. I know the fellows who are behind it, and they've got what it takes. Where there's money to be had, you'll find those who can make it grow. Money is a crop as sure as wheat or corn or barley is. And those who can plant it and make it grow are farmers. Money farmers."

"This *crop* is bound for failure," Thomas burst out. All heads swiveled toward him as silence overtook the room. "I don't know these financial experts, but at the very least, they should have put their funds in something safe and secure. A bank, for example, would have been an outstanding choice. But sinking it into something as unknown as this. . ."

"Mackinac Island is not 'unknown.'" Marie's voice broke in, and the tone in her words was fierce. Francie spun to look at her in amazement. She looked just as angry as Thomas did. "I'm sure they studied the situation, made forecasts and predictions, and looked at this every which way, inside out and upside down."

"Marie! Such language!" Grandmama Christiana fanned herself vigorously. "How very common."

Everyone began to speak at once. Aunt Dorothea and Mrs. Carlton began loudly discussing the attributes of the pie, trying to cover the arguing voices. The volume escalated until it was nearly unbearable.

Francie wanted to cover her ears, anything to make the horrible din stop. This was terrible.

Then Grandmama Christiana trumpeted over the cacophony, "Leonard, I forgot to tell you about the oddest thing. I saw ghosts in the garden the other night."

The voices fell silent, and the others at the table turned to stare at her. Aunt Dorothea cleared her throat. "You did? Are you sure? You saw ghosts in my garden?"

Grandmama Christiana shot her a withering look. "I said I saw ghosts, and that's what I meant. I saw ghosts. Two ghosts."

Uncle Leonard harrumphed. "Mother, there is no such thing as a ghost."

"Then you explain to me what I saw."

He patted her hand. "I think you made a mistake, that's all. It must have been a trick of the light."

Grandmama Christiana's spine snapped into a rigid line. "I know what I saw. There were two figures, and they floated toward each other and embraced. It was some kind of a ghostly lovers' rendezvous."

Uncle Leonard hooted. "You need to have your spectacles adjusted. You couldn't have seen a ghost because ghosts don't exist. This sounds like one of Francie's Fancies."

The family nickname for her artwork stung like a nettle, and Francie froze. She took a deep breath and tried to calm her racing thoughts, which were already overwhelmed by Grandmama Christiana's pronouncement.

Mrs. Carlton said, "You probably saw a couple who took a wrong turn on a late-night stroll. That would explain why you saw them in each other's arms."

"The breeze off the lake can be quite strong at night. Maybe you saw the shrubbery and trees moving in the wind," Aunt Dorothea suggested.

"Aren't any of you worried?" Thomas interjected. "There are all sorts of people on the island, working on the hotel or stationed at the fort, and we don't know what they're like.

Who knows what kind of unsavory intentions they might have?"

Mrs. Carlton shook her head. "I must say that I agree with Dorothea. The evenings here are quite pleasant, with that soothing lake air, and I'm sure that many people are taking advantage of the cool and refreshing zephyrs."

Reverend Carlton chuckled. "I'm sure this is a simple mistake. After all, has anyone else seen these shapes? Dorothea? Leonard? Or you, Marie? Francie, have you see anything unusual at night in the garden?"

Francie didn't dare meet Marie's eyes for fear her cousin would read the truth in her expression. Instead, she ducked her head slightly and applied herself to the diligent folding and refolding of her linen napkin.

Thomas's eyebrows knit into a tempestuous frown. "I'm sorry, but I think that you're all making light of a situation that has the potential for being quite perilous. Mr. Harris is gone much of the time, leaving only the women here in Sea Breeze. Four women—"

"Five," Francie interrupted. "You forgot Middle Meg."

"Five then. What could five women—"

He stopped as Middle Meg appeared in the doorway to the kitchen, a wooden rolling pin in one hand and a vicious-looking cleaver in the other. "We'd be fine," she said, with a meaningful glance at Thomas, who fairly quivered under her pointed glare.

Reverend Carlton coughed explosively into his napkin, and as Francie cast a curious glance at him, she realized he was trying to disguise his laughter. At last, he got control of himself. "I'm sorry, son, but Middle Meg has a point. Mackinac Island is very safe. The men at the fort are respectable gentlemen, and the workers—well, I don't know much about them, but I'm sure they're fine fellows. Plus, the construction is almost finished, and they'll be gone."

Marie reached for her teacup, and her hand shook. Her mother, who sat to her right, patted her arm. "Dear, don't worry. You are perfectly safe here; you know that, don't you?"

At that moment, Grandmama Christiana thumped her cane on the floor beside her. "Listen to that, will you? Of course we are safe. I didn't tell you about the ghosts I saw so that you would panic. A ghost can't hurt anyone."

Uncle Leonard and Aunt Dorothea exchanged glances, and he said soothingly, "Whatever is in the garden, I'm sure we are fine. But to make sure that it's nothing troublesome, I'll check the back of the house myself." Then he added, raising his voice, "Or I'll send Middle Meg, armed to the teeth, out there. Pity the poor specter that confronts her!"

Middle Meg called from the kitchen, "It'd be my pleasure, sir. I'll send that ghost right back to—"

Reverend Carlton broke in with a loud, "Let's have some of that apple pie! Why, it looks splendid!"

◆　◆　◆

"Thank you for coming with me," Thomas said as he and Francie left Sea Breeze.

"I appreciate your offer. I don't think I've ever eaten that much food." A strand of her hair fluttered across her cheek, and she tucked it behind her ear. "When you suggested a walk, at first I thought I couldn't put one foot in front of the other, but now I'm glad I did. The air smells so fresh and clean."

"I wanted to talk to you about tonight—about much more," he said. He was glad the twilight shadows masked his face, which he was sure was splotched with embarrassment.

227

"Grandmama Christiana and her ghosts!" She laughed. "Can you imagine such a thing?"

"She is certainly an interesting woman. She's quite the mixture of old-school properness and modern freedom!"

"If you were to ask Marie, she'd insist that the old school is much stronger than the modern," Francie said. "She's almost as fussy as—"

She broke off in midsentence, but he knew what she was about to say, and he finished the phrase for her.

"As I am? Is that what you were going to say?"

Francie stopped and put her hand on his sleeve. "Thomas, please don't. That wasn't what I—what I meant."

In the distance, a seagull squawked raucously, and another answered. Again, Thomas was thankful for the faint light. "I know that I am a bit rigid, and I am trying to work on that."

"I see," she said, nodding.

"I'm not sure you do." His stomach twisted—and not from the massive dinner he'd just consumed. "I'd like to talk to you about it if I could."

"Let's go into the garden. There's a seat there, and we can sit while we visit."

"What? The garden at night? And risk being attacked by the ghosts?"

She laughed softly. "Now, there you are. You're not so serious all the time!"

They didn't talk as they walked along the graveled path to the garden gate. Then, just inside the white-painted entrance, she paused. "Look, one's opening!"

She pointed toward a green stalk with a spiraled bud, which had partially unfurled to reveal white petals inside. He squinted in the darkening light to make out what it was.

"It's a moonflower," she explained, touching the plant that climbed the trellis. "It's like a morning glory but in reverse. A morning glory blooms as the sun comes up, and a moon-flower blossoms at sunset. See how it captures the moonlight?"

He couldn't resist teasing her. "You're envisioning it as a hat for a mouse or something, aren't you?"

"No, of course not, you silly man." Amusement bubbled through her voice. "It's a skirt for a moth!"

"Ah. Of course."

She motioned with her hand across the garden. "Look at this extraordinary place—Grandmama Christiana's ghosts aside. Isn't it lovely in the early starlight?"

"It is quite beautiful. Your aunt has done a remarkable job with it. I'm surprised she's coaxed as much to grow here as she has. The morning glories, for example. Aren't they found more in the south?"

Francie shrugged and smiled. "I have no idea. Aunt Dorothea is the plant expert. I'm just the audience."

Her face was radiant in the glow of the moon. A light from the next cottage cast a yellow beam across her hair, making it gleam golden.

Maybe he had been tucked away in the male confines of the university for too long. There were women who attended the school, too, but he rarely mingled with them. For the most part, his life was studying and reading and attending lectures. He hadn't had time for romance, not with his schooling taking up so much of his time.

Until now. Now he was out of school, and now, now—now there was Francie. Something odd was happening to his heart. He felt oddly poetic standing next to her, as if someone were painting abstract pictures of water and light and trees.

"Did you want to talk about something?" she asked gently.

Thomas looked down as he dug the toe of his shoe into a tuft of grass along the garden path. "The more I learn at the university, the more I wonder."

"What do you mean?"

"You have the ability to see what is not. I have only the ability to see what is. God is a challenge for me, and you can imagine what a trial it is for me as I work this out, having a minister for a father."

To his amazement, she chuckled.

"You find that funny?"

"I find it funny that you say God is a challenge for you. He is most definitely a challenge, but I suspect you mean it differently than I do."

"I do." He hesitated, searching for the words that would convey what he needed. "I want to believe, and I do, to an extent. But it's very difficult for me. I like proof. No, it's beyond that," he corrected himself. "I demand proof. I don't want to, but I do. Does this make any sense to you?"

"It does." She took his hand and led him to the marble bench. "I think I understand what you're saying. Your faith isn't as deep as you'd like?"

"Exactly. The older I get, it seems the more skeptical I get."

"Skepticism isn't all bad. It seems to me the danger is believing everything you hear."

"But there's a gulf between faith and skepticism, and I'm having some trouble bridging the two."

"Have you talked to your father about this?" Her voice was soft and kind.

How could he answer that? He had, and yet he hadn't. His father had a buoyant faith, as did his mother, and yet here was their son, unable to let his heart be free to believe.

"I want to believe, and I do," he said at last, "but I want more. I don't want to be 'Doubting Thomas' any longer."

"Let's talk to Him," she suggested.

"To my father?" He couldn't cover the astonishment in his voice. Francie barely knew his father.

"To our Father. Let's pray. Do you mind if I lead the prayer?"

He nodded his head, grateful that she hadn't expected him to do it. His prayers were short, staccato, uneasy things, not the graceful petitions of his father.

"Dearest God, we are Your own children. Our prayer is a simple one. Please help Thomas open his heart to You, to hear Your voice, to know Your face. Amen."

"That's it?" he asked. "I barely had time to close my eyes."

He knew she was smiling. He could hear it in her words as she answered, "My prayers are always brief. It helps me focus on the prayer need."

"So now, I do—what? Wait?"

"You wait and listen. Your heart will tell you what to do next."

Together they sat in the garden, listening to the night sounds, and bit by bit, he felt his frozen heart begin to thaw.

"Thomas! Are you back there? Time to go!" His mother's voice called from the front of the house.

He stood and held Francie's hands as she rose, too. "Thank you so much," he said.

Then he did something that surprised himself even more.

He dropped a quick kiss on the top of her head.

Out of his mind. That was it. He was out of his mind.

"I'm sorry. So sorry," he mumbled. "Sorry. Sorry."

He fled through the dark, leaving her alone in the garden.

Chapter 7

Francie dressed with greater care than usual. Her fingers trembled as she buttoned the ivory and peach washed-satin dress. Thanks to the generosity of her aunt and uncle, she not only had the new dress but a matching bag, shoes, and a parasol.

"Can you believe it?" Marie asked. "I'm so excited I can barely do up my own hair. Is the braid straight? It feels like it's hanging lower on the left side."

"Your hair is lovely," Francie answered. "So are you."

It was true. Marie's pale blue dress with the soft lace bodice highlighted her bright dark eyes. She looked elegant and regal and incredibly beautiful.

"I can't believe that the hotel is opening today." Francie poked a stray strand of hair back into place and sighed as it promptly fell out again. "I know it was built in lightning time, but still, it just doesn't seem possible that it's finally done. And did you hear who is coming?"

Marie leaned over and studied her eyes. "Oh, please tell me my left eye isn't bloodshot. I look like a madwoman."

"Your eye is fine. But everyone is coming, everyone famous, that is." Francie couldn't keep the excitement out of her voice. "Uncle Leonard told me that the Marshall Fields are coming, and the Armours, too!"

Her cousin stood up and nodded. "I don't know anyone who'll be there, except you, of course. Still, Papa will introduce us to some of the guests. He knows many of them through his work." She grasped Francie's hands. "Wouldn't it have been fun, though, to stay there tonight and sleep in one of those fancy rooms?"

"Oh yes!" Francie answered. "It'd be terribly wasteful but a wonderful luxury!"

"Girls!" Aunt Dorothea called from the bottom of the stairs. "Let's hurry!"

Within moments, they were all tucked inside a carriage on their way to the Grand Hotel. Even Middle Meg was along, dressed in her Sunday best.

The roads were crowded with visitors and the carriages of the summer residents, all moving in the same direction. Mackinac Island had never seen such a momentous occasion.

Soon the entire family stood on the long porch of the Grand Hotel. "Have you ever seen such a thing?" Aunt Dorothea breathed. "It's stupendous."

Around them, a crowd of elegant men and women moved in clusters of conversations. Francie had never seen such an assemblage of wealth. Women were clad in beribboned ivory and delicate lace dresses, and many of them wore plumed hats that waved above the crowd. The men, dapper in their best suits, bent their heads together in intense business discussions.

"I can't believe it," Marie whispered. "It's like a dream."

"Wait until you see them tonight," Aunt Dorothea said. "They will be all decked out with their finery."

Grandmama Christiana clutched at Francie's arm. "Be a good girl and help me to a chair. Being jostled about isn't good when one is using a cane."

"Go ahead," her aunt said. "I'll stay with Marie."

Francie led Grandmama Christiana through the assembled guests to one of the chairs on the porch. The elderly woman sank into the chair with a grateful sigh. "Bless you, Francie."

A stately woman, her iron-gray hair wound into an ornate arrangement and held in place with pearl-and-ruby-encrusted combs, paused at the chairs and put her hand on Grandmama Christiana's shoulder. "Christiana Harris!"

Grandmama Christiana smiled and held her hand out regally. "Margaret, it's so good to see you. Francie, Margaret Toller and I met years ago in Lansing. Her husband was the kindest physician I've ever known."

"He's gone to be with the Lord," Mrs. Toller said, and Grandmama Christiana nodded.

"My Barney passed on, too," she said, a tinge of old sadness in her voice. "Tell me about your life now, Margaret. Where are you living?"

The two women chatted about people and places Francie had never heard of, and her attention wandered. God had done some astonishing things for her these last months. He'd brought her from a boarding school to this marvelous hotel on Mackinac Island, where she was mingling with people whose names she'd only heard of, whom she'd never dreamed of meeting.

Thank You. The two simple words were all her full heart could manage.

As Grandmama Christiana's friend moved away to visit with other people, Marie and Aunt Dorothea joined them, their faces aglow with excitement. "Do you realize who's here?" Aunt Dorothea said. "Marshall Field himself!"

"Yes, dear," Grandmama Christiana said. "I saw him. It's been so long since I've seen him, but he's aged well, I think." Her dark eyes glowed happily. "I used to know quite a few of these people. When my dear Barney was alive, we moved in the same social sphere as many of the guests. I've seen the Armours *and* the Swifts."

"Grandmama Christiana, do you know that woman whom Papa is talking to?" Marie asked in a low voice. "I've seen her picture before, but I can't think of her name."

She gestured by moving her head in the general direction of the steps. Uncle Leonard stood beside an elegant woman.

Grandmama Christiana squinted. "I could be wrong, but I think that's Bertha Palmer. She's married to Potter Palmer, the hotel magnate." She chuckled. "Do you suppose he's keeping track of the competition?"

Potter Palmer! He was the founder of the Palmer House, the hotel that Thomas had mentioned, and here he was, at the Grand Hotel.

Francie could barely breathe. This was far beyond her expectations.

Grand didn't begin to describe the hotel, Francie thought. It was magical. Absolutely magical.

Grandmama Christiana was like a fairy godmother to Francie's Cinderella, as the two of them sat on the porch and Grandmama Christiana introduced the women of society to her. The parade of silk faille dresses with elaborate beading, waterfall overskirts, and bouffant draping, ranging from the palest tints to the most vivid depths, washed over Francie's artistic vision until her senses were drenched with beauty.

Then the evening came, and the magic grew. After a dinner that far surpassed anything Francie had ever eaten, the guests shared demitasse under chandeliered lights in the lounge.

"Are you enjoying the evening?" asked a voice at her elbow.

"Thomas! I didn't expect to see you here."

He smiled with only a trace of the old stiffness. "I wouldn't have missed this for the world. It's getting a bit close in here. Would you like to join me outside?"

"I understand that the music is about to begin," she answered. "I'm a bit warm, though, so I would like to step outside for a moment at least."

His hand on her elbow, he guided her outside, and she breathed the cool air with relief. "Much better."

"So what do you think of the Grand Hotel?" he asked.

"It's more than I ever expected. I feel as if I'm in a fairy tale. What about you? Have you changed your mind?"

He shrugged. "Time will tell. I'm trying to enjoy the evening for what it is, which is, as you say, a fairy tale. By the way, you look lovely tonight."

"Thank you. You, sir, look very elegant yourself."

Thomas touched her hand. "Francie, I'd like to—"

Music floated out of the hotel, and he let go of her hand. "Ah, the entertainment has begun. We should go back."

Together they reentered the room, and although she wondered what he had been about to say when the violins began, the fairy tale continued.

◆　◆　◆

"So what do you say now, son?" Reverend Carlton asked as they stood on the porch of their cottage. "That hotel is beyond imagination, isn't it?"

"It is." Thomas frowned in the gathering twilight. "But I don't see how they expect to fill it."

The minister put his hand on his son's arm. "This was built by two railroads and a steamship company. They want to increase their passenger use by giving folks a destination. That's why they're here on the island. The hotel is a means to the end."

"Ah! By building the hotel, they hope that more people will utilize the railroad to get here." Thomas nodded. "I understand."

"What you see, Thomas, is often only part of the story. Of course, the problem is knowing when you have the whole story and when you don't, isn't it?" He laughed. "The only simple truth is what we have from God."

Thomas tried to swallow the lump that had suddenly sprung up in his throat. "Simple? Why do you call it simple? Isn't it the most complex, involving the creation of the earth and the sea and the sky?"

"Ah, but simple it is. All God asks of us is to believe in Him and to follow Him."

"But what if someone can't—I mean, someone tries but someone just can't—get over that hurdle of a heart that doesn't accept?"

"You could talk to Him. Just talk. You can talk out loud or in your heart or however it works the best for you. Just talk to Him. Tell Him your doubts, your fears. Trust me, Thomas, it's nothing He hasn't heard before."

"You named me well. Doubting Thomas."

"Ah, but remember one thing about him. He overcame his doubt and believed in the risen Lord. Thomas put his hand in the nail-scarred hands and pierced side of our Lord and believed. You can do that, too. Just talk to God and then do one more thing."

"What's that?"

"Listen."

◆　　◆　　◆

Sleep was elusive, and Francie found herself at the tiny window again, watching the moon's dreamlight play across the garden as she relived each thrilling moment of the day. The dinner had been more scrumptious than anything she'd ever tasted, and although Middle Meg hadn't been able to have dinner with them, she'd visited the kitchen and sampled the menu.

The evening attire had been splendid. Luxurious satins and fancy clothing, jewels and gems and gold and silver draped over the guests like expensive tinsel.

She would never forget a single moment of the day.

Francie sighed happily and yawned. Maybe she could sleep after all.

As she stood up, a movement in the garden caught the silvered light, and she realized she was not the only one awake at this late hour. She picked up her sketchbook and traced out the mysterious figures as they glided toward each other, filling the last moments of the magical day with romance. Their presence in the garden was the perfect ending to a perfect day.

"Good night," she whispered to the figures. "Good night."

Chapter 8

Thomas heard their voices before they came into view. "I can't go to the fudge shop again," Francie protested as she and Marie approached Sea Breeze. "I'll be the size of—oh, look! Isn't that Thomas on our porch?"

"Hello!" the cousins chorused as they came up the steps, the morning sunshine gleaming overhead, but the smile on Francie's face faltered when she looked at him.

"I'd like to talk to Francie," he said. "Alone."

Marie didn't say anything but slipped inside the house hurriedly.

"Thomas, what's this about?"

"This." He stood up and held out her notebook. "This is yours, I believe."

"Yes, it is. Why?" Her chin lifted proudly.

His heart and his head were in the midst of a furious war. *Let it go,* his heart told him. *Take care of it,* his head argued back. He took a deep breath and plunged forward.

He opened the book and fanned through the pages. "I'll tell you what's my concern. This—and this—and this. What do you know about the mysterious figures in the garden? How could you, Francie? What if they're dangerous? They could be robbers, thieves, murderers!"

She snatched the sketchbook from him. "Robbers, thieves, and murderers don't embrace each other."

In the back of his anger, he recognized that she was telling the truth, but he forged on. "By your silence, you've been abetting them. This isn't something that your imagination created. Those shapes are real people."

"Not if you believe Grandmama Christiana." Her tentative smile died on her lips.

"That's not funny. You've romanticized what is very probably a perilous situation."

"I can't believe that I'm about to say this to you, Thomas Carlton, but be logical." Her blue eyes turned as cold as Lake Huron in November. "Think about this. Do criminals act like this, meeting in gardens and embracing? Night after night, do they do this? You pride yourself on your orderly thinking, but you've got this into a twisted mess in your mind."

He had to stop this. "Francie, I—I am—I—"

He wanted to say he was sorry, but fury was like a cold stone in his throat, blocking the words. She snatched the notebook from him and snapped, "Go."

Blindly he stumbled down the stairs and left, hating love, hating himself.

◆　◆　◆

The rest of the day hadn't gone much better. Francie's soup had spilled on her new dress at lunch, and she'd knocked over Marie's embroidery bag, sending threads and needles skittering across the floor. Then she'd gone out to the garden to draw, and Emerson, the big yellow dog, had joined her.

As she was confiding her sorrows to the animal, he'd jumped up and placed a dirty paw print on her drawing of a dragonfly with a snapdragon pocketbook.

She was glad to see the day come to a close, but she couldn't sleep. Finally she crept to her secret dormer window and looked out on the darkened garden. She smiled as she saw a familiar movement on the path, but her smile faded when she realized it was not one of the usual visitors.

This shape didn't tiptoe. Instead, it slunk along the edge of the path, furtively slipping from shadow to shadow.

Perhaps Thomas was right!

She pulled her clothes back on with shaking hands and slipped down the stairs. Grandmama Christiana was already asleep, and Aunt Dorothea and Uncle Leonard sat in the living room. Their backs were to her, as she silently sped past them.

Middle Meg wasn't in the kitchen, and Francie raced out the back door and down the path.

She sneaked up behind the figure in the rose bower, but a twig crackled under her feet, and the specter turned to face her.

"Francie?"

"Thomas?"

"What are you doing out here?"

"What are *you* doing out here?"

"I wanted to make sure you were safe," he began, "so I decided to stand guard."

"It's a good thing I don't have a rifle or a saber," she said, still rattled, "or you'd be dead."

"Francie, I'm sorry." His words tumbled over her apology.

"Thomas, I'm sorry, too."

The words weren't as important as the way their hands touched or the manner in which their eyes met. At last, they moved toward each other in unspoken agreement and kissed under the rose bower.

As their lips touched, a sound in the far reaches of the garden broke them apart, and they both sank back into the shadows.

The ghostly figures were back, gliding toward each other.

"There they are!" he said in a husky whisper, and before she could stop him, he dove toward them.

"Thomas Carlton, are you out of your mind?" Marie's voice was unmistakable.

"Leave us alone!" The male voice was familiar, and Francie gasped as she recognized it. It was the fellow in the cart who had called her cousin "Princess Marie."

Francie ran out of the bower. "Marie, are you all right? He hasn't hurt you, has he?"

"Francie, you're out here, too? No, Thomas didn't hurt me." Marie glared at him.

"Not Thomas. This man." She pointed at Marie's companion.

"Edward? Oh, my dear, no. Edward wouldn't hurt me. Edward and I—" Marie smiled up at him. "Edward and I are in love."

"I know you," Thomas said accusingly. "You've been staying in the guesthouse behind our cottage. You worked building the Grand Hotel."

It all made sense. "That's why you've been so diligent with learning embroidery—so you could see him, right?" she asked.

Marie nodded. "My early morning walks were excuses to see him. I didn't lose my embroidery bag that time either. But I have to steal time to see Edward. The hotel is done, and—"

Francie knew what wasn't said. The match was socially unacceptable.

"Don't tell my parents or Grandmama Christiana," Marie said. "Please don't."

A light flickered on in the house, and Marie and Edward vanished into the shadows.

"She should tell them," Thomas said to Francie. "Any relationship that is built on deception will falter."

"I know, but it's still kind of romantic," she protested. "Don't you see it?"

He paused, studying her. "No, I don't. I guess I'm not romantic enough for you, Francie. Not at all."

He stalked out of the garden, and Francie sadly trailed back inside Sea Breeze, fighting tears.

She didn't bother to turn back the coverlet on her bed but instead lay on top of it in the dark, thinking about how the day had gone.

"Francie, are you awake?" Marie whispered. "Can I come in? Can we talk?"

"Sure." Francie sat up and made room for Marie.

"I want to be with Edward, but he can't stay here now that the hotel is finished. Francie, he's asked me to marry him! I love him so much, and I can't bear to think of life without him. What should I do?"

Francie blinked back the tears that threatened again. "Oh, Marie, I don't think you should sneak off with him. Why can't you tell Aunt Dorothea and Uncle Leonard?"

"They'll never understand."

Francie thought of the looks that passed between her uncle and aunt, the silent messages that only two deeply committed people could share. "I think they will. They'll understand love."

"Pray with me, Francie? Please?"

"Of course. Dearest God, we ask Your guidance for Marie and for Your peaceful understanding to touch Aunt Dorothea and Uncle Leonard. Please lead Marie and Edward in a way that is pleasing to You. And, God, thank You for Your gift of love that elevates us all. Amen."

"Amen," Marie whispered. "Amen."

◆　◆　◆

Thomas walked along the path toward Arch Rock. He rarely went to that part of the island, but tonight the stark beauty of the curved rock called to him. He wouldn't run the risk of meeting someone on the way and having to be sociable, not at this time of night.

He walked along, his hands shoved into his pockets, mulling over the terrible day. Why had he argued so much with Francie? In retrospect, it seemed that he'd been purposely starting battles with her.

He knew the answer. He was afraid of loving her.

Thomas sank to his knees near the arch and opened his heart. He couldn't pray as his father did, or even as simply as Francie did. He simply pushed aside his doubts and let faith take over—let his heart speak in its own language.

A calm came over him, like restful sleep for the exhausted body, like cool water for the thirsty soul. And he knew.

He had his proof. He'd had it all along. He belonged to God. It was that simple.

A sound broke his reverie. He opened his eyes and smiled. Emerson was sprawled next to him, his head resting on his paws and snoring softly.

Chapter 9

I'm going to be as round as a pumpkin by the end of the summer," Francie objected as she and Marie headed for the fudge shop. "Already my dresses are straining at the seams."

"Oh, be quiet," her cousin chided. "It's just for the summer and—say, I think that's Edward down by the dock. Oh my, will you look at that! Thomas is with him."

"That can't be, not after last night," Francie said, "but it certainly does look like them."

"Let's go see."

Thomas and Edward were in deep conversation when they arrived, and they looked up in surprise when the women greeted them.

Thomas drew himself up straight. "I apologized to Edward, and I'd like to apologize to both of you. I was acting like a goon yesterday, and I promise that it won't happen again. Or if it does, you have my permission to bring me back to reality as directly as possible." He grinned.

Francie smiled back and turned to Marie, but her cousin was ashen. "Edward," she said in a low voice, "is that a schedule in your hand? Are you leaving the island?"

He took her hands in his. "Marie, if you don't tell your parents, there's no reason for us to go on. I respect them, and I won't do this behind their backs. We've been deceptive too long as it is."

"They're home now," Marie said.

"I'm ready if you are." Edward gave her a reassuring smile. "Shall we all go to Sea Breeze?"

◆   ◆   ◆

Francie sat on the sofa next to Thomas. She was too nervous to move as Marie and Edward told her parents and grandmother of their romance.

"And this is why I would like to marry your daughter," Edward ended.

"I see." Uncle Leonard leaned back in his chair. "Yes, I see. Well, Dorothea, what do you think? Should we let this young man take our only child?"

Aunt Dorothea turned her head away from the couple and buried her face in her hands. Her shoulders shook.

"Mama—" Marie rose to go to her, but Aunt Dorothea held up her hand to ward her off.

"No. No, Marie. No." Her voice was muffled and the words broken.

"Papa?" Marie went to her father and dropped to her knees in front of him. "Papa?"

He, too, looked away. As he did, Francie saw emotions twitching beneath his stoic facade.

Grandmama Christiana thumped her cane. "Leonard, this young man may not be the most appropriate match, but truth be told, this girl is no spring chicken. He's probably the best she can do."

Francie tried not to gasp. This wasn't going at all the way she'd expected it would, and from the horrified expression on Marie's face, she was equally flummoxed.

For a moment, all was silent. Even the sounds of Middle Meg puttering in the next room stopped.

This has to be a bad dream, and I'll wake up any minute, Francie told herself.

Then Aunt Dorothea raised her head. "We are a dreadful bunch," she said, and Francie realized that she had been laughing, not crying.

Grandmama Christiana's wrinkled lips curled into a soft smile. "I had the love of a lifetime with your grandfather. He was a good man, not afraid of work and ready to serve the Lord with his every action. Dorothea had to remind me that I had concerns about her, too, when he started courting her."

"You did? You never told me—" Uncle Leonard began, but she cut his words off.

"No parent would let a child go blindly into love without doing everything in his or her power to ensure that it was God's will." She turned to Marie. "We've known about this all along. We've just been letting you have some room to let your love grow and blossom, like one of Dorothea's flowers."

Uncle Leonard pretended to glower at Edward. "All the time, we've been monitoring it, though. Don't think for a moment we'd let our daughter run wild."

"But how did—I mean, if you—if we—" Marie stammered.

"People in love are transparent," Grandmama Christiana said. "You have no secrets. We simply wanted to make sure that you two know the love we have."

Aunt Dorothea stood and hugged them both. "We're very glad for both of you. Now, if you don't mind, we have a wedding to plan!"

Francie and Thomas left the living room and went to the garden. "That was amazing," she said to him. "They knew!"

"Do you suppose they also knew the mysterious visitors to the garden were Marie and Edward?" he asked.

"Does it matter?"

"You're so right. Sometimes we just need to stop analyzing and let love be love, don't we?"

Whatever Francie was about to say was interrupted by Thomas kissing her. As she moved into his embrace, she noticed the flutter of a curtain in Grandmama Christiana's window, and she understood. The family must have known who the specters were, but they chose not to destroy the magic of the moonlit garden, where love blossomed in the glow of dreamlight.

Epilogue

A year later

The wedding guests moved through Aunt Dorothea's garden, commenting on her skill with the blooms. Middle Meg, wearing her Sunday best, made sure that everyone had a slice of Mackinac Island fudge with his or her tea. Early afternoon sun poured over them, drenching them with golden light.

Francie, though, couldn't keep her eyes off the new addition to her left hand. The wedding ring was simple yet beautiful, and even in the warmth, it was cool and smooth.

It had been the wedding of her dreams. The small church had been filled with guests and the sweet smell of Aunt Dorothea's flowers. Reverend Carlton had performed the wedding, with Marie and Edward as the attendants. Even her parents had come back from Brazil.

They sat on the bench, leafing through her sketchbook. "Which ones are going to be in the book?" her mother asked her.

"I've selected thirty-two of them. I can't believe that *Francie's Fancies* is going to be a children's book." She smiled to herself as she thought how much pain the name had once caused her, but now it fit the drawings in the notebook. They were her fancies, born of the imaginative mind God had given her.

"We're so proud of you." Her father beamed happily. "God has done great things for you."

Uncle Leonard and Aunt Dorothea joined them. "How are you two enjoying staying at the Grand Hotel?" Uncle Leonard asked her parents. "It's quite the attraction."

Before they could answer, a yellow dog bounded into the midst of the party. Teacups and plates were righted just in time as the animal headed straight for Francie.

"Emerson, you silly dog," she said, leaning over to rub his head. "Were you feeling left out?"

Thomas laughed. "Did you marry me for myself or for my dog?"

"I said yes to you before the stableman said you could have Emerson," she said as she stood up and took his hands in hers, her heart bubbling with joy, "but I'm glad to have you both."

They stood under the bower, their fingers entwined, until Grandmama Christiana's voice broke the trance. "Does Francie know that beast is eating her veil?"

In first grade, **JANET SPAETH** was asked to write a summary of a story about a family making maple syrup. She wrote all during class, through morning recess, lunch, and afternoon recess, and asked to stay after school. When the teacher pointed out that a summary was supposed to be shorter than the original story, Janet explained that she didn't feel the readers knew the characters well enough, so she was expanding on what was in the first-grade reader. Thus a writer was born. She lives in the Midwest and loves to travel, but to her, the happiest word in the English language is *home*.

Black Widow

by Jennifer Rogers Spinola

Dedication

To Roger and Kathleen Bruner, my friends,
Bass Pro Shop partners, and writing confidantes.
None of this would ever have been possible without ya!

Chapter 1

Whoa, there, boy—easy. Easy," Wyatt Kelly whispered, tightening the reins as Samson eased his way through the squeaky stable gate in the shadows. "Not a sound. Shh. That's it." He clucked softly and pulled the large stallion to a stop, listening. Straining for any sound in the chilly, moonlit night.

A weak shiver of dry grasses rattled together in the wind, a skeletal and foreboding sound. The distant flutter of an owl's wings, the faraway squeak of a field mouse. All cold and autumn-chilly under a brilliant, frost-white moon.

The same bright moon that had hid its face in a mournful sliver the day the Cheyenne murdered his family so many years ago. Leaving their bodies crumpled on the prairie grasses and skinny Wyatt Kelly bawling his eyes out. Shaking in terror.

The only thing he'd brought with him to his uncle's ranch as a lonely child was his father's mare and gentle, loyal Samson, her only wobbly colt. Wyatt had spent his younger years crouched in the stable, talking his lungs out to Samson.

And Samson listened, blinking great liquid eyes.

The only part of his family, save the distant and skeptical Uncle Hiram, that remained intact.

"That's it, Samson," Wyatt whispered, pulling on the reins. "Quiet, old boy. We'll be back before you know it." He pulled off his cowboy hat to hear better as he turned back toward the ranch house, which lay darkened with night, its windows black.

He held his breath as he flicked the reins slightly, urging Samson ahead, step after silent step. Wincing with each slight patter of gravel under Samson's massive hooves or the faint groan of leather saddle and reins. The *clink* of metal stirrup against boot, the squeak of the chilly lantern handle.

Wyatt's palm turned clammy against the cold barrel of his Winchester rifle as he eased Samson past the log smokehouse and barns, keeping his head down and reins taut. Past the ranch hands' quarters and the long log fence, cold wind fluttering his black coat around him like a shroud. Wyatt didn't trust any of the ranch hands—none of the stable boys or Irish washerwomen. Not the sour-faced cook who turned out apple tarts and hearty stews. And especially not the mysterious Arapaho girl who'd come from a French trapper's colony in Idaho, all her Indian beads and braids hidden under her bonnet and demure white-and-blue cottons. Her cool demeanor unnerved him; Uncle Hiram swore a married girl that young and alone looking for work must be up to no good. After the gold, even.

And yet she trained horses like nobody he'd ever seen. "Jewel," folks called her—for no one really knew her name—brushed and braided and combed manes and tails, hauled feed and scrubbed troughs, poured water and broke the skins of ice that formed across the surface of the water barrels on frosty mornings. Wyatt and the stable boys would pause, mesmerized, as she trained and saddle-broke the wildest, most cantankerous colts from the end of a slim leather tether—moving in graceful circles, her long skirts and shawls swishing and beaded necklaces making a bell-like clinking, like iced branches in the winter wind.

But not even Jewel had a clue where he was headed tonight. He hadn't spoken a word—just slipped out to the ticking of the mantel clock, lifting his rifle from above the fireplace.

If only he could get to Crazy Pierre's old homestead in time to find the gold.

First. While everyone else—his uncle, the Crowder brothers, gold-thirsty prospectors—slept soundly, blissfully ignorant. Stumped once again by Crazy Pierre's insane old ramblings.

But not Wyatt Kelly. For once in his life, he'd figured something out.

Wyatt's hands trembled as Samson clipped softly down the ridge and through the grasses, leaving the ranch behind in crisp stillness. He lit the lantern, making spiny shadows across the prairie hills, and urged Samson to a slow trot as the giant teeth of the Rockies bit into the horizon. Vast and ghostlike.

Keeping his hushed secret with silent, brooding eyes.

◆ ◆ ◆

Crazy Pierre DuLac's ramshackle cabin, its roof cracked open from a windstorm, lay just over the stream and beyond the ridge—just a few miles from the Yellowstone National Park boundary. Nestled just down the ridge from Uncle Hiram Kelly's cabin, where Wyatt forked straw and scrubbed stalls and hated the stench of cow manure and dust—and, frankly, his life in general. After all, there wasn't much else he was good at, except reading dusty legal volumes, taking care of Uncle Hiram's lousy bookkeeping, settling his uncle's debts, and trying not to let the prize bull gore him.

"A silly bookworm," Uncle Hiram grunted when he saw Wyatt sitting over one of those heavy legal books or volumes of agricultural sales, peering down through his glasses and moving his lips in quiet thought. "That's what you are. You're not your father, Wyatt—that's for sure. No sir. Amos Kelly was a real man. A real man with hair on his chest."

Wyatt would bristle to himself and pretend not to notice, dipping his pen in ink and scratching out a few notes about syllogistic fallacies and mathematical equations to show the rise in wool prices versus the growth in corn equity. Trying to hide the embarrassing bloom of red that spread over his face.

But not for much longer.

Crazy Pierre, rumors whispered, had buried all the gold he'd bought from the Indians for a pittance about fifty years ago. Gold nuggets the Sioux probably stole from Ezra Kind and his bunch after they panned a wagonload of it out of ice-clear rivers in the Black Hills back in 1834—and left a frantic message for help carved in sandstone.

A fellow named Thoen found Kind's message in South Dakota in 1887, giving authenticity to the theory that the gold was real—and plentiful.

Wyatt clucked to Samson and paused to let a screech owl flap out of the way, reining in the horse when he reared slightly. He slipped his hand in his coat pocket and unfolded a battered sheet of ledger paper where he'd penned Ezra Kind's message from the Thoen Stone as accurately as he could:

Come to these hills in 1833 — Seven of us — Delacompt — Ezra Kind — G. W.
Wood — T. Brown — R. Kent — Wm. King —Indian Crow — all dead but me,
Ezra Kind — killed by Indians beyond the high hill — Got our gold. June 1834 —
Got all the gold we could carry — our ponies all got by the Indians — I have lost my
gun and nothing to eat and — Indians hunting me.

"All the gold we could carry." Wyatt repeated the words to himself in a whisper, trying to imagine the sheer quantity of gold that would weigh down seven full-grown men. He shook his head, mentally adding zeros to his wildest numerical dollar value.

Locals said that two winters after Ezra Kind scratched his note into rock, Pierre met a group of Sioux Indians hauling a frayed burlap sack full of glittering nuggets up to a trading post in Montana.

Twelve new long rifles, a thick stack of cast-off wool army blankets, and the pocket watch he'd swiped off a dead banker sealed the trade, so the legend spun—and the Indians handed over the loot to Pierre. After all, what good was a bag of glittering rocks when winter snows blew into the drought-thin teepees and the buffalo had been driven so far southeast by the Chippewa that hunters brought home little more than prairie dogs?

Pierre, in his infinite wisdom, celebrated his purchase with a drunken bar brawl in Cody. When he woke up in his straw-tick bed a few days later, he had no idea how he'd gotten home from Cody—or where he'd buried the gold.

Snows fell heavy across the northeastern corner of Wyoming during the hard winter of 1836, and March passed before young Pierre finally dug out of his cabin and tried to find where he'd hidden his stash.

And for fifty solid years, Crazy Pierre dug holes all along the East Fork River.

Lending credence to the fact that he might have been. . .well, just plain daft.

◆　◆　◆

The local folk had long given up the idea of finding the gold—if there ever was any gold at all—since fifty years was a long time for loot of that magnitude to sit around. But just before the US Army took over Yellowstone National Park, which lay just across the creek from Pierre's place, rumors began to spread that old Pierre had hit pay dirt. Or *found* it.

1886—a mere five years ago.

Folks spotted him in the saloons swilling whiskey like a madman, exuberantly buying up land and horses and dropping wads of cash. When he heard that the army had taken over the park and vigilantly hunted down poachers, Crazy Pierre boarded up his cabin, sent a sealed letter off to some relatives in the Northwest, and died in a bar fight over a card game in Deadwood, South Dakota, three weeks later.

Leaving everybody scratching their heads over the gold.

Crazy Pierre indeed. Wyatt carefully folded up the paper and slipped it back in his pocket, fingering the rusty metal key ring that clinked against the lining of his coat. Brilliant Opportunist Pierre was more like it. Folks said the pocket watch he traded the Indians didn't even work right—and the glass casing was broken.

And now, if his hunch and the battered old keys told the truth, Wyatt was about to find out.

He eased Samson under a stand of low-growing trees and quietly dismounted, turning his head this way and that to listen for any sound of mountain lions or coyotes—or worse, intruders. But he heard nothing save the wind in lonely trees, rattling thin branches against the crumbly sides of Pierre's cabin.

"Wyatt?"

He jumped, fumbling with the keys and dropping them in the underbrush. He jerked up the lantern and swiveled his head around but saw no one but Samson. Samson whinnied again nervously and pawed the ground—an eerie sound.

"Shh, old fella." Wyatt patted Samson's graying head as he snatched up the lantern, leaving his rifle tied to the saddle. "We'll be quick. You'll see. I'll be in and out of here in a few minutes, if the coffer's where I think it is." He turned back at Samson's grunt of disapproval and stroked the sleek brown flank, whispering sweet nothings in Samson's velvet ear. "And you'll get your oats when we're done. I promise."

Wyatt scrabbled in the dried grass and moss for his keys, scolding himself for being so clumsy. Why, just yesterday he'd dropped them in the stable, and it had taken him hours to frantically track them down—under a clump of straw and mud. Wyatt Kelly, the most accident-prone man alive—who once nearly bashed his head in by stepping on a garden rake.

Wyatt tucked his Colt revolver tighter into his holster and stepped over snarls of ancient roots as he strode toward the cabin, holding up the lantern. He leaned close to the broken window, darkened with age, breathing in the dank, musty smell of old boards and forgotten rooms. Mice-eaten panels and a caved-in roof.

A shudder passed through Wyatt with tingly horror as he passed his light on dusty cobwebs, which hung from the ceiling in opaque sheets, quivering in the breeze from the broken windows and roof. He trembled slightly, leaning against the mossy shutters for support.

Spiders. The thought of slender arachnid legs churned the long-eaten brisket in his stomach, making him wish he'd gone to bed without dinner. But if stalking through spiders' nests was what he had to do to find Crazy Pierre's gold, so be it. Wyatt loosened his collar, feeling nervous sweat prickle under his hat.

So long as he could keep the blood in his head and put one boot in front of the other.

Wait a second—was that a light from inside? Or merely the reflection of his own lantern? Wyatt forced his glasses deeper on his nose and leaned closer, squinting against broken glass to see better, and felt a brittle tree root give way under his boot. When he scrambled to his feet, banging his shoulder against a crooked shutter and nearly bashing the lantern against the stone-and-log wall, the light had vanished.

Wyatt turned the lantern this way and that against the shattered glass, feeling a nervous ripple down his spine.

"Calm down, for pity's sake," he scolded himself, annoyed at his shaking hands and clammy cheeks. "It's your own reflection, man. Pull yourself together and get in there before Kirby Crowder does."

Wyatt squared his timid shoulders and marched around to the front of the cabin.

Well, well. What do you know. Wyatt tamped the smooth soil at the base of the old door with his boot, that tense quiver traveling down his spine again. *Pierre's had visitors. And recently.*

The last time Wyatt had come to the cabin, windblown soil and leaves covered the threshold, piling up so deeply over the old ruin of a door that he'd had to shovel before it pushed open—and even then with difficulty.

A strand of torn cobweb inside flickered in the lantern light, blowing.

His heart thrummed as he pushed the door open with a long and plaintive creak, wishing he'd unstrapped his rifle and brought that with him, too. He held the lantern in one hand and swiped at cobwebs with the other, observing the mess: The chimney lay in ruins, a stack of broken and charred stones, and the floor had heaved and cracked from tree roots. The ancient table had tilted and smashed into the wall. An old branch still hung from the gash in the roof, splitting the ceiling open. Wyatt looked up through frosty wire-rimmed glasses, holding his breath, and saw starlight.

A rough stone staircase led down to the old root cellar, its chilly interior dank with age. Lantern light splashed down the uneven steps in bright slants, glowing against old broken barrels and glass jars. The bright red hairs on the back of his neck tingled with the eerie sensation of being watched—and yet he saw no one, heard no breath or movement.

Wyatt swiped the lantern back and forth, making shadows slant and bend, but the root cellar remained wordless and clammy. Gravelike and silent.

And then—a bump, a sound. A scurrying.

He froze on the last step, motionless. Stilling the squeaking lantern handle and swinging globe with his free hand.

But as he swiveled around, his wobbly lantern beam illuminated nothing but empty, dusty shelves. Old barrels and feed sacks in the corner. An ancient pair of boots. Wyatt kicked one, and a mouse darted out of the boot and into a crevice in the wall.

Wyatt shuddered, jumping back in disgust.

An abandoned Smith & Wesson revolver gleamed back from an empty shelf, which lay sticky with cobwebs, and Wyatt picked up the revolver in surprise. No dust on the barrel, and the stock looked well kept and polished.

Why had it been left behind? A relic from a gold digger a few years past, forgotten? It couldn't have been Crazy Pierre's. Not in such good shape, with no dust or rust.

No matter. There was no time for speculation. Not now, when he stood so close to the box that had eluded him for years.

Wyatt dropped the revolver back on the shelf, feeling his fingers tremble with excitement. He counted the rotten oak shelves, measuring over exactly two feet, and then pried out a loose board from the floor below. Then another. The next board split in his hand, crumbling with a tinny sound onto something beneath the boards.

His heart stood still as the lantern beam illuminated a dusty box.

An ancient wooden box with rusty metal braces and a lock just the right size to fit a key in Wyatt's hand.

Wyatt knelt down, his hands shaking so much he nearly dropped the precious keys in his sweaty fingers, and inserted the first key into the lock. This key ring was nearly as valuable as the gold; he'd found it with the infamous initials carved in the rough metal: PDL. *Pierre DuLac.* Or in local Wyoming vernacular, Crazy Pierre.

A rusty key ring to match the coffer. The missing link everybody'd been looking for. Men would kill for this.

He tugged and jiggled, but it held fast.

He pulled out the key and tried another and then another, but still the lock refused to budge.

Wyatt tried each of the keys again, one after the other—grunting and straining at the lock.

And. . .nothing.

Wait a second. Wyatt jerked up the key ring and shook it in the light. Three keys? He thought there were four.

Weren't there. . . ?

Wyatt counted again, feeling the color drain from his face.

At that exact moment, he heard a sneeze. A distinct bump, coming from the dank recesses of the room behind the cluster of barrels and feed sacks.

Wyatt scrambled to his feet, stumbling twice, and pulled his Colt from its holster.

"Come out now," he ordered, trying to make his voice sound sterner than he really felt as he cocked the hammer. "Or I'll blow all those barrels to bits."

Silence.

Wyatt moved closer, his boots shuffling on the hard-packed earth. A cobweb tickled his neck, and he slapped at it, trying to keep his teeth from chattering. Kirby Crowder was probably crouching back there with his posse, waiting to pump him full of lead and gunpowder.

Men had died over gold. Ezra Kind's whole group of prospectors back in 1834, including a Crow scout, had probably been murdered by the Sioux in an attempt to keep the gold in the Black Hills. And the likes of the Crowder brothers—and whatever scum they'd dug up from bars and gambling outfits—sure wouldn't think twice about slitting Wyatt's throat for a chest of gold.

Wyatt steadied the gun and eased a step closer, kicking at one of the barrels. "Come out with your hands up, or I'll shoot."

His hand on the trigger flinched, palms sweaty.

And before he could pull it, a shadowy figure rose slowly from behind the barrels, casting a terrible shadow.

Wyatt thrust the lantern forward, heart pounding in his throat.

Chapter 2

Jewel?" Wyatt leaped back, feeling the blood drain from his face as if he'd seen the ghost of Crazy Pierre himself. He reeled, light-headed. "Uh. . .Miss Jewel? Ma'am?" he corrected, trying to recall his manners as a thousand disbelieving thoughts hit him at once.

Take off your hat, Wyatt! For pity's sake. Wyatt scrambled for his brown leather cowboy hat with his free hand, gun wobbling, and clumsily dropped the hat on the floor.

"What," he stammered, "in thunder's name are you doing here?" He cleared his throat, all nerves and shaking fingers. "Ma'am?"

Wait. Shouldn't he translate? The girl spoke as much English as her ridiculous Indian pony. Arapaho, maybe, the few words he knew—or French or something? She came from a French trapper's outpost in Idaho. That much he knew, from all his wasted tutoring sessions back at Uncle Hiram's cabin—mainly trying to pry her knowledge of the gold.

But his dry mouth couldn't form any words. Couldn't think.

On a good day at the ranch he could barely meet her eyes, so graceful she was—so darkly mysterious, so confident. Oh, how he envied her ease and confidence—her uplifted chin and sparkling black eyes, meeting his for a fleeting second over the Bible pages or across the stable.

And his gaze would flutter away in embarrassment, landing on his boots or the table, or on her simple wedding band. Scurrying off like a field mouse before she noticed the ruddy glow in his freckled cheeks.

Jewel raised her head from behind the barrels, her earrings glittering in the light from the lantern, and said nothing.

"Answer me, miss, or. . .or. . ." Wyatt couldn't finish his own sentence, trying to keep the gun level and make his lips move. "Why are you here? At my uncle's, and at Crazy Pierre's?"

He blinked, feeling sweat break out on his forehead under his hat. Her appearance made no sense. His uncle's Arapaho horse trainer who bungled all her verbs and couldn't understand a lick of English? In Crazy Pierre's root cellar at midnight? Black spots swirled before his eyes, and he reached out a shaky hand to steady himself against a brittle shelf.

Jewel lifted her chin in an almost haughty manner. "My given name is Collette Moreau," she said coldly in perfect English, standing up to her full height. Hands raised. "But you may call me Jewel like everyone else. What are *you* doing here?" She nodded to the floor. "And you may get your hat."

Wyatt stared then fumbled on the dirt-littered floor for his hat. He slapped it back on his head at a crooked angle.

"I'm. . .I'm looking for something," Wyatt stammered, strangely unnerved by her calm and even accusatory demeanor. For pity's sake. He was the one holding the gun!

He jabbed the gun barrel forward, trying to keep a steady grip as his palms perspired. "How did you find out about this place?" *Wait a second.* "You speak English?" Wyatt stared, openmouthed. "I thought you could. . .could barely get out a sentence."

His mind reeled as he recalled hours and weeks of tedious tutoring, trying not to fall asleep at his uncle's brawny oak table while she stammered over the simplest of words in the thick family Bible. He'd lean his stubbly red-bearded chin in his hand and yawn, pulling off his glasses to wipe bored tears from his eyes.

"That fool girl can't speak a word of English," Uncle Hiram had said after she left, rocking back in his chair and making the wooden slats of the chair groan in complaint. *"Figures. Redskins are awful slow at learning. Which is why you've gotta work your hardest to get anything she knows outta her. You hear?"* He swept an arm around the golden-hued room. *"This is a fine ranch, Wyatt, but we'd be sitting on a gold mine if she led us to that treasure. Why, we'd be kings. You know that?"*

Now here Wyatt stood, trying to remember how that same tongue-tied girl—who had stumbled over his broken French and questions about the gold with blank eyes—had just spoken in flawless English.

"But I thought. . ." Wyatt blinked at her through crooked glasses.

"Of course I speak English." Derision flashed in Jewel's eyes. "I did go to school, you know—the mission school where I grew up—and I worked for an English doctor for a while. I've heard and understood every word you've said since your uncle hired me on the ranch. And as for the intelligence of my people, why don't you let me give you a lesson in Arapaho nouns—since you think you're so smart?" Jewel moved closer. "Truth is, you can't even say the name of my pony correctly, and I've told you dozens of times. You pronounce all the consonants wrong, and you've absolutely no tonal distinction whatsoever."

She put her hands down slowly and moved, as if in defiance, from behind the barrel, sweeping her long skirts and shawl with graceful ease.

Wyatt took a step back and kept himself between Jewel and the revolver on the shelf, trembling. "So this is your gun," he said, finally finding words. He picked it up and stuffed it in his belt. "And that must have been your light I saw. Now get your hands up, or I'll. . .I'll shoot!" He gulped the words down, ashamed. He'd sooner put a bullet through Uncle Hiram's prize stallion than this wisp of an Indian girl who worked tirelessly, frosty dawn to blue-cold evening, without complaint.

Then again, she'd probably shoot him first if she got the chance.

Jewel made a swipe for her revolver and then put her hands back up. "Of course it's my gun. You think I'd be foolish enough to ride off the ranch at night without a firearm?" She tossed her head. "You startled me. I didn't have time to grab it before you came down the stairs."

Wyatt opened and closed his mouth. "So. . .you know." His words came out hoarse. "You know where the gold is."

Jewel tipped her chin up. "As if I'd tell you."

The gun wobbled in his hand as he took another step back, strangely terrified by her fearlessness. "I mean it! I'll shoot!" he stammered, gripping the stock with two hands to keep it from shaking.

"No you won't." Jewel crossed her arms as if in defiance. "What clues can I give you if I'm dead? That's what you've been after the whole time, isn't it? With your ridiculous questions about Pierre DuLac that you thought I couldn't understand?" She pushed the gun aside. "And you've got a spider on your head. Hope it's not a black widow. One bite can disable or even kill a man."

"A...a what? A spider?" Wyatt scrubbed at his head in a panic with the crook of his arm. "You're lying."

Jewel shrugged. "Suit yourself. Odds are it's a black widow, though. They nest in dark and undisturbed places just like this."

Wyatt wavered, and nausea rose in his gut. "Where is it?" He dropped the lantern on a shelf with a clatter and slapped his forehead, nearly dropping his gun. "Get it off me, will you?"

"Give me the gun." Jewel calmly held out her hand, rings sparkling. "Before you shoot yourself."

He hesitated, his chest heaving. How could she possibly know he hated spiders? His deepest, darkest, most tightly kept secret that he'd kept from everyone, including Uncle Hiram. What was she, some kind of a mind reader, intent on humiliating him beyond reason?

"You're lying." Beads of sweat broke out on Wyatt's forehead, and he leveled the gun at her, trying not to think of webs and crawling legs. "Put your hands up."

"If you say so." She fixed her stare on his forehead and raised her hands about two inches as if in mocking. "Black widows use a poison that paralyzes the nervous system of the body, you know," she added. "Which causes incredible swelling and pain. In fact, in just five minutes after the initial bite, the venom spreads to—"

"Cut it out!" Wyatt slapped at his head again in agony, doing a little dance.

"I'm warning you." Jewel held out her hand again. "Don't complain to me if you shoot a hole in your foot and can't walk to the doctor to get an antidote."

"Fine." Wyatt smacked the gun in her hand, trying not to hyperventilate. "Get it off me, will you?"

Jewel took the gun and leveled it at him. "Thanks." And she kept the gun trained on Wyatt, spreading out her skirts to kneel on the cold dirt floor in front of the wooden chest.

Wyatt shook out his hat and hair and then slowly turned to Jewel. "You were bluffing about the spider," he croaked, watching in horror as she produced a key from the folds of her skirt. No, two keys. His eyes bulged behind crooked glasses. "Why, I ought to...to..."

"To what?" Jewel aimed the gun at him. "Hands up, please." She wagged the barrel of the gun. "And don't bother trying to use my Smith & Wesson. It's empty. See for yourself. I used five rounds on a pack of coyotes on the way over here."

In a quick second Wyatt raised his head and pictured poor Samson hobbled to a tree by his lead, fending off half a dozen coyotes—while he poked around in Crazy Pierre's basement.

"Coyotes, you say?" He glanced upstairs nervously. "Did you kill them?"

"I'm an excellent shot, Mr. Kelly." She raised an eyebrow. "Samson's fine. I'm sure of it."

Wyatt swiveled his head back and forth between Jewel and the cellar door, mouth open in question.

"How did I know you were thinking of Samson?"

Jewel's tone softened, tender almost, and she gave the faintest hint of a smile. "I've seen you in the stable, Mr. Kelly. You might not be so good with roping and branding, but you love that horse. You'd do anything for him, wouldn't you?"

Wyatt felt his fingers quiver on her revolver, nearly dropping it, as that humiliating blush of heat climbed his neck.

The gun. The gun, for Pete's sake! Wyatt fumbled with the barrel, showing an empty chamber. Six hollow clicks. "So you are out of rounds. But. . .but you're lying about one thing, Mrs. Moreau." He stood up straighter and forced himself to meet her eyes. "There's no spider. And you stole my key."

"Of course I stole your key, since you were so kind as to leave it carelessly lying around in the stable. And"—she shot him a cool look—"it matched the one Pierre sent my husband."

"Your *husband*?" Wyatt sputtered, trying to straighten his glasses and nearly knocking them off. "That's who Pierre sent the letter to?"

"Thing is, you need two of his keys to open the lock." Jewel ignored him, holding both keys together. "See how they interlay?"

Good heavens. Wyatt craned his neck to see the pattern in the keys, which made a rough "PD" in dull metal. *Pierre DuLac. That son of a gun.*

"I didn't know there was a fourth key," Wyatt muttered, humiliated at being duped.

"What did you think, that Pierre would carry around the missing key to the coffer in his pocket while the US Army was tromping right past his house?"

"The army?" Wyatt scrunched up his face. "What are you talking about?"

"Yes, the army." Jewel raised her eyes boldly to meet his, endlessly black in the flickering light of the lantern. "Didn't they settle the borders of the national park while he was still living here?"

"What are you, a history expert?" Wyatt snapped, feeling like a simpleton.

Jewel ignored him. "And Pierre wanted for all kinds of crimes? What a ridiculous idea. He was smarter than that. He planned to come back to his cabin once the army backed off, and he sent the key to my husband for safekeeping. Intending to get it later."

"Your husband," Wyatt repeated in a hollow voice, feeling doubly duped. He took a chaste step back, putting his hands up so as not to touch her. "A Moreau."

"A *DuLac* Moreau."

"Well, you're overlooking something, Jewel. Collette Moreau. Whoever you are." Wyatt pointed a shaky finger. "I knew Crazy Pierre myself. I used to haul wood for him. And key or no key, you won't find the gold in that chest." He gestured with his head. "I saw him bury this. There's no gold inside."

"Liar." Jewel jabbed the gun at him.

"Don't believe me? Pick it up yourself. It's too light to hold gold." He scooted the wooden chest with his foot, and it moved easily. "And Crazy Pierre had far more gold than would fit inside a little box like that. Savvy?" He shot her a triumphant look. "But I have a hunch there's something inside that'll tell us where to look—and I bet I can interpret Pierre's clues. I met him, remember? You didn't."

Jewel shook the chest furiously, and Wyatt watched as her bright eyes dimmed and her lips turned downward. She sat back on her heels and rested her chin in her hand.

"Maybe you're right." Jewel swallowed and looked up, her long braid falling over her shoulder. "But I have something you don't."

"My key?" Wyatt took a step closer, his fingers curling into fists.

"And mine." She clinked them both together. "Plus the actual letter Crazy Pierre sent my husband with instructions."

"Give me my key back." He held out his hand.

"No." She hid the keys in her skirt pocket. "And I've got the gun, so I give the orders here."

They were stalemated. Wyatt stood there silently a moment, wondering if he should offer peace or try to grab the gun. He flexed his fingers and then made a swipe for the gun.

Wrong choice. Jewel turned the barrel on him in a liquid second, her dark eyes flashing.

"My uncle was right about you," Wyatt spluttered, slowly putting his hands up. Feeling hot, angry blood pump in his veins. "That's why you came here looking for work, isn't it? So you could pick us off one by one after you steal all our clues to find the gold?"

"Your uncle said that? Well, that's certainly ironic." She aimed coolly at him, and for the first time Wyatt's heart pulsed with real fear. "You've both been trying to get as much information as you can from me about the gold, but you've forgotten one thing."

"What's that?" Wyatt licked his lips, wondering if he could dart up the stairs or if she'd really shoot.

"That I've been doing the same thing with you."

"But. . .but you've no right! My uncle *hired* you!"

"He hired me to train his horses. Which I've done. Exceedingly well, I might add, on such a meager salary and without heat or running water in the bunkhouse." Jewel took a step closer. "Have you ever slept a night out there? It's pure misery in the winter. The place is full of rats."

"Still." Wyatt shivered, chilled by the images of scurrying mice and Jewel aiming at his nose. "Taking a job to smoke us out is wrong. And by taking the key, you've stolen from me."

"It's not your key. It belonged to Crazy Pierre." Jewel sniffed. "And why are you hiding it from your uncle? Skulking around here at midnight instead of telling him what you're doing?"

"Because my uncle can't keep a secret to save his life. He'd tell everybody in town about the key, and I'd be shot by a dozen gold diggers trying to strike it rich." Wyatt's pulse burned. "And what business of yours is it anyway? It's certainly more my key than yours."

"It was Crazy Pierre's key, and you stole it from him."

"I didn't steal it! I found it. There's a difference." Wyatt took a step forward. "I was in Deadwood, South Dakota, buying horses, and I found it in the stable grounds. Pierre died before I could return it to him."

"Really." Jewel smiled as if in amusement.

"It's the truth, I tell you! Why would I lie?"

She studied him a moment, her dark shadow quivering against a pitted wall in the flickering lantern light. "So you *found* the key." She narrowed her eyes. "Even if I believe you, it makes no difference. I also *found* it in the stable when I happened to be sweeping up. You dropped it there like refuse, did you not?"

"Irregardless, the key was my property!" Wyatt jabbed a finger at his chest.

"Irregardless?" She cupped a hand over a laugh. "That doesn't even make sense, Mr. Kelly. It's *regardless*."

"You're wrong!" He raised his voice, sweat prickling under his hat. "I think I know English."

"Well, I think I know prefixes. And it's wrong."

Wyatt felt his fists clench in fury. Of all the nerve. "Listen, miss," he growled, trying to think of an argument that would catch her, corner her, into letting him go and handing over the letter. "That key was protected in the domicile of my uncle, and I'll have you arrested!"

He waved an arm for emphasis, bluffing the first thing that came to mind. "The last time a no-good Indian stole something from one of the ranchers in this part of the state, the sheriff had him hung. You hear me?"

Jewel paled visibly in the lantern light.

"I'll have you arrested and taken before a magistrate before daybreak!" Wyatt leaned forward and tried to look menacing. Making it up as he went along. "Why, I know all about you. All about your. . .your sordid past. You thought I wouldn't find out, but I know everything—and I'll tell it all to the judge!"

Jewel swallowed, and the revolver shook in her hands.

What on earth did I say? Wyatt's jaw dropped in surprise.

"You don't know anything about me," she hissed, taking a step closer and holding the gun out with both hands.

"I know everything." He didn't back away, determined not to lose the upper hand—no matter how he'd come by it. "And if you kill me now, it won't be the first time. You'll hang for it!"

"If you kill me now, it won't be the first time?" Wyatt halted, horrified. What did he mean by that? That it wouldn't be the first time she'd killed Wyatt? How utterly ridiculous. What, did he sleep through grammar school? He gripped his head in both hands, wondering how he managed—by sheer, bumbling luck—to mess up everything.

"Fine. Take it." Jewel thrust the revolver at him so swiftly he nearly dropped it. "You don't turn me in, and I won't turn you in. Deal?"

"Uh. . .pardon?" Wyatt craned his neck to see through smudged glasses.

"Let's just start over—you, Mr. Kelly—and me, nobody of any consequence." Jewel flipped the corner of her shawl around her shoulder, a movement that should have resonated carelessness but did not. Instead, Wyatt noticed her eyes take on a terrified cast, like a deer startled by an intruder.

"As business partners. Fifty-fifty. Everything secret. Do you agree?" She knotted her hands behind her back, and Wyatt saw them trembling.

"Fifty-fifty?" Wyatt felt the weight of the revolver in his hands, like an idiot, and quickly spun it around to face her. "Are you crazy? You lied about the spider. How can I trust you with anything?"

"Oh no. I didn't lie about that." Jewel gazed up at his forehead. "It's. . .still there. And I'm quite sure it's a black widow." She leaned forward, squinting. "Yes. Red hourglass."

And at that exact second, Wyatt felt something stir his hair. Something thin and tiny, like the brush of an insect leg.

"You were going to let it bite me." Wyatt gazed at her in accusation, his chest heaving. He'd hurled his hat and glasses across the room before clawing at his leather vest and stomping senselessly at the fleeing black speck.

Now Jewel crouched near his fallen glasses, trying to bend the crooked frame back into shape.

"A black widow, Mrs. Moreau. Really. How can I partner with you after that?"

"You were going to shoot me." She wiped the glass lens on the hem of her skirt. "I figured it was fair."

Wyatt didn't respond, checking his hair again with a shaky hand. "Partners," he muttered, turning up his lip. "How can I partner with the likes of you?"

Jewel coldly handed him his glasses, her warm fingers brushing his briefly. "How can you afford not to?"

Wyatt took the glasses with a terse nod of thanks and tried to straighten them on his face, his heart beating dizzy-fast again. Was she threatening him? After all, Jewel had obviously done something in the past that frightened her—something that made her want to forget it. Had she stolen something bigger than a key or. . .killed someone? The only bluff that made her take notice was the law. The magistrate.

Which meant. . .

Hairs stood up on Wyatt's neck as he studied her there in the dim lantern light. The keys in her hand, glinting, and her downcast eyes. The sparkling beaded earring that caught the light in colorful spots, next to the graceful curves of her neck.

"Who are you?" he whispered, holding up the lantern to see her better.

"Jewel," she replied in mocking tones. "You know my name."

"That's what people call you. But that's not your real name."

"Collette Moreau. You know that, too." She raised her face defiantly. "An Indian and a woman who can't be trusted, and who couldn't possibly learn the English language. What else do you want from me?"

"Tell me more." Wyatt didn't know if he was asking or ordering, but he couldn't pull the lantern away from her face. "Who are you? Where do you come from?"

He warily set his Colt down on a shelf next to a collection of dingy, dust-covered bottles. "Tell me the truth." He hung his thumbs in his belt loops and glanced at her, shifting his hat nervously on his head.

Jewel's head came up, and she studied him in silence.

"Look." Wyatt crossed his arms. "Everybody has a thing or two to say about you in town, and around the ranch, but nobody really knows the truth."

"The truth." Jewel gave a sad half laugh and looked away, putting her hands on her hips. "Is that what they really want?"

Wyatt swallowed, and the scarlet bandanna around his stubbly throat felt tight. "It's what *I* want."

"Why?"

He scuffed the heel of his boot in the dirt, shrugging his shoulders. "Nobody even knows your real name. Except. . .well, me. Why is that? Why are you hiding?" He waved an arm around the root cellar. "Digging around in the dirt in a cabin at midnight?"

Jewel didn't answer, twisting her wedding ring back and forth on her finger. "If you must know, I am Arapaho and French," she finally said in a tender tone, her gaze seeming to go right through Wyatt as if not seeing him at all. "I'm the daughter of an Arapaho chief, born in an Arapaho village just outside the border in Nebraska." She swallowed and looked down at her hands. Her delicate fingers, now worn from cold water and harsh soaps. "I was sold as a bride to a French trapper in Idaho when I was a young girl."

It took Wyatt a second to register that Jewel hadn't answered his question. Did she share her real name because she. . .trusted him? On some level? A wash of heat spread through his chest, and he blinked faster.

Of course not. It was probably all part of her twisted plot to pull the wool over his eyes, like everything else. He shifted his position against the shelf, keeping his gaze focused on his boots.

"How young were you?" he asked gruffly when she said no more.

"Fourteen years old."

Wyatt's hands clenched against the shelf, trying to still the angry throb in his heart at the thought of a fourteen-year-old slip of a girl being bought and sold like a mare—worse, like one of Uncle Hiram's prize cattle—for a few gold coins or some blankets.

"So what are you doing here in Wyoming?" he finally asked, clearing his throat.

"I am Hagar," she replied. "From the Bible you taught me at your table."

"Huh?" Wyatt shook his head to make sense of her words. "I mean, ma'am? Pardon?"

"Running from great injustice and much suffering." Tears gilded the corners of her eyes as she fumbled with the keys, knotting her fingers together. "I need this gold. Please. Help me find it. There's enough for both of us, if the legends about Crazy Pierre are true. And I have reason to believe they are."

"What do you mean you *need* the gold?"

Jewel turned, and a shadow covered part of her face. "I can't tell you why. But I need it. My life may depend on it."

Wyatt crossed his arms. "Well, I need the gold, too, you know."

"You? For what?"

He hesitated. "To pay back an old wrong," he said quietly, his hands clenching into fists. "I've been planning it all my life. And I'm so close now." Wyatt squeezed his eyes closed, scarcely daring to breathe. "So close I can almost feel it. After all these years, maybe I'll finally make amends for my father's death."

Jewel regarded him quietly. "I'm sorry about your family, Mr. Kelly." She spoke so softly he had to lean forward to hear well. "I know you miss them."

Emotion quivered in Wyatt's chest, and he feigned a cough to cover it, pretending he hadn't heard. "So how can I know you're telling the truth about your. . .your story?" He gestured with his arm. "You could be spinning a yarn, for all I know."

"So could you. And to answer your question, you'll just have to trust me."

"What if that's not good enough?"

"The truth is all I have, Mr. Kelly." She spread her hands wide. Cracks showed on the tips of her fingers. And before she could cover it, he noticed an ugly scar running the length of one brown forearm when her long wool sleeve fell back.

Jewel faced him there in the darkness, eyes glazed with sorrow, and something stirred in Wyatt's gut. *She has spoken the truth.*

"Well, come on then." Wyatt stuck his revolver back in his belt and reached gruffly for the wooden box. "We'd better get out of here. We'll take it with us and open it in daylight. What do you say?"

"Fine. But don't even think of opening it without me." Jewel picked up her darkened lantern and held up his, which threw gold across the dusty wood of the box. "Fifty-fifty. You keep the box, and I keep the keys." She patted her pocket. "Partners, right?"

Wyatt lifted the box, and something rattled inside. Sliding around the inside of the box with a tinny, metallic sound. He tucked the box under one arm and paused to let Jewel go first, tipping his hat by habit, and then he took the stone steps two at a time. Unspeakably grateful to leave behind the musty root cellar, which crawled with spiders and reeked of sour pickles.

As soon as he reached the top, he heard voices.

Two men's voices, filtering from the woods into the broken ruins of Crazy Pierre's house. Distant torches flickered against the trees in glances of light and shadow, splintering in long stripes against the crumbling log walls.

"Of all the rotten luck!" Wyatt hissed, ducking under the low cellar doorway and furiously brushing away cobwebs. "They've caught up with us."

"Who?" Jewel took a step back toward Wyatt.

"The Crowder brothers. They're ruthless. They'll kill us both." He put a finger to his lips.

"There are two of us and two of them. We're matched."

"Naw." Wyatt stroked his chin as a wave of nausea flitted through his stomach. "Not against the Crowders. They're crazy, both of them—and they carry more lead with them than a whole infantry. Why, I've only got a few more rounds. We're finished, you know that?"

"Can we make it outside?" Jewel stumbled over a sunken piece of flooring and caught herself against a rough-hewn chair.

"Nope. They'll see us for sure if we waltz right out the door." Dull glass in the single window sparkled in sharp shards, and the opening was too small to squeeze through without cutting himself to ribbons.

Jewel held his glowing lantern behind her to block the light. "Hurry, then. Get back down to the root cellar."

"No way." Wyatt shuddered at the thought of spiders. "There's no way out of that cellar. If they find us, we're done for. Quick!" He pushed her back, feeling his hands turn cold. "Put out the lantern."

"Give me my gun back." Jewel held out her hand.

"What?" Wyatt spun around. "It's empty! You said so yourself."

"I've got an extra round or two." She jingled her skirt pocket. "And besides, you're not exactly the best shot. I've seen you out on the ranch, Mr. Kelly. With all due respect, you can't even shoot a magpie."

Wyatt scowled, feeling his cheeks burn in humiliation. "Are you crazy? I'm not giving you your gun back."

"What, you think I'm going to stand here and let them shoot me? I'd have been in and out of this place ages ago if it weren't for you."

"You might shoot me in the back of the head and take ol' Pierre's chest for yourself."

"Better than getting run through with one of Benjamin Crowder's knives. He's not very accurate, you know."

"Fine. Take it." Wyatt pulled her Smith & Wesson from his belt and slapped it in her hand. "Satisfied? Now douse the lantern and hide behind something. Quick."

Jewel reached out greedily for her revolver. "Try not to leave footprints in the dust. Walk like my people do when they're stalking game: on the sides of your feet. Not the sole." She jerked her head up. "I bet you left boot tracks all across the floor when you came in."

Wyatt swallowed nervously.

"You did, didn't you?"

Jewel lifted the lantern for a quick look and then sighed and shook her head. As soon as she'd clicked a handful of bullets into her revolver, the inside of Pierre's cabin turned to clammy darkness.

Chapter 3

Yellow light gleamed in one of the windows, illuminating a dusty maze of cobwebs and broken boards. Wyatt flattened himself against the wall beside the crumbling chimney. Hardly daring to breathe, Jewel ducked under the rotten table.

"Get back," she whispered, whacking his toe with the stock of her (heavy) revolver and making him jump. "Your boots are sticking out."

"Get back yourself!" he snapped. His toe smarted where she'd smacked it. "I can't squeeze in here any tighter."

"Well, try. You want to get us killed?" Jewel tugged a broken board against the chimney and angled it over his boots.

Torches flickered, and Wyatt heard the whinny of horses. The *clink* of metal as someone lit lanterns and the stench of kerosene.

A figure clad in a long coat pushed open the wooden door, his lantern light shining across the ruined layers of log and stone. "I know it's gotta be around here. That's what the ol' dog said, didn't he?"

Wyatt ducked his head as he recognized Kirby Crowder's voice, and his eyes watered from the dust. He moved just enough to rub his nose against his shoulder, hoping to goodness he didn't sneeze. He'd spent all spring sneezing as a child when the wild grasses bloomed; twenty-five years hadn't changed his allergies and wimpy sensitivities much. When the dust blew across the Wyoming plains, he swelled up like a porcupine.

"Fella's lyin' through his teeth." Boots clomped against boards. "Why, I oughtta..."

The room grew utterly still, and Wyatt was pretty sure he knew what they were seeing: his boot tracks in the dust leading straight to the root cellar. His chest heaved with nauseated panic.

"By cricket." Wyatt heard Kirby's boots scuff the wooden planks as he squatted down, and something like heavy leather holsters groaned. "Somebody's been here. Looky this."

"Down to the root cellar, I reckon."

"You g'won down and see, and I'll wait here a spell." Kirby lowered his voice. "See if he comes back—whoever he is."

Wyatt eased his head around the side of the chimney to see if by some miracle he and Jewel could outmatch Kirby in weapons, but he needn't have. A shift in Kirby's stance and the clanking of heavy holsters confirmed that, yes, Kirby would shoot the daylights out of Wyatt if he even tried to draw his revolver.

Kirby cocked his shotgun, and the sharp, metallic *click* echoed through the cabin.

Benjamin's boot clatters faded down the stone steps, and Wyatt heard him holler. "There's a hole busted in the floor. Reckon they've already took it?"

"What do you mean, a hole?" Kirby must've leaned under the cellar door to see because his lantern light abruptly died into a cold shadow. "We got here before that Bradford sucker did, that's for shore. Ain't nobody else who'd know what that old Injun told us."

"Well, somebody's pulled the floor up." Benjamin's voice echoed, low and eerie. "There's a space underneath, but ain't nothin' in it."

The cabin silenced, and Wyatt felt himself convulse with a sneeze. His chest shuddered as he pressed his nose closed, and Jewel elbowed him hard in the shin. So hard he almost cried out.

Wyatt thought he saw Kirby march to the door to check outside, holding out his lantern, and then the image dissolved into watery stripes. His mouth scrunched closed. His nose tickled.

And he sneezed.

Exploded, rather.

Twice. So violently that he rocked backward, banging his head against the wall and knocking off his hat. A startled pigeon flew from the broken section of roof overhead, wings flapping.

"What in tarnation?" Kirby growled, stalking over in Wyatt's direction and hoisting his rifle. "Come out now, whoever you are, or I'll blow you to bits!"

Wyatt tried to move, but his lungs stifled, and his nose itched. He slid to his knees in misery, fumbling to keep his hold on the revolver. His glasses fell off, clinking against his boots. And he opened his mouth to sneeze again.

When he opened his eyes, Kirby lay sprawled on the floor and Jewel was raising a heavy wooden plank to swing again. Benjamin hollered and fired a shot behind her, but she ducked. The bullet glanced off a rotten section of log, making a chunk crumble from the wall.

Instead of swinging again at Kirby, Jewel whirled around and brought the plank square across Benjamin's middle without any warning, doubling him over. His lantern clattered to the floor, and she wrestled the pistol out of his hand, knocking his hand into the wall until he cried out in pain.

He lunged after her, but in a quick second she'd cracked him across the skull with his own pistol, knocking his hat off and bringing him to his knees. He struggled to get up, and she laid him out with another blow to the head. Ripping his other revolver from his belt and kicking his rifle down the cellar stairs with a clatter. Just in time to turn the pistol on Kirby, who was scrambling to his feet. Both hands grabbing at pistols in his holster.

Wyatt stood there, the revolver clenched in his hand, his knees knocking and eyes watering, unable to take his eyes off Jewel's quick and fluid movements. If he had any doubts about her ability to kill, she'd removed every one.

"Why, you little cur!" Kirby turned the barrel of his shotgun around and swung at Jewel with such great force that he struck the wall, splintering the heavy wooden barrel of the gun, shooting two rounds into the wall behind Jewel with the pistol in his left hand. "Who are you anyway?"

Jewel ducked, cocking Benjamin's pistol and leveling it at Kirby's head. "Don't worry about who I am," she retorted. "Drop your gun."

Do something, you idiot! Wyatt scolded himself. *Don't let Kirby Crowder take down a woman!*

Wyatt blinked swollen eyes, remembering how his burly father had thrown himself across his mother and two sisters for protection, wrestling five Indian braves as they tried to drag him away. The wagon burned, bristling with arrows; the prairie grasses sputtered with flames. When his father's great head finally slumped, bloodied, Wyatt counted six arrows sticking out of him—and two gaping bullet wounds.

His blood trickled down into the smoking prairie grass, a terrible rust-red.

And when they came to haul away his body and kill the others, his father lifted his hand one last time: plunging his dagger square into the Cheyenne brave's chest. Even after they carried away the wounded brave, blood and spittle leaking from his mouth, they couldn't pry the dagger from his father's dead fingers.

Wyatt had buried his face in his mother's side and bawled, terrified.

"You're certainly not your father," everyone said to Wyatt with a shake of the head. As if he wasn't smart enough to figure that out himself. Uncle Hiram thought him a fool and a skinny excuse for a ranch hand.

Wyatt felt a pang sting through his chest as he looked down at his slim, freckled hands, bony in the moonlight from the broken roof. Not great and strong and calloused from hard work like his father's. No, he was scrawny Wyatt Kelly: a twenty-five-year-old who could barely see and whose flaming red hair and glass-blue eyes had been so exotic—so alien—that the Cheyenne warrior who raised the spear to take his childhood spared him out of pity. But mainly fear.

The same fear that kept them from slaughtering the rare white buffalo. "Sacred," they called it. "An omen."

A spectacle was more like it.

And such was the reason that Wyatt even lived.

Instead of pulling the trigger, Wyatt eased backward, letting a shadow obscure his face.

Before Wyatt could plan a move, the unbelievable sound of horses' hooves thumping on the ground outside the cabin jarred him upright. He heard shouts, saw bright lights.

Sidekicks. We're done for. Wyatt squeezed his eyes closed and tried to imagine how it felt to die—and what would happen after Kirby's bullet knocked him into the proverbial Kingdom Come. Was there really a heaven and hell like the family Bible depicted in those stuffy old picture plates? Or was it just lights-out, and nothing more than eternal darkness? Sort of like being locked in Crazy Pierre's root cellar for eternity?

Oh God, no. . . . Please. Anything but that.

"This is Major Marshall from the Yellowstone National Park Cavalry," barked a voice, echoing through the half-open door. "Kirby Crowder? Benjamin? I know you're in there. Come out with your hands up, or I'll fill you both full of bullets."

Wyatt opened one eye.

The window shutters flung open, and two soldiers stood there in full uniform, light from lanterns and torches blazing against their brass buttons and cocked revolvers.

"You've been poaching elk and bison off national park property, Crowder. And about two dozen mule deer. We've been tracking you for miles. You so much as fire one shot, and we'll take you down."

Wyatt saw Kirby freeze, his pistol aimed at Jewel. Benjamin, who'd roused himself and started to climb to his feet, stood shakily.

"Better come on out," another stout voice rang out. "There are six of us here, and we'll shoot you if we have to."

By jingle. He's right. Wyatt felt his breath go out in a shaky spasm. The army ran Yellowstone now, and they were vigilant about cracking down on poachers. The last fellow who got caught poaching bison red-handed wound up in the guardhouse at Fort Yellowstone before he could reload his musket.

"You're surrounded, Kirby," called the major. "I've got men on every side of this place."

Wyatt heard whispered curses and stamping feet, and both Crowders frantically rushed around the room, probably looking for an exit or a place to hide.

The cellar. If either of the Crowders holed up down there, it could be days before the army got them out. But Wyatt couldn't move, couldn't breathe.

Over the ruins of a broken table, Wyatt saw Jewel meet his eye, giving him a slight nod toward the basement.

Me? Wyatt looked behind him to see if she was gesturing to someone else. *She wants me to block the cellar?*

Wyatt licked his lips, sizing up the shadows and shapes in the room, and then suddenly leaped around the chimney, scrambled over stones, and ducked through the cellar door. He slammed the door shut behind him, trembling as he tugged the latch to hold it closed.

"Wait a second—another one?" Kirby roared from the other side of the door, jerking it hard. "Who's this? He looks like that scrawny Wyatt Kelly fella, if I didn't know better."

Boots clattered on the floor, and bright light flooded the crack under the door. "Time's up," barked the major. "Kirby, Benjamin, drop your weapons and get your hands over your head before I count to three, or I'll shoot you where you stand."

"You, half-breed," Kirby rasped. "I'll be back, you hear me? I know where the gold's at, so don't bother getting in our way."

The major spoke again, his tone harsh and strident. "Now, Kirby." Wyatt heard someone kick the front door open followed by the sound of booted footsteps and metallic clinking of weapons.

"There's somebody else hiding in here, too," bellowed Kirby in a hoarse voice, banging on the cellar door so hard it rattled Wyatt's teeth. "And I aim to find out who it is."

"I don't care if it's Crazy Pierre's ghost. All I care about is you and your deadbeat brother. It's three in the doggone morning, and I'm sick of chasing you." Wyatt heard the major cock his revolver. "One. Two."

Kirby's guns clattered as they hit the floor.

◆ ◆ ◆

The US Army. The national park. Reality seemed to fade, ripple, as Wyatt sank to his knees.

Yellowstone, they called the park—where thunderous falls roared over a yawning chasm of volcanic rock and sulfur steam boiled up from the ground like a watery furnace. Scalding water bubbled and spurted, sometimes hundreds of feet into the air—and shimmering pools of acid carved wildly colored rings and chambers into the rock like glazed Indian pottery.

Jim Bridger and other explorers had written about "petrified birds and trees" and "waterfalls spouting upwards," all stinking of volcanic smoke, but most folks thought they were weaving tall tales. Bridger, however, spoke the truth. Wyatt had seen the geysers himself as a skinny kid, prodded along by an impatient Uncle Hiram, who wanted to show him the pits of "fire and brimstone" where he was sure the devil lived. And where "boys who disrespect their elders go, too, when they die," Hiram had added, giving an evil cackle.

Wyatt had stared, horrified, into a shimmering basin of searing water, heat bubbles breaking on its steaming surface—recalling the black-clad street preacher in Cody who'd wept and shouted about hell, hanging graphic paintings of lost souls in a smoke-filled agony that looked an awful lot like Yellowstone.

As the mists on the geyser pit lifted, Wyatt peered deep below the shivering water to an underwater pool of clearest crystalline blue—so blue the color hurt his eyes. Beyond it, streaks of red-gold and green intertwined like strands of multihued cliffs against a cobalt Wyoming sky.

"Uncle Hiram," he'd said, pointing. Breathless. "How could the devil make those colors? They're so beautiful, don't you think?"

Hiram had leaned forward, scrunching his craggy brow. "Dunno, Wyatt. Mebbe he got bored there in hell. Ain't nothin' to do but burn."

Wyatt said nothing, gazing over the railing and wondering if Uncle Hiram and the street preacher were right, and the devil made it all. Or if both of them were wrong, and by some sort of divine, comic irony, God had made the whole thing.

Wyatt had just turned to follow along the rickety boardwalk when a long snort at the far edge of the wood made him turn his head. And there, not thirty feet away, stood a colossal, full-grown bull bison—chest-deep in the hot springs, steam clouding all around him like heavenly stained glass. Two sharp horns curved toward the sky in reckless splendor.

The biggest animal Wyatt had ever seen. So strong his sinews stood out under his massive brown hide in taut lines, shaggy fur mounting around his enormous head like a king's chain-mail battle cloak. Daring anyone to disturb his respite on such a cool morning.

The bison stamped his bushy feet, shaking the water into colored rings, and waded a pace or two deeper. Mockingbirds and meadowlarks parted; aspens cringed. He snorted again and tossed his magnificent head, horns gleaming. Breath misting over the water. Huge and defiant eyes caught Wyatt's in an insolent gaze of absolute fearlessness, should Wyatt dare to challenge his majesty's peace.

Wyatt backed up, white-faced, and scrambled up the boardwalk to call for help.

But no one had noticed the bison. Wyatt stopped, peering over his shoulder. The big beast turned his head away from Wyatt, silent and aloof.

And Wyatt said nothing. Dry-mouthed. Keeping the secret to himself, a fluttering of pressed-down excitements too wonderful to voice.

But as he rounded the forested bend, seeing nothing more of the bison but a cloud of steam through the aspen leaves, Wyatt knew one thing: No devil had made Yellowstone.

It had to be God.

◆　◆　◆

Someone tugged open the cellar door, and Wyatt looked up at Jewel's silhouette against stars in the open roof. Crazy Pierre's dark and ruined house curved around her, silent.

The stench of sour pickles wafted up from the root cellar, and Wyatt thought suddenly of spiders.

"Are you all right?" Jewel knelt down and lit the lantern. The glow warmed her face and cupped hands.

Wyatt tried to raise his head, but it felt heavy.

"Mr. Kelly?" She shook his shoulder. "They're gone. You can come out now." She held up the lantern. "You should have covered me better, you know that? If it were up to you, I'd be dead by now. I think our deal should be more like sixty-forty, not fifty-fifty. But you did keep them out of the cellar. I suppose that counts for something."

Something twinkled over her head, like a spider dangling from a silken thread.

"Did you shoot the buffalo, too?" he murmured, feeling a giddy blackness in his head. "I hope not. It'll take more rounds than you've got in your revolver anyhow."

And Wyatt put his head down on the top step.

Chapter 4

Wyatt flipped the Bible page and fixed his glasses, trying to look calm and nonchalant, as if he didn't care a bit. "So you really think I fainted, Mrs. Moreau?" He watched Uncle Hiram in the rocking chair by the fireplace, dozing. His fingers steepled together and his eyes closed.

"You did faint. I didn't know you were so. . .sensitive."

"I'm not sensitive." Wyatt felt heat flare in his cheeks.

"And afraid of spiders."

Wyatt scooted his chair back in a huff, blood pulsing in his face. "That's enough. Read the next Bible story, will you?" He glared over at his uncle again, wondering if he'd been bats to invite Jewel back for tutoring. But he needed to speak to her about the gold—and by George, Wyatt wasn't the sort of fellow to slink around the ranch alone with a young girl—married or not—making the ranch hands whisper.

Jewel looked up at him with a slight smile. "It's all right, you know that?"

"What's all right?" Wyatt's brow still made two angry lines.

"To be afraid of things. To be. . .well, just like you are. There's nothing wrong with that."

Wyatt bristled, turning the pages of the Bible faster than necessary. He scrubbed a fist along his cheek, scruffy with patchy red, and hoped he could hide the blush. "Are you going to read or not?" he asked crossly.

Her gaze probed him with gentle curiosity before turning to the Bible before her. " 'Now faith is the substance of things hoped for, the evidence of things not seen,' " Jewel read aloud over Hiram's snores, her words clear and beautifully strong. " 'Through faith we understand that the worlds were framed by the word of God, so that things which are seen were not made of things which do appear.' "

"Does that make sense to you?" Wyatt stifled a yawn.

"Not really." Jewel blinked at the lines of type, following them with her finger. "Do you have faith, Mr. Kelly?"

"In what?"

"In God. In the truth of the Bible."

"I. . .I don't know." Wyatt squirmed uncomfortably. "Faith in anything seems a little impossible to me. Although I'm always interested in the truth."

"I know you are."

"You. . .what?" Wyatt scratched his red hair uncomfortably.

"I can tell you're a man who seeks the truth." Jewel leaned back and regarded him coolly. "Of course, I could be mistaken. But people do say you keep your word."

Wyatt lifted an eyebrow. "I'm not sure anybody around here has a good word to say about me."

"You're quite mistaken, Mr. Kelly." Jewel leaned forward boldly. "You want to hear truth? You could do so much more with yourself if you stopped trying to be someone you're not."

"Pardon?" Wyatt's jaw slipped.

"You've got a good head on your shoulders and your own good gifts and strengths. You don't need your uncle's approval or anyone else's."

Wyatt stared, sputtering for words. "How dare you speak that way about my uncle," he managed, his heart beating fast in his chest. "He's your superior. Your boss. He hired you."

"I never said not to respect your uncle." Jewel raised her voice slightly. "He's a good man, Mr. Kelly, and he deserves your respect—and mine. He's raised you and looked after you his whole life. But he doesn't own your future, and you certainly owe it to yourself to discover what you can really accomplish if you stop comparing yourself to someone else."

"Are you crazy?" Wyatt bristled. "I don't compare myself to anybody!"

"Yes, you do. All the time."

"Who?" He scooted his chair forward, making an ugly rasping sound. Uncle Hiram stirred, his snores sputtering.

Jewel folded her hands and glanced up at the faded tintype photograph of Amos Kelly on the mantel. "You know who," she whispered.

Wyatt abruptly got up from the table and fidgeted with something on the shelf, trying to straighten the plates with quivery hands until he knocked them together. When he sat down again, he polished his glasses a long time without speaking and then growled, "You sure do speak your mind," and stuck his glasses on his face at a twisted angle.

"So should you."

"You're wrong about all of it, you know that?" Heat climbed Wyatt's neck. "Completely wrong."

"No, I'm not."

"That's enough!" Wyatt shut the Bible and pushed it to the side of the table, his fingertips shaking with anger. "Look. If you want to talk about the gold, then talk. Otherwise we're done here tonight. Got it?"

"Fine." Jewel met his eyes without flinching. "Go ahead. You start."

Wyatt shuffled his feet irritably under the table, glancing over at Uncle Hiram's sleeping figure. "All right then. What do you think of the contents of the box?" He dropped his voice to a near whisper. "Do you think Crazy Pierre really buried it, or did someone else take what he'd originally left and replace it with something else?"

"You said you saw him bury it."

"I did, but that was years ago. Somebody might have dug it up since then." Wyatt rubbed his forehead with his fist, letting his temper cool down. And keeping his father's photograph out of his line of vision. "If it was Pierre, what was he thinking leaving nothing in that box but a rusted old set of spurs?"

"And his letter to my husband doesn't help much: '*Le trône de solitude dans la lumière de la lune.*'" Perfectly accented words rolled off her tongue like kisses. "'Throne of solitude in the light of the moon,'" she translated. "But it makes no sense to me. Pierre said something about looking under the whiskey jug if my husband was too dense to figure it out."

"Under the whiskey jug." Wyatt rested his chin in his hand. "That's pretty cryptic."

"Not only that, but Pierre wrote that letter over four years ago. Even if he left a specific whiskey jug, maybe down in the root cellar, it would almost certainly be gone by now."

"So what next? I don't get the spurs or the letter. A throne is where a king sits. Something royal? Expensive?" He raised his palms in frustration. "Or something up in the sky, like. . .like a constellation. Is that what he meant by solitude and the moon?"

"Maybe something related to a horse, then, because of the spurs?" Jewel played with the Bible page.

"Is there some. . .horse-shaped constellation?"

"What? No." Jewel stopped another laugh with her palm, and Wyatt glared.

"I'm just trying things, you know," he grumbled. "You could at least be civil."

"Wait a moment." Her smile faded. "Pegasus. The winged horse."

"Why, you're right." Wyatt ran a hand over his jaw in surprise, thinking. "No, *I'm* right. The big square in the winter sky."

"Could the big square be a box? Like the box we found?" Jewel gasped. "And one other thing. A horseshoe could look like a moon. A crescent moon."

Wyatt studied her briefly, the candle flickering between them. A bead of wax slipped slowly down, melting into a molten ivory pool.

Jewel actually hadn't shown him the letter. Who knew if she'd told the whole truth—or even part of it? "Is there anything else in the letter, Mrs. Moreau?" he asked carefully. "Anything at all?"

Jewel didn't answer, twisting the wedding band on her finger.

Wyatt crossed his arms. "You're keeping something from me, aren't you?"

"Should I?" She eyed him with a suspicious look. "If I tell you everything up-front, you could figure it out and take the entire stash yourself."

"Me?" Wyatt pointed to his chest, openmouthed. "I'd never do that."

"How can I believe you?" Jewel held his gaze. "No shrewd treasure hunter shows the landowner the full map before she asks permission to dig." The candle flame flickered from her breath.

Wyatt crossed his arms over his chest, narrowing his eyes. "You promised me fifty-fifty. That was the deal. And that means you tell me everything." He raised an eyebrow. "Partner."

"How do I know you've told *me* everything? Prove it, Mr. Kelly."

"I gave you my word, and that should be enough." He leaned across the Bible. "You admitted yourself that I'm a man of my word."

They regarded each other across the table, and neither spoke. A log snapped in the fire, sending up showering sparks. Outside the house, the wind rattled a loose shutter, which banged and groaned.

"So long as you doubt me, how can I trust you with any evidence I find? Or my ideas, or. . .or anything?" Wyatt banged a fist in his palm for emphasis. "Fact is, I don't even know who you are. What's to ensure me you won't take what I say and run off with the treasure yourself?"

"Nothing. Do you trust me?"

Wyatt studied her, his jaw tight. "Maybe. Maybe not."

"So you don't know for sure."

He picked at his nails in the lamplight. "I'd like to," he said finally, lacing his calloused, freckled fingers together. "But how do I know if you trust me? I could ask you the same question."

"Neither of us can know anything for sure." Jewel reached across the table and touched the corner of the Bible, nearly brushing Wyatt's hand. "But I'm learning a bit about faith from this book—and faith never asks me to believe foolishly or throw all my caution to the wind without counting the consequences."

Wyatt quickly put his hands in his lap. "Why, you don't mean to tell me you believe what's in here, do you?" Guilt crept up his spine like a spider skulking in Crazy Pierre's root cellar.

"Maybe." Candlelight flickered on Jewel's face, more earnest than Wyatt had ever seen her. Eyes clear and dark like a winter sky, sparkling with starlight. He looked away, pretending to study a knot in the pine-log wall.

"You think faith never asks you to believe foolishly? Look at Abraham." He flipped the Bible back to Genesis. "God told him to move to a new land—a land He hadn't even shown him—and ol' Abe packed up without a second thought. If that's faith, then forget it. It's not for me."

"No. You're missing it." Jewel pushed the Bible closer to Wyatt, and her voice took on a reverent tone, almost husky—like the one she used when training horses in her native Arapaho. "God moved with Abraham one step at a time, never asking more than His just due. You're right that God told him to move to a new land—but when he did, God blessed him. God promised him a son, and Abraham believed and waited years until it happened." Jewel smoothed the page with her finger. "God didn't throw everything at him all at once. He allowed Abraham to learn who He was, little by little, so that Abraham could make the hard decisions in the end."

"Huh." Wyatt scratched his head.

"I admire that. It took great courage on Abraham's part to believe, but also on God's—to wait and patiently reveal His character over time."

Wyatt massaged his temples, feeling like he'd just stepped in a noose. "You said you were Hagar," he said, switching subjects slightly. "How am I supposed to know that whole story isn't a lie? I don't know if I can trust you to tell the truth. About that or anything else."

"Maybe you can't." She arched a dark eyebrow. "But you can do what Abraham did."

"What, pack up and move?" Wyatt felt his patience wearing through, like a threadbare patch in his overalls.

"No. Wait and watch my character. Then you'll know whether or not you can trust me."

Wyatt leaned his elbows on the table and shook his head. "You're a Christian, aren't you?" His lip turned up slightly. "You've been pretending the whole time, just like you did with English. Why, I bet you know this whole book inside and out. Maybe you're even a missionary." He set his jaw. "Am I right?"

"What? I'm not a Christian." Jewel folded her arms. "I'm not anything. I don't know what I believe." Her eyes seemed, for a moment, sadly empty. She looked away, firelight flickering on the lines of her face. "I don't follow the gods of the Arapaho anymore. I fasted every year during the Sun Dance, and all my life I prayed to the Creator of the Arapaho who speaks through eagles. But I felt nothing. Heard nothing. Almost as if I'd died and my spirit ceased to exist."

Tears shimmered briefly in Jewel's eyes, and she blinked them back, keeping a stoic face. "When I heard the priest at the mission school speak about Jesus, the ice in my heart began to melt. And I longed to read the Bible. To soak up the stories and learn about the God who spoke not through eagles, but through people, through His Son, Jesus—and from His Book."

Her eyelashes trembled closed. "But as soon as I learned to read, my father sold me to my husband, who neither approved of women reading nor listened when I asked for a

Bible." She rubbed at a scratch on the wooden table with slender fingers. "I asked God, if He existed, to let me hear His Word for myself and see if it was true."

She looked up briefly. "And then you asked me to study English. With this." Jewel passed her hand over the pages of the Bible.

Wyatt realized he was gaping and closed his mouth.

And you only offered to teach her because of the gold. Shame on you. Wyatt shifted uncomfortably in his chair, guilt weighing so heavily on his heart that he could hardly breathe. He stared down at the slats in the wooden table until colored lines glowed behind his eyes.

The wind rattled the window shutter again, and Jewel jumped.

For the life of him, Wyatt couldn't think of a single word to say about the Bible. So he simply closed it and pushed it to the side, trying to bring his mind back to the gold. "Did the letter say anything else you feel comfortable telling me?" he asked in a gentler tone.

"It didn't say much at all, Mr. Kelly. It was a short letter. Just the key and the note, and my husband thought it funny."

"So your husband seemed to understand the letter?"

"Not at first. But after a day or two he picked up the letter and read it again, and he laughed."

"Wait a second." Wyatt looked up suddenly. "Why didn't your husband go after the gold then, if he knew Crazy Pierre died? He had the clues, and he figured out where Pierre hid the gold."

Jewel scooted back in her chair, pressing her lips together. She didn't reply.

Something awful thumped in Wyatt's chest, like the Cheyenne war drums on the field where his father died.

"Mrs. Moreau?" Wyatt leaned forward. "Your husband. Why didn't he go after the gold? And where is he? Why do you never speak of him?"

The clock on the mantel struck, and Jewel flinched. Her fingers twisted together, shaking like a leaf in the winter wind. "It's late, Mr. Kelly." She abruptly rose to her feet, sweeping her long skirts from under the table. "I think I've had enough studying for the evening, if you don't mind. Good night."

"Wait." Wyatt scraped his chair back. He crossed the room in fast strides and stood with his back to the door, throwing his arm over the latch.

"Let me leave, please," said Jewel in cold irritation, attempting to duck around him. "I've told you everything you need to know." She reached defiantly over his arm to rattle the latch.

"Why won't you tell me?" Wyatt kept his hand over the latch. "You've already told me your real name and the details about the letter. Why do you need to keep hiding?"

"I thought you said you knew everything about my past." She raised her face to his boldly, but her cheeks had paled. "You're the expert, right?"

Wyatt's heart quivered in his chest, trying to remember what exactly he'd said to call her bluff. Something about the magistrate—and something about her sordid past. "I know enough. But I'd rather hear the truth from you—and not from everybody else in town."

Jewel fingered the latch but didn't move to open the door, even when Wyatt finally stepped aside. "So they're talking about me here, too?"

"A little." Wyatt cleared his throat. "Yes." He crossed his arms over his chest.

"Do you believe them?"

He scuffed his boots on the pine floor, listening to Uncle Hiram snore in his chair.

Wind whistled around the sides of the log house, rustling grasses.

"I see." A line in Jewel's slender neck bobbed as she swallowed. "So you do believe them. Your actions show it."

"My actions show no such thing. I want the truth, and that's all."

"Why? Why do you want to know about my husband so badly?" Jewel turned to him, so close he could see the outline of each dark eyelash. "His whereabouts have nothing whatsoever to do with the gold."

"Because I won't partner with you if you're doing dirty work for someone else. And that's final."

Jewel's eyes widened in what looked like surprise—and perhaps even relief. "I'm not blackmailing anyone, or stealing, if that's what you're suggesting." She swept an arm toward Wyatt. "How do I know about you? How do I know you're honest and not working against the law yourself?"

"Because I've got nothing to hide." Wyatt spoke gently. "You talked about character earlier, Mrs. Moreau. Ask anyone about me and they'll tell you everything. No secrets."

Dark strands of hair had come loose from Jewel's braid, falling in soft lines around her ears, and he longed to brush them back from her smooth forehead. But he stuffed his hands in his pockets instead, hoping the rush of color stayed out of his face.

"Then why do you care where my husband is? What business is it of yours anyway?" Jewel's cheeks glowed an unusual pallid pink, and for a second she looked small and vulnerable there against the rough pine door. Clad in the blue-and-white cottons of a people not entirely her own and gossiped about by townsfolk she'd never met.

"Listen to me, miss. If I'm going to work with a criminal, I need to hear your side before I make up my mind." Wyatt leaned forward.

"So you can turn me in?" Something in the way she said it held a warning. A fearful quiver but with a dagger beneath.

Wyatt's heart pounded in his throat, and he breathed through his nose, trying to keep calm. Thinking through his words. "I don't want to." He spoke gently, meeting her eyes. "I truly don't."

He reached out and put a hand on her arm, trying to still the frightened look in her eyes. "Tell me. Where is your husband? You wear his ring." He gestured to her plain silver band. "Where is he, then?"

Jewel glanced down at his pale hand on her arm, but she did not pull away. "Will you believe me if I tell you the truth?"

Wyatt licked his lips nervously and then nodded.

"Fine then." Jewel closed her eyes. "My husband is dead."

Chapter 5

Wyatt lay uneasily in his bed, unable to sleep. Every whistle of wind around the corner of the house haunted him, and the steady creaking of the pine floor made him jump. All his rusty red hairs were standing on end.

If Jewel had killed her husband—a sinister guess when he put the ugly pieces together—then might she not just as easily kill him, too? A business partner with 50 percent of the goods she'd like to have all for herself?

She'd already gotten the key from him. What purpose could he possibly serve her now?

Wyatt fingered his Colt revolver under his pillow and wondered, with a tight pinch of his stomach, if he should warn Uncle Hiram—and maybe get Jewel off the ranch before she struck again. Not long ago a disgruntled cattle driver in Buffalo had set fire to an entire ranch, taking the lives of six ranch hands and nearly killing the ranch owner himself.

Was that why Jewel had taken the job? To seek out all the information she could about Pierre's gold and then get rid of the evidence?

Black widow indeed. Wyatt pulled his revolver from under his pillow and checked the chamber, then loaded in an extra round. He put the gun down and flopped back on the bed in misery, staring up at the darkened plank ceiling. He didn't want to think the worst. Not at all. Not about Jewel, with her earnest black eyes and long scar on her forearm.

After all, she'd trusted him with her name—her story. Even the contents of her private letter. Why would she deceive him now?

Or maybe the whole thing was a lie. What if her name was not Collette Moreau after all, and she was merely stringing him along—hook, line, and sinker?

Because goodness knows, he wanted to believe her.

Badly.

So much so that his stomach curled into a quivery knot, and he felt the blood rush up his neck, pulsing in his throat. He saw her standing in Crazy Pierre's root cellar with tears in her eyes, her fingers briefly brushing his as she handed him his glasses. Her dark head bent over the Bible.

She was different, this strong-minded Indian girl, from the giddy, empty-headed females he'd seen in Cody and Deadwood, swilling whiskey and banging on cheap player pianos. Fanning their ample cleavage with feather fans and giggling over ignorant jokes.

"You've got a good head on your shoulders and your own good gifts and strengths," Jewel had said at his uncle Hiram's kitchen table.

And something deep inside him wanted desperately to believe that, too.

The courthouse in Cody—that's where he needed to go. He'd make up some excuse for Uncle Hiram and leave first thing in the morning. His motives were twofold: First, to request a map of the area from five years ago, when Crazy Pierre would have written the letter. And second, to ask a few questions about a certain Collette Moreau, otherwise known as Jewel.

◆ ◆ ◆

"Mornin', Clovis. Got any news for me today?" Wyatt tipped his dusty hat and leaned against the counter. A stripe of sunlight glanced off the polished wooden desk, making his sleepy eyes wince. His room at the boardinghouse in Cody had been cold and dirty, and metal bed slats poked him in the spine all night long.

"Well, well, well. Look what the wildcat drug in." Clovis peered at Wyatt through tiny wire spectacles, which reflected the dirty window glass and city street lined with hitching posts, empty with late fall. He grinned and leaned over to shake hands. "Wyatt Kelly. Ain't seen you in a while. How's that ranch? And that uncle of yours?"

"Oh, fine. He's thinking about investing in sheep these days."

"Sheep, huh? They're a lotta work, you know. Well, I don't have any news for ya, unless you count the drunkard who got thrown in jail yesterday for walkin' the railroad track." He chuckled together with Wyatt. "What brings you to town?"

"Nothing much." Wyatt rubbed his fingers together to warm them from the cold. "But listen, I need a favor." He glanced over his shoulder and lowered his voice, leaning both elbows on the counter. "I need some maps of the land around, say, East Fork River or thereabouts—on the other side of the Shoshone reservation. Older maps." He scratched his shoulder and stretched. "How far back do you go?"

"Old maps? Why, you ain't prospectin', are ya? Or fightin' with somebody over boundary lines?"

"Don't be silly." Wyatt straightened his hat and tried to produce a posture of ease, slouching against the counter. "I'm just looking for a couple of places is all."

"Well, now, let me take a look. I'll be just a minute." Clovis adjusted his glasses and disappeared into a storage room, rummaging and pulling out boxes, and finally returned with his arms full of stuff.

"Looky here." He dropped some dusty papers on the counter. "See if this is what you want." He smoothed a paper with wrinkled hands. "Here's a copy of the map drawn by the Hayden Geological Survey when they came through the area back in 1871. All the rivers and geological features and such, and some sketches, too, if you'd like to see them."

1871. Back when Crazy Pierre was still digging holes like a mole. Wyatt straightened his glasses to see better.

"And here's a later map of the Yellowstone River area back in '81. East of here a bit. Why, close to your uncle's ranch, probably." Clovis carefully handed him a print. "Lotta details and such. The railroad lines and some businesses. Even some private property."

"Let me take a look at that." Wyatt pulled the paper closer.

He made space at the counter for an elderly man in a suit and studied the map, his eyes running over the lines and contours. Following the names with his finger. He read the tiny type from top to bottom and back up again—pausing only at a little place about ten miles from Pierre's cabin, up in the mountains. About twenty miles from Yellowstone, up against a mountain ridge.

"Clovis," Wyatt pointed to a square on the map as Clovis shuffled under the counter, "what's this place here?"

"That?" He squinted, then took his glasses off and stuck his face closer. "Why, that's old Crescent Ranch."

Wyatt sucked in a sharp breath, feeling his pulse pick up. "I remember that place. They had an inn, didn't they? A boardinghouse or something?"

"Sure they did." Clovis ran a hand over his balding head, his hairs grown as long as possible and combed over with some kind of waxy pomade. "Forgot what it was called now. Water in the well dried up and had to close everything up. Never rebuilt."

The room seemed to shimmer suddenly as if through heat waves. "The inn had a big chair in the entranceway, didn't it? Made of deer antlers or something?"

"Moose." The white-haired man in the suit leaned toward Wyatt at the counter. "Antlers from a prize moose, and the rest elk."

"You remember it." Wyatt faced him.

"Sure I do." The man's eyes were nearly opaque, like pale blue ice. He turned a knobby cane as he spoke. "That chair stood more than six feet tall—and my father killed the prize moose himself. Nobody's ever seen a bigger moose in these parts."

"Do you remember the name of the inn?" Wyatt held his breath.

"Of course. The Monarch Inn. After the butterfly." The man blinked, and those pale blue eyes seemed to drift away. "I was a boy when they built it."

Monarch. Throne. Crescent. Wyatt held on to the counter with shaky hands. "Do you know what's there now—in the place where the inn used to be?"

"What do you mean?" The man's face twisted in a sort of confusion. "There's nothing there. The whole place was boarded up like a ghost town. Been empty for years."

"Anything else, Wyatt?" Clovis carefully stacked the maps together.

"Just one thing." He tugged at his suspenders uncomfortably, not sure how much to say. "You ever hear about a fellow named Moreau? From Idaho?"

"Moreau. Moreau." Clovis passed a hand over his thin scalp, patting his long hairs into place. "French fellow, ain't he?"

"That's the one."

"A fur trapper, if I remember correctly. Mink and ermine. Made a good living up there with his kinfolk."

Wyatt turned toward the window as Clovis talked, pretending to be absorbed in a man hitching up a cart along the street. Light snow blew in thin gusts like goose down, floating and whirling.

Clovis kneaded his chin with his knuckles as he thought. "Augustin Moreau, you mean? If that's the man, sure. I've heard some talk about him."

"What's the word on him?"

"Word? He's been dead for three years."

Wyatt's heart seized up, and he felt as if the blood had stopped pumping. Turning his fingers to ice. "What, was he shot?"

"No. Bludgeoned with a metal stovepipe on Thanksgiving Day." Clovis stuck his head closer. "Funny you should ask, because just the other day the sheriff asked if any of us had seen an Indian girl in town. An Arapaho, I think. A young girl, he said, and pretty—looking for work. Said they were searching for her back in Idaho, and a few folks thought they might've seen her in these parts."

"Arapaho are good-lookin' people." A thin cowboy with cold-red cheeks and tawny, overgrown whiskers looked up from the doorway. "Tall and stately, with the nicest features you ever saw. They say the Ute Indians like to steal Arapaho wives."

Wyatt swiveled his head back and forth between the cowboy and Clovis, his mind an incredulous blur. "Why are they looking for the girl?" His heart beat so loudly he could hardly hear. "What's she done?"

"There's a bounty on her head." Clovis put the stack of papers back in a drawer and closed it. "They say she killed her husband."

Chapter 6

Wyatt stalked through the stable in a fury. His hair hung a filthy red under his battered hat, like muddy river clay—messy with wood splinters and sweat and soil. "I give up, Mrs. Moreau. I mean Miss Moreau. Whoever you are." He crossed his arms stiffly, furious breaths heaving in his chest. "There's no gold."

"Excuse me?" Jewel looked up from raking through mounds of dirty hay, her fingers pink from cold.

"Either somebody's taken it already, or Crazy Pierre's a liar." He heaved a ragged sigh of frustration. "Or maybe both."

"No, both is impossible." Jewel set the rake against a gate and offered Wyatt a stiffly dried cloth she'd hung after washing. "If he's a liar, then there's no way someone could—"

"You know what I mean." Wyatt scowled. "I'm in no mood for parsing verbs now, if you don't mind."

One of the young stable hands paused, feed bucket in hand, and Wyatt glared at him until he scampered out of sight. Then he took the cloth and sponged his dirty face, borrowing a bit of water from the water trough to moisten the cloth and scrub his filthy boots.

"Well." Jewel wiped her hands and leaned the rake against the log wall. "It sounds like you've made up your mind." Her breath misted like a fine veil, dissipating slowly.

"Look. I'm tired of these games." Wyatt snatched his hat and banged it against his boot to knock off the dirt. "I've been digging all day long, two days straight, and nothing." He slapped the hat back on his head. "Show me the letter now, or I'm calling it quits."

"You've been digging?" Jewel put her hands on her hips, and her cheeks flushed. "You didn't tell me."

"You haven't showed me the letter yet!" Wyatt flung out his arms.

"You should have told me where you thought the gold was, and we could have discussed it together. But you disappeared for five days without telling anybody where you'd gone, and what was I supposed to think?" A flicker of hurt flashed across her face, but she covered it quickly, picking up the rake again and pulling it across the stable floor in staccato strokes.

"Look." Wyatt put both hands up, trying not to look at her. Those flushed cheeks and red-and-blue beaded earrings glittering under her dark hair. "I didn't intend to do any searches without you, all right? It just happened. I was in the right place at the right time, and what was I supposed to do?" A vein in his neck pulsed. "Ride all the way back here to the ranch and ask your permission?"

"So. . .it just 'happened.'" Jewel kept her back turned. "I'm not sure how that's supposed to work. Have you ever heard of one partner digging without the other?"

"Jewel. Listen." Wyatt strode across the stable and grabbed her elbow. "Miss Jewel," he faltered, reddening and dropping her arm. Horrified at his own boldness. "Ma'am. I apologize." He ducked his head and scrubbed his dirty forehead with the palm of his hand, trying to gather his words and his sense. "I heard a few things in Cody, and I thought I'd check 'em out. The old Monarch Inn on the Crescent Ranch? Ever heard of it?"

"No." Jewel smoothed her sleeve where he'd touched her and continued raking.

"It had a big chair that locals called the 'Throne.' But there's nothing there. Absolutely nothing." He looked out over the stable, shaking with exhaustion and frustration. "I wasted my time."

"Look here, Mr. Kelly." Jewel advanced toward him, pointing her finger straight at his chest with such spunk that he involuntarily put his hands up. "You shouldn't have done anything without telling me first. I think I know where the gold is, and you didn't bother to ask."

"You know?" Wyatt stumbled backward, knocking his hat sideways against a plank.

"I thought of it after you left, and it makes perfect sense. But you haven't told me why you went to Cody."

He straightened his hat and kept his eyes averted. "On business."

"Whose business?"

"Personal business."

"Fine. Don't tell me." She folded her arms. "But don't expect any clues from me either, if you're not willing to tell me everything, fifty-fifty. You can figure out where the gold is on your own. But I think I know."

She turned to walk away, and Wyatt just stood there, hands on his hips. "They're looking for you, you know," he called after her. "I thought you'd appreciate it if I told you."

"I beg your pardon?" Jewel whirled around.

"In Cody." Wyatt dropped his voice and took a step closer. "You know why."

Jewel's face went pale, and she clapped a hand over her mouth. "You told them, didn't you?" she whispered. "You told them I'm staying here."

"I didn't tell them anything." Wyatt kicked the mud off his spurs against the hard floor, still angry.

Jewel blinked as if confused and drew back, nearly dropping the rake. She lunged for it, catching the handle before it clattered to the floor. "You. . .mean you didn't tell them I'm here?"

"Of course I didn't." Wyatt tossed the cloth over a wooden gate. "What was I supposed to say? 'The girl you say killed her husband is working at my uncle's ranch—come and get her'?"

"They'd drag me out of my bed."

"Doggone right, they would." Wyatt took a step closer, his hands clenching. "And I'll be honest. I don't know what to think of you." He pointed a shaking finger at her, hoping the ache didn't show too much in his eyes. "But let's get one thing straight. You stay away from my uncle, hear me? If anything happens to him, so help me, I'll call the local sheriff and have you dragged off to the gallows."

"I'd never touch your uncle." Jewel spoke so softly Wyatt could barely hear.

Wyatt sized her up, arms crossed. A lump swelled in his throat so tightly he had to breathe deeply through his nose.

"Don't you think I would have done something already if I'd planned to? I've been here more than two years." Her eyes filled suddenly, and she looked down at the straw-covered floor, kicking at it with a high-buttoned boot. "And I didn't kill my husband. It's a lie."

Wyatt didn't answer. He stuck his hands in his pocket and looked away, clenching a muscle in his jaw.

"You didn't turn me in." Jewel raised her head, her expression changed to one of gratitude, almost humility. "That speaks more of your belief in me than anything you can say."

"I haven't said anything," Wyatt snapped, kicking a bit of straw with his boot. "I just want the truth, and that's it."

Jewel studied him a moment, not speaking. A gust of wind blew snow flurries through an open window in the stable, and she shivered.

"It's in the outhouse."

"The outhouse? What's in the outhouse—the truth?" He scrunched up his forehead. "What in the Sam Hill are you talking about?"

Jewel glared, shushing him fiercely with a finger to her lips. "Crazy Pierre's outhouse," she whispered. "I think I've figured out the riddle."

Wyatt threw his arms up in disgust, ready to turn and stomp away, when the words fell across his memory like snowflakes: *Throne of solitude in the light of the moon.*

Moon. Crescent. *Outhouses sometimes have a crescent moon carved in the door.*

"Of all the. . ." Wyatt's face blanched, and he snatched off his hat and whacked a post with it, not sure whether to laugh or kick something. Two horses backed and reared in indignation, and Jewel scolded him, rushing to calm the horses.

"You're telling me ol' Crazy Pierre left his gold in a doggone privy?" Wyatt stalked closer.

"Throne of solitude." Jewel shrugged with a smile. "I guess they don't call him crazy for no reason."

Wyatt considered this a second, letting out a snort of laughter. "He was eccentric all right. A strange fellow. But there's no way under the sun I'm digging into somebody's privy—I don't care how long he's been dead."

"Not under, over." Jewel spoke in hushed tones. "The rest of the letter said this: *'Deux pieds en bas et lèvent les yeux.'* 'Two feet down, and look up.' Do you understand?"

"Exactly. Two feet down. I already told you, I'm not digging up a john. Got it?"

"No, no, no!" Jewel shook her head furiously. "You're not listening. Two feet down. You're thinking measurements. Crazy Pierre was thinking actual *feet.*" She lifted the hem of her skirt to show her boots. "These." She pointed. "In an outhouse, you put two feet on the floor."

"And then 'look up.'" Wyatt's voice dripped wonder. "So. . .up in the rafters?" He felt his eyebrows nearly touch his hair. "You think it might still be there?"

"I don't know. But I'd like to find out."

Wyatt faced her, his breath huffing as his mind whirled through the possibilities. Ticking off all the crazy clues one by ridiculous one.

"The spurs in the wooden box," he said hoarsely, resting a hand on his forehead. "They had crescent moons."

"Like an outhouse door." Jewel stood so still that Wyatt could see a stray snowflake catch in her hair as it blew through a crack in the log walls—a tiny white sparkle among gleaming black, like a lone star. He felt the sudden urge to reach out and brush it away, but instead he stuffed his hands in his jacket pockets.

"Let's go then." Wyatt reached over the wooden post and patted Samson's shiny neck.

"Now?"

"I'll tell my uncle you're indisposed for the evening." Wyatt straightened his hat. "First one to Pierre's gets dibs."

Jewel's eyes glowed. "I'll beat you there."

Chapter 7

Light snow whirled around Wyatt as he scrambled off his horse. He threw a wool blanket over Samson's back and gathered up his lantern, rifle, and shovels. A brooding sky hung in blue-gray layers over the pines, like translucent paper.

"Come on." Wyatt looked over his shoulder, the cold wind nearly blowing his hat off. "I don't like the way these clouds are rolling in. Looks like a snowstorm."

"If the gold is up in the rafters, it shouldn't take long." Jewel slid off her sleek Indian pony's back, her long black hair blowing. She'd tied it back with a simple velvet ribbon; Wyatt was amazed at its length and thickness. The women in Cody would pay big bucks for a wig made of hair like Jewel's.

"But do you really think an old outhouse could support the weight of, say, a hundred pounds of gold?" Wyatt finished tying Samson and shouldered his things, forcing his eyes away from Jewel and into the gray distance past Pierre's house. "And if there's as much gold as he said, it would weigh a lot more than that."

"Depends on the outhouse, I suppose." Jewel ducked her head into the wind and walked side by side with Wyatt. "The structure and the design."

Wyatt shook snowflakes off his glasses and snorted. "If it's really there, old Pierre was crazier than I give him credit for. Or smarter. Nobody in their right mind would hide gold in a privy—and nobody in their right mind would look for it."

They rounded the corner of the old cabin, and the front door creaked in the wind, swinging slightly open. Wyatt hushed, listening for footsteps or voices. "That old place gives me the creeps," he whispered, moving closer to Jewel. "I guess we are really crazy to do this."

"Maybe so." Jewel set her lips in a determined slant. "But I'm not giving up now—maybe never. I need to find this gold. I have to. It's more important than you can possibly imagine."

Wyatt looked sideways at her, lifting a thick spruce branch for her to walk past. His shovels and rifle clinked together, hollow and metallic.

"What's so important?" he asked. "Why do you want the gold so badly?"

Jewel hesitated a moment, her eyes briefly meeting his. "I need it to start over." She rubbed her nose, which had reddened in the cold. "Nothing more."

"Start over?"

"You know what they say about me. That I killed my husband. But I didn't. I give you my word." Her eyes glittered, but Wyatt couldn't tell if it was tears or wind that made them fill.

"Did you have any reason to want to kill him?"

"Many." Branches snapped under Jewel's boots.

Wyatt drew back in surprise but said nothing. The wind rattled bare tree branches together like skeleton fingers, and Jewel lifted her long skirts to step over a fallen limb.

"But I didn't kill him. His death was mysterious, all right—but I didn't do it. Although I think I've figured out who did."

"Who?"

"Someone who wanted the letter."

A shiver of cold fear tingled Wyatt's spine. "But *you've* got the letter. Do you mean somebody might be looking for you now?"

"Possibly. My husband wasn't exactly tight-lipped about secrets," she said, passing the lantern to her other hand and accepting Wyatt's arm to pass through a thicket of briers. "A little whiskey, a hand or two of cards, and he couldn't keep a secret to save his life. He spoke about the letter a week before he died, and that same week some men ransacked our house— apparently looking for the letter."

"So you think one of them did it?"

"Of course. It's pretty obvious to me, but no one would listen." Jewel shrugged. "His whole clan had always disliked and distrusted me for being *Indien d'Arapaho*, as if that made me less than human. So when he died, everyone blamed me without a second thought."

Wyatt paused and surveyed the forested stretch outside Crazy Pierre's homestead, scanning the trees for anything resembling an outhouse. His breath fogged and faded like the thin hope of comfort Jewel must have felt back in Idaho among the trappers.

"Why do you still wear his ring then?"

She shot him a dark look. "I assure you, Mr. Kelly, that a woman alone in this part of the country is far safer if she wears a ring than if she doesn't. I'm surprised you didn't think of that yourself."

"Sorry." Wyatt scratched his neck, ashamed. Until now he'd thought of Jewel mainly in labels: Indian. Female. Hired hand.

But under it all, she was painfully vulnerable. Just like himself, but perhaps more so.

"Did. . .did you love him?" Wyatt asked in a near whisper, barely managing to speak the words. He kept his burning face turned toward the cabin, shivering under his thick leather coat.

"I beg your pardon?" Jewel twisted around to see him.

He shouldered his shovels and rifle uncomfortably, and everything clattered together. "I'm sorry." He felt heat flood his face in racing pulses. "It's none of my business. Forgive me."

Jewel brushed strands of hair from her eyes with her free hand. "Did you ask me if I loved my husband?"

Of all the fool things for me to say. "I truly apologize." Wyatt rubbed his face in his calloused palm, eyes scrunched together in embarrassment. "Forget I said anything, will you?"

"No, I did not love him." Jewel's steady gaze caught his. "Ever."

Wyatt remained as still as a blue spruce, not daring to speak or even to breathe.

"He treated me as nothing but property, Mr. Kelly. I was bought, sold. He wasted our money on whiskey and women, and he beat me. Quite severely at times. Once he might have killed me if I hadn't defended myself with a pitchfork." She ran her hand over her forearm— the one where Wyatt had seen the long scar.

In a blinding second Wyatt remembered Jewel in Crazy Pierre's cabin, raising the blunt end of the pistol stock to swing at Kirby Crowder with surprising force and agility. *But she did not pull the trigger.*

"Why do you ask?" Her cheeks were red with cold.

"Huh?" Wyatt turned, too shy to look at her. "Why do I ask what?"

"If I loved my husband." Jewel turned her eyes on him, their darkness keen and penetrating.

Wyatt paused a moment, his chest rising and falling under his coat with his breath. Afraid to speak, to ruin the hush. "Did I ask that?" he stammered, painfully aware of what a short distance separated them. A foot? Six inches? Jewel's breath misted, dissolving into thin air near his cheek.

"You did."

Wyatt looked down at his boots in reddened humiliation, twisting the lantern handle and trying to come up with a reason that made any sense at all. "I. . .I have no idea."

"No one's ever asked me that before," Jewel whispered. "Thank you."

Then she reached out boldly and gave his cold hand a gentle squeeze.

◆ ◆ ◆

"Over there." Jewel pointed as they tromped through fallen pine branches and autumn-thin leaves. Snow gathered in white patches in the crooks of tree trunks.

"What's over there?" Wyatt had to force his attention away from her, willing the wild hammering of his heart to slow down. Straightening his knocking knees.

"The outhouse, Mr. Kelly."

He could still feel the fleeting warmth of her fingers against his. "Oh, that." Wyatt swallowed and crossed his arms, trying to feign nonchalance. "You're right. It sure looks like a privy to me."

Jewel strained on tiptoe to see better. Not that she was short. In fact, she came all the way up to Wyatt's chin—not a mean feat for a girl. The Arapaho were tall and stately, great warriors, and Jewel must have come from hardy stock.

"The outhouse has a stone base, Mr. Kelly. Will you look at that." She caught her breath. "And a crescent moon carved in the door."

"By gravy." Wyatt stroked his jaw. "That stone base might make it sturdy enough to hold a stash of gold, if the rafters are built sturdy. And it's solid pine log. You just might be right." Wyatt looked over at her. "You're not too squeamish to peek inside a crazy old man's latrine?"

"As I recall, I wasn't the one scared of spiders."

Wyatt scowled and pretended not to hear.

The outhouse stood in a thin stand of trees, not far from an old barn. It was a simple structure, with log walls and a peaked roof. A few shingles had come off over the years, but otherwise the outhouse probably looked much the same as when Crazy Pierre spent his days digging up the forest.

Snow blew in fast flakes as Wyatt attempted to pry the outhouse door open, tugging on the swollen wood. Jewel put down her lantern and pistol and helped Wyatt pull, and the bottom of the door creaked open, scraping across soil. Wyatt stuck his boot inside the crack and leaned against the door, easing it wider for her to duck inside.

"Do you see anything?" Wyatt struck a match and lit the lantern wick. He pushed the door wider with his shoulder and held up the lantern, straining for a glimpse of the rafters over Jewel's head. "It's boarded over." Wyatt's heart leaped. "And the board's buckling in the middle. Can you see that?"

"Look at the wood he used." Jewel leaned her hand on Wyatt's shoulder and stepped up on the wooden seating platform, avoiding the cavernous dark hole. "It's a different wood type than both the structure and the door. Here." She reached for the lantern and shined it on the joint between the wall and the ceiling. "It looks like heavy barn board."

"And nailed up in a hurry. It's a bit crooked, unlike the rest of the structure." Wyatt felt around over his head.

"See the nails over there? They're starting to pull out."

"Braces." Wyatt's voice came out in a hoarse whisper. "By George. He put braces and trusses in here."

Jewel shivered, and her teeth chattered together. "It's got to be the treasure."

"I'll break it open." Wyatt reached for his ax.

"And let it all fall through that open hole?" Jewel gasped, pointing at the shadowy toilet opening in the platform. "If you break the ceiling and rafters open, all the gold will crash down on top of us." She tapped the wooden seating platform with her foot. "You know this thing isn't very sturdy, right? And there's an open pit underneath that's probably been. . .shall we say. . .well used over the years?"

"I get it, I get it!" Wyatt stuck his head through the creaky wooden door and peered up at the roof. "We can hack the roof open, but there's no way I can crawl up there myself. I'll have to boost you up."

"All right." Jewel put her things down and pushed past him. "Hurry, though. This snow's coming down hard."

Wyatt bent down and locked his fingers together. He waited for her to step, first one pointy, high-buttoned boot and then the other, and then he boosted her up. Jewel grabbed at the edge, her fingers clawing at shingles, and Wyatt pushed her up to the roof.

Jewel steadied herself on the rough-shingled peak, her wool skirts fluttering in the wind, and reached for the ax. She brought it down hard at an angle, turning her face as splinters flew from the boards and shingles. Then again. Two brittle shingles cracked and tumbled off in pieces.

"That's it—keep going!" Wyatt shielded his eyes as heavy white flakes melted and beaded on his glasses. "Do you see anything yet?"

Jewel braced herself again and swung the sharp ax blade, and Wyatt heard the *thump* of metal cutting into wood. She hacked a few minutes, splitting open a crack, and then brought the ax down with a mighty whack.

The boards split open, and broken chunks of wood rolled down the shingled roof and into the grass.

Wyatt strained his head excitedly. "What's up there?"

"I don't know." Jewel bent and put her face to the crack and then shook her head. "It's dark, and the snow's coming down too hard. Let me open it up a bit more."

Wyatt watched Jewel's steady brown hands and felt a stab of shame at the way he'd spoken of her, tried to use her. Why, he and his uncle hadn't done much differently than her French trapper husband, who viewed her as property to be beaten.

Jewel's lips moved, her face turned toward him—and Wyatt realized she'd said something.

"Pardon?" He shook the snow from his hat.

"I said there's something here." Jewel's voice was sharp, urgent. Triumphant. "An old burlap sack full, bulging and tied at the top with twine. And. . ." She sucked in a gasp. "Something's glittering through the place where the burlap's worn through."

Chapter 8

Wyatt tried to speak, but his mouth felt dry, like he'd swallowed straw. "You're serious." His hands shook. "You're really serious. What's in the sack?" Wyatt tugged on the side of the outhouse roof as if to pull himself up, desperately wishing he could see.

"It's the gold," Jewel whispered. "Pounds of it. Nuggets of all sizes. I've never seen anything like it."

She reached into the hole in the roof and then reached down toward him with cupped hands. Dribbling a rain of gold nuggets into his outstretched palms.

Wyatt turned the gold over in his fingers, speechless. Snow sifted down on the pile of gleaming nuggets in white streaks, sticking in ornately pronged flakes and then melting into tiny water beads.

"We've. . .we've found it," he whispered. "So Ezra Kind wasn't bluffing about the gold—and the Thoen Stone's real. I can't believe it. I never thought. . ." Wyatt glanced up at Jewel. "You were right about the outhouse thing."

"A wild guess." She tucked her neck and shivered in the wind.

"A good one." Wyatt looked down again at the gold in his hand. Funny thing though—it didn't look much like gold at all. He sifted it in his fingers, watching the light gleam on the dull, brownish edges of mottled nuggets, like dirty cracked corn. The kind he might fling to his uncle's chickens without a second thought.

And to think this yellowish stuff was the metal of kings, of ancient currencies and Egyptian tombs.

He could buy a new suit now—a new team of the best horses—the best oats for Samson—repair the wagon—help Uncle Hiram pay off the rest of his cattle. Start a sheep business. By jingle, he'd run the sheep business! And books—the best books—new ones! He'd have a collection. No, a library!

And the land. . .oh, the land he'd longed for nearly all his life. Beautiful Cheyenne prairie that had nestled just out of his reach—occupied by the murderers who'd taken his family away from him. Not for sale exactly, no—but for the right price, even the US Cavalry would. . .ahem. . .negotiate.

He'd dreamed of the deed, the feel of the paper in his hands. The persuasive argument in favor of US interests, with all the right words and loopholes. The smirk of satisfaction as the judge signed his name in black ink: *"Land ceded to the United States Government, supervised by Mr. Wyatt E. Kelly."* The bang of a gavel.

He'd have his revenge after all—the last say.

Long-lost wishes and thoughts swelled up in Wyatt's throat in giddy delirium, nearly choking him.

Jewel was straining at something in the hole in the roof, pulling and twisting, and Wyatt barely had time to react when she heaved a heavy sack at him. He threw the handful of nuggets in his coat pocket and grabbed the sack before it bowled him over.

"Watch your aim, will you?" Wyatt grunted as he lowered the hefty sack to the ground. It slid sideways into a fat, lumpy pile, the threadbare patches on the sack nearly ripping open.

"You try balancing on a roof and handling a bag this heavy," Jewel shot back.

"Well, just warn me next time." Wyatt knelt and pulled at the top of the sack. Images spun through his mind: the abandoned inn outside Cody. Gold nuggets dripping through his fingers like yellow sawdust. His patched trousers, and a fat pocket full of heavy nuggets.

Time seemed to stop; the neck of the bag slipped open in a blurry haze.

"You're not going to faint again, are you?"

"What did you say?"

And Wyatt looked up in time to see a black circle opening over his head, swallowing him whole.

◆ ◆ ◆

"You're really something," Jewel was saying from the top of the outhouse.

Wyatt looked up from where he leaned against the log side of the outhouse, head bent. One arm against the wall for support.

"What's wrong with you? Have you always been this…uh…fragile?" It sounded like she was going to say the word *weak* but slipped in a substitute at the last second.

Wyatt bristled. "I'm fine, okay?" He stood up shakily and wiped his face. "Just a little vertigo is all. Why's it such a big deal?"

Jewel scooted down the outhouse roof and dangled off then let herself go. She dropped to the ground next to Wyatt and refolded her wool shawl. "It's not a big deal. It's just…" She shrugged and brushed the snow from her hair. "You're different."

"I'm who I am, all right?" Wyatt snapped. "I get overwhelmed by things, I guess. Too much emotion and not enough guts. Is that what you're trying to say?"

"I never said that." Jewel pressed her lips together, and streaks of snow fell past her face like shooting stars. "I like who you are, Mr. Kelly. The most honest man I've ever met." She raised her face boldly to his. "And you've got plenty of guts. We wouldn't be here if it weren't for you."

Wyatt knelt by the sack, not looking up at her. Incredibly thankful the brim of his cowboy hat hid his burning face. "Of course not," he fumbled, trying to pick up a couple of gold nuggets and dropping them clumsily in the grass. "You'd have figured it out already and been halfway back to wherever by now." He looked up at her with a plaintive, hollow gaze. "I guess that's what you're going to do now that you've got the gold, isn't it?"

"Maybe." Jewel knelt next to him and opened the mouth of the sack, sifting her hand through the nuggets.

"I thought so." Wyatt scooped up the scattered nuggets and dropped them lifelessly in the sack. "I guess I always figured you'd go back to your people someday." He swallowed, barely peeking over the brim of his hat to see her. Wishing he had something to offer her— to make her stay.

But she was a rich woman now, and she certainly didn't need him. Hurt seared under his breastbone, startling him.

Jewel didn't answer, turning a golden chunk between her fingers. "I said maybe," she corrected him softly, almost sternly. "But probably not. If you want to know the truth, I've already been back to Nebraska." Jewel dropped her gaze and tied the sack shut. "And it didn't work."

"What do you mean it didn't work?"

"I'm not one of them anymore, if you can understand." Jewel tucked her cold hands inside her shawl and shivered, looking positively frozen. "I lived with the French community in Idaho for years, and I'm not who I was before. I don't understand Arapaho ways like I used to. I walk differently, dress differently, even eat differently now. I've forgotten many of the old ways."

"You could learn again, I guess." Wyatt tugged on the sack of gold, the weight making him stagger off balance. Keeping his face turned away.

"I don't know if I could or if I'd want to." Jewel bent over and helped him catch a bulging corner. "I'm different now, and sometimes there's no going back. They didn't accept me and my new ways, just as they didn't accept my French mother before she died. Only this time I was viewed as a deserter, a sellout. Like an ordinary white woman who left her Indian heritage behind."

"Wait a second." Wyatt grunted, hefting the sack to the other arm. "They sold you in marriage! How can they call you a deserter?"

"Marriages and treaties have been part of our culture for generations. My marriage was no different." Jewel's boots left tracks in the snow beside his. "But they expected something impossible—that I return to them the same way I left, when I was fourteen. It can never be done."

She gave a soft sigh. "It's like Abraham in that Bible of yours, Mr. Kelly. Try as he might, Abraham could never go back to Ur."

"Of course not. He'd moved on."

"More than that." Jewel turned briefly to face him. "He'd come face-to-face with the living God, and he would never be the same." Her breath misted. "Truth and character, Mr. Kelly, cannot be undone." Her breath let out a frosty puff. "But I guess you don't have a clue what it feels like to have no home, do you?"

"Me?" Wyatt chuckled. "You think I call my uncle's ranch 'home'?"

Jewel looked up swiftly, as if in surprise—and Wyatt shook his head. "Don't get me wrong. My uncle's cared for me since I was a boy, and I'm grateful to him. I respect him as my uncle, and I will until the day I die. But I'll never fit in there. He thinks I'm a nobody—with no potential." He paused to scratch his red head under his cowboy hat. "And he's probably right. Truth be told, there *is* no place for me to go, Miss Moreau. I've lost my parents. My sisters." He swallowed, and his throat seemed to swell two sizes. "The only people I've ever truly loved in my whole life. What kind of God would do that to a boy, I ask you?" He sent a severe look Jewel's way. "Since you're so enamored with this God of Abraham?"

Jewel spoke so softly Wyatt almost couldn't hear over the quiet crunch of her boots. "The same God who gave up His own Son for you," she said, looking up briefly. "Without sparing Him or holding anything back. That's the way I see it, anyway."

Wyatt nearly dropped the bag of gold. He grunted and fumbled for it, mumbling something about the burlap being too old and too damp, and pretended not to hear her. He tramped his way through the spruce boughs toward the horses, trying to push away the image of the family Bible on Uncle Hiram's table. The words and lines, burning deep into his heart. Resonating suddenly, like the gentle thunder of wind in the pines.

THE *Valiant* HEARTS ROMANCE COLLECTION

"So what are you going to do, then, with your share of the gold?" he finally asked, gruffly changing the subject and feeling inexplicably ashamed. After all the years that Bible had gathered dust on Uncle Hiram's mantel, had he ever once cracked it open of his own accord?

"I'll use the gold to take me as far as I can go and build my own homestead. Far from Wyoming, where people are hunting for my life."

"You're right about the 'hunting for your life' part." Wyatt set down the heavy sack, groaning, and stretched his back. "So do you want to divide up the gold now or wait until we get back to the ranch? I swear I'll give you your share."

"You can stop saying that, Mr. Kelly." Jewel touched his arm lightly. "I believe you."

"Oh. Well, thanks." And he stood there like an idiot, not even moving to pick up the sack. Hands in his pockets and face hot as a griddle. Opening his mouth to say something—anything—that might make her stay at the ranch a little longer.

To forget Nebraska or her own homestead for a while.

"Let's pack it on my pony, though," she said, shivering as the wind changed directions slightly. "Bétee's saddlebags carry more than yours, and she has more space. I ride bareback."

"What?" Wyatt fidgeted in his pockets. She might as well have asked for the moon; he hadn't heard a word she said. "Sure. Whatever you say." He stepped over a clump of snowy roots and opened the pony's worn saddlebag flap.

"What about you?" Jewel helped him tighten the twine at the neck of the sack, and they lifted it together. "You've never told me what you plan to do with the gold."

Wyatt didn't answer, and his face darkened. "Catch that end, will you?" he grunted, straining to hoist up the gold to a saddlebag. "This thing's awfully hard to lift without splitting the burlap."

"So you won't tell me." Jewel shivered again, and this time her lips took on a purplish sheen below reddened cheeks as she helped him shove the sack in the saddlebag. She hopped from one foot to the other, blowing on her hands to warm them.

Wyatt took a long time adjusting the gold in the saddlebag and shaking it out to even the weight. He squeezed the saddlebag closed after three tries and strained to strap it shut then fiddled with the clasp on the buckle. "My father was killed by the Cheyenne," he said in a taut voice, not looking up. "I've hated those people all my life."

Jewel hesitated, straightening the blanket under her pony's saddle pack, which gaped at the stitches from the weight of the gold. "I'd probably hate them, too, if they killed my father."

"I loved my father." Wyatt's knuckles bulged as he squeezed the strap. "More than anything. And they killed him. Not only that, but they butchered my mother and sisters, too. I lost everybody. Everything." He shook his head. "I've got nothing left but my uncle, and he thinks I'm a shrimp. A nobody. A good-for-nothing who will never make anything of his life. And he's probably right."

"Says who? Why do you think you can't compare to your father?"

"He was a big man. Strong. Brave and bold." Wyatt scuffed a boot angrily on the grass. "I'm none of those things. Never have been. I'm a homebody. A. . .a guy who faints when he sees a spider." He shook out the pack to make more space. "I had tuberculosis as a child and was always this feeble, sickly thing. It'll never change."

"You don't have to be a copy of your father, Mr. Kelly, to be like him." Jewel poured a handful of loose gold into the pack. "You can follow his path in your own way."

286

"What path? I'm no good at anything. My father had built his homestead, produced three children, and arm wrestled grizzly bears by the time he was my age. He cut our cabin out of the woods, right under the noses of the Sioux, and made a hearty living doing whatever he pleased. If I lived my whole life, I couldn't be half the man he was." He straightened his hat. "I can't shoot. I can't really do anything well."

That was an understatement. The last time he'd shot at prairie dogs on the ranch, he'd wasted fifteen shots and not hit a single one. He did manage to shoot a window out of one of the barns, though—and Uncle Hiram pitched a fit about that.

"But there's one thing I've been planning almost my whole life."

"What?" Jewel took a step toward him.

Wyatt hesitated, fidgeting nervously with the leather fringes on his vest.

"The truth, Mr. Kelly." Jewel crossed her arms. "I'll find out soon enough anyway. You might as well tell me."

Wyatt sighed. "Listen, miss. I don't expect you to understand, but I know for a fact those Cheyenne who killed my parents—or their relatives—are sitting on a windfall of coal and natural timber. I've been studying the books for years, and that one little piece of prairie's got more than enough resources to keep the US government happy for years. I'll manage the land, and they'll be delighted to hire me for such a fair price." Wyatt stuck his hands in his pockets. "I'll finally make something of myself, after all these years. No matter what my uncle says."

Jewel's eyes narrowed. "On the backs of the Cheyenne. If they resist, the army will slaughter them, and you know it."

"On the backs of the people who killed my family." Wyatt stuck his neck forward. "And isn't that what you told me? To use my skills and discover my gifts?"

Jewel's eyes snapped with unexpected fire. "On the backs of the people who were here *first*," she corrected. "And you know that's not what I meant when I spoke about your gifts, Mr. Kelly. Not that I condone slaughtering your relatives in any way. But answer me this—is there any chance the Cheyenne you speak of had been displaced from their original homeland already? Perhaps more than once? After years of broken treaties and failed promises?"

"Of course not." Wyatt waved his hand in irritation, but he did not meet her eyes.

Her voice turned cool. "You're sure about that? Because I've heard an entirely different story. And when your family is starving and you've been driven off your designated land and hunting grounds not once but three times—all the while cooperating peacefully and signing treaties that ultimately meant nothing—it makes for ugly politics."

Wyatt crossed his arms stiffly, a vein pulsing in his neck. "You've said enough," he snapped, his words coming out thin and taut. "I get it. The Cheyenne and Arapaho help each other out, don't they?"

Jewel ignored his question, taking one step closer. "What would you do, Mr. Kelly, if your family was starving and the Cheyenne took away your land three times? Each time they found gold, or coal, or something else of value, they canceled the treaties they'd agreed on and forced you off your land—sometimes in the middle of winter?"

"I'd take them all out, one by one." Wyatt's hands clenched with anger. "If I could shoot worth a lick, that is."

"Well then." Jewel crossed her arms. "Consider that a partial explanation of what might have happened twenty years ago. The men who murdered your family deserve to hang for their crimes but so do those who forced women and children out of their beds every time someone found coal or gold on Native land. Not all of those children made it, you know." Jewel's voice turned misty. "And not all the women and elderly. What if it were your little daughter or pregnant wife who didn't make it?"

"I don't know!" Wyatt cried, gripping his head with both hands. "I'm just very alone in the world, Miss Moreau—and I despise it. I just thought perhaps you'd understand, that's all."

Jewel stared, immobile, statuesque. "I understand all right," she said coldly, folding her hands under her shawl. "You're right. You aren't half the man your father was then, if that's what you consider a good use of your life. Revenge? Blood money?" She shook her head. "None of those will bring you peace. I expected so much more from you, Mr. Kelly."

"Sometimes the truth hurts, Miss Moreau," Wyatt whispered, staring out through the trees with hollow eyes.

Then he stalked back to the outhouse to gather up his things.

"I'll pack the tools on Samson, then, since your pony's loaded down," Wyatt called after Jewel as the snow blew harder, stinging his cheeks with tiny ice particles. He tromped through the snow and picked up the ax and spades, hoping he hadn't straddled the pony with too much weight. Bétee, Jewel called her—or something like that in Arapaho—was strong and sleek, but that much gold would weigh down any pack animal.

"Miss Moreau?"

Jewel didn't answer, and Wyatt turned, looking for her. He tied the tools to Samson's saddle and looked around uneasily. Samson reared suddenly, knocking snow off a spruce bough and into Wyatt's face. He whinnied, ears flicking.

"Whoa there. What was that all about, fella?" Wyatt patted Samson's graying head and swatted the snow from his face in irritation. "You mad at me, too? Or you just impatient for your oats?"

Samson's ears pricked, and he backed up several paces, stomping the snow-softened grass and straining at the lead.

Wyatt heard something. A rustling in the trees and a scuffling. The sound of a low whistle, like a magpie.

"Miss Moreau?" Wyatt loosened Samson's lead and then the pony's, letting them drop into the snow. If a wildcat was on the loose, he'd be a fool to leave his horses hobbled to a tree, utterly defenseless.

The underbrush crackled, and Wyatt whirled around, reaching for his rifle. *Nuts.* He'd left it at the outhouse, propped up against the side when he grabbed their tools. No self-respecting man would leave his rifle lying in the snow—especially not the burly Amos Kelly.

Samson backed up and whinnied again, a fearful sound, and Wyatt reached for his Colt. Wildcats proliferated in these parts; one of his neighbors killed one as big as an ox just a few weeks ago.

"Miss Moreau? Where have you gone?" Wyatt stalked through the falling snow, his footsteps carpeted and soundless. An eerie silence filled the gray sky, save the soft rustling of the wind in the firs and the great rushing sound they made in his ears, like a stormy ocean.

Without warning Jewel whirled around a tree, putting a finger to her lips. "Shh!" she whispered, her face white and startled. She ducked her head and flattened herself against the shaggy bark, not moving. "They've found us! Didn't you hear them?"

Then the world exploded. A blast of gunpowder, and a bullet whizzed past Wyatt, blasting the limb off a tree. Needles and snow whirled around him.

"Of all the. . ." Wyatt threw himself to the ground, pressing his face to the snow. Was Jewel trying to kill him after all, now that they'd found the gold?

Footsteps crunched through the underbrush.

When he opened his eyes, he saw Kirby Crowder standing over him, raising his musket to fire again.

Chapter 9

Wyatt rolled out of the way and scrambled to his feet, hands and knees muddied and smarting with snow. Nothing made sense; not the frantic loading of the musket, nor the man in a coonskin cap who lunged after him, barely missing his jacket collar. Two other shadows crunched through the trees, and someone fired a pistol behind him.

"Kirby Crowder?" Wyatt shouted, ducking behind a tree with Jewel as another blast shook the forest. Limbs rained around him, making his ears ring. The acrid odor of black powder hung in the woods over the soft scent of spruce and snow. "I thought the army hauled you off to the guardhouse for poaching."

"I busted out," Kirby drawled, calmly reloading. "And I came back for what I intended to do in the first place—but with reinforcements. Didn't expect to find you and that half-breed gal digging the place up. You're lookin' for ol' Pierre's gold, too, ain't ya?"

Wyatt halted as he scrambled for his Colt. *"You're lookin' for. . .Pierre's gold,"* Kirby had said. Did he not see them shove the gold in Jewel's pony's saddlebags?

"You know where the gold's hid. It's the second time I seen you down here snooping around, and it'll be your last."

"Get outta here, Kirby, or I'll shoot." Wyatt steadied his voice to keep his words from shaking as he cocked his Colt. "I don't wanna shoot you, but I will. You almost blew my head off."

"You? Shoot me?" Kirby's laughter echoed through the trees. "I'm shakin' in my boots, Wyatt. You can't even shoot a prairie dog. Now come out with your hands up and tell me where that gold's at, or I'll fill you both full of lead."

Wyatt spun around to Jewel. "How'd he know the prairie dog thing?" he whispered, humiliated. "I didn't tell a soul."

"What? Forget that." Jewel smacked him. "The barn," she whispered. "It's our only hope. We're too far away to reach the horses, and they'll slaughter us out here in the open."

"How many guys are there?"

"I counted five. We're done for if we don't get to shelter—either from bullets or from freezing to death." Her teeth chattered, and Wyatt noticed a bluish sheen to her lips.

"See over there in the trees?" Jewel pointed. "Another one of Kirby's crew. They're surrounding us. We've got no choice but to move while the snow's the thickest. Cover me."

"What? Cover you?"

"Shoot, for goodness' sake!" Jewel pushed the barrel of his Colt toward the forest. "Distract them while I get to the barn, and I'll cover you while you run."

The forest curved to reveal a dilapidated barn behind the outhouse, and Jewel crawled backward on her knees. She slipped behind a shrub and then into a stand of aspens. Wyatt could barely see her; a wall of snow blew in from the north, making it almost impossible to open his eyes.

Wyatt watched her go, and a strange emptiness welled up in his chest. Jewel's strength somehow fortified him; when she was with him, she made him feel capable. Confident. Better than he was.

All he could do now was steady his shaking hands long enough to aim.

Wyatt blasted his revolver into the bushes then cocked and let the second bullet clink in the chamber. Two shots whizzed past him, and one grazed the skin of his shoulder, leaving a burned streak. Wyatt aimed, trying to see through ice-clouded glasses, and pulled the trigger. He heard a groan. A curse.

Had he really hit somebody? Wyatt lifted his head, surprised to see one of the men on the ground, holding his bleeding arm.

Well I'll be. Wyatt glanced down at his revolver in surprise.

"Wyatt Kelly, you little runt! I'll skin you alive for bustin' up my arm," a man's voice rang through the woods. "Come out now and I'll kill you quick-like. If not, you'll take whatever I decide to dish out—and I won't make it pretty."

Wyatt licked his lips and tried not to picture what the man had in mind, and instead scooted backward on his elbow and belly. He scooched to the side and fumbled in his pocket for more bullets and then hastily reloaded his Colt.

He'd just aimed through a patch of spruce limbs when somebody grabbed him roughly by the collar and threw him to the ground. Knocking the breath out of him.

Through a snowy haze Wyatt saw a musket butt raised to strike him. A hand slapped his revolver to the ground, and Wyatt clenched his eyes shut. Preparing himself for the blow and the bullet that would knock him senseless, into the arms of a God he'd only just begun to think about.

A rifle shot echoed against the trees, and Wyatt heard a yelp of pain. He opened his eyes in surprise to see the musket butt waver and fall. The man doubled over, leaning against a tree for support. Blood leaked through his shirt and coat, spattering in crimson drops on the white snow.

Wyatt gaped a few seconds, so shocking was the sight of another man's blood and the reality that he'd been granted another few seconds to live.

Run, you blockhead!

Sanity overcame his woozy senses, and Wyatt scrambled to his feet and darted into the snowstorm toward the barn.

◆　◆　◆

"Did you really shoot that guy?" Wyatt leaned against the barn door with Jewel from the inside, panting hard. The whole structure had suffered years of neglect; wind whistled through open windows, and creaking shutters flapped open in the wind. "You're a very good shot. I'm. . .well, impressed."

"Of course I shot him." Jewel loaded her rifle again and pointed it through an empty knothole in the slats of the barn wall. "And I assure you, if I'd wanted to kill my husband this way, I could have at any moment."

Wyatt took a step back. "I believe you."

"But I didn't."

"I believe you again." Wyatt's own words surprised him. But he felt they were true, the same way hot coffee warmed his insides, shaking off the chill of winter.

"Let's barricade this place." Jewel set down her rifle and pulled an old plow against the door. "My only hope is that they'll run out of ammunition, if we can hold them off long enough."

"They'll try to bust inside by sheer force." Wyatt helped her push, sneezing as dust rose up in a fine cloud. "There are five of them, you know. Maybe more."

Jewel picked up a pitchfork and shoved it sideways across the door frame, into the latch. "Then we'll conserve our ammunition and pick them off one at a time. We can do this." Jewel met his gaze. "Do you believe me in that, too?"

"I want to." Wyatt's nose dripped with cold as he knelt down beside her, pushing the plow flush against the door with his shoulder.

"No. That's not good enough. Do you believe me?"

Wyatt shoved the plow harder in place and felt a surge of strength flow from his heart. "You know something? I do believe you, Miss Moreau. I do. I will. I choose to." He felt light suddenly, relieved—as if something heavy had fallen away.

"That's it." Jewel turned to him, her face strangely lit from the inside. Eyes sparkling like deep water. "You just said it."

"Said what?"

"What I've been trying to understand about the Bible. I don't know if I believe yet, but I'm willing to." She fingered the beaded necklace around her throat. "Therefore I say 'I do'—just like a wedding."

"A wedding, you say?" Wyatt's face was so close to hers that he felt her breath on his cheek, tickling his hair. Felt his knees melting, buckling.

"Neither the bride nor the groom know the full extent of their promise when they stand at the altar," she said softly. "But they say 'I do' anyway—without knowing all the answers. Because they know it's *right*."

Wyatt's heart pounded. Madmen were shooting at him outside, and flakes were coming down so hard that if he survived, he'd be snowed in in the barn without heat and frozen into a block of ice before morning.

And yet she'd hit on something—something big.

"It's even more than that. I'm willing to believe you because I *know* you," he whispered, his breath misting. "Because I know your character. Even if I don't understand all your reasons." He tipped his face down toward hers, so close their noses almost touched. "That's what faith is, isn't it?"

Jewel lifted her eyes to his in a deep, velvet expression that unnerved him, made his heart jump. She nodded wordlessly. The world seemed to hush, silent, and Wyatt couldn't seem to remember how to breathe. How to move his mouth.

Why was she looking at him that way? *That* way?

Almost as if she. . .

No. Wyatt forced himself to think over the loud hammering of his heart. A woman like Jewel wouldn't have anything to do with the likes of him, would she?

Shots rang out over the snow—and Wyatt jumped, reaching for his holster.

His empty holster. He stuck his hand in his pocket, incredulous, and shook it out. Then the other pocket.

Wyatt Kelly, you turkey! He slapped his forehead, recalling the man who'd grabbed him by the collar and knocked the revolver out of his hand. *You've done it again! You should have grabbed your gun—and his, too—and snatched up your rifle on the way to the barn.*

"You've lost your gun."

Wyatt jerked his head up like a frightened rabbit, hands stopping in his pockets in mid-search. "I'm sorry," he whispered miserably, straightening his glasses. "I'm no good. I told you that."

"No matter." Jewel reached for a heavy wagon tongue and slid it in front of the door, pushing a stack of wagon wheels with her hip. "God can save us if He wants to. He rolled back the Red Sea and rained fire from heaven on Sodom and Gomorrah."

"But why would He save me?" Wyatt's face contorted in another sneeze. "I'm nobody. I should have died there on that field with my father."

"No you shouldn't have." Jewel stood up to see him, nearly eye to eye. "God saved you, a defenseless child, just like He appeared to Hagar the slave girl. He has plans for your life, Wyatt. Good plans—not plans for revenge. Your father lived his life. Live yours. With justice and mercy." She grabbed a wooden hoe and thrust it into his empty hands. "God will help you live out your gifts if you give Him your life."

Wyatt's hands shook on the hoe. "I'll die anyway. I can't hold off five men."

"God held off thousands of Egyptian soldiers and chariots for a band of Israelites. And so what if you die? Do it with courage, like your father."

Wyatt took the hoe, barely seeing through his crooked and smudged glasses. His heart thumped in his throat. Before he could say another word, something moved from the corner of the barn. Wooden crates tumbled to the ground, and a wagon wheel rolled in an arc until it slid to a stop against an old bale of hay.

Wyatt jumped back, wielding the hoe, and Jewel leaped for the rifle.

But not fast enough.

"Jean-François Boulé," Jewel gasped, shrinking back, pale as if she'd fainted. "What are you doing here?"

A bearded man with a scar across his cheek leaped from the jumble of crates and grabbed Jewel around the neck, shoving a pistol under her throat.

Chapter 10

"Nice speech about faith, Miss Moreau. I didn't know you were a woman of such high morals." The man smiled, and Wyatt saw ice in his eyes as he bent her over double, wrestling the gun to her head.

Wyatt raised the hoe with sweaty hands as she screamed.

"You so much as flinch and she's dead, Mr. Kelly," the man snarled in a heavy French accent. "Drop it and get your hands up right now, or I'll shoot!"

Wyatt hesitated, terrified of making a wrong decision, and Jean-François cocked the revolver. The metallic click echoed through the barren barn, and even Jewel halted, unmoving.

"Leave her alone," Wyatt growled, slowly dropping the hoe and putting his hands up. "Let her go."

"Why does it matter what I do with her?" asked Jean-François, slapping Jewel's hands away as she grabbed for her rifle. "She's a redskin, Wyatt. I should have killed her when I killed that fool husband of hers—but she was too slippery for me."

Wyatt flinched, sputtering for a response.

"Truth is, it's the letter from Pierre I want. Always has been. And I know she's got it." Jean stuck the pistol harder against Jewel's forehead. "I've been tracking her down for months, and thanks to those Crowder fellows, I've finally found her."

"Who cares about the letter?" Wyatt cried. "It'll make no sense to you anyway!"

Jean-François pulled Jewel upright, keeping the gun in place. "I'll make that decision, if you don't mind. I'm giving you exactly ten seconds to hand over the letter or tell me where the gold is, or I pull the trigger." He settled wild eyes on Wyatt. "And I'll slaughter every single person on that ranch to find it if I have to. Starting with your uncle." He narrowed his eyes into a scowl. "I know who you are, Kelly. I'll take that place apart board by board."

"The letter? Are you crazy? We already pulled the gold from the privy." Wyatt kept his hands up. "I swear. And then we packed it on her horse."

The gun wavered in Jean-François's hand, and a look of pure shock contorted his face. "You. . .you what?"

"We found the gold." Wyatt breathed too fast, light-headed, and tried to feel his feet on the floor. "He'd stashed it in the outhouse. It's all there; you can take it right off her pony. There were probably two hundred pounds of it."

Jean-François stood silent, frozen in place, eyes round as hotcakes. And then, before Wyatt could move, he began to shudder. A long, loud belly laugh, shaking his shoulders and ringing off the sides of the dilapidated old barn. Jean-François threw his head back and guffawed until he sniffled, stomping his boot as if in glee.

"What's. . .so funny?" Wyatt managed nervously, lowering his hands slightly.

"In the outhouse, you say?" Jean-François wheezed, wiping his eyes with his sleeve. "You're telling me Pierre left all his bounty in his doggone john?"

"That's right." Wyatt shrugged. "Go figure."

Jean-François laughed again, raking his sleeve across his mouth, and then leveled cool eyes at Wyatt. "I don't believe a word of it."

"I'm serious!" Wyatt's hands trembled, and sweat burned his forehead. "Ask Miss Moreau! She'll tell you. We hauled it all out and put in on her pony."

Jean-François swore in French. "You're a liar, Wyatt Kelly." He took a step forward, dragging Jewel with him. "Crazy Pierre didn't hide nothin' in no toilet, and there isn't a pony around here for miles. We've combed the place twice. We were wondering how you folks walked out here on foot in the middle of the snow."

"We didn't walk! We rode here. We tied our horses right over there." Wyatt pointed out the ruined window. "Right by the. . .wait a second." He wiped a smudge on his glasses and craned his neck. "By George. They're not there."

"No, they're not." Jean-François breathed through his teeth, leveling his pistol at Wyatt. "Are you tryin' to tell me two hundred pounds of gold sprouted legs and walked off?"

"I'm not lying!" Wyatt moved one hand just enough to push his glasses up on his sweaty nose. "We put them on her horse—a little Indian pony. She couldn't have gone that far."

Jean-François's eye twitched. "I've had enough. This thieving gal's gonna die for your stupidity—and who cares? These redskins have been a blight on our land since the day they started cutting into our fur trade. They're not fit to live."

And with that, he cocked the hammer of his revolver.

"The letter or the gold, in ten seconds. *Un*," Jean-François counted in a calm voice, his face deadly stone. *"Deux."*

Think fast, Wyatt!

"If it's money you want, don't shoot!" Wyatt cried. "There's a reason I'm trying to protect the girl. She's worth a fortune."

Jean-François's head shot up. "What?"

"There's a bounty on her head back in Idaho. A big one." Wyatt felt the blood drain from his face. He was a traitor, a rat. He kept his gaze fixed on Jean-François, not daring to meet eyes with Jewel. "She's wanted for murder—the murder you committed—and if you turn her in, they'll reward you handsomely."

Wyatt heard Jewel's sharp intake of breath, but he didn't flinch. Didn't seem to hear.

Jean-François turned Jewel to him, tipping her face up in the fading light. He turned her head from side to side, and something seemed to register in his expression, like a candle flickering to life.

"Why, you're right," he whispered. "Miss Collette Moreau from Idaho. The black widow." He grinned, showing yellow teeth. "Are they really that anxious to hang her back home?"

"You wouldn't believe how much." Wyatt lowered his voice. "I heard it back when I was in Cody. Some wealthy folks lookin' for her who've got money to burn, I reckon. And they'll pay up nicely if you turn her in alive." Wyatt moved around to Jean-François's side, keeping his hands up. "I know everything about her. I can prove she did it. Why do you think I partnered up with her from the beginning? Let me go, and I'll go in with you fifty-fifty. Or since you're the one holding the gun, sixty-forty. Shoot, seventy-thirty."

"How about I just let you live?"

Wyatt slowly put his hands down. "Not exactly the deal I'd expected, but. . ." He shrugged, avoiding Jewel's dagger eyes. "I suppose that'll work. You give me your word? You won't shoot me?"

"Nah. Not now, anyway." Jean-François tucked his gun inside his belt and turned Jewel around, eyes gleaming. "You're right, Wyatt. They say she murdered her husband in cold blood." He grinned. "You sure you can prove it?"

"I've been reading legal books since I was six. I'll have that jury on our side in ten seconds or the deal's off."

Jean-François grinned like a hungry fox. "This is almost as good as finding the doggone gold."

"So you're gonna let me go, right, boss?"

Jean-François winked. "Now you're talkin'. Fact is, folks in Cody say you were askin' about her in the courthouse, and I saw you at the sheriff's office myself." He chuckled. "Boss, huh? Not bad, boy. Not bad."

Jewel's eyes narrowed, dark and accusatory.

Jean-François adjusted the gun in his belt. "Good thing you decided to tell the truth, Wyatt, because I don't take kindly to folks tellin' me stories. You can tell a lot about a man by what kinda yarns he spins, you know that?"

"Character." Wyatt shrugged. "Just like she was saying. Anyhow, they'll pay the bounty in gold bars. Not bad if you ask me."

Jean-François's smile deepened. "I like the sound of that." He pulled Jewel's arms roughly behind her back and nodded at Wyatt. "Gimme that loop of baling twine over there."

"Baling twine? She'll bust out of that in a minute." Wyatt picked up a strand of frayed twine and rubbed it between his fingers. "You need rope. Like this over here." He tore a long section of braided rope from the hayloft pulley. "Strong stuff. What kind of a bounty hunter are you anyway?"

And Wyatt slapped a thick coil in Jean-François's hand.

◆ ◆ ◆

Footsteps tramped across the ground toward the barn, and Wyatt staggered back, willing himself to keep calm. He'd traded Jewel; perhaps Jean-François really would call it a deal and let him go.

"You find any horses or gold, fellas?" Jean-François stuck his head toward the door as Kirby Crowder pushed it open. "Wyatt here says they found a mess of it in the privy." He chuckled. "What do you make of that?"

"The privy?" Kirby grunted. "I'll be a fool if ol' Pierre hid the stash in his john." He brushed snow off his coonskin cap. "And not a sign of a horse anywhere. No hoof tracks. Nothin'."

"Of course not!" Wyatt threw up his hands. "It's snowing, for pity's sake! The fresh snow will cover up the tracks in seconds."

Jean-François waved him away. "Take care of this scum. They haven't handed over the gold or the letter, and my patience is running out."

Wyatt's jaw moved, but words stuck in his throat. "But. . .you said I could live!" he whined, turning to Jean-François. "I gave you the girl, didn't I?"

"But you lied about the gold. There's no horse on this property, and nobody's cut open nothin' inside the outhouse. The men said so. It's a lie." He bent close to Wyatt. "Character, remember? I don't take kindly to lies. But at least I have you to thank for the bounty."

And he aimed his pistol at Wyatt and pulled the trigger.

Chapter 11

The inside of the barn roared in a blast of sound and brilliance. Something whammed Wyatt in the side, and he crumpled to the ground in a puff of smoke—hay falling everywhere. Pain leaking from his side.

Three more shots blasted the barn, and a piece of lumber fell from the ceiling, crashing down on Wyatt's leg. He lay there unmoving. Not daring to open his eyes.

"That's enough, Frenchy. Save your ammo, and grab the girl's rifle while you're at it. We're liable to run into the sheriff on the way outta here, or the army, and we need to be able to hold 'em off." Kirby's boots scuffed on the plank floor. "C'mon, redskin. They're waitin' on you in Idaho."

The last thing Wyatt heard was the sound of breaking glass, and he inhaled the sharp scent of smoke and kerosene. And then the solid latching of the door from the outside.

As the door closed behind Kirby's men, Wyatt opened his eyes enough to see it: a broken lantern in flames, licking at the rotten boards and dry straw.

Heat blazed against the side of Wyatt's face before he could raise himself off the floor. The boards and scattered hay lay sticky with bright red blood, but Wyatt felt his belly and his chest with dawning surprise. He could breathe. He blinked and felt around for his glasses. Why, he could even see—sort of—through the thick haze of smoke that quickly filled the barn.

He sat up in bewilderment, wondering how he, clumsy Wyatt Kelly, who couldn't shoot a prairie dog, had managed to stay alive at the hands of Jean-François Boulé. The bullet must have grazed him, opening up a wound without penetrating any organs.

Doc might need to sew him up with a few stitches, but by gravy, he was alive.

Flames roared up the side of the barn, and chunks of loose roofing tumbled, shattering on the barn floor. Wyatt pushed the boards off his legs and jumped to his feet, holding his bloody side.

He stumbled over old rakes and wagon parts and rushed to the door as another burning beam crashed down, splintering to bits where he'd been standing. Flames swelled up in a sudden rush, like an angry bull, igniting the dry walls and hay mounds.

Wyatt rammed against the door with his shoulder, lungs choking with smoke and heat, but the latch didn't give. The windows had been boarded over long ago, like darkened eyes.

The hoe. Wyatt grabbed it off the dirty floor and swung it at the boarded window. Again and again, hacking away at wood like Jewel had chopped the outhouse roof. And just as he gasped a lungful of burning air, the window splintered.

Snow—air—wind—and a rush of exhilarating freedom! Wyatt smashed the boards with his bare hands, bloodying his knuckles, and pushed his shoulders through the opening. He lurched forward and landed in a heap on the snowy ground, snowflakes tickling his sweat-stained face as he breathed in lungfuls of air.

Just as the side of the barn collapsed with a roar, taking the roof with it.

Wyatt scrambled away from the inferno, gasping. His clothes charred and blackened, and his hair wild. No hat and no glasses. He staggered to his feet, clutching his bleeding side, and lurched to a stop just inches from a bright object on the ground, half covered with fallen snow.

Jewel's beaded earring. A tiny feather dangled from it, crusted with snowflakes.

Wyatt paused, heart flailing in his chest, and snatched up the earring from the frozen grass. The men were gone; the woods stood silent. Snow fell all around him in lonesome gusts; tree branches rattled like empty arms. They'd taken Jewel with them, and he was too late.

As usual. Bungling everything into a gigantic mess.

What could he possibly do now? Wyatt rubbed his dirty, ash-stained face in despair, turning her earring over in his blood-streaked hand.

He could still see her there in the firelight bent over the Bible. Her long black hair pulled back into a braid, earrings sparkling. Those elegant Arapaho cheekbones and black eyes, and her long, elegant neck from her French mother.

And now she thought him a traitor, too. Wonderful. Why, she wouldn't trust him for a minute if he—by some sheer miracle—caught up with Kirby Crowder and his posse. He could probably bring the whole militia and she wouldn't listen to a word he said.

Still. He had to do something—anything.

A gust of wind blew a piece of burning barn wall so that it swayed and then toppled—landing in a smoldering heap next to Wyatt. He jumped back, catching his breath, and then limped his way through the snow toward the woods to look for the horses.

Samson was gone. Thank goodness for that, or Kirby's bunch probably would have stolen him—or worse, shot him on the spot. All the gunshots must have spooked him into the next county.

But he'd promised Samson his oats. Wyatt sighed, looking down at his bleeding shirt. He might do a lot of things wrong, but he kept his word.

He called for Samson, whistled. No answer but the shrieking of wind through spruce needles and the soft sound of falling flakes. The barn smoldered over his shoulder, smoke mixing with snow and choking the sky with black haze.

Too bad Bétee was gone, too—wandering among the forested hillsides and lonesome prairie with two hundred pounds of gold strapped to her back. If someone found her at all, before the mountain lions and wolves did, they'd swipe the gold for sure.

But neither of the horses could have gone that far. It made no sense. Perhaps the men were lying; maybe they'd divided the gold among themselves and kept the truth from Kirby?

Wyatt paused there in the icy wind, remembering the way Jewel called her at the ranch. A soft, high-pitched whistle, followed by a shorter whistle, birdlike—and a terse command in Arapaho.

He stood on tiptoe and whistled. Once, then twice. And blabbered something that sounded sort of like Jewel's command. He might have been quoting the Declaration of Independence for all he knew; at least he'd tried.

He cupped his hand around his ear and tried to hear over the wind. Pine limbs tossed; dry winter grasses rattled together. Wolves howled in the distance, their ghostly voices rising and falling.

Wyatt squared his shoulders and marched into the wind back toward the barn, head down. Hoping he could survive with heat from the fire and make it to daybreak but counting his fading chances like the gold nuggets that had slipped through his empty fingers.

◆   ◆   ◆

Something whinnied softly from the forest, over the roar of snapping barn planks and crackling flames. Wyatt whirled around, reaching for his empty holster by instinct.

"Bétee?" Wyatt wiped his nearsighted eyes to see better. "Is that you?"

A blur of white and brown nervously trotted through the underbrush, head down, and nuzzled Wyatt's side. Her hot breath tickled Wyatt's ear, and he laughed. He patted Bétee's side and scratched his ear, hugging the pony to his neck.

"Well, I'll be. The gold's still here, too." Wyatt patted her bulging saddlebags and nuzzled her neck. "You're the smartest one of all of us—you know that? What did you do, hide out in the thicket until it was all over?" He combed his finger through Bétee's silky mane and gathered up the loose reins. "You might have tried to save me, you know. I'm no good to you dead."

Wyatt tried to climb on bareback, the way Jewel always preferred to ride, and caught a glimpse of the beaded earring in his hand. The feather lifeless, fluttering in the wind.

Those knotheads in Idaho were going to hang an innocent girl, and he'd helped them do it. Wyatt shook his head. If anybody deserved to die, it was Jean-François and Kirby—not Jewel.

"Why don't you ask God for a chance to stand up and be a man like your father?" Jewel had said.

A line of horse tracks led from the barn and forest toward a sparsely wooded trail. Half obscured by freshly fallen snow.

"I've no light, Bétee. No gun. There's nothing I can do, even if there were ten of me." Wyatt climbed up awkwardly and swung himself over her slender back. She was smaller than Samson; lithe. "And I'd probably faint anyway." He wiped the blood from his face with a ragged sleeve. "But by George, we're going to try. Aren't we? Even if it is impossible."

Bétee whinnied and tossed her head.

Impossible. Impossible. Impossible.

The Red Sea parting. A childless old woman giving birth. Jewel leaning over the family Bible, listening to line after line of impossible stories.

Wyatt squinted and leaned forward, trying to make out the soft indentation of horse tracks in the snow. He was blind as a mole and half frozen—nothing like the gallant Amos Kelly with burly muscles and fiery eyes.

"You are not your father," Uncle Hiram had said. So did everybody else.

But he could live and die with honor like his father.

Wyatt pulled on the reins, urging Bétee into a trot.

Chapter 12

The trail curved through the woods, through gusting wind and blinding flakes. Snow had been falling wild and thick; Wyatt leaned down and squinted hard to measure—it came nearly to the top of Bétee's hooves.

"Faster," whispered Wyatt, urging her into a gallop. "They can't be that far."

Branches flew past him, slapping him in the face, and Wyatt saw stars. The only thing he could see, ironically, in crisp detail.

Up ahead, the road curved into an open plain, white with snow. Brooding clouds hung down over the land like a mist, obscuring the trees.

And as far as he could see in a nearsighted blur, nothing else. No horses, and no Jewel. Evening began to darken, a sullen blue.

"Bétee," Wyatt spoke sharply, firmly, "we've got to find Miss Moreau. Jewel. Do you hear me? She's in trouble, and I can't see worth a lick to catch up. I want you to go as fast as you can." He leaned forward. "Do you understand?"

Bétee tossed her head, nostrils flaring, and for a moment Wyatt felt like a fool, talking to an Indian pony that Jewel had bought for a few cents from an unscrupulous dealer. Uncle Hiram nearly went through the roof when she'd brought it home. "A waste of money, that idiot pony," he'd snapped. "That girl's got no more sense than a tree branch when it comes to buying horses."

He reached forward to grab the reins and pull her to a stop, to turn back toward the homestead—when suddenly the ground began to move. Shake. Ripple beneath him.

Wyatt's legs turned to rubber as he groped to grab hold of the reins. Stars and trees and snowflakes swirled in dizzying lines, faster and faster—so fast the horse's feet seemed to lose contact with the ground. He was flying, floating.

The velocity forced his head back, chin up, and Wyatt felt his lips flap in the wind as he struggled to hold the reins, nearly losing them altogether. He groped, grasped, unable even to scream. "Stop," he croaked, his hair flying out like a madman and bottom sliding on Bétee's sleek rump. "Stop! You're going to kill me!"

Bétee didn't ease up. If anything, she flew faster—jostling Wyatt's bones and organs together in a miserable heap. He cried out as his wounded side throbbed, leaking fresh blood, but she didn't slow her pace.

Hills blurred, and snow crusted in Wyatt's hair and eyes. He choked, gasped, slid sideways. The reins slipped out of his frozen hands, and he jolted forward, grasping desperately for Bétee's mane. His fingers found her thick strands of silk and clung to them like a drowning man grasping at a floating plank.

The way the Plains Indians rode in all their glory across Nebraska and Wyoming, bareback and proud, mastering the buffalo and subduing the bear and the wolf. Until white settlers encroached on their land, making and breaking treaties. Replacing the mighty buffalo with the weak and sickly dairy cow and spreading diseases that nearly wiped out entire tribes.

His people had not been entirely hard-hearted; some sat in on war councils and traded fairly. But clashing civilizations always left someone in the lurch. Someone like Jewel, who—when it was all over—had no place to go.

Bétee leaped over a ridge like a deer, barely jostling Wyatt, and landed gracefully on all four feet, still running. She rounded the corner, snowcapped trees jutting into her path, her hooves pounding the ground and throwing up snow.

Bétee made one more giant leap, straining and puffing, and then lurched to a sudden stop.

Wyatt shouted—grasped vainly at Bétee's mane—and felt himself hurtling through space. He landed in an undignified heap, facedown in the snow, just inches from a blur that looked like Jean-François Boulé—who looked up from where he squatted, fixing a drooping saddlebag. The other horses jammed up behind him in a dead stop, rearing and snorting.

Jean-François let out a squawk and jumped out of the way.

"Wyatt Kelly?" he snarled, fumbling for his pistol and shouting in angry French. "What in heaven's name are you doing here?"

Wyatt jerked his face out of the snow and scrambled to his feet, attempting a clever reply. "Well, hey, boss." He tried to smile, his lips shaking, and held up Jewel's feathered earring—blabbing the first ignorant thing that came to mind. "You forgot something."

Muskets blasted all around him, exploding the snow into white fireballs, and Jewel screamed. Bétee reared. Wyatt lunged for Bétee's reins and pulled her to a stop, dodging whining bullets, and he ripped open the saddlebag with the tips of his fingers.

He tugged on the strap and slashed at the burlap, and out poured a rain of gold nuggets. Down into the snow, glittering in the half light of musket fire and Kirby Crowder's lantern.

For a moment utter stillness descended on the field—so still that Wyatt heard the almost inaudible clink of snowflakes hitting the buttons on his coat. Musket fire ceased. Jaws dropped, and one man slid from his horse as if in a stupor.

"The gold," Jean-François croaked. "You found it. You really found it."

Bétee backed up, snorting, and a rain of nuggets tinkled, like sifted wheat.

Wyatt hauled the saddlebags, still dripping gold, off Bétee's back and hurled them as far as he could. Which meant. . .oh, a good four feet away. They splayed in a snowbank with a smattery *splut*, facedown.

All the men leaped from their horses, shouting, and descended on the saddlebags with a flurry of boots and lantern light, knives and fists flailing. A noisy fray of grasping, hollering, and scooping up nuggets.

Jean-François pulled up fist after fist of gold, his openmouthed profile visible in the yellow glow of the lantern.

"We've hit pay dirt, boys!" Kirby exclaimed in shrill tones, digging through the snow. "We're rich!" He giggled gleefully, almost like a child. "I'll build a new cabin. Two new cabins! Buy the best horses. And thanks to Mr. Kelly, I've got a fine idea—I'll buy that Cheyenne land and open up a coal mine!"

Kirby let out a shriek of exhilaration, and Wyatt froze. *Oh no. Not the land. Not that.*

"Will you hurry up?" Jewel hissed from the horse, reaching out her boot and nudging Wyatt in the shoulder. "While they're still occupied with the gold?"

"Sorry. I just. . .sorry." Wyatt awkwardly pulled Jewel down off her horse, dropping her in the snow several times, and borrowed a knife from Kirby's saddlebag to clumsily slit her ropes. None of the men noticed; nobody even seemed to care.

"Thank you." Jewel coldly handed him the rope. "Now excuse me while I take Kirby's horse. He's the fastest of the lot; he'll get me back to Nebraska in a few days."

Wyatt's mouth dropped open. He swayed, reaching for Bétee's spotted rump to steady himself. "You're going. . .where? Back to Nebraska? But I thought. . ."

"What, that you could collect the bounty on me yourself?" Jewel snapped, jerking at a tangle of reins and leads. "Well, forget it."

Wyatt remembered—vaguely—how to talk. "You must be joking. Surely you don't think I'd follow you all way in the snow and nearly get myself shot—with my side already busted open—only to turn you in?" He glanced down at his bleeding side, which had leaked onto his pants. A few red-brown droplets stained his leather boots. "For pity's sake. I'm not going to turn you in. I told that fellow about the bounty to save your life."

"Save my life? They want to hang me in Idaho!"

"But he'd have shot you on the spot if I didn't think of something." Wyatt sneezed, sniffling as he stood there in the snow. "I'm telling you the truth."

"How am I supposed to know if I can trust you or not?" Jewel turned, her beaded neck-lace jingling.

"You said it yourself. Look at my character and see." Wyatt scrubbed a sleeve across his runny nose. "And here. I brought you your earring."

He held it out on his bloodstained palm.

Jewel swallowed, looking from his hand to his eyes. "You expect me to think this means something?" Her voice shook, and her words came out softer than he expected.

"Sure it does. It's your heritage. Your past. Part of who you are, even though you've changed and moved on. You're still Arapaho. You still carry your father's blood." He glanced over at the men digging in the snow. "And if you don't hurry up and get on your horse, it might be the earring you wear when they stand you on the gallows."

Jewel took the beaded feather and tucked it into her ear. "Thank you," she said softly.

Wyatt tried to reply, eyes fluttering, and sneezed twice. His boots and pants hung damp from snow; his teeth chattered. Smoke had stained his bloody shirt an ugly gray-black. He sneezed again, and Jewel took off her shawl and wrapped it around his shaking shoulders. Drawing him close and fitting the folds snug around his neck.

"You can't see a thing, can you?" Jewel said in a soft tone. "No matter. I'll get you home. Bétee will lead the way." She bent down and picked up the severed rope on the ground and then looped it around the bridle of Kirby Crowder's solid brown mare, whispering softly in her velvety ear.

"Miss Moreau?" Wyatt tried not to sneeze again. "Pardon, but what on earth are you doing? We've got to get out of here!"

"Right. And let those guys follow us and cut our throats? No thanks." Jewel grunted as she tied the rope and patted Kirby's horse on the muzzle. "Hurry, will you? Give me the reins of that big stallion back there so I can tether her to my lead."

"By jingle," Wyatt whispered hoarsely. "You're right. None of Kirby's men are paying a lick of attention."

"It's either that or we shoot their horses. But I'd rather not."

Wyatt scrambled for the reins, tearing a revolver from one of the saddles and tucking it in his belt. Then a rifle, and finally a slender pistol. He shook his head at the melee: Jean-François scooping up fistfuls of nuggets, Kirby frantically scooping away snow with his hat and digging in the underbrush. Laughter and fumbling in the snow, curses and brawls.

"Now, Mr. Kelly!" said Jewel, clucking to the horses and pulling the lead. "Get up behind me, and hurry!"

Wyatt reached for her hand, coughing up something bloody, and she pulled him up behind her on Bétee's rump. She gave a sharp command, and Bétee surged forward—with all the other horses on the lead trudging along obediently behind her. All laden down with packs and rifles.

Wyatt craned his neck to see over his shoulder, not quite believing what he saw. A line of horses moving forward in a blur of snow, and Kirby's men oblivious. Shouting and pushing.

Well. For a second anyway.

"What in the Sam Hill do they think they're doing?" Kirby hollered suddenly, looking up from a crouch and jerking his pistol from his holster. "Son of a gun! They got our horses!"

"Uh-oh," Wyatt whispered, ducking. "Here it comes."

Bullets whizzed past them right and left, dropping tree limbs, and the horses reared and whinnied, nearly knocking Bétee over. Wyatt yelled and held on for dear life, feeling his teeth knock together. Jewel dug her heels into her pony's side, giving an urgent command in Arapaho and making a soft sound to the other horses. Soothing and guttural, reassuring. Bétee surged forward under a thicket of tree limbs, and the other horses trotted together, faster and faster.

Ducking into the woods and down a deserted trail, until the noise of gunshots and Kirby's men died into the sibilant whisper of wind and pines.

"We made it," Wyatt said, gasping for breath. "They'll never catch up with us now."

"Not on foot, they won't." Jewel glanced back over her shoulder. "I just hope we can make it back to the ranch before they figure out a way to the nearest town and find appropriate mounts."

"They'll be too busy with the gold to worry about us, won't they?" Wyatt shivered, clutching his elbow close to his throbbing side. "In any case, we ought to call for the sheriff and turn them all in."

Jewel turned slightly, her expression icy. "And you're sure you're not going to turn me in to the sheriff, Mr. Kelly? Tell me now so I can dump you off into the snow. Because I still have my doubts."

"Of course not. You know I wouldn't, or you'd have left me back there with Kirby Crowder."

"That was a clever speech then, that you gave to Jean-François. You really checked up on me in Cody?"

"I did. And I think you should turn yourself in."

"What?" Jewel whirled around.

A branch smacked Wyatt in the face, and he saw floating lights.

"Turn myself in? You must be joking, Mr. Kelly. Mr. Boulé said it himself—they'll hang me."

"Not if you tell them the truth." Wyatt scrubbed the snow off his face and wrapped his arms awkwardly around her as he slid sideways. "It's impossible for you to have killed your husband, you know. Besides, we heard Jean-François's confession."

"What makes you say it's impossible?"

"You were in Yellowstone National Park that entire week, serving as a paid scout for a group of botanists and soldiers in southwestern Montana." Wyatt sniffled from the cold. "After all, not everyone can speak both French and Arapaho with such dexterity, along with a fine understanding of Crow and Sioux—or navigate the mountains and rivers of Montana. So very similar to the terrain of Idaho."

Jewel gasped. "How did you know about that?"

"I've been thinking about that all the way over here from Pierre's place." Wyatt groaned in pain as Bétee bumped over a snowy ridge, dropping to a trot over a frozen stream. "I saw an article about the expedition in the courthouse in Cody, and the more I consider it, the more that description of the pretty young guide sounds exactly like you."

Jewel said nothing, just pulled the reins tighter.

"The article is accurately dated, you know. None of the members of the expedition would have trouble identifying you if you came forward." Wyatt sniffled. "Fact is, if you played your cards right, you could countersue your husband's relatives for slander, demand monetary reparations and your due pension as Mr. Moreau's widow, and swear out your own warrant for the arrest of Jean-François Boulé. After all, he killed your husband and attempted to murder you. I think if we reconstruct the crime scene and his shaky alibis, we could prove it."

Wyatt coughed; his throat throbbed from smoke and cold. "Besides, you couldn't swing the stovepipe that they say ended your husband's all-too-short life."

"I'm certain I could."

Jewel's loose hair fluttered in the wind, thick and wild, like a flock of gleaming crows. Wyatt wrapped a strand around his finger and brought it to his lips, feeling something akin to delirium.

"Doubtful. With all due respect." Wyatt leaned against her shoulder and shook his head. "Not with enough force to kill a man like Jean-François did—and I could prove that scientifically, by demonstrating fulcrums and velocity and borrowing the expertise of a good physician. Although," he lifted his eyebrows, "I'm sure you could do some serious damage if you wanted to."

"Thank you." Jewel clucked to Bétee and urged her through a clearing, looking up at the clouds as if to check for any letup in the snow.

Wyatt groaned, clutching his wounded side. He sneezed again, and Jewel turned. "You're sick already, aren't you?"

"Probably. And Samson's missing." He reached into his pocket and wiped his nose on a bandana, shivering. His knees knocking against Bétee's furry side.

And before he could stop himself, his frozen knees and elbows gave way. He slumped sideways and sort of dripped off the horse, landing in a pitiful heap in the snow. Snowflakes sifting down through the pines and tickling his closed lashes.

Jewel called a sharp halt to her pony and hastily dismounted, falling to her knees beside Wyatt on the pine-needle-carpeted floor. Not much snow had fallen there; sweet scents of spruce and earth welled up in Wyatt's nostrils like heady perfume.

"Mr. Kelly." Jewel gently shook his shoulder. "Please get up. We're almost home. But if Mr. Crowder finds us here, he'll kill us immediately."

Wyatt groaned and rolled his head back and forth, too tired and sore to raise his neck off the ground. For a moment the thought of Kirby Crowder's gunshot sounded preferable to this horrible aching cold. The sharp wind and throbbing ache of his side.

"I can't leave you here." Jewel took his face in her hands. "Come. I'll help you up."

Wyatt blinked up at her, trying to juxtapose the two images: a black-haired brave raising the spear to kill his father, and an Arapaho girl lifting him, bleeding, off the frozen ground with compassionate hands. Life seemed to have reversed itself, leaving his head spinning, floating, as if under water.

"Why do you care what happens to me?" Wyatt raised himself up on one shoulder, clutching his bleeding side. "The gold's gone, you know. Our deal is done."

"Says who?" Jewel combed his red hair back from his forehead with tender fingers. "I never said I was your partner only for the gold."

"You mean. . ." Wyatt's eyes stretched open, and his tongue seemed to stick in his mouth. No woman had ever cared for him, so far as he knew. Not bumbling Wyatt Kelly with his plain face and halting speech. Not him.

"I mean I said yes to you," Jewel whispered. "To *you*. Don't you understand?"

Wyatt's heart beat fast, loud, as he reached for her.

Jewel tugged him up off the ground and helped him onto his knees then massaged his frozen shoulders until he felt warmth again. "You can do this." She spoke close to his ear, her voice deliriously sweet. "We're a team, Mr. Kelly. Partners. We share everything." She cupped his stubbly cheek in her hand. "You're not as alone as you think you are, you know. Perhaps you never have been."

Wyatt, you knothead. He tried to sit up, despising his own foolishness. Why, if he had saved a bit of gold, he might have had something to offer her—right here, on his knees—and beg her to stay at the ranch.

"I threw all the gold away," he croaked, letting her rub his cold hands in her warm ones. "I should have saved some of it for us. I could have—"

"Shh." Jewel pressed a finger to his lips. "Forget the gold."

"I could have filled my pockets before I threw that saddlebag away, and none of the men would have known the difference." He pressed shaky fingers to his temples. "Then I could have sent out a hundred men to find Samson and bring him home. I blundered that one, too, didn't I?" He reached out and rubbed a thumb across her smooth cheek, feeling his throat tighten and burn. "Why, I could have. . .could have. . ."

"Listen to me." Jewel spoke over the sound of the wind in the pines. "There's a good side to every mistake, Mr. Kelly. An excess of anything corrupts the soul, doesn't it? Take poor Mr. Crowder as an example. A year from now he'll be up to his neck in debt, with ten men at any given time ready to slit his throat over card games or liquor or property—and all the gold in the world wouldn't solve his problems."

"You're just saying that because I'm half frozen and you want to keep me alive." Wyatt let her pull him to his feet, his arm draped over her shoulder for support.

"Perhaps." Jewel led him forward, arm around his waist, and he heard her smile. "Is it working?"

Wyatt licked his chapped and split lower lip. "Maybe. Keep trying."

"You've no gold now to buy the Cheyenne land with. You can start over, Mr. Kelly. Free from revenge. No regrets."

Wyatt groaned. "No, but now Kirby has enough gold to do it. The sorry snake." He heaved a heavy sigh. "And it's my fault. It was a fool idea to begin with."

"Don't think about that now. Just hold on. We'll be home soon." Jewel eased him up onto Bétee's back, tucking the shawl tight around his shoulders. She slid on in front of him and pulled at the reins.

"But. . ." Wyatt thought hard, trying not to focus on his throbbing side as Bétee jolted down the rocky side of a creek. "I think there may be a way out of Kirby buying the land."

"How, if there are coal deposits?"

"The national park." Wyatt nodded. "That's it. There are also several rare species of wildlife and botanicals on the land; I think I can convince them to make it a nature preserve run by the Cheyenne. So long as they'll agree to work jointly with Yellowstone and comply with basic park regulations."

"With a lifted restriction on hunting, of course. Unless you want them to starve."

"Of course not. I think I can write up something so convincing that even Kirby Crowder and his gold won't do much good. Just give me a few days with some books, park regulations, and a local survey of wildlife and plants, and I'll convince them that it would be a great ecological disaster to sell the land or open a mine on it. You'll see."

Jewel actually smiled. "Why, Mr. Kelly—I'm surprised at you. You're going soft on me."

Wyatt scowled. "Well, keep it to yourself, will you?"

He gazed out through the white woods, feeling stabs of pain pulse through his side, and felt his mind drift far away—to a snow-crusted plain at the edge of the prairie. A row of rough wooden crosses that made a sob catch in his throat.

The warm tears that burned his eyes felt good—healing—and he didn't try to blink them back.

His family was gone, but he would always remember.

Always.

Until the day he died, he'd be a brother. The lone survivor.

His father's son, remembering the feel of those burly arms around his neck in a tight embrace. For he, too, carried his father's blood and his father's honor.

And that would never, ever change.

◆　　◆　　◆

Jewel turned suddenly. "You know you still have a handful of gold nuggets, don't you? The ones you stuffed in your pocket there at the outhouse."

Wyatt's emotion-hard face suddenly melted into a look of joy as he scrambled for his pocket with freezing fingers. "By George," he murmured, fingering out a handful of nuggets. "You're right."

"You can buy a new horse with it." Jewel spoke gently. "I know how you'll miss Samson. He's been your favorite ever since I've worked at your uncle's ranch."

Wyatt dipped his head, glad the gloomy darkness hid the watery sheen of his eyes. "It'd be impossible for him to survive out here alone all night, wouldn't it?" His voice came low and mournful. "Not with wildcats and mountain lions. The cold and coyotes." He sniffled, trying to keep from blubbering. "As old as he is now. He's not as strong as the young horses, but I always thought he was fine." Wyatt scrubbed his face with his palm and said no more.

"Never mind." Jewel spoke gently. "I'm sure one of the local ranchers will find him and turn him in."

"There's nothing around here for miles, and you know it." Wyatt wiped a palm across his nose. "He's a good horse, but I don't think he could find his way back to the ranch in this snow—not at his age. He'll be so lost he couldn't find his own tail."

"Perhaps he'll hole up for the night, and we can look for him tomorrow."

"You know a hungry mountain lion won't let him live that long—if we're even able to get out tomorrow in the snow. He's got arthritis. It'd be a miracle if he's still alive now." Wyatt sighed.

"Well, doesn't that God of yours do miracles?"

"Not to fellows like me, probably." He sniffled in the cold. "I promised Samson his oats," he said, jabbing a finger at his chest. "I've never failed him yet. I might do a lot of things wrong, Miss Moreau, but I keep my word, and I. . .I. . ." He wanted to say "love that fool horse," but the words stuck in his throat.

"You're a good English teacher. Isn't that what you were going to say?" Jewel spoke quickly.

"Me? Naw."

"On the contrary. In fact, I think you might make a fine lawyer. I can teach you Arapaho, if you like, and French—and you could consider legal cases and question witnesses from all over the state of Wyoming. Or all over the West, if you like. You could be a Yellowstone legal specialist." Jewel brushed snow from her long hair. "In fact, your uncle has quite a few connections in the academic world, does he not? You could go to law school. You've certainly got enough gold in your pocket to give you a good start."

"Law school." Wyatt whispered the words as if hearing them for the first time. They were magic; they rolled over his tongue. Hanging in a shiny haze like the yellow lights of the ranch, visible over the next ridge. "Law school, you say?"

"There's a shortage of lawyers in the West, Mr. Kelly. You'd be in high demand."

"Law school," Wyatt repeated, his voice thin and husky. "And you'd. . .teach me languages? That is, of course, if you'd consider me." He swallowed hard, and his mouth felt dry at the thought of Jewel bending over the table, pointing out verbs. Her slender hands guiding his as he formed the unfamiliar letters with his pen. "My Arapaho pronunciation may be a bit garbled, but I'm sure I could learn with time. And. . .tutoring of course."

"Lots of tutoring." Jewel's voice took on a lush tone. Soft, like the sleek side of a wildcat. "And it would be a pleasure to teach you. But how do I know you're not feigning your Arapaho language deficiencies, Mr. Kelly? The same way I did?"

"You can't know."

Jewel chuckled softly, sounding like sleigh bells. "Well, I'm determined to find out."

Wyatt blinked back snowflakes. He was delirious, warm and light-headed and cold at the same time.

"And your father would be proud of you, Mr. Kelly, if you don't mind me saying so."

"For what?"

"For everything you are, Mr. Kelly, and everything you will be. I'm sure of that."

Bétee slowed to a trot at the entrance to the ranch, her hooves kicking up snow in the fading twilight. Black sky curved over navy blue of snowfall, fresh and smooth on the hillsides like smoothly spread sugar. Wyatt blinked through the snowflakes at the bright front door, where his uncle stood holding out the lantern. A worried look pasted across his face.

And Samson waited obediently at the stable door, his sleek face turned toward Wyatt. Saddle empty and reins dragging. Neighing impatiently for his oats.

JENNIFER ROGERS SPINOLA, a Virginia/South Carolina native and graduate of Gardner-Webb University in North Carolina, just moved to the States with her Brazilian husband, Athos, and two sons. Jennifer lived in Brazil for nearly eight years after meeting her husband in Sapporo, Japan, where she worked as a missionary. During college, she served as a National Park Service volunteer at Yellowstone and Grand Teton National Parks. In between homeschooling high-energy sons, Jennifer loves things like adoption, gardening, snow, hiking, and camping.

Birth of a Dream

by Pamela Griffin

Dedication

A huge thanks to my critique partners and helpers—Theo, Mom, and Jane. And to my dad, remembering our tea parties of my childhood. To my Lord and Savior, always there for me as my source of strength when I feel so weak and unable. As always with every book I write, this is for You.

Let nothing be done through strife or vainglory;
but in lowliness of mind let each esteem other better than themselves.
PHILIPPIANS 2:3

Chapter 1

A harsh pounding threatened to splinter the wood of the heavy front door. Christiana's cheerful humming came to an abrupt halt, and she almost dropped her mother's good china. She spun around, her hands clutched around the plates, and wondered who could be visiting so late. Why hadn't they pulled the bell? It must be going on half past ten! No decent time for any caller.

In immediate response to her thought, the chimes rang—followed by more frantic knocking.

Pulling in a deep breath, she laid the stack of plates on the tablecloth. She wished her parents were home and that their housekeeper wasn't visiting her sister in Seattle.

"Stop borrowing trouble," Christiana scolded herself. "You're no helpless child."

Slightly encouraged, she moved to the entry hall, her hands going to her hair and smoothing whatever stray locks might have escaped their pins. She glanced at the umbrella in the stand, a possible weapon if the need should arise.

She hoped she appeared more confident than she felt.

Opening the door, she almost got her nose rapped on by an impatient masculine hand poised for another knock. Christiana blinked in surprise. The man standing there pulled back his arm in equal shock.

The gaslight from the entryway showed her visitor to be taller than her by a few inches, wearing a black hat and overcoat, lean in build. He had a nice face and rich coffee-brown eyes that looked anxious. Her mind picked up the details in the few seconds before he spoke.

"Please, miss, I need to speak with Mrs. Leonard at once," he explained in a rich, well-modulated tone.

"Mother isn't here at the moment. Would you like to leave your card? I can tell her you dropped by."

"No time for that. Have you any idea when she'll return?"

She shook her head. "I'm sorry. She went to deliver some papers to my father for the Exposition—the Lewis and Clark one that opens soon." She realized the inanity of elaborating; every member of the populace of Oregon and many from the entire nation, indeed, from around the world, knew of the Exposition.

"That's on the other side of town," he calculated aloud, "at least an hour to get there, even with taking the trolley. With all the traffic due to the Expo, double that."

She nodded, wondering the reason for his visit.

"I can't wait hours, not even one." He shoved his hands into his overcoat pockets. "Can you tell me the location of the nearest doctor?"

His gruff question triggered the alarm of comprehension in her mind. "What did you say your name was?"

He blinked. "I didn't. Sorry. I'm Noah Cafferty."

She regarded him in surprise. "You're related to Lanie Cafferty."

311

"She's my stepmother. The reason I'm here. Her time has come, and no one else was home when I arrived at their house."

Instantly, Christiana's thoughts clicked into gear. "How long ago?"

He studied her as if debating whether he should share the information. He glanced at his pocket watch. "It's taken me twenty-six minutes to find your house with her bad directions. She, um, she wanted your mother to know. . ." His face turned a shade dark, and she sensed discussing such delicate matters was uncomfortable for him. For her, it was second nature.

"It's all right. You can tell me."

"She said her water broke." He cleared his throat. "That the baby was coming."

Christiana nodded. She could wait for Mother to arrive, though with evening traffic and the distance, it could take hours. Even with the information Noah Cafferty related, it was impossible to know how far along Lanie was without an examination. Christiana had learned that for every woman childbirth was different. Only one matter was certain: Lanie would be delivering a child soon. And Christiana was the sole person available to handle the job.

"We shouldn't linger. I'll just get my coat and hat."

"Wait—*what*?" He grabbed her arm. She stared at him with her brows raised in curious question. He shook his head and let go of her sleeve. "Sorry. Wasn't thinking. This whole thing has my brain coming unscrewed."

She smiled. "It's perfectly understandable. I won't be one moment." Again she moved to collect her things.

This time he took a step inside. "You can't mean. . .you don't plan to take your mother's place?"

At his clear alarm, she nodded while turning to the hat tree for her coat and hat. She hoped he couldn't tell that she was shaking in her shoes at the idea of assuming her mother's role in delivering a baby. *And* without assistance.

She felt uncertain she was ready for this, but she had no choice. Grandmother Polly had done it at her age—and all alone, on a wilderness trail, in the middle of nowhere.

Christiana could do it, too.

◆　◆　◆

"You can't be serious." Noah eyed the young woman who looked little more than a girl. "What are you—seventeen?"

She winced at his guess, and he knew it must be dead-on.

"I assure you, Mr. Cafferty, age has little to do with skill. I've assisted my mother for the past two years. I know exactly what needs doing."

"Yes, but have you ever done it alone?"

Her anxious expression and the resounding silence gave him his answer.

"There must be a doctor somewhere close," he argued hopefully.

"Knowing Lanie as I do, I don't think she would care for the idea of one, but of course you must do whatever you feel is best."

That was just the problem. Noah had *no idea* what was best for his father's young wife. He had only thought to drop in for a visit, since he rarely came by except for the occasional Sunday dinner. It wasn't that he disapproved of his father's choice of a bride any longer. The age difference had unsettled him at first, Lanie only five years older than himself. But lately he had made a concentrated effort to accept her as family. The knowledge that Lanie's well-being and that of his little half brother or sister rested solely in his hands was nerve-racking to say the least. If he made the wrong decision, his father might never forgive him. He might never forgive himself.

"Can you tell me where the doctor lives?"

"I'm sorry. I don't know."

"You *don't know*?" He regarded her in disbelief. "How could you not know?" He shook his head. "All right, then. Have you got a telephone?"

She motioned to a nearby table. "There've been problems with it. The connection is horrid, full of static. You're welcome to try, though."

He moved toward the candlestick phone and picked it up, bringing it to his mouth while clicking the hook and putting the receiver to his ear. A series of disturbing clicks followed.

"What's the doctor's name?" he asked.

She gave an apologetic shrug. "I don't know that either. Lanie mentioned it once. She and her husband use a different doctor than we do."

"Your family doctor, then."

"He's out of town. I remember him telling Papa at church that he was going to be absent for a week, to sort out things with his father's estate."

Noah's eyes shut in dismay. Of course. Why should he expect a doctor to be available with the way this evening had progressed so far?

"You could ask the operator to connect you with Lanie's doctor—she might know who he is."

He could, *if* he could get through. Frustrated, Noah set the earpiece on its hook and the phone back on the table.

"I might not be much in your estimation," the very-young-looking Miss Leonard said carefully. "But right now I'm all you have. Once there, you can ask Lanie the name of her family physician if you feel better about doing so. I won't take offense at your lack of confidence in my skills. I just want to make sure she's all right. Her health and that of the baby are what's important."

This time, *she* rested her hand on the forearm of *his* coat sleeve.

"I don't envy your position, Mr. Cafferty, and I do understand how upsetting this is to you, to find yourself so suddenly in charge of such a monumental decision." By the grim way she said it, she understood only too well. "But I have learned in my years of assisting at births that babies wait for no one. If you don't make a decision soon, it might be too late."

Her words sounded like a death knell; he felt the blood drain from his face. He didn't know if it was the fear of arriving too late to save them or the mature manner in which the young Miss Leonard presented herself or even the wisdom glowing steadily in her gray-blue eyes; but for whatever reason, Noah nodded his consent.

"Then we should go."

"I'll just grab Mother's bag. I'll need that, too."

Noah watched her hurry away, hoping he had not just signed Lanie and little Baby Cafferty's untimely death sentences.

Chapter 2

At first Lanie showed hesitance with the idea, but when another pain gripped her middle, she clutched Christiana's arm. "Help me," she begged between clenched teeth.

Christiana patted her friend's hand, which she'd been holding since she arrived. "I know what I'm doing, Lanie. I've assisted at more births than I can count on two hands."

Brave words for as apprehensive as she felt. Yet one of many important nuggets of truth she had learned from her ancestors' journal, passed down to her mother, was to never let anyone see her fear. As her great-grandmother Adele had written, *It's in how you act that others will react. If you're worried and doubtful, the mothers will know and likewise feel the same. Keep them calm. First-time mothers are the most fearful. In all things, put your hope in God, and He will give you the peace and assurance you need to carry out this great undertaking to which you've been called.*

The journal was filled with inspiring words that the original owner left to her granddaughter Adele, Christiana's great-grandmother, and which, in turn, Adele, her daughter, Polly, and Christiana's mother added to over the years. Soon, Christiana planned also to jot down words of wisdom to share with any descendants who might seek the journal's knowledge, should they decide to take up midwifery as at least six generations of her family had done.

Christiana looked toward the doorway where Lanie's stepson watched, his expression hesitant and more than a little anxious. Clearly he had no wish to be there, but his eyes were watchful of every action Christiana made, as if he felt he must oversee in his father's place. Mr. Cafferty also had shown reservations upon first meeting Christiana's mother but was soon reassured. Had he known Christiana was the only one present at the birth of his first child with Lanie, she felt he would have shown the same anxiety as Noah. But his shadowing her made *her* nervous, and she must keep calm.

"Would you please light the kitchen stove and set a kettle to boil?" she asked, more to busy his hands at a task than because of any need to have water at the moment. By her estimation, Lanie still had some time before the baby came. But even if he had to boil five kettles of water, she reasoned the activity would help him gain some peace of mind.

"Of course. Anything to help."

Quickly he left, clomping down the stairs in his haste. Lanie's contraction passed, and Christiana took the opportunity to examine her. With Lanie only eight years her senior, the two had become as devoted as sisters during Lanie's term. Christiana read the fear in Lanie's hazel eyes as she labored to bring her first child into the world.

"Have you decided on a name?" Christiana prodded in a soothing tone.

Her heartbeat skipped to realize Lanie was closer to delivery than she'd thought. She hoped her mother would see the note she had left and arrive soon, but she doubted it. Papa would insist he return with Mother, not wanting her traveling alone at night, and he likely wouldn't be happy that she had taken it on herself to bring him his forgotten briefcase. Nor would he wish to leave the impending exhibit until all was in order. With his meticulous ways, that could take hours. She forced a trouble-free smile, grateful to see Lanie's brow also smooth.

"Clarence and I spoke of it this week. Roderick, if it's a boy. Juliet, if it's a girl."

"Those are lovely names."

Sorrow filled Lanie's eyes. "We had a row. That's why he's not here."

Wishing to keep Lanie as serene as possible, Christiana doubted the wisdom of speaking of their altercation but needed to know. "Have you any idea where your husband went?"

"Likely the gentlemen's club, playing cards or talking politics. He goes there when he's upset."

The loud clatter of banging pots came to them from downstairs.

Christiana rose from the bed. Row or no row, the father should be told his child was entering the world. "I'll just see if your stepson needs help." She squeezed Lanie's hand before going. "Would you like something for your thirst?"

Lanie nodded against the pillow. "Please. I'm so grateful you're here, Christiana."

She smiled. "Where else would I be? I'm here as long as you need me. Don't worry. You'll be fine."

Another contraction hit, and Lanie tightened her hold painfully around Christiana's hand. Christiana again sank to the bed, gently reassuring, as Lanie's face turned as red as a tomato and she squeezed her eyes shut, desperately clutching the mound of her stomach.

"Breathe, Lanie. No—don't hold your breath!"

"I'm going to die, aren't I?"

"No, you're not."

Stark terror filled her friend's eyes. She had to calm her quickly. The idea that came was foolish, counting off seconds, but it was all she could think of.

"Say it with me, Lanie: one Exposition, two Exposition, come now. Three Exposition, four Exposition. . ."

Lanie looked at her oddly but obeyed. Somehow they slowly made it to "twenty Exposition" before Lanie again rested and Christiana retrieved her reddened, nail-marked hand from Lanie's relaxed hold. That pain had come longer and stronger. Christiana feared they didn't have much time before the final moments of labor, which could take minutes or hours. She wiped the damp hair from Lanie's forehead.

"You did well. If another pain comes, do what we just did and remember to *breathe*. I won't be long."

She hurried downstairs and found Noah standing amid pots and pans of all sizes, the cupboard doors and pantry flung wide open. He turned to look at her, his eyes frantic. "Would you believe there isn't one kettle in this entire blasted kitchen?"

At her home, the pots hung from hooks in the ceiling. Here, they were stowed away on hidden shelves. If he couldn't find a kettle, she doubted she would have better success. Christiana grabbed the largest pot. "This will do. You'll have to make twice this amount and put all of it in a washbasin. Where is the linen closet? We'll need plenty of clean towels."

"I wish the doctor was here."

"If you feel it necessary, then you must call him. I'm not stopping you."

"I tried—but would you believe he's out on a call!"

His words reminded her of Lanie's husband. To send Noah out on a short errand, especially when he was at his wits' end, would be good for all of them. "Do you know the location of your father's club? He should be told."

Noah nodded brusquely. "Yes, yes, I thought of that earlier. The operator of the exchange couldn't connect me, so I went there myself—before coming to you—but Father wasn't there."

Calm. Calm. She must remain calm; she appeared the only one able to do so.

Christiana drew upon every nugget of training she'd received from her mother and the wisdom from her ancestors' journal.

Dear God, help me in my hour of need, to fight my own pharaoh of fear.

"All right. Let's just take this one step at a time. I'll start water to boil. And I'll need you to chip off some ice from the block in the icebox, small enough for Lanie to suck on." The ice would help cool her and worked better than drinking water while she was in labor. She grabbed the pot and put it under the pump as she instructed him, propelling the handle until water gushed out. Quickly she set the filled pot on the stove he'd lit and watched as he chiseled pieces of ice into a bowl. With the cupboards wide open and the glasses in plain sight, she grabbed one. "Watch the water while I take the ice to Lanie." She dropped chunks into a glass, hesitated, then said what must be addressed. There was no time for dillydallying. "If Mother doesn't get here in time, I'll need your assistance when the baby comes."

He stared at her as if she'd just told him to strike a match and set himself on fire.

"If you don't think you can do it, tell me now." She had always assisted her mother. She could not imagine accomplishing the task alone, though if she must, she would do her best.

He went a shade paler but nodded. "I'll do whatever needs to be done."

Chapter 3

Three hours later, Noah remembered his brave words, gravely telling himself, as he'd been doing all night, that he would *not* pass out. And to think, women had been doing this for centuries! After hearing Lanie's screams and witnessing her travail, he didn't see how.

No one had come, not his father, not Christiana's mother. Now Noah stood a discreet distance from Lanie, giving her what privacy he could offer while assisting Christiana by handing her whatever she asked for or giving Lanie yet more ice or his hand to squeeze to a pulp. Lanie had shown some expected awkwardness to have him there at first, but now she seemed oblivious to his presence in the room as she leaned forward, fisting her hand to the mattress, a determined look on her face as she struggled to bring her child into the world.

"Push, Lanie, push hard!" Christiana urged from beneath the tented sheet of Lanie's bent knees. "Once more should do it. I can see the head!"

The news had Noah grabbing the bed frame for support, feeling dizzy, even as Lanie let out a determined, triumphant wail and seemed to crunch the bones of his other hand.

Minutes seemed like hours before Christiana gave a happy little giggle and delivered the news they had waited hours to receive.

"She's here, Lanie. You have a baby girl."

"A girl?" Lanie breathed softly, all smiles, no trace of pain remaining on her face. "Can I see her? Let me hold her."

"Yes, of course; just a minute while I take care of things."

"What things?"

"Normal things," the young Miss Leonard calmly assured. "Nothing to worry about. Just relax."

Within a short time she brought Lanie a writhing bundle swaddled in soft toweling.

"She's quiet," Lanie said, sitting up urgently. "Why's she so quiet?"

"It's all right," Christiana soothed. "She's fine. See?"

She bent to lay the bundle in Lanie's arms. Noah's heart seized with worry as he saw the dark-blue eyes of his new half sister stare wide and unblinking from a wrinkled red face that looked up at Lanie. Apparently the baby's appearance gave neither woman alarm, though the head was misshapen. Lanie cooed to her newborn, and Christiana straightened to stand upright. Her body swayed.

"Easy." Noah rested his hands at her waist to steady her. "Are you all right?" he whispered so only she could hear, though Lanie appeared so caught up in her baby he doubted she would notice a tidal wave break outside her window at the moment.

The young midwife nodded, but he felt her tremble.

"You should sit down."

"There are things I must attend to first." She glanced at him. "I won't be needing your help any longer if you'd like to wait downstairs."

Noah just prevented himself from running for the door. He was no coward but still felt ill at ease to be thrust in the middle of such a womanly situation, one entirely out of his element. "I'll make coffee."

"That sounds splendid. I'll be down straightaway."

He held eye contact with her. Their interaction felt oddly intimate, as if they'd known each other years instead of hours, and he nodded in affirmation at her easy smile.

In his exhaustion, he almost forgot his salutations before making his quick exit. "Lanie, congratulations. I'm happy for you and Father both."

"Thank you, Noah. For everything."

He nodded and glanced at Christiana once more before heading downstairs.

◆ ◆ ◆

With everything accomplished, Christiana cleaned up while Lanie cuddled her baby. Twenty minutes had passed by the time she went downstairs to join Noah. On the landing she stopped, feeling a bit woozy. He appeared suddenly, coming from the parlor. She grabbed the banister, and he moved to her side, putting a hand to her waist to steady her.

"You all right?"

She offered a brief nod. "Yes, Mr. Cafferty, thank you. I only came down the stairs too fast."

"After all you've done, it's no small wonder that you're exhausted. And please, call me Noah. May I call you Christiana? Somehow, after tonight, formalities seem bizarre."

She felt the same way, as if she'd known this man much longer than one evening. With his hand supporting her waist, his words seemed more familiar than they actually were, but she nodded her consent.

"You should sit. I'll check to see if the coffee's ready." He steered her toward the parlor sofa, and obediently she sank to the cushion. She found it amusing that for the past few hours she had told him what to do, and now he was taking charge. She rather liked the difference.

He looked at her in concern as if she were the one who'd just given birth. "Sure you're okay?"

She wondered what her appearance must be for him to ask twice but again assured him she was fine.

Once he left for the kitchen, she sank her head back against the cushion. Her neck and shoulders ached from being held in one position too long. She felt she'd been awake for days instead of just one of them. . . .

The next thing she knew, a hand on her shoulder shook her gently awake.

"Christiana. . ."

The low, masculine voice was unfamiliar, but the soft way he spoke her name caused warm contentment to spread from the center of Christiana's being. Wearily, she opened her eyes. At the sight of Noah looking down at her with kindness, she came instantly awake and sat up.

"How long have I been asleep?" She patted her fingers at the sides of her head in a futile attempt to sweep the thick, loose tendrils into some form of acceptability, finally giving up the notion as hopeless and letting her hands fall to her lap.

"Two hours."

"*Two hours?*"

He nodded and moved away from her. "I decided you needed rest more than you needed coffee."

Disconcerted that she'd fallen fast asleep on his family's sofa, she stood and smoothed the wrinkles from her skirt. "Has my mother come yet?"

"No, but my father did, fifteen minutes ago."

"Oh?" She regarded him in surprise.

"I thought you should know. That's why I woke you. He's upstairs with Lanie."

She hated to intrude on their privacy and deliberated what to do. Since no one had wakened her before this, mother and baby must be faring well. "I should go before my parents return home."

"I would think they are home already." He gestured to the mantel clock, and Christiana's jaw dropped.

"Twenty till six? I had no idea!" In confusion she wondered why Mother had not come; it wasn't like her to neglect her patients.

"I'll take you home," Noah offered.

Christiana nodded shyly. She didn't wish to put him out—he looked just as exhausted, but she had no desire to walk three miles home in the dark by herself either.

The brisk air did little to keep her awake. Several times she found herself nodding off, the sway of the buggy rocking her to sleep. She woke with a start to realize her head lay against Noah's strong shoulder. She straightened with a mumbled apology and moved the scant distance to the edge of the short seat.

"I believe this is where you wish to go?"

In the dusky lantern light, he smiled at her, and she realized that the buggy had stopped. She looked to see she was home. She had never been so happy to see the two-story blue and white building in her life.

He helped her down and walked her to the front door.

"It's been a pleasure and an experience, Christiana. One I will never forget."

His quiet farewell seemed to hold more than what rested on the surface. It warmed her all the way up the stairs of the dark, quiet house and to her bed. Her last waking thought was to hope she might see the kind Noah Cafferty again.

Somehow, she would see to that.

Chapter 4

Christiana woke, disoriented and uncomfortable. Realizing she slept in her dress, she stripped down to her undergarments then fell back into the cool sheets. Sleep wouldn't return, but the memory of what occurred in the wee hours of morning did. And at the center was one man with whom she had shared a unique closeness while they worked as a team—more connected than she'd felt to some friends of years.

With sleep elusive, she performed her daily ablutions and dressed. While offering morning prayers, she said a special petition for Lanie and her baby, which led her to remember that her mother had never shown up at the Cafferty residence.

Curious and concerned, she went downstairs. Had something happened to Mother? Had she taken ill?

Her glance went to the entry table, bare except for a fresh vase of flowers. She then noticed the sheet of paper at the baseboard and gasped to recognize her note. She plucked it up and hurried toward the breakfast parlor.

Merciful heavens! Her mother had never seen the note! A gust of wind from the door opening must have knocked it off the table.

Looking healthy and as composed as ever, her mother poured morning tea. Not a dark hair rested out of place. She looked up at Christiana, the laugh crinkles at her blue eyes deepening as she smiled.

"Christiana?" Her smile disappeared. "Whatever is the matter, dear?"

"Lanie had her baby!"

"What?" In clear shock, her mother set down the teapot.

"Last night. I left you a note before I went there." Christiana held up the paper.

"*You* delivered the child?" Mother's soft voice contained both awe and pride.

Christiana nodded. "Her stepson came to collect me."

"Oh my. . .I trust there were no complications."

"None. I *was* frightened, though I made certain not to show it." Again Christiana thanked God for His intervention during those anxious hours. "Once I arrived, she was far into her labor. If her stepson—Mr. Cafferty—had not come by to visit, she might have been alone at the end. He assisted me, and a little over four hours later, she gave birth to a girl."

"*Noah Cafferty* assisted you?" Her mother looked startled then slowly smiled. "Frankly, I'm stunned that he didn't insist on a doctor. Lanie told me he shares the views of those who believe midwifery should no longer exist in this day and age."

Recalling their initial conversation, Christiana wasn't surprised. But surely, after being a witness to the birth, Noah would have changed his opinions. Thankfully it had been an easy delivery; not all of them were.

"I never supposed I wouldn't be with you during your first time, dear, but I have long known you were ready for the next step and just needed a boost of confidence to get there." She reached to where Christiana had taken a seat and laid her hand over hers, squeezing it before pulling away. "After breakfast, we'll visit Lanie and her baby to ensure all is well."

Christiana smiled and reached for a muffin. Scrambled eggs were in a serving dish on the sideboard, as well as sausages, but she was famished and said a quick blessing, intending to collect more once she took the edge off her hunger.

She'd not yet taken a bite when the bell cord of the front door was pulled.

Remembering that their maid was on vacation, she rose from the table.

"I'll get that, Mother."

Once Christiana opened the front door, she blinked in surprise to see Noah there. This time, no concern tightened his relaxed features, and the morning sun brought a sparkle to his dark eyes, enhancing his good looks that the night had only hinted at. For a moment she stared before she remembered her manners.

"Mr. Cafferty, how nice to see you. Lanie and the baby are well?"

"Quite. And it's Noah."

At the reminder, she felt a blush but nodded.

"Forgive the intrusion at such an early hour. I thought you might need this." He offered her mother's bag of birthing items. She didn't know she'd forgotten it.

"Thank you, yes!" She held out her hand for the bag, not realizing she still held her muffin. Her face heated further. A smile teased the corner of his lips, causing her to smile at the amusing situation as well. The warmth in his eyes eased any lingering discomfort. Again she found it odd how connected she felt to this man on such short acquaintance.

"Mother and I were just having breakfast. Would you like to join us?"

"I wouldn't wish to intrude—"

"Oh, you're not intruding!" At her effusive reassurance and his clear surprise, she added quickly, "Mother will want to meet you. She's curious about Lanie, and there's plenty to eat. Mother doesn't often bake, but when she does she gives her utmost since she loves it so well." She took the bag and held the door open wider for him to enter.

He looked puzzled by her garbled explanation. Not wishing to demolish the English language further, she didn't add that in the mode of fitting in with society's expectations for their class, her parents had hired a maid who doubled as a cook.

"If you're sure it's no inconvenience. . ." He lifted his brows, and she nodded. "Then I accept."

He took off his hat as he entered and hung it on the hat tree. She smiled shyly, setting the bag on the table before leading him through to the breakfast parlor. Her mother looked up in curious surprise. Introductions were made, and Noah was invited to take breakfast with them a second time. Christiana fixed him a plate and then her own before taking her chair across the table from him.

As they ate, Mother brought the conversation around from pleasantries to the events of the previous evening.

"Christiana told me that you assisted in the delivery of the baby."

Noah looked as if he just managed not to strangle on his food. "Yes, well, that was an experience I wish never to repeat. Your daughter was amazing, though I wish I could have located a doctor."

"Is something wrong with Lanie or her baby?" Christiana asked in concern.

"No. The baby did look more like a baby this morning—not so red—though the top of her head still looks a bit squashed."

Christiana hid a smile, recalling his wince of barely veiled horror at his first sight of an infant newly born.

"That will change," Christiana's mother reassured. "She'll look better with each day that passes."

Noah nodded. "I'm glad I chose the field of journalism. I never could have been a doctor."

"Why do you wish a doctor had been there?"

"Christiana," her mother warned softly under her breath.

But Christiana couldn't let his earlier statement go and set down her fork. "You must admit everything went well. Neither Lanie nor her baby unduly suffered."

"Yes, as I said, you were a wonderful stand-in."

His praise had the opposite effect and spoiled her satisfaction in her accomplishment. "Stand-in?"

"Since the doctor couldn't be there."

"Lanie chose to have a midwife. There's nothing wrong with that."

"It's just not natural."

"Not *natural*?" She straightened her spine in disbelieving shock and just managed to keep her tone at the same pleasant, conversational level. "Mr. Cafferty, midwives were in existence long before doctors took over. The pharaoh didn't order the physicians to kill the newborns; he told the *midwives* to do so."

His brow lifted at her formal use of his name, but even if she wasn't upset with him at the moment, she felt odd taking that liberty on such short acquaintance when they weren't alone.

"That's ancient history. We're now in a progressive era, and things must change."

"*Must* change?" she scoffed. "That seems a little dictatorial, doesn't it?"

Her mother softly cleared her throat in the manner she used to stem a rising argument. "Of course, everyone is entitled to their opinions; that's what makes life so much more interesting, don't you think?" She looked at Noah. "You mentioned you're a journalist. What paper do you write for?"

"The *Portland New Age*. They just started this year."

"And does your boss share your views on what is and what isn't natural?" Christiana asked sweetly, though she still seethed inside.

"Christiana!" This time her mother's warning whisper came more forcefully.

Noah regarded her in curious puzzlement. "As a matter of fact, he does. After all, doctors have had professional training. . ."

"Midwives are also trained."

". . .at an educational institution," Noah continued, as if she hadn't spoken. "He doesn't believe women should work outside the home in this day and age. In fact, I'm doing a story on one of those suffragist meetings this week."

"Oh?" She folded her napkin and laid it on the table. "In favor of the movement or against it?"

He smiled, but his apparent ease didn't fool her. "Totally unbiased, of course."

She leaned forward, her smile deceptively sweet. "Your own views never cloud your work?"

"I don't write editorials, Miss Leonard. I just report the news."

"As seen through your eyes, of course."

His smile slipped, and his eyes grew a trifle hard. "How else? After all, I'm the one writing the story."

"Before your arrival, I told my daughter we should visit Lanie after breakfast," her mother put in quickly, rising to her feet and picking up her plate, half the food untouched. "Forgive me, Mr. Cafferty; I have much to accomplish today. Please feel free to finish your breakfast. Christiana, a word with you."

Noah took the napkin from his lap and dropped it to the table as he rose. "I should be leaving for the office. I've lingered far too long. Might I give you and your daughter a lift to my father's house?"

"We wouldn't wish to put you out of your way."

"Not at all. His house is in the direction of the newspaper office."

"In that case, we would be most grateful. Christiana, would you please help me put these things away, dear?"

Noah excused himself to wait outside. The moment he was out of earshot, Christiana moved with what was left of the eggs to take them to the sink, but her mother clasped her arm to stop her. Knowing her mother was upset, Christiana lowered her gaze to the serving dish she held.

"Christiana, you must learn to curb that tongue of yours, especially with guests present."

"But you heard what he said. He thinks nothing of our calling!"

"While perhaps you think too much of it?" her mother suggested softly.

Christiana blinked and looked up into her gentle eyes. "Are you saying midwifery isn't important?"

"No, of course not. But are you certain it isn't wounded pride that compels you to speak so vehemently? Mr. Cafferty shares the views of most men in our society and out of it, which is why the suffragist groups formed. He's only speaking what he was taught. As are you. A difference of opinion is no cause for contention. The Lord's Word says that where there is strife there is every evil work. You would do well to remember that, dear."

Christiana restrained a sigh and gave a brief nod. They finished their chore, collected their things, and left the house.

Mother was right; Christiana knew it. Still, she remained silent on the drive, in part not trusting herself to speak but also having nothing to say. Once Noah pulled his team of horses in front of his father's home, he helped her mother down from the carriage. Christiana felt half inclined to reject his aid, but not wishing to fall flat on her face, she laid her hand in his warm one. Before he let go she felt the gentle squeeze of his fingers, which shocked her enough that she looked at him for the first time since they'd left her house.

"I'll leave you both here and wish you well," he said, his eyes never straying from hers. "I must get to the office before my boss gives up on me." He smiled in mild amusement.

Christiana felt her lips curl in the slightest grin.

"Thank you, Mr. Cafferty," Mother said. "You've been most kind."

"It was a pleasure." He nodded to her, then to Christiana, tipping the brim of his hat before he climbed back into the buggy.

"Christiana?"

At her mother's soft query from the front door where she waited, Christiana was discomfited to realize she still stood staring at Noah's departing carriage.

◆ ◆ ◆

Noah had been unable to get Christiana out of his thoughts for days. Not that he particularly wanted to, but concentrating on the sometimes sweet, sometimes fiery young brunette did tend to interfere with his work.

Like now.

He licked the tip of his pencil and jotted notes on his pad as a speaker for the women's suffragist committee stood at the podium at the front of the public hall and decried their inability to vote. He had stayed tucked in a back corner but knew he'd been spotted. A few women looked over their shoulders at him, some with curious interest while others stared in open hostility. He had not failed to notice he was the only man within eyesight and not for the first time questioned his request for the assignment. He thrived on adventure, but the idea of what must amount to at least one hundred women ganging up on one man—at the moment, the opposite gender clearly the bane of their existence—amounted to certain massacre. He imagined from the unsettled mood generated by the speaker's words that many of these ladies would like the chance to take out their frustrations against all men, perhaps using him as a target with their reticules and parasols.

Relieved when the speaker concluded her oration, Noah slipped out the door. Two women who'd spotted him managed to catch up and practically demanded his reason for being there. His answer that he was a journalist sparked questions of his views, which he politely sidestepped with his convenient response that he only reported the happenings and preferred to keep his personal opinions to himself.

They weren't pleased with his answer, and the entire walk back to the newspaper office he remembered a similar conversation he'd had with Christiana. She also had not been pleased by his responses involving a similar matter of "rights" involving women in the workplace. For that reason alone, he'd kept his distance, though he would have liked to call on her.

At the office he doffed his coat and tossed his hat in the direction of his cluttered desk then took a seat behind it. He wasted no time in transferring notes to paper. Once he'd fashioned a rough draft, he loosened his necktie and leaned back on two legs of the chair, propping his heels on the edge of the desk. So engrossed was he in what he'd written, he didn't realize someone had approached until a figure blocked his light.

Ready to give the errand boy a mild reprimand, he snapped his head up—and gaped.

He must be mistaken. Thoughts of her surely conjured the lovely mirage.

When he realized Christiana really stood there, he brought the soles of his shoes back to the floor and his chair to its original position with lightning speed, almost falling out of it. He dropped his paper to the desk and hurriedly worked to straighten his tie as he stood to his feet. He cleared his throat in an effort to recover some stability.

"Miss Leonard, to what do I owe this honor?"

She blushed a shade of soft rose. "Please, it's Christiana, remember? When we're alone I don't mind dispensing with formalities."

He glanced around the drab room of six men, the air clouded with blue smoke from his editor's pipe. No one was currently within earshot, but they were hardly alone, and his guest was receiving her fair share of looks, much to Noah's irritation.

He hid his ire with a tight grin. "Christiana, then. Do you have a story you'd like reported?" He doubted that was why she was there but couldn't figure out a reason.

"No." She bowed her head, ill at ease with whatever she'd come to say, and fiddled with

324

the strings of her reticule. "I came to apologize."

"Apologize?"

"With regard to our previous conversation. I shouldn't have judged you for your beliefs."

Amazed by her refreshing candor, he shook his head. "I wasn't completely without guilt in my responses. I could have been kinder."

"But I baited you. I was trying to influence you to approve my way of things and admit your error in judgment." She shrugged one shoulder delicately, lifting her eyes to his. "As Mother said, there will always be differing views in all matters, neither considered truly wrong—unless of course they go against God's Word."

"Yes, that's true." He returned her smile, deciding to suggest the idea that had been brewing in his head since the night he'd met her. He leaned back and sat with one hip on the edge of the desk, casually crossing his arms over his middle. "Have you been to the Lewis and Clark Centennial Exposition yet?"

"The Exposition?" She stared at him in clear confusion.

"The night we met you mentioned your father had a part in it."

"Yes, he helped arrange one of the displays for the university. He's a professor of science and dabbles with his own inventions besides." She hesitated then seemed to realize she'd forgotten to answer. "I haven't been yet, but I have every intention of attending before it's over."

"Would you consider going with me?"

Chapter 5

For a moment, Christiana could only stare.

"Why, Mr. Cafferty, are you asking if you may court me?" She responded with all the flirtatious aplomb of an experienced coquette. In reality, she was new to courtship and astonished by his invitation.

He chuckled. "If you like, Miss Leonard, yes. May I call on you?"

His dark eyes gently teased back, but his tone was sincere. She wondered what her parents would think about such a shocking notion—her attending social functions in the company of a man she scarcely knew—and wondered if society would frown on her for accepting or think her fast or loose. Mother liked him, a point in Christiana's favor. But more than that, the connection she'd felt with Noah since the night Lanie gave birth never dispersed, though she had tried valiantly these two weeks *not* to think about him. It was the knowledge that she would like to know him better that prompted her response.

"I'll need to seek my parents' permission, but I can't see why they won't allow it."

Her words came shy and uncertain. His eyes flickered in surprise as if he thought she might have refused him.

"Of course. I wouldn't dream of asking you not to follow the mandates of propriety. I look forward to meeting your father."

She smiled, relieved that he was no wolf but ignorant of how this courting matter was carried out all the same.

"This Saturday, then?" he asked quickly, as if rushing to pinpoint a date before she could change her mind. "We can spend the afternoon there."

"Yes, I should love to attend the Exposition with you this Saturday." Suddenly feeling timid, she excused herself. "I must be going. Mother is expecting me."

"Of course. Until then. . .Christiana."

The softness of her name on his tongue warmed her. Still floating with the turn of events, she left his office and met her mother at the millinery shop down the street where she'd left her deliberating on two hats. She chose not to inform her of her plans until the purchase was made and they rode home. At first her mother seemed surprised and uncertain, then gently resigned, but she did not disagree.

Her father, however, was a different story.

"Absolutely not." He pushed his plate of pie crumbs aside. "Who is this cheeky young whippersnapper? Never heard of him."

"Actually," her mother put in, "you have. Noah Cafferty is a fine, responsible young man. I told you how he helped Christiana with Lanie Cafferty, dear."

"Yes, yes, of course. But who does he think he is to swoop down on my little girl like some hungry vulture seeking a baby bird?"

"A baby bird? Really, Papa!" Christiana was accustomed to her father's overprotective attitude, but that didn't stem her indignant frustration at being thought of as a little girl.

"And he's hardly a vulture."

"Christiana, would you please bring more coffee? Your father could use a refill."

She nodded, knowing her mother wished to speak to him privately. On her return to the dining room, before she could push the swinging door open, she heard her mother's voice:

"She's no longer a child, Isaiah. We knew this day would come."

"She's barely seventeen," he spluttered.

"The same age I was when I met you," she countered softly. "And I've had no regrets."

A pause ensued, and Christiana leaned closer to the door to hear, feeling only a minute twinge of guilt at eavesdropping. After all, her future was the topic at hand.

"Lanie and I have been friends for two years," her mother continued. "She's had nothing but nice things to say about Noah."

"He's a newspaperman, isn't he? They're the worst kind."

"The worst that can be said about a journalist of his caliber is that he might be a bit too inquisitive. He doesn't smoke. He doesn't drink or engage in lewd activity. His manners are impeccable."

"It's those young gents who appear to be contenders for sainthood that are the true devils in disguise!"

Her mother gave a scoffing laugh. "What poppycock! Is it the matter of his profession that gives you concern? Or is it because he's taken an interest in your little girl?" she asked more gently. "Meet with him. Judge for yourself what kind of man Noah is."

"I intend to. And I intend to find out just what this young scalawag's intentions are toward my daughter."

Christiana let out a sigh of relief and entered with the coffee. At least Papa had agreed to see Noah, but she didn't envy Noah his first meeting with her papa.

◆ ◆ ◆

Noah stepped into the foyer of the Leonard home, removing his hat and following Christiana to the parlor. He had been in several unsettling, even dangerous situations in his short career as a reporter, but this afternoon he felt as if he were entering a proverbial lions' den, and he was the main course.

And the lion, with his curly brown beard and glaring topaz eyes, looked as if he might suddenly charge and tear him limb from limb.

Noah cleared his throat and stepped forward. "Mr. Leonard." He put out his hand. "A pleasure to meet you, sir."

His hand was ignored, and Noah dropped it limply back to his side.

"Christiana," the unsmiling master of the lair said, "please bring us some refreshment."

"Yes, Papa." Before hurrying away, she looked anxiously between them, and Noah remembered her hushed words of greeting. "Be careful what you say. He's not in a good temper."

He believed the man's order for refreshment had more to do with privacy and less to do with concern for their guest's thirst. But Christiana was worth whatever trial he must endure.

What followed resembled what Noah felt the Spanish Inquisition might exemplify sans the bizarre methods of torture. Where did he live? What did he do for a living? How much did he make a year? For what purpose had he come home to Portland? How long did he intend to stay? Did he believe in the church and in God? Endless questions, many of them personal and inquisitive.

And then the bearded lion leaned forward in his chair, his eyes intent, his mouth curled in what resembled a snarl—what reason did Noah have for wishing to court *his* daughter?

Why Christiana?

Did he realize she was little more than a child?

Mr. Leonard stated that Christiana had only just stopped playing with dolls, putting an end to his rapid-fire questions, all of which Noah had worked to answer with accuracy. At last given a chance to speak rather than respond, he said that Christiana was a beautiful, intriguing young woman for whom he held a great deal of respect and would like to know better.

The disgruntled professor sat back and crossed his legs, switching the topic to his elaborate gun collection and mentioning that he'd been an expert marksman in his youth.

Mrs. Leonard swept into the room with Christiana behind her bearing a tray of lemonade. "And not a one of those guns will fire," the lion's wife added, a lilt to her voice. "They're intended for show—a few of them my husband donated for display in Oregon's exhibit that he also helped put together. One of his weapons not at the Exposition, a musket, dates back to the Revolutionary War, originally belonging to an ancestor who lived in the colonies. Isn't that what you told me, darling?"

Her husband gave a grumbled affirmation, stating that they *might* fire, clearly not happy with the outcome of his intended threat. Noah gratefully accepted a glass from the tray and took a few gulps of the sweetly sour drink, his clothes sticking to his perspiring skin from the verbal flaying he'd just received.

"I understand you're something of an inventor?" he offered, hoping the professor would warm to the subject and temporarily forget Noah's interest in his daughter.

A light entered the yellow-brown eyes. "Yes. Among other things, I'm working on an improvement to the automatic hat tipper of several years ago."

While away at college, Noah had seen the mechanical device that tipped the hat by squeezing a bulb in the pocket of one's coat. He gratefully relaxed in his chair as Mr. Leonard spoke of other unusual inventions.

"Many inventors have their items on display at the Exposition." His eyes narrowed on Noah. "I understand it's your intention to take my daughter there this afternoon." He didn't add "over my dead body," but his glare implied it.

"Actually, sir, I thought we might all attend if you're willing," Noah quickly stated. He wasn't afraid of Christiana's father but didn't want to persist being a villain in the man's eyes. "I would be interested to see the exhibit you helped to prepare."

For the first time the lion displayed his teeth in a smile. "Excellent idea! Anna, get your things." He rose from his chair.

Mrs. Leonard regarded him in disbelief. "Isaiah, really—I just put a roast in the oven!"

"It'll keep until we return."

"Hardly. It will burn to a crisp by then and possibly take the house down with it. It takes at least an hour to reach Guild's Lake—and that was when there was little traffic, before the Exposition opened to the public. The trolleys are packed on a Saturday afternoon as it is, and traffic is horrendous. The *Oregonian* stated that visitors are coming from all over the nation—all over the *world* to attend!"

"Then since you just put the roast in the oven, it won't suffer being stowed away in the icebox and served for tomorrow's dinner."

"That's not how it works, dear. It can't be refroz—" She glanced toward Christiana, who gave her mother a pleading look, clearly of the same belief as Noah—that her father wouldn't let her attend if her parents didn't chaperone. Her mother faltered. "Oh, never mind. I won't be five minutes." She left for the kitchen.

Her father exuberantly clapped his hands together. "Excellent. Christiana, go and collect your things. We're going to the Exhibition!"

She shared a look of relief with Noah before hurrying to gather her hat and parasol.

Chapter 6

"Welcome to the Lewis and Clark Centennial American Pacific Exposition and Oriental Fair." Noah stated the full title given to the festival with panache.

Christiana stared with wonder at the magnificent sight. "It's glorious," she breathed in awe.

Noah chuckled. "May I quote you on that?"

She looked away from the layout of buildings that ringed the shimmering lake and into his dark eyes. "You're writing a story on this?"

"I'm always looking for a story—that's the life of a reporter. My boss asked me to do a piece for next week's edition. A coworker has the main assignment, but as you can see, this exhibition is huge and would take a lot of ground to cover."

Noah handed the attendant two dollars for the entry fee for the four of them.

"I think since Papa helped, he has free admission," she whispered.

Noah shrugged with a smile and slipped his arm through hers as he accompanied her through the gates.

She looked over her shoulder at the attendant, who smiled and tipped his hat to her, then looked back at Noah. "You shouldn't have to pay," she insisted.

"It's all right, Christiana. I invited your parents; it's only right I should pay for their tickets, too."

"But Papa doesn't need—"

"Christiana, please don't concern yourself. It's only fifty cents. Look around you." He motioned to the buildings nearest them. "Enjoy your time here. This exhibit will someday mark a milestone in our nation's history, I guarantee it. You'll be telling your grandchildren about it, and they'll tell their grandchildren that their grandmother saw it firsthand."

She nodded with an uncertain smile. Clearly he wasn't bothered by the idea of paying for an unneeded ticket, so she shouldn't be concerned. She doubted he had shares in a gold mine, but she hoped he wasn't a wastrel.

With her parents a few steps behind, she strolled with Noah along one of many wide, paved paths. Those in charge had done a magnificent job in giving the impression of entering an exotic land of plenty.

The greater part of the buildings, as far as the eye could see, gave an intense flavor of Spanish influence, with graceful cupolas, arched doorways, and impressive domes. Red-tiled roofs created the perfect foil against a sky of cloudless blue, and the calm silver lake, with Mount St. Helens rising in snowy grandeur in the background, topped off the lovely vista. Above the entrance, a hot-air balloon hovered, while brightly colored pennants fluttered in the breeze at the pinnacles of some structures.

They walked amid myriad groups of other exhibit-goers of every race and nation, judging from the manner of their clothing and the varied languages and accents Christiana caught snatches of in conversations. She clung to Noah's arm, slightly anxious that she might become separated from him. What must have been hundreds of people strolled the pathways and entered exhibits—and those were the ones she could see. Judging by that knowledge alone, she realized there must be thousands here today, more people than she'd ever been among in her life!

"Don't you fret." Noah patted her hand. "I won't let you get lost."

That he could so aptly discern the source of her anxiety made her regard him in wonder. "How did you know?"

"It's in your eyes. They reveal your every emotion. I'll never let anything bad happen to you, Christiana. Not while I'm around to prevent it."

Would it always be this way between them? This closeness, as if they had known each other far longer than their short acquaintance? Yet what did she truly know about Noah Cafferty? She did know that he didn't approve of her calling. At the thought, she sobered.

They took their time at each exhibit they visited. Christiana assumed the fair covered miles of ground, and it would take days to observe each site.

Italy's contribution made Christiana's jaw drop as she viewed the many marble statues that covered a huge pavilion. Of supreme artistry and skill, the graceful representations depicted the Romans of a bygone century and their gods.

Noah scribbled in a small book he carried, also talking with an attendant in charge a short distance away, while Christiana stood beside her parents and studied a statue of a Roman maiden with flowers at her feet and entwined in her flowing hair.

"If the artist had had you for inspiration," Noah suddenly said beside her in sotto voce, "there wouldn't be enough pavilions to hold his works."

Heat flashed through her face at his outrageous compliment. She looked to where her parents were, only just realizing they had moved a short distance away and out of earshot.

"Noah, you mustn't say such things."

"Why not?"

"Because. . ." Flustered, she gave a little shrug. "Because I'm not the sort of girl whose head can be turned with flattery."

"That's good to know, but I was being sincere." His eyes mirrored his words. "Your features are ten times more beautiful than that statue. I say what I mean, Christiana, which is one reason I chose the profession I did. I don't get a chance to express my personal viewpoint in my articles, but I'm honest with what I write. And I don't think much of those gents who say what they don't mean, just to get a woman's approval."

"Then you *don't* seek my approval?" she teased mildly, her heart racing with his words.

He didn't smile. "I wish for your approval more than you could know. But I'm not going to play false with you to get it."

The more he spoke, the more time she spent with him, the more she could see what an astounding man Noah was. She couldn't think how to answer but was saved the need when her father strode their way. Christiana suddenly realized how close they were standing.

"You should put that parasol of yours to use so your skin doesn't burn, my girl," her father said gruffly, narrowing his eyes at Noah.

Christiana obediently brought it from her shoulder and directly over her head, forcing Noah to step back or be impaled by the metal points.

◆ ◆ ◆

Throughout the afternoon they visited other exhibits and viewed countless items, including those by Claude Monet at the Smithsonian Institution's display. Christiana enthused over how the artist depicted light and color in his scenic paintings, finding them refreshing.

They drenched their palates with flavored ices, caught a show—one of many presented at the exhibition—and ate at an outdoor café. At each site Noah jotted notes and spoke with those in charge, and throughout the day Christiana's father continued his subtle insinuations to keep Noah and Christiana apart. Therefore it stunned Noah when he made reference to the Exposition at night while trying to explain it to Christiana, that her father, who was always one step close behind, spoke up:

"There's no use for idle words when she can see it for herself, is there?"

Noah stared at him then at Christiana in frank surprise. The same bewilderment shimmered in her eyes. He had thought her father would whisk them away as soon as the first hint of evening came, in order to separate him from Christiana—not choose to extend their visit.

At the Oregon exhibit, Professor Leonard was in his element, almost treating Noah as human as he explained to them the various objects on display dating back to the statehood of Oregon. Historical documents, geographical artwork, and elaborate inventions of technology filled the area.

"Twenty-one countries and nineteen states have exhibits here," he said. "And each state will be granted a day to publicize, with visiting dignitaries in attendance."

Noah nodded, already planning to attend on Portland Day, which the media had designated as their state's day.

"When is Oregon's day for the pageantry, Papa?" Christiana asked, putting a voice to Noah's thoughts.

"September 30th."

"So far away. . . ?"

A hint of longing in her tone prodded Noah to speak. "Would you like to come again? I'll be covering the story."

"Ahem." Her father loudly cleared his throat. "As I was saying, this display here shows how loggers felled the trees, when Portland was nothing more than forest. . . ."

Later they viewed a free motion picture, and Christiana was stunned to see people captured on film. "They were actually *moving*," she exclaimed later, as they again walked along the path. "Like numerous daguerreotypes all strung together!"

Noah grinned, catching on to her excitement. "One day you might be able to hear them speak."

Her eyes grew wider. "How?" She tried to imagine how people's voices could be extracted and put into film.

"This is the age of progress. You've seen many marvels of technology presented here. I wouldn't be surprised if not too far in the future every home has one of those touring cars or something like it—self-contained motor cabs that travel on fuel—and will completely dispense with the need to harness a horse to a buggy for each outing or even the need to have to wait to catch a crowded trolley. I mean, think of it, Christiana—before the Wright Brothers flew from Kitty Hawk two years ago in their Flyer, did you believe men would one day be able to soar through the clouds? And they successfully did so with gliders years before that.

The idea of getting off the ground has long appealed to mankind. Even da Vinci was known for more than his *Mona Lisa* or *The Last Supper*. He designed a human flying invention back in the Renaissance period."

She looked at him in curious awe. "I didn't realize you knew so much about art."

He grinned. "I learned more at college than journalism."

She gave a soft nod. "Have you ever ridden in one of those flying inventions?"

"No. But one day I will."

She smiled at his confidence. "I find it telling that mankind, as you say, has long wanted to tour the heavens and devised methods to do so. Like that, for instance." She pointed to the hot-air balloon held down by ropes and hovering over the Exposition. "Perhaps such desires arose from a deep-seated need to be close to their Creator, even an intuitive need to find God, for those who don't know Him."

He looked at her with approval. "That's a lovely thought, Christiana. May I quote you on that?"

She laughed. "Is everything a story to you?"

"Life is made up of millions of individual stories, each worthy of notice."

She smiled. "I think I like you, Noah Cafferty." Her cheeks bloomed with warmth at her words, and her eyes sparkled shyly with expectation.

"I know I like you, Christiana," he said, low enough so only she could hear.

"Mrs. Leonard!" A young woman approached them. "Miss Leonard. How wonderful to run into both of you on this fine day."

"Jillian." Christiana's mother took her hands in greeting. "How are you feeling, dear? Is this hot sun not too much for you? Wherever is your parasol?"

"I broke it earlier—got it caught in a tree branch, and it tore. Dreadful affair."

"Then you must take mine."

"Oh no, I couldn't. Besides, it's nearing sunset."

"You really shouldn't be out in this hot July sun, dear."

"My husband is taking me to one of the shows indoors. I'll be fine."

At Noah's curiosity at such an outpouring of concern, Christiana whispered to him, "Mrs. Merriweather is one of our clients."

"Clients?" He looked at her.

"She is with child."

"Ah." Inadvertently Noah's gaze dropped to the woman's waist. Her gathered and flounced skirts hid her condition well.

Christiana sighed. "You still don't approve of midwives in this century, do you?"

He chose his words carefully. "Christiana, I don't want to argue with you and spoil our lovely outing. I can't help my personal views."

"No, I suppose not. Not when you've been led to believe that way." She seemed almost dejected then thoughtful. A sudden gleam lit her eyes. "From what little I know, you seem the adventurous sort. . . ."

"Yes. . ." He let his answer trail, wary of what was on her mind.

"And you said you're always on the lookout for a story. Life is a story to you. . . ."

"You listen well," he answered in curious amusement.

"Would you be willing to do the same? To listen?"

"Pardon?"

"Jillian Merriweather is an outgoing soul, the sort who's unafraid to say or do anything. If I were to seek her permission and that of another woman who might also agree, would you be willing to interview them, to hear their reasons they chose to employ a midwife? It would be a chance to see the issue from the other end of the spectrum."

Noah had long ago learned there were two sides to each story. With the woman suffragist movement so prevalent in the news, an article of human interest might appeal to the paper's readers, though there would certainly be those opposed. His editor, for instance.

"Let me think about it."

◆　◆　◆

Christiana nodded at his answer. At least it wasn't an outright no.

If he did agree, she hoped the women would also.

Too excited with the idea to wait, she received her chance to ask when her father decided they would all attend the show. Before they entered through the double doors, Christiana urged Noah to go ahead, assuring him she would soon follow, and privately pulled Jillian aside to broach the question.

Jillian's eyes lit up like those of a child experiencing her first taste of candy. "A journalist, you say? Oh my, yes, that would be exciting, wouldn't it? Perhaps I can even sneak in a few points about why women should be allowed other rights, too."

"I don't see why not." Christiana grinned. She wasn't an active suffragist like Jillian but agreed that women should be given the right to vote in Oregon, since from what she'd read, a number of other states had acceded to the idea.

Christiana rejoined Noah, who stood at the back, waiting, her parents also standing nearby. He lifted his brow in concerned question, and she wondered what he would think of her views on the vote. She decided it best to remain silent on the matter, not wishing to begin another clash of wills and minds. The day had been too perfect to ruin it with opinionated drivel. She smiled and took the arm he held out to escort her to her seat.

The show was delightful, tasteful, the costumes from an earlier era, the singing in another language and superb, operatic in nature. Christiana enjoyed every moment sitting beside Noah in the darkened room and the respite from the day's heat.

She did wish, however, that her papa would stop glaring at her escort and hoped that he would soon grow accustomed to the idea of having Noah around, since she anticipated seeing much more of him.

Once the show concluded and they left the building, she stared with wide eyes. The Exposition had become an exotic fairy tale against an evening sky!

Small electric lights covered the framework of every building in sight, near and far, and Christiana felt as if she'd been transported to a foreign world of splendor and mystery. The dark lake served to magnify the feeling of enchantment as it reflected the multitude of lights softly shimmering above the water.

Due to the amount of time it would take to reach home with the traffic, her father soon announced it was time to leave. They had spent all day there, but Christiana didn't feel as if they'd covered even a tenth of what the Exposition had to offer.

"If you should like to come again," Noah said, sotto voce, "I would love to bring you."

Eager to spend another day in his company, she nodded at his second invitation.

"I plan to come back in two months for Portland Day."

"Oh." She tried to stifle her disappointment. She didn't want to wait *that* long to see him again and wondered how her mother would feel if she invited Noah to Sunday dinner. Would that be too forward, especially since Sunday was tomorrow?

On the trip home, Christiana pondered how she might see Noah before September. He had not yet accepted her offer to do a story, and she wondered if he would.

The perfect gentleman, he helped her on and off the trolley, finding her a seat though he was forced to stand. He kept close, to protect her from the traffic of the crowds. And Christiana felt a little more of her heart open to him with every hour in his company. Somehow she would see to it that they met again—sooner rather than later.

Once they arrived at her house, Noah helped her alight from the hansom cab her father had hired to take them the rest of the way home.

She turned to him. "I've had a wonderful day, Noah. It's been a pleasure. Thank you for asking me."

"The pleasure has been all mine."

"Christiana, are you coming?" Her father turned from walking up the sidewalk with her mother and stared.

"Yes, I won't be a moment. I'd like to say good night if I may?"

"Of course." Her father didn't budge.

"Come along, dear." Her mother eased her arm around his sleeve and gently pulled him toward the house.

Christiana hid her embarrassment with a little laugh. "I'm his only daughter," she said by way of explanation. "His only child."

"If I had a daughter like you, I'd do the same."

The gaslight flickered on near the porch, causing them both to look that direction. Her father stood in the open doorway, watching them.

Christiana curbed a sigh. "Have you given any thought to writing the story?"

Noah looked away from her father, hesitated as if considering, then nodded. "I'll do it."

"You will?" She wasn't sure if the bulk of her delight was because he agreed or because she would be seeing him again sooner than expected.

He grinned. "Tell me when and where, and I'll be there."

"Would you like to come to Sunday dinner?" The words were out before she had a chance to think about what she was saying.

His surprise was apparent by the manner in which his brows lifted.

"I mean—" Christiana thought of a way to endorse her rash invitation, making the idea up as she went along, while knowing all she said was true. "Mother will want to speak with you first. . . ." And she would definitely need to speak to Mother about the whole affair tonight! "And it would be an opportune time to discuss things." It wasn't like he hadn't shared their table before.

"Are you sure my presence at your home would be welcomed so soon?" He looked toward the porch. She directed a glance there, too, seeing her father still standing like a sentinel on watch.

"Oh, Papa? He won't mind." She doubted that, but she hoped he would soon come around. "And I know Mother will be pleased." Although she might not be happy to hear Christiana had allowed her tongue to get away from her again, in asking Noah to write the story.

"Then I accept."

"Lovely. At noon tomorrow, then?"

"Noon tomorrow. I should be going." He darted another glance toward the house then again looked at Christiana and took her hand in his, lifting it.

Christiana sensed sudden movement from the porch.

"Good night, Christiana." Noah touched his warm lips to her trembling hand then straightened, looked at her once more, and left.

Christiana felt the tingle in her fingers during her entire walk to the porch. She ignored her father's gruff demeanor and kissed his whiskered cheek. "Good night, Papa."

He patted her shoulder as she moved inside, gently muttering something she couldn't make out, but she thought she caught the tail end of his words: "At least that's over and done with."

No, Papa, not even close, she silently answered.

Minutes later, in the kitchen, once Christiana admitted her deed, her mother shook her head.

"You should have asked me first."

"I know, Mama. I was just so excited." She lifted her downcast eyes. "Although Jillian *did* seem comfortable with the idea...," she added hopefully.

"Yes, I imagine she would be," her mother mused. "She was once a thespian and enjoys an audience. Well, never mind. What's done is done." She smiled. "I, for one, like the young man and would enjoy having him sit at our table."

"Do you think Papa will mind?" A foolish question, but she felt compelled to ask.

"Don't worry about Papa, darling." Her mother laid her hand against Christiana's cheek. "It's not that he dislikes Noah. If he did, Noah wouldn't have stepped two feet from this house with you, even accompanied. Your father would have seen to that. He simply must learn to accept that you're now a young woman. You've always been his little girl."

Christiana gave a careful nod. She only hoped Papa's revelation would occur before Noah became weary of the whole ordeal to see her and lost interest in trying.

Chapter 7

Noah could not believe his good fortune. He hurried to catch up to the pretty brunette who walked ahead of him.

"Hello." He tipped his hat with a grin.

"Noah!" Christiana's answering smile assured him of her pleasure to see him, though he had no cause to doubt it after last night's invitation to a meal. Beneath her yellow parasol, her cheeks flushed a delicate pink. "You attend this church, too?"

"Yes, when I'm in town." Relieved to see that papa lion stalked nowhere nearby, he extended his bent arm. "Would you do me the honor of sitting beside me?"

Her eyes were shy as she nodded and took his arm. He didn't want to spoil the moment but had to know. "Are your parents here today?" He wanted no confrontation with her father right before the service but wished to be prepared.

"They went inside. I was talking with another woman I plan for you to interview. She wishes to talk it over with her husband first, but Jillian, the woman you met yesterday, is in absolute favor of the idea." Her words came out in a rush, the interviews clearly exciting to her with the manner in which her blue-gray eyes sparkled.

He doubted his editor would be as enthralled, but he'd told Noah, "It's the controversial issues that sell the most papers." And this idea was all that and more. Nor did Noah feel that doing this for Christiana would be time wasted, on more than one count.

"How are Lanie and the baby?" she asked as they walked through the entryway into the quiet, dimly lit building.

"They're doing well. . . ."

Inside, Noah wished for the peace to extend to his soul. Christiana's father looked shocked, angry, then frustrated as Noah greeted them and Christiana pulled him to sit beside her at the end of the pew. To his credit, her father didn't glare at him during the service, and Noah was able to concentrate on the minister's message of patience and endurance. It appeared he certainly would be learning more of that today.

The glaring came afterward, when they were again outside and Christiana's mother expressed her delight that Noah would be spending the afternoon dining with them. By her father's initial reaction of surprise, he guessed it was the first he'd heard of it.

As his wife gently nudged her husband toward the direction of their vehicle, Noah walked with Christiana a short distance behind.

"Your father didn't know I was coming?"

"Oh, he knew. Mama told him last night."

"He seemed surprised."

"I think he feels Mama should be on his side in all this. I mean—" She looked at him, embarrassed. "He doesn't understand her reasoning at times. But then, not all couples agree on everything, and it doesn't change their feelings for each other. Does it?" Her face flushed rosy, and she looked away. "Oh, look, there's Maribelle. Doesn't she look nice in that blue feathered hat. Hello!" She gave a little wave, and Noah looked toward the departing carriage and the redhead waving back, wondering who Maribelle was and why Christiana thought he should know her.

By the time they all reached the Leonard home, Noah following her parents' buggy on his horse, Christiana had calmed from whatever so unsettled her. Her father, however, had not.

While the two women worked in the kitchen, Noah sat in the chair across from the uncharacteristically silent, but still glaring, bearded lion, all the while wondering if he was to be the appetizer. His few attempts at conversation were truncated with deliberate monosyllabic answers that prevented further discussion.

Once Mrs. Leonard announced that dinner was ready, Noah practically leaped from the chair.

The lion remained quiet during the meal, concentrating on his food. His kind wife was gracious, bringing up the Exposition and the displays that appealed to her. Christiana was talkative as well, darting looks at Noah as she spoke, and Noah managed to converse with both women, eat his meal, and keep a wary eye on the sleeping lion.

"What did you like best, sir?" Noah surprised himself and the others by asking.

Mr. Leonard looked full at him, narrowing his eyes. Noah swallowed hard.

"Portland's exhibition, of course," he declared as if that should be obvious.

He then went into another recounting of each item on exhibit and those who helped him put it together. Noah could almost hear the collective sigh of relief from the ladies as the master of the den relaxed and spoke of the topic he enjoyed best.

The atmosphere around the table lightened considerably, and the dessert of lemon meringue pie was a pleasure.

"I thought we could sit outside on the porch and discuss the interviews," Christiana said to Noah.

"Interviews?" her father suddenly barked. "What interviews? It's too hot outside."

"That sounds like a splendid idea, dear," her mother said. "I'll bring lemonade."

"What blasted interviews?"

"Noah plans to interview a few of our clients for a piece he's writing in his newspaper," Mrs. Leonard said in the same mild tone.

The look in Mr. Leonard's eyes impaled Noah, like a moth pinned to a board. He could almost hear his mind issuing the angry words: *That is why you have an interest in my daughter—to use her for your paper?*

"Actually, it was my idea. I thought it would be splendid for Noah to get the midwife perspective from our angle." Christiana quickly rose from the table and looked at Noah. "Shall we go outside?"

"There's nothing wrong with the parlor!"

Noah couldn't imagine trying to concentrate on what Christiana said to him with a threatening pair of topaz eyes focused on him the entire time.

"There's nothing wrong with the porch either, dear."

Mr. Leonard brooded. Noah stood to his feet and thanked Christiana's mother for the meal, uncertain if the matter was settled but not wishing to wait around to ask.

He followed Christiana to the porch and took a seat next to her on the glider, leaving a socially acceptable amount of space between them. Movement caught his attention. He looked toward the house.

Christiana's father stood at the window and stared from between parted curtains. The lemon curdled in his stomach, and Noah curbed the insane urge to let out a miserable laugh.

Christiana also turned to look. "Pa-pa...," she enunciated in a softly pleading fashion.

He didn't move away, but a pale, slender hand appeared at his sleeve. He turned his head to answer then moved aside, and the drape fell back in place.

Christiana sighed. "He's really a very nice person. Everyone at the university loves him, both his students and the other professors."

"Ah." Noah smiled politely, unable to say much else.

"Yes, well, Mother and I will be visiting Jillian on Tuesday. Does that work for you?"

"I don't expect you to arrange your appointments around me," he teased lightly. "I'll make it work."

"I'm still waiting to hear back from Mrs. Radcliffe. There's also another lady I'd like to ask—she gave birth a little over two months ago. I think she also would be amenable to the idea."

"What about you? Are you amenable to it?"

"Pardon?" His enigmatic smile made her heart turn over.

"To an interview."

"You want to interview me?" she squeaked nervously.

"Of course, since the article will be based around your work. Any objection?"

"No, I just didn't think you'd want to. . ." Flustered, she let her words trail off as she watched him pull a pad and pencil from his pocket. "What—*now?*"

He chuckled softly. "Can you think of a better time? A reporter's always working, Christiana. The news stops for no man."

"No, of course not. . ." She just didn't realize *she* would be the news.

"Relax." His voice was soothing. "If we were getting to know each other, we would ask questions, right? It's the same sort of idea."

"Is that what we're doing?" She offered an uncertain smile.

"Well. . .yes."

"All right then." Her smile grew more confident. "How do we do this?"

"I'll ask a question and you answer. Like. . .how long have you done this sort of thing?"

"Midwifery?" At his nod, she continued: "I started assisting Mother when I was fifteen, almost three years ago. My first actual delivery, I told you, was Lanie's. Mother said that she long knew I was ready for the next step. I just had to know and exert the courage to try—oh, but don't write that! That's just a minor confession for the getting-to-know-you part of this."

He grinned, crossing out what he'd last written. "And your mother? How long has she been involved?"

"Since before I was born, I imagine. I don't remember her not being a midwife."

His brows arched. "How does your father feel about your mother engaged in a job that could interfere with her duties at home?"

Christiana resolved not to take offense at the question; he was conducting an interview, after all. She wondered if he should ask Papa then immediately thought better of it. "He has no problem with what Mama does. There are no true duties that she's taken away from. We have a maid and cook, though she's on a vacation of sorts, visiting her sister who's ill. While she's gone, Mama is tending to meals and keeping house."

"Hmm." He jotted something down.

Christiana wasn't sure she liked the sound of his *hmm*.

She straightened her spine. "As long as the home is well kept and the husbands and children don't starve, I see no reason that women, no matter their social status, cannot be allowed to work outside the home. Do you?"

He looked up from writing to smile. "I'm not the one being interviewed."

She let out an irritated breath then chided herself. She already knew his answer; it matched what most men thought. She couldn't fault him for a gender-shared attitude.

"What interested you in the occupation?"

"Oh, it's much more than an 'occupation.' It's my godly calling. My grandmother, who took the Oregon Trail, and her mother before her, and even before that, into several generations, all were midwives. My mother gave me their journal filled with advice to those who followed after them, along with their bits of inspiration. Would you like to see it?"

"Yes, but later. Why do you consider it your calling?"

She struggled with how to explain. "It's nested inside my heart. Every mother is special to me and every child born. Helping to bring life into the world is an exhilarating experience—sometimes frightening. But each time I look at a newborn's face, I wonder how anyone can question the existence of God. Midwifery keeps me humble, and yet at the same time confident that God watches out for His own." She made a mental note to jot that down in the journal also, for her own wisdom to share.

He nodded slowly. "I can understand that, having just been through the experience—and never wanting to go through it again."

"It's a good thing you weren't called to be a midwife, then," she teased.

"Or a doctor."

He posed other questions, his responses polite, when asked, but also letting her know he didn't agree, and in her frustration she spoke without thinking: "Since you're clearly not in favor of women working outside the home, I suppose you're also opposed to women gaining the vote?"

"I never said that. As a matter of fact, I think women should be given that right."

She blinked at him like an owl. "You do?"

"Certainly. Most men opposed are worried that if women are given the vote, the first thing they'll do is revoke liquor, because of the existence of the women's temperance groups. Since I don't drink, it doesn't affect me either way." He grinned.

She was still fighting disbelief. "You support women voting but are against them working?"

"A vote generally takes place once a year. Women who work do so every day. Some women neglect their families to work."

"And what about those women—like my mother—who don't? I agree with you, families should come first. Mother is adamant about that. They are the ones God gave to us, aren't they? But some women have no choice. They must work in factories or secure whatever means available to live and help support their families. It's been that way throughout history."

He gave a short nod. "Poverty has been around since the days of Moses, long before that. There are always extenuating circumstances. But I speak of those who have no need to work and do so out of desire alone."

"Like my mother?" She couldn't help the bitter edge to her tone.

He sighed. "From all I've seen and heard, your mother isn't one to neglect her family."

"She most certainly is not."

"I know. I was agreeing with you. Christiana, I don't want to argue about this. Can we just get back to the interview?"

She nodded, struggling to control her wretched temper. "Yet despite Mother's good example, you are still opposed to the idea in general?"

His silence provided her answer.

"I imagine that once you marry, you won't allow your wife to work?" Her face warmed. Where had that question popped from?

"She won't need to."

"But if she should wish to?"

He stared at her a long time. Christiana held her breath, wishing she could retract the question, though her heart raced to hear his answer.

"I was raised by my father and his father before him to believe that women shouldn't work outside the home. So no, I wouldn't wish my wife to work."

His answer given, Christiana felt worse. She gave a little nod and looked him in the eye. "As I said, I consider midwifery a godly calling, one that's been in my family for generations, and especially necessary to those mothers who prefer a woman tending them. I don't plan to quit anytime soon, if ever."

"And if your husband should disapprove?" he asked softly.

She swallowed hard. "If he is of that opinion, then I would save us both a good deal of grief and never marry him in the first place."

The silence grew so thick she could hear the flies buzzing off the porch. They stared at each other a long time, Christiana's heart beating fast.

Noah flipped his pad closed. "Thank you for the interview. I think I have all I need." He stood up.

She bounced up from the glider, sending it into motion. "Do you wish to see the journal?" She didn't want him to go, as foolish as it was to wish he would stay.

He hesitated as if he might refuse but nodded. "Yes."

"I won't be but a moment."

It would be more polite to invite him back inside, but she didn't want her father's beastly attitude to scare Noah away. She slipped into the house, located the journal, and hurried back outside, handing it to him.

He eyed the plain worn cover and opened the book to the first yellowed page. He read for a moment then looked up. "Would you mind if I borrowed this? I'd like to read it in my own time. I'll take good care of it."

"I know you will." She hated letting it go, even for a few days. It was hers to do with as she pleased, since her mother had given it to her on the eve of her seventeenth birthday— wishing to share the wisdom of it with Christiana now, as she had then told her, rather than after her death. Christiana looked in the book every morning after her devotions. Both always helped her outlook for the day. Still, if reading it would help Noah to understand. . .

"Yes, all right."

He closed the journal. "If you would rather I didn't take it. . ."

"No, that's fine. I trust you, Noah."

◆ ◆ ◆

Long after they said their farewells, the tender but sad look in Noah's eyes lingered in her memory. Did that look mean he saw no hope for a future for them? Perhaps Christiana *was* rushing things—they had known each other a matter of weeks—but she couldn't help how her heart felt. And it was immersed in Noah.

Christiana approached her father where he sat in the parlor. Immediately he took off his reading glasses, slipped them into his pocket, and laid down his book.

"Ah, Christiana, how are you, my girl?"

"I could be better," she said, taking a seat across from him.

"What seems to be the problem?" His bushy brows slanted downward. "That Rafferty fellow isn't giving you grief, is he?"

"It's Cafferty, Papa. Noah Cafferty. And he's not the one causing me pain. You are," she admitted softly.

He glanced down at his lap, his face going stony.

"What is it about him that you dislike so?"

"He's a reporter, isn't he? And they're not good news."

She didn't smile at his wry pun. "You're judging Noah based on a generalization of men in his career? Is that fair?"

"Blast it, Christie, I don't need this from you, too!"

He reverted to her girlhood name for her, a sign that he was troubled.

"Papa. . ." She moved off the chair and sat on the floor beside his, as she had done when she was little. She laid her hand over his large one. "You're never going to lose me. I'll always be your little girl at heart, even after I marry and make a life of my own."

Moisture made his eyes shine. He swallowed convulsively. "No man will ever be good enough for my little girl."

"One man has to be. You *would* like me to know the joys of marriage and, one day, childbirth, as I see women experience all the time, wouldn't you? I want to know all of that, all of what Mama had. I don't want to be an old maid."

He sighed. "You're barely seventeen."

"No, Papa, I'm approaching eighteen. This Christmas."

He shook his head softly. "Time is a cursed villain that robs us of life so quickly."

Alarm made her eyes widen. "You're not ill?"

"No, I'm right as rain. Forgive an old man his reminiscences, Christiana. It seemed only yesterday I bounced you on my knee, and now you speak of bouncing your own children on your knee. . . ."

"Time doesn't have to be the enemy, Papa. Grandmother Polly wrote that time is a gift to be treasured and used wisely. Only then will the treasure hold true value."

He patted her hand. "Your ancestors were wise."

"Just because I'm growing up doesn't mean we won't have other moments to hold dear. Different, but just as special. One day you'll be bouncing your grandchild on your knee, creating a new and beautiful memory."

His gaze sharpened. "You're not *that* interested in this boy, are you? You've only just met!"

"I don't necessarily mean Noah. . . ." She avoided the question. "It's much too early to consider that. Just please, won't you lower the shotgun always aimed his way and give him a chance? For me?"

He looked at her long and hard then let out a weary sigh.

"For your sake, I'll try, Christie. I ask one favor in return. Don't grow up too quickly? Don't throw out your dolls and tea set just yet?"

At his hopeful response both knew to be impossible, for time had a way of rushing things along, she stood and kissed his cheek. "For you, Papa. I'll try. I promise to keep my dolls." She wanted to pass them on to her daughter. "As for the tea party. . .would you like to have one with me? For old time's sake?"

"You're a sweet girl to humor a pathetic old fool," he said gruffly.

"Pathetic? No. Not a fool, either, and certainly not old. We had such fun with our parties, didn't we? We talked of everything under the sun—well, what was then my sun. All those things important in my little-girl world. And this time I shall make *real tea*, since I'm now old enough to use the kettle."

"Yes, do that. I look forward to it." He picked up his book again and glanced at the table then at his lap then at the floor. "Have you seen my glasses?"

"Right here, Papa." She plucked them out of his pocket and set them behind his ears with a grin then scurried to the kitchen. She hoped this revisit to a dear childhood memory would help ease her father's heart and make her transition into womanhood a little easier for him to bear.

Chapter 8

Noah stared at the words of the journal's final written page.

The women of Christiana's family were strong, courageous, full of hopes and dreams. None of them considered midwifery true work but instead their godly calling, as if they were doing a great mission for the Lord's people.

He looked at the last entry, the ink newer and bolder than the others. This entry bore a different handwriting than the previous ones, the letters graceful and flowing, and there was only one small notation from this last writer to add to the journal. Christiana, no doubt.

I have learned that to fear a problem takes a greater toll on the heart and more effort than it does to trust for the best, even the miraculous. My first delivery was solo and frightening in that respect, as it was thrust upon me. I received help from an outside source, who proved invaluable, but I could not escape the reality that if anything went wrong, the consequences would be upon my shoulders to bear. As the poor woman, a dear friend to me, was in such travail, the revelation suddenly came: I was not the one in charge. I was merely God's handmaiden, His chosen vessel, and it was through me that He would make His glory known. I only had to allow Him to do so, to trust in His power, and to submit to His greater authority. With that new understanding, everything fell into place and I was no longer afraid.

Noah stared at the entry for some time. He'd been unable to get Christiana out of his thoughts all week, since he'd last seen her. It was foolish, he knew. To think of her in any capacity other than friendship would be disastrous; she had made clear her feelings on the subject of women and work. So had he. He was not one to form a dalliance with the ladies as some of his associates did. He wanted to find a woman to make a life with, to share his home and his name. It would be a *mistake* to continue to see her.

But every time they met, he found something else about her he admired, and this journal entry was no exception. A godly woman, humble, but strong of spirit and willing to stand her ground—wasn't that what he always hoped to find in a wife? Yet the very tenacity he admired in her worked in opposition to what he'd been taught by his father. His mother died when he was three, so he'd never gained her insight.

Looking at the time, Noah grabbed his coat and hat and drove his buggy to Christiana's home. His heart gave a little jump as she came through the door. The sunlight hit her face, giving it the luster of a pearl. Her eyes were glowing, her smile for him.

He managed to peel his attention away from her and greet her mother as she came behind, her loveliness a mature version of her daughter's beauty. He helped both women into his buggy.

"Am I that late?" he asked, curious that they had not waited for him to ring the bell.

"I was watching and thought I'd save you the effort and us some time," Christiana said with a little smile.

Clearly she was sparing his feelings. He knew he was at least five minutes late, the writings of the journal having captured his interest.

Jillian Merriweather proved to be a colorful character to interview. After showing Noah an album of old photographs from when she'd taken the stage and telling of some of her more memorable endeavors as a singer, she moved right into the subject of women's right to vote. As if she were the interviewer, she asked Noah's opinion. She was as shocked as Christiana had been to learn he had no opposition to it—did they really view him as so hardnosed?—then his interviewee asked if he would be in favor of speaking at a women's meeting. Remembering the last suffragist gathering and his feeling of being a trapped and despised beast with the women approaching for the kill, he adroitly evaded the topic and moved to the reason for his presence there.

He asked various questions, also urging her to speak freely, jotting notes all the while. "To sum it all up," he said at last, "why do you think the occupation of midwifery is so vital to maintain in this progressive era of our nation?"

She laughed at that. "Oh, I can give you plenty of reasons, Mr. Cafferty, but the chief one for me is that most midwives have been through the ordeal. Men have not. Mrs. Leonard knows the pain involved, being a mother herself. I am more inclined to trust my body to a woman who knows what it *feels* like to experience all one does during pregnancy and childbirth than I am to a man who cannot begin to imagine all of what occurs."

Jillian Merriweather also had a flair for complete candor. Noah busily jotted, his face going a shade warmer at her expressive words.

Once the interview ended, he thanked her and went outside on the porch to wait. Jillian had been so excited to be interviewed, she asked to do that before her checkup, though they had planned it the other way around.

As Noah waited for the Leonard women to join him, he went through his notes, his mind weighing all he had learned against all he'd been taught.

◆　◆　◆

A week and a half after the first interview, Christiana again waited for Noah to arrive. He had been quiet after speaking with Jillian, when he took Christiana and her mother home. Polite. Kind. But quiet. At church the past Sunday, he had been the same.

It frustrated Christiana that he'd not shared his feelings with her, and she hoped today would be different. She would *make* it different!

She would be going alone. Her mother was needed at home to make Papa's lunch, as she'd done every day since the term ended and the university closed. That should make Noah happy—to see firsthand that her mother put her family before work.

Once he arrived, this time she waited until he came to the door. Her father came in from the parlor and gruffly shared a few words with him. But to Christiana's relief he did not interfere with her going alone with Noah, though he did tell her mother he could see to lunch himself and she could go along, too.

"Yes, dear, I've seen how well you cope in the kitchen," she gently replied and looked at Christiana. "Be sure and tell Helen that I'll visit her tomorrow. Her time is nigh, and she might wish to know information you cannot give."

Christiana reassured her mother, and Noah drove her to Mrs. Radcliffe's.

The woman's time was not only nigh, but after her appointment and in the middle of the interview—she doubled over in sudden pain.

Noah was out of the chair and by her side before Christiana could blink.

"Mrs. Radcliffe, are you all right?" he asked.

She looked up, horrified. "I think the baby's coming. I had light pains this morning, but I thought it was indigestion. They weren't like last time and went away after a few hours. . . ."

Christiana immediately took charge, helping Mrs. Radcliffe out of her chair, Noah on the other side of her. They walked with her to the bedroom, and Noah helped ease her to the bed.

He turned to Christiana. "A phone?" he asked hopefully.

Mrs. Radcliffe, still suffering through her pain, gritted out, "We have no phone. Neighbor does. Across the street."

"You're going to call a doctor?" Christiana took him aside and whispered so the woman couldn't hear.

"I'm going to call your mother."

Christiana nodded in gratitude. She felt more assured as a midwife since Lanie's delivery, but assistance was always better, and Noah had often made it clear he didn't wish to repeat the role he once played.

"The twins. . . ," Mrs. Radcliffe muttered.

Noah sharply turned. "You're having *twins*?"

Christiana hoped she wouldn't have to try to catch him since he looked about ready to fall.

"Mrs. Radcliffe *has* twins—Mark and Mary—three years old. They're sleeping."

"I can't leave them alone. They'll be up from their nap soon. And my husband won't be home from the Expo for some time."

"Leave it to me, Mrs. Radcliffe. I'll call Mrs. Leonard, and then I'll watch the twins."

"Don't you have to report to the office?" Christiana wondered if he had any idea what he had just signed to. He had seen how many hours labor could take, and they had arrived toward the end of Lanie's travail. Yet Christiana also could see no other way.

"You don't have to do that," Mrs. Radcliffe said. "Mrs. O'Brien, my neighbor across the street, said she wouldn't mind watching them when needed."

Noah nodded in relief and headed for the neighbor's house. The elderly Mrs. O'Brien, kind as she appeared, barely held on to the door as she opened it. One look at her bleary eyes and reddened nose and Noah realized he might be sitting with the twins after all.

"Feeling a bit under the weather," she admitted when he asked about her condition in concern. "Not to worry, dear boy. I'll be all right."

Once Mrs. O'Brien heard the news, she led him to her phone. First, Noah called Mrs. Leonard, who assured him she would come immediately. Second, he called his boss. He had to hold the earpiece away from his ear at the man's irate reply, but the crusty geezer had developed a reputation for being a hardnosed editor. Noah often suspected that beneath beat a softer heart, and he found proof of it when the man told him in a quiet voice to do what he had to do to help the women.

Thanking the widow O'Brien, he settled his hat more firmly on his head and approached his newest challenge—entertaining two three-year-old children.

Surely that couldn't be as much of a strain on the mind and emotions as the one time fate had forced him to become a midwife's assistant.

◆   ◆   ◆

To Christiana's relief, her mother soon arrived. Helen Radcliffe's labor pains came more intense at this stage than Christiana would have expected, but after a first child that sometimes happened. To her absolute shock, her mother quietly told her she would assist and Christiana would deliver. Knowing that her mother sat near helped to ease the sudden lurch of dread, which then faded when she remembered she'd done this once before. She had learned then that God was her supplier to give her all she needed. They prayed for the mother and the child and for guidance and prepared for the long wait.

While Christiana fed Mrs. Radcliffe ice chips, she wondered how Noah was faring. The twins woke up two hours ago, their excited voices heard on the opposite side of the door. As Mother encouraged their patient, Christiana glanced out the bedroom window, shocked to see her answer: Noah pushing a wheelbarrow with both children inside. Absent of his sack coat, his shirtsleeves pushed up to the elbows, he careened back and forth over the lawn while the towheaded tots squealed in glee, the girl holding to the sides of the wheelbarrow, the boy in front of her, clapping his hands.

Mrs. Radcliffe's latest spasm of pain subsided, and she also turned her head to look. "He seems like a fine young man," she whispered to Christiana.

"He is," Christiana said somewhat dreamily as she watched Noah with the twins.

Mrs. Radcliffe soon had another pain, and Noah was temporarily forgotten.

Six hours and twenty-three minutes later, Tobias Radcliffe entered the world. Squalling and red, he was not one bit happy about it, until he found solace in his mother's waiting arms.

Exhausted but pleased that there'd been few complications and both mother and baby were well, Christiana left the bedroom to find more towels to clean up. She came to a sudden halt as she entered the parlor.

Thoroughly mussed, Noah sat sprawled on the sofa, his head back and eyes closed. Mary also slept and clung to his middle, resting her head on his chest. Mark sat on the other side of Noah, wide awake and holding a bowl of what looked like applesauce. He pulled the spoon from his mouth and held it out to Christiana. "Wan' some?" he asked. Applesauce spotted the two children and Noah, as well as the sofa and floor and anything else within the vicinity of Mark's waving spoon.

Her heart twisted in amusement at the tender sight, and in that instant Christiana knew: she had fallen deeply in love with Noah Cafferty.

Chapter 9

Three weeks had passed since Mrs. Radcliffe delivered her son. In that time, Noah interviewed one other expectant mother, spoke with Christiana twice more at church, and immersed himself in the news stories his editor assigned to him.

He told himself he wasn't avoiding her, but that was a lie. Since she had opened the door to his frantic knocking on that first night, what seemed ages ago, she had disrupted his well-ordered, long-conceived notions with her opposing views. She had shaken the tenets of his male existence with every nuance of her feminine personality. When he closed his eyes at night, it was her bright, intelligent eyes and coy smile that he saw. And when he opened them, she was always the first thought on his mind. He was, in a word, hopelessly and completely besotted.

He prayed over his dilemma and spent hours poring over her journal, which he had yet to return. He spent equal time recalling how perfect Christiana was in her role, how happy she had been with giving herself to others. His interviewees had all offered diverse but sound reasons why they preferred a midwife. He would be a heel to ask Christiana to quit what she felt God had chosen her to do, what Noah had seen with his own eyes—a fearsome task he doubted that many, if any, men had experienced, save for Eve's husband, Adam, and the physicians, of course. And he had witnessed her confidence each time she spoke of her vocation.

At last, coming to a decision, Noah gathered his notes. He stayed late at the office and spent the next two hours writing out his story. His editor showed surprise the following morning but to Noah's relief agreed to print it in the next edition. He hadn't been sure what the crusty man would say to Noah's unusual approach.

But it was really Christiana's reaction that concerned him.

◆ ◆ ◆

Christiana opened the door to Noah. Her heart gave a little jump of delight to see him. It had been so long!

"Noah, what a pleasant surprise. Come in." She held the door open.

"Actually, I was hoping you might come outside. I have something to show you."

Her heart beating fast at his peculiar behavior, she nodded and closed the door behind her.

"Since your father doesn't get the *Portland New Age*. . ." He held out a newspaper. "Page two."

She felt she should apologize for her father reading a rival paper and almost admitted that she'd bought every newspaper of his since they met, just to read his articles, but his serious expression stalled further comment.

Her eyes narrowing in puzzlement, she opened to the page, giving a little gasp when she read the title and byline: MIDWIFERY IN THIS PROGRESSIVE ERA BY NOAH CAFFERTY.

Excited, she read the succinct article, creatively written, citing the interviews with quotes and bringing up the controversy, touching on it from both angles. But it was the personal addendum at the end, which she had never seen him use in any of his articles, that had her mouth drop open in shock:

> *... I have always been led to believe that women should not work outside of hearth and home, and in some cases, I still adhere to that belief. However, after spending time in the Leonard women's company while witnessing the differences they make, the lives they touch, and the skills they possess, I am convinced no physician could have done a worthier job. It is this reporter's belief that midwifery is still as important as it was thousands of years ago. In conclusion, perhaps the true progression of our era is to open our minds to novel ideas, not only in technology but also with regard to our women in society.*

Stunned, Christiana looked up and blinked. "I don't know what to say."

"Say you'll go with me to the Exposition again. This weekend."

She gave a soft laugh, slightly shaking her head no then nodding yes in confusion.

"I stayed away because I didn't think it would be fair to either of us to continue seeing each other after you made your position clear. I've had time to consider, and that"—he glanced down at the paper she still held—"is my answer."

Tears welled in her eyes. "Are you saying. . . ?"

He took the newspaper from her and dropped it to the ground, taking her left hand in both of his and holding it up between them. "I am saying, my dear Christiana, that one day I hope for the honor of calling you my wife. I have found that a life without you is no life worth living. I am hopelessly in love with you, you understand. So now I must ask, is there a chance you might put me out of my misery and agree again to let me court you?"

Her smile grew with each moment of his nervous avowal, and her heart soared at his declaration of love. "Oh yes, Noah, I think there is much more than a chance."

His bright smile soon faded. "And now, to ask your father's permission."

Both of them glanced at the window to see the curtain remained closed.

"One step at a time," she said softly, bringing his hands still clasping hers to her lips, the caress landing on this thumb.

She felt a little shock as he moved his hand so that his fingertips brushed her jaw, tilting her chin. A thrill surged through her at the anticipated touch of his warm lips on hers.

Their first kiss. . .

His, a kiss of promise. Hers, a kiss of hope.

And the first of many to come. . .

She would see to that.

Epilogue

Two years later

Noah's father-in-law slapped him on the back, keeping his hand there in comfort. "She'll be fine, son. The good Lord knows she and her mother have plenty of experience at this sort of thing."

"Yes, I know. You're right." But this was different. . . .

This was Christiana.

"I think I'd like more lemonade. Fill your glass, sir?"

"You don't need to be taking care of me. Just relax."

"I feel better when I'm active," Noah admitted, and the older man nodded in understanding.

Noah headed to the kitchen. It had taken six months into his yearlong courtship with Christiana before he became comfortable around the gruff professor, and two months after their marriage before they became friends. While he felt relief that he was no longer considered the enemy, he had bigger problems at the moment.

Instead of lemonade, he found himself chipping ice into a glass. He had thought that *being there* was the greater trial—but not being there, not knowing, was ten times worse.

This was Christiana!

Uncertain of his reception, he approached the second landing and hovered at their bedroom door. She panted heavily then softly moaned and clutched her distended belly.

Propriety was the least of Noah's concerns as he rushed to her side and knelt on the floor near her.

"Noah?" her mother said in surprise from the foot of the bed.

"I thought you might need assistance." His eyes remained on his wife's glistening face. He smoothed the tousled hair from her damp brow as the pain subsided, her strained features slackening in relief.

"This is most unusual," her mother said.

"Yes, I know." He never looked away from Christiana. "But I've done it before."

Christiana smiled tenderly, her eyes glowing. "I want him here, Mama."

"I love you," he whispered, kissing her hair, her cheek, her lips.

"And I love you. . . ." She stroked his cheek with her hand. "Are you sure you're up to this? You did say you would rather be boiled in oil than go through this again."

"I'm the reporter who writes about supporting novel ideas, if you'll recall. I don't think it gets any more novel than having the father at the delivery." He grew serious. "I *want* to be here, Christiana. I want to be here for you. . . ." His hand lowered to spread gently across the mound of her stomach. "For our child."

She nodded, a tear slipping from her lashes. He kissed it away.

"Well, you won't have much longer to wait," Anna Leonard said with a smile. "I think my grandchild will soon make an entrance."

At the announcement, both excitement and dread filled Noah, but he was determined. Five months into their courtship, when he knelt before Christiana in her mother's rose garden and proposed, he never dreamed he would have succumbed to this.

He held his wife's hand through the worst of her travail, fed ice chips to her in between pains, even sat behind her to help support her when the big moment loomed nearer. Somehow he didn't pass out, though he wanted to weep when Christiana's pains came stronger, and he wished he could take all of her suffering away.

He ceased to breathe as she gave one final push. As long as he lived, Noah would never forget the astounding sight of glimpsing his daughter enter the world, caught in her grandmother's hands. Then and there, he silently vowed that his little girl would always know love and safety. He would protect her with his dying breath, and woe to any rapscallion who ever made his baby girl cry....

For the first time, he understood what Christiana's father must have felt upon meeting Noah.

"She's perfect," Anna said.

"A girl?" Christiana asked with a tired smile.

"A girl," Noah confirmed, his eyes falling shut while he held Christiana against him and kissed her hair, thanking God for the gift of his wife and child. After a moment, he moved away, helping her to lie back among the mound of pillows as he stood to his feet.

Once he straightened, Anna held the infant out to him.

He stared at her in shock.

"You wanted to assist," she said quietly, slipping the featherlight bundle of soft femininity into his arms. "Please take your daughter while I finish things here."

Within the blanket, his child's face was cherry red, her head a trifle squashed, but Noah saw nothing but beauty. Huge blue eyes. Dark hair. Ten fingers. Ten toes. Two tiny hands and feet...

"Noah?"

"...And do let your wife see."

Noah had been so immersed in gaping at the miracle of his daughter that he had not moved. At Anna's teasing prod, he smiled in sheepish apology to Christiana. Carefully, he handed the precious bundle over to her mother.

"Oh, Noah," she breathed. "She's wonderful.... I think she has your beautiful mouth."

"And your eloquent eyes," he added, lowering himself beside the bed.

Christiana tilted her head to rest against his shoulder as they gazed with awe at the culmination of their love.

"Hello, my little Pollyanna. Your papa and I have waited so long to see you. Your grandparents, too. Oh, the life you will have, the love you will know! And when you're older, you'll have tea parties with your grandpapa, and lovely strolls with your papa and me, and your papa will tell you such exciting stories. We'll teach you all you could ever wish to know...."

Noah wasn't sure, but he thought he saw his baby girl smile.

PAMELA GRIFFIN lives in Texas with her family. She fully gave her life to Christ in 1988 after a rebellious young adulthood and owes the fact that she's still alive today to an all-loving and forgiving God and to a mother who steadfastly prayed and had faith that God could bring her wayward daughter "home." Pamela's main goal in writing Christian romance is to help and encourage those who do know the Lord and to plant a seed of hope in those who don't.

Home Fires Burning

by JoAnn A. Grote

And the bow shall be in the cloud; and I will look upon it, that I may remember the everlasting covenant between God and every living creature of all flesh that is upon the earth.

GENESIS 9:16

Keep the Home-fires burning,
    While your hearts are yearning,
Though your lads be far away
    They dream of home;
There's a silver lining
    Through the dark cloud shining,
Turn the dark cloud inside out
    Till the boys come home.

—From *Keep the Home-Fires Burning,*
by Lena Guilbert Ford, 1915

Author's Note

H*ome Fires Burning* is set at the World War I military hospital at Fort Snelling in Minnesota. For years before the war, the Red Cross had kept a roster for the surgeon general of qualified nurses who agreed to work for the United States military in times of emergency. Women responded wholeheartedly to the United States' need for nurses in World War I. In March 1917, just before the United States entered the war, 403 nurses were on active duty. On Armistice Day, November 11, 1918, 21,480 women were members of the Army Nurse Corps.

No nurses were killed by enemy fire in the war. Even so, the first United States war casualties were two nurses. The Base Hospital Number 12 unit was aboard the SS *Mongolia* on its way to Europe in April 1917, when one of the ship's guns misfired, killing the two nurses and wounding a third.

Most Army Corps nurses who died in World War I were victims of the epidemic of influenza commonly called the Spanish flu. Almost all of the 102 nurses the surgeon general reported as dying overseas during the war were killed by the flu. One hundred twenty-seven Army Corps nurses died of the Spanish flu while serving in home-front military hospitals.

More American servicemen also were killed by the flu than by the enemy in World War I. The disease killed more than 500,000 American civilians and servicemen, more Americans than died in all the wars of the twentieth century.

Following the war, home-front military hospitals centered their efforts on helping wounded servicemen rebuild their lives. When a Red Cross nurse joined the Army Nurse Corps, she was technically no longer a Red Cross nurse but a member of the military. In many people's minds, the Red Cross was so interwoven with the Army Nurse Corps that they were one organization. Captain C. Arthur McLeod praised the work of nurses in World War I with these words: "We breathe a prayer of thankfulness for her presence among us—bend down in fullest veneration of her marvelous work and challenge the race to find her equal. ATTENTION!!! The world! Salute the noblest creation of the boundless love of God for His creatures, perfect and imperfect—the Red Cross Nurse."

JoAnn

Prologue

P*ray.*"
Glorie Cunningham's eyelids flew open. She stared into the dark of the nurses' quarters and held her breath, listening. There was no sound but the even breathing of the nurse in the next bed and the clock on the bedside table.

Had the voice been part of her dream? Unlikely. In the dream she and her brother Fred were playing together as children.

Fred. The fog of sleep evaporated from her mind. Fear gripped her, squeezing her heart. Fred was in France, on the western front. She shut her eyes tight against images of inhumane conditions on the battlefields and the terror of attack.

I should be there, not serving on the home front. From the time America joined the war it had been her desire to nurse at the front, as her Grandmother Lucy Cunningham had done in the War between the States.

Pray. Glorie prayed—prayed for Fred and the men who fought with him, and the doctors and nurses who cared for the wounded. She prayed until she fell again into a restless sleep, exhausted from her twenty-hour shift caring for soldiers on the home front who were battling the Spanish flu.

◆ ◆ ◆

October 14, 1918
France

"Busy evening, huh?"

"I'll say," Johan Baker yelled in response to the soldier beside him.

The enemy had kept a steady barrage of fire directed at the artillery. The cold and rain and mud and worn-out horses didn't help the Americans, who were trying to get shells to the large-gun positions. On top of that, today the division experienced some of the heaviest fighting since its arrival in France, and that was saying a lot for the tough Rainbow Division.

A screeching shell sent the two soldiers heading pell-mell toward a trench, slipping and sliding in the mud. Johan dove into the hole headfirst. He rolled over. Where was the soldier he'd just spoken to? Johan popped his head up over the edge of the trench. Twenty yards away, on the edge of the makeshift road, the shell burst. *P–bl–uup.* The typical silly little sound didn't do justice to the toxic cloud of gas that rolled out.

He shoved off his tin helmet, forced his gas mask over his face, and slammed his helmet back on, all the time scanning the slope. Where *was* that man? A shell bursting in the distance outlined the soldier, stuck in mud up to his knees and not wearing his mask.

Johan slithered out of the trench and over to the man. He grabbed the soldier's gas mask. The soldier pointed to a puncture. Johan's chest deflated. The mask was useless. The cloud would reach them any second. There wasn't time to get his companion out of the mud and find another mask.

Frustration ripped through him. He tore off his own mask and started pulling it over the man's head. "No!" The man struggled against it.

Johan let go, grabbed the soldier's damaged mask, and rolled away from him. He stuck a handkerchief in the puncture. It wouldn't help much, but it might give him a minute or two. The cloud was on them. *Too late.* The words blazed through his mind as he tugged the mask over his face. He slid into the trench and looked back. Thank God, the soldier had put on the good mask.

Chapter 1

The whistle warned him.

Johan dove into a nearby shell hole. He pressed his body against the mud wall, making himself as small a target as possible. *Little good it'll do if that bomb has my name on it.* He grabbed the gas mask attached to his belt. The hose was torn. Despair washed over him. He shoved his face between his arms until he felt the cold earth against his cheek, could almost taste the mud.

Someone shook him. He shoved the hand away from his shoulder.

"It's all right. Nothing can hurt you anymore." The soft voice filtered through the explosions and screams of battle. The gory scene disintegrated. Johan opened his eyes. His mind registered the fact that he'd been dreaming, but his heart still thumped hard and fast against his ribs. That battle was a dream, but the battle that landed him here at Fort Snelling had been real. The knowledge prevented relief on wakening.

Two identical women in their early twenties stood beside his bed. Identical red hair swept neatly back from identical freckled faces. Two pair of identical green eyes stared at him in concern and sympathy. Either the dream continued or he was seeing double.

He rubbed his eyes with his thumb and index finger, then looked again. The women were still there, both dressed in white, one wearing a small nurse's hat.

The woman beneath the hat smiled. "Your vision is fine, Lieutenant Baker. There are two of us. I'm Nurse Gloria Cunningham. This is my twin sister, Grace Holt."

He recognized the gentle voice that had drawn him from the dream.

Grace held up her left hand and wiggled her red-tipped fingers. A diamond flashed, reflecting the sudden amusement in her eyes. "Mrs. Daniel Holt."

Johan grinned. "For a moment I thought the war left me with double vision. Seeing two of every beautiful woman wouldn't be a bad way to go through life." As usual, his voice, the legacy of mustard gas, came out as though he was a frog with laryngitis.

Grace smiled and shook a finger at his not-so-subtle flattery.

The edges of Nurse Cunningham's lips hinted at a smile. She held up a white pitcher. "Would some ice water taste good, Lieutenant?"

He nodded. Clear, cold water still seemed a luxury. In France there'd never been enough to drink, or bathe in, or for the field hospitals' needs. Filthy water, on the other hand, was everywhere, especially in the trenches.

Johan's fingers met the nurse's lightly when he took the glass. The simple touch sent a jolt of awareness through him. He'd been too ill from the gassing to pay the nurses in France much attention. *Why, I haven't held a woman's hand since leaving for France,* he realized.

That was not the place to allow his thoughts to travel. Half the hospitalized doughboys fell for their nurses. He wasn't going to be one of them.

The water felt good on his throat. His voice had returned only a few days ago, and he'd talked too much today. When he indulged in speaking, he paid for it with searing pain. But who could refrain from cheering a mite when the Allies were finally victorious?

His gaze followed Nurse Cunningham as she turned her attention to the soldier in the next bed. He glanced up at Grace. "Twin nurses; that's unusual."

"I'm not a nurse." Grace waved her hand toward her sister's back. "Glorie's the Florence Nightingale. I'm but a humble Red Cross volunteer." She lowered her lashes.

Her feigned modesty brought a chuckle from Johan. A Red Cross girl. He should have recognized the high-buttoned white dress, but she wasn't hiding that fabulous red hair she shared with her sister beneath the traditional Red Cross headpiece.

The captain in the next bed peered around the nurse. "A Red Cross girl brought us lemonade in the middle of a battle. You'd have thought we were on the beach at Cape Cod, for all the notice she gave the bombs and bullets. Red Cross girls are okay in my book."

The patients who overheard him agreed, giving Grace a "hip-hip-hooray!" She flushed with obvious pleasure.

Johan observed the captain with reservations. He wondered how Captain Smith had ended up in the next bed. Johan avoided Smith whenever possible. He was an intelligent, loyal officer, but his hatred of Germans extended way beyond German soldiers. Still, Johan agreed with the captain's appreciation of Red Cross girls.

"Why aren't you out celebrating Armistice today with the rest of the city?" the captain asked.

Grace propped her fists on her hips and gave him a saucy look. "What better place to celebrate than among the men who won the peace and took the curl out of Crazy Bill's mustache?"

Her implied praise of the doughboys and belittling reference to the kaiser brought huzzahs and cheers from the patients.

A moment later, a thin soldier with brown hair parted in the middle and a black patch over one eye, broke into song. "Johnny is marching home again, he's finished another fight." Before the end of the second line, most of the soldiers had joined him.

Singing was beyond Johan's capability. To try it would be to tear open the lesions in his throat, which were finally beginning to heal.

Listening to Joe's patriotic enthusiasm brought a lump to that throat. Joe would never again see with the eye beneath that patch, but that fact didn't lessen his love for his country.

A doctor walked into the room, wearing a typical olive green army medical officer's jacket. Johan's gaze immediately sought his shoulders and standing collar for brass; a lieutenant colonel, likely the top medical officer on the post. Johan's back stiffened and he started to sit up, then remembered he didn't need to snap to attention in a hospital bed.

A toddler in a yellow dress entered hand in hand with the doctor. Her hair was hidden by an oversized Red Cross headpiece. She tugged her hand from the doctor's and marched down the aisle separating the two rows of white metal beds. Her arms and knees pumped as she sang the popular song with the soldiers.

Patients continued to sing, their eyes dancing with laughter.

Johan's gaze immediately sought the quiet Nurse Cunningham, to see her reaction. She was speaking to another patient, her lips close to his ear because of the din. The patient's eyes were bandaged. Johan couldn't hear what she said, but when the patient laughed, Johan was sure she'd described the little girl's march.

He liked the nurse's thoughtfulness. There were two other nurses in the ward, but something about Nurse Cunningham's sweet reserve caught his interest.

The little girl stopped beside Grace and grasped the blanket at the bed's edge. Her blue eyes looked right into his. "Hewwo."

"Hello yourself, Miss." It was easy to see from the girl's round face that she belonged to Mrs. Holt or Nurse Cunningham. His heart skipped a beat. Why hadn't he thought to look for a wedding band on the nurse's hand? *You're out of practice, Soldier,* he scolded himself, then remembered he'd pledged not to fall for her.

"I'm 'Lisbeth. Who're you?"

"Elisabeth." Grace spoke in that warning voice mothers use to gently let their children know their behavior isn't proper.

The mother, he thought before answering. "Johan."

"Lieutenant Baker," Grace corrected.

He held out a hand to Elisabeth. "You can call me Johan."

She shook his hand gravely. "You talk funny. Do you have a cold?"

"Elisabeth." This time Grace's warning was louder.

Johan ignored Grace and smiled at Elisabeth. "Something like that." He caught Grace's glance and nodded at the doctor the girl had walked in with. "Is that the honorable Daniel Holt?"

Grace shook her head. "No. The military wouldn't take Daniel. He had scarlet fever as a child. It left his heart too weak for fighting."

"Are you wearing your mother's Red Cross hat, Elisabeth?"

She nodded and stroked the white cloth as though it were silky hair. "Isn't it pwetty?"

"Very pretty." Wisps of short red hair curled out from beneath the white cap, framing the cherub's face. The symbolic red cross was slightly askew in the middle of her forehead above curious eyes. The folds of the hat hung down her back like a veil.

"When I don' feel good, Mommy weads me stowies. Would you like me to wead you a stowy?"

It brought a lump to his throat, which made talking even more difficult than usual. He nodded.

"I'll bwing my stowies."

Grace indicated the notebook she carried. "I'm making a list of soldiers' requests. I visit the hospital regularly as part of my Red Cross duties. Is there anything I can bring you?"

A hunger ate at his insides, just looking at her pad of paper. "A sketch pad, please, and some charcoal pencils if you can find them."

"I'll find them." Her pencil scratched across her pad. "I'm quite the detective when it comes to searching out things for our men."

Nurse Cunningham stepped quietly up beside Grace. He liked the graceful way the nurse moved. She laid a hand gently on his shoulder and smiled into his eyes. His insides turned to mush. A hint of spring flowers lightened the hospital's disinfectant odor.

"You need to stop talking for awhile, Lieutenant, and rest your throat."

He nodded. At least he didn't need to communicate with sign language and paper and pencil the way he had for awhile. The first two weeks, he'd been blind as well as mute and couldn't communicate at all.

She lifted her hand. He held back the absurd desire to grasp it and ask her to stay, to simply talk to him awhile, talk about anything at all. He just wanted to look in those sweet eyes and hear that reassuring soft voice.

Instead, he watched her leave the ward with Grace and Elisabeth.

What was the nurse's first name? It started with "G" like Grace—Gloria, that was it. Gloria reminded him of a sky filled with angels singing praises to God. A nice image but too noisy for someone as quiet as this nurse. Glorie, the name Grace called her, suited her better. The two looked alike, but talk about opposite personalities!

Johan laid back on the bed, suddenly exhausted, amazed at how it tired a body to fight for health. His gaze drifted over the white-walled room. The sense of light and cleanliness rested him after the year of mud and filth. Everything here was white: walls, ceiling, floor, metal beds, bedside tables, nurses' uniforms, sheets. Clean sheets were a luxury barely known in the field hospitals in France.

The quiet was heavenly. No bombs, no machine guns, no rifles, no train or ship engines. The usual hospital odors had already dispelled the fragrance of flowers Nurse Cunningham carried with her, but even the smells of the hospital were preferable to the sweet, sickening smell of gas.

He'd gone to war with the attitude expressed in the popular song: "We won't be back 'til it's over Over There." He'd hated coming back before it was over. *But today is Armistice Day. The buddies I left behind are done fighting, too.*

A peace came over him. His muscles relaxed against the mattress as he drifted toward sleep. He was home. The war was truly over.

Chapter 2

Once out of the ward, Elisabeth spotted another nurse she knew and sped down the hall to say hello.

Glorie moved quickly to the wall and sagged against it. She wrapped her arms over her chest, trying to hold in the pain that threatened to burst through.

"Are you all right?" Grace's voice mirrored the worry in her eyes.

"Yes." Glorie didn't feel "all right." Waves of sympathy and horror washed over her, threatening to knock her off her emotional feet. But she had to be "all right" for those brave men. "It's just. . .so much at once. These men—our first overseas men arriving, 150 of them, men who went away strong and healthy, and now. . ."

Grace rested a comforting hand on Glorie's arm. "You're exhausted, that's all. You were up before dawn helping prepare the celebration for the wounded, whose train arrived with them at eight, and you've been working with them all day since then."

"The wounded." Glorie repeated the words softly. "Before this, patients were the ill or accident victims, never 'the wounded.' "

"You're just tired," Grace repeated. "Things will get better."

Things wouldn't get better, of course. Glorie knew it, and she knew Grace did, too. More wounded would arrive every week until the hospital was filled with them, twelve hundred or so.

It was true she was tired. The influenza epidemic had worn out all the staff, not only here, but in civilian and military hospitals around the world. The first person to die of the flu in St. Paul was a lieutenant here at Fort Snelling. The hospital had overflowed with patients. St. Paul was closed down because of the flu. Restaurants, churches, schools, pool halls, saloons—all were closed in an effort to keep people from gathering in places where the deadly disease could easily spread.

At least the places were ordered closed. Today people flooded the streets, celebrating Armistice.

The first overseas men had been scheduled to arrive at the fort back in September. The flu changed the plans. Finally the flu here at the fort had abated to the point that it was believed safe to allow the wounded to be brought in. The few remaining flu patients were in a separate building, the fort's contagious-disease ward.

"We nurses encouraged our flu patients to get better so they could go overseas to fight, Grace. Did you know that?" A shiver ran along Glorie's spine at the memory. "We'd stand in the middle of the ward and call out, 'Where do you go from here, boys?' and they'd answer in a batch, 'Over There.' None of them made it over there, of course. The war ended too soon for that."

"They wanted to go. They knew what might happen."

Glorie shook her head fiercely. "No. They wanted to be heroes to impress their friends and families and girls. They were frightened of dying in war, though they blustered that they weren't. They didn't want to die at home of the flu. I doubt they believed they'd return like the overseas men here today."

"No one thinks horrible things will happen to them. Soldiers aren't alone in owning that illusion."

Glorie pushed herself away from the wall. "For most of the world, the war is over. For me and the rest of the medical staff, our war is just beginning."

"Excuse me."

Glorie turned toward the male voice with the heavy German accent. Blue eyes danced in a middle-aged man's narrow, deeply wrinkled face. Beside him a woman with round red cheeks and blond hair had equally happy eyes.

An answering smile spread across Glorie's face. "May I help you?"

The man doffed his hat and held it against his chest. "Our son is here. He's back from the war, a patient, Lt. Johan Baker. Do you know where we can find him?"

"He's right through these doors. Let me show you." Glorie opened the ward door.

The couple followed, thanking her. The mouth-watering aroma of fresh-baked bread brought Glorie's attention to a large basket the woman carried. A white linen towel covered the contents. "Oh, he can't. . ." Glorie hesitated. She'd started to tell them Johan couldn't eat solid food yet. How much did they know about his injuries?

They hurried past her and down the aisle toward his bed in the middle of the ward. She trotted after them, smiling at their eagerness.

The conversation and laughter of the other patients died as the soldiers watched the couple approach their son. They stopped beside his bed. Johan was sleeping again. The couple's gaze moved from Johan to Glorie. She saw fear in their faces. *They don't know how he was injured,* she thought. "He's only sleeping. It's fine to wake him, but you mustn't let him talk much. His throat is still healing from the lesions caused by mustard gas."

Mrs. Baker's eyes widened.

"It will be fine eventually," Glorie rushed to assure her, "but for now he needs to let his throat rest. As you might imagine, he's had a hard time keeping quiet and not celebrating the Armistice."

The Bakers' faces relaxed into smiles.

"Why don't you wake him?" Glorie suggested to Mrs. Baker.

The woman set the basket on the floor, laid a hand on Johan's shoulder, and leaned close to say in a soft German accent, "Johan, it's Mother."

Johan moved slightly in his sleep. A small smile formed.

Mrs. Baker shook his shoulder lightly. "Wake up, Son."

This time Johan obeyed. The surprise in his eyes was greater than when he'd awakened to see Grace and Glorie. He bolted to a sitting position and threw his arms around the woman's neck. "Mother!"

Glorie blinked back sudden tears. Even through Johan's scarred throat, even though it was barely more than a cracked whisper, the word held a world of love.

"Father, you're here, too!" The men gripped each other's hands. Tears streamed down all three faces.

Glorie turned discreetly away. The room had gone from its first hushed notice of the couple to complete quiet. She glanced at the men. Each one watched the meeting. Tears sparkled in more than a few eyes. A couple of men dashed away tears from their cheeks. One corporal pulled out a khaki handkerchief and blew his nose loudly.

The men who earlier appeared tough, courageous, even cheerful in facing the future with the handicaps war had bestowed on them watched the family wrapped in each others' arms. *This is what they're all waiting for—to be home, all the way home, with their loved ones.* She swallowed the lump the scene brought to her throat and unnecessarily started down the row straightening blankets. It wouldn't do for the men to find her staring at them.

"Hip-hip-hooray for you, Johan," one soldier whispered through a throat as scarred as Johan's.

Only Glorie heard him. "Amen," she said softly.

She glanced back at Johan. His mother, beaming from ear to ear and with eyes only for her son, was seated on his chair. She held one of his hands in both her own. A soldier climbed out of bed and brought another chair for Mr. Baker.

Glorie continued straightening blankets and began a conversation with two soldiers. The other patients cleared throats and turned away to give the Bakers privacy.

Even so, Glorie heard pieces of the family's conversation. Johan's questions were those of any family member away for a time—about relatives and friends. The news that an uncle had died in the flu epidemic brought a stillness to the room again, but only for a moment.

Mr. Baker told how the family dog carried one of Johan's shoes everywhere he went. "Even sleeps on it, like a pillow."

Glorie thought she wouldn't be surprised to learn that Mrs. Baker, too, kept something of Johan's with her all day and all night. Glorie herself kept a picture of her brother, Fred, on her bedside table.

She started back toward Johan's bed. She hated to cut the visit short, but Johan shouldn't be talking so much. When she'd almost reached them, she heard Johan say, "Where's the bread? It isn't my imagination that I smell it, is it?"

Mr. Baker grinned and lifted the basket. "We made your favorite sweet buns."

Mrs. Baker folded back the linen towel and displayed the golden bread.

Johan reached for a bun. Glorie grabbed his hand and smiled at his parents. "I'm afraid Johan can't eat that yet. He's on a liquid diet until his throat is better."

"Can't I keep it just to smell?" Johan gave Glorie such a beseeching look that she laughed out loud.

"I'm afraid not, Lieutenant. No doubt you have strong willpower, but these wonderful buns would be far too tempting for any man."

He pretended to pout. "I dreamed of these during every one of those meals of beans and mush in France."

"We own a bakery, Nurse," Mrs. Baker explained. "My husband's people have been bakers for generations. That is why our name is Baker."

"Our son will not be a baker." Mr. Baker lifted his chin in pride. "Johan will be attending the university."

"Schooling won't take away what you taught me," Johan said. "I'll still make a great batch of bread." The last word was strangled in the beginning of a cough that continued for too long.

His parents leaned toward him, concern written in their eyes.

"I'm afraid you must end your visit for today. Johan, Lieutenant Baker, must rest his throat." Glorie felt a wave of color flood her face. The nurses never called any of the soldiers by their first names. She tried to cover her slip with a question for his parents. "Do you live nearby?"

"Not far," Mr. Baker replied. "Our bakery is in downtown Minneapolis."

"As soon as I can eat solid food, I expect a basket of buns and bread each day," Johan challenged. Again a cough erupted, smothering the smile his words brought to his mother.

"That won't be too long," Glorie assured while pouring a glass of water from the pitcher on the white bedside table. "If he learns to stop talking so much." She smiled sweetly at the dirty look he gave her across the glass he accepted.

Mr. Baker took the basket from his wife and set it on the chair. "We'll leave this for the other patients."

Glorie hesitated. She wasn't sure it was fair to share it with only a few, but she didn't want to hurt their feelings.

"We don't want anything made by a dirty old Hun," Captain Smith spat out.

Glorie spun to face the man sitting up in the next bed. "Captain!" Hatred burned in his eyes and so changed his features that she barely recognized him.

He grabbed a bun from the basket and hurled it. It bounced off the wall and hit Mrs. Baker's cheek.

"Stop!" Glorie yanked back the basket before the captain could reach another bun.

A roar came from behind her. A second later Johan burst from his bed. He lunged toward Captain Smith.

Glorie tried to throw herself between the two. The basket which made her hands useless added to her effectiveness as a barrier.

Other patients hurried to the fray. Joe grabbed Johan's arm, and two men pressed Captain Smith back against the mattress.

"You can't insult my folks that way." Johan's attempt at a yell came out a scratchy growl.

Glorie's own throat hurt for the pain she knew he must be feeling, both physically and emotionally. "Lieutenant, please, remember your throat."

"She's right," Joe told Johan. "Besides, the captain outranks you. We might be in a hospital, but we're still in the army."

The satisfied glint in Captain Smith's eyes sickened Glorie. There wasn't an officer of higher rank in the ward at the moment. Surely that wouldn't allow him to get away with such behavior. "Assault on a civilian isn't acceptable no matter what an officer's rank." The command in her voice surprised her.

It obviously surprised the captain, too, from the look on his face when his gaze jerked from Johan to her.

Glorie hurried around the end of Johan's bed. Mrs. Baker held a hand to her cheek. Tears pooled in her eyes, but they weren't tears of joy this time. Mr. Baker had an arm around her waist. "Are you all right, Mrs. Baker?"

"Yah."

"We're used to worse than this." Mr. Baker glared at Captain Smith. "We didn't expect it from the soldiers Johan fought beside."

Glorie walked with them out into the hall. "I'm so sorry Captain Smith ruined your visit."

Mr. Baker shook his head. "To see our boy back, to know he is going to be well. . .nothing could spoil that."

"He isn't our boy any longer, Father," Mrs. Baker said softly. "Didn't you see his eyes? He has his father's eyes now, old eyes, the eyes of a man who has seen too much." She turned her hands palm up and stared at them. "When I fed him as a babe, he'd hold my little finger. It filled his entire hand. When he was a toddler, I'd wrap his blond curls around my fingers when I brushed his hair." Her sorrow-filled gaze met Glorie's. "Our boy went to war, but a man came home."

Mr. Baker laid an arm around his wife's shoulder. "Come, Mother. Let's go home."

Glorie held out the basket.

"You share it with the other nurses."

"Thank you."

Their steps were slow and they leaned against each other, a different image than the eager couple who'd arrived a short time ago.

The memory of Johan's face when Captain Smith shot his ugly words and threw the bread cut into Glorie's heart. She sighed and sent up a prayer for both young officers.

The war was over, but it left a bottomless lake of hate behind. She and the rest of the medical staff would give their all to help the soldiers' bodies mend, but only God could mend men's souls.

The Bakers disappeared around a corner, and Glorie threw off her dismal thoughts. She hurried to the ward station. Relief flooded over her when she saw the ward officer there. She described the situation between Captain Smith and Lieutenant Baker.

"I'll take care of it," the ward officer assured her. "Wouldn't you know trouble would break out between officers and not enlisted men? Poor example, I'd call it."

The next morning Glorie found Joe assigned to the bed Captain Smith previously occupied. The captain now resided in the bed at the far end of the row. This wasn't a permanent answer, of course, but at least it put some distance between the barb-throwing captain and the lieutenant.

Johan managed a smile when she approached his bed, but he didn't attempt to speak. She could see by his eyes that he was in physical pain. All the talking and yelling yesterday likely tore at the throat lesions that had begun to heal. Her own throat tightened in empathy as she took his wrist to check his pulse.

When she returned later, she brought a pad and pencil. "In case you want to say anything," she said, handing them to him. She poured aspirin powders in a glass of water for him. It wouldn't alleviate all his pain, but it would help a little.

Glorie dreaded changing the dressings on the blisters caused by the mustard gas, but it had to be done. She was as gentle as possible. Still, she wondered whether her attempts were clumsy and knew they were hurtful. The blistering was similar to that experienced with first- or second-degree burns.

The blisters had broken on his trip from New York to St. Paul. Now it was important to prevent infection from setting in. She knew if that happened, it would add five or six weeks to his recovery. As usual with mustard gas burns, the blisters were the worst in places where there was the most body friction, like the armpits and behind the knees.

He flinched when she removed the last old dressing.

Glorie gasped, dropped the dressing, and stepped back. "I'm sorry."

Johan scratched something across the pad, then turned it toward her. In bold capital letters he'd written *OUCH!*

A giggle escaped her. Guilt followed on its heels. "I'm sorry," she repeated, though she couldn't discipline her grin.

He smiled back.

She returned to the dressing with a lighter heart, knowing he'd intended to make her laugh. The pain she'd caused him was real; she'd seen the glint of a tear at the corner of one eye. Yet he wasn't about to wallow in his pain or allow her to feel guilty about it.

Her exposure to the effects of gas warfare made her profoundly grateful for the thousands and thousands of peach pits scouts had collected during the war. The pits had been ground and used in making gas masks. She'd grown so tired of eating peaches and canning peaches and even *seeing* peaches that she'd remarked to Grace, "I'm surprised God made them yellow instead of red, white, and blue."

Treatment of the blisters required frequent dressing changes. The second time Glorie changed them, Johan showed her two sketches. The first was a stick man with a sad face. An arrow pointed from a notation to the man. The notation said, "Me after weeks on a liquid diet." The second sketch was a handsome, muscled, smiling man beside the words, "Me before the liquid diet."

She chuckled and reached for the first dressing.

He scribbled something else. She glanced at it. Beside the sketch of the handsome man he'd written, "Aren't you going to tell me how good-looking he is?"

Her gasp was a mixture of surprise and laughter. Turning her gaze and hands to the dressing, she replied with intentional primness, "Mother always said, 'Handsome is as handsome does.' "

When she chanced a glance back at his face, he was grinning.

On night duty, Glorie discovered that Johan wasn't the only patient experiencing nightmares. Every night at least a half-dozen men thrashed about or awoke screaming. She'd hold their hands, bathe the sweat from their faces with a cool cloth, and speak to them in low, soothing tones until they fell back asleep. But their screams awoke others who lay tense, staring into the darkness, not needing sleep to produce nightmares.

Glorie stopped in surprise beside Johan's bed a couple of days later. He was sitting up, his sketch pad resting against his knees. His face was covered with white cold cream. He'd exaggerated and thickened his eyebrows with a charcoal pencil. A clownlike broad band of a red smile covered his lips and more. "What on earth. . . ?"

Johan's eyes glinted in a smile. He lifted his hands, opening them wide to frame his face, and she saw that he wore white gloves. He pointed to the next bed. Joe wore the same gloves and face covering.

Joe pretended to hit a badminton shuttlecock to Johan. Johan hit it back. Joe returned it. Johan slapped a hand to his forehead, as if he'd been hit. A white finger scolded Joe.

"You're mimes," Glorie exclaimed in delight. The other nurses and most of the patients joined her in laughing at Johan and Joe's show. After the game of volleying, they performed a tug of war until Johan was tugged out of bed. He brushed himself off thoroughly, while casting dirty looks at his gleeful opponent.

"Charlie Chaplin better watch out or you two will replace him as America's favorite comedian," Glorie quipped when Johan finally settled back into the bed. "Before we change your dressings, we'd best get that cold cream off your faces. The cream isn't good for blisters, you know. Good thing the blisters on your faces are dried up and almost healed." There wasn't the friction on the face skin that caused such severe blistering elsewhere, she remembered. She leaned closer to Johan's face, studying his clown mouth. "Where did you get the lipstick?"

He jotted down the answer.

"From Grace. So my own sister is plotting with you. I can see I'm going to have to watch the two of you like a hawk."

The clown smile grew very wide.

◆　◆　◆

The days soon fell into a routine for the medical staff and patients at Fort Snelling. Each morning, promptly at seven—or 0700 in army parlance—the nurses entered the wards. Any fatigue or self-centered pettiness they possessed fled in the face of the patients' situations and cheerful courage in facing their wounds.

The nurses awakened the soldiers with sunny greetings, took vital signs, and wheeled in curtained dividers that were placed between beds for privacy when the patients were bathed. Then came the more challenging duties. Changing dressings was the most painful task, for both patient and nurse.

Convalescing soldiers often preferred to sleep in, but such laziness wasn't allowed. "Muscles need use to heal properly. You want them built up nice and strong for the girls back home, don't you?" Glorie wasn't above needling. Her approach usually brought the desired result. The chaplain doubled as the athletic officer. He made sure the men who were physically able exercised daily, building up their strength slowly.

Next the nurses prepared for the ward officer's 0900 inspection. After the ward inspection, the nurses brought meals to the patients unable to eat in the mess hall.

Each week, another 150 men came for reconstruction and convalescence. *Reconstruction is such an impersonal word,* Glorie thought, wheeling a patient in a high-backed cane wheelchair to a physical therapy session. *It's a term for repairing buildings, not bodies.* Yet that was the term coined for the medical help she and her coworkers provided the soldiers.

Aides in dark dresses and white aprons took over for nurses and doctors in the physical therapy rooms. A soldier flirted with a smiling aide while she massaged his arm. Glorie waited while another soldier completed his hot water treatment, his leg in a tall, round canister that looked like a metal wastebasket. The patient she'd wheeled down would receive the same treatment on a leg amputated just above the knee.

She wheeled another patient back to his ward. They met a group of ambulatory convalescent patients returning from an outdoor exercise session, not looking at all like patients in their sweaters and wool slacks.

One of the men grinned at her patient. "How do you rate, Tom, riding and with a beautiful woman at your service? I've only these ugly doughboys for company."

The wheeled man spread his hands and shrugged his shoulders. "Ugly attracts ugly, and good-looking—"

The men hooted and continued on their way.

The patients' good cheer continually amazed Glorie. They seldom allowed themselves the luxury of self-pity, and they didn't treat each other with pity, either. She and the other nurses followed the men's example to the best of their ability.

After delivering the man to his ward, Glorie headed for the officers' dayroom. Grace was scheduled to read to some of the blinded men and had asked Glorie to join them if she could get away. Their war duties kept them so busy, they seldom saw each other, compared to Glorie's prenursing days.

She was thankful for the busy hours. The joy of Armistice had tarnished with news that her brother Fred was missing in action in the last offensive. She swallowed the painful lump of fear, said a prayer, and forced her thoughts away from the worst.

Her steps slowed when she neared Johan's ward. She hadn't seen him in almost two weeks, not since she'd been reassigned to surgery. She often wondered whether the humorous soldier was healing well. Unless he had another episode with the callous Captain Smith or his friends, Johan's throat and blistering should soon be healed well enough for him to be discharged. She felt a slight twinge in her heart at the thought.

She toyed with the possibility of stopping to say hello but tossed the idea aside after a moment. Fraternizing with patients was discouraged. Patients often developed fond feelings for their nurses.

Glorie sighed and forced herself to pass the ward doors. It wasn't the patient whose heart was endangered; it was hers. She wasn't sure why Johan drew her interest more than any of the hundreds of other men, but he did. Certainly his humor helped, though other men joked and teased, too. Whenever she recalled his face and voice when he'd greeted his parents, the memory warmed her like a blanket. It was like a gift, seeing his heart open in that intimate way. All the patients were courageous men, but few allowed others to see their vulnerable side. Perhaps Johan would have hidden his emotions if his parents hadn't surprised him.

Outside the officers' dayroom she stopped to take a deep breath and put on a smile. She could hear Grace's musical voice through the door. When Glorie entered, the first person she saw was Lt. Johan Baker, seated in a leather mission chair near the stone fireplace. He glanced up. A smile leaped to his eyes, sending shivers of joy through her.

He and the other officers started to rise.

Glorie shook her head. "Please, continue with what you are doing."

Their activities were varied. Captain Smith and a major played chess in one corner. Another major read a book. A lieutenant sat at an oak table writing a letter on familiar YMCA stationery that bore a printed heading which stated that he was proudly serving in America's armed forces. A deck of cards in the middle of another table showed how others spent time. The new tune "Everything Is Peaches Down in Georgia" filled with cheer the corner where a nurse and colonel looked through the record collection beside the Victrola.

A calendar hung above the Victrola, picturing a child Elisabeth's age with short blond curls. Beneath her image was the caption, "Guess what Daddy bought me for my birthday. A Liberty Bond!" Glorie tried to imagine Elisabeth happy about a bond for a gift and failed.

Grace's voice rose and fell while she read the day's *St. Paul Pioneer Press* to a blinded captain. She and the captain were seated in overstuffed chairs near the fireplace.

Elisabeth rose with a gasp of delight and raced to Glorie. The white veil of a miniature Red Cross headpiece Grace had finally made the girl floated out behind her. Glorie knelt to receive the little girl's hug. "Hello, Elisabeth. Are you having a good time?"

"Yes. Muvver is weading, so I must be quiet like my kitty when she naps," Elisabeth informed her in a stage whisper. She took Glorie's hand. "Come sit with me."

Glorie followed obediently. Elisabeth sat on the rug before Johan's chair. She indicated that Glorie was to sit down beside her.

Immediately Johan stood and waved his sketch pad toward his seat. "Take my chair, Nurse Cunningham."

"I'm accustomed to sitting with Elisabeth, thank you." She lowered herself as gracefully as possible beside her niece, trying to ignore the awareness of Johan's presence, which made every movement feel exaggerated and clumsy.

Johan sat down beside them, crossing his legs.

"Shh." Elisabeth held a stiff index finger to her lips.

"Sorry," he mouthed.

"Your voice sounds much stronger," Glorie whispered.

"I've a lot of practice whispering," he said with a straight face.

She giggled. "I meant when you spoke normally."

"The doctors say they'll discharge me any day now. My throat and the lesions are almost healed."

"That's wonderful."

"Here's some great news, everyone." Grace raised her voice for the entire room to hear. "Sugar allowances have doubled. We're now allowed eight teaspoons a day. It's about time. I'm simply wasting away with so little sugar and real flour. Soon Fuelless Mondays, Meatless Tuesdays, and Sugarless Fridays will be behind us. But they were worth it. It says here that Minnesotans saved thirty-six million pounds of sugar and three million bushels of wheat for the Allies. Hooray for us!" She returned to reading articles for the officer beside her, and her voice moderated. The others in the room returned to their occupations, too.

"You've bobbed your hair," Johan remarked, studying Glorie.

Her hand went to the marcelled waves framing her face. "Yes. I thought it would be easier to care for now that I'm so busy."

"I like it."

His approval warmed her, and she ignored the thought that it shouldn't give her so much pleasure.

Elisabeth tired of not receiving their attention. She leaned toward Johan. "Are you done drawing me?"

"Almost." He added a few strokes. "There." He handed the pad to Elisabeth.

She beamed in delight. "Look, Aunt Glorie."

The sketch caught Elisabeth's intensity as she comforted a bandaged doll in her arms. "You're very good," Glorie told him, her gaze and emotions riveted on his sketch.

He took the tablet from her without comment.

Glorie lifted the real doll from Elizabeth's lap. "What happened to your baby?" It appeared almost mummylike, with only its porcelain cheeks and a few stray brown curls peeking out from the gauze.

"She was wounded in the war." The statement came out short and matter-of-fact.

"Is she a soldier?" Johan asked.

"No, Silly." Elizabeth shook her head vigorously. "Girls aren't soldiers. She's a nurse."

Glorie wondered where Elisabeth came across the idea the war endangered nurses the same as soldiers. True, the flu epidemic killed many nurses. Those near the front lines were sometimes injured, but none had been killed in battle.

The Victrola sent out a new song. Elisabeth jumped up, eyes gleaming. "That's my favowite song. K–k–k–katy," she sang as she skipped across the room to the couple playing records.

Glorie glanced at Johan, and they shared a laugh at the girl's enthusiastic rendering of the popular tune. When the laugh died, they were still staring into each other's eyes. Glorie wondered what he thought and felt inside, in that place with war memories he didn't share with anyone. She had the sudden, aching wish to hold him, her arms absorbing all the awful pictures, all the horrible and painful memories.

It almost took a physical effort to pull her gaze away. Her cheeks felt warm. Had he seen her thoughts in her eyes?

"Are you changing the doll's dressings?" Johan's teasing tone made her aware she was picking at the doll's bandages.

"Grace says she tore up an old sheet for Elisabeth to use, as she's bandaging everyone and everything. She bandaged their cocker spaniel." She liked the chuckle that rewarded her tale. "That wasn't the worst of it," she continued. "A few nights ago, while her father napped after dinner, she wrapped his feet—wrapped them together. Grace had to cut the makeshift bandages off."

The chuckle became a guffaw. "Wish I'd seen that. Did you know I met her husband? Daniel is one of the volunteers who take us restless convalescing soldiers for Sunday drives. I liked him."

"He's a fine man." Glorie sometimes envied Grace her pleasant married life, with a man who thought the sun rose and set in her and a daughter who lit up her heart. *But I've never met a man I wanted to spend my entire life with,* she thought. *Besides, if I'd married, I wouldn't be here now, helping the soldiers. Grace gave up her dream of nursing for a dream more important to her, building a life and family with Daniel. Until I meet a man I'm that crazy over, I won't marry.*

Johan took the doll from her and looked down at it as though it had secrets to tell. "The men love it when Elisabeth visits. In France, when a little girl was in the hospital she was injured. The war wasn't limited to soldiers."

Glorie's chest constricted at his words. She closed her mind against the image of children with the same grievous wounds as the soldiers at Fort Snelling.

"The day always seems brighter after seeing Elisabeth," he continued. "Have you noticed the way the mood seems lighter in a ward when she's there? She reminds us of that sweet world waiting for us when we leave here. Perhaps we're selfish, grasping for the life she brings." He ran a thick index finger over the wrapping binding the doll's head. "No child should see all the carnage she's seen here."

"No one any age should see or experience it." Glorie stopped his finger, laying her hand lightly over his. "Children are stronger than we think. The children in France have seen worse things. Wouldn't it be wonderful if the Great War turned out to be what President Wilson called it, a war to end war?"

"An end to war. I wish we could make that happen." His voice was low, the passion causing it to reverberate like distant thunder.

"That'll be the day." Captain Smith's harsh comment crashed through the world that had included only Glorie and Johan.

Glorie snatched her hand away from Johan's. The gesture that had been only a natural reaching out to comfort another, suddenly appeared forward and ugly when reflected in the captain's glaring eyes.

The captain's lip curled. "The whole world fought together to put Germany out of business. As long as one German remains alive there won't be a chance peace will last. The Allies shouldn't have agreed to peace. We should keep fighting until the earth is wiped clean of filthy Huns."

Glorie could see Johan struggling to keep his temper. Music continued to roll out from the Victrola with inappropriately cheerful lyrics, but everyone but Elisabeth was watching the two officers. Glorie wanted to lay her hand on his again, to tell him the captain's taunts weren't worth challenging, but she clenched her hands tightly in her lap and sent up a prayer instead.

"You're right that Germany was the aggressor," Johan said through tight lips, "this time."

"You can't weasel your fatherland out of guilt just because there are wars your country didn't fight in."

Johan pointed to a print on the wall beside them, a picture of an American Indian warrior slumped on the back of a horse after battle. "Your fatherland was the aggressor against this nation, wasn't it?"

Captain Smith snorted. "You can't compare the two."

"Why not?" Johan asked softly. "The English and French wanted to take the land from the American Indians. The Germans in this war wanted to take land from the French."

"Are you saying the Germans were justified in invading France?" The captain braced his arms against the back of a chair and leaned toward Johan. Glorie sensed menace in the line of his body.

"No." Johan stood up, the bandaged doll hanging from one hand. "I'm saying evil doesn't exist only in the people of one country. I'm saying a war started for the wrong reasons doesn't justify condemning an entire people for all time, doesn't justify forgetting the good things they've given the world."

Glorie hadn't been aware that the colonel had left the Victrola and now approached them, until he spoke from behind Johan. "Put a lid on it, officers. There are ladies and a child present. If you want to continue your private war, do battle elsewhere."

"Yes, Sir." The captain's back straightened.

"No need for battle, Sir." Johan's eyes challenged Smith to refute him.

"That's right, Sir." Smith's look said the words were a lie.

When Smith had left the room, the colonel faced Johan. "A word of warning: Take care how you express your feelings about the war. I know you are a loyal American and fought hard for us, but there are those who won't take that into account. They'll remember that your people came from Germany and interpret your words according to their preconceived ideas. They want someone to blame for their sons coming home like this." He rested his left hand on the prosthesis that replaced his right arm. "As you said, this time it's Germany's fault."

Color drained from Johan's face. "Right, Sir. Thank you, Sir."

"Germany's a long way away," the colonel continued. "You're here, so you're an easy target."

"I was born in America," Johan told him. "My parents immigrated from Germany right after they married. Both have brothers and sisters living in Germany. At least, we hope they are still alive. We haven't heard from them since before the United States entered the war. I have cousins who fought for Germany. Neither I nor my parents have met them, but they're family, my parents' nieces and nephews. Over there, when we were shooting at the enemy,

I might have been shooting at my cousins. I never thought it right that Germany invaded Belgium and France, but other Americans don't understand what they asked of German-Americans in this war. No one should be asked to make such a choice."

Glorie's throat tightened in sympathy at the pain in his voice.

The colonel's expression didn't change. "It's a nasty choice, no question about it. But remember, one of your cousins might have launched the gas shells that put you here, Lieutenant." He gave a sharp salute and left the room.

Glorie was dimly aware that the others in the room had gone back to their activities. Grace's voice picked up a news story again, the paper crackling as she adjusted it. The other nurse asked Elisabeth about her favorite songs. The officers at the chess table murmured across the playing board.

It's impossible to live in Minnesota and not be aware of the German-Americans' mixed sympathies, Glorie thought. Almost a quarter of the state's population were born in Germany or Austria, or their parents were born there.

Glorie rose to stand beside Johan and cleared her throat. "I have friends who Americanized their names after the war started."

"Denying their heritage? My family refuses to consider our ancestors shameful."

She wondered if he was turning his anger at Captain Smith on her. "They only wanted others to know they're loyal Americans," she said, "and to avoid trouble."

His gaze studied hers until she thought she would quake at the intensity. "Do you believe it's acceptable to deny your family and your history?"

"I can't judge them. I've not faced that choice, nor have I faced the awful choices you did."

"If I'd chosen not to fight for our country, for the United States, what would you think then?"

The question seemed silly to her, asking what she would think if he were someone else. She wanted to duck her head to hide her smile, but he might interpret that as avoiding his gaze. "That depends. Would you choose to support Germany because of your heritage or because you believed Germany right in invading its neighbors? Did you enlist in the American army because you live in America or because you believe the Belgians and French and all other people have the right to choose the leaders who will govern them?"

His eyebrows drew together in a frown. For a moment he looked confused. Then he laughed. "You should be a diplomat."

"I think that quality is required of nurses."

"Thank you for reminding me of the true questions."

"You always knew them." She knew it was true. Yet it was equally true that he and millions of others had been forced to make a horrible and costly choice.

"Tomorrow's Thanksgiving," he reminded her. "Will you spend it with your family?"

"No. I see my family often since they live in St. Paul. I offered to work to free someone else to spend time with their family. My grandparents are coming for the holidays. They live in Virginia. I haven't seen them in years. They arrive this afternoon and are staying through Christmas." She didn't tell him they'd decided the family needed each other over the holidays while they dealt with their fear and grief over Fred.

"I've never met my grandparents." Johan gazed out the window.

"I'm sorry. I can't imagine life without grandparents."

"We've other things to thank God for tomorrow." His cheer sounded forced. "The Armistice, naturally. But also, I've been off that liquid diet for a week and a half, so I plan to enjoy that turkey and dressing." He wiggled his eyebrows and rubbed his palms together in anticipation.

Glorie burst into laughter and pointed at his hands. The forgotten doll danced from them.

Chapter 3

Glorie glanced at the clock on the wall as she hurried down the hall toward the door; three o'clock. She'd have time for a short nap before helping get trays ready for the evening meal. She couldn't imagine that the patients would be hungry after the huge Thanksgiving meal this noon, but a hospital was nothing without a schedule.

The outside door opened just as she reached it, letting in a rush of chilly air tinged with the sharp scent of autumn leaves. "Surprise!" Grace, dressed in a khaki military-style coat, threw out her arms and grinned like a cat who'd just finished a bowl of cream. Behind her stood an elderly couple.

Glorie rushed to throw her arms around first the lady and then the slender gentleman. "Grandmother Lucy. Grandpa Jere. What a wonderful surprise." She pressed her lips to her grandmother's soft, wrinkly cheek, then to the tougher, though just as wrinkled, cheek of her grandfather. "I didn't think I'd see you until Sunday. I can't tell you how jealous I was of the rest of the family for your company."

Grandmother and Grandpa's Virginia-accented greetings were almost drowned in Grace's excited, "They wanted to see where you worked. Grandpa Jere wanted to visit some of the soldiers and thank them for their sacrifices. So I offered to bring them. I knew you'd love the surprise. Won't it be fun to show them around?"

Glorie's gaze took in the couple. Grandpa was tall with a lean, narrow face. Grandmother was slightly on the rounded side. She looked comfortable, the way Glorie always thought a grandmother should look. Her hair was still long; it was pulled back in a bun. Silver waves framed her face. "We haven't seen you in five years. Grace and I agree, it was the most wonderful summer of our lives, staying with you at Hickory Hill. We felt like Southern belles. Remember the way Grace and I tried to adopt your wonderful Southern drawls? We were such children."

"Northern or Southern, you're both beautiful belles in my book," Grandpa Jere insisted.

"Let me look at you." Grandmother took both of Glorie's hands and stood back. Glorie beamed and waited patiently while Grandmother's gaze traveled from the pert white nurse's hat to the simple white dress to the sensible shoes on Glorie's tired feet. Grandmother's hand shook slightly as she touched a fingertip to the gold U.S. on one side of Glorie's shawl collar, and the medical department's gold caduceus with ANC superimposed in white enamel on the other side. "We hadn't such fine uniforms in the War between the States."

"You didn't have uniforms at all, my dear." Grandpa's dry remark set Glorie and Grace giggling out of all proportion to the humor, simply because it was lovely to be with the couple again and enjoy the way they were together. Grandpa teased Grandmother Lucy relentlessly but always with a sparkle in his eye and never with a cruel undertone.

"Let's start our tour." Glorie slipped one arm through Grandpa's. "Stop us whenever you feel the need to rest a bit." Grace hooked elbows with Lucy and the four started off.

The couple obviously was awed by the up-to-date equipment such as the X-ray machine.

"It's invaluable," Glorie told them. "Every day we've a couple of men who take bismuth meals and then are fluoroscoped so the doctors can determine problems from gunshot wounds to the abdomen."

Grandmother Lucy pressed a hand to her waist and her eyes grew large, but she didn't comment. Glorie suspected she was remembering abdomen wounds of soldiers she'd nursed.

The two surgery rooms looked pristine today. "This is the hardest duty, but rewarding beyond measure," Glorie told them. "It takes three doctors and six nurses to handle the surgeries. Eighty percent of our patients require surgery. We're only able to do a couple each day. The Carroll-Darkin treatment is used in all operations for diseased bones. If there's the slightest chance an old infection is recurring, the doctors do another operation. That way gangrene can't do its dirty work, and the wounds heal faster."

Next she showed them one of the two lab wards, which looked barren and cold with its stark metal furnishings. The microscopes, set where the sun shone through uncurtained windows, were life-giving. To Glorie the room looked empty without the white-aproned doctors bent over the microscopes. Only a skeleton crew remained at work today. "The labs are specially equipped to keep the detailed bacterial counts necessary for treatments."

The physiotherapy ward was next. "You've a separate ward for everything." Lucy sighed. "I wish we'd had all these modern wonders available during the War between the States."

A wave of sympathy rolled through Glorie. She wished much more could be done for her patients, but they had much better medical help available than when Lucy and Jere helped the men when their generation fought.

Glorie listed all the areas of medicine represented at the fort. "General surgery; orthopedics; eye, ear, nose, and throat; electro-hydro and mechano therapeutics; dental surgery, nerve surgery, and X-ray. Oh, and there's a separate building for contagious diseases. Of course, when the influenza epidemic was at its peak the entire hospital overflowed with cases."

"Everyone at Hickory Hill had it." Jere placed his arm over Lucy's shoulders. "So did Jinny and her husband. Lucy brought them to Hickory Hill. Lucy here nursed us all, and the servants and some of the neighbors, too, until the grippe dropped her in her steps."

"You did the same." The woman wasn't about to be put on a pedestal.

The fondness in Grandpa Jere's eyes as he looked down at his wife tugged sweetly at Glorie's heart. *All couples should love this deeply and this long,* she thought.

Tears sparkled on Grace's long lashes. Glorie wondered whether she was hoping that she and Daniel had such a long and lovely life ahead together as the couple standing before them.

Jere shook his head. "I don't know why a couple of old codgers like us made it through."

"This strain acts strangely," Glorie admitted. "The strong young men and women who usually weather the grippe with a few days discomfort—they are the very ones who are most likely to die from the Spanish flu." The strain had swept the busy army posts, killing thousands of the United States' strongest men when the world needed them most. Glorie had seen more die than she cared to remember.

"Did you lose any nurses from it?" Lucy asked.

"None of the nurses at Fort Snelling. The army's training school for aircraft mechanics has its own hospital. Three nurses died there. For some reason I never caught it, despite the fact that I often worked when I was so exhausted that I wondered if I was sleepwalking."

"They say the flu hit the boys over there hard, too." Jere's jaw tightened. "As if they didn't have enough to fight."

"It spreads so easily and rapidly," Lucy said. "I'm surprised your hospital isn't closed to visitors."

"The flu is waning," Glorie reminded her. She shivered, suddenly cold, and wished she was wearing a sweater over her uniform. "St. Paul has allowed all businesses to reopen and children are back in school. The city officials feared that the way people filled the streets in their spontaneous Armistice celebration would cause a sharp rise in the flu rates. The number of cases did increase, but not at the rates feared."

"Then we can visit the wards?" Jere asked. "I'd consider it an honor, meeting some of these men."

"I'd like to meet that special young man Grace told us about, the one who's stealing your heart, Glorie." Grandmother's face was a study in innocence.

"Gra—ace." Glorie forced the name between clenched teeth.

"What?"

Glorie forced a smile for her grandparents. "There's no special young man."

"Of course there is." Grace leaned toward Jere and Lucy and dropped her voice to a stage whisper. "The air between them positively crackles. He's a delightful man. You'll like him."

Glorie rolled her eyes.

A smile pulled up the corners of Grace's mouth. "I notice you haven't asked the name of the young man I've mistakenly identified as special, Sister."

The implication that he hadn't needed identification heated Glorie's cheeks in a telltale blush. "Don't be silly." She darted a glance at her grandparents. They didn't say a word, but their eyes danced with amusement.

Grace slipped her arm through Grandpa Jere's. "Let's visit one of the wards."

Nonchalance wasn't easy to assume when her heart raced in anticipation, Glorie discovered. It was obvious the ward Grace had in mind was Johan's.

Laughter met them in the hallway like a barrage long before they reached the ward doors. "The movie must still be showing," Glorie informed the others. "We don't have a screen, of course, so it's shown on the ceiling. It's the new Charlie Chaplin film. Charlie is a rookie soldier. He single-handedly captures the kaiser and the crown prince. I saw it earlier today in one of the other wards."

The letdown of disappointment mixed with relief for Glorie. Her spirits always lifted when she saw Johan. She'd love for him to meet her grandparents. But she and Johan were only nurse and patient. Well, perhaps a little more. After he was discharged, they'd never meet again. She hoped impulsive Grace hadn't said anything inappropriate to him, hinting a certain nurse had her cap set for him, for instance. Grace was a dear, but she didn't understand why Glorie liked to keep her life more private than Grace kept hers.

They met other Thanksgiving visitors and patients in the hallways. When the group entered another ward, they saw visitors dressed in their Sunday best seated beside many of the beds. Grace and Glorie went from one bed to another, introducing Jere and Lucy and wishing each man a happy holiday. Glorie found herself wishing they'd visited Johan's ward, after all.

Grandmother Lucy wanted to see Glorie's nursing quarters, but Grandpa Jere wanted only a chair and a cup of coffee. Grace assured him she would find him both.

Glorie and Grandmother had the quarters to themselves. The other nurses were either on duty or out on holiday. Grandmother looked about, commenting on the few personal and impersonal belongings before sitting down on the neatly made-up, narrow bed with its thin mattress. She pulled out a pearl hat pin and laid her fashionable, wide-brimmed hat down, then patted the army green blanket beside her. "Now, sit down and tell me about your life as an army nurse."

The words poured out, describing the experiences and feelings of the two-and-a-half weeks since the overseas men had arrived. "I felt cheated when I was assigned here, Grandmother. I desperately wanted to work near the front. The men there needed help most, I thought. My friend Julie is near the front. She went over with the medical corps from the University of Minnesota. She told me of her assignment when we met for dinner one evening. I was so jealous, I made up an excuse to leave early. I'm ashamed to admit it, but I did." Glorie took an envelope from her bedside drawer. "Here's her description of the first batch of wounded she saw."

She opened the letter with its familiar YMCA letterhead and read:

> The injured came in a like a flood, over six hundred in twenty-four hours. Most walked from the battlefield, if you can call it walking, the way they reeled and stumbled. They leaned on each other when necessary, using sticks, when they could find them, for canes. Gassed men came in single file, cloths bound about their streaming eyes, each man with his hand on the shoulder of the man in front, the blind truly leading the blind. The ambulances only had room for the worst cases, usually meaning men without limbs or who were in danger of losing shattered limbs. The sheer numbers with horrifying wounds took its toll on our hearts and minds. It took stern stuff to turn from the continuing stream of wounded and concentrate on helping the person in front of you. And throughout all of it, the constant sound of guns and bombs.
>
> I wish you could see these brave doughboys of ours. All shot to pieces yet telling us to help their buddies first, and all the time talking about getting back to the front.
>
> The worst, for both the medical staff and the soldiers, is knowing there are more injured boys where no one can reach them out in that awful no-man's-land between the armies.

Glorie looked up from the letter. "When I first read this, I thought how blessed she was to be stationed where she could help these men. Her work sounded so. . .noble. I wanted to be there if Fred was injured. But even though many boys I know are over there, for me the wounded she wrote about were faceless."

"And now they aren't." It wasn't a question.

"No." The word came out a whisper. "Now when I read these words I see the men in our wards struggling toward the hospital, or worse, lying helpless in no-man's-land, not knowing whether help will reach them in time. It's because some of the wounded here laid in the mud and filth so long that they've lost their legs and arms."

"It sounds like the war Jere and I were in. The weapons change, but war remains the same."

Grandmother stared out the window, but Glorie knew she saw the battlefields and hospitals of her own generation, not the bare tree branches swayed by raw November wind.

She isn't fragile, Glorie realized. *She's old but still strong.* Strength seemed to seep into

Glorie's spirit at the thought of Grandmother Lucy and Grandpa Jere and thousands of others of their generation who had experienced war's carnage and survived to live happy, useful lives. *My generation will, too.*

Grandmother turned her gaze back to Glorie and took one of her hands in both her soft ones. "One of the men you see when you read this is Johan."

"Y–yes." She stared at Grandmother Lucy, too surprised to be embarrassed. "How did you know?"

"When the War between the States separated Jere and I, and I didn't know whether he was alive or dead, I saw him in the face of every soldier I nursed."

"Today you might be scolded by your medical superiors if they heard that," Glorie teased. "We're to keep our contact with the patients impersonal. Some of the nurses manage that by joking and laughing with the men. Others are brusque and businesslike, concentrating on the treatments, as though the patients are toy soldiers to be rebuilt instead of humans with emotions as well as flesh and blood.

"When I was taking my nursing course, one of the doctors invited me to dinner. I was flattered. I chattered on about how much the profession means to me, how deeply I'm affected by suffering. He said, 'If it's so hard for you to be around the suffering, why do you want to be a nurse?' Can you believe it, Grandmother?"

"What did you answer?"

"I said, 'How could I be anything else?' "

Grandmother's arms encircled her. Glorie felt the older woman's soft cheek pressing against her own. "Yes, that is the right answer. That is the answer in every true nurse's heart."

When the embrace ended, Glorie said, "I wonder if reconstruction nursing isn't by nature more personal than other types of war nursing."

"How do you mean?"

"When the first overseas men arrived, they were almost drunk on the joy of the war ending and returning as heroes. They never spoke of their wounds as anything but a minor difficulty to be overcome. I suspected much of it was bluster. The longer the men are here, and as more and more arrive, the more I see that every patient has emotional problems, too—what are called the spiritual wounds, I guess. Especially the amputation cases. The greater the physical wound, the deeper the unseen wound. The men are terribly afraid of the changes their disabilities will cause in their lives."

"Are you able to help them?"

Glorie hesitated. Were she and the other nurses helpful? "It seems the men respond best if we neither pity them or treat them like heroes beyond the reach of ordinary men. Of course, we let them know we honor them for their courage and sacrifice."

"It sounds like a difficult balance to find. And your friend Johan, does he have these invisible wounds you speak of?"

Glorie looked down at her hands. "He has deep wounds, Grandmother. His greatest wound is bitterness. He's not angry with the Germans; he's angry that he was forced to fight against them. It's not that he thinks the Germans were right to invade France and Belgium," she hastened to clarify. "It's that so many don't understand that for him and other German-Americans, they had to chose between their countries, to make war on their own people."

Grandmother Lucy nodded slowly. "Yes, that is always a hard choice."

"I. . .I was afraid you would think he's awful for feeling that way."

"Awful?" Surprise filled the wrinkled face. "Many people felt that way during the War between the States. Jere had a terrible time choosing which side to serve on. Didn't we ever tell you how Jere's father almost disowned him when he decided to serve with the Union?"

"No. I just thought. . ." Glorie paused, revelation striking. "I'm embarrassed to say that I thought it natural he was with the Union army. I suppose it seemed like the 'right' side, since I was raised in the North."

"Jere and Grace will wonder what happened to us. There is something I want to tell you before we rejoin them."

The reluctance in her tone made Glorie draw back slightly. "What is it?"

Grandmother's fingertips gently touched a small pin on her round collar. "This."

Glorie leaned forward and studied the image of a small, old-fashioned lamp. The brooch was made of metal, polished to a soft luster. "It's lovely. It looks old. Is it an antique?"

Her question brought a soft chuckle from Lucy. "I expect you would think so. Jere gave it to me sixty years ago, on my fifteenth birthday. He made it himself, fashioning it after a lamp he'd seen in a picture of Florence Nightingale. You see, he knew of my dream to follow in her footsteps."

"How special." Glorie was aware once more how deeply her grandparents cared for each other. *What a blessing it must be to find someone you love that much, and who loves you back the same.* A painful twinge of envy twisted her heart. Would she ever experience that? Johan's face with his teasing blue eyes and wide smile flashed into her mind. She pushed the picture away. She mustn't allow herself to daydream their friendship into something it wasn't.

But the picture returned, and the longing remained.

"It's the pin I want to tell you about," Lucy went on. "Ever since you went into nursing, I've planned to pass this pin along to you."

Glorie gasped softly and pressed her palms to her chest. "To me?"

"I'd hoped you would wear it close to your heart, as I have, and pass it along to your own daughter or granddaughter one day. But now I've decided to leave the pin to Grace."

"Oh." Disappointment filled Glorie's heart.

"Grace confided in me this morning that she'd also dreamed of becoming a nurse. Then she met Daniel and gave up her dream of nursing to marry him. She's not sorry for her choice, as I'm sure you know. She is completely in love with that man, and darling Elisabeth is the light of their lives. But Grace feels useless next to you."

Surprise straightened Glorie's spine. "Useless?"

"When she sees the wounded and knows you have the skills to help them and she doesn't. . ." Lucy spread her hands, palms up.

"She fills every minute with helping others. Hasn't she told you about her Red Cross work? She visits soldiers here, reads to them, writes letters for them, does shopping for them. She spent untold hours making surgical dressings. And even remade shirts for the soldiers when the army changed the uniform regulations, which was a great sacrifice, since she hates sewing."

Lucy smiled. "Yes, she's thrown her heart into helping the soldiers. That's why I decided to give her the pin. I realized you won't be allowed to wear it when you're in uniform. Grace can wear it. I hope it will be a reminder that her efforts are as much a gift as any nurse's. From your defense of her, I know you will understand."

"I think it's a wonderful idea." Glorie gave her a quick hug.

"I want to give it to her tonight, instead of leaving it to her in my will. I want to see her face when I pin it on her." Lucy stood and replaced her hat. "I would have joined the army as a nurse in this war, if they'd allowed me to." Her eyes danced with a merry smile. "Unfortunately, the army only accepts nurses between twenty-one and forty-five, so like Grace, I joined the Red Cross and made dressings. My favorite work was recruiting nurses."

As they left the room, Lucy continued, "Did I ever tell you about the time I met Clara Barton? It was one of the most memorable days of my life. It happened in Washington, and. . ."

Chapter 4

Glorie was assigned to Johan's ward that evening. She saw him look casually toward the door when she entered. Then he did a double take, and a grin brightened his face. A smile leaped to her own in return, but she made herself casually stop at each man's bed until she arrived at Johan's in turn.

"You haven't had a shift on our ward for quite awhile." Johan's tone was a mixture of censure and gladness.

"I've been assigned to surgery most days. Did your parents visit today?"

"Yes. Better than last time."

She understood that he meant no one had said anything unkind in their presence, and she was glad for all concerned that it was so.

Three beds later, she discovered she was humming. Even a short encounter with Johan left her happy.

At the ward desk she filled out paperwork, then made a final check of the ward toward the end of her shift.

Johan, dressed in his uniform, showed up at the desk minutes later. "I can't sleep. Will you walk with me when you're off duty?"

Shocked at his boldness, she could only stare at him.

"It's not against the rules for an officer to ask a nurse to walk with him," he reminded her.

Like Johan, Glorie and most of the nurses were lieutenants, though most patients called them "Nurse" or "Sister." Glorie liked it that way. The men treated the nurses with respect whether they called them by the proper army titles or not. She couldn't quite imagine a patient saluting every time a nurse passed his bed.

"It's not against the rules," she agreed, "but fraternization between patients and nurses is discouraged."

His grin blazed. "Did the bachelor doctors make up that rule?" He leaned against the desk. "I won't be a patient long. I'm only asking you to keep me company on a platonic walk around the hospital halls."

In the end she agreed. She'd wanted to all along.

They chatted in low voices as they wandered the dimly lit, empty halls. He told her of his parents' visit, and she told him about Jere and Lucy.

"They sound interesting. I wish I'd met them."

She was glad he didn't know of Grace's attempt to arrange that or Grace's comments on Glorie's feelings for him.

At the end of one hall, they stopped beside a tall window overlooking a wide, tree-lined green. The moon shone brightly down, casting tree shadows across the manicured lawn. "I wonder if we'll have snow for Christmas," Johan mused. "I like a white Christmas. Do you?"

"Yes. I love snow." She leaned her forehead against the cool glass. "My brother, Fred, used to pummel Grace and me with snowballs. We'd fight back, but our aim wasn't as accurate as his."

"This is the first time I've heard about a brother. How old is he?"

"He's. . .I don't know." Glorie closed her arms tight over her chest, trying to keep back the pain gripping her.

"You don't know? What kind of sister doesn't know her brother's age?" Johan teased. He traced a frosty outline on the windowpane with his index finger.

Glorie had to swallow twice before she could explain. "Fred's birthday is November sixteen. He's twenty-one now, if he's alive."

"If. . ." Johan swung to face her.

"He. . ." She swallowed again. "He was declared missing after the last offensive." She shut her eyes tight in a vain attempt to keep back the threatening tears.

Then Johan's arms were around her, and her cheek pressed against the wool of his coat. "Oh, my dear, I'm so sorry," he whispered into her hair.

Her heart cracked open, and the tears spilled. She clung to him, sobbing. "I've tried so hard to believe he's all right, but I'm so horribly afraid."

"Of course you are. Anyone would be." One arm held her close about the waist, while a hand cradled the back of her head. She felt a kiss pressed against her hair, just above her ear. "Cry it out, Dear. It's all right."

His spoken invitation wasn't necessary. She was bawling uncontrollably, the sobs racking her body.

When they subsided to a small shower and she'd used up both their handkerchiefs, part of her was appalled at her behavior. She always did her crying alone. She never broke down like this in front of others. Yet it hadn't felt strange or embarrassing. It felt. . .comfortable. It was too much to understand how sharing her grief with him could feel that way. She set it aside to examine later.

He led her to a flight of marble steps. She didn't resist the arms he kept about her, drawing her close when they sat down. The crying had drained her of energy. Exhausted, she laid her head against his shoulder. He rested his cheek against her hair. It felt so peaceful, so right, together with him this way. She wasn't sure how long they sat like that—not speaking, not spooning, just being together. She had the sense he was praying for her.

"Fred was with your division," she said finally, breaking the silence. "He was. . .is one of the Gopher Gunners with the 151st artillery, the Rainbow Division."

"I don't remember a Fred Cunningham. Of course, there are a lot of men in our division. We might know each other by face."

"I keep telling myself 'missing in action' doesn't mean dead. I know it might mean that, but it could mean other things, couldn't it?"

"Of course."

Had he hesitated before answering? She didn't want to believe it. "He could be a prisoner, couldn't he?"

She felt him nod, his cheek mussing her hair.

"Or wounded. Maybe he's unconscious and the people at the hospital don't know who he is. That's possible, isn't it?"

"Yes, Dear."

Glorie pressed her cheek harder against his shoulder and rested her hand on his chest.

"Sometimes I don't think I can hope anymore. Other times, I don't know how to go on if I don't hope."

"Did Fred ever write you about the rainbows?"

"I know the Gopher Gunners are part of the Rainbow Division."

"Because of the division's name, we gave special meaning to nature's rainbows. We all knew the biblical story of the rainbow, how God gave it as a promise after the great flood. 'And the bow shall be in the cloud; and I will look upon it, that I may remember the everlasting covenant between God and every living creature of all flesh that is upon the earth.' When we'd see rainbows, we'd take them as a message of hope. They showed up at some pretty strategic times.

"The first was in June, when we left Baccarat and headed for Champagne and our first battle. The next was July 15, when the regiment started attacking north of Chateau-Theirry. Then September 12, when the division went over the top at the start of the Saint-Mihiel drive. We won the battles and the war."

The names were important names in the war. Like most Americans, she'd followed the troops' movements through newspaper reports. It seemed the Rainbow Division fought in all the major battles after its arrival in France.

This man beside her, with his arms around her and his uniform beneath her cheek, had been in those battles, which would be listed in history books for generations, perhaps for centuries. He'd returned injured, but he'd returned, and was almost restored to health now. If he could come through it all, couldn't Fred, even if he was missing in action?

If it's not already too late. The words hissed through her mind.

Reluctantly, Glorie pushed herself away from Johan. "I should go back to the quarters. If it weren't a holiday and so many nurses away on leave, I'd probably be in trouble. It's way past lights-out."

He walked with her down the steps and to the outside door. There his arms encircled her once more, and she leaned against him trustingly, not wanting to leave. His lips touched her temple in a soft, warm kiss. Then his fingers were beneath her chin, lifting it gently. His gaze searched hers with a question. She shyly smiled her answer.

His lips were gentle against hers. Glorie closed her eyes, welcoming the beauty in the lingering kiss. She wanted to stay in this place forever, this place of tranquillity and hope.

"When you think of Fred, remember the rainbows," Johan whispered as she stepped into the night.

◆　◆　◆

St. Paul citizens spent Thanksgiving rejoicing over the war's end. Victory Sings across the country celebrated "thanksgiving for the triumph of right, birth of universal freedom, and dawn of a new day." St. Paul's Victory Sing brought together almost five thousand people. Some ambulatory patients received passes to attend the sing with relatives or Red Cross volunteers.

Glorie heard about the celebration from Grace. "The people sang their hearts out, Glorie. 'America,' 'Battle Hymn of the Republic,' 'America, the Beautiful,' 'Star Spangled Banner,' and a host of our generation's songs, like 'Keep the Home-Fires Burning' and 'Pack Up Your Troubles.' The reverend from St. Mark's spoke. He said—let me think a moment, I want to get this right—okay, he said, '1776 marked the birth of the nation. 1861 marked the reconstruction of the nation. 1917 marked the birth of the nation's soul.' Isn't that beautiful?"

Glorie did think it beautiful.

So was Grandmother Lucy's lamp brooch which Grace now wore. Glorie commented on it, and Grace told her how much she loved it. "I almost forgot," she added, "Grandmother sent this box for you, Glorie."

Glorie took the box back to her quarters to open it. It was a cedar box, hand carved. Inside were old letters and a journal. A note from Grandmother said they were letters Jere had written her during the War between the States and the journal in which she'd written letters to God. "I thought you might enjoy reading them," Grandmother wrote. "If you wish to share them with Johan, you have our permission to do so."

It was tempting to share the news of Johan's kiss with Grace. She and Glorie seldom kept secrets from each other. But Glorie wasn't ready to share this one yet. She wanted to savor the memory of it, the sweetness of it.

Glorie was glad she was assigned to surgery Friday and Saturday. She longed to see Johan, but she didn't know how she'd hide her fondness for him from other patients if she was working in his ward. It was a lesson in discipline, keeping her focus on the surgeries.

Saturday afternoon, she and the rest of the surgical team came out exhausted from a grueling eight-hour operation. A nurse met them with grim news. Five patients had come down with the flu that morning. Already fifteen were suffering from it. All were removed to the contagious-diseases building.

The staff exchanged weary glances. Fear bubbled up in Glorie's chest like chemicals in a test tube, hot and sudden and overflowing. No one said the removal had come too late. But everyone knew it.

By Monday, St. Paul and Fort Snelling were caught up in another wave of the deadly Spanish flu.

Chapter 5

The building set aside for contagious diseases was overflowing within the week. Wards in the regular hospital buildings were set aside for flu cases also. Those who worked with the flu cases weren't allowed to work in the other wards.

The hospital, according to plan, had spread since it opened in September until it encompassed the entire fort. Now the fort was quarantined.

Still the flu spread.

Surgery cases were postponed, except in the most serious gangrene cases. The strictest care was taken to avoid exposing those who had recently had surgery. Precautions were also taken to keep gassed patients apart. As the flu spread, it became more difficult to protect these patients.

Every time Glorie approached Johan's ward, the fear she struggled to keep under control threatened to overwhelm her. She'd studied a lot about the gas used in war since the overseas men started arriving. It was believed that mustard gas didn't harm the lungs, as did chlorine and some other gasses that were common in the early years of the war. Already it was known that soldiers attacked with these gasses often had lingering asthma, and bronchial and heart problems.

She never thought she'd be grateful for anything related to Johan's experience with mustard gas, but now she was grateful the gas wasn't considered more harmful. Still, the knowledge of gasses' long-term effect was in its infancy. If he caught the flu, could his lungs fight off the resulting pneumonia that killed so many of its victims?

Ten days into the second influenza wave, Glorie stood outside Johan's ward gathering her courage. Her hand on the door, she sent a prayer heavenward. She straightened her shoulders, took a deep breath, forced her lips into a smile, and entered the ward.

She avoided eye contact with Johan while exchanging comments with other soldiers as she walked between the two rows of beds. She made a point to talk to a couple of soldiers who she knew were in a depressive state.

Johan, like most of the ambulatory soldiers, was in uniform during the day. When she reached his bed, he was seated with his back against the headboard's white metal bars, his sketch pad on his knees.

"May I see what you're sketching, Officer?" Glorie hoped her tone was appropriately light and impersonal. She always tried to act professional when in the ward with Johan. It was a difficult task, with the comfort of his arms and tenderness of his kiss filling her memory. She'd had a lot of practice hiding her attraction to him. Since the surgery ward was basically shut down, she'd been reassigned to Johan's ward.

Now he gave her a grin that was anything but impersonal and allowed her to see the page. He'd sketched her plumping the pillow of the patient across from him.

"I'll never understand how you capture a person or a scene in only a few quick strokes," she complimented.

"Have you seen his caricatures?" Joe slid off the neighboring bed to stand beside her. "I like them best." He glanced down at the sketch of Glorie and the patient. "Hey, that *is* good."

Johan jerked a thumb in Joe's direction. "The resident art critic."

"At least I give you good reviews."

Glorie liked Joe's constant easygoing nature. "I agree with your opinions, Joe, but I haven't seen the caricatures."

"Show her the ones of President Wilson and Kaiser Bill," Joe urged.

Glorie raised her eyebrows in surprise. "There's a likely combination."

"Didn't you hear that Wilson's going to Paris to join the peace-treaty talks?" Joe asked.

The pages of the sketchbook rustled as Johan flipped through them. A moment later, he handed the pad to her. She burst into laughter. Joe was right. Johan had captured both the famous and the infamous with the expertise of a professional political cartoonist.

"Nurse Cunningham."

"Yes?" Glorie spun around to see which patient was calling for her. "Oh!" Her ankle twisted beneath her. She reached for the bed to steady herself. The sketch pad fell to the floor.

Joe grabbed her arm. "Are you all right, Nurse? Guess I shouldn't have left my shoes where someone could trip over them."

"I'll say," Johan growled. Glorie felt his hand at her back. "Did you hurt your ankle?"

"No, I'm fine." The ankle did hurt, but only a smidgen. All the attention embarrassed her. She knelt to pick up the sketch pad. It was lying open, upside down. Some of the pages were bent. "I hope I didn't ruin any of your drawings, Officer."

She smoothed back one of the pages. "Uuuh." The picture drew her breath from her like a vacuum. Her stomach felt as though she'd been kicked by a horse.

Johan grabbed it from her and snapped the pad shut.

Her gaze darted to his. Her breath came quick and hard.

He stared back at her, his eyes black. "A patient is asking for you, Nurse."

Glorie rubbed the palms of her hands down the sides of her skirt and tried to calm her runaway heartbeat before turning to find out which patient had called to her. The nurse-smile that was as much a part of her now as her uniform slid into place.

The soldier didn't need her nursing skills. His blankets were tangled around his feet, and with one arm it was difficult to release them. Most of the other patients in the room could have helped him. Glorie suspected he only wanted the attention of a woman. She chatted with him about homey things while straightening the bedding.

When she was done, she moved to the center of the ward. "May I have your attention, men?"

It took only a couple moments for everyone to stop what they were doing and look her way.

Glorie caught her hands behind her and gave them her most radiant smile, looking at any of them but at Johan. "I stopped in to let you all know that I've been reassigned again."

A groan went up in one large wave.

Gratitude toward them for appreciating the service she'd given them surged through her. "I'll be working in the flu wards, so I won't be able to visit you for awhile."

"Ah, no!"

"Don't go there!"

"Tell them we won't allow it."

"Now *there's* a reason to get the flu."

She held up her hands in laughing protest. "I've enjoyed working with you all. When I'm free to visit again, I'll stop back to this ward and say hello to any of you who aren't discharged."

She left the room without looking back.

She'd only gone a few feet down the hall when she heard the ward door bang open and steps falling hard on the marble floor behind her. A strong hand grabbed her shoulder. "Glorie, wait, please."

Immediately she stopped and looked up at Johan. "I'm sorry. I didn't mean to do it. The sketch. I didn't mean to invade your privacy." There was so much more she wanted to say. Her chest hadn't stopped aching since she'd seen the picture. It was only a moment, but she was sure the scene depicted was etched in her mind for eternity—the battlefield as only those who had been there had seen it. The horror of what he'd seen, what he had lived among, had leaped from the page.

He started to pull her close. A nurse passing by shot them a sharp and disapproving glance.

Johan took Glorie's arm and ushered her around a corner where they could be alone. He dropped back against the wall and pressed the palms of his hands over his eyes. "You weren't meant to see that. No one was." His voice was gruff, almost as coarse-sounding as it had been when she'd met him. "I thought if I put it on paper, maybe. . .maybe I could get it out of my head. Out of my nightmares."

She slid her arms around his waist, pressed her cheek against the rough wool military jacket covering his chest, and hugged him as hard as she could. She didn't say anything. What could she possibly say to take away the images he lived with? She only tried to surround him with her love and prayed silently for his healing.

He dropped his hands from his eyes and wrapped his arms around her so tightly, she wondered if it was possible she might break. She felt a tear against her hair and squeezed her eyes shut to keep back her own tears.

Glorie didn't know how long they stood that way. She wasn't about to move if he needed to draw strength from her. Even if the head medical officer for the entire fort walked by, she wouldn't budge.

After a long while, Johan's arms loosened. He sighed, ruffling her hair. "You always smell like spring flowers. Much better than the antiseptic hospital odors or mess-hall food."

"Anything would smell good next to them." She forced a lilt to her voice, though her emotions were still gripped by the pain he'd allowed her to share.

His chuckle released some of the tension. A wide fingertip slid along her chin line, sending a shiver through her. Barely touching her skin, the fingertip continued its path to her eyebrow, across her cheekbone, and on to the edge of her lip. She closed her eyes, relishing his touch.

His kisses traced the path he'd blazed, his lips as light as gentle raindrops against her skin. They left her breathless. When his kisses reached her lips, they lingered there, long and sweet. They felt like a promise.

When his lips left hers, they moved again to her hair. She sighed with contentment and tucked her cheek against his shoulder.

"Do you have to take the assignment to the flu wards?"

The question jolted her back to the reality of their world. She nodded, the wool scratching against her cheek.

"You'd say so even if it weren't true. You're like one of Uncle Sam's doughboys. When duty calls, you answer, and give 110 percent."

"I won't be able to see you until the epidemic is over."

Neither spoke for a few minutes. Glorie wouldn't allow her thoughts to dwell on what might happen. Instead, she memorized the feeling of shelter in Johan's arms and the strength of his chest rising and falling beneath her cheek, so that she could keep them with her while the flu war separated them.

Johan cleared his throat. "I started reading your grandmother's journal from the Civil War last night. It's fascinating. War and people don't change much, I guess. When I first reached the front in France, I wished someone waited for me back home, a special girl, like you." His embrace tightened slightly in a squeeze. "Later I was glad there wasn't a girl to mourn if I didn't make it back. Then I came home and a miracle happened. I met you. Now we're in the same hospital, and we'll be as far apart as Lucy and Jere during the Civil War."

"God brought them through it and they found each other again." Was she assuming too much, saying that? Surely not, when he'd just told her she was special to him.

"I'll be praying for you, Glorie. Remember the rainbows."

His arms tightened around her waist. "Don't let it get you." His voice broke on the words. "Don't let that flu bug take you from me."

◆ ◆ ◆

Johan's chest felt like a shell hole when he returned to the ward half an hour later. The thought of Glorie heading into a ward filled with Spanish flu patients terrified him. His mind flashed a picture of her in a doughboy's tin hat, going over the top with a thermometer in her hand instead of a gun.

Was this what it was like for the women and families who waited at home for the soldiers who went to war? And he'd thought the soldiers were the ones who had it tough.

He flopped onto his bed, setting the springs creaking. Snoring came from close by. Joe was taking a nap.

Johan rolled onto his back, picked up his sketch pad, and started paging idly through it. He paused at a picture of Elisabeth asleep in Grace's arms. It was one of his favorites. He was crazy about Glorie. If they ever married, would their children look like Elisabeth?

That wasn't a safe path to follow right now.

He flipped through a few more pages. A flash of red, reminiscent of gory battlefields, stopped him. His heart skipped a beat. *It can't be.*

The familiar sweet yet metallic scent told him it was blood. It had only been applied to one page, the caricature of Kaiser Bill. "Hun Lover" was written across the kaiser's face in an American soldier's blood.

Johan's gaze darted about the room, searching for the perpetrator. Some men slept;

some visited together; some read; three were playing cards.

Only one man paid Johan any attention. Captain Smith's dark gaze met Johan's without wavering, without smiling, without smirking. *There's nothing in his eyes but hate,* Johan thought. He was certain Smith was the guilty party. He couldn't have pulled it off without at least a couple of other men seeing him do it, but Johan doubted anyone would go against the captain to tell about it, except maybe Joe, but Joe was asleep.

Johan made his shoulders relax. He ripped out the offensive page, balled it up, and tossed it into the wastebasket beside his bed. The blood had soaked through a number of pages. One by one he removed them, the sound tearing through the deceptive quiet.

Chapter 6

The second wave of influenza was like reliving a nightmare.

The wards overflowed with sick soldiers. Most recovered after three to five days. Some died within forty- eight hours of the first symptoms. The healthiest-appearing men often were the ones who didn't make it.

Usually the onset was sudden. A headache, a general sense of not feeling well, then chills or fever. Within a few hours the temperature shot to 101 degrees or higher. Fevers lasted three to five days. A cough developed, short and dry, lasting a week or two beyond the flu itself, if the person was fortunate. Back and leg muscles and joints ached, causing the patients the most distress of any of the symptoms. Eyes watered and swelled. A few patients experienced nausea and vomiting.

The medical staff had little to offer the patients, other than to attempt to keep them comfortable. Isolating them was necessary in an effort to contain the disease as much as possible. Quinine and aspirin powders reduced some of the symptoms but didn't cure anything. Keeping the patients hydrated with water and juices and nourished with any food the patients could be convinced to eat was important.

Everything the patients touched needed disinfecting: blankets, handkerchiefs, bedclothes, eating utensils. The staff couldn't keep up with the demand.

During the first wave of influenza in October, enlisted men stationed at the fort while waiting to be called overseas were drawn into service at the hospital to help nurse the ill. Now there were no enlisted men to call upon. The overseas men at the hospital for reconstruction and convalescence were in no shape to help with flu victims. The dozen doctors and 120 nurses had only themselves and the Almighty to rely upon. And when the doctors and nurses began falling ill, the pressure increased. Neither nurses nor doctors were available from other hospitals, or even from training schools. Everywhere the need exceeded the supply, not only at Fort Snelling.

Red Cross volunteers helped out, as they did everywhere in every emergency. Even though most hadn't any medical knowledge, they could perform many of the necessary mundane procedures. Until they too fell ill and became patients.

Glorie was glad she didn't see Grace among the Red Cross volunteers. She didn't want Grace bringing the disease home to her husband and Elisabeth, or to their parents, or Grandmother Lucy and Grandpa Jere.

Even in the midst of the flu battle, Glorie always had an awareness of Johan. He wasn't foremost in her thoughts, but the knowledge of his caring was like a soothing background melody. When she allowed herself a moment to dwell on him, it was with a prayer that he be saved from the flu.

Time sheets and schedules were forgotten. Everyone worked until they were too fatigued to move and then worked awhile longer. Glorie and other nurses bandaged their ankles to help them keep going when they'd been on their feet too long. She became adept at recognizing staff members behind their gauze masks.

It wasn't the flu that killed, but the pneumonia that often followed the flu. When the patient appeared to be recovering, he was in the most danger. Glorie came to dread the cheerful patient with a heliotrope coloring to his skin. The combination was a sure sign that the patient wouldn't be alive in twenty-four to forty-eight hours.

The wards were never silent, even in the middle of the night. Even when nurses and volunteers weren't hurrying in and out, or urging patients to drink more fluids or take their medicine, or changing bedding, or bathing patients, the flu's dry cough was constant.

It was only two days before Christmas when Glorie walked into a flu ward, stopped short, and rubbed a hand across her eyes. Surely she wasn't seeing right; it was only fatigue causing the illusion that a masked Johan bent over one of the beds, sponging off a patient's face.

He wasn't an illusion.

Nausea threatened to overwhelm her. She fought it down. She'd faced so many fears the last few months, but seeing Johan in the midst of the flu victims. . .

She rushed to him, dodging a Red Cross girl whose arms were piled with clean towels.

Glorie reached to lay a hand on Johan's arm but hesitated at the sight of the patient in his care. "Captain Smith."

Johan turned. The blue eyes above his mask were heavy with fatigue.

"How long has he been ill?"

"A few hours. Complained of the headache about 0900, according to the guy in the bed next to him. He's running a fever already. He's sleeping now."

"That's probably the best thing for him."

"Joe's ill, too. I brought him down here an hour ago."

"Oh, no. Johan, we need to talk. Come out in the hall, will you?"

They walked quite far down the hall, searching for privacy. Glorie launched into her attack before they stopped walking. "Why didn't you let the staff bring him down here, Johan? It's dangerous for you to be in this ward." She hated the way fear slid her voice up the scale.

"Joe has been sleeping in the bed next to mine since Armistice." His voice was low and soft. To Glorie it sounded as though he was trying to quiet a hysterical child. It only added to her upset.

"But here everyone has the flu. Everyone except the staff, and I'm not so sure about some of them."

"The flu's everywhere, Glorie. Everyone knows we're short on nurses here now with so many down sick. I've more strength than most people in this hospital. I can't just sit up there on my bed and try to protect myself when I can do something, anything, to help."

She stamped her foot in frustration. "Don't you understand? The gas may have weakened your lungs. You mustn't take the chance of getting ill. If you develop pneumonia, you could die."

"I'm not going to—"

She covered her face with her hands. "I couldn't bear it if anything happened to you. . . ."

His hands were warm and strong on her shoulders. "Nothing's going to happen to me. I caught the flu when I was in France, before I was gassed."

Glorie lowered her hands as far as her chin. "Are you telling the truth or just trying to comfort me?"

He grinned. "Both."

"This is no laughing matter, Lieutenant."

His chuckle filled the hall.

It infuriated her. "Why are you laughing?"

His arms encircled her waist. "Are you always going to call me Lieutenant when you're angry with me, using that upset-mother tone of voice?"

She pressed her palms to his chest and shoved him away. "Why won't you be sensible? You shouldn't be holding me. I've been exposed. And I'm not so sure catching the flu once means you won't get it again."

"Glorie. . ."

"Oh, do go back to your bed." Frustrated, she started back to the ward. Her view of a Red Cross girl heading toward her carrying a pitcher grew hazy, cleared, and grew hazy again. *I must get some sleep soon,* Glorie thought.

She bumped into a table filled with glasses, then grasped it to steady herself.

From a great distance she heard Johan call her name, deep and slow like a Victrola record running down. Her knees seemed to dissolve. She heard something crash. Then she was falling into a deep, soft, foggy sea.

Chapter 7

A white curtain separated the cots of ill nurses from the ill soldiers. A dozen of the 120 nurses at the fort had developed the disease.

Johan refused to leave Glorie's side, except when modesty demanded, despite urging by doctors and nurses to rest. The second time the doctor checked on her, Johan made a quick trip to the ward where Joe and Captain Smith were located. Both still fought fevers. The captain ignored Johan when he stopped.

"Guess he'll never forgive you for being born German-American." Joe paused, then continued in an uncertain tone. "So, have you forgiven him? Couldn't believe you helped him down here."

Hands in his trouser pockets, Johan looked over at the captain's bed. "I've had a lot of time to think about the war. None of us were raised to kill. People think the hard thing about going to war is risking your life. They forget our country asks us to put aside everything we've been taught and take lives. It's easier to kill if you can hate the people you're fighting." He shrugged, self-conscious at opening up this way. "I expect that's what's happened to the captain. A person is an enemy or an ally, no gray lines. Easier that way."

Johan tried not to act rushed while talking with Joe, but as soon as possible he hurried back to Glorie, stopping at his ward to pick up his Bible and the cedar box with Jere and Lucy's letters that Glorie had lent him. The twenty minutes since he'd last seen her seemed like a lifetime. There was no change in her condition.

He sat beside Glorie's bed, praying for her, loving her, trying to will strength and health back into her body. Her collapse had sent fear spiraling through him, fear as strong as anything he'd experienced on the battlefields. Twelve hours passed before she slipped bleary-eyed into consciousness. She struggled to get out of bed, grabbing her hip, which he knew ached like those of all the flu victims. "I can't lie here. The men need me."

Johan pushed her gently back onto the mattress. "You can help them best by getting your strength back."

"But there aren't enough nurses."

"Take care of yourself, then you can take care of them."

The head nurse repeated his words a few minutes later, invoking her rights as a superior officer to turn the suggestion into a command.

Johan tried to temper the joy that flooded him at Glorie's awakening. He knew it was only the beginning of her fight.

He bathed her face with a cool, damp cloth.

"That feels good. Have I scolded you yet for staying with me?"

Her question surprised a short laugh from him. "Not yet."

"I must be even sicker than I feel. You shouldn't be here."

"You're too weak to chase me away. I'm staying."

"I suppose it's too late anyway. If you weren't sufficiently exposed to the virus before, you are now. If you get sick, Johan Baker, I'm going to be awfully mad at you."

"I'll take my chances, Beautiful."

She groaned and pushed back her hair. "I know what patients look like when they feel like this. It should be against hospital rules to let you see me when I'm ill."

Johan laughed softly, glad she had enough energy to make the feeble joke. He lifted one of her hands and touched his lips to it. "Your face is beautiful to me, but even if it weren't, it wouldn't matter. It's your beautiful heart I love."

Her feverish eyes searched his. "Love?"

He nodded.

She sighed and closed her eyes. "What a nice word." Tucking his hand against her fever-heated cheek, she fell back asleep.

It didn't matter that he grew uncomfortable sitting on the hard oak chair with his hand in hers. He wouldn't remove his hand if a bomb struck. He shifted the rest of his body as best he could time and again the next couple hours, while reading more of Jere's letters to Lucy and Lucy's letters to God one-handed.

It wasn't until morning that Johan thought to call Grace. Lucy answered the telephone. She thanked him for letting the family know about Glorie, assured him that someone would visit if allowed into the wards, and asked him to tell Glorie they were praying for her.

By noon Glorie was coughing up blood.

The tired-looking doctor stepped out from behind the curtain around her bed where he'd been examining her and spoke to the impatiently waiting Johan. His gaze focused over Johan's shoulder instead of meeting Johan's own gaze. "Pneumonia's setting in."

The fever built. Glorie drifted in and out of consciousness, sometimes hallucinating, sometimes moaning in a manner that tore at Johan's heart. Her medicine was changed to quinine. Terror at the evidence of the flu's power twisted his insides into painful knots. Johan found it difficult to concentrate on the letters, journal, or Bible.

He bathed her face repeatedly. It seemed to soothe her, and that soothed the aching around his heart a little. He combed her hair, though she remained unconscious of her surroundings, simply because he knew she disliked looking unkempt.

He almost prayed himself out. It was difficult to avoid the temptation to try to make a deal with God, even though he'd seen on the battlefields that such deals seldom appeared to work. He wouldn't let himself think what life would be like if she didn't make it.

Hours later, strains of "Silent Night" filtered through the patients' moaning and coughing and the clatter of dishes from dinner served in bed. The music startled Johan. Carolers were singing in the hallway. *It's Christmas Eve,* he remembered. A night for miracles. Would there be any miracles in the hospital tonight?

"Lieutenant Baker?"

"Yes?" Johan rose politely and held out his hand to the tall, slender old man standing with his hat in his hand at the end of the bed.

The older man's grip was firm. "I'm Jere Cunningham, Glorie's grandfather."

"Glorie will be glad to see you. I wasn't sure family would be allowed in. But, maybe it isn't safe for you to be here."

"I've had the flu. Besides, it was important to me to see Glorie tonight." His gaze rested on Glorie's face.

"She's sleeping right now." Johan was thankful she wasn't tossing and turning. He knew it would hurt her grandfather more to see her in that state.

Jere removed something from his pocket and held out his hand, palm up, toward Johan. "Why, that's the pin your wife gave Grace, isn't it?"

Jere nodded. "Grace died this afternoon."

Shock muted Johan.

"Her husband, Daniel, died a few hours earlier," Jere continued, "right after we received the news that Fred, Glorie's brother, is alive. I guess the good Lord gave us the gift of that news to strengthen us for what came next."

"We didn't even know they were sick." His senses reeled. Bubbly, compassionate Grace, gone. *How will I ever tell Glorie?*

"When Grace fell ill, she made us promise not to tell Glorie. Grace didn't want her sister to leave the men here when her nursing skills were so needed."

"Elisabeth?"

"The flu didn't strike her hard. She's already getting past it. Getting past the other will be the fight." Jere sighed deeply. "Almost losing our grandson in the war, losing Grace. . .I had to come see Glorie. Not to hit her with the hard news, just to sit with her awhile and pray for her."

Johan understood that to the depth of his bones. He indicated the straight-backed oak chair that had been his home the last two days. "Won't you sit here, Sir?"

Johan retreated a few feet away to give Jere privacy. He watched the older man take Glorie's hand and knew he was talking to her heart-to-heart, though not out loud.

He wanted to tell Jere he'd learned so much from his letters, written during a different war. He recalled what Jere wrote near the beginning of that war, when he joined the Union army. *"I can't support the South, but neither will I fight against the South. I told the officer in charge, 'I am strong and can obey orders. I can be a litter bearer and help bind up wounds. But my beliefs will not allow me to bear arms.' "*

Johan had learned about that war in school, but he hadn't understood it was about people choosing sides against their own families and friends. He hadn't realized that other people had faced the kinds of choices German-Americans had in the Great War. Now he knew it wasn't about choosing who you'll be against; it was knowing what you are for, as Glorie had reminded him. Glorie, Grace, Lucy, and Jere all chose to be for healing, even in the middle of war.

I choose healing, too, Johan thought.

Healing of a different sort. President Wilson had a plan for a new kind of world with an organization to help nations choose to live in peace instead of war: the League of Nations. It seemed to Johan something the King of Peace would like. *That's what I want to do, help the world live in peace.* He'd try going into politics. Maybe be an ambassador one day or, better yet, part of that League if it became a reality. Wherever he ended up, he wanted Glorie beside him.

Jere left before Glorie awoke.

Johan was sitting beside the bed, turning the lamp pin over and over in his hand, when dawn's first light filtered through the windows and Glorie opened her eyes. Joy leaped in Johan's chest when he saw that her gaze was clear and true, without the haze of fever. "You had company," Johan greeted her return to the waking world. "Family. You have good news. Fred is alive."

Even the fever couldn't keep the joy light from her eyes. "What happened to him? Is he home?"

"He's staying in Europe with the occupation troops for now. He was injured in the last battle and found unconscious. Who knows why the news didn't get back to your family. He's fine now."

"What a wonderful Christmas present."

"Yes." He waited until a round of coughing passed. "Grace wanted you to have this." He placed the pin in her hand.

"Why, it's the pin Grandmother Lucy gave her."

"Yes. Florence Nightingale's lamp. A symbol of healing."

"How nice of her to lend it to me." Another round of coughing racked her.

Johan cradled her hand, kissed her palm beside the pin, and said yet another silent prayer. When she was stronger, he'd tell her about Grace and Daniel. "Will you marry me, Glorie? As soon as you're well?"

"Yes, oh yes, my love." The glow in her eyes lit his heart. "But, would you mind very much if we wait until Fred is home? I want all my family at our wedding."

"Of course we'll wait for Fred."

Glorie yawned and blinked. "I suppose it's awfully poor etiquette for a girl to fall asleep when she's just received a marriage proposal, but I don't think I can stay. . .awake. . .any. . ." Her eyes closed. Her hand went limp in his.

Fear struggled within him. The fever seemed to have broken, but it would take awhile to recover from the pneumonia. He remembered God's rainbows and made himself concentrate on the future he hoped he and Glorie would share, man and wife, raising Elisabeth, and working together for healing in the world.

◆　◆　◆

Johan continued to pray and hold fast to his dreams of the future during the anxious days which followed. When Glorie showed definite signs of improvement, he teased, "It wasn't the fever talking when you promised to marry me, was it?"

Her lashes lowered against still-pale cheeks, then rose to reveal green eyes sparkling with love. "I thought perhaps I'd hallucinated your proposal. I couldn't ask without being immodest."

He chuckled and drew her into his embrace, rejoicing inside at the gift of this woman's love. At the sound of a nurse's voice nearby, he released Glorie reluctantly. She leaned back against the pillows, smiling in the January sunshine. "I'm so happy. It hardly seems possible the war is over, Fred is alive, and you and I found each other here."

"All answered prayers." Johan sent up another silent prayer. So far she'd accepted Grace's absence as a wise precaution in avoiding the flu. He took Glorie's fingers in his, rubbing his thumbs lightly over the back of her small hands, wishing there were a way to prevent the pain he was about to inflict. Sorrow for her burned within him. "But Grace. . ."

"What about Grace?" Her green eyes smiled in question.

"God has called Grace and Daniel home."

Glorie stared at him as if she didn't comprehend.

"It was the flu. I'm sorry." His voice cracked on the words. He gathered her into his arms.

She clung to him as he gently rocked her. After a long time she whispered, "Poor Elisabeth. I want to raise her, Johan."

"Of course we will raise her, Dear. We both love her already."

Healing tears came. Gradually Glorie's tense body relaxed against him and she slept. Johan gently lowered her to the pillows. His vision blurred. How like her to be more concerned with Elisabeth's pain than her own. The realization that Glorie's love for Elisabeth would help heal Glorie's own loss brought him peace. And he would be with her every step of the way, from the storm of heartbreak to the rainbow God had promised.

Epilogue

May 8, 1919

L ook, a rainbow!"

A collective "Ooooh!" went up from the crowd waiting at the railroad station for the returning Rainbow Division. The spring shower that had made the brilliant colors bridging the sky possible was instantly forgotten.

Glorie squeezed Johan's arm and met his glowing gaze. Elisabeth was held tight in his other arm. "Uncle Fred will be home in just a few minutes, Elisabeth. Watch for the train."

"I hope your parents saw that rainbow," Johan said as he stretched to look over the heads of the crowd. Many people carried flags, making it more difficult for Johan to see. "I guess it's no surprise that we've managed to lose them. There must be forty thousand people here."

A stranger saw the wound stripes on Johan's uniform and asked to shake his hand.

A whistle blew.

"Here it comes! Here comes the train, Aunt Glorie!" Elisabeth's eyes were wide with excitement.

Glorie clung tightly to Johan's arm as the crowd jostled in anticipation.

The engine chugged into view, draped with rainbow-colored ribbons. An engineer leaned out the window waving an American flag for all he was worth. A sign stretched across one of the cars announced, "Minnesota's Gopher Gunners." The crowd let up a roar of welcome.

Everything was tumult and noise. Men in khaki almost fell from the train in their eagerness to find family and friends. A corporal threw his arms around a tiny gray-haired woman. "Ma!" An older man blinked back tears, pounding a private's shoulder and repeating, "Well done, Son, well done." Dozens of grinning doughboys shook hands with everyone they met, whether they knew them or not. A burly sergeant stopped beside a woman wearing a black crepe armband, removed his hat, and thanked her.

Tears clouded Glorie's eyes at the sight of a Red Cross girl in a broad-brimmed hat weaving through the crowd handing soldiers oranges and chocolates, which were accepted with a polite "Thank you, Miss" and stuffed into pockets while the soldiers continued looking for loved ones. Glorie touched a gloved finger to the lamp pin on the lapel of her Army Nurse Corps jacket, a strict violation of the dress code. Then she dashed her tears away. This was a day for rejoicing.

For a split second Glorie saw Fred's face on the train steps before he dropped into the sea of people. She waved her handkerchief frantically. "Fred! Fred Cunningham!"

"Fwed!" Elisabeth repeated, waving her hands in the air at no one in particular.

Their calls were lost among thousands of other calls.

"Which way?" Johan yelled in Glorie's ear. They pushed through the crowd in the direction she'd last seen Fred.

Suddenly he was there. "Sis!" His arms enveloped her, sweeping her off her feet. Their exuberant hug knocked her hat askew.

Elisabeth allowed him a brief hug, suddenly shy now that she was face-to-face with him.

Grinning, Fred held out his hand to Johan. "You must be the man who won my sister's heart." His lower jaw dropped, a shocked look on his face. "Why, it's. . .it's you!"

Mystified, Glorie looked from his face to her fiancé's. Johan's face had the same shell-shocked look as Fred's.

"You!" Johan repeated.

A moment later the men were slapping each other on the back. "I wondered what happened to you," Fred said, "but I didn't know your name so couldn't ask."

Fred turned to Glorie. "You've some man here. A group of us were surprised by a sudden shelling. Gas bombs, you could tell by the sound of them. We headed for a trench, reaching for our gas masks on the way. The area was nothing but mud. I fell, rolled a few feet, stood up, and started forward. I stepped in just the wrong place and found myself up to my knees in mud. I grabbed for my gas mask. Evidently when I fell, the mask hit something sharp, for there was a hole in it."

He jerked a thumb at Johan. "This soldier sees what's happened, pulls off his own mask, and shoves it on me. I protested something awful, but caught in the mud like that, I couldn't get away. He yanked my mask out of my hands. I saw him stuff a handkerchief in the hole in my mask, slip the mask over his head, and take off down the trench as fast as he could away from the cloud of gas that was rolling toward us with the speed of a locomotive."

Johan shrugged, his face ruddy. "I wasn't exactly a hero."

"You are in my book," Fred declared.

Glorie's gaze met Johan's embarrassed one. "In *my* book, too," she quipped lightly. A sweet peace washed over her. War and evil weren't as strong as people thought. Love was stronger. Johan taught her that in helping Fred. The nurses who voluntarily risked their lives to help the wounded proved it, too.

Nothing was as strong as love.

If you would like to read the story of Elisabeth finding love as a nurse during World War II, please see "A Light in the Night" by Janelle Burnham Schneider in A Sentimental Journey Romance Collection—*available now.*

JOANN A. GROTE lives on the Minnesota prairie which is a setting for many of her stories. Once a full-time CPA, JoAnn now spends most of her time researching and writing. JoAnn has published historical nonfiction books for children and several novels with Barbour Publishing in the Heartsong Presents line as well as the American Adventure and Sisters in Time series for children. Several of her novellas are included in CBA bestselling anthologies by Barbour Publishing. JoAnn's love of history developed when she worked at an historical restoration in North Carolina for five years. She enjoys researching and weaving her fictional characters' lives into historical backgrounds and events. JoAnn believes that readers can receive a message of salvation and encouragement from well-crafted fiction. She captures and addresses the deeper meaning between life and faith.

Bayside Bride

by Kristin Billerbeck

Dedication

To my grandpa Arnold Bechtel,
my first knight in shining armor,
who taught me what it was to be spoiled!
And to the Highway Community and its members
for keeping me grounded
and for always pursuing God's Truth in
a place where it's often hard to find.
And finally, to Colleen Coble
for being my "adult conversation" each day
and helping me hone the writing craft.

Prologue

Josephine Mayer looked to her younger sister, afraid that her teary eyes gave the news without words. "It's done. Father has married her." Jo tossed the letter aside and hugged her sister.

Claire sniffled on her shoulder. "She stole everything we have, Jo. She took Mother's wedding gown, the family chest, and now our father."

"It's all possessions, Claire, nothing more. Father is not gone; he will return to us." Jo tried to be stoic for her sister's sake, but she understood the enormity of their father's actions. It meant nothing would ever be the same. Adulthood would come much earlier than they had planned.

Claire couldn't hold her emotions as easily. "Father will be back, but it will never be the same. Marian should have been married in Mother's gown. Instead she married in gray wool while that *creature* took the gown. It was our gown," Claire wailed. "Generations of brides, our legacy, gone. Does that woman have no heart at all?"

"I'm sure she was only doing what she thought would please Father." Josephine looked to the floor, afraid that her eyes would give away her own struggling emotions. "We just have to remember to keep it to ourselves and not let Grandma Faith know. Her health is far more important than a box with some keepsakes in it."

"The dress probably hung well above Agnes's ankles, she is so unbearably tall." Claire clicked her tongue distastefully, pulling away. "I can only hope Dad remembered the beautiful vision Mother was in that gown." Claire picked up a silver-framed photo of their mother in younger, healthier years. "I'll have this waiting just in case he's forgotten." She placed the photo on the cherry hutch near the front door. The reminder wouldn't be missed by Agnes; nothing ever was.

Josephine garnered contempt for her new stepmother, but she held her tongue for Claire's sake. Harmful words served no purpose now. "Mother would have gladly let her heirlooms go, if it made Father happy."

"Father will never be happy with *her*, Jo. How can you even think such a thing? He only married her to give me a mother while he's working on the rail. A railroad man with children needs a wife, I suppose." Claire, although only thirteen, was an astute child. Sometimes too intelligent for her own good. "I suppose it's all my fault. Father couldn't possibly love Agnes."

"Practicality often makes up for a lack of love, Claire." Jo knew better than to condescend to her little sister, but Claire needed a legal guardian. At seventeen, Jo wasn't quite old enough. The irony of her age only fueled her annoyance.

Claire stamped her foot childishly. "Father gave away Mother's only legacy because Agnes is an old maid! No dressmaker would fit her with such a fine gown of white lace without laughing hysterically. Seed pearls indeed, on a woman her age! She probably looked like a man in Mother's beautiful dress."

"Now, Claire, we mustn't be disrespectful. This is our new stepmother, whether we like it or not. Father provided for us the way he saw fit." Jo tried to be the voice of reason, though it pained her. "We shall welcome her into the house just like the day Father brought her home as the hired help." Jo squared her shoulders, determined to make the best of the situation. Their father's job as a railroad man took him away from them most of the time. He didn't have time to provide food *and* his presence. Unfortunately, he also hadn't the time to see Agnes for who she really was—a selfish, vindictive woman with her own agenda.

Jo would make the best of it, if only for Claire's sake. Jo would take the rail pass her father's job provided and pave a way for them. Their new stepmother certainly wouldn't take responsibility. Agnes would continue on as before, acting the proper mother for Father's eyes, and turning into a raving madwoman when he left. A virtual battleground awaited, unless Jo did something to change it.

Jo would find refuge with their sister Marian in California. She hated leaving Claire alone, but the quicker Jo earned her own money, the quicker Claire would be free of Agnes. Any other alternative was only temporary.

Once Claire was settled, Jo would send for the wedding chest. Certainly, their father wouldn't deny them their heritage, the last vestige of their mother. Agnes would be powerless if their father took charge.

Claire's head snapped up. "This means you're leaving, Jo, doesn't it?"

"It's the only way, Claire. I'll go west and send for you as soon as I'm able. It's time. One less daughter in the house will make things easier for Agnes. Perhaps she won't have as much to be bitter about."

"I can only hope," Claire answered.

Jo swallowed hard. They could *both* only hope.

Chapter 1

February 1929
San Francisco, California

Jo fell onto the ragged davenport. "Nothing. There's no work out there, Marian. Everyone wants me to be older, widowed, or the mother of six to qualify for work. What am I going to do? Every day I'm out here, Claire is on her own with Agnes. Maybe I should just go back on bended knee and finish school."

Marian folded the tiny cloth diapers and placed them neatly on the shelf. "Times are tough, Jo, and if I'm to believe my husband, they are only going to get worse. There are lots of men out of work, and certainly they take precedence over a single woman. Some of them are veterans of the Great War. Would you rather have families go without?"

Jo looked at her squalling nephew and cringed. "No, of course not."

"Then be thankful for what you have." Marian, although only twenty-four, seemed so much older and wiser. In Michigan, Marian had been full of energy and excitement, but here she was simply focused on her next task. Aged already with flecks of gray in her brown hair and just trying to make ends meet. Jo wondered if that's what lay in wait for her, as well—a hard life etched out in laundry and keeping house for a humble man and his baby.

Jo scanned the one-room flat she shared with Marian, Mitch, and Davy. She was thankful. She just planned things differently. She expected immediate work, to bring Claire out within a month or so, and to have a flat of her own. Instead, reality was a far cry from expectation. As it turned out, she was lucky to have a spot on this rickety davenport in her sister's one-room apartment.

"Oh, Marian, of course I'm thankful." Jo picked up Davy. The baby gurgled in delight. She snuggled her face into his sweet-smelling head, tickling him into an unrelenting giggle.

Marian smiled. "Must you do that? You'll get him too excited for his nap. Besides, you have work to find. You can't give up now; we need the money with an extra mouth to feed."

Jo grimaced in guilt. "Oh, Marian, I know, and I'm so sorry. I won't be a liability much longer. I'll find something soon, I promise. I want Claire out here and away from Agnes more than you know. Mitch works hard enough for his family; I don't want to burden you anymore."

Marian shrugged. "God's timing, Jo. Not yours. Times are tough, and Mitch doesn't mind. We like the extra set of hands for Davy, and we're not suffering any more than the next man. At least we're happy. By the way, set an extra place. Glen is coming for dinner."

"Glen?"

"He's our upstairs bachelor, a carpenter's apprentice, and he just loves to play with Davy. He lives with his sister and her husband, but they don't have children yet. Glen comes down every once in a while to give them some privacy and keep that little man busy." She smiled at Davy, and he cooed lovingly at his mother.

"And I don't suppose this has anything to do with me, your unmarried sister?" Jo prodded. She lifted the baby, and once again, Davy squealed happily.

"Glen's not in a position to marry, Jo. He makes three dollars a day as a carpenter's apprentice. He's only in step two of the four-step process. He doesn't even come home until the last streetcar passes. He's coming to spend time with Davy. That's all. If I was trying to arrange a marriage, I'd let you know first."

Suddenly Jo's eyes sparkled, and a smile flickered. *Marriage.* It hadn't occurred to her before, but perhaps that was the way out of this hopeless mess. San Francisco was a city full of wealthy bachelors from families who had made their money long ago and new entrepreneurs. The city was teeming with money. Jo just needed to find where it was hidden. *It is just as easy to fall in love with a rich man, isn't it?* She'd just find one who went to church and shared her values. It was the perfect, and probably the quickest, solution. A new resolve hidden in her heart, Jo went about setting the table with a happy whistle.

The doorbell rang promptly at six. Jo went to the door, rolling her eyes at the thought of a dinner guest. Mitch worked hard enough each day, but now he was expected to feed the neighbors, too? Her emotions wrestled themselves when she got a glimpse of the simple carpenter from upstairs. Glen Bechtel smiled, and Jo felt her world shift. The full array of his perfect white teeth shone.

Glen displayed the physique of a man who did physical labor for a living: broad shoulders, strong, long legs, and an expansive chest, tightly surrounded by a clean work shirt. His appearance was hard to ignore, especially when combined with clipped, blond Nordic locks, and a carved jawline. All in all, Jo would have to say he was the most perfect-looking specimen of a man she'd ever seen. *Too bad he is so poor*, Jo thought wistfully. Maybe it wasn't quite as easy to fall in love with a rich man. Rich men usually didn't develop the picture-perfect physique of a man who did strenuous labor. Jo chastised herself for thinking such ludicrous thoughts.

"You must be Jo," Glen said, placing a work-roughened hand in hers. "You're as pretty as your sister." His eyes went past her and rested on the baby as he walked knowingly into the flat. "But not quite as sweet as my boy, here." Glen scooped Davy up into his arms, and the child wiggled his chubby little hands in euphoria. "Davy, what has my boy been up to all day?" Glen put the baby on the floor and settled himself next to him, playing a silent game of patty-cake. "Smells great in here, Marian."

"Thanks, Glen; it's almost ready. Mitch will be home soon."

"No hurry. Davy and I have some catching up to do, don't we, Peewee?"

Jo remained at the front door, her gaze lost in the confusion of the situation. Jo had never seen a man take such an interest in a baby. *It's unnatural,* she mused. Crossing her arms and finally shutting the door, she watched the two together as Davy giggled constantly.

"Ahem," Jo abruptly coughed. While no raving beauty, she wasn't used to being ignored. And she didn't like it one bit. "Mr. Bechtel, my sister tells me you're a carpenter's apprentice."

"That's right," he answered without looking up. "I'm working up at the Linton estate on Nob Hill. Doing a little add-on and finishing work for the family."

"Estate?" Jo asked as casually as possible. "Is there a *Mrs.* Linton?" Jo caught Marian's glance at her, as though her older sister knew exactly what she was thinking. *Am I that transparent?*

"Oh, that's right, you were looking for work, weren't you?" Finally, Glen looked up from the baby and focused his gray-blue eyes on her. She forgot what she asked momentarily, and couldn't possibly think of an answer to his long-forgotten question.

"Are you still looking for work, Jo?" Glen repeated.

"Work," she felt her head nod. "Yes, I'm still looking for work."

"Why don't you take the streetcar with me tomorrow? I'll introduce you to the house-keeper, and you can see if they're in need of a new girl. They seem to go through house girls pretty regularly. The Lintons are very private folks. Can't say I ever see much of them, but their son is around quite a bit."

"Their son? Does he have a nanny? Where are his parents most of the time?"

"Their son is about twenty-five, Miss Jo." Glen laughed. "He hangs around the estate quite a bit. He's a nice chap, too, a regular joe, very interested in the building going on at the house."

Jo's ears perked. "A son. Of course, they'd have a son. About twenty-five, you say? Yes, Glen, I'd love to go to the estate tomorrow. What time should I be ready?"

"I leave about six in the morning to catch the streetcar."

"Perfect." And it was, too. Young Mr. Linton was the perfect age and had all the qualifications she required. He was rich, unattached, and about to meet his match.

Chapter 2

Six A.M. was an ugly hour. She emerged from her flat, bleary-eyed and grumpy, only to be met with the Nordic's big, expressive frown. Glen stared at his watch. "I said six."

"Close enough," she groaned.

"Not for the streetcar. Mussolini couldn't run a better system. Come on." He grasped her hand and bolted up the hilly San Francisco street, dragging her along behind him. By the time they reached the car, Jo needed to bend and catch her breath. But the crowded streetcar jolted, and Glen grabbed her to keep her from pitching off the side. He helped her into the last available seat, and they rode cattle-style up the long, arching hill. *Who would have thought all these people would be up at six in the morning?*

"Do you have a problem with mornings?" Glen asked, his burly arms crossed.

"Only that they start too early for my tastes." Jo's eyes fluttered shut. *Must he talk so much? It's far too early to be engaged in conversation.*

"I can't recommend you for any job with the Lintons if you have trouble with mornings. They'll need a good, hardworking girl, not a spoiled princess. I daresay they've had enough of them. I'm not going to put my neck on the line for you. I've worked too long for this job. If I lose my apprenticeship, I lose my future. Here," he dropped a quarter in her hand. "You can catch the next streetcar back." The streetcar lurched to a stop, and she was thrown into him. He began helping her off the car before she realized what was happening.

"No!" She climbed clumsily back up into the cab. "No, I need this job! I'm sorry, I'm sorry I was late."

His jaw was set. His steely blue eyes unwavering. "It's not your tardiness that's the problem. It's your attitude. You've never worked a day in your life, have you?"

Jo thought back to all the chores Agnes forced on her after school. The soaps that dried out her hands, the iron that often burned her, and worst of all, the constant darning of the endless mountain of socks. *It had to be cheaper to buy more socks!* She knew what it was to work.

Jo put her hand on Glen's. His rough hand flinched under her touch, and she felt something she didn't care to examine further. A connection with the hard-hearted carpenter she felt to her very soul. She caught her breath, remembering her situation. "I'll work, Glen. I promise I won't let you down. I'll be on time, and I'll work harder than any girl they've ever had. Just please give me the chance to prove myself."

He stared again. With an icy look from his blue eyes, he warned, "I've only got one shot to be a carpenter. There are four stages, and I'm only in stage two. If I ruin my apprenticeship, I can kiss my trade good-bye. A man without a trade is destined to failure as times get tougher."

"I'm a hard worker, Glen. Grandmother Faith always commented on that. When my mother was ill, I took over many of the chores." Jo swallowed hard. "Even more of them when my stepmother came to live with us."

"Frankly, you haven't shown me you know how to work, Miss Mayer. Your sister Marian knows how to work, so I'm assuming you've seen it put into action at some point. But so far,

I've only seen the spoiled princess in action." His eyes continued to assess her, and she unconsciously crossed her arms in front of her.

She couldn't help but wonder if he was right. Her mother had spoiled her, and when Agnes came, her own pride had intervened when she was asked to do something. Perhaps she was spoiled, but she hated the thought. A spoiled woman could never earn enough to care for herself and Claire. If she was indeed spoiled, things needed to change, and quickly.

"No, Glen! You've got the wrong girl. I'm a hard worker, or at least I can be. I came here from Michigan by myself so I could earn enough money to bring my sister Claire here. I want to learn how to earn my own living. If I've been spoiled, it's only because I didn't know any better. Please take me to the Lintons'! I won't let you down, I promise."

His expression was unwavering. His narrowed eyes scanned her, as if checking her for honesty. How could she make him understand how badly she needed this job? How badly she needed to bring Claire out and make a life for herself? Of course, she'd never let him know her true plans for meeting the young Mr. Linton, but she wouldn't let that stop her from working hard. She didn't examine why his opinion meant anything to her, but his negative assessment stung. She had no wish to ruin Glen's reputation or her own.

"I'll recommend you on one condition," he finally said.

"What's that? Anything, Glen, anything."

"If you get hired, you keep the job for an entire year, doing your best regardless of the circumstances. No matter what happens, do we have a deal?"

"A year?" she stammered. "Why would you care if I stayed a year or not?" His requirement simply didn't make sense. What would require such a promise? She was incredibly uncomfortable with the condition, but considering her remaining options, she didn't know if she had a right to protest.

"Because, Jo, in my estimation, a man, or a woman in this case, is only as good as his word. When you're hired for a job, you do it until completion. That's what the Bible preaches, and that's what I believe. If you're willing to make the commitment, so am I, otherwise...," he trailed off, leaving her to decipher his final meaning.

"But what if—"

"A year, Josephine," he answered resolutely.

Jo thought about her options. They consisted of going back to Michigan a failure, continuing to take food from her nephew Davy's mouth, or taking this job for a year. A job, which may or may not exist when she reached the top of the hill. For now, that was only a possibility.

"A year," she relented, holding out her hand to shake on the deal.

The electric streetcar ambled up the last hill, chugging desperately to the city's highest point. She knew sweeping views of the sapphire blue San Francisco Bay were all around her, hidden behind the shroud of morning fog. Stepping off the car, Glen took her hand in his and helped her from the vehicle. He smiled at her, and for a moment she forgot there was any conflict between them at all. There were only his shining eyes, his gaze warmer now, and his masculine carriage.

His chivalry quickly disappeared, however. Carrying his metal lunch box in one hand and his toolbox in the other, he took off at an unnatural pace up the stifling grade. Jo scrambled to keep up.

The stately homes of Nob Hill reeked of money. Elaborate columns and Victorian details provided a sight unlike anything Jo had seen. If times were hard, it certainly wasn't apparent here. They stopped in front of a stylish three-story stone mansion.

"Now, Mrs. Houston will want to know you're coming. She doesn't like surprises. Wait out here," Glen said. "I'll check whether she's willing to see you this morning."

"Mrs. Houston? Who's Mrs. Houston?" Jo was looking forward to meeting Mrs. Linton, and hopefully being introduced to her son.

"She's the housekeeper, Jo. Rich people don't bother with the likes of us." Glen snorted.

"They don't?"

"Wait here, I'm going to be late otherwise." Glen disappeared behind the house, leaving Jo alone on the sidewalk. She looked up at the enormous house, removed her hat, and patted her carefully created bun. Reality struck with the thick, icy fog. She had about as much chance of marrying the wealthy, young Linton chap as she had of being struck by lightning in a city where it was rare.

"Are you waiting for someone, Miss?"

Jo was startled by the voice. She turned to see a dapper young gentleman sitting in a shiny Duesenberg with all the windows rolled down. The man maneuvered the auto against the curb, twisting the wheels until they ground themselves into the curb on the steep street to keep it from escaping. He emerged from the car dressed in a tuxedo, a camel's hair overcoat, and velvety black top hat. Tipping his hat elegantly, he spoke again, "Good morning. Mr. Winthrop Linton at your service." His voice was a low growl, as though tinged with intention.

Jo stood up straight, smoothing the folds of her thick, wool skirt. She had dressed in her finest that morning, but suddenly she felt as raggedy as a street urchin. Winthrop Linton's finely tailored clothing was just another reminder that he was well out of her reach. His charms were an eerie reminder that she wasn't versed in fine society. Her marital aspirations disappeared as quickly as they'd appeared.

"Miss Josephine Mayer," she stammered.

"What brings such a young beauty to my doorstep this fine Wednesday morning?" Under his top hat, Winthrop Linton boasted a mop of curiously sloppy brown hair. He had light brown eyes and nondescript facial features, including a complete lack of chin. Jo scrutinized his face again, but there was no shadow or clothing across his face, he simply lacked a chin. Although small in stature, his dress made him appear bigger and more important.

"I, um, I was waiting to speak with Mrs. Houston about a job," she blurted nervously.

"Well then, you must come in, she'll be waiting." Mr. Linton took her arm and began leading her up the front path. Jo now understood enough to know her presence would not be welcome in the front parlor at such an early hour.

She tried to pull herself from his gentle grasp. "No, Mrs. Houston doesn't know I'm coming. I mean, I haven't been invited in yet."

"Nonsense. I'm inviting you in. I think you're a ripe little beauty, and Mrs. Houston always hires such plain-Janes. It would be nice to have an ornament for a change. Come in." With one final tug, Jo was standing in the extravagant foyer. The marble entryway, covered by a domed, glass ceiling, was larger than Jo's entire flat—a family of three could have easily lived in the foyer.

"Glen Bechtel is asking—"

"Ah, so you're Glen's girl." Winthrop Linton clicked his tongue. "Well, I've had enough of my girlfriends wag their tongues over him; it's only fair he should end up with a beauty like you." He crossed his legs at the ankles and leaned against the great mahogany banister.

"I'm not Glen's girl, I'm just a friend," Jo said hastily. She didn't want him to think she was unavailable. "He lives in the flat upstairs."

"Winthrop, is that you?" an operatic voice called. A large, elegantly dressed woman who appeared to be about fifty years of age came down the stairs. Her deep violet clothing shuffled with the sound of expensive material and was clearly styled in the latest fashion.

"Yes, Mother. Come see who Mrs. Houston's hired." Winthrop Linton wore a devious grin as his mother lumbered down the great stairwell.

Mrs. Linton scrutinized Jo, then summarily ignored her presence. "Were you out all night again, Winthrop?"

"Oh, Mother, you know the parties hardly begin before sunup. I had a marvelous time." He kissed his mother's cheek, and her expression immediately softened.

"When it's time for you to take over your father's business, you won't be able to keep such hours, Son."

"Nor will I, Mother. Mother, this is Miss Josephine Mayer. She is a friend of our own Glen Bechtel. The carpenter?"

"Well, Miss Mayer, I'm sorry Glen didn't explain certain things to you, but the hired help uses the rear door and stays out of sight of the family. Otherwise, well, otherwise we might not be the genteel sort of family we are. We'd be common, do you understand?"

"Yes, Mrs. Linton. I understand perfectly. I'm sorry to have bothered you this fine morning. If you'll just point me in the right direction, I'll be happy to find Mrs. Houston." Jo felt a shaft of irritation that Winthrop had placed her in such an awkward position, but if it helped her get the job, she was grateful.

"Nonsense, I'll take you. I'll meet you in the dining room, Mother." Winthrop once again took her arm chivalrously and led her to the back of the extensive house. "Sorry about Mum, Sweetheart. I'm afraid she's living in a very Victorian age. She hasn't quite realized we are all of equal stature here in the twentieth century."

When they reached the cavernous kitchen, Glen was waiting with a scowl. He stood beside a particular-looking, stout woman who simply appeared angry. "Mrs. Houston." Winthrop placed a kiss on her irate forehead. "I met this little woman on the sidewalk in front of our home. It appears she's looking for work. You'll take care of her, won't you?"

"Yes, Sir," Mrs. Houston replied curtly. Her eyes thinned at Jo. "I'll take care of her, indeed."

The disappointment in Glen's eyes could not have upset her more. He had placed his job on the line for her, and however misinterpreted, she had risked his apprenticeship with her folly. Why hadn't she told Winthrop she was walking to the streetcar or something else? Remembering the inane thoughts of marriage to a wealthy magnate that she'd entertained, she wondered if she hadn't done it on purpose. Perhaps her own foolishness had led her here. Another dead end for work, and now Glen, her only connection, was upset by her foolishness.

She reached for Glen's broad shoulder. "I'm sorry, Glen, I didn't—"

He flinched and pulled away. "I've got work to do. Here's a quarter for the streetcar." He tossed it at her, and his crystal, gray-blue eyes disappeared as he backed out the door.

"You haven't got the sense of a puppy if you don't know enough to use the service entrance," Mrs. Houston bellowed. "And I promise you no work. This is my house, and I run it accordingly. Mrs. Linton understands that. She trusts my worthy opinion."

"Yes, Ma'am. You're right, and I'm so sorry about my entrance. I wasn't thinking."

"Well, you'll have to learn to think if you plan to work here. Girls without a lick of sense mustn't work for me."

"Ma'am?" Jo questioned.

Mrs. Houston sighed. "It isn't every day we see the likes of a worker like Glen Bechtel. You're a bit too attractive for the job, but if Glen is your beau, I can't say you would be tempted by the likes of Winthrop. If Glen recommends you, I'm capable of forgiving one mistake, but let it be your last."

"Yes, my last mistake. Absolutely, Mrs. Houston." Jo knew better than to correct the housekeeper about Glen, but she'd also probably hear about it later.

"You'll begin today with dusting and bathroom shining. You'll receive two dollars a day, six days a week, with Sundays off." Jo nodded pleasantly, trying to keep her disappointment at the low salary from showing. "I'll get you a uniform immediately, and Miss Mayer. . ."

"Yes, Mrs. Houston."

"The Lintons are a very private family. You'll keep your presence out of theirs, do you understand? No more appearances in the family rooms when they are present unless you are called as a servant."

"Yes, Mrs. Houston." Jo's joy over employment was overshadowed by Glen's frustration with her. She fingered the shiny quarter in her hand, knowing the owner of it cared enough to get her back home, but that was probably all he cared. She'd make him understand her mistake. Certainly, he wasn't unreasonable.

Chapter 3

Every muscle in Jo's body ached. Darning socks was child's play next to scrubbing bathroom fixtures with a vengeance. Mrs. Houston was a stickler for the smallest details, and she noticed everything. If there was the slightest smudge, Jo was forced to scrub the fixture as though it hadn't been touched. She found herself cursing indoor plumbing by the time the day was up.

Glen met her at the back door. "How was your first day?" His voice was far too cheery, his muscular body unmatched by the day's work.

She nearly fell into his arms as an answer. Her weary body clamored for the sanctity of her bed, and the idea of the trip to the streetcar overwhelmed her. "Good," she replied feebly.

He laughed out loud. "You don't look all that good. Mrs. Houston has exacting rules, but she'll soften up. Once she knows you're capable."

Jo's legs buckled underneath her as she tried to walk down the steep hill toward the streetcar. Glen noticed her stumble and gave her a pitying glance. He tucked his metal lunch box under his arm—the same arm that held his heavy toolbox. Then he took her hand and held her up by just his presence.

"Is this why you said a year? Does anyone make it through the first week?"

He chuckled. "Oh, Jo, you're just not used to hard work. Give your body two weeks to adjust, and you won't even notice anymore. I think if you work for a year for Mrs. Houston, there won't be a challenge you can't meet."

"Will my arms look like yours?"

Glen had his work shirt folded above the elbows, and the material stretched precariously where it needed to hold his muscles. "I don't think so, Darlin'."

He helped her to the streetcar stop. Jo thought she'd cry at the sight of the full cabin; her body ached with desire to sit. Luckily, a gentleman gave up his seat, and Jo thanked him profusely.

"Seriously, Jo," Glen said, leaning over her, "I know the Lintons aren't an easy family to work for, but I think you'll find if you stick it out, it will be worth your while. They've been so good to my boss and me. They've kept us working for nearly two years now. Soon I'll have my carpentry apprenticeship finished, and I'll be able to go wherever I want. The union is paying about eight dollars a day now."

"Where is it you want to go?"

Glen shrugged. "Nowhere in particular. I'm happy with my life here. I'd like to move out of my sister's apartment, though. That flat can get awful cramped with three of us."

"Try it with four," Jo replied miserably.

"I doubt you'll care how crowded it is tonight."

"That's the truth. I'm exhausted."

"Tomorrow will be easier."

The streetcar rolled to a stop, and Glen hopped off, holding up his arm to help her down.

As she stood, Jo found out just how sore she was and tumbled off the streetcar. She fell into Glen's arms, and his lunch box clattered onto the street. He pulled her to the safety of the sidewalk before returning for his dented lunch box. As he put the contents back into the box, Jo smelled the stench of strong drink. Prohibition made the alcohol scent even more obvious since it had been so long since she'd smelled it. She looked around her nervously to see if there were other witnesses, but only she seemed concerned.

Glen looked up with a guilty shrug. "You wouldn't believe me if I told you." He placed a broken bottle back into the lunch box.

Jo's strength returned. "I don't want to know anyway." She dusted herself off and walked resolutely toward their building.

"Wait, Jo. It's not what you think."

What else could it be? Jo had long since heard of men addicted to strong drink during Prohibition, but she'd never met one. "You're carrying liquor in your lunch box?" Jo's downcast head just shook. "I can't believe it, Glen. My sister trusts you."

"Please just let me explain. Winthrop—"

"You yourself told me the Lintons don't socialize with the likes of us, and now you're going to try to blame this on Winthrop?"

"No, I'm not blaming Winthrop. Just please let me finish."

"Never mind. The less said, the better. Just stay away from Davy, or I'll tell my sister you carry strong drink to work. I doubt she'd want a drunk near her child." Jo slammed the door to her apartment, scarcely hearing Glen's last protest. It was well known that men who drank must have frequented the illegal speakeasies, and flappers, or loose women, were known to be there as well. Jo was indignant. She knew speakeasy life was a form of rebellion that many young people had taken to, but she wouldn't have believed it of Glen. Not unless she'd seen it for herself.

"But it's not mine, Jo!" Glen called through the door.

"Not mine. As though someone would carry an illegal substance for someone else." She answered in a whisper, rolling her eyes. The recent Valentine's Day massacre in Chicago had shown Jo vividly that alcohol was nothing to play with. Just days ago, seven men, who thought they were undergoing a routine police inspection, were killed in cold blood by a rival bootlegger.

"How was your first day, Jo?" Marian's tired expression tried to muster up some enthusiasm.

"It was fine. I'm tired, but I'll survive."

"Where's Glen? He was coming for dinner." Marian shut the oven door, wiping her brow with a dish towel in her hand.

"You don't want him here, Marian. He's not the right sort to be around Davy. Debauchery is contagious, after all."

"Debauchery? Jo, I don't know what's gotten into you, but Glen is not capable of such a thing. Your hard day's work has gone to your head. Now go upstairs, apologize, and bring him back here for dinner. We're having pot roast. It's his favorite. Besides, his sister will be looking forward to the quiet night with her husband."

"I will not go, Marian. He's. . .he is simply not the man you think he is. Trust me. Just please trust me."

"Jo, you always were so dramatic. You'll be starring with Gary Cooper one of these days in those moving picture shows," Marian said through clenched teeth. "Go upstairs and bring

Glen back down here. Mitch looks forward to their evenings and their card games." Marian wiped her hands on her apron, clearly frustrated with the conversation.

If only Jo could tell Marian what she knew. Glen got her the job, and she owed him her silence. If he wanted to ruin his future with strong drink, that was his business, but she wouldn't let him near Davy. But neither could she afford to lose this job by offending him. Not now. Claire could come out within six months if pennies were counted. Free rail fare would make only room and board necessary. Although the money would be tight, they'd manage.

"Jo, I mean it," Marian barked.

Jo let out a heaving sigh. "Does Mitch approve of alcohol?" she hissed.

"My husband has never taken a drink in his life, and neither has Glen. Go upstairs and get him."

Jo reluctantly climbed the concrete steps, only to find Glen sitting on the stair landing. He didn't even look up when she approached. "What are you doing out here?"

"My sister made a special dinner for her husband. I'm trying to give them some privacy." He looked up, his steely blue gaze meeting her own. "Why can't you just listen? I listened to you when you came through the front door with *Winthrop*." Glen dropped his head again. "You are so spoiled, and you're just determined to think the worst of people."

Jo, incensed by his accusation, railed at him. "I'm not spoiled. Cut that out! I worked hard today, and you know it! Don't try to turn this back around on me. Liquor, last time I checked, was illegal in this country. You are carrying it around in your lunch box like it was apple juice. What would my sister think if—"

"Your sister would think there was some misunderstanding, because your sister doesn't jump to ridiculous conclusions."

"Ridiculous? You still smell of it, how ridiculous is proof?" She sniffed again. "Ninety proof!"

"You know, I could jump to some conclusions of my own. Like how you managed to worm your way in the front door with Winthrop Linton easily enough. The servants' entrance wasn't good enough for you, was it? You know, Winthrop has a notorious reputation with the ladies."

"Funny, that's what he says about you."

Glen's crystal blue eyes thinned. He stood up, walking toward his apartment door. "Is it?"

"Where are you going? My sister wants you for dinner!"

"What do *you* want, Josephine?" He came close. Uncomfortably close. She felt herself gulp, and she made the motion to square her shoulders. Unfortunately, they didn't heed her call.

"I want to understand what people see in you. What do you do to fool them into thinking you're a decent guy? We both know better."

"I am a decent guy," he replied softly. He was still close. She trembled in his proximity but tried to hold her uncompromising stance. She couldn't let him know he affected her. Besides, what was it her sister said? He was a carpenter's apprentice, with three dollars a day to his name. She rolled her eyes.

"A decent guy who just happens to carry liquor in his lunch box?"

"Yes," he answered. "Now, what about you? You tell me you're not spoiled, where's my proof?"

"Your proof is that I'm here in California. I'm earning enough to bring my sister out here, and then I'll support her, too. Would a spoiled brat do that?"

"Depends," he answered, crossing his arms, "on why you want your sister out here. What are you three running from? All three sisters come to California with times as tough as they are?" he asked treacherously.

"I'm not running from anything. I'm simply trying to give my little sister a future. The one she deserves. The one our mother would have given us if she'd lived." Jo had had enough of this conversation. "Dinner's at six-thirty." She started down the steps, but she felt his firm hand grasp her arm. His touch startled but intrigued her, and she halted. Looking into the depths of his eyes, she tried to see his villainous ways, but there was nothing—only purity, in clear blue, gazing warmly at her.

"You know there's a reason for that alcohol flask, don't you, Jo?"

Jo crossed her arms. She assumed as much, but she wasn't willing to relent. She wanted an explanation.

"I think you and I have a lot in common."

"I doubt it," she answered curtly, but her heart didn't agree with her snappy mouth.

"Still, you agreed to a year with the Lintons. You're not going to back out on your promise when your sister gets here, are you?"

"I promised. I'll be there for a year."

"No matter what?"

"Within reason," she answered.

"That's not what you promised. You should know me well enough to know I wouldn't ask anything of you that would compromise yourself."

"On the contrary. I don't know you at all, Glen. You play cards, carry liquor, and have the face of a Boy Scout leader. I haven't figured you out at all."

He laughed aloud. "There's nothing to figure out, Jo. I'm just a simple carpenter's apprentice going to work every day and trying to make a future for myself."

"Somehow I find that hard to believe." And she did, too. Hardworking carpenter's apprentices didn't carry liquor in their lunch boxes. Glen made her swear she'd keep *her* job for a year, yet by his very actions that day, he could have lost his own position.

"Winthrop said the ladies—"

"Winthrop says a lot of things, Jo. The sooner you learn to ignore most of it, the safer you'll be. If he ever gets too close, you come to me, do you understand?"

Jo laughed, "Winthrop's a gentleman, Glen."

"Gentlemen ignore the hired help, Jo, and it's worse when they don't." He skipped the steps beyond her, never looking back. Jo simply shook her head. *They lived in America, not in the caste system of India.*

Chapter 4

Glen and Jo rode the streetcar to work silently the next day. She felt his disdain, and he probably felt hers, so they both opted for silence. Glen apparently thought she was a foolish girl who couldn't handle herself with the likes of Winthrop Linton, and Jo thought he sought his place in the bottom of society too readily. Submission was not something that came easily to Jo, and she found Glen's easy example of it pathetic.

The great house looked so spectacular from the front, it was hard to fathom such darkness dwelled within. Jo shivered at the memory of Mrs. Houston's cold reception and Mrs. Linton's outright refusal to acknowledge her. Winthrop drove up the street, honking the horn of his Duesenberg at the unholy hour. Once again, the young, enigmatic Winthrop appeared perfectly attired after his long night.

"Good morning, Glen. Good morning, Miss Mayer." The young man tipped his hat chivalrously, and Jo couldn't help her sideways glance at Glen.

"If gentlemen ignore the hired help, someone forgot to tell Winthrop," she whispered through clenched teeth.

"Winthrop is an exception. He's from a different generation than his parents. *He* believes in the American dream, but his parents are still in the Victorian age. He's watched many of his friends die from the postwar flu epidemic. Money is not a separator to him. Trust me, Jo, it's not that way with his parents. It won't do you any good to be mingling with the likes of Winthrop. His mother would have you shot down faster than an enemy biplane." Glen smiled as well, giving the impression they were having a perfectly amiable conversation.

Winthrop slurred inaudibly and stumbled forward. Glen rushed to catch him, and Jo realized that young Winthrop was decidedly drunk. His eyes were glassy and he wore a careless smile. He tried to say something else, but she heard only sputters of sound.

"Jo, go get to work. Mrs. Houston will be expecting you," Glen shouted. Jo averted her eyes, which is really what Glen meant. She scrambled up the back steps and entered.

"Good morning, Mrs. Houston." Jo gave a slight curtsy.

"Good morning, Josephine. There's coffee brewing if you're of a mind to drink it." Mrs. Houston had already assembled the elegant breakfast for the family and kindly had left a few scraps of bacon for Jo next to the coffee. "You'll be working hard today so be sure and eat up. We can't have you withering away to nothing." Mrs. Houston maintained her solemnity, but she must have had a heart. To consider Jo's hungry and tired state defied that callous front.

Jo inhaled the rich coffee aroma and took a cup from the cupboard. "Thank you, Mrs. Houston. The coffee smells divine. It's so frightfully cold out there. I didn't think Michigan had much competition for its winters, but that ocean fog just cuts right through a person."

"Drink it up quickly. I'm going to teach you to serve today. You can practice on Winthrop. Most likely he'll be needing coffee this morning, and he's not particular if you make a mistake." Mrs. Houston clicked her tongue. "Perhaps after some practice you'll be ready to serve Mrs. Linton tomorrow."

"Yes, of course, Mrs. Houston."

The older woman assembled a perfect tray, complete with orange juice, a coffee cup, two eggs, and three strips of bacon. "Now, there will be a sideboard in the dining room. Set the tray on the sideboard and serve the coffee first. There's a silver pot waiting over the warmer. Serve from the left. Pick up from the right. Winthrop takes his coffee black. After he's been seated with his coffee, you may set the warm plate in front of him. Don't bother to ask him what he wants, he won't be of a mind to care. If he needs anything you don't see in the dining room, come back to the kitchen, and I'll help you. All right?"

"Yes, Mrs. Houston." Jo's confidence waned. She would have actually preferred scrubbing bathroom fixtures to being thrown into proper serving techniques. Of course, her mother had taught her manners, which fork to use, and all that, but actually serving for an upstanding San Francisco family was beyond her mother's skills.

Jo watched the orange juice shake and sputter as she headed toward the dining room. "Head up, Josephine," Mrs. Houston called.

Jo straightened and followed voices into the elaborate dining room. The walnut-paneled room was laden with crystal electric lights, though the general darkness of the fog and day still dimmed the room immensely. Jo was shocked to see Glen sitting beside Winthrop at the great table. It didn't coincide with his "hired help" persona. She did as Mrs. Houston asked and placed the coffee in front of Winthrop. He and Glen were looking at plans for some type of building project—the same schematics Glen had with him on the streetcar. At least, Glen was trying to interest Winthrop in the plans, but the weary man only wanted to sleep. She placed the plate of food alongside the schematics.

"Would you care for coffee, Mr. Bechtel?" Jo asked sweetly. Glen nodded and she poured him a cup. "Cream or sugar?"

"No, thank you." Glen watched her for a moment, clearly hoping she'd leave. Something about his determination caused her own to muster. She settled in at the sideboard, rearranging items that didn't need to be rearranged.

Winthrop smiled his drunken smile her direction. Obviously, he had little interest in Glen's plans, or business of any sort. Winthrop just watched her dreamily. "She's such a peach," he slurred in Glen's direction. "I like good-lookin' women."

Glen nodded as if to tell her to leave, but she didn't. She lifted up the coffee urn again, hoping to refill Winthrop's cup. The poor man was in such a sorry state. His glassy eyes couldn't quite focus on her, but he gave her a sloppy smile anyway. Suddenly, Winthrop collapsed into his plate, his face a mass of yellow eggs when he finally turned to breathe.

"Winthrop!" His mother's opera-tinged voice bellowed.

"Help me get him out of here," Glen whispered. Jo wiped Winthrop's face with a white linen napkin while Glen lifted the load up, throwing Winthrop's lifeless arm around his shoulder. "Get the door, Jo. The back door!"

Thinking Mrs. Linton would come in and find the unwholesome scene, Jo ran toward the door and let the two men out quickly. "What do I tell Mrs. Linton?"

"You'll think of something. Get the plans!"

Without thought, Jo rolled up the schematics and hid them in the sideboard. Just as she shut the cabinet, Mrs. Linton's shrill voice addressed her. "Is there something you're looking for?"

"I was just making sure there was enough silver on the table, Mrs. Linton. Teaspoons are a necessity." Jo cringed at the mistruth. Why was she covering for Glen? Mrs. Linton had to have some idea of her son's behavior if he came home in the morning every day.

"Tell Mrs. Houston I'm ready for my meal. *She* can serve. Did young Mr. Linton dine yet? He went to bed so early last night."

Jo's eyes rested on the plate of smeared scrambled eggs. The white of the china shone through where Winthrop's face had been, while much of the breakfast entrée rested on the crisply ironed tablecloth. "Yes, Mrs. Linton. He wasn't very hungry." Jo's eyes widened.

The older woman looked at the mess, and back at Jo. "Well, no wonder. What type of slop is that for breakfast? Please ask Mrs. Houston to come in here presently. I'm sure she can find something useful for you to do."

Jo nodded. "Yes, Ma'am." Jo would probably get her walking papers that very day, and then what would she do? This was all Glen's fault. He should have just left Winthrop to deal with the consequences of drink. Jo hurried back into the kitchen. "I'm sorry, Mrs. Houston. I'm afraid I ran into Mrs. Linton, and I didn't impress her with my serving."

"Never mind, Dear. I'll deal with Mrs. Linton. You start with the dishes. We'll work on serving again this afternoon before lunch."

If there is an afternoon for me, Jo thought solemnly.

"Psst. Jo!" Glen's roguish frame filled the doorway. "Did you get the plans?"

Jo put a finger to her lips. "Shh! Mrs. Linton is in the dining room. You're going to get us both fired."

"Jo, you've got to get those plans. Mrs. Linton cannot see them. Please," he pleaded. "If not for me, do it for Winthrop. You seem to like *him*."

"Fine," Jo relented. "But only because I owe you both my job, and if you're up to something illegal, you ought to be ashamed for bringing me into it. I'll get them when I clear the dishes. Now get out of here before someone sees you."

He flashed his perfect teeth, with all the charm of a silent movie star. Jo pursed her lips, trying to remain unaffected by his captivating grin. "I owe you, Jo. I'll make it up to you, I promise. If Mrs. Linton asks where Winthrop is, tell her he's out back overseeing the building."

"I doubt Winthrop is overseeing anything."

"No, he's awake, and he's watching us build. I'm not asking you to lie, Josephine. I'm asking you to protect Winthrop. Give it a few weeks; you'll understand."

"Winthrop doesn't strike me as the type of man who needs protecting."

"He will, Jo. Just give it time. Thanks!" Glen planted a kiss on her cheek and shut the door without another word. Jo unconsciously touched her cheek. She should know better than to be affected by Glen's touch, but someone forgot to tell her pounding heart.

"Haven't you started the dishes yet?" Mrs. Houston's disapproving glare shamed Jo.

"No, Mrs. Houston. I'm sorry. I'm getting to it right now."

"Well, get snapping, my dear. There's no place for idleness in this household. Mrs. Linton opted for only coffee this morning. She's finished in the dining room. You can clear the dishes and put the table back to right. Then, come back and finish these dishes."

"Yes, Ma'am." Again Jo curtsied in deference. She doubted it had any effect on Mrs. Houston, but her working situation was precarious enough without being proud.

"And Josephine," Mrs. Houston continued, "the last girl was fired for associating with Winthrop. Make sure you keep out of his way, especially where Mrs. Linton is concerned."

"Of course, Mrs. Houston." Jo cleared the dishes from the table, filling the tray with the unused, elegant bone china. Jo sighed at the sight of it. *Bone china.* Marian and Mitch struggled for each day's provisions, and they still managed to feed her and Glen, too. Pot roast, no less. It couldn't be said that Marian didn't know how to run a proper home. It simply wasn't right that bone china went unused and prepared meals uneaten. All this waste sickened her. But she knew if she said anything about it, Mrs. Houston would have her gone before the day was up. The wealthy had room to waste.

Checking to her left and to her right, Jo opened the sideboard and took out the rolled plans. She was tempted to look at the contents but thought ignorance might be best. She was in enough trouble, and Claire was waiting in Michigan. Waiting for the money and the means to come to California.

Jo tucked the plans under her arm and opened the door. "Glen," she whispered. The hammering outside stopped, and Glen appeared.

"You're an angel," Glen said smiling, taking the plans from her. "I'll see you tonight. I may be a little late, but wait for me. I don't want you on the streetcar alone at night."

"I'll be fine," she protested.

"Wait for me," he commanded, and she saw something in his eyes she couldn't refuse. Everything about Glen Bechtel was a mystery. From what he was building out in the garden, to his liquor-toting lunch box. But for some reason, getting on the streetcar without him seemed dire. As much as reason pointed in one direction, her heart was taken in another. Glen's soft blue eyes and gentle touch with those around him made it impossible to believe he was up to no good even though all the evidence was stacked against him. Marian's good opinion had something to do with it. Marian wasn't easily taken in. She had a discerning nature.

"I'll wait," Jo answered.

"Good. I promised your sister I would not let you get on the streetcar alone."

Jo's heart plunged. Glen's chivalry went only as far as duty. "I'll wait in the kitchen," she added solemnly.

Chapter 5

Disgusted by the events of the day, Glen hammered with a vengeance. His aggression was well served by his job today. Winthrop Linton was an exasperating chap—too dainty to be useful, too strong-willed to be silent. Glen's jaw clenched remembering Jo's concerned look for the drunken Winthrop.

Glen would never understand women. Seems they were all taken in by those sweet, schoolboy looks of Winthrop's. Young, idealistic women had no idea the trauma that lay beneath his easy façade. Winthrop was a broken man; useless to his powerful father and yet trying to forge a place for himself before it was too late.

Maybe it was the money that fooled them. Women seemed to think money changed things—that it solved problems. The Linton household was a prime example that it simply wasn't true. Money just caused different sets of problems. Turmoil reigned in that household. Jo would see it quickly enough, if she hadn't witnessed it already with Winthrop's continual drunken state. Jo would soon relish her place in simple society. Not that he was without feelings for Jo. The school of hard knocks was no place for a girl of seventeen. Glen had admired men of means at one time, too. But never again.

Glen wished he could teach her the lesson without her having to see it for herself, but it wasn't his place. Glen promised Jo's sister, Marian, he'd look after Jo until she figured it out. An easier promise he'd never made. He'd feel responsible for any young woman in the Linton household. Josephine Mayer was special, though. He'd known that from the first time he'd laid eyes on her.

Glen was a man of few words. He didn't know how to describe the rush of feelings Jo sent through him. Jo wasn't a beauty queen, but she cast some kind of spell. She was an average woman of petite stature, yet solidly built for her young age, with dark brown hair always swept up into a neat bun. She had the lightest of green eyes. Something about her defied her average looks. Men were simply attracted to her. She had that magnetism that just made a man want to know more, as though an intriguing slice of heaven hid within. Certainly Winthrop was not immune, and neither was Glen.

He laughed aloud at the ridiculous notion of pursuing such a romantic thought. Josephine was a mere baby. Only seventeen and in need of a big brother's protection. She was too young to marry. He was too poor. Three dollars a day and a lifetime debt he couldn't shake. Courting was the last thing on his mind. Or at least, it should have been.

Glen drove the last nail of the day. One swift whack and the nail was embedded firmly into the redwood. He packed up his tools and headed toward the kitchen. He knocked. "You ready?" he asked as Jo opened the door.

She nodded. "Good night, Mrs. Houston."

"Night, Dear. See you in the morning. Don't forget about the party tomorrow night," Mrs. Houston called.

"No, Ma'am, I won't." Jo shut the door behind her and smiled up at Glen.

"Party?" Glen tried to hide his nervousness.

"Mr. and Mrs. Linton are entertaining business associates tomorrow. I have to work late tomorrow night. They said if it runs too late, Winthrop can take me home."

"No!" Glen shouted. "I mean, I'll wait for you. I have some extra work I can do. I have just one more thing to learn before I graduate to the next step. Step three of my apprenticeship."

"That's nice, Glen, but it's not necessary. The streetcar will have stopped running by then, and I've put you out enough. Mrs. Houston said the parties go well into the night."

That's not all they do, Glen thought. He took Jo's hand to help her down the steep walk, and rubbed her hand. It felt like sandpaper. She pulled her hand away, hiding it in her pocket.

"I had to shine the silver today," she explained. "The cleaning mixture was harsh on my hands."

He watched her in the fading sunlight, and they faced one another. Her pale green eyes filled with tears. Clearly, this wasn't how she imagined life. Glen unconsciously brushed a loose tendril of hair behind her shoulder. Her neatly arranged bun was now a mass of tangled confusion. She'd never looked more attractive—her vulnerability, her beauty, it all hung between them like an unspoken whisper of love. With it came the realization that she would be as irresistible to Winthrop tomorrow night as she was to Glen that very moment. Glen felt a shaft of guilt. He'd promised Marian to help get Jo work, but at what price?

"Jo, maybe this job is too difficult. Maybe you ought to think of looking elsewhere," Glen suggested.

"When would I go look for another job? I have to be there at six-thirty in the morning, and I'm not home until just about the same time in the evening. I need to focus on Claire, not myself. She has it harder than I do, Glen."

Only two days of work, and she was ravenously unhappy. Who could blame her? She looked bedraggled. Her hands were a chapped mess. The real Josephine Mayer was wilting away behind a disciplined servant's body. If she kept this up, she'd be an old maid before she was twenty.

Glen's guilt got the best of him. "I know, Jo. I'm sorry. I'm sorry I got you into this mess." He placed an arm around her, and they began walking again.

"Sorry? Glen, this is the only hope of work I've had in a month of being here. I have no experience, no references. I'd have nothing without your help. Neither would my sister, Claire. When she comes, Glen, it will be because you helped me. Even if I was too stubborn to realize it at first."

For the first time ever, Glen left his toolbox, his very livelihood, out in the work shed. He prayed they'd still be there in the morning, but he also felt a responsibility to have a free hand for Jo. Last night she'd been so bone tired she could barely lift herself onto the streetcar. Today, he'd be there if she needed him.

"I thought you were a spoiled child who was looking for easy work. I didn't realize you really knew what it meant to work for a living."

"Marian gave me no dreams about what it's like out here. I knew when I came that making the money for Claire and myself would be difficult. Life at home was worse, Glen, or I wouldn't be here. I just pray that my coming out here is helping Claire manage." Her voice dropped a bit. "I hope she's staying free of the strap."

Glen wondered what kind of woman their father married. Certainly Claire, at thirteen, would have outgrown the strap. Josephine's eyes were filled with apprehension. Glen knew life after the war wasn't easy; he knew many children who'd gone to work to help their families. It was different with girls, he thought. Young women should have been sheltered. He felt a bolt of anger toward Jo's father before remembering the man was only doing what he needed to do to provide for his family just like any other man in America. Work was hard to find, and war was looming in the rest of the world. The war to end all wars had done no such thing.

"Your father's only doing what needs to be done," Glen said in support.

"I know, Glen. So am I. Father and Agnes are bound to start a new family soon. After that, it will be too late for my sister. Claire will be expected to stay and care for the baby. She'll become nothing more than the family maid when that happens. I'm certain of it. Won't it be ironic?" Jo said with a sarcastic laugh. "My father will have hired a maid for his daughters, only to have his own daughter become the maid's maid."

"You have to look at Marian's life, too, Jo. Life isn't much different on your own. It's no picnic right now for the workingman. We scrape and struggle to keep food on the table while the rich get richer. They make sense out of all those stock numbers, and we are just thankful to have their scraps and to build their office buildings and houses."

Jo's eyes softened, and she faced him again. "I know, Glen. I don't blame my father one bit. President Hoover has big plans for this country. He said no American shall ever starve, and look what he did for the Allies. He kept them fed without ever rationing portions in America. I know we can expect things to get better soon, but until then, I feel responsible for Claire."

Glen admired her optimism, and he wished he shared it. In July of '28 he'd watched the Lintons panic over a big stock market drop. This gambling was a false economy, and he worried its days were numbered. When the rich suffered, the poor were bound to suffer more.

"I'm waiting for you tomorrow night, Jo. The party may go late, but I'd just feel better knowing you got home safely."

"But, Mrs. Houston said—"

"I don't doubt Mrs. Houston, and I don't doubt their good intentions, but all the same, I'd like to see you home."

She smiled. It was the first time he'd ever seen her smile in a way that he felt was meant for him. "I'd like that too, Glen."

Chapter 6

Jo's hands trembled as she held the letter. *More bad news. I just can't take any more bad news, Lord. Please let things be getting better for Claire.* Jo ripped open the envelope on the crowded streetcar, ignoring prying looks from standing passengers.

Dearest Jo,

How I wish I were older. How I wish Father would let me come to California and supply for me there. I took your advice. I'm trying so hard to make Agnes happy. I am doing the wash after my schoolwork and have even taken to preparing some of the family meals, but nothing seems to please her. When Father is off the railroad line and here, things are almost worse because he does not give her enough attention. Or so she tells the ladies at afternoon tea. Grandmother Faith has been here a time or two, and I've been very careful to shelter her from the true happenings here. Her health is very frail, I'm afraid. I'm dreadfully sorry for my lamenting. I know things are tough for you, too. It is just that I'm so anxious to see you and Marian and especially to see precious baby Davy. I miss you all and long for the time when the Lord sees us together again.

Love, Claire

P.S. Mother's wedding chest has miraculously returned to the house. Agnes keeps it in her room. She's taken down the pictures of Mother, and I cannot seem to find them any-where. I'll find a way to get the chest, Jo. If it kills me.

Jo's eyes closed as she heard her name called. "Josephine! It's our stop." Glen roused her from the correspondence, and Jo stepped off the car at the last possible moment. "Is every-thing okay?" He took her hand, and she felt herself pulled off the street.

Jo's words surprised her. "I'm simply not making enough money, Glen. I think I need another position." Jo stuffed the letter into her apron pocket, looking to Glen for some kind of answer. As if he had one.

"Jo, you're lucky to have this job. They're not easy to come by these days."

"Oh, I know, Glen. I know." Jo knew better than to feel sorry for herself, but she battled to fight the tears in the back of her throat. Life was tough for everyone right now. Everyone but the rich. However, she knew Claire was enduring the strap at home. She could read be-tween her sister's lines, and she knew Claire's quest for the wedding chest could only lead to more trouble. Some legacies, no matter how treasured, were best left alone. The Holy Grail of her family—that would be all that remained of her mother's gown and family Bible, but certainly Grandma Faith would understand.

"Is there anything I can do?" Glen stopped on the street corner and gazed at her. His blue eyes seemed to offer her everything, yet she knew he had nothing. Nothing except three dollars a day and a rent payment to his own sister.

Biting her nails, Jo tried to think of a way. "No, Glen. There's nothing that time and a savings account won't cure. My sister Claire will be here. I just have to be patient."

Glen reached over and gave her a small kiss on the cheek. "God will provide, Jo. His timing is perfect."

"It doesn't feel that way today." His kiss was gentle and fatherly, but Josephine felt so much more within her. She stirred at the sight of his concerned brow, and suddenly wanted to kiss him. To let him know everything would indeed be okay. She couldn't explain why his gentle kiss and concerned words soothed her so, but they gave her courage. The more she looked into his sincere expression, the more she knew there had to be an explanation for the liquor. She should have taken that explanation when it was offered.

"Sometimes, God's timing doesn't always feel right." Glen smiled again. His perfect, rugged smile highlighted his strong features. "I'll wait for you out at the work shed. Come out when the party is finished."

"I will." Jo let his hand go and walked into the Linton kitchen, thoroughly aware of Glen's eyes following her.

◆　◆　◆

Preparing for a party made the workday feel even longer. Minute details seemed so unimportant when Claire was suffering. Both Mrs. Houston and Mrs. Linton put everything to the test. Jo wished to burn their white gloves over the perfectly arranged logs on the fireplace. Everything had a proper arrangement, and Jo wondered if rich people noticed such details as how the fire logs lay.

"Josephine, did you get the glasses down from the dining room cabinet?" Mrs. Houston's voice called.

"Yes, they are on the table. Where shall I put them? In the kitchen?"

"Heavens no. We can put them in the bar now. I'll get the key."

Jo looked up for a moment, only to shake her head. She must have misunderstood. Bars were illegal in prohibitionist America, and although the eighteenth amendment was controversial, it was still the law. "Mrs. Houston? Where did you say I should put the glasses?" Jo walked into the kitchen, wiping her hands on her apron.

"Silly me," Mrs. Houston laughed. "In the bar, Dear. I'm going to open it soon. The guests will be arriving, and we'll want to be prepared. Mrs. Linton will stand for nothing else. You did bring your clean uniform for serving, right, Josephine?"

"The bar, Ma'am?" Jo was still lost in Mrs. Houston's first comment. Were the Lintons setting up a bar for the party? Would Jo be put into a real speakeasy? The thought sent her heart racing like an out-of-control streetcar down a steep San Francisco grade.

"Josephine, you didn't think a state-of-the-art mansion like this would be without a bar, did you? You're not uneasy about the drinking, are you? Certainly you know that refined people take to the privilege of mirth. Although, these days, we can only get that rotgut from Canada, so we have to mix it with juice. People of society have a right to their pursuits, and why shouldn't they? Simply because a few do not know how to enjoy such things in moderation and with decency?"

Jo was too naive; she had no idea people of "refinement" pursued what her mother had fought so vigilantly to end. "Mrs. Houston, they must be aware of the law. The Volstead Act declares that the purchase and consumption of alcohol is illegal." Jo straightened her shoulders. She may have been innocent, but she was not ignorant.

"For the common folks, perhaps prohibition is necessary. I can see why when so many are dependent on their working men for their livelihood, but for the upper echelons of society, Josephine, you must see that they have a right to their pursuits."

"Why? Are they above the law?" Jo heard the indignation in her voice and bit her lip to keep more angry words from escaping.

Mrs. Linton appeared, laughing while covering her mouth discreetly. "We have a temperance league member on our staff, do we? You know, young lady, if the police find nothing wrong in our actions, neither should you. Rest your conscience, Dear." Mrs. Linton opened a locked closet, and to Jo's astonishment, a fully stocked speakeasy appeared. Bottles of every size and color filled Jo's view. She felt in the pit of her stomach a sickly, filthy feeling.

The room was newly built behind a great mahogany wall. Glen's apprenticeship had probably been spent building it. *The plans,* she thought. *The plans he was hiding. Were they for another speakeasy elsewhere?* Was Winthrop involved in building more of these dens of iniquity? Worse yet, was Glen? This must have been why he asked for her year's service.

Unwillingly, Jo walked somberly into the small room. It was a miracle she hadn't noticed it before, for the stench told of its oft use. Polished to a shine, Mrs. Houston herself must have seen to its care. Gold faucets and mirrored shelves reminded Jo of her mother's words: Sin is usually wrapped in a pretty package, never forget that.

Winthrop appeared at the doorway, and for once, he was strikingly sober. Jo's eyes must have appealed to him for assistance, because his comment suggested they had. "Mother, I don't think it's proper for Jo, a young woman of genteel upbringing, to work this party." The use of Victorian language was not lost on Jo. Clearly, Winthrop made a profession out of deceiving his mother. And it obviously worked. "Why don't you hire one of the men from the club? I bet Jo has never even heard of a cocktail, much less served one."

Mrs. Linton's outrage at Winthrop's suggestion was obvious. "Because, Winthrop, Josephine is our employee, and as such she is expected to work our social gatherings." Her stuffed chest stuck out just a bit farther than normal. Jo had no idea why Winthrop would try to help her, but she appreciated it just the same and remained quiet, knowing the young man would get much farther with his mother than she. Winthrop wasn't deterred by her dominant reaction.

He shrugged. "It doesn't matter to me, Mother. I was just thinking about you. If you have any thoughts of matchmaking tonight, you might want to keep her out of the way. You know how Dad's associates can be around the hired help. The young *female* hired help." He stated the last with special emphasis. "Seems to me you've been in trouble with some of the wives before, especially when their husbands part with their money during the evening." Winthrop scanned Jo up and down. "And none of those women were anything to look at, whereas Jo here. . ." Winthrop began to take a glass down from the wall, when his mother slapped his hand.

"Don't touch that. You know better." Mrs. Linton opened her mouth to speak to Winthrop but snapped it shut quickly. Then she hobbled off, mumbling to herself. "I'm going to call someone from the club. I'm sure this simpleton has no idea of the latest cocktails anyway. Her serving skills are still appalling. What was I thinking?"

Mrs. Houston followed hurriedly behind the mistress of the house, and Jo was left alone with the youngest Linton. His lecherous gaze was gone, replaced by an apparent longing for the odd-shaped bottles in the bar.

"Thank you, Winthrop. I don't know why you did that, but I appreciate it. My mother would have been appalled if I worked such a party."

"No need to thank me, Jo. Glen told me the favor you did us yesterday, with the plans. I certainly appreciate it. Mother and Father would never understand my plans. They think I'm destined for the family steel business, but I have other ideas. Big ideas."

"What are they, Winthrop? Do you mind my asking?"

He laughed. "Nothing to worry your pretty little head about. Let's just say it's going to be very profitable. Say, Glen's planning on working late tonight; would you care for a ride home? Have you ever ridden in a Duesenberg?"

"Glen was planning to work late to see me home. I think I'll try and catch him now." Jo looked to the door as if it was her escape from sin. The one God had promised to provide. Her hands trembled as she approached the door. Winthrop may not have done her any favors after all.

Winthrop grasped at her arm and cooed his words. "I'll get you home safely, Miss Jo. I haven't had any complaints yet." He grinned, then winked almost imperceptibly. "Besides, I saved you from working at our den of iniquity tonight."

"I suppose you did, but Glen made special arrangements. He promised my sister to see me home, and I'd hate for Marian to worry." The door was so close, she longed to lunge for it and find Glen. Yet the opening was fading from view. A virtual black tunnel darker than a miner's pit.

"You know, Jo. Working the parties is in your best interest. The revelers often have a few too many cocktails, and then they tip big. You might have made fifteen dollars or so." Winthrop's face curved into a half-smile, and Jo felt herself swallow hard.

"What were you saving toward?"

Fifteen dollars. That was more than a month's rent on her sister's flat. It was certainly enough to get Claire out to California. The tunnel disappeared when the door opened and late afternoon light streamed in, blinding Jo. Glen closed the door and stood in the doorway, his blue eyes staring warily at her.

"I finished up early." Glen looked at Winthrop, and then back to Jo. "I'm ready to take you home as soon as Mrs. Houston is finished with you. I won't be staying late after all."

"How did you know I wasn't working the party?" Jo searched both the men for answers, but they seemed to be having a silent conversation that didn't involve her.

"I'll wait for you outside," Glen answered.

Winthrop said nothing of the ride in the Duesenberg, and so Jo ignored the offer and followed Glen outside. "Glen, Winthrop says I might make fifteen dollars in tips if I worked tonight." She didn't hide the hope in her voice, or what that money might accomplish.

"He did, did he?"

"What do you think, Glen? Fifteen dollars is a lot of money."

"I think you either have a conviction or you don't, Jo. I suppose it's your place to decide. I'll wait for you if you want to work the party, but I won't support you. I know what Marian would have to say about it, and I would never go against a woman who cooks like Marian."

"I do have a conviction; drinking is illegal!" Jo cried. "But fifteen dollars, Glen! Claire could be out by the end of the month, and I could have a place of my own."

"Where would you come up with the rent for next month, Jo? Did you think of that?"

"I make enough to support Claire and myself if we lived frugally, I just needed a stash to get us started. This could be the answer to my prayers."

"You could make a lot more than fifteen dollars, depending on what you're willing to do, Josephine Mayer."

Jo slapped him hard across the face. "How dare you!"

Glen grabbed his reddened cheek. "Convictions are something you stand by despite the cost, Jo. If it's worth fifteen dollars for you to forget your convictions, you go right ahead. I won't stop you."

"How dare you lecture me! You carry liquor in your lunch box. Are you going to stand here and preach at me?"

Glen pulled his billfold from his back pocket and casually pulled out a twenty-dollar bill. It was more money than Jo had ever seen at once. "Take it. Don't worry, I earned it. It's mine fair and square. Take it and bring Claire out here before you do something you regret."

"Where did you get this kind of money?"

"I earned it, like I said. Now take it, and let's go. Tell Mrs. Houston you'll see her in the morning."

"I can't take your money!"

"But you're willing to take it from a gang of drunken, rich fools? Take it, Jo! Before you take it from someone who expects something in return." The disgust in his voice held her riveted. He turned and walked resolutely to his work shed. Soon, the consistent pounding emanated from the room, a constant reminder she was back at the beginning with Glen Bechtel.

Chapter 7

Jo fingered the bill in her hand as she slowly returned to the kitchen. She had what she needed to bring Claire to California, so why did she hesitate? She could pay Glen back with some of her savings, and give him the balance soon. So why this annoying guilt?

"You can leave now," Mrs. Houston huffed.

Jo stuffed the bill into her apron. "I'm sorry, Mrs. Houston. I didn't know alcohol would be served. I—"

"Just never you mind. Let me tell you something though, Missy, for your own good. Wealthy people live a life of privilege. We have no right to judge them. They are our bread and butter. The sooner you learn that, and get over this high opinion of yourself, the better off you'll be. You're a maid, not even a housekeeper, Josephine, and with that attitude of yours, it's all you'll ever be."

Jo looked to the floor. "You're wrong, Mrs. Houston," she said gently. "I don't think I'm better than anyone. I simply am trying to be the woman I promised my mother I'd be. I can't do that and serve liquor when she fought so valiantly to keep it from America. I can, however, scrub floors with dignity." A surge of guilt rose in her throat. After all, Jo had considered the offer. She'd considered it seriously and may have given into the temptation had it not been for Glen's discerning words.

"It's a good thing you appreciate washing floors, Missy, because it's all you'll ever do." Mrs. Houston's hands left her hips as she prepared the last of the appetizer trays.

"Do you want me to leave, Mrs. Houston? For good, I mean."

Mrs. Houston only huffed, her patience clearly waning for what she considered Jo's self-righteous indignation. Mrs. Houston walked away without another word. For now, Jo had a job, but she had no idea how long it would last. Glen was right, though; a conviction was nothing unless you really stood for something. Jo mumbled a prayer and left it to God. She wouldn't be anxious for something she couldn't control. Embarrassed by her behavior in front of Glen, she longed to make her peace with him. To let him know she was ever so grateful for his reason.

The sun had long since hidden itself behind the hills of San Francisco. Darkness filled every crevice of the Linton exterior. Only a lone light in the work shed shone as a beacon, calling her to it like a lost ship in the night. Silence greeted her, and she wondered if Glen was still there, or if he was angry with her, too, and left. She approached the work shed and heard voices. She peeked around the door frame, her eyes wide at the discovery.

"I got her out of the party, Glen. I can't promise any more than that. My mother runs this house as she sees fit." Winthrop Linton's sober voice hit her like a fist. His sobering words, even more so.

"Your mother runs this house as you tell her to, Winthrop, and you know it. Jo needs this job, and she needs to keep her reputation. She is not your typical flapper with bobbed hair and naked knees. You can't drink all night with her and dispose of her presence easily. She's young, Winthrop, and full of goals and aspirations. I won't let you harm her."

Jo bit her thumbnail at the realization—she was the topic of conversation. She didn't know whether to run or listen closely. Curiosity won and she leaned in closer.

"It seems to me you haven't much choice in what I do." Winthrop snorted. "In case you've forgotten, you work for us, too."

"In case *you've* forgotten, Winthrop, I know your secret. You can threaten me all you want, but if you want your secret kept, you'll find a way for Jo to keep her job. Your money means nothing to me. You ought to know that by now."

"What do you care about her, anyway? You've got enough missies following your every move. What's so special about her? I daresay a few of the society women would come down a notch or two to have you for awhile."

Glen shoved his hammer into his toolbox, the loud clanking breaking the unbearable night silence. "I don't know what she means to me. Nothing so special, I guess. I just want her safe because she's my responsibility. I promised her sister."

"You're quite the promise keeper, aren't you, Glen?"

"Winthrop, I've been a friend to you. I know you can't see that from your viewpoint, but you need to get right with God. You think only money has power. Understand this." Glen ground his forefinger into Winthrop's chest. "I haven't kept your promise because I feel compelled by my employment. I can get carpentry work at the presidio. I've kept your secret because I care about your eternal future. You can scoff at that all you want, but I will leave if you pursue Jo. And your secret won't go with me. She's an innocent, Winthrop. Find another hobby before someone gets hurt. You've got time to make things right."

"I only offered her a ride home."

"Don't fool with me, Winthrop. We both know what your rides home mean. I'm going to get Josephine, and I'd appreciate my money."

Winthrop held out cash, and then snatched it back when Glen reached for it. "Did you make her promise to be here a year, Glen? Did she fall for your ridiculous requests?"

"Give me my money, Winthrop." Glen held out his palm, his face red with anger.

"Who's taking advantage of her really, Glen? She knows I don't intend to marry her." Winthrop reluctantly handed Glen another twenty-dollar bill. In return, Glen handed Winthrop a clear glass bottle with a honey-brown liquid inside.

Liquor. Jo bit her fingernail clear away at the ends. Glen did have liquor, and worse yet, he sold it to a drunk. Right in front of her eyes. What was all that talk about getting right with God? *How could anyone handing alcohol to such a troubled man be right with God?*

"You're taking advantage of her, Winthrop. Don't try to fool yourself into believing anything else. Your hero image in front of your mother, your concern for her welfare at the speakeasy. . .I know what it all really means. I've watched you before, remember? I think of Jo as a little sister, nothing more."

"I saw you kiss her, Glen. You're going to deny that, too?" Winthrop's smile curved up one side of his face.

"I kissed her. It didn't mean—never mind." Glen latched his toolbox, shoved the twenty into his billfold, and headed for the door. Jo raced down the walkway near the entrance to the house.

She pulled the twenty-dollar bill from her own pocket—the one Glen had handed her earlier. What was the difference between this money, and her "tips" had she worked the party? It was blood money, and she didn't want it—and she didn't want this job. She'd learned that much this evening. She had no reason to keep her one-year commitment to a man that bootlegged liquor. She'd go back to Michigan and beg Agnes for her old room. She'd see to it that she and Claire were cared for under Agnes's nose. Even if she did have to endure the strap occasionally.

"Jo?" Glen's tone was normal again. Smooth and gentle, not excited and angry as he'd been speaking with Winthrop. Jo tried to regain her composure, to act innocent of the conversation.

"Yes?"

"Are you ready to leave? I am finished in the shed. Anything else can wait until Monday. I imagine no one will be too fond of the hammer tomorrow after the party." He smiled slightly, and his straight teeth appeared. Glen appeared to have everything to offer a woman, maybe not money, but everything else. He was charming, handsome beyond compare, and chivalrous to a fault. What a pity it was all a desperate illusion. She'd heard by his own admission she was nothing special, and she supposed it was true. She was seventeen, uneducated, with little talent and fewer means. Being no great beauty, her youth was her only asset, and it wouldn't last long. She could hardly blame Glen.

"Why did you keep Winthrop from driving me home? Did you think I was unable to handle myself? That I am so inept at life I could have fallen prey to such a drunken man?"

Glen looked behind him nervously, putting his hand in the small of her back and forcing her down the path. "Let's not discuss that here."

Once at the sidewalk in front of the mansion, she stopped him, placing her hand on his chest. "No, we need to discuss it. I am not staying for a year here, Glen. I'm not even finishing the week. I'm going home where I belong, to take care of Claire and deal with my stepmother like I should have done from the beginning."

Glen's jaw flinched, but there wasn't even the slightest twinkle of surprise in the blue of his eyes, which reflected the streetlight. He'd been expecting her resignation, that much was obvious. She pulled his twenty-dollar bill from her pocket again. "Here, I won't be needing this, but thank you for your generosity."

She felt him grab her hand, forcing the bill back into her pocket. "Take it, Josephine. You deserve it. Get back home and make a life for you and Claire, but get out of this city. It will corrupt you faster than a bootlegger's man."

His eyes avoided her, and she touched his cheek, her finger tracing his jaw. She wanted— no, she needed, a reason to believe that his words to Winthrop were a lie. They'd shared something in their kiss. She couldn't believe the alternative. "Is that what happened to you, Glen?"

He raked his rough hands through his clipped curls and specks of sawdust released themselves. Little pink shavings fell to his feet. He slapped his hands together. "No," he finally said. "It isn't what happened to me, but I've seen it happen to a lot of men. There are so many temptations, so little cash for the workingman. If you're satisfied with the simple life, it seems fine, but if you have an ounce of ambition, postwar America can be harsh."

"So what's your ambition, Glen?"

"To finish my apprenticeship and be a full union carpenter, then build myself a little house at the edge of the city near the streetcar. That's my dream. Ain't much, is it?" He laughed.

Jo felt as though she was listening to his very soul speaking. There was no façade, no foolish games playing out. Glen really was a simple man. *A simple man who dealt in liquor*, she reminded herself. But his honesty, the true blue of his eyes—in them she saw nothing but a man she wanted to know more about; to be with for a long time to come. The honey-brown liquid faded into the deepest banks of her memory. Something else was filling her mind.

"What is it you want, Josephine? Have your dreams changed since coming here?"

"Woefully so," she said while keeping her eyes on his. Her breath left her, and she waited for his kiss, but it didn't surface.

"Here." He handed her another twenty-dollar bill. "Take this and get home to Michigan."

"I–I don't want to go back to Michigan."

"You just told me you did. What is it you do want, Josephine?" He said her name in a whisper, and she knew he felt the sparks between them, like one of the electric streetlamps that reflected in his blue eyes.

"I promised you I'd work a year in the Linton household, and I know I sound flighty, but I'm going to work that year, Glen." How could she tell him her convictions all stemmed from the concern in his blue eyes, from her desire to be near him? She forced the twenty into his large hand, and he grabbed her wrist with one hand. She felt his other trace her cheek, and she looked up to see the emotion in his eyes. He bent toward her slowly, and they shared a kiss. First, a small gentle touch to the lips, and then something far more passionate. She anticipated more, still gripping the money in her hands, but throwing her arms around Glen's wide neck. She tried to kiss him again, but he pulled away.

"Go back to Michigan," he said sternly. "I have nothing to offer you. Those two twenties you hold are all I have to give a woman."

"I don't want your money, Glen. I want answers. Why do you work in this creepy house? Why don't you finish your apprenticeship elsewhere? Why did you ask me to work for a year in that mausoleum?"

"Because I made promises. Promises I have to keep."

Josephine stepped back, her shoulders straight. "Then I have promises to keep. I promised to keep working here, and I will, Glen. I'll make you bring me here every day, and I'll figure out what your secret is. I know how you've been looking out for me, protecting me. Something is going on, and I intend to figure it out."

Glen turned from her. "There's no deep mystery, Jo. You've seen too many Gary Cooper movies. I'm just a workingman of no importance whatsoever. Any secrets I have aren't worth two nickels rubbed together."

"Kiss me again and tell me that." She baited him, not allowing his eyes to leave hers.

He just cleared his throat, looking back at the house. "Let's go, Jo. Before we both lose our jobs."

Chapter 8

Marian, you must know where he gets this kind of money." Jo flashed the forty dollars in her hand. A king's ransom for the residents of Eighth Avenue, indeed. Jo moved her gaze to the sleeping Davy and lowered her voice. "I've seen him with liquor, Marian. Is he a bootlegger?"

Marian's hands kept busy. "Heavens no, Jo. He's probably just saved the money. He's a hard worker, and he's been working for a long time. Take it and send for Claire. Glen wouldn't have parted with it if he needed it, and he wouldn't have had liquor without a reason. I've fed that man two nights a week for years now. Not once have I ever smelled liquor on his breath. It's not the sort of thing you can generally hide, Jo."

"You think I should take it then?" Josephine's mouth dropped open. It was so unlike Marian to suggest charity. This was charity, wasn't it? "I thought you wanted us to work for everything we have."

"Glen doesn't want anything from us, Jo. He knows we have nothing to give, and he's been a good friend to us, especially to Davy. I wouldn't question a man who has a heart for children as Glen does. He probably feels for young Claire, alone in that house with a madwoman. Take the money; you can pay it back. We'll do what we can as well. Mitch has just been saying it was time to get Claire here, too. Her letters are sounding more and more desperate. It's just too bad we have to sneak her out here, rather than using Father's free rail pass. But Claire is so young, and Agnes would never let her come without a fight. Agnes would miss the live-in maid she's created."

"I'm going to wire her the money first thing in the morning, Marian!" Excitement fluttered in Jo's chest. Perhaps she hadn't accomplished things the way she planned, but Claire would be out of danger. The money was a simple loan; if Glen's conscience had something to worry about, let his heart be troubled, not her own. His image raced through her mind: his steely blue eyes, his intense work ethic, his three-dollars-a-day salary. None of it made sense, but she pushed such thoughts away. Ignorance provided her a clear conscience and her sister's safe delivery.

Since it was Sunday afternoon, Glen would be arriving for dinner soon. His church got out a bit later than their own, and she used the time to help Marian in the kitchen before freshening up at the sink. She wished there was a way to thank Glen for his generosity, but she felt he probably preferred her quiet gratefulness.

At his knock, she opened the door to see him standing before her with a black eye. The blue of his pupil shone brightly against the dark purple splotch surrounding his upper face. "Glen!" she exclaimed. "What on earth happened?"

"Come on outside, Jo. I don't want Davy to see me like this. It will probably frighten him."

"Davy's sleeping," she explained. "Let me get you a cold compress to put on that. It looks dreadfully painful."

"No, just please come outside, Josephine. I want to talk to you." He looked around at

Marian. "Alone, if you don't mind."

Jo followed him outside, intrigued by the nature of his visit, but fearful at the same time. If he was going to tell her the money came from an illegal source, she'd have to give it back—and she was so set on Claire's arrival. She closed the door behind her. They sat on the landing, as they now did every night following the dinners they'd shared in Marian's home.

"What happened?" She allowed her fingers to gently touch the swelling.

Glen flinched at her touch. "I'm in trouble, Jo."

Her stomach turned at the admission. "Do you need your money back? I have a few more dollars saved in the house—can I help you in any way?" She took his hand without thinking, only wishing there was a way she could dissipate his troubles as easily as he'd done for her.

"No, it's nothing like that, Jo. It's Winthrop Linton. This shiner was intended for him, and far worse, I suspect. Apparently he used my name to hide some business dealings from his father. He's dealing with dangerous men."

Jo shivered at the admission. Glen wasn't the dramatic sort. If he said dangerous men, it probably meant far worse than he was allowing. Thinking back to the recent Valentine's Day massacre in Chicago by bootlegging thugs, Jo was consumed by the thunderous beating of her heart. If there were any doubt left as to how she felt about Glen, it was gone now. The thought of him in trouble sent her mind stirring. She wanted nothing more than his protection, his safety. She'd do whatever to ensure it.

"What can I do, Glen? Please, tell me. Can I talk to Winthrop?"

"I want you to quit at the Lintons'. I'll help you find something else, but I want you out of danger, Jo. Once those men figure out I'm not the one they are looking for, they are bound to come looking for Winthrop, and I don't want you near there."

"But, Glen, I need that job to support Claire. Do you want me to go back to Michigan? Certainly Winthrop has kept his wits to keep his identity sealed."

"Certainly he has. Unfortunately, he's used my name to do so. I came to tell you we can't be in contact with one another anymore. Whoever these men are, they'll be watching. If they think you're important to me, well—"

She stumbled over her words. "*Am* I important to you?"

"Too important for me to get you involved in this."

"Tell me the truth, Glen. Are you selling liquor? Is this your mess and not Winthrop's? It won't change anything between us. I just need to know. Even if you did something illegal, I know where your heart is, by the fact you gave me that money."

He studied her face, the disappointment evident in his expression. "I'm a man of God, Josephine. I take that title with the utmost seriousness. I haven't done anything illegal, I promise you that. And as for us, there is no us. You've got to stay away from me. I'm moving out this week to protect all of you from whatever, whoever is out there. This is my bed. I made it that fateful day when I listened to Winthrop Linton."

"Tell me what you've promised Winthrop. What are his plans? What is his secret? Tell me, Glen, please!" She pleaded with him, longing to know what kept Glen at arm's length, and why he made her promise to work a year and now was begging for her resignation. Nothing made sense anymore. Least of all, her impassioned desire to kiss this man and gently touch the throbbing purple bruise around his eye.

"It is for your own good you know as little as possible. I'll explain your absence to Mrs. Houston tomorrow."

"I won't be absent tomorrow." Jo faced him, conviction in her eyes. "I'm bringing Claire out this month. I've already written the telegram for the wire. I need this job, Glen." Jo's nose prickled with the urge to cry. "If you can't give me a good reason to quit, I certainly won't."

"You don't need this job, Josephine. Go home and live with your stepmother. Surely your father or your Grandmother Faith I hear you speak of—certainly she could help you."

"No, Grandmother has an infirmity. She's had it since she was young, and it's only gotten worse with age. I can't worry her over such a small thing. I haven't even told her the wedding chest she passed to my mother has been taken." Jo shook her head. She'd long since decided her grandmother's health was too frail.

"Her granddaughter's well-being is not so small. Tell your grandmother, Jo. Or better yet, your father. Claire shouldn't be your concern. Not at your young age."

"What is happening to this world, Glen? This seems such a lost generation, with the women cutting their hair to obscene lengths, illegal alcohol is so readily available, and now, a man begins teaching we evolved from monkeys and are not of God. What's next? I just don't understand, Glen. Is there no truth left in the world? I want to bury my head in the sand and protect my sister's precious Davy from ever growing up and seeing the corruption we've created."

"Josephine, no. Don't cry." Glen leaned over and kissed her gently. Their lips met in a firestorm of emotion, and soon their kiss developed into a passionate encounter. The importance of breathing suddenly paled in comparison to his light touch. She allowed her hand to follow the structure of his face, to hold him before her, willing him not to leave her again.

"No!" He pulled away, just as he'd done that night on the Linton walkway. When would he admit he loved her? That they were meant to be together? She tried to kiss him again, and he stood. "The Bible says to be anxious for nothing. Take that advice, Josephine, and run with it. Run back to Michigan and live your fate." He headed up the street toward the streetcar, and she followed him desperately.

"No, Glen. Please don't leave!" But he was out of her sight before she finished her plea.

◆　◆　◆

Glen rushed to the moving streetcar, dashing on it like some kind of Buster Keaton movie poster. Glen focused on the floorboards, ignoring the curious looks and whispered talk over his beaten appearance. He looked as though he'd been thrown out of some speakeasy, and he knew the hushed voices said so. This was the will of God? Glen shot a glance at the clouded sky.

Why, God? I heard Winthrop's cry for mercy, and I tried to help him. For what? Now I've lost Jo's trust, probably my job, and Winthrop's own parents think I'm corrupting their boy. I can't make him listen to me, Lord! Only You can do it. Only You can humble Winthrop to see his need, but will You? Or will You let me fall into this trap?

Glen rode to the end of the line and stepped off the streetcar without a destination. He had nowhere to be, nothing to do, but he couldn't stay with Josephine any longer. Josephine, and her trusting eyes and willing heart. He couldn't even beat his anger out on the hammer today. It was Sunday. He walked toward the rocky cliff where the bay met the Pacific Ocean and looked at God's magnificence.

The wild surf beat the shore with one unrelenting explosion after another. God's power took on new meaning when watching the strength of the waves, the reminder that He was indeed in charge. The ferry to Sausalito sailed and returned multiple times before Glen knew what he had to do. It was time for Winthrop to quit hiding behind his mask. It was time his parents knew the truth, and Winthrop prepared for the inevitable. The men who came after Glen had only offered a warning; the actual punishment would be far worse.

With renewed resolve, he rode the streetcar up to the Linton mansion. His presence would not be welcomed on a Sunday, but some things were more important than formal etiquette. Knocking on the door, he waited for Mrs. Houston. To his surprise, Winthrop himself answered.

"What happened to you?" Winthrop stepped back at the hideous sight of Glen's purple bruise.

"You should ask me what happened to you. This was intended for you."

Winthrop's small frame trembled as he opened the door wider. "Come in. Go on into the study; we can talk there." His voice was hushed.

Turning, Glen witnessed the true Winthrop, the one behind the fine clothes and shiny Duesenberg. The Winthrop who cared nothing for people except as a means to get his way. Winthrop was more like his father than he'd ever know. The sight of him hurt Glen, even while filled with compassion for the sickly man. In the end, Glen felt a raw disgust.

In the past, Glen focused on the need, the spiritual dryness that the rich young man possessed, but today he could only see the sin, he could only feel the pride. Vanity emanated from Winthrop's pores, and he wasn't about to admit his need. Not to Glen, or God, or anyone else. The time had come for the games to stop.

"I'm done, Winthrop. I tried to show you God's love by helping you make something of yourself. But you've squandered my help. You've chased the almighty dollar, and I'd hoped it would impress your father, that you might be seen as some type of success before your time came. Now I know I've just wasted my time. You haven't appreciated a thing I've done for you, or you never would have given my name to those thugs."

An evil grin inhabited Winthrop's features. His lackluster chin and crooked smile came alive with malice. "I've seen you look at Josephine, Glen. You don't fool me for a minute. You've impressed her with my money. I saw you throw a twenty at her just last night. You see how dazzled she'll be by your measly three dollars a day. You've got no choice, Glen. Here." Winthrop held out the formal currency-like piece of paper which was so familiar to Glen.

"No, you get it yourself. I've done nothing illegal. I only tried to help you. A useless cause I see now. God knows your heart, Winthrop. Don't forget it. Even if you fool the entire city of San Francisco, you'll never fool Him."

"Do you think your God scares me? Your God is only a substitute for the power of money. I can buy and sell your God, Glen. He's only a figment of your imagination. A crutch for those of you who can't make it in today's world. We'll see how religious your little girlfriend is come Monday when she's fired."

Winthrop's threats held little power over Glen any longer. Glen had managed to pack away a tidy sum with his extra work. He had invested it in the stock market, made a killing on steel, pulled out the cash, and had enough to support a wife. Certainly not in grand style, but in the simple life he'd always imagined. He'd sent Josephine back to Michigan, but if she didn't go, he'd know God kept her there for him.

Now if only Josephine would trust him again, if only she'd be his wife, they'd find a way to make it. He'd tried to tell himself she was only a flight of fancy, too young to be a bride. But her kisses had crumbled that wall he'd built—her kisses and her stolen glances. When she could have been looking at Winthrop, in his impressive suits and fancy Duesenberg, her eyes always followed Glen in his simple denim jeans and wrinkled shirts.

Chapter 9

Mrs. Houston's coldhearted stare burrowed right through Jo's heart. Jo tilted her chin and returned the gaze blankly. There were no words, and none were necessary; Jo's employment was terminated. She curtsied before the older woman, not giving Mrs. Houston any more ammunition. Inwardly she winced as she slowly traipsed the walkway and the door slammed behind her. Mentally, she counted her meager savings at home in the coffee can. With no way to support Claire, Jo would have to focus on finding work, not on Glen. Failure decimated what she had left of confidence.

She couldn't return to Michigan now that Claire was on her way. She silently blasted Glen for leaving her in such a fix, but she was unable to stir up any anger. She knew he was only trying to protect her. Feelings of betrayal didn't surface, only an inexplicable longing for the muscular carpenter who had stolen her heart.

◆　◆　◆

Summer ended quietly amidst the evergreen trees of San Francisco, and still Glen remained absent. She prayed for his protection every day. Finally, it dawned on her that Winthrop Linton might know where her love was and help put an end to her misery. Claire was due any day now, and Jo so wanted to share her arrival with Glen. One morning, after finishing the laundry and offering to go to the grocery, Josephine took the familiar streetcar route to the Nob Hill mansion in search of Winthrop, and, hopefully, some answers.

She drew in a deep breath and knocked on the front door, praying that Mrs. Houston wouldn't answer. Winthrop appeared. His face was white as stale snow and his weak features more sallow than ever. He splayed his bony, feminine fingers across the doorjamb.

"Well, Josephine. I see you couldn't stay away." He smiled, forcing her to gaze upon his small, sickly teeth.

"Can we talk somewhere privately, Master Linton?" She strained to use his proper title, to bow to his station in life, but it made her sick to her stomach. His adamant trust in himself and in his own power was more evident than it had once been, and his false confidence in his power over her made her want to laugh.

"I knew you'd be back. Not much work out there, Miss Josephine?"

She strode past him to the dining room, knowing he'd follow. Even in her long, green corduroy skirt, the kind everyone wore, she knew she interested him, and she'd use that to her advantage today. If she'd learned anything during her time in San Francisco, she'd learned she wasn't completely powerless. Certainly not to a weak-minded man like Winthrop Linton.

"I didn't come to speak to you of a job. My brother-in-law is doing fine financially, and we're managing just fine. I came to speak to you about Glen."

"Glen?" Winthrop casually fixed himself a drink. "Do I know a Glen?" He tried to look down on her, to appear haughty, but Josephine stood to her full height. Although petite, she still towered over the spineless little man.

She walked toward him, forced the crystal glass from his hand, and plopped it on the shiny dining room table with a thunk. "Don't play innocent with me, Winthrop. I didn't come here for a job, and I don't want anything you have to offer. I just want to know what you did to give Glen a shiner. Besides hide behind his name, of course. Where is he? Tell me, Winthrop, or I'll tell those men at the apartment, the burly ones who have been looking for Glen, *who* they are really looking for. I think they would actually pay handsomely for the information." She watched his arrogant smile disintegrate into fear. "They might make my money woes go away completely, possibly?"

The familiar sound of a hammer caught her attention, a steady beat she'd know anywhere. Winthrop's anxious eyes gave way to recognition, and Josephine ran for the door. Winthrop tried to stop her, but his frail frame was no match for her determined self. She was at the door before he finished the thought. She flew down the steps to the work shed.

"Glen! Glen!"

The hammering stopped, and his steely gray-blue eyes met hers for the first time in months. Every emotion melted except one, and she ran toward him. He dropped his hammer and his muscular arms came around her tightly, clutching her in an embrace she once only dreamed about.

"Josephine!" His hands ran through her hair desperately, and he pulled her face back, looking at her momentarily, before she felt his firm lips on hers. All sense of decorum was lost as she returned his kiss frantically, searching for a way to tell him how she missed him. Her kiss grew firmer when words wouldn't come.

"Well, isn't this cozy?" Winthrop's voice tore them apart and Josephine's eyes threw daggers. Winthrop. The man who'd kept them apart all this time, who'd stolen precious moments from their love affair.

Before she spoke, Glen put a hand to her mouth. "Winthrop, I told you how I felt about Josephine from the day you first fired her."

"Winthrop fired me? I thought it was you, Glen. To protect me, remember?" Jo's face twisted in confusion.

"Is that what he told you?" Winthrop laughed, that obnoxious, weasel-like giggle she'd heard one too many times when he came home in the mornings, drunk. "How many women have heard that line and believed it?"

"That's enough, Winthrop! I've lived this lie of yours long enough. Leave us." Glen stood to his full height. "We have some things to discuss."

"Not at my expense you don't. You're not telling her the truth, or I'll—"

"You'll what, Winthrop?" Glen's eyes narrowed, and Winthrop cowered behind a brick pedestal decorating the garden. At that minor show of strength, Winthrop left them alone, retreating for the safety of his mansion.

"Where have you been, Glen? We've been worried sick. Even baby Davy looks for you when I take him outside." Her concern soon grew to feelings of betrayal at being left behind. "How could you just leave us and come back here—when you had me fired from a job I swore I'd keep a year?"

"Sit down, Josephine." She found a place on a dusty sawhorse and did as he asked. His expression was grave, his words slow. "I was prepared to leave town, to let Winthrop get himself out of his own mess, but then God spoke to me. Clear as day, He said I wasn't done here. I heard Him tell me not to desert Winthrop in this time of need. I couldn't go, and I couldn't explain it to you for your own good, but the time has come."

"Yes," she agreed.

"Do you know what this is?" He pulled an official-looking slip of paper from his back pocket. It had the appearance of currency but was headed by the title line "Original Prescription Form for Medicinal Liquor" and was attached to a stub reading the same. On the bottom it read in block, dollar-bill letters: National Prohibition Act.

"A prescription for liquor?" Fear rose in her like an untamed fire. "Are you sick, Glen? Is that why you had the liquor in your lunch box?"

"Not me, Jo. Winthrop. It's cancer. First they thought it was tuberculosis, but his cough subsided, and now they feel it is cancer. They gave him a year to live, just about the time when you started."

"That's why you wanted me to stay?"

Glen only nodded and continued. "He's been in a lot of pain, and they've given him prescription liquor to fight it. I've been picking it up for him at the drugstore so his parents wouldn't worry. I've been hoping my witness would show him that God's love wouldn't desert him. That's why I'd hoped to keep order in the house during his bout, but that was not to happen."

"Glen, there's enough liquor in his house to keep him drunk for years. Why would he need a doctor's prescription?" Jo shook her head, trying to make sense of the nonsense. Winthrop, although pale as a sheet, appeared in fine spirits when sober.

"His parents don't know about the illness. He's been building a neighborhood of small tract houses for the working folk with my help. That's how he planned to make his money from the allowance his parents provide him with. He wanted to succeed before he succumbed to the disease—to prove to his parents he was more than just an ornament to take over his father's steel business."

"Why the thugs? He had to be involved in some nasty business to have those kind of men after him. You're telling me it wasn't the liquor?"

"No, Winthrop borrowed heavily to keep building the houses after the stock drop in July. He didn't go to a bank to keep his father from knowing. It turned out to be a bad decision. Luckily, I'd made a little money in the stock market and was able to help him out."

"So you're out of trouble? And you still deserted me?" Jo stared into Glen's eyes, looking for the deception she felt. His answers only brought up more questions. "How could you allow me to lose my job?"

"I was worried, Jo. Really. Those men meant business, and I wanted you safe. I figured the forty dollars would keep you set for awhile until you could find something else."

"I used that money for my sister, Glen, to bring her to California. She's finally able to come after months of arrangements. You left me with meager savings, and no earning potential whatsoever. How could you do that to me? To my family?" She stamped her foot, embarrassed by her childish behavior, but too upset to care.

"I was trying to earn enough money to buy one of the houses, Jo. I took my carpentry test, and I'm in the union now, thanks to Winthrop, and making eight dollars a day! I cut the lumber here all day for the project downtown."

"Well, that's just fine for you. In the meantime, I'm stealing food from Davy's mouth in that cramped flat! Not to mention Claire is—"

"So we could be married," Glen continued.

Josephine stammered, "Wh–what did you say?" She looked up in hopeful anticipation.

"I said I wanted to buy the house so we could be married, Josephine. I love you. Maybe I've done an awful job of showing it, but I want you as my wife. My sister told me you hadn't left for Michigan, that you'd sent for Claire. I took that as a sign you cared for me, too. Was I wrong?"

"No, Glen. I love you, too, but what about Winthrop? What about his threats?"

Glen looked to the floorboards and pulled her into the shed deeper. He whispered, "I'm afraid Winthrop isn't going to be with us long enough to make many more threats. Pray for his soul, Jo. That's what we must do, and we must try not to upset him. He plans to tell his parents this very night. I tried to leave so many times, but God kept holding me back, forcing me to stay. He needs me right now, Jo. I know it's hard to see with his obnoxious behavior, but he's hurting. He aches with physical pain but even more with spiritual darkness."

Glen's eyes filled with tears as he spoke, and Jo had never seen a more beautiful sight. How could she have ever doubted him? "I'll marry you, Glen. Whenever you're ready, I'll marry you."

"It won't be long now, my love. Give Winthrop no pity, only your prayers."

"I will; you can count on it. I'm going to the station to pick up Claire tonight."

"I'll be home to you soon. Claire and you will have a quaint little house within the next couple months, and hopefully Winthrop will have a room prepared for him by our Lord."

She embraced Glen with all her strength, overwhelmed by the fact that her family would soon be intact. The new family which God had fashioned of His own hand.

◆ ◆ ◆

Jo arrived at the station, anxious and thrilled for her sister's arrival. She babbled incessantly while Glen just watched her happily. Running alongside the train, Jo searched the windows for a sign of her sister, but slowed her pace eventually when the appearance didn't come. When the last traveler disembarked, a shudder of fear overcame her. She ran to the conductor and was directed to the office.

"My sister was supposed to be on that train. Is there another train due?" Jo's voice shook. Glen smoothed his hand along her back trying to comfort her, but it was of little use.

"You Josephine Mayer?" The office man's chin jutted toward her.

"Yes, yes, I am." Jo nodded.

"Letter for you, over there in that trunk."

Jo turned to see her mother's beloved wedding chest, hand-carved and filled with memories, lying isolated in a forgotten corner of the station. "Glen, that's my mother's trunk! The one Agnes stole from us." Josephine shook her head. "But how did Claire get it, and where is my sister?"

"Let's go find out." Glen held her shaking hand. Jo was overwhelmed with tears at the sight of the old chest.

"This chest meant so much to my mother and my Grandma Faith." Jo reached and opened the chest. A letter lay on top of the treasures within, treasures which included the seed pearl gown worn by generations of brides before her. Jo ripped open the letter with abandon.

Dear Jo,

I'm sure you're wondering where I am by now, and the answer is, in case you haven't guessed, I'm not coming. Grandma Faith found out what I was up to and asked Agnes for the chest back, saying she was in need of memories of Grandpa. Even Agnes couldn't refuse her. I've decided to live with Grandma for now. She could use the company, and I could certainly stand to get away from here. She was very angry with both of us for not telling her our situation. Anyway, I used the money you sent me to pack the chest and ship it to California. Marian tells me there's a husband in your future, and I knew you had to have the dress. I only wish Marian had had it as well. Wear it and think of me, dear sister. I love you.

Claire

Jo wiped the tears from her eyes and fingered the delicate fabric of the elaborate wedding gown. "It's all too much!" She stood and Glen took her in his arms.

"No, Josephine, it's all from God, and He never holds back in good gifts."

"Like our little house on State Street?"

Glen smiled. "Yes, just like that. Now that the stock market has crashed, work will be even harder to come by."

"Poor Mr. Linton." Jo looked to the fancy chest below her, thankful her own treasures would last.

"Mr. Linton is just lucky Winthrop invested outside the stock market. Winthrop finally got what he wanted— his father's respect."

"And God finally got what He wanted—Winthrop's heart."

Jo snuggled into Glen's firm chest, knowing whatever lay ahead, she'd weather it all with Glen at the helm under God's direction.

Epilogue

Josephine wrapped her wedding gown in cotton and placed it carefully back into the box. As she did so, she added a letter as each of her predecessors had done:

To My Future Generations,

Times are very hard as I write this letter. Most of America struggles to put food on the table, and we are, gratefully, unscathed by the Great Depression. I don't know if times will warrant anyone wearing this elegant gown again, but know whoever reads this letter as my descendent, I have prayed for you and the generations that come after you. This gown meant everything to me at a time when marriage itself was a financial stretch. It was a piece of my beloved mother given back to me. While the gown may go by the wayside, I pray that your faith in our Lord and a godly husband will not. May God richly bless you, my daughters, wherever He leads you.

Josephine Mayer Bechtel
Married August 14, 1929

Enclosed in this chest, I've added a piece of colored glass that is so popular in our day. It is not expensive, nor will it probably ever be, but it meant a great deal to me when Glen brought it home. The pattern is called cabbage rose, and the pitcher held a place of great honor in our home.

KRISTIN BILLERBECK is a bestselling, Christy-nominated author of over 45 novels. Her work has been featured in *The New York Times* and on "The Today Show." Kristin is a fourth-generation Californian and a proud mother of four. She lives in the Silicon Valley and enjoys good handbags, hiking, and reading.

JOIN US ONLINE!

Christian Fiction for Women

Christian Fiction for Women is your online home for the latest in Christian fiction.

Check us out online for:

- Giveaways
- Recipes
- Info about Upcoming Releases
- Book Trailers
- News and More!

Find Christian Fiction for Women at Your Favorite Social Media Site:

 Search "Christian Fiction for Women"

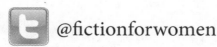 @fictionforwomen